Hummingbird Memories

9-27-2012

To Lela, my Desert
Vagabonds friend.
Here's wishing you all
the best in life. End just
remember, like in the book,
always stay young at heart.
Love, Margie

Hummingbird Memories

Margie House Neal

Library of Congress Control Number: 2012906145
ISBN: Hardcover   978-1-4691-9573-5
                  Softcover   978-1-4691-9572-8
                  Ebook   978-1-4691-9574-2

This book was printed in the United States of America.

To order additional copies of this book, contact:
Xlibris Corporation
1-888-795-4274
www.Xlibris.com
Orders@Xlibris.com
114354

This book is lovingly dedicated to the memory of my wonderful parents, Gordon and Virginia House, whose Christian lives were truly an inspiration.

Part I

Prologue

Heavy coastal fog was rolling in when I glanced out the kitchen window this morning. It lay like a thick, fleecy gray blanket that seemed to smother our small town. But in spite of the morning gloom, I felt that I had to get out of the house. I hurriedly rinsed out the cereal bowls and loaded them into the dishwasher, and opened a can of cat food for Patches, Buster, Roxie, and Slinky. Three of the cats were purring loudly and rubbing my legs, while Slinky, the stuck-up, stand offish feline, watched from a distance. I had the house to myself that day, and I enjoyed that, mostly because I appreciated the solitude. The TV was off for a change, and that's because my husband had left the house early. He was helping a friend drywall his garage and that would be an all-day project. Since we were both retired, I was kind of looking forward to having the day to myself. We had been married for 48 years, and had known each other since we were in high school, so there were days when we'd just had too much togetherness and could use a break from each other.

I grabbed a warm jacket and a scarf from the hall closet, headed out the door and down our steep gravel driveway. It was early June, but was still quite chilly on the Oregon coast. I was a southern California native, and even though we had lived in the small town for nearly 20 years now, I really hadn't acclimated to their damp weather. Any time we had guests come for a visit, they would always exclaim over the beautiful, lush, green landscape, but I was quick to tell them that we paid a price for all that beauty. The price was plenty of rainy, cloudy, damp days, and if it wasn't rain, there was fog and just plain gloom to deal with, even in the summertime.

I reached the end of our driveway and turned left on the small access road, which was lined with spruce trees, and then after passing the magnificent myrtle wood trees about 100 yards down, I crossed the main highway and reached the sandy stretch of beach. The ocean was fairly calm that morning, and I could hear the mournful sound of the foghorn way out past the breakers.

The salt smell of the ocean and the brisk air was invigorating, and I took some deep breaths. If only I could get rid of the gloominess and the sadness I was feeling. It didn't help that we'd had no sunshine for the last two weeks. I had always been a sun person, and I really missed the sunshine. The past year had been a most difficult one. Our oldest son had moved away about a year ago. He'd lived in Eugene, Oregon, which was only about 200 miles from us, and our two families visited each other fairly often. Our little granddaughters were real sweethearts, and we loved seeing them. But our daughter in law was from Tennessee, and she missed her life and family back home, so they had relocated there. Our other two adult children already lived in other states, so we didn't really get too much time with any of our grandchildren. We had a total of five.

The more shattering incident that had taken place this past year was the death of my father, Charles Hummer. He'd always been so healthy, but he was 89, and slowing down. My mother had died five years before, and Dad never seemed to be quite the same after that. Oh, he kept busy with church activities, and square dancing, and seemed to have a full social schedule at all times. But we kids knew how much he missed our mother, his wife of 60 years. His favorite activity was working as a docent for the Nature Conservancy, which was located up in the foothills behind his southern California hometown. He truly enjoyed leading a class of school children on nature walks, pointing out the various wildflowers, and the flora and fauna of the area. He was very familiar with all 48 miles of trails, and up until about two months before his death, walked all the trails at least once a month. After the loss of my mother, I had called Dad every few days, and went down to visit as often as I could. Now it had been nearly a year since Dad had passed, and I truly missed him.

Of course most everyone at my age had to deal with the deaths of parents, but that didn't always make it any easier. As I walked along the beach I thought that I probably needed more activities to keep me busy and get my mind on other things. I did volunteer at the local hospital on Monday mornings, and worked in a third grade classroom one afternoon a week, and was in charge of our library at the Senior Center. I also worked out at the Curves in town on a steady basis.

But maybe there was more I could be doing. My husband and I both talked about volunteering at the local animal shelter, but with our love for animals, we'd probably be adopting more and we didn't really need any more than the four cats, two dogs and three goats we already had.

After about an hour of walking on the beach, I headed back to our house, stopping at the mail box at the end of our driveway. Noticing a thick envelope with a return address of "Reunion Committee" lifted my spirits greatly. Sure enough, it was an invitation to our high school class reunion, which was to be held in August. Of course I had figured it was going to happen, since I had been on Facebook for the past year, and had reconnected with some of my friends from school. There had been talk of a reunion; however, I just wasn't sure if or when it would actually take place. But now, it was official. What was just incredibly hard to believe, though, was that it was to be our 50th. Where did that number come from??? Where had all those years gone? I can remember being overwhelmed by three small children (two in diapers at the same time, and not disposable ones either) and then before we knew it, the little ones were teenagers, and giving us much grief. And now here we were, 50 years away from our days back in high school. Some years in the past, one of our neighbors had attended his 50th, and both my husband and I had thought that sounded so ancient. Now here was another 50th Reunion just right around the corner. And it was ours! Unbelievable!

Two months later, I was boarding a plane headed for southern California. I found a seat by the window and settled in for what would be about a two hour flight. My younger sister, Pam, would be picking me up at the San Diego Airport. I would be attending the reunion by myself, since my husband had sprained his ankle at the last minute. I had made plane reservations for us both, and he was sorry that he was unable to go with me. His sprain was a bad one, but we were very lucky to have some wonderful neighbors who would be helping around the house, and checking on him constantly. They had joked about my trip, saying, "You're just going to be seeing a bunch of old people!" Well, my former classmates might look older, at first sight, but I had to believe that in their hearts and minds, they were still young, the way I was. There was no way I was going to cancel that trip. I had missed our 40th class reunion, and I really wanted, more than anything, to attend this one. I'd had some wonderful friends in high school, and, although I'd kept in touch with some, there were others I hadn't seen in years. Also, when a person gets to their 50th, one doesn't know how many more there will be.

How those four years of high school had flown by. I'd had some of my happiest days, and some of the worst days of my life. I could be feeling on top of the world at times, and then way down in the dumps just a short while later. People who say that the best years in a person's life are the teen years, are wrong however. All the years since then, for me anyhow, were much calmer, much more peaceful.

I thought back on about the crazy years that followed high school, that turbulent decade of the 60's. The Cuban Missile Crisis took place when I was in college. A little more than a year after that was the assassination of John F. Kennedy, the president that I had so admired at the time. There were several assassinations in that decade, Malcom X, Bobby Kennedy, Martin Luther King. Later on in the 1960's, many of the younger generation were turning to drugs, and the music was considered more acid rock instead of rock and roll. I had read that there were some who believed that more social change occurred in the United States in the 1960's than in any other decade in the 20th century. There were also claims that the 60's may have been the beginning of the end for the last innocent generation. It made me feel good to know that I had been a part of that generation.

Once we were up in the air, and knowing that the plane wouldn't be landing for at least two hours, I got comfortable, and began to go back over the years. I had plenty of time to think about the past, about my high school years, my younger self, and about all the huge changes that had taken place in the world since those long ago days. I made sure my cell phone was powered off, turned on my IPod, and sat back to relax, and to ponder about the classmates I would soon be seeing, and to reminisce about those golden days, those innocent times back in high school.

Hummingbird Memories

Chapter 1

Elaine Hummer got off her bicycle, laid it gently down at the side of the road under a eucalyptus tree and plopped herself down next to it. "I don't know about you," she said, "but I'm exhausted. I need to take a break now or I'll never make it over the next hill."

"Oh, don't give up now," Natalie Irby told her. "We're almost there. Whose idea was this bike ride anyhow?"

"I guess I have to take the blame for such a crazy idea," Elaine groaned. "I didn't know it was so hot out."

"It must be at least 95 in the shade," Natalie remarked, wiping her perspiring forehead. "We've only got one more hill to go. Come on, Elaine."

Elaine slowly climbed back onto her bicycle with a disgusted sigh, and after several minutes of strenuous, uphill pedaling, they'd reached their goal-the green and shaded cemetery which overlooked their small hometown of Ellington. The girls leaned their bikes against the iron fence, pushed open the gate, and sank down into the cool green grass inside, sheltered from the sun's rays by an umbrella tree.

"I think the cemetery is the only green spot in the entire town," noted Natalie, glancing around.

Elaine didn't reply. She was catching her breath and enjoying the awesome view.

Armedia Valley was approximately 30 miles long, its western boundary formed by low, sloping hills which separated the valley from the southern California coastline. To the east, opposite the coastal range were higher, steeper peaks which sheltered the valley from the hot winds of the vast Mojave Desert on the other side. Toward the southern end of the valley the two mountain ranges dwindled into insignificant hills, only to rise again to form a similar valley, and to the north the mountains narrowed to a pass.

Located at the north end of the valley, not far from the mountain pass, was the town of Armedia, the valley's namesake and largest community. The town was definitely a melting pot. Jewish people liked the mineral water, Mexicans found work in the numerous orange and olive groves in the area, the black and the white people simply resided there because it was the place of their upbringing.

On a sloping hill at the west end of town stood the faded, pink stucco high school which overlooked the surrounding homes and a dwindling lake. Armedia wasn't a large town, with a population of approximately 3500, many of which were retired people living there for their health. Thus the high school remained one of the smallest in the fast-growing state. Armedia Valley seemed to be the only area in Southern California which wasn't growing by leaps and bounds. The school had an enrollment of 450 which included pupils from the smaller surrounding communities.

At the south end of the valley, among rolling hills, was High Bluffs, a rough clay mining town. Fifteen miles to the north lay the farming community of Ellington. To city dwellers it was an extremely small town, having a scant population of 975 residents. Everybody knew everybody else. Gossip spread like wildfire over back fences, and tongues wagged knowingly at sewing circles and committee meetings. Ellington was bursting with organizations: Farm Bureau, 4-H Club, PTA, Boy Scouts, The Ladies Aid Society, The Garden Club, and Methodist Youth Fellowship, to name a few. It had a Catholic and a Methodist Church, and elementary school, a general store, a post office, and even a Town Hall (which was actually a house donated to the town for that purpose). Most of the inhabitants made their living farming. Some worked at a nearby hot springs resort, while others found employment at Camp Pendleton, a Marine Base about 40 miles away.

Ellington was spread out over a large area, dissected by Main St. Covering the north end were large fields of wheat, oats, barley and rye. Cattle grazed in alfalfa pastures. Eucalyptus, tamarack, oak and poplar trees lined some fields, while neat white fence posts surrounded others. Expansive horse ranches nestled in the foothills. In the center of town was Barney's General store, containing everything from liniment to lawnmowers. On the next corner was Bub's Place, a small run-down bar and cafe. The next block held the gray Catholic Church, and also a gas station, a favorite haunt of the Ellington boys. Further down the road was the white, old fashioned Methodist Church. Toward the south end of town was the tiny post office, and Debbie's Diner, another popular spot for young people. Here Main St. curved to the left and went east and then south toward High Bluffs. Continuing from where Main St. turned was First St. which went south out of town, and dwindled into a dirt road leading up into the foothills of the coastal range. On the west side of town was an old grain elevator that had been constructed back in 1918, but was still being used. The elevator stood 80 feet high, like a sentinel, overlooking the small farming community.

It was an unusually warm day in late summer. The ocean breeze which frequently cooled the town through a gap in the mountains was not present. Nothing stirred. Heat waves shimmered up from the golden stubble of grain fields.

"Isn't it strange that we like coming up here to the cemetery?" Natalie asked. "Some people might think we're kind of weird."

"Well, like you said, it is green and it is cool, and our town doesn't have a park," Elaine responded. "Besides this is a nice quiet place to start our diaries. I'm just trying to think of a dramatic way to get started." The girls had recently bought big notebooks which would serve as diaries for the next four years, from the time they started high school until graduation.

"Good idea of yours," commented Natalie as she flipped through the empty pages. "I wish I knew how it will end." She flipped over to the last page. "Four years is a long time. No telling what might happen in between."

"We'll probably be starting out in college," Elaine said.

"How can you be so sure? How do you know you'll be going to college? Maybe you'll get married instead."

"Not till I finish college. I've always wanted to be a teacher or nurse or airline hostess or a writer anyhow. I think I'll probably be about 25 before I get married."

"That sounds about right," Natalie said. "But that doesn't mean I'm not interested in boys."

"Of course not!" Elaine added emphatically. "Just think of all the cute guys we'll meet once high school starts. I can hardly wait til I start dating!"

"My folks say I can't go out with boys until I'm 16," moaned Natalie. "Two years seems like a long time to wait. I'll just have to find a way to get around that." Her parents had always been quite strict, especially her father.

"I haven't really discussed that with my folks yet," Elaine replied, staring dreamily into the sky. "They always say that the years from 14 to 19 are the best in a person's life. And our teen years have to be simply wonderful. We don't want anything to go wrong." She leaned back against a tree and began to write in her diary, the first entry of many to follow. She was a slim girl of medium height and had a small, heart-shaped face featuring bluish green eyes and a sensitive mouth that was usually smiling. Her glossy brown hair was pulled back into a pony tail. She wrote:

> "Dear Diary, the day seems momentous-the beginning of my diary for the next 4 years, my high school years. As I thumb through these empty pages, I am filled with curiosity as to what they will contain. I really haven't the slightest idea what the future holds for me. Life is like a book, except one can't look ahead to the last page to read how it all ends.
>
> I live in a very small town on a poultry ranch. I've lived here since I was three, and there isn't one person in Ellington that I don't know. I love this town, but I'm really anxious to get out and meet new people. I graduated from elementary school 3 months ago with 6 other girls and 8 boys. Two of the girls, Natalie Irby and Beth Hathaway are my closest friends. Nat just moved to town a year ago, but Beth's family has lived here even before we did. They raise cattle. The boys around here are very childish, and I've known them all for ages. I hope to meet some other guys at Armedia High. Our freshmen class will have about 100 students instead of just 14.
>
> One thing about Natalie is that she always seems to attract the boys. She's lucky that way. She has pale blonde hair and a great figure that looks good in a sweater, and I feel rather ordinary compared to her. But hopefully things will change and my bust will get bigger as time goes on.
>
> Going back to the subject of boys, there is one boy in Ellington that does interest me, however. His name is Warren Fawcett, and he is our minister's son. I've had a crush on him for the past year, but he doesn't seem too interested in girls. He's a year ahead of me in school, but I still see him around since we both belong to Methodist Youth Fellowship. Our youth group has been pretty small lately, but we're hoping to find some new members this fall.

This year has to be a really great one." With that she laid down her pen and got up to peer over Nat's shoulder in fun. "Go away, Nosy." Nat pushed her playfully. She was a petite girl with straight blonde hair that hung almost to her waist.

"Are you almost finished" Elaine asked. I have to get home and gather eggs. Are you coming to Youth Group tonight?"

"My folks will probably think of some reason I can't go. But I'll try," she added, picking herself up from the grass. They mounted their bikes and rode down the hill in the Sunday afternoon heat. Natalie went straight toward Main St. while Elaine turned right on First, and then down the long dirt driveway that led to the house.

Her family's home was a low, rambling stucco structure of pale green. Surrounded by lawn with a garage on the right and patio on the left, it made a pleasant scene. Roses and camellia bushes, carefully tended by her mother, bordered the front of the house. A tall honeysuckle hedge separated the back lawn from rows of chicken pens and kept them hidden from view.

Charles and Lois Hummer were sitting out on the back patio lawn swing drinking lemonade. "Hi Honey, how was your bike ride?" her father asked. Without waiting for an answer he added "You'd best get out and get those eggs gathered before they get too warm." He was tall and pleasant looking with a gentle face, blue eyes, and hair which was graying rapidly from his years of hard work to build a successful poultry ranch.

"There's lemonade in the frige, so help yourself," Lois Hummer suggested. She was a calm, easy-going woman, slim for her years. She had wavy blonde hair and soft blue eyes, framed by glasses.

"Good idea," Elaine said, walking into the house, which was cool compared to the heat outside. She stopped in the bedroom she shared with her younger sister to hide her diary under her mattress. Elaine felt that sharing a bedroom with Pam presented a real problem. Pam's bed was strewn with clothes, comic books, candy wrappers, a baseball and bat, and several stuffed animals, much worse for wear. Her bulletin board above her bed featured pictures of dogs, cats, horses, and child stars.

Elaine's bed was uncluttered except for a few stuffed animals. Her bulletin board was covered with pictures of popular singers: Elvis Presley, Pat Boone, Frankie Avalon, and the Everly Brothers. In the corner was a small candid snapshot of Warren Fawcett. Between the beds was a long, low bookcase that also sufficed as a nightstand. It contained the familiar classics of *Little Women, Anne of Green Gables, Dorothy and the Wizard of Oz, The Bobbsey Twins,* and *Nancy Drew Mysteries.* Elaine was an avid reader. On the opposite wall from the beds were desks and a bureau. The wallpaper in the room featured pink rosebuds while pink dotted Swiss curtains hung at the window. Beige chenille bedspreads completed the decor.

Elaine headed out to the kitchen for some refreshment. Her brother Russ, age 12, was seated at the dining table. He was a tall, slim serious fellow. His glasses made him look shy and studious, which he was, unlike his two sisters. He was busily drawing a truck for his little brother. Pam was belatedly washing the lunch dishes. She was small for her 10 years with her brown hair in a pixie cut and freckles scattered lightly over a dainty face, a face which was frowning at Elaine. "I'm just about finished with the dishes, and you're getting another glass dirty."

"Oh like washing one more little glass is really going to add to your work load? And when you're done here, you can go clean up your side of the room. It looks like a cyclone hit!"

"You're just way too picky," Pam retorted.

"Let's not argue," suggested Peacemaker Russ.

The youngest of the Hummer clan, two year old Timmie, sat under the table, frantically scribbling crayon onto a clean white paper. He was a chubby, towheaded boy with big blue eyes. "Hey, 'Laine,'" he cried, extended a grimy finger in her direction, "See my twuck!" He waved the paper in her direction.

"Timmie, that is a great truck."

"Someday, he'll be drawing big diesel trucks like me," Russ said. "Take a look at this."

"Not bad, Russ. You're pretty talented at drawing."

Elaine went outside, crossed the back yard with its swing set for Timmie, and went through the hedge opening. She stood and surveyed the eight rows of chicken pens with disgust. She'd had her egg-gathering job ever since she was in 5th Grade, and now it was a habit with a firm foundation. Every day around four o'clock she was automatically prompted to go collect eggs, rain or shine. She went to the large aluminum building which served as a storage house for chicken feed and a packing house for the 6,000 eggs gathered daily. Carrying 10 wire egg baskets, she made her way to the first row of pens and began her menial task. Russ had already done his egg-collecting for the day, and Pam would be starting to help soon. They earned a small amount of spending money for helping out, a dime a day for each row. Beyond the rows of chicken pens were 30 acres of fertile land, now covered with hay stubble.

Charles Hummer had bought the property back in 1945. He had been born and raised in San Bernardino County and later went to UCLA where he majored in Engineering. Lois Hummer had lived all her young life in Illinois, but came out to California to attend UCLA, and it was there that she met her future husband. They were married in 1941 but were separated shortly after because of the war. After Charles had served in the Navy, he came back to Long Beach and found an engineering position with a large, prestigious company. But by the time a year had passed, he realized that was not the job or lifestyle for him. Taking a Sunday drive out to the country, he stumbled on 40 acres of farmland for sale. It was only a matter of time before he moved his wife and daughter out to the small town of Ellington, where he began the uphill undertaking of starting a poultry ranch. His parents and friends were skeptical the idea of his leaving a comfortable home and giving up a good position in the city to undertake a project about which he knew relatively little. At that time the only building on the property was an old ramshackle barn that had been built in the early part of the century. The remainder of the land was just weeds, a few eucalyptus trees on First Street, and three palm trees near the dirt driveway. The first year he was there, Charles had built a small house using wood from a chemical plant in Orange County. He was able to get the wood for free in exchange for the labor of tearing down the chemical plant. After the house, came the building of chicken pens, followed by the aluminum feed building. Just two years ago, Charles had a new home built, a large, rambling ranch house. He had done well in the past twelve years.

After her egg chore was completed, Elaine hurried to the house to get ready for the church youth meeting, or MYF for Methodist Youth Fellowship. She put on a white blouse and full print skirt over a couple of freshly starched petticoats. After adorning her pony tail with a blue ribbon and applying lipstick, she was ready.

"I hope you have a good turnout tonight," Lois said to her daughter as Elaine left the house to walk to her friend Beth's, on the way to the small church in town.

A refreshing breeze was blowing across town, making the air more pleasant. The golden grain fields, the eucalyptus and tamarack waved softly. The sun was lower in the sky, but still shining over Ellington's purple mountains on the west side of town. An occasional cricket was chirping, gearing up for the evening concert, peacocks in the distance called in shrill voices, and cows were lowing. Elaine, enjoying the sounds of the pleasant summer evening, stopped at a large wooden ranch house a short distance from her home, and knocked on the door. Beth Hathaway answered with, "Hi, I'm almost ready. Come on in." She was an attractive girl, slightly overweight, with brown eyes and curly brown hair.

"Well, how's our Elaine doing today?" boomed Mr. Jack Hathaway in a hearty voice. "How are your folks? Surviving the heat? Are you losing any chickens?"

"Not so far. We have a sprinkler system installed that keeps them cool," Elaine answered.

"I'll stick to cattle," Jack said. "Heat or blizzards, they can withstand anything."

"As if we'd ever get any snow out here," scoffed Beth. "I'm ready. Let's go, Elaine."

"Are you all set for school?" Elaine asked, as they headed north on First Street.

"As ready as I'll ever be. I've been sewing like mad-a dress, a blouse, and two skirts."

"You're so talented. I wish I could sew as well as you do."

"You had sewing, two years of it, in the 4-H Club," Beth pointed out. "I can remember the first garment we made. It was a skirt, made from those printed feed sacks that we got from the grain elevator."

"Oh, yeah, my old feed sack skirt," laughed Elaine. "I think Pam still has that in her closet. But in spite of my 4-H sewing, I still don't sew well. I'm just not the domestic type."

"Well, you're good at other things. You can write stories. You'll probably be another Louisa May Alcott. After you're famous I can tell everyone I used to know you. Not to change the subject, but it's hard to believe we'll be starting school tomorrow," Beth said. "We've waited so long."

"It doesn't seem like that long ago when we were starting First Grade," remarked Elaine. "The first time I saw you, you were behind your mother crying."

"What a memory you have. Well, I'll be just as scared the day high school starts, only I won't have anyone to hide behind. Initiation Day is what's got me worried."

"Oh, I think that will be a ball."

"I'm sure you won't think so after the seniors smear you with lipstick and make you bow down to them," Beth retorted.

"If the senior is a cute boy I don't think I'll mind one bit."

"Speaking of cute boys, look who is waving to us," teased Beth as they approached the church.

"Hi there," a friendly, masculine voice called out. Elaine looked up and saw Warren Fawcett smiling at her as he set out chairs on the lawn in front of the parsonage. He was tall with brown hair and an athletic build. "It's such a nice evening I thought we could have our meeting outside."

Adam Irby, a high school senior and brother of Natalie drove up, but Nat was not with him.

"Where's Natalie?" Elaine asked him.

"How should I know? Am I my sister's keeper?" he joked. "I think Mom needed her at home. Too bad she doesn't know how to get out of work the way I do. I'm just smart and conniving."

"And very modest too," Beth added.

"Okay, what am I missing?" asked Lucy Snowball, who had just arrived. She was a tall, slim redhead the same age as Elaine and Beth. Elaine thought she was appropriately named, since she had a great sense of humor like the actress Lucille Ball, and also the red hair.

"Not much since these guys never have anything worthwhile to say anyhow," remarked Beth, taking a seat. The rest of the group followed suite.

"Shall we get started?" Mrs. Fawcett asked. The pastor's wife was a small, dynamic woman, dearly loved by Ellington's young people. Most of the time, she led the discussion at the meetings, and once in a while her son was in charge.

I'd better take role first," joked Warren. "I don't want to miss anyone since we have such a large group."

"Well, at least you five are usually always here, and are really interested," Norma Fawcett said optimistically. "That's what counts. Small groups are easier to work with anyhow."

After a discussion on witnessing for Christ, the group made plans for recruiting new members, and for a swimming party, and argued over that would have the program for the next meeting (no one really wanted that job). Mrs. Fawcett then served refreshments. Elaine was sure she had never seen anyone eat as much as Warren.

"Well, it looks like tomorrow is the big day for you girls," Reverend Fawcett remarked. He had come out of the house to join the group.

"Mere Freshman," scoffed Adam. "Just wait til Initiation Day," he added threateningly. "I'll have you girls carrying my books, shining my shoes, doing—"

"You'll be sorry," Lucy interrupted.

"Oh, no. If you are insubordinate to a senior you'll be sent to Kangaroo Court at the frosh assembly. Then *you'll* be sorry. I can't wait to get back at Natalie for all the times she's been such a pesky little sister," Adam retorted.

"Oh, it's going to be a fun day," stated Warren.

"Well, I'm not so sure I want to go to high school after all," Elaine said.

"Shame on you guys for scaring such sweet girls," Reverend Fawcett said.

"Sweet?" asked Warren sarcastically. "I don't think so!"

"Well, I have to be getting home," Beth remarked. "I'm in the middle of a big sewing project, and I'll probably be up til midnight to finish."

"I'll drive you girls home," offered Adam.

"I'll ride along," Warren offered. This was a pleasant surprise for Elaine. Since he was already at home, he didn't really have to go along for the ride. The five climbed into Adam's old blue Ford, the girls in back. "See you later," Warren called to his parents as Adam swung around and headed down Main St. "Hey, Adam," he asked, "How about if we stop for something to eat?"

Adam looked at him with scorn. "We just had chips and dip. And you're hungry again? Where do you put it, man?"

"I can't believe you're still hungry," Elaine said from the back seat.

"Lady, I'm always hungry." They drove into the parking lot of Deb's Diner and the five sat in a back booth. The girls only wanted cokes, and Warren and Adam ordered hamburgers.

"Well, this is all very nice," Elaine said. "An added benefit of MYF."

"An extra bonus," remarked Adam.

"The others will be sorry they didn't come," Beth stated.

"That's their tough luck," Warren said. "Too bad more girls didn't show up. Then we could have had the pleasure of taking them *all* home."

"Too bad more guys didn't come to our meeting. Then we could have had a choice of who to ride home with," rebuked Lucy.

"Ohh, that was a low blow," Adam responded.

Elaine was enjoying the banter. She was hoping that Warren would ask her out sometime, now that she would be in high school. She had never been on an actual date because of the lack of fellows and the lack of activities in Ellington. She ardently hoped that high school would be different.

"Well, we'd better get you girls home now," Adam was saying. "It must be way past your bedtime."

"It is rather late for freshmen to be up," Warren added.

"You guys are not very amusing," Elaine told them.

"We weren't trying to be, I assure you," Adam stated. They dropped Elaine off at her home with the parting words of "See you tomorrow in school, Freshie!"

Chapter 2

At 6:00 a.m. on Monday Elaine was wide awake without the help of her alarm clock. She had an hour and a half to get ready for school, and it took her just that long. After bathing and dressing she hurried out into the kitchen.

"Good morning, Honey. You look very nice," Lois told her, as she bustled about the kitchen. "I guess you'll be eating earlier from now on, won't you?"

"I can get my own breakfast, Mom, so you won't have to get up earlier.

"No, no, I want to make sure you get a good breakfast every morning. Besides, you know I'm usually an early riser. It certainly looks like nice weather for the first day of school," she added, glancing out the window at the cloudless sky. She set a plate of scrambled eggs, bacon and toast before Elaine. Elaine wasn't really crazy about scrambled eggs, but she ate horridly and ran back to her room to recomb her hair and put on lipstick and eyebrow pencil.

"Goodbye, Dear, I hope you have a wonderful day," her mother called as she left.

"Now don't go getting into trouble the first day," Mr. Hummer added jokingly, just coming into the house from feeding chickens.

"Well, that fateful day has finally arrived," Elaine said to Lucy and Beth as they waited at the corner by the gas station, at one of the designated bus stops. "But I have butterflies. Suppose I walk into the wrong classroom or something?"

"Don't worry about it," Lucy assured her. "There will probably be a lot of freshman making dumb mistakes today."

"Oh, thanks a lot. You're a real comfort."

The bus stop was occupied by chattering students. Girls were in freshly ironed garments, while the fellows wore immaculate shirts and jeans or corduroy slacks. The bus came from the south, already having picked up the High Bluff students. It made another stop and Natalie Irby boarded along with a few others. She sat with Lucy behind Elaine and Beth. "That looks like a rough crowd in the back," she whispered to the other girls. "I don't know about those kids from High Bluffs."

The fourteen mile trip to Armedia didn't take long, although the bus made several stops along the way. At last it turned into the circle drive in front of AUHS. Students were streaming from several buses parked out in front. The 4 girls climbed the steps leading into the lower hall of the main building. Across the street from the school, beyond the drive in restaurant, was Lake Armedia, sparkling in the sun. It was slowly dwindling, due to previous years of drought.

"We have a nice view of the lake from here," commented Elaine.

"But look at this building," Natalie said. "It definitely needs a new paint job."

"Complaining already? Beth asked. "At least wait until you've been here awhile."

"We still have 20 minutes to go until the assembly," stated Elaine, glancing at the hall clock. "What do we do until then?"

"Stand around and look wise," advised Lucy. "Act like we know what we're doing."

They strolled casually down the lower hall, looking nonchalantly at the trophy case. "Hey, look who got a trophy for best sophomore athlete last year," Natalie exclaimed, pointing to the inscribed name, Willie Bannister. The girls all knew that he was one of Armedia's most popular boys. Nat and Elaine had met him earlier that summer at the Armedia Roller Rink, and he had skated with both of them a few times. Elaine knew that her friend still had a big crush on him. "Willie is so cute and so much fun," Nat said wistfully. "But sadly I hear he's going steady with Megan Frye now. Adam told me that she'll probably be the most popular girl in the freshman class. He says she's really cute. I know I'm not going to like her."

"Well, the four of us aren't so bad either," remarked Lucy. "We'll be making our mark on this place in no time. Those other girls had better watch out!" Everyone laughed.

They left the darkness of the lower hall and went out into the sunshine onto the student square next to the cafeteria. The area was dominated by upperclassmen, confident, laughing and talking. Everybody seemed to know everyone else. Students were having late breakfasts of donuts and milk, couples were holding hands, and guys were flirting with girls. No one was aware of the four girls.

"That must be Megan Frye," stated Elaine, recognizing her because of the boy at her side. Megan was a slim girl with a great figure, blonde hair in a pipe curl pony tail, and blue eyes which gazed into those of debonair Willie Bannister. He had his arm around her waist.

"Oh, there is DJ!" cried Beth. "A friend at last! It's good to see someone we know in this crowd. Let's go talk to him!"

DJ Morrison was a cocky kid of a boy who had been one of their fellow grammar school graduates. He was well-liked because of his jovial, outgoing personality. He lived in Ellington on a small melon farm. "Well, hello, girls," he greeted them with a mouth full of donut. "Am I glad to see you sweeties. You're a sight for sore eyes. I feel like I'm all alone, not a friend in the world."

"We didn't see you on the bus," Elaine stated.

"Where are all your Ellington buddies?" asked Natalie.

"I haven't found them yet. No idea where they might be," he added dramatically.

"Poor lonesome DJ," Lucy said. "Anyone have a handkerchief? I think I'm gonna cry."

"Everything went horribly wrong this morning," continued ham DJ, enjoying his audience of sympathetic listeners. "I got up late. I missed breakfast and I missed the bus. Woe is me!"

"DJ, you should be in Hollywood, not in high school," Beth told him.

He put his arms around the girls which proved to be difficult with a soft drink in one hand and a donut in the other. "Please don't leave me, girls," he cried. "You're my only friends."

"DJ, watch it, you're spilling coke on me," Nat said crossly. Suddenly he handed her the drink. "Here, you can have it. I gotta run! I see my good buddies! Bye! "And he hastily headed up the stairs to the classroom area, nearly knocking down a senior couple and a teacher in his flight.

"What a nutcase," laughed Lucy. "He acts like he's still in grade school."

They climbed the steps at a much slower pace, meeting Adam Irby and several other seniors. He passed without any greeting or acknowledgement whatsoever.

"Well, how rude can you get?" Beth asked rhetorically.

"Oh, he wouldn't stoop low enough to speak to us," said Natalie.

"Freshmen don't get treated like this all year, do they?" Elaine asked.

"I certainly hope not," remarked Lucy. "I guess they accept us after Initiation."

"Hey there, how're you guys doing?" asked a friendly, bright-eyed girl as she passed. She smiled at the girls as if they were long lost friends.

"That's Vicki Bannister, Willie's sister," Nat informed them. "She's a freshman too, one of us."

"Then she's a friend," Elaine said. "It sure comes in handy to have an older brother, doesn't it? You seem to know a lot of people around here."

"Oh Adam can be helpful at times, I guess," admitted Natalie.

The rings of the assembly bell rang loudly and clearly across the campus, officially opening school for the year. Students from all over Armedia Valley filed into the gym on the second floor of the main building. The upperclassmen sat in the front half of the gym, while the freshmen and sophomores sat on the right and left aisles in the last halves of the rows of chairs, keeping in tradition with the AUHS assemblies. The gym smelled of fresh paint and floor wax. Elaine, Nat, Lucy and Beth found seats next to Vicki Bannister and Megan Frye. The students were chanting their class yells. The Senior voices rang out loud and strong, and then the Juniors, louder yet. Even the sophomore chant boomed out with gusto. As their yell ended a dead silence fell upon the gym and everyone turned to look encouragingly or tauntingly at the freshmen. "Freshmen-rah!" a few voices called half-heartedly. The gym rang with laughter and catcalls. The crowd grew quiet when the student body president stepped out on the stage to lead the flag salute. It rang out 450 voices strong. The principal's brief, welcoming address followed. The teachers were introduced and the students were given their class schedule cards.

"Oh, this is terrible," Elaine moaned. "I have Algebra first! My favorite subject—ugg!"

"You should have signed up for General Math like we did," Lucy pointed out.

"Well, we all have Spanish and PE together," remarked Elaine, "but it doesn't look like I have you guys in any of my other classes. Not good! I'll have to go by myself." The bell rang, dismissing students to their classes.

"You'll survive without us," Lucy remarked as she left with Beth to find their first class. Nat, who had been talking to Megan and Vicki, introduced them to Elaine who was still complaining about her schedule. "I'm not even sure how to find the class," she moaned.

"Algebra?" Megan and I are going that way," Vicki was saying. She smiled at Elaine. "Come along with us. We'll either find it together, or get lost together, but there is strength in numbers."

Elaine had a really good feeling about Vicki with her warm brown eyes and friendly, dimpled smile. Megan Frye also seemed friendly and interesting. "I hear that the Algebra teacher is really cute," she was saying. "He's also the football coach."

"Maybe he will be more interested in football than Algebra," Elaine said hopefully.

"Speaking of football, isn't it neat that Willie's going to play quarterback this season?" Megan said. "Willie's my steady," she explained to Elaine as they turned into the lower hallway.

"So I heard."

"But he's my brother and is a big pain," Vicki stated.

"We've been going together exactly two months, one week, and five days," Megan said.

"Are you going with anyone?" Vickie asked Elaine.

She had to admit that she wasn't. "I'm just looking around."

"Me too," remarked Vicki, as they reached the large old fashioned classroom with its scratched desks. Mr. Carr, a tall, dark young man sauntered into the room, carrying a football.

"Good morning," he said. "The name's Carr. Since this is First Period, I know some of you aren't going to be too alert, especially since some of you have been able to sleep in all summer." He then proceeded to call roll, noting the boys who played football. "Our first game is only 10 days from now, and we've got a lot of work to do before then." He handed out the Algebra books, assigned them the first chapter, and discussed football the remainder of the period.

Elaine's next class was Spanish. She found her way to the right classroom where she met Beth, Lucy, and Nat. The teacher, Mrs. Mendoza, was very tall, slim and gray haired. She looked like the type that would take no nonsense from anyone.

"Well, *Buenos dias, clase. Como esta ustedes?* Now let's hear you answer in unison, '*muy bien gracias, y usted?*'"

They answered in this manner and DJ was heard to mutter from the back row in sarcastic tones, "Oh my, how cute!" Of course the comment was followed by laughter from the class, and Elaine knew that DJ Morrison would be the life of every class and the pet peeve of every teacher. Mrs. Mendoza was not about to put up with him.

"Young man, in thees class we have respect for the teacher and for the other members of the class. We do not make eensulting remarks. You hear?"

"Yes mam," the irrepressible DJ said with a bold grin. Mrs. Mendoza chose to ignore him.

A mid-morning break followed. Elaine found Vicki since she was sure she could not locate her next classroom by herself. It was the Art classroom. "I can't figure out where Room 22 would be," mused Vicki. "Let's ask these guys," she added, indicating a couple of good looking Seniors.

"I never heard of Room 22," one said with a gleam in his eye. "Have you, Kellogg?"

"Nope," Kellogg shook his head solemnly. "Must be some mistake."

"Too bad," said the first boy. "But I think that room was blown up during the war."

"Actually, it blew up when Lippie got mad and threw a cherry bomb at the class."

"Oh, Paul, a big help you are," Vicki said. "You just have explosions on the brain. Thanks loads, but we'll find it on our own."

They laughed. "Well, we really tried to help you ladies in distress. Just call on us if you two are ever in need of anything else. We aim to please. Just call for the Big Four."

"We'll call out the Marines," Vicki retorted. "Who needs you?"

Elaine was laughing heartily at the remarks flying back and forth, and wishing she could have thought of something clever to add to the banter. She always felt tongue-tied and bashful around boys. Vicki seemed so confident and sure of herself. "Those guys are cute," she remarked.

"Oh yeah, they're cute all right, and they know it too. That's Duane Kellogg and Paul Newberry. They call themselves the Big Four, along with two other guys. They're the most popular guys in the Senior Class . . . . and the wildest. They're friends of my brother, and treat me like a little sister, unfortunately."

"I hear most of the Senior Class is pretty wild," Elaine said.

"That's true," agreed Vicki. "We're really in for a rough Initiation this year."

When they finally located the art room in one of the bungalos at the back of the main building, they were 15 minutes late.

"Well, it looks as if the lost sheep have finally found their way to the fold," Miss Lippert greeted them. "Come and join the class, girls." They took seats in back of the room. She looks like an interesting teacher, Elaine thought. She was young, in her 20's, but dressed in an old fashioned manner in a long dark skirt. Her hair was cut "as though she's put a bowl over her head," Vicki later declared. Horn-rimmed glasses added to her role. However, she seemed very nice and had a good sense of humor. The students had long since nicknamed her Lippie.

Following Art, Elaine walked to English with DJ. "That Lippie is cool," he remarked in complimentary tones, "even though she does look like she came from outer space. But I am most definitely not looking forward to English class. It's going to be rough with old lady Teague."

"Yeah, you'd better be on your best behavior in her class."

"Hey, wait up," called a voice from behind them. DJ then introduced Elaine to his buddy from Armedia, Shawn O'Dell. He was a slim fellow Elaine had seen in an earlier class.

"Hello there," he said in a low, drawling voice. "So you're from that hick town of Ellington."

"Her family has a big chicken ranch," DJ explained, "and she lives in a chicken pen."

"DJ's dad owns a melon ranch," Elaine retaliated," and DJ lives in a cute little melon patch."

"Well, I live at the bottom of Lake Armedia," joked Shawn, "and I just come up every so often to check things out." By now they had reached their destination, and their chatter stopped abruptly. They quietly found seats. The freshmen were all very still, and not a sound was heard from them.

Mrs. Teague sat calmly at her desk waiting for the last bell. In spite of her diminutive size, the high school students feared and respected her more than any other teacher. Now she surveyed the class with ice blue eyes, and remarked in a calm voice, "My, what a quiet, well-behaved class. You're much better than my sophomore classes. I don't expect you'll be this way for long though." She chuckled to herself. "Once you get used to the newness of high school, you'll probably drive your teachers crazy." There was nervous laughter from the class. She continued, "I suppose you've heard that I'm the toughest teacher at this school. You've probably heard also, that I yell at people and throw things." She laughed. "I only threw something once and that was several years ago." She picked up at small gavel on her desk and gazed at it lovingly. "Yes, I did throw this at some character who seemed to think that what he had to say was more important than what I had to say. Naturally my aim was off, but I certainly scared the poor boy. And I broke the handle in the process. Yes, this little gavel is what keeps order for me. You are the only freshman class I have this year. I know, you're probably wishing you could be in one of the other frosh English classes. But in case you don't realize it, all of you had high scores on your achievement tests in English. And I am expecting great things from you, class."

Elaine was secretly glad to have Mrs. Teague for English because she knew she would learn from such a dynamic person. English had always been one of her favorite subjects, and she hoped to impress Mrs. Teague with her ability to write. She also hoped to do what many students deemed impossible-get an A on a report card.

English was followed by lunch. The student square was crowded with hungry teen agers waiting in line. Elaine, Beth, and Natalie, loaded down with hamburgers and soft drinks, made their way to the shady lawn beyond the circle drive, which overlooked the lake. Vicki joined them. "Megan is having lunch with Willie, so I thought I'd join you," she explained.

They discussed events of the day, teachers, students, and the coming Initiation Day. Everyone agreed that it would be rough. "My brother is making all kinds of threats," said Nat.

"So is Willie," remarked Vicki. "But he is only a Junior, and won't be able to get away with much. Of course he'll try. All the kids that have to ride buses will get the worst of it, they always do."

The bell rang shortly and Elaine went alone to her Geography class. Everyone was totally unfamiliar to her and she felt very much alone. Mrs. Gimple, the teacher, was an elderly, seemingly frail little lady with white hair and a high—pitched voice. Her manner seemed friendly but cautious. She took the entire class period explaining how useful geography would be. Elaine sat daydreaming about all the good times she would have in high school, and all the new friends she hoped to make. She was sure her next four years would be simply wonderful. There would be lots of social activities, and there would be dates. She thought of all the new friends she had met already. There were two girls across the aisle from her who looked as if they would be fun to know-a Hispanic girl with dark hair and eyes named Alma, and Karen, a petite, auburn haired girl who seemed very sweet.

The last class of the day was Physical Education in the gym. A young British teacher, Miss Morgan, taught the class which had over 60 girls. After giving instructions on gym clothes to purchase and assigning lockers, Miss Morgan dismissed them in her crisp English accent.

Initiation Day dominated the conversation on the homeward bus ride. The fateful day had been set for Friday. Elaine wondered how she could be both dreading it, and looking forward to it at the same time.

Chapter 3

"This stupid sewing machine is on the blink again," Elaine called to her mother. She angrily set a pair of scissors down and leaned back in her straight chair. It was the third time in the last half hour that the ancient Singer sewing machine had sewed nothing but tangled up knots, and Elaine's patience was wearing very thin.

"Calm down, Honey," Lois Hummer soothed as she walked into the bedroom. "Remember, this machine once belonged to my grandmother, so it's been around for quite a few years. You really have to treat it with kid gloves. I've owned it since my grandmother died, and that's been, oh, about 25 years or so. You really have to use patience and kindness with it, lots of TLC."

"Well, it's no wonder Beth can just whip up outfits in the blink of an eye," Elaine remarked, "her sewing machine is only a couple years old, and it does practically everything."

Little Timmie toddled into the room pulling a squeaky wooden train. "I want some waisins, Momma," he asked in a tone pitched to that of his train.

"How about looking after him, Elaine," Lois remarked "while I untangle this, and give you a little break from sewing?"

Elaine gladly handed her the red, orange, and brown print which was destined to become a sheath dress for school. She was in the process of adding more clothes to her already full closet. She gladly obliged her mother and took Timmie by the hand. "Come on sweetheart, I'll get a little snack for you."

"I not sweetheart," he shrilled indignantly. "My name is Timmie Hummer!" Elaine laughed and hugged the little boy. His blonde hair looked so cute, freshly cut in a butch. Freckles were beginning to appear on his snub nose. Elaine handed her little brother a handful of raisins and found a couple of oatmeal cookies for herself. She was pouring herself a glass of Kool-Aid when Pam came in from the front porch, carrying her hula hoop, and humming *That'll Be the Day*, a current Buddy Holly tune. She was small and looked very fit. Elaine envied her natural ability for athleticism and her tan which seemed so easily acquired.

"I just made a new hula hoop record," the younger girl announced, "and kept it going 116 times."

"Wow, that's pretty good."

"I would have done even better if Timmie hadn't come along and stood in my way just then. Hey, save some Kool-Aid for me."

Elaine found that her mother had the sewing machine running smoothly and had sewn a couple of seams. "You can get started on the facings now," She said, handing the dress to Elaine. "And by the way, don't forget that Daddy's birthday is coming up in a couple of days."

"Oops, I did forget. How old will he be?" Elaine wanted to know.

"You shouldn't ask your parents questions like that anymore," smiled Lois. "He'll be forty."

"Gee?" exclaimed Elaine, glad that she had many years to go before she reached an age as ancient sounding as forty. "I have an idea, Mom. Let's not say anything about his birthday all day, so he thinks we've all forgotten it. Then at dinner we can surprise him with his favorite dinner, cake, and presents."

"That sounds like a good idea. We'll warn Russ and Pam ahead of time, and we don't need to say anything at all around Timmie. Maybe we could even have a family outing like miniature golf or something," Lois went on to say. "We haven't done anything together as a family for a while."

As much as she loved her family, Elaine had begun to dislike going places with them lately. She wasn't exactly sure why she felt uncomfortable on family gatherings, but figured it was a teen age feeling, and she just wanted to be independent of them. She felt that her parents didn't really understand her, nor did they make any effort to do so, and she felt she didn't have anything in common with members of the family anymore. She got along with her two brothers, however. She enjoyed talking over school activities with Russ. He was only two years behind her in school and he was mature and intelligent for his age. His chief interest was photography and he never went anywhere without his camera and flashbulbs. He also active in the Ellington Boy Scout Troop, working on different merit badges.

Pam was a different story, and the two girls did their share of quarreling. It was hard for them to share their bedroom. The age span of four years was mainly responsible for their varied interests. At present Pam was active in sports of all kinds, and she also had a love for animals. She had a couple of rabbits which she was raising for her project in the local 4-H Club.

Lois Hummer's main activity was the little white Methodist church. She taught a 2nd and 3rd Grade Sunday School class, she was secretary of the Ladies Aid' Society, and she was the church pianist. Between the church activities and her work on the farm, she kept very busy. She was thrilled when Reverend Warren Fawcett and his wife, Norma had been assigned to the church several years ago, for the congregation had been steadily growing since their arrival.

Her husband, Charles, was also active in church, and on several different committees. He enjoyed listening to classical music, he was an avid reader, and he enjoyed traveling. He had taken the family on several trips to scenic national parks. He was also a very hard worker, and at times the responsibility of the farm laid heavily on him.

The surprise birthday party didn't go exactly as planned, however. When Elaine arrived home after school on Wednesday, only Russ was there, and he had some sobering news.

"Mom and Dad aren't here," he explained as Elaine walked in through the door. "They had to go to Armedia to take Pam to see Dr. Fox. "She got creamed big time at school today!"

"What are you talking about? What happened?"

"It was the last recess and some kids were out on the baseball field, mostly bigger kids, but Pam was in the game and she was the catcher, and one of the 8th graders was up at bat, and I don't really know how it happened, but when he swung the bat back, it hit her smack in the face. I guess she must have been standing too close. I was on the other side of the playground when it happened, but all the kids that saw it said there was blood all over, and that it was really scary. Some of the girls were crying." And Russ was crying too, as he ended the account of what had taken place.

Elaine felt her stomach drop as Russ relayed what had happened at school. The three older Hummer kids were a hardy bunch, and didn't have to make many trips to the doctor's office. She said a silent prayer that Pam would be okay. She deeply regretted the argument she and Pam had gotten into just that morning before school.

"I have to go gather eggs now, and I am doing half of Pam's row," Russ was saying. "You're supposed to the other half of Pam's row after you finish yours."

After finishing her egg gathering chore, Elaine remembered that today was her dad's birthday, and began looking around in the kitchen to see if her mother had had a chance to make the cake, and had it hidden somewhere. She didn't find it, but she did find the recipe for a basic applesauce cake, so she thought she should get started on it. They always had an abundance of homemade applesauce, and she was able to find the other ingredients in the cupboard. She was busy mixing and stirring when she heard her parents' car drive up. She went running outside to see her little sister.

"Well, we had quite a scare today," Charles was saying, "But our little girl is tough, and she's going to be okay." Pam was getting out of the back seat. The front of her shirt was splotched with blood and she had two of the biggest, blackest eyes Elaine had ever seen.

"Nothing was broken, thank God," said Lois. "This is one of those accidents that looked so much worse than it actually was. But, Honey, you're going to have to take it easy for a while," she added to Pam.

"But I don't want to take it easy, that's no fun," Pam was complaining. "My headache's almost gone, anyhow. And it was my turn to be up at bat next in the game, and I never got to."

'Well, maybe we can find something to do together for the next few days," Elaine told her as she walked her into the house with an arm around her. "We could play *Sorry* or *Go Fish*. Those are two games you always like to play."

"We'll see," remarked Pam, a bit suspicious of the sudden attention Elaine was showing her.

Mr. Hummer's surprise party was carried out successfully. However, Timmie almost gave it away. He was in the kitchen when Elaine pulled the cake from the oven. "Oh, boy," he cried, clapping his small hands. "I like cake. Can I have some pwease?"

"It's for Daddy's birthday," Elaine told him. "And you can have some for dessert." She was rather proud of the cake she had made. It smelled wonderful, and was only a little lopsided.

"Goody. I'll go tell him to come and eat now so we can have our cake."

"Don't you dare, Timmie," Elaine commanded, pulling him away from the kitchen door. "You'll spoil the surprise. Here, you can lick the spoon. And we'll eat as soon as he is done with the chores."

When Charles came in he was pleasantly surprised to see his favorite dinner of hamburgers, corn on the cob, and fruit salad on the table, and his place surrounded by home-made cards and gifts. "In all the excitement, I forgot I even had a birthday today," he said.

"Open dat one, Daddy," said Timmie, pointing a chubby finger to a small package he had helped wrap.

"Let's eat," suggested Russ. "I'm really starving and it has been a long day."

Chapter 4

"I think the whole concept of Initiation Day is way over the top," Lois was saying at the breakfast table on Friday morning. "Those seniors are just carrying things a bit too far. I would think the school would want to put a stop to the whole thing. I can't believe what you're wearing today!" Elaine looked as if she had just gotten out of bed. She wore her father's striped pajamas, a pair of old beat up slippers, and a polkadot necktie. Her hair was charmingly arrayed in eight ponytails. Make up was forbidden to the girls.

There had been an assembly the day before, and the seniors had handed out printed sheets which gave the frosh instructions on how to dress and what to bring. "The boys have to wear nightgowns and bedroom slippers, and have their hair in pin curls," stated Elaine.

"Gee, I am so glad I'm not in high school," muttered Russ, buttering toast. "But what if the boys are wearing a crew cut like I have? It's just too short to make pin curls."

"I guess I'll find that out when I see them today."

"I think Initiation Day sounds like a lot of fun," Pam remarked. "I hope they still have it when I start high school."

"Oh, you'll get your turn," Elaine told her. "With your two black eyes right now, you would fit in."

"Yeah, too bad Halloween's not here yet. I would make a good spook without any make up at all." She was taking her accident in stride.

"Well, if they'd put as much emphasis on schoolwork as they do on this hazing, think how much better off everyone would be," Charles observed between sips of coffee.

"I'd better get going," Elaine said reluctantly, "although I hate to leave the house."

"Don't forget your cookies for the seniors," her mother said, handing her a paper bag.

"Too bad you didn't put arsenic in them," Russ suggested, "or maybe Ex-Lax. Yeah, that's even better."

"Russ, the things you come up with," his mother said. "Good-bye and good luck today, Honey," she added, giving Elaine a big hug.

The freshmen at the bus stop were a sight to behold. Lucy's short, stubby pigtails were tied with brightly colored ribbons. Beth was in matching teddy bear pajamas and slippers. DJ wore a pink flannel nightgown with fuzzy red slippers.

"I hate to say this," Elaine told him, "but your colors clash."

"Oh, I'm so sorry about that," he said dramatically, "and by the way, your tie doesn't do anything for those p.j's either!"

Adam Irby, his sister Natalie, and Warren arrived about the same time. "Hey, boys and girls, you are looking lovely today," Adam called. He handed the girls each a cloth. "Beth, I want you and Elaine to start shining my shoes. There's a couple specks of dust on them. And Lucy, sweetheart, here is a whisk broom. My path needs sweeping off. Get busy, peasants." He produced a camera and started snapping photos, while the girls tried to turn their backs to him.

"We aren't at school yet", Beth said rebelliously, "and we're not shining your shoes til we get there!"

"Oh, but the day starts right here and now," stated Adam, "and you guys will wind up in Kangaroo Court for impudence if you don't go by the rules."

Other seniors were joining in the fracas. They grabbed DJ and a couple of other boys and smeared them mercilessly with lipstick.

"Was it this crazy last year?" Elaine asked Warren.

"Oh, yeah," he said. "I wouldn't go through that again for anything. "And this is nothing compared to what happens once you get on the bus."

"Speaking of buses, here it comes now," added Adam, looking down Main St. "I bet all the seats will be filled today, since most of us who usually drive are riding the bus to get in on all the fun."

The freshmen were made to crawl down the bus aisle and bow to each senior as they passed. At the rear of the bus they had to sing the Mickey Mouse song at the tops of their lungs

"Now we're going to have a little party with good things to eat," said a senior as if talking to small children. He passed out hot peppers to the huddle of frosh. Those who refused the delicacies were given mustard shampoos. All the freshmen were eventually.

"Have some cantaloupe," said another, pushing melon halves, seeds and all, into boys' faces.

"How about some whipped cream to go with your hot peppers?" suggested another, squirting the creamy liquid into their hair and faces.

"Boys! Take it easy!" shouted the bus driver from up front. "And don't make too much of a mess!"

"You heard what the man said, Freshies," they were told. "Now get down there and clean up this mess you just made! Put all the garbage in this bag." They halfheartedly obeyed.

After a seeming eternity the bus reached the high school. A huge crowd of students had gathered at the steps of the main building to take stock of the bedraggled 9th Graders. Elaine, Beth, Nat, and Lucy ran toward the washroom. "They told us it would be rough," Lucy pointed out, "but I didn't think it could possibly be as bad as all this! I'm scared!"

"Me too," wailed Beth, scrubbing her face with a wet paper towel. "And the day is just beginning. I've got mustard running down into my eyes and cantaloupe seeds in my hair."

"Most high schools have forbidden initiations like this one," Natalie told them. "Armedia is one of the few schools left that hasn't put a stop to it." Her father was on the school board.

"Well, if the school board does ban initiations, they'd better wait til we are seniors and have a chance to get even," Elaine said grimly as she rinsed off the sleeve of her pajama top.

The day seemed endless. At the mid-morning break everyone gathered out on the student square, the center of activity. The seniors in all their glory were requiring their slaves to do all sorts of ridiculous stunts. One senior had brought a chair with poles fastened to it, and four husky 9th graders were ferrying him around in it. Elaine found Vicki struggling in vain to carry a stack of books belonging to members of the Big Four. She was completely smeared with lipstick and had egg yolk on her face.

"Hi Elaine," she called merrily, "are we having fun yet?"

"Hey, you," Paul Newberry called to Elaine, "get over here and help your friend with these books, and don't be slow! Chop chop!"

Elaine gladly obliged. Waiting on such good looking fellows was almost a pleasure.

"Where are the cookies you were supposed to bring?" Duane Kellogg growled, dropping books into her arms.

"They already got eaten up by greedy senior boys like you," she retorted saucily.

"Well you should have brought more in the first place," Paul told her.

"I didn't realize you guys were such bookworms," remarked Vicki, noting the variety of books.

"Us? Bookworms? Are you kidding? We just got these so you could lug them around for us," Duane sneered.

"You girls have to find us at lunch," Paul said. "We'll need someone to stand in the lunch line for us. Meet us at the end of the lower hall. And don't be late! Got that?"

The girls walked back to Art class laughing. In spite of their complaints, they didn't mind playing slave girls to the Big Four. "Isn't Megan a sight to behold?" Vicki asked. Chained to Willie by a ring around her ankle, and in p.j.'s several sizes too large, she did look amusing. Willie was doing his best to protect her from the hazing of the seniors. "They'll get even with him for that at the assembly," Vicki added.

During the lunch hour the entire school gathered out on the front lawn. The frosh had to roll peanuts with their noses across the lawn under the sprinklers. They sang and danced for everyone, and they participated in water balloon fights and egg fights. The principal came down and demanded a stop to the egg fights. He looked rather perturbed, but no one paid much attention to him.

Elaine was fanning Kellogg and Newberry as they lay comfortably on the grass. Vicki was feeding them their hamburgers. "I think your class is getting the worst initiation the seniors have ever given," Newberry stated.

"I wouldn't doubt it," said Elaine.

"That's because we're the wildest class," Duane said proudly. "The principal isn't going to like it one little bit. What do you want to bet that all initiations will be stopped after this one?"

At the assembly after lunch a few freshmen were called up on the stage to perform various stunts. The sophomores and juniors, who had interfered, such as Willie Bannister, were called up on stage also, and smeared with lipstick. The assembly was followed by a watermelon feed and a tug-of-war with the sophs who won with ease over the tired and bedraggled freshmen. The tug-of-war officially ended the day's hazing.

"Now if I can just wash all this gunk out of my hair before the dance tonight," Elaine groaned as she, Beth, and Lucy got off the bus that afternoon

"That was the meanest thing the Student Council could do," Beth said. "Why do they have the welcoming dance right after Initiation? We'll all be an absolute mess!"

"My mom isn't going to let me in when she sees me," Lucy laughed.

"It sure would be nice to have a date for the dance tonight," said Beth wistfully. "But I hear Armedia boys don't date much."

"Especially not at the first of the year," Lucy pointed out. "Besides, I hear that everyone goes stag to the welcoming dance. Better way to meet guys. By the way, are we still riding up to Armedia with Adam tonight?"

"That's the plan," said Beth. "But it's complicated. A few days ago Natalie asked Adam if he would drive us four girls to the dance. Of course Warren would be going too, but Adam's car will hold six. However, I just found out that Nat won't be going. You know how strict her folks are. But Adam will still take us; I just talked to him on the bus."

"It would be really nice if they wanted to take us, as in a date," Elaine said, "since you sort of like Adam and I sort of like Warren. But all we are to them is Freshmen."

"They have known us for too long," remarked Beth. "They think of us as just friends."

"Maybe that's not such a bad thing," Lucy said. "Let's just concentrate on Armedia boys tonight at the dance. I met some really cute ones today."

"When you looked so cute yourself," Beth laughed. "And that reminds me, we'd all better get home and start washing all this stuff off."

Elaine finally got herself cleaned up after shampooing her hair three times, and scrubbing her face with all the energy she could muster. She put on a white sleeveless blouse with a Peter Pan collar, a pleated skirt, and saddle shoes with thick white socks, since the dance was to be a sock hop.

Promptly at 7:30 the boys arrived in good spirits. Elaine was the last to be picked up. The girls rode in the back seat. "Well, you look very different from when I last say you, Warren was saying, "and you smell better too."

"You try smelling good with cantaloupe juice and mustard all over you," Elaine retorted. "Besides, Adam wouldn't have let us in his precious car if we'd looked like we did several hours ago."

"That's for sure," Adam agreed. "But you girls made it through, and it are all behind you now, just a fond memory that you'll always carry with you. I got some good snapshots to show you once I get my film developed."

The conversation flowed freely and it didn't take long for them to arrive at the high school. "We're going across the street to the drive-in," Adam stated as he pulled into the parking lot. "Do you girls want anything to eat?"

"I just had dinner and I'm not at all hungry," said Lucy.

"Well, we certainly are," Warren replied. "See you later at the dance."

"That was just a sneaky way to get rid of us," Beth laughed, as they climbed the stairs to the dimly lit gym. "But I don't care, really. I want to meet lots of guys tonight."

"How can anyone be hungry at a time like this," Elaine asked. She had butterflies in her stomach, and was nervous about how the evening would turn out. Her first high school dance had to be really wonderful. They reached the gym, gaily decorated with red and white streamers. A huge sign read "Welcome Frosh."

"Yeah, that was a warm welcome all right," Beth said.

"Go on in, girls," Coach Carr told them at the door. "It's free for all Freshmen. You are Freshmen, aren't you?"

"I have the battle scars to prove it," said Lucy.

Once inside they joined Vicki Bannister and Alma Mendoza, the dark haired girl in Elaine's Geography class. "Hi! Join the wallflowers," she said with a laugh.

"Gee, how do we rate that compliment?" Elaine asked.

"This is what you would call segregation," stated Vicki. The guys stood in small groups at the far end of the room by the door. All the girls were at the opposite end of the room by the stage and record player. Only a few couples were dancing. At the beginning of the dance Elaine met more girls than she did boys. She was just getting acquainted with Alma, who was as much fun as Vicki and Megan were. Karen Gillespie, a quiet auburn-haired girl joined them. She was also in Elaine's geography class.

"What is that crazy DJ Morrison doing now?" Elaine asked, seeing movement out of the corner of her eye. He was decked out in a straw hat, a brightly colored shirt, and Levis. He was going up onto the stage behind the curtain, followed by Shawn O'Dell, in cut off Levis and a sweatshirt.

"No telling what those two are up to," Karen said. "I've known Shawn all through grammar school and he's always been kind of goofy."

"Same with DJ."

"How did they ever get into the dance dressed like that?" Alma asked. "They must have had to sneak in somehow."

"It's really surprising how childish many of these guys are," Beth stated. "I thought they'd get away from all that in high school."

"It's just mostly the Freshmen," Vicki said. "The Juniors and Seniors are the neat guys, well, most of the time anyhow. And I wish they'd ask us to dance."

"Ohh, that's a great song," Lucy was saying as *Jailhouse Rock*, Elvis Presley's latest song came on. It was a fast song with a good beat. The main problem with the fast songs was that hardly anyone danced to them. A few black couples were the only ones, and they were all good dancers. After that came some slow music, and gradually more couples began circling the floor. Elaine danced with various boys, all lowerclassmen. She was wishing that Duane Kellogg or Paul Newberry would ask her, but they were far beyond her reach. They only danced with popular girls, like Vicki and Megan (when she wasn't dancing with Willie). She was having a good time, however. She liked the records that were being played: *Love Me Tender*, another Elvis song, *The Great Pretender*, by the *Platters*, and *Earth Angel*. They were all songs that were currently very popular with teen agers. Adam and Warren had come back and she danced with both of them. Warren was a good dancer, although he told her he didn't dance much. Elaine couldn't help liking him, tall and husky, with a warm smile. He was holding her close and she was enjoying every minute of it.

Suddenly the music stopped and every light in the gym went out, leaving the students in complete darkness. Several girls screamed. "I always thought this was a cheap high school," Adam was heard saying, a few feet away. "They didn't even pay their light bill."

"This must have something to do with why DJ and Shawn were going backstage a while ago," Elaine exclaimed suddenly.

"That's where the switchbox is," Warren said. "Wouldn't you know that DJ would be in on something like that?"

"I hope they don't get caught and get in trouble," remarked Elaine. The lights suddenly came on again, as did the record player, and dancing was resumed as if nothing had happened. She danced with Warren two more times, which made her happy. But she noticed he also danced with Lucy and Beth about the same number of times. And he didn't talk to her that much. He seemed to have more to say to Adam than he did to her. The boys were arguing about how soon man would reach the moon.

"I say it will be a good 15 years," Adam stated. "They couldn't possibly do it before that."

"Oh, but they could," disagreed Warren. "All these scientists and engineers have to do is to hit on one little thing that will start the ball rolling."

"Who cares?" Beth whispered to Elaine, "just so the spacemen don't reach us first," she added jokingly.

"At least Adam and Warren act their age, not like children," Elaine replied.

She was very tired as she climbed into bed later that night. It had been a week of activity, stress, excitement, and emotion.

The entire month of September was filled with new activities. Elaine joined the Future Teachers of America and the Girls Athletic Association. She became a reporter for Armedia High's newspaper. She had wanted to work on the yearbook staff, but found it impossible to squeeze it in with all her other activities. She had been secretary of the Ellington MYF for the last two years mainly because no one else wanted the job. The small group met regularly every Sunday night. Sometimes there were seven at the meetings instead of just five. Natalie showed up once in a while, and DJ came when he didn't have anything else to do.

Thus the sunny month of September came to a close as the days gradually grew shorter and the nights more crispy-cold, and Elaine reached out for new horizons in her young, inexperienced life.

Chapter 5

The month of October turned out to be rather frustrating for Elaine. She missed several days of school because of the Asian flu. There was an epidemic of influenza sweeping across the U.S. that fall, and nearly half the students were stricken with it at various times. Elaine might have missed some classes, but she didn't miss out on school news, since she was on the phone every evening with Natalie.

"The classes sound like TB infirmaries because of all the coughing," Nat told her. "I just feel lucky that I haven't caught it so far."

"Well, I'm glad I'm almost over it. When I first came down with it, everything on my body was aching like crazy. I haven't felt this sick since I had the measles last year."

"Oh, I remember that," Nat said. "You were so upset because Elvis' first movie came out, and all of us girls went to see it, and you missed out on *Love Me Tender.*"

"Well, I saw it later but it wasn't the same, being the last one to see it. At least Mom took pity on me, and she and I and Pam went to see it after I got better. Your immune system must be working pretty well. You don't usually get whatever is going around."

"I'm tough," Natalie stated. "And you know what else? My dad doesn't let me go all the places the rest of you girls go, so I'm not around all the germs."

"Except in the classroom where everyone is coughing," Elaine laughed. "Why is your dad always so strict? Your mom doesn't seem to be that way."

"I think that if it were just up to her, I'd be able to go places, but my dad is a different story altogether. And I'm not waiting until I'm 16 to date. You know how your teen years are supposed to be some of your best years? Well, it's just damn unfair that I have to be sitting at home instead of out having fun. I'll figure out a way to sneak out. You watch!"

"Well, maybe your dad will have a change of heart one of these days," soothed Elaine.

Elaine was glad when she was able to return to school after four days of being at home. She was working hard at catching up. She was finding that Algebra and Spanish were very difficult classes for her. She could not for the life of her remember how to find the unknown answer X. It was hard for her to realize that she would have to work the problem backwards. In Spanish she had a good memory for vocabulary, but when it came to verb conjugations she was at a loss. She mostly enjoyed the rest of her classes, however.

"If you want my opinion, I think you're taking on too much this first year," her mother told her a couple of weeks later when they were cleaning up the kitchen after dinner. "Why don't you drop something?"

"Oh, Mom, I can handle everything. Future Teachers only meets once every two weeks during lunch period. And I like staying after school for GAA. That's only once a week and we play basketball or volleyball, and I still manage to get home on the late bus and get the eggs collected. Russ and Pam don't have to do it for me."

"I'm not sure why you're even in GAA," Lois remarked. "You're not the athletic type. I guess you enjoy it though."

"I do enjoy it and all my friends are in it."

"Are you going anywhere this weekend?" her mother asked.

"Well, I wanted to go to Desert Palms this Friday night for the football game," Elaine said meekly, knowing what her mother would most likely say.

The expected explosion came. "Desert Palms! That's almost one hundred miles away! That will be a really long trip! Think of how late you will get back!"

"But everybody is going," Elaine pointed out. "We all go on the rooter's bus together. It's going to be loads of fun. And I've missed the last two football games." Elaine was disgusted. How dull life would be if she did everything her parents wanted her to do.

"I don't like you going so far away, Elaine. And you just got over the flu not that long ago. You can't afford to miss any more school. After all, you're just beginning high school and you have three more years to have fun and go to games and other events. We'd like to see you concentrating more on your studies instead of thinking about how much fun you can have. I'll have to talk this over with your father."

"Talk what over with me?" Charles asked, coming into the room.

Much to Elaine's surprise, her father overrode her mother and gave his permission for her to go. "However," he told her, "When it's report card time, I want to see A's and B's on yours. You're really going to have to keep your nose to the grindstone on your school work."

"Thank you, Daddy," his daughter said, giving him a hug. "I will work really hard."

The rooters' bus going to the Desert Palms game on Friday night left Ellington so early that the sun had not yet disappeared behind the coastal mountains. Elaine and her friends were sitting toward the back of the bus discussing the usual topic, the Armedia boys.

"It's really disgusting they don't date, but just mostly hang around with each other," Beth was saying. "I really don't get it."

"Well, there is one guy who dates," said Megan proudly.

"Willie is an exception," Alma pointed out. "Most of the guys don't even dance at the school dances."

"They stand around in their little wolf packs discussing their cars, or guided missiles, or who is having the next beer party, and telling dirty jokes," stated Vicki, thinking of her brother's friends.

"Well, we girls stand around in our little hen circles and what do we discuss?" Megan asked. "Clothes, songs, hair styles, and boys. And maybe we don't tell dirty jokes, but we do gossip, which is just as bad, if you ask me."

"Well, maybe we wouldn't be if we were talking to guys," stated Vicki firmly. "They could pay more attention to us."

"I don't see why *you* are complaining," Lucy told her. "You seem to be friendly with every guy in school."

"That's just the problem. I'm like everyone's baby sister, and I get treated as such."

"Even that would be an improvement for me," Elaine said.

"Tell us, how did you hook Willie anyhow?" Karen asked of Megan.

She shrugged. "I guess he was just ready to be hooked."

"My dad told Willie to go out and find a girlfriend, so he'd quit hanging around with his buddies and getting into trouble," Vicki joked, ducking Megan's playful punch.

For the crowded students on the bus, the trip was long. But no one seemed to mind. They sang to pass the time: "Give a cheer, give a cheer for the boys who drink our beer, in the cellars of Armedia

High." *I've Been Workin' on the Railroad, Oh You Can't Get to Heaven, Ninety Nine Bottles of Beer,* their alma mater, and others.

As the bus rolled onto the streets of Desert Palms, the occupants grew noisier, and began cheering loudly: "We're from Armedia, couldn't be prouder! And if you can't hear us, we'll yell a little louder!" They waved to the band and drill team bus just behind them. Their bus pulled into the high school parking lot and the students wasted no time in getting off and finding seats in the bleachers. The girls had dressed warmly in anticipation of a cold evening, but the weather was even colder than they had expected. A howling desert wind blew gusts of sand in the girls' faces, and the sting of the air was sharp. Their heavy coats and wool capris pants didn't even seem warm enough. "Next time I'm wearing gloves and a scarf," Elaine said.

"I'm Little Red Riding Hood," Vicki remarked, pulling the hood of her crimson car coat over her head. "But now all I need is a wolf." Her comment brought laughter from the girls.

Elaine was thinking how lucky she was to be around this group of girls. Megan, Vicki, Karen, and Alma seemed to be some of the nicest girls in school, and they had quickly welcomed the three girls from Ellington into their group. Megan Frye, without trying, seemed to be the leader of the group. She was a girl with a mind of her own, having definite opinions on every subject. When Elaine had first met Megan, she had the opinion that she was a frivolous blonde, with little on her mind. But, to the contrary, Megan was a very ambitious girl. She already decided on a college and a major. She was encouraging Willie to go to college, and she was discouraging him from his aimless evening wanderings with his friends.

Vicki Bannister was the liveliest girl in the group. She was always ready with a joke, and kept those around her laughing constantly. Her warm brown eyes and dimpled smile were her assets. Her good natured ways and easy-going manner endeared her to those around her. She was unlike her best friend Megan in view of the fact that she never planned ahead of time and never worried about anything until it happened.

Karen Gillespie was small with a well—proportioned figure. Elaine didn't know her as well as the rest of the girls. She seemed to be a sweet, quiet girl, intelligent and well organized.

Alma Mendoza acted like the scatterbrained "nut" of the group. She could be loud at times. Alma was usually the first one to try out the new fads such as putting a blonde streak in her dark hair or wearing the new, pointed toed shoes. She never seemed to worry about grades and she never seemed to have any problems. Her favorite topic of conversation was boys.

"Gosh, I am numb already," Karen shivered, "and the game hasn't even started yet."

"It's going to be a long night," added Alma.

"If we were playing football we'd keep warm enough," stated Beth.

"We should go down and do warming-up exercises with the team," Elaine suggested, indicating the Armedia players, who looked big and husky and yummy in their red and white padded uniforms. The girls bought programs and noted the differences in weight and in size of the players on each team, and also realized that the Desert Palms had more players.

"They have twice as many players as we do," complained Vicki.

"And they all look like really big guys," Beth stated.

"Everybody keep an eye on Number 6," Megan told them. "That's my Honey, and he's going to do great things." Adam Irby was Number 22, a halfback. Warren Fawcett was one of the few sophomores on the team. He was a center, Number 74. Duane Kellogg and Paul Newberry were also team players that Elaine knew, if only slightly.

"Will the audience please stand for the National Anthem, played by the Desert Palms High School marching band," requested the announcer from his booth. Once the onlookers were standing, complete silence reigned in the stadium. Then the familiar strands of The Star Spangled Banner prevailed.

The Armedia team kicked off. A Desert Palms halfback caught the ball and started running it toward the goal line, but was tackled on the 30 yard line. The audience sat down. Elaine didn't understand very much about football, but tried her best to keep up with the game. When the cheering crowd around her grew silent, she judged that Desert Palms still had the ball, although it was sometimes difficult to tell. Desert Palms eventually inched closer and closer to the goal. Then an end from the opposing team caught a pass from the quarterback, weaving and dodging the players that were trying to tackle him. He was quick but Warren Fawcett was quicker. He made a flying tackle and stopped the player on the eight yard line. Armedia cheered, but now Desert Palms had a first and goal. In the play that followed, their quarterback was stopped again. Now the players were so close to the goal line that it was difficult to tell just how just how close, or where the ball was, but Desert Palms finally managed to carry the ball over the line and make a touchdown.

"Block that kick!" everyone yelled. The ball landed outside the goalpost bars, so only six points were made.

The spectators stood for the next kick-off, and Desert Palms kicked the ball into the hands of Adam Irby. His long legs skillfully dodged the opposing players, and he managed to run the ball for 36 yards, to the 45 yard line, accompanied by loud cheering. "First in ten, do it again!" yelled the crowd. And Armedia did it again, gradually working their way down. Desert Palms' defense was good, however. Duane Kellogg kept making incomplete passes intended for the receivers. By the time Armedia's 3rd down came, they lined up and kicked a field goal. At the end of the first quarter the score was 6-3

The second quarter began with Desert Palms running the ball. An unfortunate fumble caused their loss of the ball, however. Then on Armedia's second down, the game seemed to come to a standstill. Both teams were gathered in a small circle.

"Oh darn, someone must be hurt," Beth cried. "Hope it's not one of our guys!" But there were no injuries. The girls were relieved to learn that the game was stopped only because one of the players had lost a contact lense.

"How funny," Vicki exclaimed with a laugh. "Excuse me folks, but I think I misplaced my contact lense. It's somewhere in the grass on this little field. Watch where you step now!"

"Talk about a needle in a haystack," said Elaine, "that's way worse."

The game resumed, and it wasn't long before Desert Palms made another touchdown, and the extra point. Armedia got the ball, but was then penalized 10 yards for clipping.

"What's clipping?" asked Elaine.

"I think that's where they get hit from behind," Megan explained.

"Well, I think that was a lousy call," stated Alma. "That referee needs glasses."

"One-two-three-kill the referee. Three-two-one-kill the other one," chanted the rooters, who were growing discouraged. But the referees called several other penalties on Armedia as the game progressed. By the time the half rolled around, the scoreboard read 20-3. The girls all went to the concession stand and fortified themselves with hotdogs, popcorn, and hot chocolate. They needed to get up and move around anyhow to get warmed up.

"I can't believe that none of us thought to bring blankets," Lucy said, as they settled back down on the bleachers. "I guess we'll know to do that next time."

"Ohh, this hot chocolate tastes wonderful," Karen said, sipping slowly. "Here we sit stuffing ourselves while our guys are running themselves ragged for the glory of our school."

"Well, they don't have to play football," Vicki said matter-of-factly. "The only reason Willie plays is because my dad says he has to keep out of trouble, or he'll become a juvenile delinquent or something."

"Vicki, will you stop telling everyone such horrible lies about Willie," Megan reprimanded. "People might start believing you."

"Sure they will. So what?" asked the irrepressible Vicki.

Desert Palms started off with the ball in the third quarter. The quarterback handed it off to the running back, who fumbled it. The crowd watched, tensed, as Adam who was just in the right place at the right time, intercepted it, bringing wild cheers from the rooting section.

"That Adam is such a neat guy," Beth whispered to Elaine.

"What exactly happened," she asked. "I'm cheering, but I'm not really sure why. It's so hard to keep my eye on the ball."

"Adam just recovered a fumble, you big dope." Beth told her, "So we have the ball now. Maybe you need glasses," she added. And Armedia kept the ball as they worked down toward their goal line. Then Paul Newberry caught a pass from Willie and headed toward the goal line. Unfortunately, Armedia's blockers couldn't keep him from being tackled. The gun went off ending the third quarter. No points had been made.

The fourth quarter went very fast. Desert Palms made another touchdown and an additional point from the kick, making the final score 27-3.

The disappointed, half-frozen Armedia High rooters went slowly back to their buses. The warmth of the bus felt wonderful, after sitting out in the cold, but the trip home was long, and much quieter compared to the trip into Desert Palms. Tired students dozed in their seats, some even sleeping in the aisle, having been drained of all their energy. As they came back into Ellington the bus driver stopped as close as he possibly could, without leaving Main Street, to each person's home or driveway. It was about 1:00 a.m. when Elaine stepped off the bus, and it felt extremely dark, and lonely and quiet. She watched the tail lights of the bus round the corner and disappear into the night, and her heart began pounding faster. She had to walk about half a block on First Street before turning into the Hummer's long drive.

It's blacker than the ace of spades out here," she thought. "Why didn't I bring a flashlight? That would have been the smart thing to do." Ellington, being an unincorporated town, did not have any streetlights. And she could hardly see her hand in front of her face. There was only a thin sliver of a new moon in the western sky. She wished she could run, but there was always the possibility she could trip on a rock or step in a hole. The silence was very unsettling. She never knew the little town could be so deathly quiet. Every darkened bush and tree seemed to be a potential hiding place for a Boogeyman. She turned into the long driveway, which was about half the length of a football field. She picked up her pace a bit. "If it were a few hours later (or earlier in the morning)" she thought, "at least then there would be roosters crowing." She was over halfway down the driveway. The porch light at the house had been left on, and nothing ever looked more welcoming or friendy. Uh-oh, something was touching her ankle, and her heart dropped. Oh, it was just Boomer, the coal black kitty, the family pet, rubbing her legs. She gathered up Boomer in her arms, in a hug, and ran the last few feet, shutting and locking the back door of the Hummer home behind her.

*   *   *

The MYF continued to meet every Sunday evening, but the attendance of five or six was at a standstill. Warren suggested a Halloween party, an idea which was met with approval. Beth volunteered her family's barn, and the group made plans to clean and decorate Hathaway's barn on Saturday morning, the day of the party. Hopefully some new members could be recruited at the party.

Friday night, however, was Halloween. Elaine, Beth, and Lucy did not want to miss out on the "Trick or Treating" fun although they were older than most of the spooks and goblins out on the town that night. Actually the trick or treating was just an excuse for them to roam around Ellington and get into mischief, although they would most likely observe others doing the misdeeds than actually doing some of their own. They met at Elaine's home wearing car coats and ugly masks. Beth's younger brother was with them, so he and Russ could trick or treat together.

"Glad to see you girls wearing masks," Charles Hummer joked. "That way you won't scare people as much."

"Very funny, Dad."

"Yeah, you don't want anyone to have a heart attack when they see your real face," Russ remarked.

"Gee, Russ, do you think you're going to get a lot of candy or something?" Elaine asked, noticing his enormous shopping bag.

"Well, Billy's got a pillowcase, which is even bigger," Beth said of her brother.

"You boys won't even be able to carry all your loot home," Charles stated.

"There is a lot of rough stuff going on in Ellington on Halloween," warned Lois. "You girls need to be really careful. I wish you'd reconsider and go with us instead." She was driving Pam and a couple of her friends around

"Oh, Mother, we wouldn't have any fun going with those punks."

"We wouldn't want you anyway," retorted Pam, adjusting her witch hat.

"We'll be all right, Mrs. Hummer," Beth said. "We're armed." She produced a squirt gun and flashlight from her pocket.

They left the house and went down the driveway, turning left on First Street. "Look what I've got left over from July 4th," Lucy said, reaching into her pocket for a package of firecrackers.

"I'm glad you didn't let my mom see those," Elaine remarked. "Let's throw them at some of the older guys around here."

"Not a good idea, then we'd really be in big trouble," Lucy replied. "I'm not sure what we should do with them yet. But we'll think of something."

"I wonder what the town will look like by tomorrow morning," Beth mused. "Probably sitting in ruins." They turned left on Tamarack Street and stopped at a few houses for candy.

"That car seems to be following us," Elaine said, walking faster. "Let's turn around and get back onto Main. It's too dark around here."

"We could wait in the grove till they pass," suggested Beth, indicating a small grove of eucalyptus trees on their right. She and Elaine ran into the grove as the car approached. Lucy, unafraid, followed them more slowly.

"Lucy, run!" Beth and Elaine called in unison as the car slowed way down, and a watermelon came crashing into the shrubbery, just missing Lucy by inches. Laughter and catcalls were heard from within the car as it sped down the street. The girls sank down on the dry leaves laughing.

"That was a close call for you, Lucy," Elaine sighed, her heart pounding in spite of their laughter. "Who were those guys anyhow?"

"I didn't really have time to get a good look at them," Lucy said, out of breath. "Probably Armedia boys. They drive down this way to do their dirty deeds because they don't have cops around here. This town seems to be a magnet for all the mischief makers in the valley."

"I bet there'll be someone patrolling the town tonight," Beth predicted. "They're wising up."

"They should be, after all that mess around here last year." Shhh, what's that?" Elaine whispered suddenly. They could hear the crackling of dry leaves not very far away.

"Someone is over there in the bushes," Beth said, panic stricken. Then there was a sudden flash and the loud boom of a firecracker. The girls screamed and then they heard DJ Morrison's snicker. He was with two other boys. "Bet we scared ten years growth out of you," DJ was saying, as they doubled up with laughter.

"Now would be a good time for you to use your firecrackers," Elaine whispered to Lucy, who had thought the same thing and was pulling them from her jacket pocket.

"I never thought the day would come when I'd be glad to see you guys," remarked Beth. "But I am now. Stick around. It's too scary for us to be wandering around alone, and too many weird things are happening out there." The girls were trying to distract the guys, as Lucy backed up a bit to discreetly light the fuse to her firecrackers.

"Well of course strange things are happening. What do you expect? It's Halloween! What are you? Chicken or something?"

"We have to get going," said DJ. "We've got important business to attend to at the grammar school. Like soaping some windows. We're even gonna leave a little present on the front steps—pumpkin pie in the form of banana squash!"

"You guys are so juvenile," Beth said disgustedly.

"Well, we get a lot more fun out of life than you girls do," they responded. "We'll see you later. Don't do anything we wouldn't do."

"Boys will be boys," remarked Elaine. "Hey, what happened with your firecrackers?"

"They must be too old or something," was Lucy's answer, as they headed out of the grove and back toward Main St. "Nothing happened when I lit the fuse. What a letdown."

A few minutes later, in front of Barney's General Store, they came across Warren and Adam, up in a tree of all places. They wouldn't have even noticed the guys, except for the fake sounding bird calls they were making.

"And what are you two trying to pull off, may I ask?" Beth wanted to know. "Aren't you a little old for tree climbing?" The boys laughed gleefully but said nothing.

"Can you believe this mess?" Lucy exclaimed, pointing to the sidewalk in front of the market. It was covered with squashed melons, pumpkins, and overripe tomatoes.

"Looks like DJ and his cohorts have been this way," Elaine said. "What a waste!"

"Who? DJ or the melons?" Adam asked, climbing down from the tree. "I guess they can afford to lose a few spoiled melons, since they grow them on their ranch."

"The police aren't doing a very good job of patrolling around here," stated Beth.

"Most of the force is up in Armedia," Adam informed them. "There have been rumors of a fight. Kellogg and Newberry's group against the Mexicans."

"Oh really?" Lucy asked eagerly. "Take us up there, Adam. We want to see what's happening. We always miss out on stuff."

"Oh, there's probably not a thing happening," Adam said. "You know those guys, they're all talk and no do. Besides, what do you think we are—some kind of taxi service?"

"Hey, Elaine, come here a minute," Warren called, as he dangled a rope from the branches of the umbrella tree. "Pull on the rope."

"I'm not dumb enough to fall for your little trick, Warren. You think I want a bucket of water dumped on my head?"

Warren laughed as he slid down from the tree. "It really wasn't intended for you. DJ and his buddies are bound to come back by this way, and since those guys are all so nosy, they won't be able to resist pulling the rope."

"How funny," Beth exclaimed. "It will serve them right for all the mischief they've done tonight."

"What's even funnier," remarked Adam, "is that a dozen cracked eggs are in that bucket, instead of water. We just bought some eggs real cheap from your dad."

"He probably had no idea what you would be using them for," Elaine laughed. "He did tell me that DJ asked him if he could buy some rotten eggs, and Dad told them he never has any rotten ones, that they are all fresh."

"Well, the nice fresh eggs are sitting up in that tree just waiting to fall on someone." They doubled up with laughter.

"I hope no innocent little kid comes along and pulls that rope," Lucy said.

"We'll stay behind the store building and keep an eye on things," Adam said. "You girls are welcome to join us if you want."

"Uh-oh, here some a cop car," said Warren. "They're an hour too late. Let's move it. I don't want them to think we're responsible for this mess." They all hurried behind the market as the patrolman drove slowly by shaking his head at the cluttered sidewalk and street.

Fifteen minutes later DJ and his companions came by, casually smoking cigarettes. "Wait til old man Withrow sees that school building" one of the boys was saying. "But that was a close call. We got out of there just in the nick of time."

"Hey somebody left a rope in that tree," JD pointed out. "And I just now had an idea what we could do with it." As he reached for it, one dozen eggs came tumbling down, shells cracking, covering the boys with a sticky, gooey mess. "Oh shiiiiittttt!"

The group behind the store didn't wait to hear any more, but hastily climbed into Adam's car, before they were discovered, and quickly turned down D St.

The girls felt that their Halloween night had been rather enjoyable. The MYF Halloween party the following night also turned out to be fun. Hathaway's barn had been cleaned out that morning. Bales of hay were moved around and set in corners. Fake cobwebs and spiders were strung across the high ceiling (and a few genuine ones as well). Skeletons danced from the black and orange streamers, and black cats pranced. The traditional tub of apples was on the floor, and apples hung from strings. Eerie glows came from jack-o-lanterns.

There was a surprisingly good turnout, considering Ellington was in a more remote part of the valley, and that the normal MYF group was small. At the beginning of the party, no one had any idea who anyone else was. Elaine had told no one what her costume would be. She had a rubber mask with a sad hobo's face, and her hair was tucked under an old hat of her father's. She wore his old plaid shirt and an ancient pair of overalls she had found at the Goodwill Store. A pillow helped to fill them out. She wore a sign that featured a popular saying from a current song, "I got hit with an ugly stick." When the party first started, she felt very much alone, not recognizing anyone. No one was saying much for fear of being discovered. But Elaine disguised her voice and went around hitting everyone with her stick. One costume which had everyone puzzled was a "dead man" with a grotesque green face. He was being carried around on a stretcher, and sheets were draped from the stretcher (which was nearly six feet high) to the floor. After the unmasking, Willie Bannister was revealed as the "dead man." He had carried a light weight board perpendicular to his body, and even with his head, which he tried to hold back in lying position. The sheets had hidden the rest of his upright body. He had won first prize for his cleverness and originality. Megan and Vicki were clowns named Tweedle Dum and Tweedle Dee. DJ had been some sort of Frankenstein. "Not far from his natural self," someone had said.

After the unmasking they played a few active games, and then roasted hot dogs and marshmallows over a small fire behind the barn. Of course that was followed by the telling of ghost stories around the campfire.

Elaine thoroughly enjoyed the party. She only wished that Warren would think of her as more than a friend, and would ask her out. Her freshman year would be a complete failure if she had to remain dateless for all the games, parties, and activities.

Chapter 6

Report cards came out in early November. In spite of Elaine's promise to her dad to study hard and get all A's and B's, things didn't exactly work out that way. She got C's in Algebra, Spanish, and Art, and B's in English, Geography, and P.E. Elaine was frustrated. In grammar school, it had been so easy for her to get good grades. But high school was a whole new ballgame. She felt really bad as she handed her report to her father, and hoped he wouldn't be too upset. "Well," he mused, "the good news is that you have room to improve. I know you are trying to learn new study habits. It does make a difference if you have good study habits and know how to take notes in class."

"I feel like I let you down," Elaine said glumly. "Algebra is hard because Mr. Carr doesn't really explain things too well, and usually ends up talking about football, his favorite subject." Mr. Carr gave the students a short assignment at the beginning of every period which didn't take them long to complete. Then they would talk among themselves while Mr. Carr would discuss football with the guys on the team. He wasn't always predictable, however. Once he bawled Vicki out for talking and made her cry. He was continually ordering Shawn O'Dell out of the class because Shawn wasn't afraid to talk back.

Every time Charles heard about Mr.Carr's class he grew most indignant. "What kind of schools do we have nowadays?" he would ask his wife as if she were responsible. "Sounds like all they do is play football, have band practices, pep rallies, and dances. I'm going up and talk to the principal about this Algebra teacher. This is what we pay taxes for? It's no wonder the Russians are getting ahead of us!"

"I think maybe I should start tutoring you in Algebra," Charles was saying. He had studied engineering in college, and had a mathematical background.

"That's a great idea, Charles," Lois praised him. "I think that would help a lot." Elaine wasn't so sure about that, but she agreed to give it a try.

If Elaine wasn't learning much algebra, she certainly felt that Spanish made up for it. Mrs. Mendoza expected perfection from her students and drilled her class continually. Once in the classroom, they could only speak in Spanish.

Art Class was thoroughly enjoyable, even if one was not artistically inclined. Elaine and Vicki "relieved their pent-up emotions," as they put it in their colorful paintings of "modern art."

"Add this to your picture," Shawn suggested, turning around and adding a large brown spider. He and DJ nearly drove poor Miss Lippman crazy with all their antics. In spite of her old fashioned appearance, she had a good personality and was a teacher the students termed a good sport.

During lunch period Elaine's group of friends sat out under the pepper trees on the front lawn, basking in the sunshine, which was still warm for the November. The main topic of conversation was the traditional Turnabout Dance, sponsored by the Girls Athletic Association.

"It's going to be on Wednesday night this year," Megan was saying, "the night before Thanksgiving vacation starts. I hear there is going to be a really good band. Now is your chance to grab a date, girls. Anybody want to buy a ticket?"

"I don't know if I want to ask a boy," Vicki remarked. "After all, they don't seem very enthusiastic about taking us out."

"I'd feel silly asking a guy anyhow," Karen said in her quiet way.

"Besides, who wants to spend money on them?" asked Beth.

"Well, I'm going to pop the question to someone," announced Alma. "There's such a big choice of guys around here that I'll have to put all their names in a hat and draw one. I wonder who that lucky fellow will be?" They all laughed.

Elaine was quiet as she thought about asking Warren. But he didn't seem interested in her, except as a friend. She wondered if he would change his mind about her if he saw her in a semi-formal looking feminine and pretty. It was worth a try, she decided.

The other subject everyone was discussing was Armedia's homecoming festivities. Besides the football game were the

Homecoming Parade, the Rooters Bonfire, and the nominating of two princesses from each class.

"You'll all have to vote for me of course," joked Alma, tossing her head and preening.

"As Freshmen, we'll have to have a really good float for the parade," Megan remarked, "just to show the rest of the school."

The bell rang and the girls walked slowly up the steps. As Elaine opened her locker near the classrooms on the upper landing, a white envelope fell out. It was addressed in typewriting to her, so she opened it. The message inside was also typed. It ready: *Dear Elaine, I've had my eye on you for a couple of months now. I think you are pretty cool and cute too. You would be surprized at how much I know about you. I know that you live on First St. on a chicken ranch in Ellington, mailing address Rte. 1, PO Box 58. I know that you were with your family playing menature golf on a Sat. night a couple of weeks ago. As you can probly tell, I get around. I may know a great deal about you, but I would really like to get to know the real you. We have one class together, and just from our one class, I can tell that you have a great personalty and are a very sweet girl. But there is no way I can meet you. I have 2 left feet and don't dance much, so meeting you at a dance is out. I don't have my drivers license so I can't take you out. Looks like I'll just have to be content with seeing you in my faverite class. So long for now, Your Secret Admirer.*

"What is it?" Vicki asked, looking at Elaine's puzzled face. "Did you get some bad news?"

"Oh, you have to read this," she exclaimed, handing Vicki the note.

"My gosh, this is too much" Vicki laughed. "Do you have any idea who it is? I'll say one thing; he sure can't spell worth a darn. It is kind of neat though, getting a secret note. You'll have to work on finding out who he is. See you later."

Elaine couldn't figure it out. She wondered if he was someone she knew, playing a trick on her. But then she wondered why anyone would go to the trouble, if they already know her. How did he know her address? In Geography she passed the note to Karen who was thoroughly puzzled, and to Alma who laughed out loud and received a reproving look from Mrs. Gimple. They had to postpone their discussion of the note, since the teacher was keeping an eagle eye on them.

The girls were involved in a volleyball game in P.E. As they raced for the locker room and the showers, Vicki called out, "Guess who has a secret lover?"

"Mr. Anonymous himself," added Lucy.

"Looks like we have a real Mystery Man," Megan said to Elaine. We girls will have to get on the ball and find out who the heck this guy is."

He remained an unsolved mystery however. And as far as Elaine's affairs of the heart were concerned, she was only interested in Warren. Because of him, she rarely missed going to church, or to the MYF meetings. To her, he was perfect in every way. He was intelligent and ambitious; he had a good personality, was good looking, and was well-liked. Elaine sat daydreaming about him on a rainy Sunday afternoon. She was sitting on her bed, trying to concentrate on *Ivanhoe* for her English class. She gazed out the front bedroom window at the raindrops slowly trickling down the glass, the wet lawn beyond, the shining shrubbery, and the cloud-filled sky. She decided that if she got the chance at MYF that night, that she would ask Warren to the Turnabout Dance. The dance was more than two weeks away, but several of the girls already had dates. Beth was going with Tom. Vicki had given in and asked Paul Newberry. Alma had asked a junior boy; Karen was going with a guy she liked in her band class. Megan, of course, was going with Willie. Natalie, Lucy, and Elaine were the only girls in the group who had not asked anyone. Natalie's parents were not allowing her at attend anyhow. Elaine felt much sympathy for her friend who was never allowed to have much fun. She had a feeling that Natalie would rebel sooner or later.

Elaine took extra care in getting ready for MYF that night. She was frustrated with her hair, which wasn't cooperating at all. "You sure do look dressed up," Pam remarked, coming in from gathering her share of eggs. She was dripping wet. "I bet you're getting dressed up just for Warren."

"Oh, Pam don't be silly! I don't care one bit for Warren!"

"Then why is his picture on your bulletin board?"

"Oh, I put that up a long time ago, when I liked him."

"And you still do," the younger girl persisted stubbornly.

"Why don't you go jump in the lake," Elaine told her, leaving the room.

The number of MYFers had become a bit larger since the Halloween party. There were eight in attendance that night. The subject of the discussion, led by Mrs. Fawcett, was "Taking a Stand" and dealt with various temptations teen agers face on drinking, smoking, and premarital sex. At the present time Elaine was sure she would never be faced with any of these temptations. Her girlfriends didn't smoke or drink and she figured that many girls in her class didn't either. However, she wasn't so sure about the older girls. There were rumors of parties where girls had made fools of themselves because of too much liquor. And she didn't have to worry about how to conduct herself on a date, simply because of a lack of dates. She almost wished she had that to worry about. She was somewhat consoled by the fact that some of her best friends were faced with the same problem. She brought herself back to the present, and to Norma Fawcett's words, "It is so hard for young people to be different, to go up against the crowd, to withstand peer pressure. If one of you went to a party where drinks were being served, could you, as a good Christian refuse, although all your friends were drinking?"

"But that's not a problem if you run around with a nice bunch of kids," Lucy pointed out.

"You're absolutely right," Norma said. "Being in with a good group of friends is most important, probably more than half the battle. But some of these temptations are something you're definitely going to run into later on in high school, and most definitely in college."

"I've been faced with decisions like that," Warren said gravely. "Especially with my buddy Adam around. This guy is a bad influence," he added with a twinkle in his eye.

"Are you sure it isn't the other way around?" his mother asked, and everyone laughed, for they all knew that Adam was a very clean cut guy, and a good Christian. It was a wonder, Elaine thought, since his father was an atheist. Adam ended the discussion with a prayer: "Dear Lord, guide us in our footsteps as we meet these temptations in our everyday lives, and help us to realize that it is You we must follow, not the crowd. Give us the strength and courage to be a witness for You, so that we may influence others to follow You. In Christ's name we ask this, Amen."

"And please, dear God, give me a chance to ask Warren to the Turnabout Dance, and please let him say yes," Elaine prayed silently.

After the meeting Elaine and Beth went out to the church kitchen to prepare the cocoa and cookies. Elaine was sure that Warren would be there in a moment, since he was physically unable to stay away from food. The girls had it all planned out. Once he came into the kitchen, Beth would make an excuse to leave so that Elaine could ask him the question that had been bothering her for days.

"But what if he turns me down?" she asked.

"Don't be silly," Beth said crossly, mixing chocolate powder. "Why in the world would he turn you down? I'm sure he'll be glad to take you. The four of us will double date, and we'll have a great time. He likes you, I know. He's always asks you to plan MYF activities with him."

"Big deal. Why doesn't he ask me out then?"

"Well, you know he is saving money for college. He isn't taking out anyone else. Adam certainly isn't beating a path to my door either."

"It doesn't look like Warren's going to come in here," Elaine said. "Sounds as if he and Adam are having another one of their discussions."

"It's all a case of mind over matter," they heard Warren say.

"Then where does the law of gravity come in?" asked Adam. "That has to be considered."

"I'll prove it to you," Warren said stubbornly. "Dad, you've seen this work, haven't you?"

"It can be done," Reverend Fawcett agreed.

"Elaine, could you come here for a minute?" called Warren.

The girls exchanged puzzled glances. "Wait till we get the food ready," she called back.

"Oh, just leave it. We need you right now!"

"This I can't believe!" Elaine exclaimed, rinsing off cookie crumbs. "Whatever Warren is trying to prove must be awfully important. I never thought I'd see him not interested in food."

They went back into the church social hall. "Okay, who is the lightest?" Warren was asking. "You are, Elaine. Have a seat in this chair."

"Hey, what are you up to?" she asked skeptically, although glad enough to be the center of his attention. "I don't know if I want to be in the middle of this."

"This is a trick I saw done at MYF Camp last summer," explained Warren. "It's supposed to prove that with concentration, anything is possible, a case of mind over matter. All you have to do, Elaine, is relax. Adam, you and Lucy stand on her left side, and Beth and I will stand on her right side. The object is for all of us to pick Elaine up in the air, each of us using only two fingers."

"Don't you dare drop me," Elaine told them.

"First we have to really concentrate," stated Warren. "Everybody, place your hands flat on Elaine's head, one on top of the other, like—so. That's it. Now gently press down."

"What's this supposed to prove?" Lucy asked.

"Builds up pressure or something. Now when I count to three, let's all concentrate on getting her up into the air." He folded his hands but extended his two forefingers. "Each of you fold your hands this way when you pick her up. Put your two fingers under her knees and arms, and lift when I say 'three.' "

With their hands on Elaine's head, they concentrated for several seconds. Then Warren counted. Their hands quickly changed positions and within a matter of seconds they had boosted Elaine nearly three feet into the air with considerable ease, and then gently let her down.

"Hey, that was fun," Elaine cried. "I felt like I was almost weightless."

"You did feel light as a feather," Warren told her. "See, it worked," he said triumphantly to Adam. Of course several others wanted to try after that.

The last person they tried lifting was Reverend Fawcett, who was not a small man. They managed to lift him also, but with somewhat less ease than the others. The girls then served refreshments. As the group prepared to leave, Adam asked Warren if he wanted to ride along while he took the girls home and maybe stop at the diner. Elaine was holding her breath, knowing she would have a chance to ask Warren if he decided to go for cokes. But she was disappointed.

"Sorry, can't make it tonight. Teauge is having a big English test tomorrow, and I'm not ready. Have to hit the books tonight." Elaine and Beth exchanged looks of disgust.

Monday morning Elaine found another note in her locker. This one was handwritten in an angular scrawl, and its contents were similar to the first note, misspelled words and all. "This is a real mystery," cried Elaine to the girls who were standing around her locker. "I am dying of curiosity."

"Aren't we all?" Lucy asked. "Put a note on the front of your locker saying 'Mystery Man, please reveal yourself. I must know. I'll go out with you if you'll just tell me who you are.'"

"That would be the ultimate of all blind dates," Natalie said.

"He might be some nerd," Beth said. "If he weren't, he wouldn't be so secretive about the whole thing, and would just ask you for a date like any normal guy."

"I'm beginning to think there aren't any normal guys in this school," Karen said.

"If you did know his identity, you could ask him to the dance," Vicki said. "By the way, did you ask Warren yet?"

"I've been trying, but I just haven't had the chance."

"Call him up, for heaven's sake," advised Megan.

"Oh, I couldn't do that."

"Your Mystery Man must be a freshman," mused Karen, still puzzled. "Aren't most of the guys in your classes freshmen?"

"I suppose only a freshman would do something that juvenile," said Elaine.

"We need to get all the freshmen boys' handwriting analyzed," Vicki suggested.

Elaine was secretly just a little flattered by her unknown admirer. It proved to her that at least one boy from Armedia High was interested in her. And just maybe he was someone cute. She could always dream that he was anyhow.

The freshman class began plans for their Homecoming Parade float. The class president had come up with the idea of building a Sputnik, named after the Russian satellite which had been the first to recently circle the globe. Members from each class stayed after school every day that week in order to complete their floats by Friday. They also worked on them during the lunch hour and mid-morning break. Teachers permitted students who were caught up in their work to go help on the float during class time. The freshmen project was out behind the school bus garage. Its skeleton was a jeep completely covered with chicken wire. Each small hole was filled with a red or white napkin, spread out to cover the wire. On top was a platform where the two princesses would sit. That coveted honor went to Megan Frye and a girl from High Bluffs. The motto in front of Sputnik read "Out of This World."

Classes were excused on Friday afternoon for the big event. A horseback rider carrying the American flag led the parade through the streets of Armedia. The Senior float followed, then Junior, Sophomore, and then the little Freshmen Sputnik, which brought cheers from those watching the parade. The high school band followed, riding in the back of a truck, and looking very festive in their new red and white uniforms. Behind the band were several more floats from other school organizations. Last of all were the cars. Elaine and Beth were riding in Adam's car, crowded between Adam and Warren in the front seat. They had helped decorate the car with red and white streamers and pom poms. Elaine was still hoping for a chance to ask Warren to the dance, but the car was too crowded for her to even consider that. DJ and Shawn and two 2 more boys were squeezed in back, and were throwing confetti from the windows and shouting at every girl they passed. Adam was getting rather annoyed with them.

Armedia's triumph of 13-0 over their opponents at the football game that night climaxed the homecoming events. The freshmen had still another victory when their red Sputnik with its white lettering and two antennas received first prize.

Elaine was bound and determined to ask Warren to the dance, and it had to be at MYF the following Sunday no matter what. Again, the group was a little bigger than usual. Two sophomore girls who didn't normally attend, showed up that night. It seemed to Beth and Elaine that Adam and Warren were doing a lot of flirting with the new girls.

"Well, I certainly don't have the MYF spirit tonight," Beth was saying as they prepared onion and bleu cheese dip. "Nobody would miss us at all if we weren't here!"

"Oh, you two," said Lucy. "Those girls are new here, and the guys are just trying to make them feel welcome."

"Hush, Warren's coming," Elaine whispered.

"What do we have to eat tonight?" asked Warren as he came into the kitchen and grabbed some chips. Elaine's heart beat faster. If only Beth and Lucy would leave. She telegraphed the message to Beth, who in turn, bumped Lucy.

"We're going to serve everyone," she said casually, as they walked out with the food.

"You and Beth have done a really good job on always being responsible for the food," Warren was saying warmly. "I mean that's the only reason I come," he added jokingly.

They both laughed. This is my chance, Elaine thought, looking up into his attractive green eyes.

"You won't have to worry about refreshments for the next two weeks," Warren told her. "We'll be going to the Armedia MYF next Sunday, and we won't be meeting the following Sunday."

"Why not?"

"Our family is going up to Santa Barbara for Thanksgiving vacation, and we probably won't be back til Sunday evening. We have family up there that we haven't seen in quite a while. It should be fun. We'll be leaving on Wednesday right after school is out. My dad is having a guest speaker preach that Sunday."

"Oh," Elaine said weakly. She couldn't have cared less if Warren had said that DJ Morrison would be preaching on Sunday. All she could think of was the fact that Warren wouldn't be around on Wednesday night to take her to the Turnabout Dance. Her stomach felt as though something inside was rotating. Warren was looking at her rather strangely, and she handed him another bowl of chips to distract him. "I'm sure your family will have a great time in Santa Barbara. Now, let's go eat," she added, walking into the church social hall.

Chapter 7

Elaine was spending the night with Natalie on the Wednesday evening before Thanksgiving. She always enjoyed staying there. The Irby farmhouse had been built back in 1918, and was three stories high. It had been bought and sold several times before the Irby family had purchased it in 1956. Of course the upkeep on it was enormous and there was always something in need of repair. But in Elaine and Nat's opinion, there were some unique, fun features like the dormer windows, the dumb waiters, and secret closets in unexpected places. Nat's room was on the third floor, and from her dormer window, one could see all over the valley.

"I just love this room," Elaine was saying. "You have such a great view up here, you can play your records loud without disturbing anyone, and you have all kinds of space."

"Yeah, I kind of like it," answered Nat. "When we first moved here, both Adam and I wanted this room, so Dad flipped a coin and I won. But it was a little scary at first, being up here all by myself. When we get those big Santa Ana winds, like we've had the last couple of days, the tree branches outside scratch the window, and of course it sounds like someone's trying to get in. And the other disadvantage is that there's no bathroom on this floor. When I take my shower I have to be sure and bring everything I need with me."

"Yeah, that could be a problem," mused Elaine. "But another plus is that you don't have to share the room with your sister." Nat's sister, Cheryl, age 12, was the youngest of the Irby clan. "I would love to have my own room. Pam is very messy, and besides I have no privacy at all."

"The other room across the hall from this one is full of junk right now," Natalie pointed out. "But my mom is in the process of cleaning it out, and then she's going to make a studio out of it for her photography. It won't be hard to make a darkroom out of the big closet in there."

"Your mom is really talented at taking pictures. I bet she likes her new job with the Armedia newspaper. The Armedia Appeal is a good paper for a small town."

"Oh, she loves it," answered Nat. "By the way, how about some music? I just got two new records: *That'll Be the Day* and *Great Balls of Fire.*"

"Sounds good to me," Elaine said. "Buddy Holly and Jerry Lee Lewis. I only want to hear fast songs tonight. Nothing slow or romantic. Don't even want to think about guys tonight."

"I agree. We can find plenty of other interesting topics to discuss. And we have some good snacks. When we go downstairs, we'll bring back Fritos and dip, pretzels, and chocolate ice cream. Oh, and we have some of those Spanish peanuts as a topping for the ice cream."

"Sounds yummy."

The house was quiet as the girls slipped down the stairs in their pajamas to raid the kitchen. Of course Adam was at the school dance; Mrs. Irby and Cheryl were already asleep. Mr. Irby was in his study off the kitchen. He worked out of his home, Elaine knew, doing something called consulting, whatever that was. "Time for a little midnight snack?" he asked coming into the kitchen.

"Yeah, we'll probably be up until the wee hours, so might as well get some nourishment," Nat said.

"I'm surprised you're not at the high school dance," he said to Elaine.

"Well, I thought I'd pass on this one," she told him cheerfully. "There will be plenty more to go to later on."

"Well, I definitely agree on that. You certainly don't need to rush things. And as lovely as you girls are right now, at this age, you'll be fighting the boys off when you're older," Mr. Irby stated emphatically. Elaine was glad to get back up the stairs, away from him. He was a very nice looking man and friendly to her when she visited Nat, but he always made her nervous. She didn't know why.

As the night wore on, the conversation flowed freely. Elaine didn't spend nearly as much time with Natalie at school, or at school related activities, but the two girls always enjoyed each other's company, and the conversation was never dull.

"You know, I think I'm adopted," Nat was saying, as they sat on the thick rug in her room, sorting out some of her records.

"Now why on earth would you think that?" Elaine asked. "You and Adam and Cheryl all have brown eyes and blonde hair. That's just a weird idea."

"Well, I just don't feel a connection with the rest of my family at all," Nat said. "I can't explain it, but this feeling is always there. I'm writing a story about a girl who is adopted."

"You'll have to let me read it when you're done," Elaine told her. "But as far as you being adopted, I think it's just your overactive imagination at work. I'm sure they would tell you if you were adopted. Besides, you take after your mom, being good at photography. Ohh, what is that rattling? That really sounds spooky!"

"I told you earlier, when the wind blows like this, the window rattles. Nothing to worry about!"

"Well, I wonder how the Turnabout Dance is going," Elaine remarked. "It's probably nearly over by now. I hope Beth is having a good time. She really likes Adam."

"I'll let you in on a little secret, and you can't tell anyone," Nat said. "My brother only likes Beth as a friend, and I happen to know that for a fact. He's interested in a junior girl. But we can't tell Beth because it would break her heart."

"I think that Warren's feelings for me are just platonic too," Elaine said. "Why is it that we get crushes on these guys? Seems like I can't help myself. I've been interested in guys ever since Third grade when DJ and I kissed out in the barn. You know barns are good places for secret stuff."

Natalie laughed heartily at that. "You mean this all began with goofy old DJ? That's just hard to believe!"

Elaine also had to laugh at herself. "Yeah, I guess that is kind of funny. By the way, do you still like Willie Bannister? Even though he is going steady with Megan?"

"No, I think I'm over that. But there's a guy from High Bluffs who has ridden the bus a couple of times, Ty Ramirez. He is really cute, and dark and mysterious looking. I guess he usually drives to school, 'cause I don't see him on the bus."

"Oh, I know who you mean. But I think he kind of has a wild reputation."

"I really don't care about that," Nat said yawning. She sat up all of a sudden. "I'm getting tired and I really don't want to go to sleep yet. It's only 11:30. What else can we talk about?"

"I don't know, but I'm getting tired too," Elaine said.

"Oh, I know. You know how I don't really agree with my dad on any subject? Well I do on this one thing. I've told you that he's an atheist? I think that I am too."

Upon hearing this announcement, Elaine sat up in bed. "Oh, you can't be," she remarked. "You need to start going to MYF again. We have some good discussions there."

"Well, there are just too many bad things going on in the world and if there is a God, and then He should be doing something to stop all the evil. But it just keeps going on and on. There are always wars, and murders, and—"

"But when He created people, He gave them free will," interrupted Elaine. "So they make the choice to do good or to do evil. And just think about this universe. It all didn't just get here by accident. God created it all, and He had a plan. Talk to Adam about all this."

"I have, and he hasn't convinced me yet. But I should start going to MYF again."

"We'd better get to sleep. I have to get home early tomorrow to help Mom with our turkey dinner. I'm so glad we're having turkey instead of chicken this Thanksgiving. There is such a big difference."

*   *   *

Winter had finally set in. Of course winters in southern California were much milder than in other parts of the U.S. The trees were completely bare, and the air was cold and dry. There were quite a few windy days too, and no one liked the wind. The air crackled with static electricity. All of Armedia Valley looked dry. Two days of rain in November had produced the only moisture the valley had received in several months. The farmers glanced up at the overcast sky every day and prayed for rain. But no rain came, although the clouds did not disappear.

Elaine was out of school with a cold. It was a Friday morning and the house was quiet. The younger children were in school. Her mother and Timmie had gone to the store. Charles was out feeding the chickens, and Elaine could hear the clang of the feed buckets. She reached for a tissue and turned up the volume on the little radio that sat on her bookcase. She had been in a bad mood off and on for the last two weeks, and couldn't seem to get rid of the blues. Christmas would be coming soon and she was truly hoping to snap out of her funk. She had quarreled with her parents, and with Russ and Pam. She had found fault with her clothes, her hair, her teachers, and her friends. Her grades had been slipping. Thanksgiving Day had found her miserable instead of thankful.

Lois, back from the post office, interrupted her gloomy thoughts by knocking on the bedroom door. She came in with a letter for

Elaine. "It looks like a card," she said as Elaine tore open the large white envelope. Inside was a card, a beautiful, glazed Christmas card covered with flowers. A sentimental verse was written inside, and the words "Guess Who" were signed at the bottom in an angular scrawl. Elaine's first thought was that it was from Warren. But of course he wouldn't be sending her sentimental cards, she knew. Then she remembered her unknown friend who slipped notes into her locker through the ventilation slits. She hadn't heard from him for a while. She told her mother about the Mystery Man.

Well, how interesting," Lois remarked, sitting on the bed. "You'll have to hire a detective to guard your locker, and report any mysterious people lurking around it."

"I just can't figure out how he manages to find out so much about me, like my address and other things," Elaine said. "And if it's supposed to be a joke, then he's going to a lot of trouble for just a joke. He must be from Armedia," she added, noting the postmark on the envelope. "We girls decided that he's a freshman, since he mentioned in one note that he has one class with me, and I have mostly freshmen in my classes. But he must be some sort of drip or he would reveal himself."

"Well, I don't know about that. Maybe he is just really shy."

"Oh, I really don't care," Elaine added crossly. "Boys make me sick! All of them, and so does school! I wish this cold would last and last so I would never have to go back!"

"Oh, Honey, now you're acting childish. Where did all that come from? It's no wonder you caught this cold with your negative attitude. My goodness, this isn't like you. You need to look on the bright side. You have so much to be thankful for."

"And what would that be?" she asked sarcastically.

"If you can't figure that out, I'm not wasting my time telling you."

"Hi, 'Laine," Timmie called out, running into the room on his chubby little legs. "I got some gum at the store. Want some?"

"Thank you Sweetie."

"We both have colds, don't we? That means we should get lots of candy cause we're sick."

"Timmie, you're hilarious," his mother told him. "Come on, Honey, I'll get you some orange juice."

By the time Elaine had gone back to school, she became too involved in various activities to concentrate on her own problems. The holiday season was rapidly approaching. It seemed that Christmas came earlier every year. The Spanish class was learning Christmas carols: *La Blanca Navidad Llega, Noche de Paz, Pueblecito de Belen*. The Art class was excused every day to go to the gym to paint scenes for the Christmas program. Elaine enjoyed that kind of work. They were painting the rolling hills of Bethlehem. The Future Teachers of America had a project of collecting toys for needy children. Elaine stayed after school to help. Then she would come home on the late bus and gather eggs in the twilight, since the days were rapidly getting shorter. She would study for a short time after dinner and then fall into bed from fatigue. She'd been too busy with her studies to go to MYF lately. Deep down, she knew she'd been rationalizing, by telling herself she couldn't go because of homework. Then Mrs. Fawcett, knowing of Elaine's writing talents, called her and asked her if she would write a Christmas play for the Junior High Sunday School class to put on. She had a book report due in English and a map project for Geography, but she told Norma Fawcett that she would think about ideas for a play.

"One more week til vacation," she thought wearily, sinking onto her bed one night. She'd been so busy she didn't have time to think about being miserable. "And that's the way I'm going to keep it," she decided.

On the last day of school before her vacation she opened her locker and found a nicely wrapped Christmas package. "Oh no! One guess who this is from!" she cried to Beth.

"The Mystery Man of course. But how did he ever get your locker combination?"

"I haven't the slightest idea. But that makes me mad. I haven't told anyone my combination."

"What's all this?" asked Vicki and Megan, joining them.

"The Mystery Man strikes again," Beth told them.

"It says 'Do Not Open until Christmas,' but I'm not waiting," Elaine said, ripping into it. Inside was a 1.98 box of Sees chocolate candy. "Ohh, yummy," she said, passing it around. "I love chocolates."

"How thoughtful," Vicki remarked with her mouth full. "He does more for you than Willie does for Megan and they know each other."

"Oh, hush," Megan said to her.

"I'm just really puzzled," Elaine said. "How is he opening my locker? I don't feel like I have any privacy anymore. It's scary. This guy must be some sort of a mind-reader."

"The office would have your combination, but of course they wouldn't give it out to anyone," Megan pointed out.

"Well, maybe he's in cahoots with someone who works in the office," suggested Vicki.

"You could report it to the office, and they would probably give you a different locker," Beth said.

"Maybe I will if it happens again." She passed the chocolates a second time.

"I just thought of something," said Vicki brightly. "They pass chocolates at engagements. Maybe this is his way of telling you he wants to become engaged." Their laughter rang down the hall.

Friday passed quickly with shortened classes and a Christmas program at the end of the day.

Elaine felt so relieved that school was out, and she had made big plans for her two weeks of vacation. She had been neglecting her writing since school had started, so she figured she would have to write some stories during her time off. Also her room needed a good cleaning, if only she could get Pam to cooperate. Her family had plans for her also. There were household chores to do. The floors needed mopping and the windows needed washing. Charles needed her and Russ to help with vaccinating chickens, a job Elaine especially disliked. But every nine weeks a row of chickens needed to be vaccinated from chicken pox. The fowls also had to be debeaked. Their beaks would be shortened by a special machine, a debeaker, so that they would not peck each other to death, as chickens are prone to do. "At least I'll have some money for Christmas," Elaine thought wearily, after several hours of "stabbing" chickens. Her hands and wrists were covered with chicken scratches. Lois, Russ, and Elaine alternated with each other on the vaccinating job, with Charles always doing the debeaking.

She had completed the play for Mrs. Fawcett, the theme being "Christmas in Many Lands." Elaine had written about a Scandinavian family's Christmas. The program was to be put on in a few more days, which didn't leave Norma Fawcett much time. But Elaine knew how capable this dynamic little woman could be. There was nothing she could not accomplish.

On Wednesday Elaine and Pam set up the artificial Christmas tree in the corner of the living room. It was very old, and not very full, but was always fun to decorate. The girls wanted their parents to either buy a real tree, or a new artificial tree, but their wishes seem to fall on deaf ears. However, decorating the tree was a task they always loved. Timmie helped but all the ornaments he added were clustered together at the bottom, so they had to rearrange them when he wasn't looking. "I'll put the Nativity scene up on the mantle, and you can finish with the icicles," Elaine told Pam.

Elaine had just finished taping their Christmas cards around the fireplace when the phone rang.

"It's for you, Elaine," Pam called from the dining room. "It's a boy," she added loudly as if no boy had ever called Elaine before, which was almost the truth. Elaine wondered if it was Warren. He sometimes called about MYF. She rushed to the phone.

"Hi there," said a drawling, totally unfamiliar voice.

"Hello, who is this?" she asked nervously.

"Don't you wish you knew?" he replied in teasing tones. "How did you like the candy?"

"Oh, it's YOU! The candy was great. But who are you? And how did you open my locker? And how to you manage to find out so much out about me?"

"Curiosity killed the cat."

"But I'm not a cat, and I have a right to know!"

"I miss seeing you every day at school," the voice said, changing the subject.

"Well, maybe I would miss seeing you if I knew who you were," she told him, taking the phone from the buffet, and into her room. She was thankful for the long cord. "Where are you calling from?"

"From the moon."

"Well, I must say, you're coming in loud and clear, for being so far away. Oh, can't you give me an idea of who you are? Like what grade you're in, or what class we have together?"

"Nope, sorry."

"Well, I think you're mean. Will I ever know who you are?"

"Yeah, I'll surprise you one of these days. In another month or so I'll be getting my driver's license, and I'll take a little drive down there to see you."

"I can't wait another month to find out your identity. Be sweet and give me a little hint."

"It's much more fun to keep you guessing."

"We call you the Mystery Man," Elaine told him.

"Who calls me that?"

"All my girlfriends. They know about you. And they all liked the candy, by the way."

They talked for 20 more minutes, but Elaine got no other information from him. He was easy to talk to, she decided. As soon as she hung up from him, she called Beth, and then Natalie.

"Do you realize you've been on the phone for over an hour?" her mother asked as she bustled around the kitchen. She was making a special fruitcake for Charles, who was a church board meeting that night.

"That was the Mystery Man, Mom. He's coming down here in about a month when he gets his license. Of course, I had to call Nat and Beth, after finally hearing from him in person."

"Well, it will be nice to meet this fellow, I guess, after all this cloak and dagger stuff."

The following night the church group went Christmas caroling. Sixteen enthusiastic carolers seated themselves on bales of hay in the back of Beth's dad's pickup truck. They were dressed warmly in heavy coats, scarves, and gloves. Elaine and Beth were seated near the cab of the truck next to two boys who were visiting Ellington as guests of one of the elderly church members. The girls paid extra attention to them, since they felt that they should make strangers feel welcome. At least that's what they were telling themselves. Adam and Warren were sitting with two girls who had recently started coming to MYF. The truck took the carolers to isolated homes of the elderly, and to homes of the sick and shut-ins. A few people, with tears in their eyes, stepped to the door to thank the group. Elaine could not imagine herself ever being old and decrepit. She loved being young and healthy, full of life and enthusiasm. There was so much to life, she thought, and so much to be thankful for. The truck then drove south, down to High Bluffs, which was even smaller town than its sister town, Ellington. Only the business district was bigger; it had several bars on the main street. "Let's stop at Joe's Nite Spot," someone suggested.

After they had "made the rounds" they drove back to Ellington, to the Hummers, for hot chocolate and cookies. After their time out in the cold, the warm house felt very inviting. The group swarmed into the living and dining room area, seating themselves as close as possible to the blazing fire in the fireplace. Elaine made sure that Bill, her out of town guest, had plenty to eat. Warren could fend for himself.

Tuesday was Christmas Eve. After an impressive candlelight ceremony at church, the Hummers had their own ceremony of singing and reading the story of Christ's birth from the Bible. At 8:30 Elaine's mysterious friend called to wish her a Merry Christmas. They talked for a half hour until Lois asked her to get off the phone.

"I wonder who he is," Pam said to Elaine. "It must be fun to get secret phone calls and notes."

"It is. I like him already and I don't even know him."

"I wish we could have opened our presents tonight," said Pam, changing the subject. "We never have much time in the morning."

"I know," Elaine agreed. "We tear into one present, and barely look at it and then we're on to the next one. We always have to leave here so early to get to Grandpa and Grandma's house and visit with everyone, we barely have time to enjoy just being home." Every year on Christmas they made the trip to Redlands to the stately home of their paternal grandparents. It was always very festive, and there were plenty of cousins, aunts and uncles to see.

"But we always get such good presents there," Russ remarked. "Grandpa and Grandma are the best present picker-outers in the whole world."

"Is that the only reason you like going?" Elaine asked her younger brother. "That's very juvenile."

Elaine went to her room to get ready for bed and to write in her diary. Pam was sleeping so she went into the dining area to write. She looked over the past pages filled with her hopes, her dreams, and her life. And there were still all those blank pages left to the future. But her wildest dreams or her most vivid imagination could not foresee the heartaches or the happiness the future would hold. She went to the sliding glass door and pulled the curtain, looking out at the dark trees silhouetted against the night sky, and the vast, lonely field beyond. A star shone brightly over the poplar tree, reminding her of the immortal star that had lighted the way for the travelers and led them to the Savior of the world 2000 years ago. The familiar, sweet tones of *Oh, Little Town of Bethlehem* were playing on the radio, and tonight the tiny town of Ellington seemed so still and peaceful, that it could have been the holy city itself.

Christmas morning everyone except Elaine was up and stirring around 6:00. It was always hard for her to get up early, even on Christmas. She finally staggered out to the breakfast table in her old blue bathrobe, her hair still in rollers.

"Well, look what the wind blew in," greeted Russ.

"Hi, good looking," Charles said. "Merry Christmas!"

"Can we start opening presents, Daddy?" Pam was asking.

"That big wed one is mine," Timmie stated, pointing under the tree.

"I'll be Santa and hand them out to everyone," offered Russ.

From her parents Elaine received a lovely green dyed to match sweater and skirt set. Russ gave her a gold locket; Pam gave her perfume, and Timmie a book of assorted lifesaver candies. Russ was busy taking pictures, Pam was admiring her horse statuette, while Lois was trying to get a squirming Timmie dressed. At last they left for Redlands. It was a beautiful, sunny day, so as they neared their destination, they saw a typical southern California scene: lots of neighborhood children out on the sidewalks, riding new bikes or new scooters, or playing with their Christmas toys. Finally they pulled up in front of a beautifully kept up, older home. Parked outside were 1957 and '58 Chryslers and Buicks, new and shiny. The Hummers arrived in style, in their well-worn station wagon.

"All our relatives are so rich," Elaine complained.

"So are we," noted Charles. "We have almost 9,000 chickens. Nobody here can beat that."

Two cousins came running out of the house to greet them. The morning passed quickly between visiting and opening gifts. Charles had a younger brother and sister, both married and with families. There were also great aunts and uncles there. Every year dinner was served at a long, elegant table in the formal dining room. Elaine was the oldest of the nine cousins, and they always ate in the kitchen dinette area. There was always much clowning around at the table, and much laughter. This year Elaine and her cousin, Lynne, who was a year younger, were invited to sit at the big table. The two girls felt very grown up sitting at the long table which was beautifully set. But it wasn't near as much fun as being with all the cousins, and they had to mind their P's and Q's of course. The dinner consisted of roasted turkey, a ham, corn soufflé, sweet potato casserole, assorted fruit salads, cranberry relish, and homemade rolls. The sumptuous meal was topped off with mincemeat, pumpkin, and peach pie.

The remainder of the day was spent in visiting. Elaine always enjoyed seeing Lynne, although she seemed very knowledgeable and sophisticated. Her family lived in Huntington Beach. She was up on the very latest style of clothing, and always acted as if she knew everything. According to Lynne, she went to the best Junior High in all of California. Of course Elaine's glowing descriptions of Armedia High were so vivid that her friends would not have recognized the school.

The remainder of Christmas vacation passed quickly. Elaine did some babysitting for neighbors across the street. She had not yet had a chance to write on her stories, so she put away her half-filled notebooks. "Until summer," she told herself.

Lucy had been planning a New Year's Eve party. She was inviting all the same group who went to MYF, plus a few of the kids from Armedia, like Megan and Willie, and Vicki. Most of their friends from Armedia did not have transportation to get there. Adam was there with Rosemary, a junior girl with big blue eyes and smooth brown hair cascading down her back. Beth, it appeared, was having a good time joking with DJ and his friends, who had arrived late, carrying a large box of mistletoe. They proceeded to tape sprigs of it to the ceiling.

"Don't look now, but there's mistletoe over your head," DJ said to Warren, who was dancing with Elaine. She wished ardently that

Warren would take advantage of the situation, but he just laughed and said, "Elaine would slap me if I tried to kiss her." And what could Elaine say to that? That was the only time Warren danced with her, but at least he danced with several different girls, not just one. And as the group rang in 1958, Elaine wondered what the New Year would bring.

Chapter 8

When Elaine started back to school after the holidays, she tried to be aware of the boys who might have been the Mystery Man. She looked around in each class, and tried to match up voices, since now she had spoken with him twice on the phone but she couldn't figure it out. Each time she opened her locker, she expected to see a note. However, none appeared. She was very glad to be back in school, however, and to be with all her friends again. But not glad for homework, of course. Homework always seemed more difficult than usual, after not having any for a while. The teachers were most unsympathetic about assignments. Elaine came home every day laden with books. Semester finals were looming ahead and she was worried about her grades. She had received an unsatisfactory notice in Spanish just before vacation, and her parents were most unhappy about that. She probably would have been grounded, except Christmas activities were coming up at that time, and Charles and Lois felt that it would have made for a sad Christmas. So she was struggling to bring up her Spanish grade. She stayed up quite late one evening studying at the dining table. So it was difficult for her to wake up the next morning when she realized her mother was talking to her.

"Elaine, Honey, wake up. I need to talk to you," Lois was saying as she gently shook her daughter.

"Wha—what's going on, it's still so dark out," she muttered groggily.

"I know, I know, it's only 5:00 in the morning. But I have to leave in a little while." It was then that Elaine noticed that her mother was dressed in her beige wool suit that she very seldom wore. "During the night I got a phone call from Chicago," Lois explained. "It was from Grandma Thompson. She told me that Grandpa had a stroke last night and is in the hospital. As you know, he hasn't been well for quite some time, and I need to go back and see him. He probably doesn't have too much time left. Charles is driving me to LA International Airport, and I'm flying back to Chicago. We have to leave pretty soon. Charles is on the phone right now talking to Mr. Hobbs about feeding the chickens this morning. And I'm planning on calling Sue Hathaway to see if she can keep Timmie for a few hours until your dad gets back from LA. I feel bad about leaving you with everything, taking care of the house, the cooking, and the responsibility, but I really do need to go and see my father."

"Mom, it's all right," Elaine reassured her. "After all, I'm fourteen now, and I know we'll get along just fine. We did okay when you were in the hospital having Timmie, and we were all younger then."

"I'm sure you children will be okay." Lois tried to smile bravely. I don't know when I'll be back. Probably in a week to ten days. Now I have to go and take care of some last minute details."

Elaine began to cry softly in the darkness. She knew she would miss her mother terribly. And it was all so sudden. The upright, orderly world in which she was accustomed to living had been turned upside down. She felt so sorry for the heartache her mother would have to go through. Lois Thompson had been born and raised in Chicago. She had an older brother, John, who had been a pilot in the Air Force. He had married a Chicago girl in 1943, and they had one child, a son named Scottie, who was born in a year later. World War II was going on at that time, and John was killed that same year when his plane was shot down. Elaine had a distant memory of a trip back to Chicago when she was about four. Her mother had taken her and Russ back on the train. She had very few recollections of it however, except that she was always thirsty on the train, and that the trip covered miles and miles of prairie. She also remembered a huge, old house with numerous stairways and a dark, musty cellar. Another tragedy occurred in the family in the summer of 1949, when her cousin Scottie was six. His mother had contracted polio, a disease which seemed to be ravaging the country at that time. The dread disease had taken her life. Scottie was also affected by polio, but his case was not as severe. He was left with a withered leg. He was fortunate that he had two loving grandparents who took him in. They had given him a determination to show the world that, though he had a disability, he was certainly not helpless, nor was he self-pitying. A few years ago Elaine's grandparents had come out to California for a visit. Elaine's grandfather was a cheerful, white haired man who was very handy with tools, had a great sense of humor, and was a wonderful storyteller. Grandma Thompson was also white haired, and she was a bundle of energy. Elaine recalled that she was like a magician in the kitchen. She could whip up almost anything from almost nothing. And her hands were never idle. She was always crocheting or doing needlepoint. Lois didn't exactly take after her mother in that area, but then Lois had numerous farm chores that kept her busy.

Elaine wished that she could see Scottie again. Her cousin was a remarkable human being. When he was visiting them, he seemed to get around faster on his crutches than the Hummer kids did on their two legs. He had never complained, but was always happy and cheerful. He was very intelligent and had an unending curiosity about everything. Of course only a few short years later, in 1955, Dr. Jonas Salk had found the cure for polio, but a bit too late for Scottie, Elaine was thinking.

Elaine decided she needed to get up and start doing something to help. She set the table and got out breakfast cereal. She hugged her parents good-bye as they were leaving. "Sue will be over around 8:15 this morning to get Timmie," Lois told Elaine. "And she'll give Russ and Pam a ride to school at the same time, since it's raining cats and dogs. And Mr. Hobbs will be here in a little while to feed the chickens."

"I should be back early this afternoon," said Charles, "before you kids get out of school."

As they left, Russ came strolling into the kitchen. "Poor us, we're going to have to be eating your cooking for the next few days," he teased.

"I think you'll survive somehow. And Pam's going to be stuck with doing dishes a lot, since you and I will be helping Dad pack eggs."

"Mother said I will need to take care of Timmie too," Pam remarked as she sat down at the breakfast table. "I think it's going to be a busy week.

By the time Elaine was dressed for school, life in the Hummer house was getting rather chaotic. Russ had been outside, and came in with muddy footprints and was dripping all over. Timmie was fussy, as he was prone to be in the mornings. "I want Momma," he wailed, holding up one sock and shoe. "I don't want Pam to dwess me."

"Pam is going to be your Momma for a few days," Elaine told him. "And you have to do what she says. Your Momma went back east on a big jet plane."

"Like my toy jet?" Timmie asked with interest.

"What state would she be flying over now?" Pam wanted to know.

"They're probably just now getting to the airport," Russ told her. "And why are you dressed like that? That skirt is really big for you." Pam was wearing one of Elaine's old skirts that she really hadn't grown into yet. It was way too long.

"I don't care. We're having folk dancing at school today, and I'm wearing this! And you can't tell me what to do!" she stormed at Russ.

"Well, then go ahead and look like a dork," Russ told her. "Dork, dork, dork!"

"Am not!" she retorted, giving Russ a shove. Timmie's cereal bowl was overturned in their scuffle, and Cheerios went all over the floor.

"And I told Mom that we would be fine," Elaine thought grimly, as Timmie's howls grew louder. "Russ, go get the dustpan and broom and clean this mess up! Pam, get Timmie another bowl of cereal. I have to leave to catch the bus now, and Sue Hathaway will be here in another 20 minutes. You guys have to behave, and you need to be ready when she gets here. Do you think you can handle that?"

"Yes, Ma'am," Russ said with a salute. Pam didn't answer since she was pouting. Elaine hastily finished her orange juice, grabbed her books, and was out the door. She was thankful it was Friday, so that she would have the weekend to rest up from school and get organized. The rain was still coming down steadily and the students were huddled together under the roof of the gas station. Elaine was glad to tell all her troubles to Beth and Lucy who were duly sympathetic.

School seemed long and tiresome, as it always did on rainy days. Elaine hadn't done her Algebra problems correctly, and she goofed up on a surprise quiz they had in Spanish. At noon she found she'd forgotten her lunch money and had to borrow some from Natalie. It was good to sit down and relax in the warm cafeteria. Macaroni and cheese, one of her favorites, was being served. It was some comfort to her that her friends weren't in a particularly good mood either. Even the usually jovial Vicki was grumpy. "Rain, rain, rain," she said glumly. "I know the farmers need it, but I'm sick of it. And if it's not raining, it's cloudy and gloomy."

"And I can't find my raincoat," remarked Karen. "I left it somewhere this morning. Maybe it's in the gym."

"That gym floor is a mess," Lucy stated. "Someone's going to have to do something about that before the basketball game tonight."

"Is everybody coming to the game tonight?" asked Megan. She seemed to be the only happy person in their group.

"I probably won't be," said Elaine, and proceeded to explain why.

"Gee, I feel sorry for your family with you doing the cooking," Megan told her. But no one laughed at her attempt to be funny.

"I hear they're having a noon dance in the gym," Megan remarked. "Are we all going?"

"Where's Willie today?" Elaine asked Megan. "You're usually with him at lunchtime."

"Haven't you heard? We broke up last night," Megan answered flippantly. "He thought I was flirting with Duane Kellogg. So we ended up in a big argument. He can be so childish at times."

"Boys are such a pain," remarked Beth. "We'd all be better off without them." She was still upset because Adam had a girlfriend now. "Don't worry about Willie," she told Megan. "There are plenty of other fish in the sea."

"Oh, I'm not worried," Megan said loftily. "I'm going to the basketball game with Paul Newberry tonight."

"You don't waste any time, do you?" Lucy said to her.

Beth and Elaine trailed behind the rest of the girls as they walked to the gym. "It's just amazing about Megan," Beth was saying. "Everything is so effortless for her. She breaks up with one guy, and Presto!! There's another one right there for her to go out with. No down time at all."

"I know. It's just not fair. Some girls have all the luck," Elaine complained.

Elaine came home that afternoon to a messy house, floors tracked with mud. Beds were unmade, dishes were unwashed, and clothes and toys were strewn all over. It gave her a headache just to look at everything. Before she could even start on the house, she had her daily chore of collecting eggs. How she hated doing that in the rain. She found Pam sitting on the pack porch struggling with her rubber boots. She was near tears. "That darned Timmie," she exclaimed. "He's been in his room quite a bit this afternoon, and he was really quiet, so I thought he was being very good. Well, he went and scribbled all over the wall with his crayons. Now I have to clean it up. Daddy was really mad."

"Daddy is just upset because Mom is away," Elaine said. "Don't worry about the mess. I'll help you clean it up after we do the eggs. Where is Timmie now?"

"He's out in the feed room with Daddy. He's not going to let Timmie out of his sight," Pam explained.

The girls walked out past the back lawn, past the honeysuckle hedge, and into the aluminum feed building, which smelled of damp mash. They picked up the wire egg baskets and carried them out to the chicken pens. "Don't worry about the eggs getting wet," Charles told them, "because there isn't much we can do about it. Just leave the baskets under the nests, out of the rain, when they're filled." The aisles between the rows of pens were soggy and muddy, and rainwater ran off the tops of the nests onto their hands and wrists as they reached in for the eggs. The task at hand was most unpleasant in bad weather. After the eggs were all collected, Charles went around on his electric feed cart and gathered up the baskets.

The girls were glad to get back into the warm house, and headed to the fireplace to warm up. Russ, who already done his egg collecting was contentedly watching cartoons on TV. Elaine turned off the TV, and let him know that there was work to be done. "I need you to go around and get some of this stuff picked up, and then you can start on the dishes," she told him.

"Not my job," he said. "Pam has to do the dishes."

"No arguing. You need to get busy, or I'm telling Dad. Pam and I have another job to do." By scrubbing hard with Ajax, she and Pam got most of Timmie's handiwork off his wall. Preparing dinner was the next item on her list. She was glad her father had taken a package of ground beef out of the freezer to thaw. Hamburgers patties were one meal she knew how to cook. She also opened a package of frozen corn. Russ had washed the dishes, she noticed, but it was a sloppy job in her opinion.

At dinner Charles told the family that their mother had arrived safely in Chicago. Other than that, no one seemed to have too much to say. The meal was okay, Elaine thought. There was celery and bread to go along with the hamburger patties. For dessert Elaine served a simple box pudding, butterscotch, a bit lumpy, but passable. They had Lois' homemade oatmeal cookies to go with it.

"This pudding looks like throw-up," commented Russ.

"Yeah, looks like thwow-up," echoed Timmie.

"Russ, you can leave the table for that," his father said.

"But I was just kidding."

"It wasn't really funny. Your sister worked hard on this dinner. You can go to your room."

"Dad, are you going to need me to help pack eggs tonight?" Elaine asked him.

"No, not tonight. They're still too wet. But you'll have to get up early tomorrow to help. Russ can help me at 6:00, and I'll need you about 7:30. After the weekend, Mr. Hobbs will be helping me with the egg packing. It's just too much for you kids when you're in school." Mr. Hobbs was the elderly neighbor across the street, who always seemed to be there to help when there was an emergency.

"If you don't need me tonight, then can I go to the basketball game?" Elaine asked him. "Lucy's parents are going, and said they would take Beth and me."

"Is Pam going to do the dishes?" her father asked.

"You mean I have to clean up this mess all by myself?" Pam cried in anguish.

"Maybe we could both do it in the morning," Elaine suggested.

"I guess that will work," said her father wearily. "I hope you don't get home too late tonight, because you're going to have a busy day tomorrow."

It felt especially good to be out of the house, Elaine thought as she sat in the packed bleachers of Armedia's gym and watched the fast moving game. Their basketball team had won every game so far. (The football team hadn't fared so well, winning only three out of eight games.) Tonight's game was a close one, however, and the girls cheered so loudly, they were hoarse by the end of the game. Armedia had won with a score of 63-60. There was a dance after the game, but the girls had to leave before it started, since they had ridden with Lucy's folks. The rain had decreased to a drizzle as they drove home.

Saturday was an early day. Packing the eggs took about two hours. It was a chore that Charles and Lois had to do every single day, rain or shine, no matter what else was going on in their busy lives. Sometimes they did the egg-packing in the evening, sometimes in the morning. The eggs were taken from the baskets and put on a conveyer belt which sent them through a cleaning device. Next they rolled down and were machine sorted by weight. Elaine's job was to pull the eggs from the basket and put them on the trough, where they rolled into the cleaning machine. Charles took the eggs that rolled down after being weighed, and packed them accordingly, small medium or large. They didn't have to do any candling, since the company that bought the eggs handled that.

After she helped pack eggs, Elaine washed the dishes from several meals back while Pam dried. Pam swept the kitchen and dining room floor while Elaine vacuumed and dusted in the living room. She even put Timmy's room in order which was a task in itself.

The following day she was glad for the warmth and solitude of the small sanctuary of the Methodist Church. In the quietness she prayed for the safety of her mother so far away, for her grandparents, and for help her family to get through the following week. She went to MYF that night. She hadn't been for a few weeks. The group had grown somewhat larger. To her dismay, Elaine found that she still had feelings for Warren. When she was not around him, the feelings weren't nearly as strong. After the meeting Warren came up to Elaine with a question. "I was wondering if you'd be interested in going to MYF camp in June?" he asked. "I've gone for two years in a row now, and I wouldn't miss it for anything. It's really a worthwhile experience, one you'll never forget."

"I'd have to think about it," she replied. "What's the cost of it?"

"About $35.00 for the week. Maybe that sounds like a lot, but the MYF will be doing some money making projects for those who want to go. I'm hoping we can get a large group to represent Ellington, and we'll probably have a bake sale or a rummage sale to make money. By the way, where has Beth been hiding herself?"

"I guess she's been busy," Elaine replied vaguely. She thought to herself, how naive of Warren, doesn't he realize that Beth quit coming because his buddy, Adam has been seeing someone else?

The next week passed slowly. Everyone was getting tired of Elaine's cooking. Over the weekend they had received casseroles from two of the church members, but they were on their own after that. Monday they had macaroni and cheese from a box, which was okay. Tuesday she got ambitious and fixed spaghetti with meat sauce, but the pasta was a little gooey. On Wednesday she fixed cube steaks which she found in the freezer. Also on Wednesday they got a call from Lois, who said that her father had passed away the evening before, and she would stay in Chicago for the funeral on Friday, and would be flying home on Saturday. On Thursday, Charles took the family out for dinner in Armedia, and they ended up ordering hamburgers and French fries, and enjoyed every bite.

Lois got home on Saturday. It was wonderful to see her. She and Elaine had a long talk on Saturday evening. She told Elaine all about her plane trip, about her stay in Chicago, and said that her father had died peacefully, with his wife and daughter there with him.

"Now Grandma and Scottie are all alone in Chicago," Elaine remarked.

"They're thinking about moving out here to California."

"Really? That would be wonderful!"

"It would be, wouldn't it? They have no other close family back east, and Mother needs to sell that house. It's way too big for the both of them, and it's so old, it always needs maintenance. It's in a commercial part of the city, and the property is probably worth more than the house."

"Where would they want to live, if they moved out here?"

"I'm hoping they would consider Ellington as a possibility. Scott will be starting high school next year, and since he's on crutches, I think he would do better at a small, friendly high school, not some really big one with over a thousand students."

"I think Ellington would be the perfect place for them," Elaine cried with enthusiasm.

"We'll pray that it works out," her mother said.

Chapter 9

Elaine was seated at her desk trying to study for her final exams. But there were so many distractions, it seemed to be an exercise in futility. The TV was on in the living room and she could hear laughter and jokes from a comedy. And Russ was teasing Timmie in the other room and the little guy was fussing. Pam was cleaning out her side of the closet, and though she was trying to be quiet, she wasn't succeeding. Elaine could hear clicks and creaks and rustling. Pam had two years' accumulation of clothes, boxes, toys, magazines, and junk.

"Do you think I should get rid of this jump rope?" Pam was asking Elaine.

"Sister, Dear, that is your decision to make. You need to get rid of a lot of stuff, just because you don't have the room to keep collecting the way you do. But no more questions, please. I really need to study right now."

"Well, okay."

When report cards came out, her grades were better than they had been last time. She got a C in Spanish and B's in all the other subjects except English. To her delight, she had gotten an A—from Mrs. Teague. She was thrilled beyond words. And she felt she hadn't really deserved a B in Algebra, that Mr. Carr had just been kind. Charles had been tutoring her for a while, but that didn't work out too well. She just didn't understand the way her dad was explaining it to her, and they both ended up frustrated.

The month of January had passed and Elaine did not hear from the Mystery Man. She was disappointed. "I guess he's found someone else," Natalie said dramatically. "He could have at least written you a

Dear Mary letter." The girls were having their nightly gabfest on the phone.

"Now I'll never know who he is," wailed Elaine.

"Oh, you probably find out one of these days."

"By the way, did you hear that Megan and Willie are back together?"

"Megan acts as going steady is a child's game," Nat said cattily.

"Well, I know what you mean. But I think you still dislike her because you used to like Willie."

"That's all in the past now, yesterday's news."

The month of February brought record setting rainfall. Mr. Hobbs, an old-timer who had lived in Ellington for many years, said he had never seen the river running that high. The school bus plowed through puddles on the highway as it made its way from Armedia to Ellington to High Bluffs. Elaine disliked riding the bus, since it was usually crowded-three to a seat. Today she hadn't been able to find a seat except near the back, where the High Bluffs group usually sat. The older boys were often smoking and swearing. Even the girls seemed rude, giving Elaine dirty looks. She was glad when a seat next to Beth became vacant, and she moved up to sit next to her.

"If this rain keeps up," Beth remarked, "we'll all be floating out of here in canoes. I've heard that the Ellington River is running for the first time in years."

"Yes, it's higher than it's ever been, a new record."

After Elaine finished her chore of collecting the cold, wet eggs, she called Beth and they made plans to walk down and see the river before it got too dark. They met at the corner; both bundled up, carrying umbrellas, and wearing high boots. The rain had slowed to a drizzle however. They walked up Oak Street, the same road that eventually led up to the town cemetery. From the top of a small hill, they could see the raging river. Its muddy waters raged across Oak Street, swirling rapidly over sticks, logs, and other debris that had been caught in its current. It was approximately 30 feet wide, but the girls had no idea how deep it was. It flowed south toward High Bluffs.

"Just look at how strong that current is!" Beth exclaimed. "Strange as it seems, someone could easily drown in it."

"I'd hate to fall in." Elaine shuddered. "Look at how it keeps taking dirt from either side and causing the banks to cave in."

"They need to have a bridge across it," remarked Beth. "The people who live in the foothills have to drive way up to the other end of town, since the only bridge is up there."

"Some of the roads going up to the foothills are too flooded out to even get to the bridge. I guess some of the people just get stranded."

"I heard that yesterday some guy was stupid enough to try to cross right here in his car. Of course the river was running much slower then. He got stuck up to his axle. Someone saw him and came and got my dad and he pulled him out with his truck."

"Warren told me that he and Adam would like to take a raft down the river to High Bluffs, after it slows down of course."

"That would be a fun adventure." stated Beth. "Well, it's getting dark fast, we'd better head back."

On arriving back at the house, Elaine saw Russ and Pam coming through the back hedge. Their boots were covered with mud, and Russ was carrying Timmie, who was crying. He had no shoes on, only his socks, which were completely muddy. In fact his overalls were splashed with mud up to his waist. Pam was carrying his blackened rubbers and shoes. She and Russ were laughing so hard they could hardly walk. "We were out in the field walking around in a mud hole," she explained to Elaine, "and it was really a mess, and we almost got stuck in it. Then Timmie came along and wanted to play in the mud too and we told him not to because his boots weren't high enough."

"But of course he wouldn't listen to us and walked right into the mud and got stuck. When we pulled him out, his shoes and boots stayed right there in the mud," added Russ.

"You quit laughin, you," Timmie said furiously, pounding Russ with his small fists. The four siblings were quite a sight as they walked into the house. The rain was starting to come down hard again.

That evening after dinner the phone rang, and it was the Mystery Man.

"I haven't heard anything from you in quite a while," Elaine was saying.

"Oh, so you missed me, huh? I was wondering if that would happen if you didn't hear anything from me. I've been busy, working on my car so that I can drive down and see you. I just got my license a couple of weeks ago. Are you doing anything on Sunday afternoon?"

"Not that I know of. But I can't make a date with you. I've never even met you."

"Yes, you have. You just don't know it yet."

"You know what I mean," she protested. "Girls just don't make dates with guys they don't know."

"We know other just by talking on the phone. Besides, it's not as if we'll be going somewhere. I'll come over to your house and meet your folks, and everything will be just fine. But if you really don't want me too, I won't trouble you anymore. It will be just like we never met. Because of course we haven't," he laughed.

Elaine's curiosity was getting the best of her. "Do you know how to find my house?"

"Are you kidding me? In Ellington, that little podunk town? Of course I can find your house. No one can possibly get lost in Ellington! I'll be there Sunday afternoon about 2:00, okay?"

"All right, I'll see you then." After Elaine had hung up the phone, she was overcome by nervousness. Of course she called Beth right away, who was excited for her.

"I am so glad you're finally going to meet this guy," she said. "I hope he is really good looking and really nice."

Her mother seemed pleased. "He sounds more original that most of the boys. He really got your curiosity up with the mysterious notes and somehow getting the candy into your locker."

"Yes, I have to find out how he did that."

"He probably some weird dork or nerd," Pam said, drying dishes.

"Pam, don't be so disagreeable," her mother scolded her.

Of course Elaine's mysterious secret admirer was the topic of conversation at lunch in the cafeteria the following day. "Any bets on what he looks like?" Vicki joked.

"Look out your window when he drives up," suggested Alma, "and if you don't like his looks, have your mom tell him you're not home."

"Oh, but that's so heartless," Karen said. "Now that you've made the date, you have to be brave and go through with it."

"Beside, my mom is too honest. She would never lie for me."

When Elaine got home from school that day, Lois was very excited. "I got a letter from Grandma Thompson today, and she has a buyer for the house in Chicago, and she wants to move out here to Ellington. I am so happy!" she exclaimed, hugging Elaine. "The escrow will go through in about 45 days. Scottie's schoolwork is advanced enough so he shouldn't have a problem transferring schools. It's going to be our job to find a rental house for them. Rentals are pretty cheap around here."

"Oh, Mom, that's exciting news. I'm so glad they're coming."

"So am I," Russ added, coming into the room. "Scottie's a real swell guy for a cousin. And he knows so much about radio and electronics that he can teach me."

"When are they coming?" Elaine asked.

"It will probably be near the end of March. Like I said, the escrow will take 45 days. In the meantime, they have a lot of packing to do."

Sunday was a cold, damp day, but Elaine wasn't paying much attention to the weather. She thought she would look too dressed up in a skirt so she wore her plaid capris, and a white long sleeved shirt.

"A dress would look nicer," her mother frowned. "Your dad and I will probably be asleep when he gets here. But we'll be up later to meet him." She and Charles never missed their daily afternoon naps. "Have fun," she said, going into her room.

Elaine sat at her desk listening to the radio. She had given up trying to study. What if he doesn't come, she thought. What if this whole thing is a joke? But promptly at 1:45 she heard a car drive up.

"Want me to answer the door?" asked Pam, peeking out their bedroom window. But she was too late to see him since he was already at the front steps. "His car is ugly." Pam stated. "It's pea soup green and splattered with mud."

"Well, of course it's muddy," Elaine shot back. "It's raining, you dope."

Pam went to answer the door, and Elaine suddenly wished she were 100 miles away. Pam came back to the room with a smirk on her face and her hand in a thumbs-down motion, and Elaine went to meet the Mystery Man. He was standing by the front door. He was slightly taller than she was with curly, reddish brown hair. His blue eyes were framed by horn-rimmed glasses, and freckles spotted his round face. Elaine recognized him as a boy in her Art class. She knew he was a sophomore and that his name was Alvin Minegar. Of course the kids at school had re-named him Vinegar. She didn't think of him as the creep that Pam had described him, but he was certainly not her idea of a good looking guy.

"Well, hello," she said. "We know each other from Art class. So I finally meet the Mystery Man."

"That's me," he said nervously, "in the flesh. Very nice house you have here."

"Thank you. Let's go over and sit in the chairs by the fire. Did you have any trouble finding your way here?"

"In this town?" he scoffed. "It was a cinch."

He settled himself down in a comfortable chair. Elaine wished he hadn't come. She didn't like his looks, she didn't like his throaty chuckle, and she didn't like his big brown overcoat, which was out of style as far as she was concerned. But as they chatted, she realized that he could be pleasant, and somewhat interesting to talk with.

"By the way, how did you find out so much about me" she asked him.

"Oh, that was simple enough. My sister, Abbie, works in the attendance office. She's a senior. She looked up all your information in the office files. It took some persuading on my part. And she said she absolutely couldn't give me your locker combination. So she opened it up for me herself. As you know, it was only opened once."

"Well, I guess the mystery is solved. When did you get your driver's license?"

"I turned 16 at the end of January," he said, "and got my license a few days later. It sure is nice to be able to drive where ever I want to go now."

"Yes, I'm really looking forward to the Driver's Ed class next year. Mr. Sharpe's a pretty cool teacher." The conversation flowed pretty easily, and Alvin seemed comfortable in the Hummer living room. So comfortable, in fact, that he stayed the entire afternoon. Lois and Charles, up from their naps, came out to meet him. Elaine had to excuse herself to go gather eggs. She was rather disgusted that Alvin didn't offer to help. But he stayed on and chatted with her parents. She came back from her chore to find him discussing chickens with Charles. She wished he would leave.

"Are you busy tonight?" he asked her.

"Yes, I'm going to MYF," she was glad to tell him.

"Methodist Youth Fellowship, huh? I used to go to the Methodist church in Armedia, but I haven't been in quite a while. Mind if I tag along?"

"Of course not," she answered, minding very much. She wondered what Warren would think. She excused herself to dress for MYF, and a few moments later Beth called.

"Hi, I couldn't wait any longer. I had to call you. So who is the guy?"

Before answering, Elaine looked around for Alvin. He was in the dining room eating a cheese sandwich Lois had fixed for him. On Sundays the big family dinner was always at noon, after church. They just had sandwiches in the evening. She took the phone into the bedroom. "It's Alvin Minegar."

"Never heard of him. Is he cute?" Beth asked.

"No, but he's nice, I guess. He's coming to MYF tonight."

"That will show Warren you're not sitting around waiting for him. I think I'll come too. It's been awhile since I've been there. And I want to see this this Alvin character. Ohhh, I just thought of something. Is that the guy they call Vinegar?"

"One and the same. And he's a character all right."

There was a good sized group at MYF that night, and Elaine didn't think Alvin fit in too well. But of course that was the first time he'd been there, she thought. Much to her dismay, Warren seemed to like him. "I've seen better," Beth whispered to her frankly. "But he could be worse too, I guess." On the way home he asked Elaine to the movies next Saturday night. And she accepted, since she didn't have anything else to do. Besides, two good movies were playing: *Jailhouse Rock* with Elvis, and *Raintree County* with Elizabeth Taylor.

Chapter 10

"I think this is just the cutest little house," Lois was saying. "We couldn't have found a better place for Grandma and Scottie." It was a warm, sunny Spring day, and she and Elaine were walking into the little house on Elm Street, their arms full of curtains which Lois had made. The yellow shingled cottage was well shaded by two large popular trees. Once inside they could smell the fresh paint. The floor had just been varnished, and the windows were clean and sparkling.

Elaine explored the living room and kitchen with delight, and then went to the bedroom. "Scottie will like this room," she called from the east side of the house. "It has two big windows and will catch the morning sun. It's so cheery."

"And it has built in shelves for all his radio equipment," added Lois. "Just think, they'll be here in a few more days!"

"It's going to be a long drive for them, especially pulling a trailer," Elaine remarked.

"Yes, it will. Grandma said it's only a small trailer, though. She is bringing some family heirlooms, dishes, and kitchen essentials, and anything of sentimental value. She did have a few things shipped out here. They will need to buy some furniture though. Come on and help me with these curtains."

Together they put beige draperies in the front window, sage green ones in Scottie's room, and light blue ruffled Priscillas in Mrs. Thompson's room. The kitchen windows were done last, and looked very cozy, framed with red and white checked curtains.

"That makes a big difference already," said Lois with satisfaction.

"I hope Scottie likes it out here," Elaine remarked.

"I'm sure he will. He's the type of boy who would appreciate a town like this. I think he'll like your MYF too. By the way, how does Alvin like it?"

"Okay, I guess. He only goes because I go."

"Well, you're setting a good example."

"Alvin's been here every Sunday for the last three weeks. And he stays and stays. And mostly all he talks about are his rabbits, and the dumb steer he's raising for his FFA project. He just gets boring after a while. I'd like to have some time to myself on Sunday afternoons, but he always shows up."

"Well, it's good practice for you to talk to him and be interested in what he has to say," Lois said as they went out the front door.

"Maybe so, but he doesn't listen to anything I have to say. He just talks about himself, and then he's always telling these corny jokes. And I do get tired of hearing about his animals."

"But you live in a farming community and you're bound to meet guys whose main interest is animals."

"There are many guys in school who have other interests and hobbies," stated Elaine. She stood on the driver's side of the car. "Can I drive? It's only a few blocks."

"You know you can't till you get your license next year."

"Mom, you're such a stickler for all the rules," her daughter complained as they drove home.

Later in the day Warren drove up to the Hummer home to buy two dozen eggs. "I got a letter from MYF camp," he told Elaine. "It's going to be in the San Bernardino Mountains near a beautiful lake. It's from June 15th to June 22nd. We'll all be in cabins under the pine trees."

"It does sound really great," Elaine told him.

"And as I said before, we'll have some money making projects in the next couple of months. You can also apply for a job in the dining hall. That's what I'm doing. You may not like doing KP all week, but it's worth the fun of camp." He gave her some paperwork and left. She was relieved to find that her infatuation for Warren was gradually diminishing.

Alvin had asked Elaine out again for that Saturday night. As she dressed for the date, she decided that this would be her last one with him. She had seen all of him she ever wanted to see, and he bored her to tears. Not only that, but the high school students had a tendency to believe any couple they had seen together more than once were going steady. The talk at school had Elaine and Alvin paired off already. All her girlfriends had had a good laugh when they heard that Alvin

Minegar was the Mystery Man. And, unfortunately for Elaine, he wasn't a fellow who kept his mouth shut. In just a few weeks he had told many people that Elaine was his girlfriend.

"Alvin Minegar!" Vicki had exclaimed. "You know how to pick 'em, Elaine." The girls had been waiting in the shower line after PE.

"But he picked me, I didn't pick him! And I don't even want him!"

"Poor Alvin," stated Alma. "You're going to break his heart."

"He's a character in Art class," Vicki remarked. "He's constantly drawing pictures of his pet rabbits. And he drives poor Lippie crazy because he's always spilling paint. He has no coordination whatsoever."

"Elaine Minegar sounds really nice," Alma said daringly. Elaine had chased her into the shower for that, and had turned the water on her, even though she still had on her bra and panties.

The sound of the doorbell brought Elaine back to the present. Alvin had arrived on time and they left for the movies in Armedia, one of the few sources of entertainment in that town. As they drove home, Alvin told her of his plans to enter his steer, Sebastian, in the county fair next month. "He's sure to win a prize," he added. "He's a real good animal."

"And then you're going to sell him to someone who will eat him," Elaine said.

"Well, that's what he was raised for-food. He'll bring a good price at the fair. You're a farm girl, so you how it works."

"Well, sure, our chickens get killed when they don't lay. But I couldn't stand to ever chop their heads off, like my mom does, or to clean chickens. Yuck! And if I raised an animal from a baby, like a calf or a piglet, it would be too hard for me to ever think of eating it, or even selling it for food. Killing animals is one thing I really hate about farming. Guess I never would have been a good pioneer woman."

"You're such a softie," he said. He drove down the driveway and turned off the ignition. He always wanted to sit in the car after a date, while Elaine was always anxious to go in. "My folks would like to meet you. You'll have to have dinner at our house sometime." Elaine couldn't think of anything that sounded worse. But she could not bring herself to heartlessly tell him that she didn't want to see him anymore.

"I probably won't be able to come down here until later tomorrow, maybe about 5:00," he said. "I have to clean my rabbit pens. Those rabbits sure are messy. And after that I should study for the Geometry test old man Dumpke is giving. Or maybe I'll just get by with a cheat sheet instead."

"I was just going to tell you that I won't be here at all tomorrow," Elaine lied. "I'm going somewhere with my folks."

"Gee, that's too bad. Where are you going?"

Nosy, Elaine thought, quickly inventing another lie. "We're going to visit my grandparents in Redlands."

Alvin looked very disappointed. He cleared his throat. "Uh, I was going to ask you this tomorrow, but I'll ask it now instead. The sophomores are getting their class rings in another month, and I was wondering if you would wear mine?"

He was asking her to go steady. Elaine's answer was prompt.

"Alvin, I like you for a friend. But I'm not interested in going steady with you or anyone else right now. I appreciate your asking me, but that's just the way it is."

"I was afraid your answer would be no," he said sadly. "Is it anything I've done?"

"No, not at all. I just don't want to go steady right now."

But Alvin didn't give up easily. He continued to call her up and to pay unexpected visits. Elaine was thoroughly disgusted with him when the weekly edition of the high school paper came out on Friday. It was during lunch break when Lucy came back from the Student Square with a copy of the paper. Once she started reading the song dedications, she squealed "Oh no! Listen to this: to Elaine H. from Alvin M: *You Are My Destiny*. How touching! I'm sorry, Elaine. He just doesn't know when to quit." Elaine had thought it a great song, but now she never wanted to hear it again.

"Alvin and Elaine sound so cute together," Beth teased.

"You marry him, and you'll have steaks every night, if he keeps raising steers," Vicki pointed out.

"Rabbits too," added Alma.

"Be serious, how am I going to get rid of him?"

"Have you tried arsenic?'

"Volunteer him as the rider in Russia's next Sputnik."

"You're all such a help," she sighed sarcastically.

Grace Thompson and Scottie arrived by the end of the week, and Elaine was glad to help get them settled, not only because she was excited that they were here, but it took her mind off her troubles with Alvin. In the space of about two weeks, they were settled comfortably in their new home. Lois, Elaine, Pam, and Russ spent as much time as they could spare to help. Charles fixed the broken step on the back porch. Scottie seemed thrilled with his new home and environment.

He was a slim boy, slightly taller than Elaine. He had a shock of brown hair and deep brown eyes. He was very good looking, Elaine thought, except for his disfigured leg. But she noticed he was able to get around on his crutches fairly well. Russ was helping him with his radio equipment. Her grandmother, short, plump, and white haired, bustled busily about the house, getting organized.

"I can't believe how quiet it is around here," she kept saying. "It was hard for me to get to sleep the first few nights, because of the quiet. I'm just used to so much more noise."

"I know we're going to like it here," Scottie said. "Everything is so pretty and green."

"Well, it's not always this green. We've had a lot of rain this spring," Elaine told him. Ellington did look especially beautiful right now, Elaine thought. The town had a freshly washed look and the recent rains were responsible for the growth of greenery and abundant wildflowers in the foothills.

"What's the high school like?" asked Scottie.

"Very small, very friendly. Everybody knows everybody else. But that's not always good because nobody minds their own business," she added, thinking of Alvin.

"I'm glad it's friendly. There were 250 eighth Graders in my Junior High back in Chicago. When I started school here in Ellington, I couldn't believe how tiny it was. Only 14 eighth Graders, and after going there only a week, I know all of them. Unbelievable! Not to change the subject, but what's up there?" he asked, pointing to the coastal mountain range, silhouetted against the sky.

"Mostly brush," said Elaine. "And there's a small stream running down from the mountains into our river here in town."

"There's more up there than meets the eye," Russ told him. "There's a Boy Scout Camp back in a valley. There is a big cattle ranch all over those mountains. The ranch has thousands of acres. And there are lots of hiking trails that crisscross all over the place. My dad loves going hiking up there."

"Do you think I could go hiking with you guys sometime? I went hiking with my scout troop back home, and I even kept up pretty well," said Scottie.

"Good for you, Scott," Elaine cried. "We'll have to get a hike together real soon."

After that conversation, they planned a welcoming hike and picnic for Scottie. Elaine, Beth, Lucy, Russ, and Scott found themselves walking up Oak Street toward the mountains. The river, which had been so wide and treacherous a few weeks ago, was now just a stream, very easy to cross. The girls had doubted Scottie's ability to hike, but he was excited about going, and seemed to enjoy it more than anyone. "What a great view!" he exclaimed as they passed the cemetery

"Just wait tell you see it from the top," Elaine told him. Oak Street narrowed into a thin, winding dirt road, no longer accessible to cars. Russ wanted to leave the group and try a steep trail that branched off to the left.

"It's a shortcut to the top," he explained, "and I've been on it with Dad a few times, so I won't get lost. I know exactly where it goes. I want to get some snapshots of the area.

"All right, we'll meet you in about an hour," Elaine told him. The girls and Scotty followed the trail for about a half mile, meandering through manzanita bushes, bunchgrass, and Engelmann oak trees. Wildflowers of every color were popping up everywhere. They came to a clearing about 20 minutes later and another trail that branched off, this time to the right. "Does this trail go up to the top?" Scott asked, indicating the wider one on the right. "If so, it might be better for me."

"You can't go alone, you don't know the way," Elaine said. I'll go with you."

"No, let me," Beth volunteered.

"No, I will," said Lucy, as she moved quickly to his side. "I've been on this trail before. We'll meet you at the top for lunch."

"I like that-having three girls fighting over me," Scottie grinned. "Home was never like that."

"You're so good looking," Lucy told him. "I bet all the girls fight over you."

"Careful," Elaine warned. "He's conceited enough as it is."

"Not me. See you later," he called, as they started up the trail.

After fifteen minutes of continually beating the brush back from the trail, Elaine and Beth wished they had taken the wider trail, since they were making little headway through the chaparral. They were constantly sliding backwards and getting scratched by manzanita branches. Twenty minutes later they had reached the small plateau, where a full view of Ellington could be seen. The rest of their party hadn't arrived yet. The contrasting fields, different shades of green and brown, gave a patchwork quilt look to the valley below. The river bed was nearly dry except for the small, brown stream winding slowly and aimlessly toward High Bluffs. Silos in the distance stood straight and tall. A thin sliver of roadway was off in the distance. The view from the top of the plateau was always breathtaking, Elaine thought. What was not so nice was evidence of previous hikers at the top, the usual debris of pop bottles, candy wrappers, and cans. There was a flag flying in the breeze, represented by a white sheet on a pole. A number of initials were carved and written on the pole.

"Well, now we know, this is the fastest way up here," Beth said.

"I've been here in 1954, 1955, and 1957," Elaine said, looking at past records of her presence there.

"And now we can add 1958 to that. Oh, here comes Russ now," stated Beth.

Lucy and Scottie arrived shortly after that, and the five young people sat down on various flat rocks to feast on ham sandwiches, pickles, apples, cookies and cokes.

"I can't think of anything worse to drink on a hike than coke," Scottie said. "Plain old water is best. And Ellington has the best water."

"I haven't heard you make one complaint about this town," Beth told him. "And I don't think I've ever had anything really good to say about it."

Scottie Thompson seemed to thrive in the small town. He had such a zest for life and was always full of enthusiasm. He looked for the best in everything and found it. He just seems so much happier than I am, Elaine thought, even though he knows he'll never be able to walk again without the help of his crutches. And even though he'll always be a cripple. How she hated that word. But Scottie had found the secret of true happiness somewhere along the line, and it showed in his brown eyes and his radiant smile.

Chapter 11

Easter vacation came and went rather quietly. Elaine tried to look for ways to earn money for camp. She did some babysitting, helped with vaccinating chickens again, and worked at the MYF bake sale. The weather was unseasonably warm for late April. One afternoon Elaine, Russ, Beth, and Billy, Beth's younger brother, got on their bikes and rode out to Ellington Hot Springs Resort, which was about three miles from Ellington. They usually made this excursion in the summertime, but the weather was warm enough for it right now. By the time they got there, they were always hot and perspiring, but then they cooled off by going swimming in the resort's big pool. For twenty five cents they could go swimming all afternoon. It was mostly older adults who were there, coming from all parts of the state, but there were usually a few of the younger generation from Ellington there.

After Spring Vacation life resumed its normal course, the same dull routine, Elaine thought. She was already making plans that would fill the long, hot summer days ahead. Her week off had just been a little taste of what it was like to slow down, sleep in, and be a little lazy. She knew that during the summer, however, she would miss all her friends from Armedia. They were becoming a very close knit group. One day during the lunch break when the girls were sitting out on the lawn in their usual place under the trees, Megan had a suggestion. She always seemed to be coming up with good ideas. "I've been thinking of having a slumber party sometime soon," she said. "I'd like to invite all of you, plus a few others, maybe eight girls altogether."

"How about a few boys?" joked Alma.

"Of course only you would come up with an idea like that," Elaine told her.

"You haven't heard all my idea just yet," Megan went on. "Right before the slumber party, I'm having a boy-girl party, and I'm going to invite twice the number of guys, which would be 16 guys."

"Ohh, that sounds like a good plan," stated Beth.

"A two to one ratio. I like those odds," Karen remarked.

"And since boys are socially about two years behind girls at this age, I'm going to invite mostly upperclassmen, like Willie and his friends."

"Willie doesn't have that many friends," Vicki joked.

Megan ignored this and went on. "I definitely don't want any freshmen boys there. They are way too juvenile."

"Remember that time DJ and Shawn turned off the lights at the dance? Soo childish," said Beth.

"I just want men at my party."

"Well that leaves out my brother," remarked Vicki, still teasing.

"We'll have to invite Alvin for Elaine," suggested Alma.

"Don't do me any favors. Besides, he doesn't fall into the man category."

"That's for sure. Has he bothered you lately?" Vicki asked her.

"Oh, he still calls up in the evenings and tries to talk for hours about nothing. I finally told him I couldn't talk on school nights. But I'm running out of excuses for not going out with him."

"Just tell him the truth, that he needs to leave you alone," Megan heartlessly advised.

A light breeze blew over the girls and they suddenly grew quiet as they sat, looking down the sloping hill and across the street, past the drive-in, to the sparkling waters of Lake Armedia, which was now over halfway filled.

"It's so nice to have our lake back," Karen remarked, "for the first time in five or six years."

"Summer's going to be fun what with water skiing, boating, and swimming on the lake," said Megan. "And it will bring people to Armedia, and help our economy"

"But Beth and I will be stuck in Ellington away from all the action," moaned Elaine.

"Well, by next summer we should have our driver's licenses," Beth pointed out. "We can come up here whenever we want."

"We will have our licenses, but we still need a car," remarked Elaine.

"You mean you'll actually miss us this summer?" Alma asked.

"We'll write to you."

"Maybe Alvin will come and keep you company."

"Honestly, you guys, I am getting sooo tired of being teased about him," she told the girls. "It's not even funny anymore."

"But it's such fun to tease you," Megan remarked.

The MYF group was making plans for camp. It seemed that everyone was interested in going, but they all had the same problem Elaine had, getting the money together. Elaine had submitted the paperwork for camp, along with a 5.00 deposit, and had received notice that another 5.00 would be subtracted from the total sum if she would take a job in the dining hall and help serve meals. The MYF had money in the treasury that would help send everyone to camp, but of course the amount allotted each person depended on how many from the group would be attending. She sincerely hoped that Alvin would not go because she knew she would have no fun at all if he did. He still came to the MYF meetings, although sporadically. He stopped to pick her up first and then he took her home afterwards. Then he sometimes stayed as late as 9:30 or 10:00 in the evenings when she had other things to do. Her parents, who had liked him at first, were beginning to feel rather annoyed with Alvin. He had a way of dropping in at mealtime and he never knew when to leave. Elaine had dropped more than merely subtle hints to him, but he remained oblivious. Whenever he asked her out, she told him she was busy.

"What are you doing Friday night?" he asked her one morning at her locker. "My sister and her boyfriend are going into Hollywood to the Cinerama Theater, and we could double date with them."

Elaine wished that she liked him better, since he was always asking her on such interesting sounding dates. "It sounds like it would be fun, but I'm busy that night."

"Busy? What are you doing?"

"I'm going to a party that Megan is having." She knew Alvin would know she didn't have a date for Megan's party. It was a real disadvantage at Armedia High, that everybody knew everybody's business. If she had a date for the party, Alvin would have known because he always managed to find out everything about her. She sometimes wondered if he'd put the FBI on her trail.

"Wouldn't you rather go and see Cinerama than go to a party?" he prodded.

"I already promised Megan I would help with the party, and besides, my parents aren't going to let me go off to Hollywood. They don't even know your sister's boyfriend, or what kind of driver he is." That happened to be the truth, because her parents were always concerned about her getting into a car with a guy who was a careless or reckless driver or a speed demon.

"Could I take you to the party then?"

Elaine thought fast. "It's a slumber party," she said.

"Well, that sounds like fun. But I wouldn't want to go to that since I'd be the only boy with a bunch of giggling girls. Elaine," he added as they walked down the steps toward the Student Square, "sometimes I get the idea that you don't want to go out with me."

How right you are, she thought, "It's just that I'm really busy these days. Besides, like I told you one time, I want to go out with more than one guy only, you know, play the field."

"Who else do you go out with?"

"You know what? You can be really nosy sometimes."

"Not being nosy, just interested."

She couldn't fib about Armedia boys or Alvin would be questioning them. She hated to lie, but had little choice. "There is a guy from San Diego, a sailor that I date once in a while."

"A swabbie, huh? Is he bigger that I am?"

"Yes, he's over six feet tall."

"Well, he must be an okay guy if you really like him. I do think a lot of you, Elaine."

"Well, thank you," she said, ardently wishing she could act in a way that would make him think much less of her.

The party on Friday night wasn't exactly the kind of get-together the girls had hoped for. Megan's sister, Marie, who was a junior, had wanted a few of her friends at the mixed party and at the slumber party later. Marie was a cute little brunette who was much more sophisticated than her younger sister and she ran around with a rather wild group. Another problem with most Armedia Valley parties was the fact that news of every party leaked out and filtered among the students, and as a result, many came uninvited. And there was usually some alcohol around somewhere.

Since Marie and Megan Frye were well known around Armedia, there was a large crowd present, and many of the guests smelled of liquor. Cigarette smoke permeated the air. There wasn't too much dancing. Most of the guests and crashers stood around in small groups, going in and out of the house. Elaine and Beth judged that 50 or 60 people had been there sometime during the course of the evening. Megan was furious. "This certainly isn't the kind of party I had planned," she whispered to Elaine. "I told Mother I didn't want any of Marie's friends here, but she didn't listen to me. This is all Marie's fault, and now she's drunk. She makes a great hostess," she added sarcastically, glancing at her sister on the couch who was curled up in the arms of Duane Kellogg, making out with him. "The guys aren't bringing beer into the house, but they keep going outside to their cars to drink. It's so disgusting!"

"I'm sure the slumber party will go better," Elaine comforted.

"Not if Marie and her little clique are here," Megan said disgustedly. "And even Willie is drunk. He's such an idiot when he's had a few drinks."

Elaine was glad that most of the freshmen didn't drink, although she realized that some would by the time they were older. She wasn't having a particularly good time at the party. She had danced with a stout Hispanic guy with beer on his breath and a tall thin boy who held her too close. She perked up when Ty Ramirez asked her to dance. He was a very good looking guy, and was Natalie's secret heartthrob. Of course Nat wasn't there, but she knew she would tell her later that she had danced with him. "We had a close call on the way over here," Ty was saying.

"Why, what happened?"

"Well a bunch of us were drinking, and we made a couple of stops on the way over here to talk to other people. We were cruising over to another party when the cops pulled us over. We thought we were cool, since we'd all finished our beer, and threw out the bottles. But we'd forgotten at our last stop, that some dummy had put two six-packs of Hamms on top of the car."

"So you were driving down the street with beer on the roof of the car?" Elaine asked, amazed. "I don't believe it!"

"Yeah, pretty stupid, huh?"

"Whoever did that must have felt like a real idiot. So what did the cops do?"

"When they pulled us over, they were both real friendly like and we just all had a conversation. But then they said 'you know you can't be driving around with beer on top of your car,' and they took it off, and emptied out all the bottles on the ground. What a waste of good beer and a couple of bucks." He pulled her closer and began humming the Hamms beer commercial "From the land of sky blue waters . . ."

Elaine was laughing at his story when she saw Alvin walk into the room, and her smile quickly faded. After the dance with Ty, Alvin stuck by her side for the remainder of the evening. At least he hadn't been drinking, and he was in a very good mood. He was telling Elaine that his steer had won a blue ribbon at the county fair, which took place just last week.

"Of course I had a feeling he was going to win. He weighed almost one thousand pounds, and sold for 38 cents a pound, and also received Reserved Champion FFA." Elaine really wasn't too impressed, although she tried to act as if she were. She was relieved when, finally at midnight, Mrs. Frye made the announcement that the party was over.

Twelve girls helped straighten up the living room, picking up half full punch cups, and chips that had fallen everywhere, and then they filled the room with blankets and pillows. Marie's group was over closer to the dining room area while Megan's group was by the front door. They ate, chattered, and listened to records. They played a game called Blanket, and they played cards. Willie and a couple of his friends came back, but they weren't allowed in the house. By the time the mantelpiece clock had chimed 3:00, most of the girls had dropped off to sleep.

Elaine, Megan, and Vicki sat by the fireplace, still talking and telling each their life history almost. Megan and Vicki, having lived in Armedia since kindergarten, knew the past of many of the high school students, and Elaine liked hearing the stories they told. Megan also liked to predict the future of everyone. She had her own pretty well planned out. "Willie and I will get married in June of 1963 after he graduates college. And I'll be finishing my last two years of college after that."

"How do you know you'll even like Willie by the time you graduate from high school?" Elaine asked. "I mean, how can you be so sure?"

"That's what I keep asking her," Vicki said.

Megan shrugged. "I just know. Deep down I just know that for a fact."

"That's five years from now," Elaine mused. "I wonder what we'll all be like by then."

"We should have a reunion," stated Vicki. They lay back on their pillow, staring dreamily into the dying embers of the fire, wondering what life's next five years would hold for them.

Chapter 12

The Gay Nineties was the theme of the MYF Ice Cream Social that the group undertook as a money maker for camp. It was a big project for the small group to carry out successfully. The afternoon of the social had arrived and the young people were carrying tables out from the church social hall onto the back lawn.

"It would be just our luck to have rain this evening," Adam remarked, as the sky clouded up.

"We need a positive outlook," Norma Fawcett told him as she handed out tablecloths to the girls.

"I think the Gay Ninety's idea is fun," Lucy said. She looked cute in her high necked, long sleeved blouse, and long skirt. Elaine wore a long, mauve colored formal of her mother's, not a fashion of the 1890's, but ancient enough, Lois had said. Her hair was pulled back into a bun with curls hanging down on each side of her face. The evening was pleasantly warm, and a good sized crowd turned out for the event. The youth group waited on the customers while Mrs. Fawcett and Mrs. Hathaway made up the sundaes, banana splits, root beer floats and other ice cream delights. Later there was a sing-along, with songs of that period, like *Down By the Old Mill Stream, Sweet Evangeline,* and *Bicycle Built For Two.* Elaine's Grandma Grace told her later that she'd had a wonderful time. "I was born in 1890," she said. "So I have wonderful memories of that era when I was growing up, the long dresses, the hairstyles, the manners everyone had. It was all so much more formal." Elaine tried to picture what life must have been like back then, and what her grandma had been like as a young girl.

The group had made 50.00 after paying for the ice cream and the other foods. Combined with the 30.00 they had make from the bake sale a few weeks ago, the MYF treasury could contribute 8.00 for each camper. (Ten from their group would be going.)

Elaine celebrated her fifteenth birthday the middle of May. She'd wanted to have a party, but after seeing how Megan's turned out, she'd decided a party would have been a bad idea. She settled for a family dinner. Grandma Thompson and Scott were there too of course. And Natalie was there, since she would be spending the night. Lois fixed her favorite dinner: pork chops, ambrosia salad, corn on the cob, and apple pie ala mode for dessert.

Later Elaine and Nat were in the bedroom reminiscing over the past year. Lois had arranged for Pam to spend the night at the home of Dodie Fawcett, which was most convenient for all concerned.

"Have you kept up your diary?" Elaine asked her.

"I got bogged down around Christmas time. Oh, I still write in it, but I've skipped a few weeks here and there."

"It's hard to keep it up every day. But I've only missed a few entries. I have to keep it up if I'm going to be a writer."

"That's for sure. When are you going to start your book?"

"This summer. All my friends are going to be characters in it."

"Good. Make me and Ty have a red hot love affair."

"I can do that. I'm not putting Alvin in the book at all."

"It will serve him right for being such a jerk. I bet you'll miss seeing him this summer."

"What do you mean miss him? He'll probably be driving down here all the time," Elaine stated, throwing a pillow at Nat. "Oh, by the way, he had some news for me today, some really good news. He's not going to camp, since he just got a job at the skating rink. I'm so happy about that. Also I have to show you what he gave me for my birthday." She went to the closet and pulled out a large box, showing her a fuzzy, spotted leopard, the school mascot. A big red bow adorned its neck, and its green glass eyes gleamed at the girls.

"Oh, he is just precious!" Nat exclaimed, cuddling the stuffed animal. "He's so huggable."

"I really should have given it back to Alvin," Elaine said. "But I just couldn't. He is too cute. So since I accepted it, I had to accept a date with Alvin tomorrow night. But the fact that he's not going to camp is the best gift of all."

"One thing I'll say for him is that he can pick out nice presents," Nat admitted.

"My family can pick out nice presents too," Elaine added, her thoughts going back to dinner that evening. After she'd opened her gifts, a charm bracelet, a wallet, a beautiful little music box from her grandma and Scott, her father handed her an envelope. In it was a check made out to MYF Camp for the amount that she still needed. She was ecstatic.

"Well, we think that camp will be a really great experience for you," Charles had said.

Before her think too much about camp, however, there were still three weeks of schools and finals to get through, and there were numerous ends of the year activities. The Spanish classes took a trip to the Huntington Library in San Marino. The GAA had a swimming party. The seniors were busy practicing for the graduation ceremony.

Elaine felt as though she didn't know much more about Algebra than when she came into the class back in September. Of course, now that football season was over, Mr. Carr didn't discuss that subject as much, but he didn't discuss too much Algebra either. Because of his negligence of the subject, he hadn't earned the respect of his students. Vicki disliked him immensely ever since that day he had made her cry in class. Shawn O'Dell still slept in back of the room, and also continued to talk back to Mr. Carr, calling him Mr. Ford, Mr. Chevy, etc. Elaine was in a cold sweat worrying about the final. Mr. Carr was very unpredictable. He might have an easy final as he had last semester or he might have a much more difficult one. So far Elaine had averaged a C in his class.

She was improving in Spanish, but just slightly. Out of all her teachers, she disliked Mrs.Mendoza more than any other, although she had found out during the year that Alma Mendoza was the niece of the Spanish teacher. She never seemed to show any feelings for members of the class, or show a sense of humor at all. She seemed to dislike DJ Morrison more than anyone else, but he constantly annoyed her by eating in class or listening to the small transistor radio that he kept hidden in his shirt pocket. The final in that class consisted of an oral report, completely *en espanol*, and the students were dreading it.

Art was one class in which everyone could relax. Miss Lippert had them working with clay, and her pupils were enjoying themselves immensely. No one had a desk in Art, but sat at big tables. Elaine and Vicki sat in the back of the room with Shawn O'Dell. The tables had pipes for legs. The pipes were screwed to the top of the table, and the end of the pipe curved around to the edge of the table. Elaine, in deep conversation with Vicki, absent-mindedly stuck her finger into the pipe. Her finger had been sticky because of the gooey modeling clay, and she suddenly realized that it was stuck in the tight hole. She twisted and turned, and pulled as hard as she could, but it would not budge. How silly of me, she thought, this is something a kindergartner would do, not a high school girl. She was beginning to get a little panicky. She finally whispered her predicament to Vicki who burst into laughter rather loudly. She tried to help, but was laughing too hard to be of much use. By then Shawn had realized the situation, and was also laughing and making his usual inane comments.

"You're going to be stuck here for life at this table, Elaine. It's going to be a long hot summer for you. But don't worry, I think Lippie will take pity on you and bring you food and water."

"You're such a comfort, Shawn," she told him. By then Alvin, at the next table had come over to assess the situation. Elaine was beginning to really worry, and she thought her finger was beginning to swell a bit. She didn't want Miss Lippert to hear of her predicament, because then the entire class would know of the dumb stunt she had pulled.

"They may have to amputate that finger," Shawn was saying. "Is there a doctor in the house?"

"What's all the commotion back here?" Miss Lippert asked, coming back to their table. "How are you guys doing on your clay modeling? Why it looks like you haven't even started," she added reproachfully. Vicki took one look at Elaine's stricken face and quietly explained the problem to Miss Lippert. A grin spread across the teacher's face, but then she grew serious, and suggested putting Vaseline on Elaine's finger. She thought she had some in her desk. Elaine was thinking that her finger was too tightly jammed into the hole, that Vaseline could only be put on the end of it, so how would that help? By this time the entire class was aware of the situation, and everyone was looking toward the back table or standing around it. She hated Alvin's chuckles.

"Why did this have to happen in the same class with Alvin?" she whispered to Vicki. "It will be spread all over the school before noon."

"Don't worry about it," comforted Vicki.

Suddenly there were five short rings of the bell which indicated a fire drill. Instead of lining up, as they usually did, the students looked around, puzzled. "There's no doubt about this, you're going to stay here and burn," Shawn told her grimly.

"It's only a drill, Stupid," Vicki told him. "And I'll stay here and burn too."

"Class, class, you know the procedure for a fire drill," a rather worried Miss Lippert told them. "Line up and leave in an orderly fashion, just as you always do." Suddenly she had an idea. "Shawn, you and Alvin pick up your end of the table. Vicki, you help with this end. We'll have to carry it outside. Everyone will think we're crazy, but it's the only solution." It was a clumsy attempt at first, especially getting through the door of the Art bungalow. That took some maneuvering. Going down the steps was also a bit tricky. They were trying to carry the table outside with dignity, acting as if this was a natural procedure of a fire drill. But when they saw the curious stares of other students, they nearly choked with laughter. Elaine violently threatened anyone who told others about her predicament. She hoped that, from a distance, no one could tell what was wrong. They had reached the grass now, where they were "safe" from fire. Shawn had somehow dragged a chair outside with him also. He calmly sat down on it and began playing with the modeling clay which was still on the table.

In answer to the queries of the others, he replied, "Had to take this table with me so I could finish my clay modeling. Lippie will beat me if it's not done."

"You bet I will, Shawn, "Miss Lippert teased.

"You should be thankful that we saved your life, today, Elaine," Alvin told her.

"You owe us big-time for all our help," Shawn added.

"You can both go jump in the lake!" she told them.

"Okay, class, fire drill's over. Let's carry the table back. I'm going to find a janitor. He should be able to help you, Elaine," Miss Lippert said to her.

After the friendly, elderly janitor had dismantled the table, Elaine was able to free her finger. It was swollen, but free from captivity. She never lived down her misadventure though. Everyone in the entire school had heard about it by lunchtime.

Final exams came around and Elaine did better than expected. The much feared Algebra final consisted of ten easy problems. At the end of the year, report cards would be mailed out instead of going home with the kids, but Elaine knew what she had received in each class, about the same as last semester.

The yearbooks, *The Armedian* were distributed and signed. The girls sat out under the pepper trees for the last time as freshmen. They were busy signing yearbooks.

"This is kind of sad," Elaine said. "Seems like were just starting school a couple of weeks ago, and now it's almost over."

"Well, you might be sad," Karen told her "but I'm really looking forward to summer."

"Actually, so am I," Elaine said. "I'm going to MYF camp later this month, and that should be a lot of fun."

"Here, sign your John Hancock on my annual," Alma told her.

"Whatever you do, don't ask DJ to sign," Vicki told the group. "He told me he didn't want to sign it because everybody always wrote the same thing and it was a waste of time, but, dumb me, I kept insisting. So he did finally. He took up an entire page writing DJ in huge letters, and drew an ugly little man at the bottom."

"Well, he wanted to do something different that you'll always remember," Lucy told her.

"Yeah, no one can really forget DJ," Elaine said. "They might try to forget him, but they can't."

"He does have a point," Megan pointed out. "Everybody mostly always writes the same thing: to a great kid, it's been fun knowing you, have a wonderful summer, blah, blah, blah."

"Oh, well, it's one time when everybody has something nice to say about everyone," Karen remarked.

"Just think, tonight is graduation," Megan said. "Next year Willie will be graduating. How sad."

"Cheer up, maybe he'll flunk," Vicki comforted.

"In three more years, that will be us," Elaine said.

"I heard that Paul Newberry had a really wild party for some of the seniors," Alma stated. "Everyone got drunker than skunks."

"Wonder if our senior class will be like that," Beth mused. "Hope not."

"Doesn't the lake look pretty?" Lucy asked, and they turned to look out at the silvery-blue waters, shimmering in the sunlight.

"Wouldn't it be nice to go swimming right now?" Alma asked.

"We could go wading," Megan suggested.

"It's the last day of school," Vicki pointed out. "Let's do it. Who cares if we're late to class?" They stacked their yearbooks and assorted other belongings together in a pile by a tree, and headed down to cross the street to the lake.

The last period of the day an awards assembly was held, long and uninteresting for the freshmen, who received few awards. Alma's twin brother, Lenny, was mentioned for awards a couple of times, as was Greg Okamota, a popular Japanese boy that was in Elaine's English class. Karen Gillespie's name was called too for an award. Her friends clapped loudly for her. After the awards, the student body president made his last appearance on the stage. He excused the seniors first.

They made their way out of the gym, some slowly and reluctantly, some eagerly. They all looked rather fatigued after their grad night vigil, and breakfast. A few girls looked as if they were almost in tears.

Next the juniors moved up to the senior section and gave their newly acquired senior yell. Then the sophomores moved, and finally the freshmen moved to the soph section across the aisle. At last they gave a yell that rang out full and strong, a yell of confidence and pride. That was the end of the assembly and the end of Elaine's freshman year.

Chapter 13

Two weeks into summer vacation Elaine found herself packing her suitcase for camp. Her bed was covered with freshly ironed blouses, a couple of dresses, T-shirts, Capri pants and Bermuda shorts. Beth and Lucy were calling her every twenty minutes to compare notes on what items should be packed. On Sunday afternoon the group drove up into the San Bernardino Mountains to Camp Whispering Pines. Warren had part of the group in his car, and Marvin and Dorothy Snowball, Lucy's folks were driving the three girls and Scottie. "You girls are just so excited, you're chattering like a bunch of magpies," Mr. Snowball said to them, as they sat in the back seat. "Scottie here, can't get a word in."

"Oh, I'm okay, Mr. Snowball," Scottie told him. "I'm just enjoying the drive."

After about an hour, they began climbing into the foothills, then into the mountains. Pine trees began to pop up, a few here and there at first, and then the landscape became thick with them. Mr. Snowball was behind Warren's car, and followed him onto a side road which had numerous switchbacks. After one more turn onto a dirt road, they at last reached the camp's entrance, marked by a large sign, which was bordered by pines. Everyone scrambled out of the cars.

"Oh, the air always smells so fresh and fragrant in the mountains," Lucy was saying.

"This is the place," remarked Warren. "The first thing we need to do is register. That will be over there at the lodge." They said goodbye to Lucy's parents and headed over toward a large brown building built of logs with a huge stone chimney.

"Wow, there are some sharp looking chicks at this camp!" exclaimed DJ, watching the assortment of blondes, brunettes, and redheads running around in shorts and T-shirts, carrying their suitcases.

"And some good looking fellows too," Elaine added. After a short wait in the registration line, they were given name tags with a number on the back, camp schedules, and cabin assignments.

"Oh, no, we're in Cabin 13," Beth cried.

"Don't be so superstitious," Warren told her. He had some of the boys helping carry the girls' luggage and sleeping bags. The girls had brought twice the luggage the boys had. "After we deposit all your junk at your cabin, then we're going across the creek to ours. That's the boys' section across that little creek."

"This camp is really segregated," Lucy remarked. "Guess they want to make sure that no monkey business will be taking place." Everyone laughed at her remark.

The small, bubbling brook divided the campground neatly in half. The lodge and chapel were on the side with the girls' cabins, while the dining hall and swimming pool were more or less in the boys' area. A large meadow, filled with wildflowers and tall green grasses covered the soft, sloping hills behind the cabin area. There was beauty everywhere. As they climbed to the top of the hill, they could see a small lake in the distance.

They reached Cabin 13, and the boys went on their way. The cabin was a small, plain building with three sets of wooden bunk beds and one table.

"Well, nothing fancy about this," Beth commented. "Where's the bathroom? I don't see one, just a sink in the corner."

"Bathrooms must be in a separate building," said Lucy. "No place to put our clothes, though. Guess we'll just be living out of our suitcases."

"There are some big cubbies over on that wall," Beth noticed. "That's where our clothes will go."

"I wonder what our roommates will be like," Elaine mused, glancing at three beds, already made.

"I would guess this girl is a real nut, judging from her bedspread and hat," Beth remarked. The spread on a top bunk was a bright orange, red, and purple checked comforter, and the straw hat sported only one decoration, a miniature beer can on the brim.

"And she's going to wear that around here?' asked Lucy. "At a Christian camp?"

"I have a feeling she and DJ would make a good pair," Elaine said. She set her stuff on the bunk beneath the made up one. "I have to have a bottom bunk, since I once fell out of a top one."

Suddenly they heard a thud and a clatter outside the door. "Ow!" a voice cried. They opened the door and found a girl sitting on the ground at the door's threshold. She had obviously just fallen down and was a sight to behold. She had the reddest hair Elaine had ever seen, and it was blowing wildly in the breeze. Her cute round face was dotted with freckles. She was wearing oversize, comic sunglasses, faded Levis, a cotton shirt, and a gray beanie was perched atop her wild hair. Assorted items lay strewn around her: Mad magazines, a tennis racket, a transistor radio, and a guitar case. Her sandals had slipped off when she fell, and she wriggled her bare toes, looked up calmly at the three girls with a big sunny smile. "Hello," she said nonchalantly. "You must be my roomies. I'm Dottie Snell from Long Beach. And these two," she added, gesturing to the giggling girls behind her, "are Moe and Sandy."

Moe was a petite brown haired girl, and Sandy was a tall girl with sandy colored hair. The Ellington girls introduced themselves, and everyone helped Dottie up, and then helped with her belongings. "You've never met anyone, tile you've met Dottie," Sandy told them. "She is a character. And she's terribly uncoordinated."

"I'm not really, I just slipped," Dottie told them as she climbed to her top bunk.

"Dottie, you've brought so much junk you could spend a year here," Moe stated, handing her a box, which contained a partial rock collection.

"Don't forget to water your begonias," Sandy told Dottie. "Oh, you should see Dottie's begonias," she said to the girls in a mock serious voice. "They should win a prize at a flower show."

"Really? Where are they?"

"Under your bed," Dottie told Elaine.

"Well, why did you bring them to camp?"

"I'm going to plant them outside the cabin," was the answer, "and make our yard look pretty."

"Of course, why didn't we think of that?" Beth asked.

"I pity you having a bed beneath Dottie's," Moe said to Elaine. "Last year her bunk came crashing down, but luckily no one was underneath at the time."

"I guess maybe a top bunk would have been safer," Elaine said.

"Is Moe a nickname for something?" Lucy asked her.

"Well, my full name is Florence Moe, but I hate the name Florence. And of course the nickname Flo sounds silly with Moe. Flo Moe sounds like a detergent or something. So I just have everyone call me by my last name. It's easier that way."

A knock resounded on the frame of the open door. "Hello everyone. I'm your cabin counselor, Pat Weston," called a tall young woman. "I'm in cabin 14, just next door if you need anything. What are your names?"

After they had introduced themselves and Pat had left, Elaine said, "I thought every cabin had to have a counselor."

"No, thank goodness,' Moe exclaimed. "The cabins are in groups of three, two small ones, with a big cabin in the middle with enough beds for nine girls and a counselor. Last year we were in the middle cabin with the counselor. She was always kind of grumpy too. It was no fun, let me tell you."

"We lucked out this year," Sandy stated.

"Oh, no, there's a spider up here, a big one," Lucy squealed from her bunk.

"It's only a daddy-long-legs," said Dottie. She jumped down off her bunk, climbed onto Lucy's, and knocked the offending spider into her hand with a magazine and tossed it out the window. Elaine could hardly believe her eyes. She didn't know any girls who would touch a spider. Dottie amazed her.

"That's one advantage of having our Dottie for a roomie," Sandy pointed out. "She's not afraid of anything."

"She had a snake in the cabin last year," added Moe. "Our counselor nearly had a heart attack."

"That was pretty funny," Dottie agreed. "And remember when I put a lizard in Patty Tyler's bed?"

"Patty Tyler would win the wimp award hands down," Moe told the others. "She didn't come with us this time. We had a ball last year, and we will this year too."

"What are these numbers for on the back of our name tags?" Elaine asked.

"Your number determines what group you'll be in for the week," Moe explained. "They try to mix everyone up, so you meet more people that way. There are about 300 kids here at camp, and they're divided up into about 20 groups. When you meet for the first time, each group has to pick a name. And then you're with that group for sporting events, your craft sessions, and your Bible study."

"I'm glad we're rooming with someone who seems to know the score around here," Beth said.

"I should know," came the answer. "My mom has been a counselor for the last four years." The girls compared numbers, and none of them had the same number. "I told you everyone would be mixed up," declared Moe. "We'll all be going our separate ways with our groups."

The girls were unpacked and settled by 3:30, and according to the schedule, they were to meet at 4:00 in the lodge. There they rushed around getting signatures for a get-acquainted game: a counselor wearing purple and green socks, a boy who is over six feet tall, a girl with green eyes, and a boy from San Diego. After that there was an opening meeting in the lodge. The camp faculty, consisting of counselors, speakers, and song leaders was introduced. Then each church group was introduced. The Ellington group was proud of their matching blue and green T-shirts, although they weren't the only group with that idea. Following the meeting, Elaine and the others who had jobs in the dining hall had to go there to receive instructions about work. She was thankful that Dottie was working there also.

"I know just about half the kids here," Dottie was bragging, as they climbed the hill to the dining hall. "One reason is that our bunch from Long Beach has the biggest MYF group up here. A little bird told me that the fellows from our church are going to serenade our cabin tonight. That is if I'll loan Danny Settle my guitar, which I probably won't do because he can't be trusted with it. Maybe he can find some other sucker to loan him one instead." She paused for breath, and Elaine saw her chance to get a word in.

"Did you work here in the dining hall last year?"

"Yes. It's loads of fun and the work isn't really hard. All we do is set and clear tables mostly. And if the serving bowls or the milk pitchers at our table get emptied, we get up and get more for everyone."

They walked inside the large dining hall with its knotty pine walls and two rows of 18 tables on either side of a large aisle. Each young person was assigned a table for which they were responsible. Elaine looked around at the others. There were some interesting looking fellows she hoped to meet at some point. Dottie began talking to one of the boys she seemed to know. Elaine noticed that his name tag said Danny Settle. He was slightly taller than Elaine with deep set blue eyes and brown hair in a Napoleon-style haircut. He wore a straw hat, a bright shirt, and cut-off Levis. He looked to Elaine to be the type of boy with loads of personality. A small, but noticeable scar on his jaw made him even more attractive.

"Well, hello there, cutie," he said to Elaine. He was studying her nametag. "And where, may I ask, is Ellington?"

"Oh, it's out in the sticks. Nobody has ever heard of it."

"Nowheresville, huh?"

"That's about it. No excitement, nothing to do, very peaceful."

"It's anything but peaceful around here. Right Dottie?" he asked.

"Come on, Elaine," Dottie was saying, "it's almost time to eat and we need to get our tables set." They finished just in time, since teen agers were swarming into the dining hall. She and Dottie hurried to set steaming bowls of food on the tables. Danny was working in the dining hall also. DJ and Scottie seated themselves at Elaine's table, and Dottie asked Elaine to introduce them to her. Once the entire group was seated everyone quieted down long enough to sing a grace, and then the chatter began again.

After dinner the campers went back across the little bridge to the Greek theater which overlooked the meadow. The song leader, a black man whose face radiated love and good will, led them in group singing. Their 300 voices rang out across the camp. The singing was followed by the reading of a humorous camp newspaper and more announcements. The sunlight gradually faded from the grassy meadow as the sun slowly disappeared behind the mountains, leaving the area bathed in twilight. The pine trees were standing at attention, silhouetted against the pale sky. The first star appeared over the trees, giving the landscape an air of serenity. Logs had already been placed in a big fire pit down in front, and the campfire was lit once darkness descended upon the area. The evening speaker was a petite little lady from San Diego, and she delivered her message with warmth, humor and enthusiasm. Elaine was thrilled by everything the evening program had to offer. She felt a warm glow as the group sang *now the Day Is Over*, which was last on the evening's agenda.

As the teen agers walked back to their cabins, to the haunting sound of *Taps*, Scottie and Warren caught up with Elaine. "Well, what did you think of your first day here?" Warren asked.

"It was really amazing," she told him. "I was at 4-H camp a few years back, and it was fun. But I think this camp is much better . . . It's in a beautiful place and I'm meeting some interesting new friends. Are you enjoying it, Scottie?"

"I'm having a ball so far," was his answer. "And there are plenty of good hiking trails around here."

Before getting ready for bed, the girls went next door to the counselor's cabin for devotions, then back to their own cabin. The girls then walked over to the bathrooms to get their showers. They felt just as comfortable with their new companions as they did with their high school friends.

"That Warren Fawcett is a certainly good looking," stated Moe. "Does he have a girlfriend?"

"No, he's just friends with all the girls," Elaine told her. "I had a crush on him for a long time, but he only thinks of me as a friend."

"I think your cousin is cute," Sandy remarked. He sure gets around well for being on crutches."

Once they were back in their cabin, tucked into bed, the same discussion about boys went on. It felt so familiar to Elaine; she almost thought she was back at school on the front lawn at lunch.

"So what about DJ," Dottie asked. "Does he have anyone special?"

That question brought laughter from the three Ellington girls. "DJ—a girlfriend? No way!" Beth laughed. "He thinks he's cute, but he's just a goof-off, and doesn't have a serious bone in his body."

"Well, I'll tell you who I think is absolutely fascinating," Elaine said, "and that's Danny Settle. There's something about him that really intrigues me. Must be his blue eyes, or that scar maybe."

"Don't fall for him," Moe advised. "Lots of girls have, and have gotten hurt. He's the biggest flirt I know, and he has a different girlfriend every week almost."

"Shhh." Dottie interrupted. "Did you guys hear something outside?"

"Don't try to scare us like you did last year," Sandy told her. "It's most likely your overactive imagination."

"As I was saying," Moe continued. "Danny has a girlfriend back home, an older woman. She's 17."

"What year is Danny in school?" Elaine asked.

"He'll be a junior. But he's nothing but a big clown, sort of like DJ, from what you guys say."

"Speaking of DJ, did you guys know he and Danny are in the same cabin?" Dottie asked.

"Oh, that cabin will be falling down before the week is over," Moe stated. "I pity the poor guy who is their counselor." In the silence that followed, a suppressed laugh was heard just outside the window. Dottie, who had closest access to the shade, pulled it up and looked out. And there, squatting down next to the cabin wall were Danny and DJ and two other boys, all doubled up with laughter. The boys stood up to look in the window.

"What's the big idea?" Moe demanded in a stage whisper. "You guys are supposed to be in your cabin after lights out. If you get caught, you'll be in big trouble, and we probably will too."

"We were going to serenade you," one of the boys said.

"But then we found your conversation so interesting, that we hated to interrupt," Danny added, looking at Elaine. She suddenly became conscious of her thin summer nightie, and pulled the covers up around her. She was even more embarrassed when Danny added, "No need to do that."

"We been havin' a ball up here," DJ said. "After the program tonight we raided some chick's cabin and took all their—their—"

"Unmentionables," Danny put in.

"Yeah, that. And then we tied them—"

"Just wait til you see the flagpole tomorrow," Danny interrupted.

"This is any MYF camp," Sandy told them. "And you guys are acting like a bunch of hoods."

"Well, it was their fault because they didn't lock their door," DJ said, putting the blame on the girls.

"Besides, we are getting a counselor tomorrow," a tall blonde fellow said. "So then we'll have to settle down, but we wanted to have some fun first."

"Hey, we'd better split," Danny said, noticing the beam of flashlights across the creek. "I think they're having a cabin check." He winked one of his fascinating blue eyes at Elaine, and then they were gone.

The next morning came far too early for most of the campers. Bugle call was at 7:00, breakfast was at 8:00, followed by cabin clean-up and inspection. At 10:00 each camper went to their special group for discussion or Bible study. Each group voted on a name and Elaine's group chose "Pinecones" as their name. Elaine didn't think that was very original, but it got the most votes. Lunch was followed by an hour's rest period. It was strange, no one felt that they needed the rest, but half the girls in Elaine's cabin had fallen asleep. She was writing postcards to Pam and Natalie. The afternoon was filled with various forms of recreation: swimming, hiking, volleyball, tennis, and crafts.

Elaine was looking forward to her KP duty in the dining room because she knew Danny would be there. She blushed every time she thought of how he had heard what she'd said about him. Before dinner she put on a pretty summer sundress of pink plaid material with spaghetti straps. White sandals and a flower in her pony tail completed her look.

"I wish we didn't have to wear dresses for dinner," Dottie was complaining. "After all, this is camp, and we're supposed to be roughing it. I'm much more comfortable in my Levis."

"That's because you're not a lady," Moe teased her. She was sitting on her bunk reading a Mad magazine. "Our group played Warren's in volleyball today," she told Elaine. "But they won because they have a lot of tall people in their group."

"Is everyone going to the square dance after the campfire program?" Sandy asked.

"I didn't even know about it," said Beth.

"It was just planned today."

"Sounds like fun," Lucy said.

"It sounds pretty square to me," mumbled Dottie. "I'm not going."

As she was setting the tables for dinner that night, Danny came up to her and put his arm around her. "You sure do look yummy," he whispered in her ear. "Do you still think I'm absolutely fascinating?"

Elaine blushed and smiled at him teasingly. "No, I think you're terrible," she retorted.

Danny looked at the artificial rosebuds on her pony tail. The clip they were on was coming unfastened, and with a swift gesture he pulled the clip from her hair and put it in the pocket of his Hawaiian print shirt. "And I'm not giving it back until I get an apology and a kiss," he said.

"Apology? For what?" she asked innocently.

"For saying just now that I was terrible. And for believing all those stories Moe was telling about me last night."

"Let's get those tables set," the dining hall counselor told them. "You can do your talking later."

Danny sat across from Elaine at the dinner table. She didn't want to admit to herself that she had a crush on him. But she was so attracted to him. She found his haircut, his smile, and his mannerisms irresistible. She loved his voice, which sounded like that of the comedian, Jerry Lewis. She liked the animated expression on his face when he was talking, which was constantly. His conversation was usually about past mischievous escapades in which he had participated.

"And none of us got to bed until 2:00 am," he was saying between bites of Salisbury steak.

"What were you doing all that time?" Moe asked.

"We were acting out a real wild play on Ben's tape recorder. It was a riot."

"I can just imagine," Sandy said dryly.

"Our counselor arrived today so that ends all our fun," Ben said.

"And get this," remarked Danny. "His name is Cecil Kunkle."

"That's nearly as good as Alvin Minegar," Beth told Elaine.

"And they probably call him Vinegar," Danny said. "Who is this character anyhow?" And Beth and Lucy proceeded to tell him in spite of Elaine's protests.

"That guy was very persistent, but I don't blame him," Danny stated, looking intently at Elaine.

His remark and his look made Elaine all shivery inside, but she kept telling herself that she did not plan on coming to a Christian camp just to fall for some guy. When she saw Danny later that evening with his arm affectionately around another girl, a very cute girl, her resolve hardened not to get sucked in by love, or what she thought was love.

"I know we'll have a dynamic program tonight," Moe told the girls as they walked to the campfire program. "Our minister is speaking, and his talks are always very interesting."

As they sat down in the Greek theater, Danny squeezed in by Elaine. "It's supposed to get colder tonight, and you can keep me warm," he said, snuggling up next to her, "or I can keep you warm."

She felt really good sitting next to him throughout the evening. But when Reverend Stokes began speaking, he caught her attention. The topic of his talk was "Following Jesus."

"Tonight I'm going to give you several examples of how people's lives have changed when they turned their lives over to the Lord," he said. He went on to tell about a teen ager, 14, who lived in Los Angeles. "Bob had been raised by a well-to-do family, had parents who were active in the community and civic affairs, but were so busy with their careers and other pursuits that they weren't paying attention to where their only child was headed. He was becoming friends with some older fellows whose primary interest was seeing how much damage they could do and how much trouble they could cause. They were almost a gang, these long—haired hoods with leather jackets and switchblades. These parents were too tired or preoccupied at night so notice that Bob was keeping very late hours after he had been riding around and drinking half the night. All the signals were there, but the parents just didn't see them. Another problem for Bob was that his folks were becoming quite distant from each other, and it looked as if a divorce was in the works. Bob had one friend, a bit older than Bob, who was an upstanding young man and a good Christian. We'll call him Sam. Sam kept trying to influence Bob to stay away from his low life buddies. One night an event occurred that changed everything. Bob was riding around with his one true friend, with Sam doing the driving, when suddenly another car pulled out in front of them and the two vehicles collided. Sam was killed instantly. Bob just had minor injuries, and spent maybe one night in the hospital. He was just really overwhelmed, and kept wondering why his life was spared, but not Sam's, who was such a good Christian. He did a great deal of soul searching. About that same time, his parents got divorced, and he moved with his mother to a different area. But he began going to church and to a youth group and ended up as a born-again Christian. He figured that the Lord had a purpose for him."

Elaine was intrigued by the story, but Danny seemed rather fidgety, and he disappeared into the crowd on the walk back to the cabin area. Moe nudged Elaine. "Did you know that the star of that story you just heard was Danny Settle?"

"Oh, no way!" she answered.

"Yes, it was Danny. He truly did almost belong to some gang when he lived in LA."

"Oh, my gosh, that is so incredible!" Elaine cried. "Did you know him then?"

"Oh, no. I didn't meet him until a couple of years ago when he began coming to our Long Beach MYF. Then his story gradually came out, little by little."

"That really was a good program tonight," Elaine remarked. "I love that song *Kum Ba Yaa.*"

The square dance which followed the campfire program was fun. The caller was calling only easy, very basic moves. Moe was happy because Warren was in the same square as she and Elaine. But Danny didn't seem to be around. Scottie was sitting on the sidelines watching the dancers, and Sandy was sitting with him, and the two were deep in conversation.

As the girls walked home after the dance, Elaine wondered where Beth and Lucy were. Moe was noticing that Dottie was also missing. "I hope she's staying out of trouble," she said.

"You know, it seems as if we've already been at camp for days and days," Sandy observed.

"I know, and it's really only been two days," Elaine said. "I don't even want to think about it being over. We have to make the most out of our days we have left."

When they reached the cabin they found Beth writing a letter and she looked happy. "I had a headache earlier, so I didn't feel like going to the dance. But Ben walked me back to the cabin and we talked for awhile. He seems like a really nice guy. But I haven't seen Dottie or Lucy at all."

"I wonder what those girls are up to?" Moe said anxiously. "I guess we'll have to go next door for devotions without them. Pat's going to wonder where they are." The girls weren't very devout at devotions that night. They made excuses for the missing roommates. They were back in their cabin getting ready for bed, and Moe was saying "I hope they don't have a cabin check tonight."

"They usually do," Sandy pointed out. "Pat will probably be here by 11:00 to see that we're all tucked in like good little girls."

"Do you think they're in some sort of trouble?" Elaine asked while brushing her teeth.

"Dottie wouldn't be Dottie if she weren't in trouble of some kind," Moe stated. "It just follows her naturally. But she usually gets out of it somehow." The girls stuffed pillows and jackets into the two empty sleeping bags so it looked as if the girls were actually in them. But just before 11:00, there was a noise at the door, and in came a calm and collected Dottie and a rather abashed Lucy. But before any questions could be asked, the counselor's tap was heard at the door.

"Here's Pat. Into bed quickly," Moe commanded in a hoarse whisper. Dottie was like lightening, climbing quickly up onto her bunk. Apparently she was used to tense situations. Lucy was a bit slower, and slid under her covers, just as Pat opened the door, checked, and smiled a good night.

"Okay, out with it! Where were you?" the girls asked after Pat had left.

"We had fun, didn't we, Dot?" Lucy asked.

"We went for a little moonlight hike. There were only us two girls and four guys, very good ratio," Dottie sighed happily. "Lucy and I were on our way back here after the program, since only squares go to a square dance, and DJ came up and said the boys from Cabin 9 wanted to take the girls from Cabin 13 on a hike in the moonlight."

"Well, you just made it back by the skin of your teeth, "Moe said.

"Where did you go for your hike?" Sandy asked.

"We just walked around the big meadow and up the hill a little way," stated Lucy. "And I met the dreamiest guy."

"What boys were there?" Elaine wanted to know.

"The same four guys who were sneaking around outside our cabin last night," Lucy said.

"That DJ is a real kick," remarked Dottie.

"That's because he's a nut like you are," everyone told her. "You two just have a lot in common."

Elaine wished she could have gone too. She sincerely regretted not being with Lucy and Dottie when they met up with the boys earlier.

"By the way, Elaine, Danny was disappointed that you weren't on the hike," Lucy told her. "He said he has something for you."

"What's this?" asked Beth. "I didn't know there was anything between you two."

"There isn't," Elaine said. "He took my flower hair clip and needs to give it back."

"Well he gave me a note to give you," Lucy added, pulling a torn, crumpled page from her pocket.

Elaine eagerly took it and began reading it with the use of her flashlight. *Hi Cutie, How are you doing? I sure missed you on the hike tonight,*

*specially since there was a full moon. Do you still want your hair clip back?
I'll give it back on one condition, that you'll be my date for the scavenger hunt
tomorrow night. Love, Danny*

Elaine's heart was singing as she put the note under her pillow.
The other girls tried to find out what he had said in the note, but
Elaine told them it was none of their business, and said she wanted
to go to sleep anyhow. She was happy and excited thinking that the
good looking, popular Danny wanted to date her, and she had sweet,
cotton-candy dreams that night.

The following evening was perfect. Danny sat with her again at
the campfire program, and then they were together for the scavenger
hunt, walking around together holding hands. Of course he was
constantly flirting with other girls, but that was to be expected. Boys
were flirting with her too. Warren looked at her with new respect.

The remaining days of camp went by with lightning speed. There
were so many enjoyable and humorous events that made up for
wonderful memories. There was the time the gong rang at 2:00 am and
everyone was roused because they thought it was a fire alarm, and as it
turned out, Danny and DJ were not the culprits of that prank. There
was the item in the camp newspaper that was rather embarrassing,
that Cabin 13 was found to be the dirtiest of all the girls' cabins. (That
was due to Dottie's rock collection). Another Dottie mishap that
occurred was when she leaned too far out the window talking to some
boys, and as a result, fell out the window breaking a pane of glass. She
wasn't hurt, but the roommates had to take up a collection to pay for
the glass. There was an afternoon hike with the girls of Cabin 13 and
the boys of Cabin 9 where they all got lost and barely made it back in
time for dinner. It was believed that the boys knew where they were
the entire time. That same the evening the counselors took over KP at
dinner to give the campers a break, and Danny and DJ had made of
tower of dishes and glasses nearly two feet high on the table.

Then there was the more serious side to camp, informative and
informal discussions on Disarmament, Capital Punishment, Teen Age
Morals, and Improving Your MYF. There were fascinating discussions
on God, and Life after Death. Elaine wished that Natalie could have
come to camp, since she would have definitely benefitted by some
of the discussions. Best of all, and most inspiring were the campfire
programs. There was a feeling of togetherness as the campers sang
together, and there was a feeling that Christ was there also, among
them, surrounding everyone with His wonderful love.

Love was definitely in the air the last evening of camp. There had
been a candle lighting ceremony at the campfire program. All the

campers and the entire staff had formed a huge circle, a friendship circle, and each lit the others' candle until a ring of light spread around the circle, cutting off the darkness. It was symbolic of each person taking the love of God they had found at camp back to their families and back to their communities, and spreading this love.

After the ceremony Danny and Elaine took a short walk through the meadow, which was covered with dew. They were both silent, realizing that camp was almost over. Elaine found that Danny usually was silent when he was alone with her, which wasn't often. He was always very talkative when surrounded by others and he liked to be the center of attention. Elaine realized now that he was much more bashful when it was just the two of them.

"Have a chair," he said, indicating a large boulder. They sat there close together, her hand in his, gazing at the stars. Finally Danny asked, "Do you remember the campfire program talk on Monday night?"

"Of course. It was about the boy whose life changed after he was in a wreck and his friend died."

"He was talking about me."

"I know."

"I was just out of control at that time, and my folks were having a lot of problems. I didn't even think about God or religion or anything like that. My friend's name was Joey, not Sam, and when he was killed, man, that was just so hard. He was such a great guy, and had so much to offer. I'll always wonder why it was Joey, and not me, who had to die. I think about that every day of my life," he added, touching his scar.

"Maybe God is using him where he is," Elaine said softly.

"Oh, I'm sure of it." They sat and looked at the stars for a while longer. He turned to Elaine and said earnestly, "I'm so glad I met you, Elaine Hummer. Camp just wouldn't have been the same without you. I really mean that. You're my sweet little hummingbird. I am going to miss you sooo much. You'd better write to me when you go home."

"Oh, you can count on that," Elaine promised. "I am good at letter-writing. But I don't want to talk about going home. It makes me too sad."

"I'm sorry. We'll just think about tonight, about right here and now," he said, turning to her and pulling her into his arms and kissing her with passion. And Elaine knew, without a doubt, that this was her best memory of camp, really her best memory of the entire year.

Part II

Chapter 14

This is the life, thought Elaine, as she swung comfortably back and forth in a hammock, which was stretched between two pine trees. The shrill hum of insects penetrated the thin mountain air, and tall, sturdy Ponderosa pines waved softly as the mountain breeze filtered through their needles. The September air was cool and pleasant in the shade, although the sun shown down warmly on the campsite.

The Hummer family was on their annual summer vacation. It was rather late in the season since Charles had not been able to leave the farm until just before Labor Day. He had had difficulties in finding someone to take care of the chickens for the brief week that they would be away. Their neighbor, Mr.Hobbs, usually filled in, but he'd recently had some health issues. However, Charles had finally found a family which he felt was responsible enough to run the farm for a week. They packed up their 54 Ford station wagon, which pulled a small utility trailer behind, and left Ellington at 4:00am on a Sunday. They traveled through San Bernardino, then over the mountains, followed by a long stretch of desert. They stopped for breakfast in Barstow, and then drove for miles without seeing much of anything except desert. There were a few tiny towns with their unattractive, run-down gas stations and cafes, with the hot desert sand blowing through them constantly. Elaine had wondered, upon seeing them, who would want to live out in the middle of nowhere. By late afternoon, they had traveled through a small, green corner of Utah, and then followed the road south into Arizona, where they began climbing the mountains, and heading toward the North Rim of the Grand Canyon. A campsite in the park had been easy to find, since most families had already taken their summer vacations.

Today was their 5th day at the Grand Canyon. Charles, with his love of hiking, had kept the rest of the family occupied, taking them on his long jaunts to see the many wonders that the national park had to offer. Yesterday they had walked partway down Bright Angel Trail, which led to the bottom of the canyon. Actually, Elaine would have been content to see the glories of the canyon from the rim, since she was not too fond of long hikes. But her father had always insisted that she would miss some of nature's wonders if she stayed at the campsite. Today, however, only Charles and Russ were hiking, just a short jaunt that wound through part of the Kaibab Forest which dominated the national park and an entire section of Arizona.

Lois was catching up on some reading, Timmie was making a fort under the picnic table, and even Pam was relaxing for a change, reading a book from the Black Stallion series. Elaine was enjoying the peacefulness of the campground. In previous years they had vacationed at the height of camping season, and tourists swarmed the area. Today there was only one other lone tent in sight, and its occupants were nowhere around.

Elaine was reflecting on the summer that was just coming to a close. She had come home from camp feeling as if she was on Cloud Nine. It had been such a great experience for her, and she had enjoyed the new friendships she had made there. She felt more spiritual, and renewed vows to try and stay closer to the Lord, and put Him first in her life. She also spent a great deal of time thinking of Danny Settle, and how much she had enjoyed kissing him. In her mind, she reviewed many, many times, the wonder of being young, and the thrill of Danny's lips on hers the last night of camp. He said he'd write, she thought. And every day in July Elaine would walk to the post office, but there was never a letter from him. She kept reminding herself that it was only a summer romance, and it didn't mean that much. Elaine had written to him twice. Finally, in August a letter came. It definitely sounded like Danny, full of flowery and romantic phrases, but she knew deep down that being romantic and being flirtatious was second nature to him, and that he probably already had another girlfriend at home. Moe had written also, saying that Danny talked about camp and about Elaine, but he also was dating another girl. She cried at times, missing him so much, and she had almost stopped listening to the radio because it hurt to hear a song that she and Danny had heard together at camp.

Another reason for her sadness that summer was that the Fawcett family had been transferred to another church. They had left Ellington in July. She missed Warren's friendship, she missed little Norma Fawcett's interest in her, and she missed Reverend Fawcett's loving ways with his congregation. She realized, however, that in the Methodist Church, ministers get transferred every few years. The Fawcetts had been transferred to a much larger church in San Diego, and it was a good opportunity for them. Elaine had cried and cried at the farewell get-together that was held for them. With a loving arm around her, Norma told her that good-byes were just inevitable. "Some good-byes will be only for a short while," she had said, "while others will mean good-bye forever. This is a good-bye for a short while, because we will be back to visit. San Diego isn't that far away." The last MYF meeting followed the farewell party. Elaine, Lucy, and Beth were in tears most of the time, because it wouldn't be the same at all. Adam would be leaving and going off to UCLA in the fall. There would be a few new high schoolers joining the group. Warren was on a roll, hugging and kissing the girls good bye. He had been bolder that way since camp. When everyone at camp said their good byes, there was a great deal of hugging and kissing.

During the summer, visiting ministers had preached at church. A different preacher each Sunday hadn't helped unify the congregation, and the attendance had waned. A new minister and his wife, Reverend and Mrs. Graham were scheduled to move into the parsonage sometime that week.

Elaine had spent most of the summer writing stories. She had two notebooks full of short stories and poems. She sorely missed her friends from Armedia, and frequent letters had flown back and forth between the two towns. She rocked tranquilly back and forth in the swing, daydreaming. School would be starting probably only a couple of days after they would arrive home from their trip. What would her sophomore year be like? Sometimes Elaine felt that she was growing up entirely too fast, and yet there were times when she wished she were already an adult, without all the problems of a teen ager and the obstacles to overcome. The teen years could just be too challenging at times, and that phase of life between childhood and adulthood was definitely not an easy one.

During the afternoon, Elaine and Pam, having nothing else to do, took the long walk to the camp store, which seemed rather empty and quiet, without the usual excited tourists milling about. Even the lodge was being closed up for the winter. "It's too lonesome around here," Pam remarked as they left the store with popsicles and picture postcards. "We need more activity."

"Well, I guess the South Rim is more popular, and stays open longer," Elaine told her, "but they have to close earlier up here at the North Rim. It will start getting cold here soon."

"Why didn't we camp at the South Rim then?"

"We've already been there, so I guess Dad wanted to try here. But I'm getting anxious to get home. I've got ironing to do for school, and I have things to get organized."

"Well, I'm just tired of camping. My air mattress leaks, and I keep waking up at night."

"I know what you mean," Elaine said. "Last night I woke up, and found I was almost sleeping on the ground. I think I stayed awake half the night listening to the wind blowing through the trees, and to all the owls hooting. It was a little spooky."

"I think the forest where we're camping is real nice, but I just don't want to stay here for two more days."

By the time they were back at the campsite, Charles and Russ were back from their hike. "Did you girls get rested up from yesterday's activities?" Charles asked.

"Sure did," Elaine answered. "I got some letters written, and I'm all caught up in my diary."

"Sounds dull," said Russ, consuming a baloney sandwich.

"Well, hiking isn't the most exciting thing I've ever done," Elaine told him.

"Nothing exciting ever happens on our vacations," complained Pam.

"Sure it does," said her father. "You nearly fell over the edge yesterday. Wasn't that enough excitement for you?"

"What day will we be leaving for home?" Elaine wanted to know.

"Are you anxious to get home already? I thought we'd leave early Sunday morning, but we wouldn't get back until really late that night."

"But Charles, school starts on Monday," Lois protested, "and the kids will be really tired from the long drive, and getting home so late."

"It wouldn't hurt for them to miss the first day of school, I guess," he remarked.

"But Dad, I really need to get back and see all my friends," Elaine protested. "I don't want to miss out on the first day of school."

"I don't care if I miss," stated Pam sadly. "My best friend won't be there, and I miss her so much." Dodie Fawcett had been Pam's closest friend for the past few years.

"I thought you wanted to get home," Elaine told her. "Now you're changing your tune."

"If we stay, we can get one more hike in," Russ said.

"Stay, stay," Timmie added, running around the campfire ring.

"Well, Elaine, I guess you and Mom have been outvoted," Charles said.

That evening at sunset the family walked out to Bright Angel Point. The sun cast long shadows over the world reknown spectacle. The vast, yawning void before them was revealing in all its splendor its many hues of lavenders, blues, siennas, grays, browns, greens, and purples. Far in the distance, perhaps 20 miles to the other side, Elaine thought she could see the South Rim. Always a romanticist, she wondered what mysteries had been uncovered in the depths of the canyon. What secrets had it been concealing in its chasms for centuries, ever since the waters of the mighty Colorado River had made her conquest of the land? The force had shaped the land to its own will as the river waters dug deeper into the submissive soil, leaving behind a vast,undescribable gulf, a thrill and a wonder for mankind to see. Elaine wondered if, in the centuries that followed, the ocean would rise up and cover forever the breathtaking, overwhelming beauty and the solitary loneliness, and the mysteries that lay in the depths of the Grand Canyon.

The sun had set now, leaving the canyon in twilight, leaving all the little inhabitants, friendly and unfriendly, to go to their homes in the rocks and gullies, and crags to sleep for the night. For the nocturnal creatures however, it was time to awaken and start their hunting. It was a silent, thoughtful Elaine who walked back through the cool evening breeze with her family. A few hours later she was glad to be in her flannel-lined sleeping bag under the heavy canvas tent, for the nights were cold, and sometimes the temperature dropped below freezing. She didn't see how her father and brother stayed warm, sleeping outside in their hammocks. Tonight the wind was howling louder than usual, but it finally lulled her off to sleep.

Hours later she was awakened by the steady patter of raindrops on the canvas overhead. Opening the door of the tent, she could see nothing outside, except for inky black darkness. Suddenly a flash of lightening illuminated the entire area, revealing the swaying pines, which were thrashing against each other. Thunder sounded seconds later, echoing and re-echoing with a tremendous roar across the walls of the canyon less than a half mile away. Charles and Russ, immediately wide awake, were moving their sleeping bags hastily into the car. The rain began to come down harder and harder, almost in torrents now. Thunder and lightning continued to boom and flash around them. Charles ducked into the tent to see if everything was all right. But Lois, Timmie, and the girls were warm and cozy in the waterproof tent.

"Well, how's this for excitement?" he asked Pam. "It's just what you wanted, right?"

Pam yawned sleepily. "It's pretty exciting all right," she agreed. "We don't get storms like this at home."

"This tent is holding up pretty well. So far it's dry in here, and the wind hasn't blown it down yet. But I'm in favor of pulling up stakes and leaving. This storm probably won't be letting up for awhile, so maybe we should pack up and get out of here. What do you think, Lois?"

"Of leaving right now in the middle of the night? I think it would be hard to drive in this torrential rain, and in the dark. It's only 3:00am, and won't be light for a few hours."

"But everything will be soaked and covered with mud, if we don't pack up right away." He stopped suddenly, listening to a new sound. "Isn't that hail?"

Elaine stuck an inquisitive hand out the tent door, and was instantly pelted with large, stinging hailstones. "I'm in favor of leaving," she said.

"Hey, Dad," Russ called from the darkness. "Come help me get these hammocks packed into the car before they get soaked."

"I think it's too late to worry about everything getting muddy and soaked," Lois commented, as Charles went back outside. "It won't be any wetter a few hours from now when daylight comes."

Charles came back into the tent with two boxes from the picnic table. "I'm putting these in here to dry off. However, it looks like we won't be leaving til morning after all," he added sheepishly. "I just checked the gas gauge, and we're almost on empty. The service station down the road opens at 7:00, I think. For now I'll bunk in here with you guys. At least my sleeping bag is dry on the inside."

Elaine slept very little during the next few hours. She found the sounds of the storm fascinating. Traces of the long-awaited dawn began to appear and the dark of the night faded gradually. The rain was slowly decreasing. They were all up by 6:00, folding blankets, sleeping bags, putting belongings into suitcases. Anything that was dry was loaded into the back of the station wagon, while the tent, and other wet and muddy items were placed into the utility trailer. Before leaving, they went to the edge of the canyon for one last look, but found it completely covered over with clouds.

The trip home was long and tiring. When they stopped for gas, they realized that a tire was going flat, so they had to wait for it to be changed. In just under an hour they were on their way. The immense forest on either side of the highway was a bright green and sparkling under the gray, heavily clouded sky. After they had left the Kaibab Forest behind, they began traveling through the Navajo Indian Reservation. Elaine could see the shabby little hogans of sticks and adobe through the rain. She wondered what the people who lived in them would be like. Going at a steady pace, they reached Flagstaff around noon. The town was being pelted with hailstones. After a quick lunch they traveled on, finally making their way out of the storm area. They went on through Kingman, then Needles. The longest, most tiring part of the trip was after they had left Needles, California. They were surrounded by the late afternoon desert heat. All the car windows were down, but hot air was blowing into the car. Outside was mile after mile of endless desert. By 8:00pm they had reached Barstow, still almost three hours from Ellington. The number of cars headed the opposite way, going to Las Vegas for the weekend was amazing. Miles of cars drove toward them, and it was easy to see how someone could get hypnotized while driving at night with an endkless line of headlights coming on and on and on. After Barstow, the Hummer kids fell asleep, and did not awake until they heard the welcome words, "Wake up, we're home finally!" All Elaine could do was thankfully stagger into her room, open the windows, and fall into bed.

Chapter 15

"It's really good to be back," Elaine was saying to Beth and Natalie the following evening. "The best part of a vacation is coming home." It was Saturday evening and the three girls were taking a walk around their home town, enjoying the pleasant evening air and the long shadows that the sun was casting upon the town. "So what's been going on around here?" asked Elaine. "What have I missed? Anything world shaking?"

"Well, things have been in an uproar at our house, what with Adam getting ready for college," Natalie told her. "It's like Cheryl and I are non-existent right now, and everything is all about Adam. But I told him, now that he is leaving, I want his room."

"But you have such a cool room up on your third floor," Elaine remarked. "I thought you liked it."

"It has its advantages," Nat stated. "But it gets cold up there in the winter, and there's no bathroom on that floor. I just think I need a change."

"Adam took us up to the skating rink last week," Beth told Elaine. "Ty Ramirez was there, and he skated with Nat several times. I think that made her night."

"Heck, it made my whole week," Nat laughed. "He is really a cool guy. But if my parents ever find out that I like a Mexican guy, I'll probably be grounded forever."

"You've been interested in him for most of last year," Elaine noted. "And so what if he is Mexican? He's really cute, and a really nice guy, and that's what counts in the long run."

"Yeah, my folks are just prejudiced. One great thing about our school is that blacks, whites, and Mexicans get along really well. Race doesn't seem to matter." The girls doubled back toward Lucy's house to see if she was finished eating dinner yet. Their timing was good and she came out to join them.

"Hi," she called. "How was your trip, Elaine? Meet any cute guys?"

"No, and it doesn't bother me one bit. I am swearing off guys for now." That statement was met with laughter from everyone.

"I think we've heard that before, Elaine," Beth said. "I bet you'll be falling for someone as soon as school starts again. Warren is out of the picture now, and Danny was just a camp romance. Wonder who the next lucky guy will be?"

"There's always Alvin," Lucy remarked. "Poor Alvin, he must feel so rejected."

"Oh, he called me during the summer and came down here a couple of times," Elaine told them. "But I said that I had met someone at camp, and that we were going together now, and he said if he ever saw Danny, he would beat him up."

"Give me a break," Beth said. "He couldn't even beat up his little sister!"

"By the way," Lucy said, as they passed the white Methodist Church, "the new minister and his wife got moved in last week. My mom and I went over to see them, and took them a casserole. And they are the cutest couple, Reverend and Mrs.Graham, although they asked me to call them Chuck and Cathy. Can you imagine calling a minister by his first name? Of course they're very young. Chuck is only 22. He just graduated from college in June, so he still has to go to seminary before he can be an ordained minister. Cathy is only 21. They just got married two months ago."

The girls walked to the north end of town and then cut across the river to the west side, and parted ways at Natalie's driveway. "Don't forget that Adam's taking us to the beach tomorrow," Nat said. "We'll be leaving early, around 9:00."

"Sounds good to me," Elaine said. "Our last fling of the summer."

At home Elaine found her mother baking cookies and chattering happily about the new minister. "Oh, Elaine, I wish you could have been here to meet them. They just left. They had heard they could buy eggs cheap from us. And we had the nicest visit. Reverend Graham and his wife are the cutest couple. They must be in their early 20's. They were just married in June. This is their first church, and they are so enthusiastic about having their own church."

"I bet I won't like them as well as I did the Fawcetts," Elaine said, reaching for a freshly baked cookie. "Ouch, that's still hot."

"You leave those alone. They're for dessert. Now how can you say such a thing about the Grahams? You haven't even met them yet?"

"I just don't see how they can be a great as everyone seems to think they are." Elaine knew in her heart that she was just trying to be contrary. And she figured that she probably would like them once she'd had a chance to meet them.

"I invited them over for dinner tomorrow after church."

"Oh, but I'm not going to be here. I'm going to the beach with Adam, Natalie, and the girls."

"So you're going to be missing church? I don't like that."

"We'll be leaving in the morning. It's our last outing of the summer. And you know I don't miss church very often."

"Well, I'm really sorry you won't be able to meet them tomorrow."

"I have a feeling I will be meeting them soon enough, since our family is always so active in church," Elaine remarked.

*   *   *

On Monday morning the four sophomore girls from Ellington climbed the steps of the main building, full of confidence with their new status.

"Hey, the building has been painted," exclaimed Beth. "It's about time."

"But look at the color," Elaine remarked. "Did you ever see such a bright shade of pink?"

"It's icky," stated Natalie. "Sure stands out though."

They strode past the trophy case, through the lower hall, and out into the sunshine of the student square, feeling as if they belonged. It wasn't long before they ran into Karen Gillespie and Alma Mendoza, and they began to catch up on the news of the summer. Megan Frye and Vicki Bannister joined their group a few minutes later. Megan was still wearing Willie's class ring on a chain around her neck, and Vicki was also wearing someone's ring.

"Okay, who's the lucky guy?" Lucy asked her.

"It's Paul Newberry. Of course he graduated last year, but he's still around town," Vicki explained. "And he still hangs out with Willie sometimes. We've only been going steady for about a month."

"Karen has a new boyfriend too," Megan stated. "Tell them your news, Karen."

"Well, I've been going out with Greg Okamota." Greg was one of the few Japanese students in school. He had been voted Sophomore Class president, was on the football team, and a straight A student. He was very popular, and had a great sense of humor.

"That's great, Karen," Beth said. "I think Greg is a really cool guy."

"Oh, we have the cutest new guy in our class this year," Megan informed them. "His name is Phil Santini, and his father is the new school principal."

"Well, I've heard that he's going to make some changes around here," Alma said. "like having a closed campus, seven periods in a day, instead of just six, and maybe no more Initiation Day."

"Oh, that's terrible," Elaine remarked. "Our class has to get even for the way we got treated last year! He can't take that away!"

"Even if we have to break the rules, we'll get even somehow," said Nat, always the rebel.

"By the way, Elaine, I really like your hair," Karen told her. "It looks good in a brush-up." The ring of the assembly bell interrupted their conversation, and the girls found their way to the gym and sat proudly in the sophomore section. They gave their class yell with vigor. The freshmen across the aisle from them did not fare as well.

"Well, Elaine, how's life out in the sticks of Ellington?" asked a deep voice on her right. Elaine turned and looked into the green eyes of Shawn O'Dell, a boy who had been in some of her classes last year. He was short and slim, and was known to be quite a cut-up in class. He sometimes ran around with DJ Morrison. The two of them could be a lethal combination at times.

"What do you mean, the sticks of Ellington?" she retorted. "That is one very busy little town." It was strange how everyone like to cut down Ellington.

Elaine listened vaguely to the new principal's speech, thinking more about all the conversations of the morning. The speech was the standard opening speech of the year: "If we all cooperate and work together—," "School standards in the past have been—," "I'm not going to change but a few of the rules and regulations," "This is the last wonderful year for you seniors," "I'm sure we'll all get along just fine." Elaine was glad when it was over and the teachers were introduced. There were only six new teachers this year. The assembly ended and the students were released to go to their classes.

"Last year at this time we would have been going to Algebra," Elaine remarked as she, Megan, and Vicki walked to the Home Economics class.

"Don't remind me," shuddered Vicki. "I hope to never have another teacher like Mr. Carr, or another class like Algebra."

"I liked him," Elaine said. "Maybe we didn't learn much, but the class was fun. We did learn something about football, however."

"You just like him because he is young and good looking," Megan teased.

"Did you see who we have for Geometry?" Karen asked, joining them.

"Good old Mr.Dumpke," Vicki said happily. "His class should be a cinch from what I've heard. He's the easiest of all the teachers, although he acts like he'll be really strict."

They had reached the Home Economics room and seated themselves at a table. Mrs. Jenson was one of the new teachers, and was young and very attractive. Elaine knew at a glance that she would like her. She seemed anxious to please. She announced to the girls that they would start the Good Grooming Unit the following day, and gave them the rest of the period to discuss what they wanted to cover in class. Elaine, Megan, Vicki, and Karen, being the only sophomores in class, felt confident among the timid freshmen girls.

The bell rang, and Elaine and Karen went dismally to their Spanish class together.

"I could do without this class," Karen whispered to Elaine, as they seated themselves as close to the back of the room as possible.

"It's not a very big class this year," Elaine remarked, noticing the number of empty seats.

"Well, naturally," Greg Okamota said from across the aisle. "She flunked out almost everyone last year, or scared them so much they decided not to come back."

"Aren't you glad you passed?" Elaine asked. "Now we have another year of fun in here."

"Oh, I can't wait," he joked.

Mrs. Mendoza called roll in her deep voice, and then passed out brand new Spanish books to the class. "You'll like these," she said. "They have big vocabulary lists in the back, and some very interesting stories, *en espanol* of course."

Third Period was Sophomore Science with Mr. Sharpe. He had a reputation for orderly class sessions and stiff tests, but he taught with humor and warmth. He announced that they would cover Drivers Ed the first semester and Health the second semester. Phil Santini sat several seats in front of Elaine. She noted that he was very good looking with black hair and dark eyes and an engaging grin. He looks like fun, she thought as she watched him empty the contents of Lucy's purse onto his desk while Mr. Sharpe's head was turned. Lucy was trying not to laugh out loud.

Physical Education was Fourth Period with Miss Morgan in the gym. "This class will be a ball," Vicki was saying as they tried out their new combination locks. "All our friends are here, and very few upperclassmen."

During lunch the girls returned to the familiar spot on the front lawn under the pepper trees. "Well, here we are again all set for another year," Megan said. "Did everyone have a good summer? I know Karen and Elaine did."

"It had to be a guy," Alma said to Elaine. "Come on now, spill it. I want all the juicy details." Elaine was only too glad to oblige, and Danny and camp dominated the conversation for the next few minutes.

"Looks like she forgot about poor Alvin," laughed Vicki. "He's left in the dust."

"Hello, Cousin," Scottie Thompson called from the rock wall that lined the circle drive. He was with a group of freshmen boys.

"Hi, Scottie," Elaine called. "Come over here and meet my friends."

He climbed over the wall as quickly as his crutches would allow him, and slowly walked over to the girls. Elaine, proud of her cousin with his good looks and sparkling personality, introduced him to her Armedia friends, since he already knew the Ellington girls.

"He gets around really well for being on crutches," Karen remarked as he walked back to his group of friends.

"Yes, he does. He had polio when he was younger, but he's quite a remarkable guy, and always has a really positive attitude. He doesn't let his handicap slow him down at all," Elaine said.

Elaine's Geometry class was after lunch. Mr. Dumpke was a short man in his fifties with iron-gray hair combed back in an English style. He looked very serious and business-like, and didn't crack a smile at all. He talked for the entire class period on how hard his students would have to study to keep up with everything, and how easy it was for A's to drop to F's. Under the wall clock was a big sign in black letters that said "Time is passing, are you?"

"From what I hear, he's quite the bluffer," Nat whispered to Elaine.

"Yes, I think his bark is much worse than his bite," she answered.

"You two young ladies in the second row, I won't tolerate any whispering," he told them sternly. "We have a great deal of work to cover this semester, and everyone's attention needs to be up here in front."

Study Hall, which followed Geometry, was in the cafeteria, and was a very large class, consisting of about 40 or 50 students. They were scattered at tables around the room, all talking at once. Mr. Caldwell, who was in charge, didn't seem to mind the commotion. The students knew he could have perfect order if he requested it, since he was the Dean of Students and highly respected.

Elaine sat in back of the room eagerly talking to Megan about Danny. "He was just so much fun, and the all the boys were outside our cabin until about 1:00 am. And he was the best kisser and—"

"Yakety, yak yak," Phil Santini interrupted. "Let me in on this conversation. Sounds like a story out of *True Romance.*"

"Eavesdropper! Get out of here!" Elaine told him, waving her Spanish book at him.

"Help! Under cover!" Phil cried, as he ducked.

"I'd advise you not to hit him," Greg said from across the table. "His head's so hard you'll probably break the book in two."

Elaine was laughing as the bell rang. School was really going to be fun this year, she thought as she and Megan walked to their English class.

"It might be a problem having English the last period in the day when everyone is all tired out," Megan said. "I can't get over the idea of seven periods in a day. It's just too many."

"Our dear Principal Santini's idea," remarked Elaine. "Every pupil should have a Study Hall, he says, but I have a feeling we won't be able to get much studying done in such a big class."

"I'm going to change over and try to work in the library during 6th Period," Megan stated.

She had Mrs. Teague again for English Literature, and noted that DJ and Shawn were in the class, as was Greg, Phil, and Alma's twin brother Lenny Mendoza. Mrs. Teague gave her opening speech to a quiet, well-behaved class. No one spoke out of turn, and when she called roll, you could hear a pin drop. Elaine wondered if she would be throwing her gavel at DJ this year. She started daydreaming, thinking of Danny with his outgoing, flamboyant personality, and wondering if he was a problem for his teachers, and what classes he would be taking in school.

The following Sunday Elaine finally met the new minister and his wife, and in spite of her resolution to remain loyal to the Fawcetts, she found them absolutely irresistible. Reverend Charles Graham preached the most interesting sermon she had ever heard, and it had a good deal of appeal for the youth. And he was good looking too. Chuck, as his congregation called him, had blond hair in a crew cut, blue eyes, a husky build, and an ever prominent grin. He looked like a football player, Elaine thought. Cathy was very attractive, tall and slim with dark hair. After the church service, Elaine shook hands with both of them.

"So you're the other Hummer," Chuck said heartily. "We've met everyone in your family except you, and I must say it's a real pleasure meeting you!"

"Why don't you drop by the parsonage this afternoon, Elaine," Cathy was asking. "We haven't had too much of a chance yet to visit with the youth. We need your feedback on MYF, plus it would be a good time just to get to know you."

So Elaine found herself in the Graham household that afternoon. There were still boxes to be unpacked, and the house wasn't too well organized, but Cathy offered her some ice tea and homemade cookies. "I didn't make them," she said. "The congregation has made sure we are well fed while we are settling in. I can see I'll probably gain about 20 pounds while we're here." Elaine had been feeling bashful around her new acquaintances, but she soon got over that. Chuck and Cathy were a couple of characters, she decided.

They asked her many questions, about MYF, about high school, and about Ellington. She began telling them about her hometown, about the problems of a small country town, and the problems of a small high school.

"How is the boy situation?" Cathy asked frankly.

"Well, good guys are rather scarce around here," Elaine told them. "And most of the fellows I've met at high school don't seem to have much ambition."

"That's the trouble with small towns," Chuck remarked. "We both grew up in the city, and opportunities for young people are much greater there."

"Still, I think there are advantages to growing up in a small town where you know everyone," Cathy pointed out.

"Except everyone knows everyone else's business," Elaine said. "You can't keep anything a secret around this town. For example, when I was in 1st or 2nd Grade, I always wanted to go barefoot, and I wasn't allowed to. So when I was walking to school, I used to take off my shoes and socks, and walk barefoot to school, in good weather of course. I'd only done that for a few days, when our neighbor, Mr. Hobbs, who had seen me going barefoot, told my mother about it when he saw her in the store."

Chuck and Cathy laughed heartily at her story. "But it also sounds like everybody watches out for everyone else, which is good. You don't have that in the city," Cathy said.

"Did you go to MYF Camp this year?" Chuck asked.

"I did, and met some really great people, both girls and guys. I was going with a guy from camp, but that's all over now," she added sadly.

"Summer romances are usually short like that," Cathy said understandingly. "It's not easy being a teenager. They always say a person's teen years are the most wonderful years in a person's life, but I don't agree with that at all. There is a lot of heartbreak involved. Most everyone at that age is looking for security, and they think the only security is in going with someone. And it's really rough when you get your heart broken, believe me. I know that from experience."

"You have to watch out for some of these fellows, Elaine," Chuck advised. "They all have the biggest lines they'll try to get you to believe. But they usually don't mean a word of what they tell you. It's just a phase guys go through. It's a feather in their cap to get a girl to believe all the sweet nothings they tell them, just to get their way with them."

"Of course you never did anything like that," Cathy said jokingly to her husband with a fond look.

"Well, I haven't gone out enough yet to tell the difference between the truth and a lie," Elaine said honestly. "But everything is so disillusioning at times. I can look forward so much to something, like a party or a dance, or an event, and then it turns out to be nothing. After a while I wonder if everything in life is nothing but a big let-down."

"God has a plan for you, Elaine, just as he does for everyone," Cathy told her. "Don't lose your faith. Just keep on looking forward to everything, and embrace life. It all works out for the best."

Don't lose your faith, Elaine thought, on her walk home. She wondered how many times in the next few years that she would have to repeat those words to herself.

Chapter 16

Elaine engaged herself wholeheartedly into numerous school activities. The Sophomore class, the biggest in school, had their first meeting. Greg Okamota led the class in a discussion of what type of float they would have for the Homecoming Parade, and asked for ideas on possible money making projects. Phil Santini was elected as Class Treasurer, since the girl who had been elected at the end of their freshman year had moved away during the summer. During the course of the meeting Elaine found herself on the sophomore dance committee, the football program committee, and an agent for collecting class dues.

One item of business that was brought up at the meeting was Initiation Day. The new principal had followed through to some extent on getting it changed, Greg was explaining to the class. "I know you don't really want to hear this," he said, "but the Initiation Day that we had last year is a thing of the past. I know we got the brunt of the worst Initiation ever, but going forward, there will be no whipped cream, or mustard, or ketchup, or anything else messy." There were collective groans and mutterings heard from everyone in the room. "Of course we wouldn't have been able to participate anyhow, since only seniors could do that, but, like all of you, I was looking forward to just being a bystander, and watching all the freshmen get creamed," Greg continued. "The good news is that there will be an event called 'Slave Day' which will be this coming Friday. For three dollars, any student can buy a freshman and can dictate how they want them to dress for that day. Then that person will have to be their slave for the day. So you don't have to be a senior to participate, and have a slave.

The money from people in our class will go into our treasury, so there's good money raising activity right there. I'd say it's a pretty great deal. Three friends could go together, and for just a buck you could have a slave for all three of you." Of course many questions followed. Elaine, Nat, Lucy, and Beth decided to go in together to buy a slave.

It was fun for the Ellington girls to be on the other end of the hazing. On Friday morning they were busy snapping pictures of the freshmen at the bus stop, who were wearing everything from raggedy clothes to pajamas and nightgowns. The slave the girls had purchased was from Armedia, so they didn't get to start their bossing until they got to school. Names had been pulled at random to make everything fair. The girls enjoyed having a slave. It was a freshmen boy who carried their books and swept off their path, and stood line line for them at the cafeteria without too much complaining, but the day seemed quite tame compared to last year. "We were such a mess at the end of the day," Lucy remarked

"Yeah, Adam took all those pictures of us last year, and it was unbelievable," added Natalie.

Friday night at the first football game of the season, Elaine, Lucy, and Beth got off the rooters bus in Armedia, and went to the office to pick up football programs and change from Mr. Sharpe, the class sponsor.

"Why do you always wear that hat to football games, Mr. Sharpe?" Lucy asked boldly, referring to the black derby he was wearing. (Being outside the classroom made a great deal of difference between student and teacher.)

"You don't like my hat? It's a good hat—keeps my ears warm," growled Mr. Sharpe, pretending to be insulted. "Besides it's traditional."

"We win the game if he wears it," joked Elaine.

"Well, it looks like a Wyatt Earp hat" Beth remarked.

It seemed like a beautiful night for football, since the weather hadn't gotten really cold yet. It was just cool and crispy, with a slight breeze blowing. Elaine loved the football scene: freshly mowed grass dissected by the white lye yard lines, the huge lights at each end of the field illuminating the night to seeming daylight, the brightly glittering scoreboard. She was proud of the job the sophs had done in decorating the goalposts with the red and white crepe paper streamers. At the opposite end of the field were the blue and gold streamers of the opposing team, Madison High. The stands on both sides of the field were rapidly filling up, and it was gratifying to see a good deal of red and white on Armedia's side.

Beth and Lucy took their programs to the other side to sell while Elaine wound her way among the Armedia rooters. Her friends called her over, and most of them bought programs.

"Willie is Number 6," Megan informed Elaine, who wasn't particularly interested. "He's playing quarterback again this year." She was sitting with Vicki, and Paul Newberry.

"Lainy! Hey Lainy, over here!" came the call from the very top of the bleachers. She made her way up to the top, where DJ and Shawn were sitting. "You're going to give us free programs, aren't you, since we're your buddies?" they asked.

"That's what you think," she retorted. "Twenty cents for two programs. Fork over your dimes. No freebies. And the name is not Lainy, and don't you forget it."

"OK, Lainy Hummingbird," Shawn said.

"Hummingbird, that's a good one," DJ said, handing her a quarter. "And you can keep the change."

Other cries of "Lainy, up here!" were heard. It looks like they started something, she thought. She sold all her programs in the next ten minutes and sat down with Karen and Alma, as the crowd began yelling for the Armedia players who were just running out onto the field. Several guys from their class were on the team: Phil Santini, Greg Okamota, and Lenny Mendoza.

Armedia played poorly that night, and lost the game 20-0. The boys on the team looked sad and discouraged as they walked off the field.

"Are we in for another bad season this year?" Megan asked. "Last year we won three out of nine games, but Coach Carr said this should be a better season."

"But he doesn't always know what he's talking about," Vicki scoffed.

"I'm going down and walk Willie off the field," Megan said. "Maybe each of us should find a player to walk with, give them a little encouragement."

"It might scare them," Lucy said. "If I had the nerve I would find Phil, but he's probably already surrounded by a crowd of girls."

The girls had reached the field by now, and Lucy did find Phil, and Beth and Elaine walked with Woody Stuart, a tall, husky blonde headed guy, who had several classes with them. To be encouraging, the girls both told him that he played a good game.

"Yeah, all fifteen minutes while I was in," he said sadly. "I wish I had played a good game."

The after-game dance was sponsored by the sophomores. Elaine and Vicki, as co-chairmen, had given it a theme, the Kick-Off Dance. Streamers of brown, yellow, and orange had been hung in various places in the gym. The floor had been varnished to a gleaming surface.

"This is the only gym floor I know of where kids can dance with their shoes on," Karen said.

"Don't forget, this is the oldest school in the county," Beth reminded her. "They gave up on having a nice gym floor years ago."

Elaine wasn't paying any attention to them, since she was watching the door to see which guys came in. She was hoping four certain boys would show up, since she had to admit she was slightly interested in them. There was Woody Stuart, who she considered really cute, Lenny Mendoza (Alma's twin) who was a very smart guy with a great sense of humor, Shawn O'Dell, who was always clowning and made her laugh, and Phil Santini just because all the girls were interested in him. If any one of them would ask her to dance, it would make her happy.

"I got a few people lined up to sell tickets," Vicki was saying to Elaine, "so we won't have to. I'm good at delegating."

"Where's Paul?" Elaine asked her.

"Oh, I think he'll be here a little later," Vicki told her. "He has to have his time to be with his buddies. You know how that is. Gee, I hope this dance won't be a drag."

"The after game dances last year were always drags," Beth complained. "None of the boys really care about dancing. They just come for something to do."

"Well, I think there are too many dances," Lucy stated. "After awhile they are nothing special. The only reason we keep having them, is certain organizations want to earn money."

The majority of the fellows refused to dance to fast records. They merely stood and watched the few brave souls who would. It was disheartening to the girls. A few of the black students got out and danced to the fast songs, and they were all really good.

"Hi, Cuz," said Scottie, as he joined the group of girls. "Are we having fun yet?"

"It's good to see you here, Scott," everyone told him.

"Can you do me a favor?" he whispered to Elaine.

"What's that?"

"Well, I want to learn to dance, but I'm not really sure that's possible, with my crutches and all. But I thought maybe you could come over sometime and teach me to dance, and just see if it's even doable in my situation."

"Of course," she told him. "I would be glad to help you. We could give that a try tomorrow."

Alma Mendoza joined the group. "Hi everyone, what's this, the old maids' circle?" she joked. "Looks like this place is starting to fill up."

The football players were starting to come into the gym now. Greg came over to be with Karen, and Elaine saw Lenny and Woody coming in. Woody had looked really cute in his football uniform she thought, like the typical all-American boy. He was in nearly all of her classes and seemed quite friendly toward her. He looked very nice that evening and was wearing a blue bulky sweater with brown cords. A slow song came on the record player, and this seemed to be a simultaneous signal for the guys to ask a girl to dance. Elaine found herself dancing with a freshman boy a couple inches shorter than she was. The record *One Summer Night* had been popular last summer, and it really reminded her of Danny. But she managed to smile and joke with her partner. She later danced with DJ, for old time's sake, and Shawn, who had her laughing the whole time. Finally Woody asked her to dance. He was teasing her about her lack of knowledge in Geometry class.

"You seem to be having a good time," Lucy said later to Elaine. "Bet you haven't thought of Danny once."

"No, not once," Elaine lied. "And I see you've danced with Phil a few times."

Lucy didn't answer, but just smiled a big, beaming smile.

"Oh, here comes our lovable Algebra teacher," Vicki interrupted with a whisper.

"Hello, girls, what's up?" came Coach Carr's friendly voice.

"We're discussing an important subject," Alma told him.

"You must be talking about the male species. From my astute observation, that's about all girls talk about these days," He turned toward Elaine. "Didn't I have you in my Algebra class last year? Yes, I remember. You were the girl I never called on because every time I did, you'd get real embarrassed, and blush and stammar, and then you wouldn't come up with the right answer after all."

"Oh, I wasn't that bad," Elaine said blushing.

"Yes, you were. You're just bashful, but that's okay. What grade did I give you anyhow?"

"You gave me a C," she told him. "And I think I deserved better than that," she added boldly.

"Then why didn't you come up and ask for a B?"

"Oh, I was afraid of you last year," she said demurely.

"Yes, a teacher has to keep his students walking the chalk line," he joked, walking away.

Much to Elaine's dismay, Alvin Minegar came up and asked her to dance just then. He looked skinnier than ever, and freckles stood out on his pale face. He was wearing a shirt that was several sizes too large for him. "What have you been doing lately?" he asked. "And where have you been hiding yourself? We don't have any classes together this year, so I don't get to see much of you."

"Oh, I've been pretty busy," she answered briefly. During the remainder of the dance she had to hear about Alvin's rabbits, his steer, and his chickens, a recent addition to his livestock.

"My Rhode Island Reds are real good chickens," he stated. "They're tremendous egg layers, and are also good eating. Maybe your dad should try raising them instead of White Leghorns."

"Well, I think that my dad, with his many years of experience, knows a lot more about raising chickens than you do." The nerve of him, she thought. But nothing seemed to faze the unflappable Alvin. He begged her for a date, but she gave him another well-worn excuse. After the dance he stood by her in a proprietary manner, which made it seem as if they were together. She was saved by the captain of the football team, Ty Ramirez, who asked her for a dance.

"I think I rescued you," Ty told her. "Natalie has told me about your problem with Alvin, so I should get points for being a knight in shining armor."

"You do get points, Ty. Thank you for being such a nice guy. By the way, you played a good game tonight, even though we lost. I was sorry about that."

"You win some, you lose some," he said. "There's always another game coming up, so I don't sweat it." He smiled and pulled her closer. "Where is Natalie tonight?"

"Oh, you know the usual problem she has about getting out of the house. She's working on her dad, and hopefully he's relenting a little bit, but it's terrible the way she is always stuck at home."

"Nat is a really sweet girl," Ty stated. "It's a shame her folks aren't more understanding. I sure would like to date her, but Mr. and Mrs. Irby would never go for that."

Chapter 17

Natalie Irby was curled up on the couch in the small family room of their home watching a rerun of *I Love Lucy*, which was usually a very funny show, but she wasn't laughing. Her younger sister Cheryl was sitting on the floor, very engrossed in the program. Natalie's emotions ran the gamut of anger at her father, and excitement about an event that had taken place in the last 24 hours.

Earlier in the week Natalie had approached her father about being able attend the high school football games with her friends, but her request was met with the usual stubborn resistance from her dad.

"Dad, I will be 16 in March, and I just don't see why I'm not allowed to go hardly anywhere. I make decent grades at school, and I work hard for them, and it seems like I should be able to get some enjoyment out of school too. You know the girls I run around with, and they're not the type who get in trouble or anything. Lucy, Beth, and Elaine have good reputations."

"That may very well be," was his answer, "But at this age people, can change in a hurry. There are just lots of temptations out there right now. I thought we'd agreed that you need to wait until you are 16, before participating in school activities, and 17 before you start dating."

"I don't remember to agreeing to any such thing," she had said angrily. "I feel like life is just passing me by, and everyone else is having all the fun."

"Girls your age don't make good judgments about most things," he responded. "And I don't think you realize it, but you're becoming a very beautiful young woman, and I don't want those young, hormone crazed hoodlums taking advantage of you. Boys that age have only one thing on their minds. And your high school has such a mix of people. When we moved out here to the country, I didn't realize the number of niggers and spics that are in school with you. It's just unbelievable. And knowing you, that's who you would fall for. You still have much of your life ahead of you, nearly three years of high school left, and then four years of college. I think with a little more maturity on your part, you'll be able to handle any situation that comes along." He stopped and put his arm around her, caressing her shoulders.

Natalie pulled away from him, upset. "Oh Dad, you're just not giving me enough credit. I can handle myself right now, and you and Mom have taught me the difference from right and wrong. And I'm not even asking about dating right now. I just want to be allowed to attend some of the school activities with my girlfriends. What could possibly be so bad about that?"

"Well, right now you're needed at home," Mr. Irby replied. "With my hours working out of town, and your mother's crazy hours working for the paper, it's nice to have you here with Cheryl. You're a big help around here, and we need you to keep things running smoothly."

"But Cheryl is 13 now, and she's old enough to stay by herself if she has to. I know girls the same age as she is who babysit on a regular basis."

"I think we're at the end of this discussion, Sweetheart," her father said calmly, patting her behind as he walked out of his study. "We've had this talk before, and I'm sure we'll have it again when you turn sixteen."

Natalie was furious as she went upstairs to her room and slammed the door as hard as she could. When Adam had left for college, she had moved into his room on the second floor. It had less character than the attic room, but more space. She still had some boxes of books to unpack, so she started unloading them onto the bookcase. How she missed Adam. Her older brother had always been a calming influence on her, and now he was at UCLA, and wouldn't be home until Thanksgiving, most likely. There were times when she just couldn't stand being around her father. He was such a racist, she thought, and just acted so self-righteous at times. Her mother was much easier to talk to, but then she always ended up in agreement with her husband.

Cheryl interrupted her thoughts, and brought her back to the present. "I'm going to pop some popcorn? Do you want some?"

"Sure, that sounds really good. Put plenty of butter on it."

Natalie went back into her reverie. Early yesterday morning, Elaine had called her with a message from Ty Ramirez. She had seen Ty at the Friday night dance, and he had given Elaine his phone number and told her to have Natalie call him. Nat was ecstatic after getting off the phone with Elaine. But what was she going to do about it? As happened, things worked out really well for her. Her father had to go back to Los Angeles on business, and he wouldn't be back for a few days. He left on Sunday afternoon. Her mother had one of her migraine headaches and went to bed. Nat knew her mother's migraines usually lasted nearly 24 hours. She called Ty on Sunday afternoon and made a date with him for that evening.

As she dressed for her date, butterflies were fluttering around in her stomach. She had had such a big crush on Ty for many months now. He was so good looking and so popular with everyone, and he was captain of the football team, no less. A quick check in her mirror told her that she was looking especially good. Her long blonde hair wasn't flying all over for a change, and her face looked happy, and her skin was clear, though slightly flushed. Her sweater and skirt clung to her in all the right places. Cheryl stopped by her room and peeked in.

"Lookin' good, Big Sister," she said. "If Mom needs you for anything, I'll cover for you. I'll either tell her that you went to bed early, or you're in the shower, or something. And I'm pretty sure she won't be getting up any time soon. Where are you guys going, anyhow?"

"Ty said something about going to the movies. I should get going right now. I'm going to meet him at the end of the driveway. It's good that Mom and Dad's room is at the back of the house, even though Mom probably won't be looking out the window anytime soon, but if she does, she won't see me getting into his car."

"It is just so ridiculous that Dad has to be so strict all the time," Cheryl complained. "When I start high school next year, I want to be able to go places, and I probably won't get to."

"Yeah, we girls are really gonna have to stick together and stand up against the folks. Thanks, Cheryl, for your help," Nat said, as she left the house. The date with Ty had been beyond wonderful. He was such a gentleman, going around and opening the car door for her. They had found lots to talk about as they drove up to Armedia to the movie theater. The first movie, *Bridge on the River Kwai,* was quite suspenseful, and they were really engrossed in it. They didn't really see a whole lot of the second movie because they were too busy necking. Since they were sitting in the back row of the theater, they knew they weren't disturbing the other movie goers.

"You're so beautiful," Ty told her as they sat at the end of her driveway as their date came to a close. He was kissing her fingertips. "I can see why your dad worries about you going on dates. He just wants to keep his little girl at home."

"Oh, let's not even talk about my dad. It has been a really great evening and I don't want anything to spoil it." The radio was playing *To Know Him Is To Love Him* and moonlight was filtering through the car window, lighting up Ty's handsome face.

"Baby, when can I see you again?" Ty was asking. "I've had so much fun I don't ever want this night to end."

"Oh, Ty, I don't either. And I can't answer your question. Of course we can see each other at school. But I don't know when I'll be able to sneak out again. It just worked out really well this time. We'll have to wait and see what happens."

"You're my prisoner of Zenda," Ty remarked, referring to a really old movie. "It's just my luck to fall for someone who's not allowed to date. But that makes you all the more desirable, do you realize that?" Natalie's answer to that was to run her fingers through his thick, black hair and to kiss him hungrily. There was no more talking after that.

Chapter 18

As the weeks passed, Elaine found that she was thinking less and less of Danny, and was enjoying her classes and her Fall Semester at school. She was having fun with her various school activities and she was studying harder than she had done last year (or maybe she was learning better study habits.) Mid quarter tests were coming up and Elaine's goal was to make at least three A's, which would make her eligible for the California Scholarship Federation. She was pretty satisfied with all her classes, except maybe Spanish II which was just as difficult as it had been the previous year.

In her first period class, Home Economics, the girls had started on sewing. Elaine loved the large, sunny sewing room with its neat sewing machines lined up in a row, but she didn't like the actual sewing that much. She was making pink, cotton over blouse, and had sewed a simple dart wrong for the third time.

"Poor Elaine," Megan said, half teasing, half sympathetic. "But really, I don't see how anyone can have as much trouble over a dart as you do. I think you just daydream too much." Megan herself was an excellent seamstress. She had already finished the required blouse, and was laying out black corduroy designated for a jumper.

"I've never been too good at sewing," Elaine complained. "Beth is just like you, she can practically sew anything with her eyes closed. Part of my problem is our sewing machine at home. It's an antique, and never seems to work right. But I would love to be better at this, because it would be great to be able to make a lot of my own clothes."

"Well, we have a much newer sewing machine at my house," Beth said from across the table.

"Just keep on trying," Megan advised. "Practice makes perfect. I've been sewing for years. She indicated the corduroy. "After I finish the jumper, I'm going to make a semi-formal out of pale blue chiffon. It will take a while, but will be finished in time for the Turnabout Dance."

Elaine laughed. "If I started on something like that, it might be done by *next* year's dance. However, I do already have a dress to wear for this year's dance." Elaine went on to tell her about a package that had arrived in the mail from a friend of her mother. The friend had two girls older than Elaine and Pam, and she occasionally sent her daughters' hand-me-downs to Elaine and Pam. The clothes were always very high quality and showed little wear. The recent package had included a semi-formal dress of pale yellow taffeta. It featured baby doll sleeves, a full skirt, and a square neck trimmed with lace. "I was so excited when I saw it," Elaine continued. "Of course the dance is more than a month away, and I have no idea who I should ask this year. I'm not sure I even want to go."

"Oh, but you have to go," Megan stated. "I think there are some better choices of guys this year. Of course it's harder for you girls in Ellington because of transportation. Most of the guys our age don't drive yet. That's why it would be better to ask an older guy."

"I don't know the older guys that well," Elaine remarked.

"Let me think about that," Megan mused. "I'll see if I can come up with some ideas for you."

"Sounds like we have an Abigail Van Buren in our midst," Vicki joked.

In Spanish II Elaine was in a thick fog, just like she had been in the preceding year. But she wasn't too worried about it, since nearly everyone else was in the same boat. The verb conjugations of the preterit and conditional tenses were just too much for her. Once, after giving a test in which the highest grade was 72 %, Mrs. Mendoza asked the class why everyone seemed to be having problems. Woody explained the feelings of the class perfectly when he said, "Last year's class was such a confusing experience for us that during the summer we formed a mental block against the subject."

"Well, I'll have to try and erase that block," Mrs.Mendoza said softly. The students were noting with surprise, how much kinder and more pleasant their teacher was this year. Elaine was proud of the way Woody had expressed the feelings of the class. He was never afraid to offer his opinion on any subject, and was respected by teachers as well as students because of his frankness. She had also heard from Alma (the niece of Mrs.Mendoza) that her aunt had had some personal problems the previous year.

Mr. Sharpe made Sophomore Science a very interesting class for most of the students because of the variety in class sessions. One never knew what to expect when he walked into the classroom. Sometimes he would ask questions on the current chapter, pulling the student attendance cards which were in his hat, all mixed up. Elaine always panicked when she had to unexpectedly answer a question, because she hated reciting aloud. Also, there were a lot of boys in the class, which made her more nervous being the center of attention. One day Mr.Sharpe looked around the room, and spotted Elaine sitting unobtrusively behind Lucy. "Elaine Hummer," he boomed. "You're an agent for collecting class dues aren't you?"

"Yes."

"Well how many students in this class have paid their dues so far?"

"Um, about four, I guess."

"You guess? Don't you know for sure?"

"Yes. Four people have paid their dues."

"That's not a very good number. I can see that the sophomore class isn't going to get anywhere at this rate," Mr. Sharpe said. "And it's my duty as your class sponsor, to see that this class gets on the ball. Elaine, how about you getting up and giving a little pep talk about class dues?"

At this request, Elaine suddenly broke out into a clammy sweat. Her heart began pounding and her knees began to shake. "Shouldn't a pep talk be the class treasurer's job?" she asked meekly. She was sure Phil, the treasurer, was much more qualified to speak than she was.

"Nope, get up here, Elaine!" ordered Mr. Sharpe.

"Speech, speech," Phil grinned, looking back at her.

Reluctantly she made her way up to the front of the room. "What kind of sophomore class is this?" she asked rather weakly. "Let's get busy and get our dues paid. If no one came up with the money, why, where would we be? All the other classes would outdo us, and we certainly don't want that!" She was on a roll now, and her voice was stronger. "We'll be needing money soon for the Homecoming Parade float, and we want to build up the treasury for the prom next year, and of course we want to have plenty of money by the time we get to our senior ditch day. And Greg Okamota and Phil Santini, as class officers, of all people, you should be the first to pay your dues and set a good example!" Amid clapping and laughter, she went back to her seat, making a face at Phil.

"Did you hear that?" Mr.Sharpe asked. "Better pay up or the entire class will be after you."

"I haven't got my allowance yet," Phil was saying. Greg was reaching into his pocket for some cash.

"I have a question," Shawn said from the back of the room. "Has Elaine paid her dues yet?"

"No, but I am right now," she answered, as the class roared.

Physical Education class followed, and all the girls enjoyed P.E. with affable Miss Morgan as the instructor. The girls were learning how to spike a serve in volleyball, and how to make pyramids in tumbling exercises. The pyramids were constantly collapsing, and Elaine, being on top because of her lightness, would usually take a spill onto the mat. Miss Morgan also had them doing calisthenics the first ten minutes of class, so they were getting quite a workout.

Geometry, after lunch was a peaceful, sleepy, and undemanding class. Elaine understood little of the subject, but her lack of knowledge did not bother her too much, since she knew Mr. Dumpke liked her, and would grade accordingly. He usually left the room during part of the class period, and everyone would become very lively. Woody enjoyed tormenting Elaine by drawing cartoons of her on the back board, labeling them 'Lainey', much to her dismay. Sometimes she went back to erase them, and would get into an argument with the irrepressible Woody. One day she didn't quite manage to get back to her desk before Mr. Dumpke returned to the room. He calmly handed her a stack of blank paper and told her to write 500 times "I will not waste time on Woody." The class thought Mr. Dumpke's penalties were most amusing, although elementary.

Study Hall was her favorite period. It was completely wasted as a study period, however. As long as the sunny October days remained warm, Mr. Caldwell let members of the class meet out on the lawn behind the cafeteria. Elaine, Lucy, Karen, Greg, Phil, and Shawn, and Lenny sometimes sat in a group under the pepper trees and talked. Elaine usually did more listening than speaking. The conversation wasn't as gossipy compared to girl talk. With guys in the group there was more joking and teasing.

"I was riding around Ellington on my motorcycle about a week ago," Lenny was saying. "I never saw such a dead town. Nothing going on at all."

"What day were you riding around?' Elaine asked.

"Oh, I think it was on a Sunday morning."

"Well no wonder you didn't see any activity," Lucy told him. "Everyone was either still asleep, or in church. That's where I was anyhow."

"Well I'm glad to hear you are a good little girl," Phil said. "I haven't been down that way yet. But I hear that it's mostly swampland,

and there are no phones or electricity, and that mail is still delivered by pony express."

"That's about right," replied Lucy, "we're just pioneers down there. I chop wood and go and hunt animals to put food on the table. You should make your way down there sometime and see how the other half lives."

"I just might do that sometime," Phil stated, looking at her intently.

The walk to English class after Study Hall was just a short way, and the group always went together. Once class started, however, they had to forget everything else, and concentrate on Mark Twain and Victor Hugo under Mrs. Teague's stern glare. She was a good teacher, and Elaine found that if she listened, she got a great deal out of the class.

*   *   *

Later that day, on the bus ride home, Lucy confided in Elaine and Nat that she was going to ask Phil to the Turnabout Dance. "I think he is so cute, and so much fun," she said. "But even though it's a month away, I suppose I should ask him soon, because I think a lot of the girls are interested in him."

"You're right," Nat told her. "The sooner the better. And while we're on the subject, Elaine, I have a really big favor to ask of you."

"And what might that be? Anything for you, my friend."

"Well, I was thinking that maybe I could stay at your house the night of the Turnabout Dance. Now that Ty and I are a couple, I'll be going to the dance with him of course, and he could pick me up at your house. My folks won't have to know a thing about it, and I won't even be telling them a lie, I'll just tell them I'm spending the night at your house."

"Yeah, that would probably be okay," Elaine told her. "But aren't you forgetting something? I haven't yet figured out who I'm asking. Your plan just won't work if I don't have a date."

"You still have a thing for Danny, don't you?" Nat asked.

"I do still miss him, but I'm trying to focus on other guys."

"Well, you need to get with it, girl. You must have someone in mind," Lucy told her."

"I know, it's really strange, because last year all I could think of was asking Warren, and now he's moved away, and I don't even care anymore. Life is funny that way. I sort of like Woody, since he's cute and fun. I also think Lenny Mendoza would be interesting to get to know better. And I always laugh a lot when I'm around Shawn. He is such a character."

"Well, if you want my opinion, you should ask Woody," Nat told her. He's friends with Ty, and he probably doesn't have his license yet, so you and Woody could go with Ty and me."

"I don't know if Phil drives, either," Lucy was saying. "The dance should be really nice this year. Did you hear what its theme will be? It's Starlight Fantasy. Doesn't that sound romantic? They've set the date for November 26th, the evening before Thanksgiving holiday."

Elaine was deep in thought as she gathered the eggs that afternoon. It's all so strange, she reflected, how in the short space of a year, something so terribly important then, is completely forgotten now. Here I am laughing at my heartbreak of a year ago. It certainly is crazy to like someone so much that you think you want to be with him more than anything else in the whole world, and are devastated if he doesn't like you back, and then a few months later you don't even care. It is absolutely senseless. But I guess that's part of growing up. The more she thought about asking Woody, the more the idea appealed to her.

She talked about Woody at the dinner table that night. "You would like him," she told her parents. 'He's intelligent, well-mannered, and has a good personality. Oh, and he plays football."

"Well, that's most important," Charles joked. "You can't like a boy who's not a football player. Heaven forbid!"

"Oh, Daddy," she said.

"I'd love to meet him," Lois said. "And I'm sure I'll have a chance to when he takes you to the dance."

"Pass the potatoes please," said Russ, with his mouth full.

"You mean *if* he wants to take me," Elaine corrected. "I still have to ask him."

"Momma, I want some gravy," said Timmie.

"Think positively," her mother told her. "Of course he'll take you.

"Please pass me the salt, Pam," Charles requested.

"Why don't you ask dorky Alvin?" Pam suggested, passing the salt. "He would take you."

"Do you have to mention him?" Elaine asked. "I wouldn't ask him if he were the last guy on earth!"

"Could I have some more salad?" Russ asked.

"I think there's a two-way conversation going on here," Charles said. "I'm getting confused." Everyone laughed.

"Well, we don't want to hear about Elaine's crummy boyfriends," Russ complained. "Gee, I'd hate it if a girl asked me to one of those silly dances."

"You'll change your mind soon enough, Russ," Elaine told him.

"I hope not for a while yet," Lois said, wiping gravy off Timmie's face. "Children grow up much too fast these days. I'm glad I still have a baby left."

"I'm *not* a baby," howled Timmie, splattering mashed potatoes as his spoon came down hard on them.

"Hey, it's time for *Huckleberry Hound* cartoons," Russ cried, jumping up from the table. "Dad, why don't we get a color TV set?"

"So you can watch cartoons?" asked his father, laughing. "We have enough expenses without a color TV. We have two girls constantly needing all kinds of stuff, Russ here growing like a weed, and just look at Timmie there, eating us out of house and home."

"Yes, we all eat as if this were our last meal," Lois added.

"You're not kidding," said her husband. "Look at that little man shovel in the food!"

And they all laughed when Timmie cried, "More jello."

"Lately we've been rather short on money," Charles continued in a more serious tone. "Egg prices have gone down. The small poultry ranches don't stand much of a chance with bigger ones popping up all over the state. At this time of year, everyone is hard up. The farmers around here are struggling. And we desperately need some rain. Things are really getting dry."

"We certainly have had a long heat spell," Lois added. "Lovely weather, but more like July than October."

"One good thing about warmer weather is that you don't freeze at the football games," Elaine later told her mother as they were clearing the table. "Did I tell you that Woody plays football?"

"Yes, you did. And now may I offer a word of advice? You'd better not say too much around school about Woody. You know how gossip spreads at that school. You wouldn't want Alvin to hear that you like Woody. He might try to cause some trouble."

"Oh Alvin couldn't do a thing," scoffed Elaine. "He just likes to bluff. Did you know he offered me advice on what kind of chickens Dad should get?"

"That's all I need, some punk kid trying to tell me how to run my business," Charles said from behind the newspaper.

On Halloween night Elaine, Beth, and Lucy rode the Rooters Bus to the town of Ralston for the 7th football game of the season. Armedia had not had a good football season so far; their standing was two wins and five losses. There were some who said that the lack of school spirit was part of the reason that Armedia was on a losing streak. Ironically, as the team kept losing, spirits grew worse, and game attendance grew worse. At the Pep Rally earlier that week, the cheerleaders had depicted a funeral for the departed school spirit. Members of the football team had carried Spirit's large, black coffin up the gym aisle to the tune of Chopin's funeral march. But the clever little skit didn't help attendance that night, in spite of the fact that Ralston High was their big arch-rival. Hopes were high that they would have a win tonight, and get back their Victory Bell. But once they were seated on the bleachers, Megan told the other girls that one of their best players couldn't play because of a sprained ankle, and another player had an injured hand. "We seem to have a lot of injuries this year," she added.

"We still have Woody, Greg, and Lenny," Elaine said. "And your Willie, of course, and Ty."

"Don't forget Phil," added Lucy.

"Yes, but the sophomores just don't have the experience," Vicki replied.

In spite of the importance of the game with their rival team, Armedia's bleachers were not as full as usual. "Maybe because it's also Halloween," Megan said. She told the girls jokingly that Willie had wanted to tip over outhouses instead of playing football that night. The five girls sat huddled close together under blankets drinking hot chocolate. It had turned cold the last few nights.

The Ralston team made two touchdowns the first quarter. Halfway through the second quarter they saw Woody and a Ralston player throwing punches at each other, and both players were benched. Elaine watched Woody as he angrily threw his helmet on the ground. She could imagine how badly he must feel. The other sophomores were playing more than usual since the team was so small. And then Willie was injured.

"Oh, no, not Willie!" cried Megan.

"Not another injury," moaned Beth. "Our team must be jinxed." But Willie's injury, whatever it was, wasn't that bad, since he went back into the game the third quarter. And no one else was hurt, except the spirits of the fans. The bouncy little cheerleaders were doing their best to keep the team spirits up, and to keep the rooters happy and enthusiastic. During the fourth quarter, Armedia managed to get a field goal. But by then, Ralston was four touchdowns ahead. The final score was 35-3 at the end of a long, discouraging night.

"Well, so much for getting our Victory Bell back," Vicki said glumly on the way back to the bus. There was one cheerful thought in the back of Elaine's mind. The game on Halloween marked the end of October, and time was drawing closer for the Turnabout Dance.

Chapter 19

Fall was definitely in the air. The leaves on the tall poplar trees behind the Hummers' garage had turned a brilliant yellow and orange. The grape arbor leaves, once a vibrant green, had changed to a dingy brown, and clung tenaciously to the branches. The November sky remained a bright, cloudless blue, and frequent groupings of geese flying in V-shaped formations were seen heading south for the winter. The nights were crisp, clear, and cold, sometimes with temperatures below freezing. Frost warnings were issued nightly for the sake of the orange growers. The dry weather continued, and on the nights when the temp was above freezing, people had to deal with the wind. The strong north winds, the Santa Ana winds, as they were called, blew fiercely for days at a time. Farmers in the valley needed rain desperately, if only to clear the air of the dust the gales created. On bad days the surrounding hills were seen through a haze of dust that had once been the topsoil of the now badly eroded land around the valley. Lake Armedia was slowly drying to a sticky, stinking bog of mud and rotting fish. All of Armedia Valley, all of southern California wished for rain.

Elaine spoke to her school counselor about working as a library assistant with Megan in place of Study Hall. Since the weather had turned cold, Study Hall was inside again, but the class was noisy and distracting. Elaine had thought it would be most interesting to work in the school library. Having secured her counselor's permission, Elaine made the transfer. She liked the cool, quiet bungalow building and found it much easier to study there. She and Megan were busy for a few days cataloging books, most of which were fifteen years old with thick covers and small print. But Mrs. Coyne, the school librarian, was ordering new fiction, which made Elaine happy since she was an ardent fan of fiction. And she enjoyed working with the vivacious Megan, who always seemed to be the first to know out about every detail and every person who had anything to do with Armedia High.

She informed Elaine that Principal Santini hadn't been getting along too well with the teaching staff, or the Board of Education members. It was rumored, Megan said, that Dean Caldwell was planning to break his contract and quit, due to problems between the dean and the principal. Elaine liked the tall, friendly man with the warm smile, and thought he had some good ideas for school improvements. However, she knew very little of what went on behind the scenes. And it was hard for her to know what to believe because false rumors spread so quickly around the school, and around the valley.

Friday night Armedia actually won their football game, and everyone was exuberant. Excitement was in the air that night. Elaine was happy because Natalie had been at the game, and now the dance. She confided to Elaine that her father had had to fly to San Francisco on business, and that she had finally convinced her mother to let her go. And after the dance the girls were going to Vicki Bannister's for a slumber party. So spirits were high that evening, and everyone was in a wonderful mood. Elaine was a little envious of Nat however, who danced every dance with Ty. More of her friends had boyfriends this year. Vicki was with Paul Newberry, Karen with Greg Okamota, and Lucy seemed to be with Phil for most of the dance. Elaine danced with DJ, Shawn, Lenny Mendoza, and with Woody. But Woody danced with several other girls too.

After the dance, eight girls rode in two cars headed for Vicki's home in the hills above Armedia. The Bannister house was a large, gray, rambling Cape Cod house set back from the road, and was surrounded by trees. Vicki took the girls out behind the house to Willie's room where they would spend the night. It was quite spacious, and far enough away from the house that all the noise from the girls wouldn't disturb the rest of the family.

"Poor Willie," Karen giggled. "He had to evacuate because of a bunch of girls."

"Definitely not poor Willie," stated Vicki. "He got the better end of this deal. Mom made him clean this room earlier this week, but I don't think he did that good a job. I had to go behind him, cleaning and mopping, and stuffing some of his junk out of sight. And I'm sure he'll be around some time tonight just to bug us."

"Well, lock the door," Beth suggested. "We want fair warning if anyone comes in."

"Oh, for sure I am locking the door," the hostess said. "It's kind of lonely out here."

"I noticed that there aren't any houses close by," Elaine said.

"That's true," remarked Vicki. "I hate to stay here alone at night. The last time I did, I swear I heard someone trying to get in the front door. And there is a maniac around here. He's our nearest neighbor, and lives about a quarter mile down the road."

"You're kidding," said Lucy, fascinated.

"I kid you not. And our neighbor on the other side, about two blocks away, is Phil Santini's family. They just moved in this summer."

The girls plunked themselves down on top of their sleeping bags, eating chips, dips, and cookies. A radio was turned on, and the usual slumber party atmosphere was achieved. Later the lights were turned off for ghost stories. Alma, who had a talent for storytelling, began. "This is called 'The Wreck of Bernadette,' so sit back and listen."

"Sounds like it's about a ship," Nat said, popping a pretzel into her mouth.

"Well, it's not. It begins in a college. An old professor dies and bequeaths his body to the anatomy class for study and research. Some of the boys in the class took a hand from the body and gave it to the girls to scare them, but they didn't scare that easily, however. The girls got together and decided to put the hand in Bernadette's room. She was a really beautiful girl with long, flowing black hair, but she was very, very timid. Well, the—" A loud scream interrupted the story, and confusion reigned.

"We need the lights turned on!" someone shouted.

"What's going on?" Alma asked, cross at having her story interrupted. Finally Vicki reached the lights, nearly tripping over Megan and Beth in the process, and switched the lights on. The disheveled girls sat up, feeling rather silly. The clock ticked off 1:00 am.

"Who screamed?" Megan asked. "Just when the story was getting interesting."

"Did anyone else see what I saw?" Karen asked. "I'm the one who screamed, but I swear that I saw a white face looking in the window! I know it wasn't my imagination!"

"Come to think of it, I saw something too," Nat added.

All eyes turned toward the window, but nothing could be seen except for the black sky with a few twinkling stars, and the outline of a tree branch. Nothing was stirring outside.

"I wouldn't put it past Willie to be trying to scare us," Vicki said. "He's probably laughing his head off right now." She went to the window and pulled the curtains. "There, that's better."

"Can we get back to my little tale?" asked Alma. "I'm just getting to the good part." Everyone said yes, but there was an argument as to whether or not the lights should be turned out. At last they went out, and Alma proceeded. "Those girls took that withered old hand into Bernadette's room and laid it on her pillow, under her bedspread. Later Bernadette came back to her room, and of course they expected to hear a scream, as she was getting ready to go to bed. But instead, there was only deathly silence. After about half an hour, the girls went into her room. There was no sign of Bernadette or the hand. The girls began to panic, and started to search everywhere in her room. Upon opening the closet door, they finally found her. She was all hunched up, sitting on the top shelf of her closet. Apparently she had gone completely insane. Her eyes stared glassily into nothingness, and her once beautiful black hair had turned completely white. She just sat there, chewing on the withered hand!"

At the startling ending, loud screams penetrated the silence. Suddenly there was a knock at the door, which prompted more screams, followed by silence. Then they heard Willie's voice asking to be admitted. His big frame filled the doorway.

"You girls are terribly noisy," he remarked. "We can hear your screams all the way up to Phil's house. Noise carries at night." He stepped aside so Phil could enter.

"We decided to join the party," he explained with a grin, as he helped himself to chips.

"And eat up all our food," Megan complained. "By the way, were you guys at the window about ten minutes ago?"

"No, we've been over at Phil's in his garage all this time," Willie stated. But no one believed him. The boys sat down unobtrusively in the corner and listened to the conversation. Vicki and Megan had come up with one of their frequent brainstorms.

"As you all know," Vicki began, "there is one social club in Armedia for girls. It's Greek and quite exclusive, with mainly Junior and Senior girls in it. I think they mostly drink at their social get togethers, and don't do much of anything to help anyone. I thought we should start a different type of club, more of a service club with projects for helping out in the community. It would have to be a non-school organization though. And we don't want to be snobbish about admitting other girls, but we mainly want nice girls."

"It sounds like a fabulous idea," Lucy said. Everyone shared her enthusiasm.

"May we join?" Phil asked.

"Seeing that it's a girls club, I guess you can," Megan told him.

"What an insult! I'm not hanging around here any longer. Let's go, Willie," and with that, the boys departed.

"There are eight of us here tonight," Megan said. "We can be the charter members. We have to decide on a name, first of all. We need to elect officers, and we need a sponsor, membership cards, and ideas to raise money."

"I'm sure my mom would be a sponsor," Karen said. "She has often said that it would be nice to have a girls' service club in town." They voted on the name *Collettes*, and Vicki was elected president. Their first project would be a rummage sale, they decided, to raise money for Thanksgiving dinners for needy families in the area.

The clocked off 2:00 am, and some of the girls were getting sleepy. Elaine, Megan, and Vicki went into the main house to get some banana cream pie from the refrigerator.

"I'm just not sleepy at all," Megan said once they were in the cool, dark kitchen. "I think I could stay up all night. Everyone always gets tired too soon."

"Well, the three of us can sit up and talk," Elaine told her.

Five minutes later the girls walked around to the back of the property, back to Willie's room. The dry leaves crackled as they stepped quietly over them. Elaine was shivering from the cold. Suddenly Megan gripped Elaine's arm hard. "Look over there," she whispered, pointing to an old oak tree across the dirt road. The outline of a man, not 20 yards away, was barely visible on the moonless night. He was leaning against the tree, smoking a cigarette, and his face was turned toward the girls. They didn't wait to see any more, but turned and ran with lightning speed around the building, and into the safety of the warm room, locking the door behind them. They quickly explained to the dozing girls what they had seen, and that roused everyone again.

"I told you guys earlier," Vicki said breathlessly, "that there is a weirdo who lives down the street. He's very eccentric, and sometimes takes night walks around the neighborhood. He could be a prowler, or he could be the Peeping Tom we saw earlier. I really don't know if that face at the window was the boys tricking us, or if it was that man." It took a while for the girls to calm down. They kept imagining all sorts of weird noises. They were sure they heard a baby crying until Vicki convinced them that it was just peacocks down the road.

"I wonder if anyone else in this neighborhood is getting any sleep," someone said. At last they calmed their jumpy nerves by singing songs: *Lonesome Valley, I come to the Garden Alone,* and *Do Lord,* and others. And one by one, they fell asleep.

*   *   *

By Friday of the following week, Elaine had not yet asked Woody to the Turnabout Dance. Every time she saw him there were too many other people around. "You are the biggest chicken I know," Nat told her. "A little bird told me that Mary Lou Wright is thinking about asking him. Please just do it before she beats you to it. Hey, I'm a poet, and don't know it."

"That's easy for you to say," Elaine told her., "Now that you're going with Ty, it's not a problem for you. But I have an entirely different situation. What if he turns me down?"

"That is not going to happen," Karen told her. The girls were standing at Elaine's locker after fifth period. "He likes you. He's always staring at you in class. He's probably just too bashful to ask you out."

"But he doesn't have a car," Elaine said.

"Let him worry about the transportation," Nat advised. "Besides, I already told you that you guys could ride with me and Ty. Problem solved. And, speaking of the devil, Woody just went around the corner to his locker, and he's all by himself. Now's your perfect opportunity."

"Good luck," Karen whispered, as the two of them walked away.

Elaine wished she had never heard of the Turnabout Dance. He heart was pounding so hard she could scarcely breathe, her knees were shaking, and her mouth felt dry as sawdust. Before she could change her mind, she walked quickly up to Woody and said, "Hi, Woody, I need to ask you about something. I was wondering if you'd go to the Turnabout Dance with me."

Woody reached into his locker for a book. It seemed like a long time before he replied. "That sounds like a really cool idea. I don't have a car, but I think I can work something out, and find someone to double with. Thanks for asking me." He smiled at her as he left for class.

Elaine stood still, weak and relieved, and then delirious with joy. He'd said yes! Mrs. Teague, who happened to be walking by, broke into her reverie. "The second bell has already rung. You'd better get to class right now, young lady," she said, clapping her hands twice. "Run!" she added. And as Elaine ran on light feet toward the library, she felt more like she was flying.

The following week was filled with various homecoming activities. The students got out of class to work on their floats for the parade. The sophs were using Mr.Okamota's flatbed truck, and had built a castle of heavy white cardboard around it. The girls were busy drawing black squares on the cardboard to make bricks. The slogan, "Gateway to Victory," was painted in front of the castle drawbridge. Ivy and flowers were draped around the door, and on top of the tower, built with two by fours, was a platform where the princesses would be sitting. The parade through town was a spectacular affair, and created publicity for the homecoming game which was coming up that night.

A large crowd turned out for the game that night, only to see Armedia lose their ninth and last game of the season. It was most disheartening to see how hard the team tried that night. In fact they almost tied the game. The score was 7-0 for most of the game, in favor of the opposing team. In the fourth quarter, Armedia had possession, and Willie was carrying it for a touchdown. But just as he neared the goal line, he was tackled by an opposing player, and down he went. Was he over the line? The crowd stood breathless, and then shouted in relief and joy as the ref's hands went up to signal a touchdown. Unfortunately, Armedia's conversion failed, and they lost the game by a point. The girls were crying as they watched the boys walk off the field, not even waiting tilt the Alma Mater was sung. "Oh, Armedia, we hail to thee, ever loyal and faithful we will always be—."

The week before the Turnabout Dance went by rather slowly. The girls were up to their ears with plans for the dance, and were hardly aware of what was going on in class. Elaine and Nat were going ahead with their plans for Nat to spend the night at Elaine's that night.

"Mom and Dad are completely clueless," Natalie told her as they stood in the lunch line.

"And I've persuaded Pam to sleep on the living room couch that night, because we'll probably spend half the night talking about the dance once we get home," Elaine said.

"I'm just so glad that you convinced Beth to ask Scottie to the dance," Nat remarked. "She just had no idea who to ask, and I think they'll have a good time, just going as friends."

"Yeah, that worked out really well. You know, I got together with him at the first of the year, because he wanted to see if he could learn to dance with his crutches. It wasn't easy, and it's kind of awkward, but he can move around a little for a short time anyhow."

The girls started getting ready way ahead of time, since they wanted to take their time, and they were sharing a bathroom. They each took a shower, and just about used up all the hot water. They did each other's hair. Nat's hair was easy, since she wore it long and straight. Elaine's had grown out since her brush-up, and Nat had curled it in soft, glossy waves which framed her face. A stiffly starched petticoat went on over seamless nylons, and then she pulled the yellow taffeta dress carefully over her head.

"That color looks really good on you," Nat told her. "It goes well with your brown hair. I would just look washed out in yellow."

"Well, royal blue is definitely your color," Elaine stated. "I know you borrowed that dress from Megan, but you look sensational in it. Ty will fall madly in love with you."

"Isn't it strange, how I didn't even like Megan very well last year, and now we are good friends," Nat said. "It was really sweet of her to loan me this dress. I feel really good in it too."

Lois knocked on the door just then. "Headlights are coming up the driveway," she said. "Once we meet Ty and Woody, I know your dad will want to take some pictures of you girls and your dates. And you are both looking really lovely, by the way."

"I'm glad your parents and mine aren't that close," Nat whispered to Elaine. "Otherwise they would want to be sharing pictures." That was true enough, Elaine thought. Mr. Irby didn't really involve himself in Ellington's activities. However, Nat's mom, Jackie, attended some of the activities, but mainly as the local photographer. It made Elaine a bit uneasy, as she thought of what could happen if Natalie's parents found out why she was spending the night. But as she heard the ring of the doorbell, she pushed that thought right out of her mind. She didn't want anything to spoil the evening.

Introductions were made to her parents, and then Woody handed her a corsage of white gardenias and peach colored roses in a cellophane covered box. After posing for pictures, the four of them climbed into Ty's 55 Chevy, which sparkled like a new penny.

"I don't think my car has ever been this clean and shiny," Ty said as they headed up the road to Armedia. Half an hour later when they walked into the gym, they were amazed at the transformation. Royal blue satin parachutes were hung across the ceiling. To carry out the theme "Starlight Fantasy," glittering stars were attached to the parachutes. Star covered panels hid the dingy walls, and big paper moons hung from the basketball rims. Girls in their pastel party dresses and freshly scrubbed boys in their suits and ties were seated at tables positioned around the room. The band, ensconced on a transformed stage was playing *Til There Was You,* but no one was dancing.

Elaine was thinking how nice Woody looked in a gray suit and a burgundy tie, as the four of them sat down at a table. He seemed to be enjoying himself with Elaine.

"Every year this crummy gym gets harder to camouflage," he said. "But I hope nobody gets wise and pulls the cord to those parachutes," he added glancing above them. "It wouldn't be too good if they all came tumbling down."

"Your dress is about the same color as the parachutes," Ty told Natalie with a smile. "If they fell down, I would never be able to find you. Bet you didn't plan to match the decorations."

Phil and Lucy, who looked beautiful in a dress of green satin, stopped by their table to say hi. Willie and Megan were right behind them.

"Hey, Phil, you clean up good," Elaine told him.

"And that green is a beautiful color on you, Lucy," complimented Natalie. "Goes really well with your auburn hair."

"Oh, Wood-man," Phil gushed. "I just love that brown, or whatever color, suit you're wearing, and it does *SO* much for your dishwater blonde hair and your red eyes." He had everyone laughing.

"Well, what about me?" Willie asked, sticking his foot out. "Aren't these shoes just to die for?"

"Us guys just look so spiffy tonight," added Woody, waving his hand in front of his face. "And look, here comes Newberry. Never thought I'd see him in a tie."

Vicki looked very pretty in a bright turquoise dress, but Paul was already tugging at his tie. "I don't know how some of these jokers wear a suit and tie to work every day," he complained. "I don't even know if I'll last an hour in this get-up."

The next hour was full of lively conversation and laughter. Beth came in with Scottie, and they sat with Elaine, Woody, Nat, and Ty. Vicki, Megan, and Lucy, and their dates were at the table next to them. The band began playing a slow number, and many couples got up to dance. Woody was a good dancer, and they danced smoothly and in perfect rhythm. As he held her close, Elaine closed her eyes. She could smell the luscious fragrance of her gardenia. She wished the song would never end, but it did all too soon, and they walked back to the table holding hands.

Elaine asked Woody how he managed to get such good grades all the time, since she knew he had been in the California Scholar Federation last year.

"Oh, I'm just good at snowing the teachers, I guess," he laughed. "Especially the women teachers. I just give them my puppy dog eyes look. Like this," as he batted his eyes at Elaine. "It works like a charm."

"I'll have to try that," Elaine said. "But somehow I don't think I can work that with Mrs. Teague. She'll see right through me. English has always been my best subject tilt now."

"I suppose Spanish is your best subject now."

"Don't even mention that class!" she scolded. "Do you really want to know what my best subject is? Library," she told him.

"I bet you really work hard for that grade. Every time I go there you and Megan are either eating snacks, or reading *Mad Magazine,* or gossiping."

"What? Me gossip?" she asked. "Besides I've seen you in Geometry, and you certainly don't try to improve your mind in that subject. The hardest thing you do in that class is to scheme with Phil on how to get hold of one of the tests that poor Mr.Dumpke unsuspectingly puts in his top drawer."

"How do you happen to know where he keeps his tests?" Woody asked grinning.

The evening wore on, and Elaine was enjoying every minute of the dance. Woody was a good conversationalist, and the two of them covered many subjects. At 10:30 the Football King and Queen were crowned. Ty Ramirez was chosen as king, and Barbara Larson, a Junior, and a cheerleader was crowned queen. The boys mentioned that they did not like Barbara's "balloon" dress. It was pink chiffon over pink satin. Living up to its name, the dress ballooned out to the hips, and then was tight, gathered by a wide, pink satin ribbon. "Looks like her belt slipped," Woody said. Dresses like Barbara's were being worn on the covers of *Vogue* and *Seventeen*, but most Armedia High girls weren't wearing them, and it was Elaine's opinion, from the remarks the fellows were making, that the girls wouldn't ever be wearing them if they wanted to dress for the opposite sex.

Natalie confided to Elaine that she was having a wonderful time, and that she was really proud of Ty, who sat up on the stage looking very good. "I don't want to see this night ever end," Nat said. "It's really magical." And Elaine had to agree.

Later on Ty and Woody exchanged partners for a dance. "I'm really glad that you and Nat worked it out, and had her stay at your house tonight, so she could go with me," he told her. "She is a great girl, and we don't get to go out very often."

"I'm glad it worked out too," Elaine replied. "It has been a really fun evening for all of us."

At midnight the dance ended. Once they got back to Ellington, they stopped at Deb's Diner for hamburgers and milkshakes. The boys walked them to the door at Elaine's home. Woody gave her a quick goodnight kiss, but it was a bit awkward because Ty and Nat were locked in each other's arms for what seemed an eternity to Elaine. Boomer, Hummer's black cat, came around, rubbing on their legs, and Elaine picked him up, while Woody petted him. The girls felt a bit like Cinderella as the car drove out the driveway. They went in and the first thing they did was to put their corsages in water. All night long her room was filled with the deep fragrance of the gardenia corsages.

Chapter 20

Thanksgiving dinner at the Hummer home was over. It had been complete with the traditional turkey, cornbread stuffing, mashed potatoes, green bean casserole, cranberry sauce, a molded fruit salad, homemade rolls, and pumpkin and mincemeat pies. Two extra leaves had been put in the dining room table, since Charles's parents from Redlands were there, as well as Grandma Grace and Scottie. After helping in the kitchen clean up, Elaine sat and visited with the grandparents.

"How is high school going this year?" her Grandpa asked her.

"It's going pretty well," Elaine answered. "I am really enjoying it so far."

"That's good to hear. You must be taking some interesting classes," said Charles Hummer Sr.

"More likely, it's a fellow she's interested in," her grandma replied knowingly, winking at Elaine.

"Well, that's true too," Elaine confessed. "But it's so hard to know when a guy is interested in me because some days they can be real friendly, and flirting with me, and the next day, they just ignore me. It's very frustrating."

"I do think we had it much easier back in our day," Grandma Grace said. "Don't you agree, Maxine? Back then if a young man was interested, he had to get permission from the girl's father to court the girl. So then his intentions were known."

"Yes, it took out a lot of the guesswork," Maxine said.

"And girls usually didn't kiss a boy until they were practically engaged," commented Grandma Grace.

"Wow! It definitely is different these days," Elaine remarked.

"Yes, those were certainly the good old days," sighed Grandma Grace, reminiscing. "Why I remember going to the World's Fair in St Louis with my family when I was about 13 or 14. It was 1904, I believe. That was when they introduced a new kind of treat, the ice cream cone. They called it the World's Fair cornucopia."

The two grandmas were trading stories, while Grandpa snoozed in the Lazy Boy recliner. Lois was on the phone and Charles was selecting a record, a Mozart symphony, for background music. Elaine asked Scottie if he had enjoyed the dance the night before.

"Hey, it was pretty cool," he said. "Beth and I are just friends, but I had fun with her. The GAA really outdid themselves on the decorations. That gym was well disguised. And the girls all looked pretty darn sharp wearing their party dresses. Did you have a good time?"

"Yes, I did. Woody can be a lot of fun," she replied dreamily.

Pam came bouncing into the living room just then. "Guess what?" she said to Elaine. "The Fawcetts are in town, so I'll get to see Dodie. In fact she will be spending the night with me for the next three nights! She is my best friend, and I will be so happy to see her!"

Lois entered the room, explaining that Reverend and Norma Fawcett were visiting from San Diego, and staying at the home of one of the elderly parishioners, and that they would be coming for a visit the following day. Elaine volunteered to sleep on the couch so that Pam and Dodie could have the girls' room. She took her diary and went out into the back yard, since the weather was still reasonably warm for late November. The grape arbor was now completely bare of its leaves, and the white paint on the trellis was peeling off. But Elaine was oblivious to any flaws in her surroundings, just as long as she had privacy. She wanted to write about the dance while everything was still fresh in her mind.

A soft breeze blew through the treetops and crackled the few dry leaves left on the trees. Geese down the street were honking loudly. Crickets were chirping in the field beyond the Hummer yard, and the occasional sound of a meadowlark was heard between the shrill calls of the neighbors' peacocks. A faraway rooster crowed. They were all typical sounds of fall and Thanksgiving, and of peace and security in the small country town.

The quiet was shattered suddenly by a noisy blue Ford coming up the driveway, and Elaine recognized it as Adam Irby's car. Adam, Warren, Nat, and Beth called to her with gusto. Warren's little sister, Dodie, climbed out of the car and went happily to greet Pam, who had come out of the house by then.

"Hey, Adam," Elaine called to him. "You're home from college! And it's good to see you, Warren! Is this old home week, or what?"

"Come on and get in," Adam said to her. "We'll cruise round. Warren and I have to make the most of our short visit to town, and this way we can all catch up on what's going on."

"MYF just isn't the same without you two," she was saying to the boys.

"But the new pastor and his wife are a lot of fun," Beth added.

After checking with her family, Elaine climbed into the car, and they began driving around. Warren looked very good, all fit and tanned. He explained that he had been learning to surf since moving to San Diego. Adam said he had been enjoying life at UCLA, that there was a lot of studying, but college life was really great. He had just gotten into Ellington that morning. The girls were chattering about what was going on at high school, and everyone was talking a mile a minute. It was fun catching up.

After the busy Thanksgiving break, school settled down in much the same old way for everyone. The subjects were just as difficult, and teachers gave even more homework than they had before. Woody's manner toward Elaine was much the same as it had been before the dance, except he seemed a bit more self-conscious around her, a fact that bothered her a great deal.

One December day Alvin Minegar came into the library with his big loose leaf notebook. He greeted Elaine in his usual cheerful manner, and told her that he would be doing research for Agriculture I on "Soil Erosion." Elaine was hoping he could finish his project as quickly as possible, but he didn't seem to be in much of a hurry at all, and spent most of the time talking to Elaine.

Gone With the Wind by Margaret Mitchell," Alvin said, noting the book she was trying to read. "Have you seen the movie?"

"Yes."

"It was okay, except a bit too long for my taste. I'll take a good western any day. And I don't like love stories."

"Well, I do," she said crossly, anxious to disagree with him.

"And, speaking of love, how is Woody Stuart?" was Alvin's next question.

"Woody? What does he have to do with anything?"

"Well, I kind of got the impression that you liked the guy. After all, you did ask him to the Turnabout Dance."

"Well, you got the wrong impression. We're just friends," Elaine said, trying to dismiss the subject.

"That isn't what he says."

Elaine took the bait on that remark. "Well what is he saying?" she asked anxiously.

"He thinks you're a real sharp chick and would like to take you out again." But a mischievous gleam in Alvin's eyes gave him away.

"Alvin, you're lying. Just do me a favor, and get lost, okay?"

"Well, looks like I proved my point that you do like Woody, or you wouldn't be so interested," Alvin said, picking up his books from the check-out desk and leaving.

"I can't stand him," Elaine said furiously to Megan. "I wish he'd just leave me alone."

"He certainly doesn't know how to mind his own business," Megan stated. "The other day I heard him asking Woody if he'd had fun with you at the dance."

"Oh, no! What did he say?"

"He just told Alvin that it was none of his business, and to get lost. Alvin must hear that a lot."

"One thing I hate about small schools is that everyone has their nose in where it doesn't belong," Elaine stated. "I am so sick and tired of it."

Megan had to agree. "News and gossip travels faster than lightning around here," she added.

On Friday noon the school paper made its appearance. The girls were reading it in the cafeteria over fish sticks and tossed salad.

"This reminds me of the breakfast table," Vicki laughed. "Everyone has her head buried in the paper."

"Ohh no!" was suddenly heard from the depths of Elaine's paper. She pointed disgustedly to a small statement in the gossip column that read: Woody S. and Elaine H. have been seen together quite a bit lately. Could this be a new romance?

"How corny," Elaine said. "I'm sure that Alvin put that in the paper. He's on the staff, you know."

"That sounds like something he would do," Karen said.

"Woody won't like it one bit," Elaine sighed.

"Well, if he's interested in you, it won't bother him," Alma stated with finality.

"By the way, who is going to the Snowball Dance?" Vicki asked.

"I hadn't heard about that one," Beth said.

"The Student Council is sponsoring it," Megan said. "It will be semi-formal too."

"I'm not sure if I can get Paul to dress up again," Vicki said. "He did a lot of complaining last time."

That Friday, after school the newly formed club, the Collettes, had their first meeting. Eight lively girls met at Megan's home in Armedia. Vicki, very businesslike, called the meeting to order. "Our first project is to write a constitution," she explained. "Our vice president could appoint a committee to—"

"I have an idea," Alma interrupted. "Why don't we—"

"You spoke out of turn," Vicki said. "Elaine, as secretary, why don't you take down names of everyone who speaks out of order? At the end of the meeting everyone will be fined a nickel for each time they speak out of turn."

"More money for the flat treasury," Natalie said.

"That's a fine for you," Elaine told her.

"And for you too, Elaine," Vicki told her. "Just write the names down, but don't talk."

By the end of the meeting, the treasury was a few dollars richer. In spite of the interruptions, a committee was assigned to write a constitution, and the girls selected the type of pin they thought appropriate. It was to be an emblem of a heart, a cross, and an anchor. The club's motto was Faith, Hope, and Charity. After the meeting the girls posed for a picture, since Jackie Irby was there to take pictures for the Armedia Appeal.

Elaine, Beth, and Lucy rode home to Ellington with Nat and her mother after the meeting. They were discussing the wildfire that was burning in the mountains between Armedia Valley and the coast. All the conditions were right for fire. The mercury had been as high as 88 degrees on some days, and December that year was known to be the hottest and driest in southern California's history. It was hard to believe that storms were taking place back east. The valley's one and only rain had taken place way back in October.

Consequently, when a brush fire started in the dry hills behind Armedia, no one was too surprised. This fire, supposedly started by someone's careless cigarette, raged over parched brush, spreading over a considerably large number of acres. There were 20 miles of hills between the valley and the ocean, and the fire was blackening this range of land with rapid strokes. It had also worked its way south, more than halfway to Ellington. Depending on which way the Santa Ana winds blew, it was possible that the blaze could reach the Marine base that was located southwest of Ellington. The acrid smell of smoke permeated the air, and valley residents could see a pinkish glow over the hills once the sun went down. It was fortunate that the inferno was mostly in a wilderness area, but there were a few homes that had been destroyed. Over 2000 men were fighting the blaze, and one had been killed.

When Elaine got home that evening it was after 5:00 pm, and everyone was gone. Lois had left her a note that the family had gone to a PTA Dime-A-Dip dinner. The house seemed unusually quiet. Elaine went outside to do her egg gathering chore in the deepening twilight. The smell of smoke was getting to her, and she was glad to get back inside. She was fixing herself a chicken spread sandwich and a glass of milk, when Natalie called.

"Christmas is certainly rolling around fast this year," Nat was saying. "It doesn't seem possible that it's almost here."

"Only 13 days left," Elaine answered. "And that Snowball Dance is in a week, but it doesn't look like I'll be going. I think everyone in our group is going, except you and me and Beth. Of course I don't know what I would wear anyhow. It seems like they shouldn't have planned two dressy dances so close together."

"Well, I just feel lucky that I got to go to the other dance," Nat was saying. "I felt like Cinderella at the ball, with Ty as my prince."

"You're lucky to be going steady with him," Elaine told her, "even if you have to be really sneaky about dating him."

"I really love him, Elaine. I've never felt this way about any guy before. He's good and sweet, and he makes good grades, and he is loads of fun to be with," she declared vehemently. "But I just hope my folks don't find out. So far, I've been lucky. And guess what? Yesterday I spent all afternoon and evening with him. I told Mom I was going to Karen's to study, and then have dinner, and then go to the school play with her family. Well, Mom wanted to know their phone number. I hadn't expected her to ask that. So I gave her Karen's number, except I changed one digit, and then I kind of, sort of misplaced the phone book. She really got upset with me this morning because she called their house, and it was the wrong number of course."

"And your dad is out of town again?"

"Right. So anyhow, after school Ty and I drove around Armedia and he showed me the garage where he works part time. He's saving up for college. And then we went to a really nice restaurant on the other side of the lake, Antonio's. And after that we drove up to a look-out spot by the lake and we parked for a while."

"You didn't!" Elaine exclaimed, delightedly shocked. "Oh, Natalie!"

"My parents would flip if they knew. But I don't care. And I love Ty. He's an angel, and he treats me really well. We did a lot of kissing, and things got pretty hot and heavy a few times too. We really steamed up the car windows."

Elaine was amazed at the turn of events in her friend's life. She felt suddenly cheated. "Nothing neat ever happens to me. I lead the dullest life," she complained.

"Well, you had Danny at camp," Nat told her. "And at least your parents don't treat you like an infant. If my mom were home right now, I couldn't be telling you all this. She'd probably be listening in on the extension. She had to go out this evening to an event the PTA is having, some Dime-A-Dip dinner, whatever that is."

"It's a fund raiser for the PTA, sort of like a potluck. People bring casseroles, or salads, or desserts, and then you can eat there. Whatever you put on your plate costs a dime for each serving. It's a pretty cheap way for the whole family to eat. By the way, Nat, I just thought of something. I hope your mom and my mom don't run into each other. I mean, what if they do, and my mom mentions the Turnabout Dance when you were just supposed to be spending the night with me? You know this town, how everybody talks to everyone else? I hate that! You can't keep secrets at all around here."

After the family had gotten home that evening, and Lois wanted to speak to Elaine in her room, Elaine figured that her mother had indeed, spoken to Jackie Irby. Lois was really upset, and Elaine's heart dropped to her stomach.

"I just can't believe that you would do something that sneaky," she said, "and go behind my back, when you knew how Natalie's parents are. And can you imagine how I felt when I said something about the dance to Jackie, and she didn't know anything about it? You should have seen her face. Of course she wanted to know the name of Natalie's date, and I guess she doesn't like Ty Ramirez very well, because she got even more upset when I told her. You really put me in a bad spot, Elaine."

"Oh, Mom, I was just trying to help out a friend whose parents are unreasonably strict. I wanted to see Nat have a good time for a change. I can see now why it wasn't such a good idea, and I am so sorry that I made you look bad to Jackie. But really, she shouldn't be upset with you because you didn't know anything about the situation at the Irby's. I'm sure that Jackie is very mad at me now, and I probably won't ever get to have Nat over here again, or go over to her house." Elaine was almost in tears, thinking of the dire consequences of her error in judgment. "I just feel badly for Nat most of the time because she doesn't get to lead a normal life, and have the fun activities that most teen agers do."

"Well, I do think her folks are way over the top with all their rules and regulations," Lois said, "but that's not our call to make. Maybe they have their reasons for being that way, and now that they know you've interfered, they may not let her run around with you anymore. And I know that would be far worse than any punishment I can dish out. Still, you're going to be on restriction for two weeks and no phone privileges either. Sorry, but that's how it's going to be." And Elaine was in tears for the rest of the weekend, and also very apprehensive, thinking about what was going on with Nat and her family.

Chapter 21

On Monday morning Elaine boarded the bus, hoping that when it came to Nat's stop, they could sit together, but there were no empty seats at all, and she had to go all the way to the back with the group from High Bluffs. The girls who always sat in the back were usually rude, and snickering, and made her feel like an outcast. She didn't get to speak to Nat until the bus drove up into the circle drive at school.

"So what's going on?" she asked Nat. "I've been worrying about you all weekend. Now your parents know everything, and I feel like it's my fault."

"Well, my mom is pretty upset with me," Nat explained. "But wonder of wonders, I don't think she said anything to my dad about my sneaking around. But now I'm not allowed on the phone at all. Of course I can't go anywhere, but that's not anything new, is it? But so far, she hasn't told my father what happened, and he was what I was the most worried about. He's just acted so weird lately, and so possessive of me. He just walks into my room without knocking, which has been kind of embarrassing at times. I wish now that I had stayed in the third floor room, farther away from everything."

"Well, I'm so glad that he doesn't know about Ty."

"Oh, me too. He'd probably send me away to a private school or something," Nat said. "And I know I'll find a way to sneak out. This isn't going to stop me from seeing him."

On Friday, the last day of school, everyone was in a festive mood. The girls made candy in Home Ec, the Spanish class had a party, and Mr. Sharpe's class had a test in Sophomore Science. "I don't think old Sharpe knows how to spend a holiday," someone grumbled. The students hurried out of English last period to find that the wind had come up during the 50 minutes they had been inside, and the fire had cast a thick haze of soot and ashes over the high school campus. All of Armedia Valley lay under a heavy, gray blanket. Through the smoke and ashes, the disc of the sun was barely visible.

"Well, this beats the Los Angeles smog," joked Woody.

"The fire hasn't reached this side of the hills, has it?" asked Elaine.

"Let's hope not," Karen said grimly. "But if the wind keeps blowing this way, there are so many homes up there that will be right in its path."

"They've planned for this," Greg said. "They've bulldozed firebreaks all over the place, back behind the homes. It might look worse right now, but I've heard that it's about seventy percent contained."

Elaine felt very miserable and very sorry for herself, staying home that night watching *77 Sunset Strip* on TV. She was babysitting Timmie, since her parents had gone to visit some friends, and Russ was spending the night with Scottie. Timmie was already in bed, and Pam was chattering away on the phone. School was out for two weeks, and she wasn't even really excited about that. She was thinking that tonight was the Snowball Dance, and most of her friends would be all dressed up, and the gym would be decorated beautifully, and everyone would be having fun. Of course she realized that even if she did have a date for the dance, she was grounded, so she wouldn't have been going anyhow. She had heard, through the grapevine that Woody hadn't asked anyone else either. Most all her friends were going, except Nat of course. Beth was going with a Junior boy, who had asked her just a few days before the big event. She wondered at the concept that a person's teen years were the best years in one's life. Someone certainly didn't know what they were talking about, when they said that, she thought. She was beginning to realize that life was made up of conflicts, of reaching goals, of overcoming fears, and of solving problems. Elaine went to bed early that night, thoroughly disgusted with life, and love, and the pursuit of happiness.

*   *   *

On Saturday morning Elaine woke up in a much better frame of mind. Christmas, her favorite holiday, was just a few days away. She loved all the festivities, the lights, the carols, the mystery and the secrets, and of course the true meaning of Christmas. Even though she was grounded, she would still be able to go caroling with the MYF. (Her parents usually made exceptions for church activities.) And she would have some extra time for her writing during the holiday vacation. For the last year she had been trying to write a novel about a girl in a small town. She wrote in spurts. For a week she would use all her spare time to write, and then she would bog down and burn out. She fared better at writing short stories and poems about life and about her problems. She had written one poem about her gardenia corsage, which was now carefully pressed in her high school scrapbook. Her poetry was hidden under her mattress along with her diary. She spent the morning writing letters in Christmas cards, and later took the short walk to the post office. She had had instructions to come right back home, after the two block walk, so she felt very lucky to see Beth on her front porch stringing some Christmas lights.

"Hi," greeted Beth, jumping up. "Isn't this crazy weather? Here I am wearing shorts in the middle of winter. Did you hear? The fire is almost out. It's something like ninety percent contained!"

"It's about time," Elaine said. "Can you stop for a few minutes and walk to the post office with me? I'm supposed to go pick up our mail and come right back. No dilly-dallying, Mom said. So seeing you is really great. And I have to hear all about your date and the dance last night. But talk quickly."

Beth laughed as they made the short walk. "The dance was fine, and Rodney seems like a nice guy. We have a lot of laughs together in Study Hall. I don't know if he'll ask me out again or not. But as far as dances go, I had more fun at the Turnabout. Most all of our friends were there last night, except Vicki wasn't. Megan told me that she and Paul broke up. What a shocker, huh?"

"Well, that is a surprise," Elaine stated, opening the Hummer mailbox. When she saw the top letter, she gave a small cry of excitement. "Ohh, look, it's from Danny!" It was a Christmas card with a letter, full of dashed and exclamation points. Danny wrote just like he talked.

Dear Elaine, Merry Christmas! Now that's original, isn't it? How are you Sweetheart? Please don't faint from shock that I'm finally writing-you know how the sight of a pen scares me. Actually I've just been busy with school, my part time job, etc. etc. I know, I know-that's not really an excuse. You'll never realize how much I miss you, and how I miss the wonderful times we had at camp! Wasn't it a real blast?? It wouldn't have been the same without you, though, my little Hummingbird! I can hardly wait til next

summer rolls around. You have to promise me that you'll be at
camp again. Please write me back soon-I miss you very much. I
promise to answer your letter this time-I really do! Love always,
Danny.

"My little Hummingbird?" laughed Beth, as Elaine finished
reading the letter to her. "That's really corny. Did you already send
him a card?"

"It's right here in this batch," Elaine answered. "And I didn't really
write a whole lot to him, and I'm not writing him again either. I did
write letters to Moe, Sandy, and Dottie," she added, dropping the
cards into the slot.

On Christmas Eve, Elaine sat curled up on the couch in front of
the fireplace, watching the dying embers in the fireplace. She knew
she needed to put more wood on, but was getting sleepy. The clock
chimed 10:00. Their family had had their traditional Christmas Eve
earlier, singing carols around the piano, and then Charles had read
the Christmas story from the second chapter of Luke. Then her
parents had to go out to the egg building to pack eggs, since they
didn't want that chore on Christmas morning. The younger children
were all asleep. *Silent Night* was playing on the radio. When she heard
Christmas carols, she always felt a wonderful sweetness connected
with God, with love, with the past and the future. Even though her
life felt mixed up about half the time, the Christmas carols gave her
a beautiful sensation, and she wondered if most people felt that way.
She wondered what it would have been like to live back in Biblical
times, and to have known that infant who came into the world to
save it. She wondered at times when she said her prayers, if God
actually heard her and paid attention to her desires, as trivial as
they sometimes were. It was hard to understand how He could really
care about tiny Elaine Hummer, a mere speck in the huge universe,
especially since there were two and a half billion other people in the
world, many with problems way worse than hers. But then she would
think of the wonderful universe, and all the other planets out there
in space, and of her home, and family, and friends, and she knew,
sure as the stars above, that God did care for her and love her. She
felt secure in knowing that He would guide her to a wonderful life
if she followed Him and tried to do His will. With that thought the
last one in her consciousness, she fell asleep on the couch to wait for
Christmas morn.

She was awakened by Pam around 6:30 a.m. "How come you're sleeping out here on the couch? Did you see all the presents under the tree?"

"How could I, since I just woke up?" her sister asked sleepily. "It's still dark out. Why don't you go back to bed? It's too early to open presents now." She burrowed under the blankets her mother had apparently put over her the night before. But she had a feeling that the day had started already. By then Timmie had padded out into the room in his flannel sleepers.

"Are all those presents for me?" he asked, his eyes like saucers.

"No, you spoiled child," Pam told him. "Santa brought presents for all of us. Hmmm-I wonder who that big one is for," Elaine heard her say. "Shucks, it's for Russ."

"Which one's for me?" Russ was asking, as he entered the room, wide awake.

A few hours later the living room was a shambles of bright wrapping paper, ribbons, toys, and other newly acquired belongings. The day was filled with the usual excitement of going to Redlands for the Christmas Hummer Family Reunion. It was good that they had a station wagon, because this year Grandma Grace and Scottie went also, even though it was a bit of a squeeze in the car. Visiting with all the relatives was great fun, as usual, and the dinner, as always, was wonderful. Elaine and her cousin Lynne were relegated back to the kids' table in the kitchen this year, since Grandma Hummer had to find room for three more adults at the formal dining table. The girls really didn't mind however, even with the burping going on and the bad manners some of the cousins exhibited. Everyone was really wound up, and there was plenty of laughter at the table, along with a couple glasses of spilt punch. Elaine and Lynne tried to keep the rest of the crew in line, but that turned out to be an impossible task. "I don't think I ever want to have kids," Lynne told Elaine, laughing.

Elaine was happy to be home afterwards, listening to music and looking over her gifts-black Patton T-strap shoes from her parents (all the rage of the teen set at the time), a blue angora sweater, some books, a couple of 45's (one record was a new song called *Rockin' Around the Christmas Tree* by Brenda Lee, and the other was *The Twelfth of Never* by Johnny Mathis.) One gift from Grandma Hummer, who was always up on the latest styles, was a sack dress of orange and brown plaid. The girls at school were just beginning to wear the shapeless dresses, and Elaine hoped she could get up the nerve to wear hers.

She knew Woody's opinion of them, however. But since he really isn't too interested in me at this time, what do I care, she thought.

Timmie interrupted her thoughts. "Laine," he said, digging into the debris beneath the tree and coming up with a plastic airplane, "would you help me fly this?"

"You know how, Timmie. Just throw it up in the air, and it should fly."

"But the wing came off."

"You don't waste any time breaking your Christmas toys, do you, Sugar? Go and get me some glue from the kitchen drawer."

"But I didn't break it," he cried, getting frustrated. He was overtired from a long, exciting day.

"Never mind, just bring me the glue."

"It's about his bedtime," Lois said, coming into the room. She stopped as the doorbell rang. "Now who could that be at this time of night?"

As Elaine worked on the broken plane, she heard Chuck Graham's hearty laughter in the kitchen, and Cathy's light, twinkly laugh. She was glad they had dropped by, as she always enjoyed seeing the cute couple. And she had to admit that even though Chuck was married, and a minister, she did have a slight crush on him. He was fun to talk with, and was always teasing Elaine.

"Well, Merry Christmas, Elaine," he boomed cheerily, entering the living room. "You look real cute in that blue sweater and skirt. Matches your eyes."

"Thank you," she replied, blushing.

"Looks like Santa Claus was good to you. But I see you're playing with plastic airplanes now," he added, noting the red toy in her hand. "I always did wonder about you. How about a toy dump truck? Or maybe you'd prefer a bag of marbles."

"Don't get smart. This is Timmie's plane, and I'm fixing it for him."

"You don't have to lie to me, Elaine," teased Chuck. "I understand. Remember I'm a minister."

"I do forget sometimes," she retorted.

"Well, did you get everything you wanted for Christmas?" he asked, changing the subject.

"Just about."

"What do you mean, just about? I'll bet I know what you would like. How about a six foot, 180 pound, blonde haired, blue-eyed guy? I'll bring you one."

Elaine was laughing heartily. "Okay, Santa, bring him on," she said, going along with him.

"Be right back," Chuck said, striding back into the kitchen.

"That Chuck is sure a nut," Elaine told Pam, who had just come in from the girls room.

"Yeah, I heard him," Pam giggled. "Wouldn't it be a kick if he really did bring you a cute guy?"

The door from the kitchen swung open again, admitting Cathy, pert and pretty as ever. "Hi, girls, Merry Christmas! How is everybody doing?"

"Hi Cathy. You didn't know you were married to Santa Claus, did you?"

"What do you mean?" she wanted to know.

Before Elaine could answer, Chuck came back into the room, followed by a husky fellow a little taller than Chuck. He had very blue eyes, blonde hair in a crew cut, and an engaging smile.

"Elaine, this is my nephew, Jeff Chadwick," Chuck said with a grin. "My little nephew," he added jokingly. "Jeff, this is Elaine Hummer and her sister Pam."

Elaine was blushing furiously, thinking of the trick Chuck had played on her. "Hello, nice to meet you," she said bashfully.

"Jeff is out here for the holidays," Chuck explained. "His family was here for the day, but they left just a little while ago. Jeff thought he'd like to stick around and see what Ellington is like, and then we'll be driving him back in a couple of days."

"There really isn't a lot to see around here," Elaine remarked, trying to think of something clever to say. "Where are you from?"

"Oh, I'm a desert rat."

"He lives out with the cactus and Joshua trees and desert tortoises, and jack rabbits, and sand, lots of sand."

Jeff pushed his uncle playfully. "Well, any way you want to look at it," he grinned, "my hometown is bigger than Ellington. What do you do when the sun goes down?"

"Oh, we manage to keep busy," Chuck stated. "By the way, are you doing anything this evening?" he asked Elaine.

"Nothing special. Why?"

"Thought you might like to come over for some hot chocolate, and Christmas goodies," said Cathy. "We got a Monopoly game for Christmas and it's more fun if four play. Thought maybe you could come over and help break it in."

Elaine liked the idea immediately. Jeff was very good looking, and she always enjoyed Chuck and Cathy's company. She wondered how old Jeff was. He looked about 20, and she decided that wasn't too old for her. And her two weeks of restriction had just ended the day before, but even if it hadn't, she felt her mother would have let her go, since how much trouble could one get into being with your minister and his family?

She was feeling bashful at first, but after she had been over at the Graham home for a short time, her bashfulness departed. The four of them were soon in a frenzied game of Monopoly.

"Hey, you landed on my property," Jeff told Chuck. "Don't try to sneak by without paying the rent, you free-loader. Fork over the forty-two bucks you owe."

"What do you mean forty two bucks? I don't—"

"Would you like to see the deed?" Jeff asked. "You have to watch my uncle," Jeff told Elaine. "Minister or not, he has a tendency to cheat at Monopoly. He's always been that way."

"Ha! Don't listen to him. Oops, Cathy, looks like you have to go to jail," Chuck pointed out.

"That won't stop me from collecting rent on my railroad," she told him. "You'd better be careful where you land."

After over an hour of a hilarious game, Elaine and Cathy went out to the kitchen to fix some snacks, and Cathy asked Elaine what she thought of Jeff.

"He's really neat," Elaine said. "And that husband of yours certainly was sneaky about introducing us. Very clever of him!"

"That's my Chuck," Cathy laughed as she briskly stirred milk and powdered chocolate together. "But he didn't even really plan it that way. We just went over to your house to buy some eggs for breakfast. On the way over, we told Jeff about you and naturally he was interested in meeting you. He really is a nice guy."

"How old is he?" Elaine wanted to know.

"He is sixteen, and is a Junior in high school."

"What high school does he go to?"

"Desert Palms. Do you know where that is?"

"Desert Palms!" exclaimed Elaine. "Our school plays football with them! They're one of our biggest rivals. Oh, that is too funny? Does he play football?"

"I believe so," Cathy answered.

"Both times when our school has played them, we lost by a lot," Elaine said. "Their players always seem so much bigger than ours do, and so much tougher. So what is Jeff like?"

"He's a lot like Chuck. He's fairly easy going and fun loving, and is always up to something. Chuck says he is kind of bashful around girls, though."

"I don't believe it. Does he have a girlfriend? And how long is he staying with you?"

"Only for a couple more days. We'd hoped he could stay til New Year's but he has a job, so he has to get back. And to answer your other question, no, I don't think he has a girlfriend."

"Hey," Chuck called from the other room, "are you women having a convention in there? Or are you making the cookies from scratch, or just eating up all the goodies?"

"We're coming," Cathy called back.

Elaine was enjoying herself thoroughly, and was having more fun than she'd had in quite a while. She hadn't thought of Woody at all, even though Jeff kind of reminded her of Woody, with his football player build and his coloring. It was getting late, and Elaine mentioned that she should be getting home.

"You want to drive her home, Jeff?" Chuck asked.

"Sure, no problem. But how? On a bicycle?"

"Oh, I forgot, you don't have your car here." He tossed a key ring to Jeff. "Here, take mine."

Elaine talked to Jeff about football on the way home. "I remember going to Desert Palms on the bus last year, and your team beat ours so bad. That was a discouraging night. And you guys had so many more players than we did, and looked so much bigger. Then we girls nearly froze to death, sitting on the bleachers."

"It gets cold out on the desert in the fall," Jeff said. "We do have a pretty good team. I think we only lost two games this year. So what high school do you go to?"

When she told him, he remembered the game. "This year we traveled to Armedia. But I didn't play in that game. I had a pulled hamstring and had to sit the bench for that one."

The car pulled into the driveway and stopped in front of the house. Jeff turned off the ignition and sat for a moment, looking at Elaine. "I had a really good time tonight," he said seriously. "I can see that I will be visiting Uncle Chuck a bit more often, that is if it's okay with you?"

"That would definitely be okay with me," was her answer.

Elaine spent the remaining days of her vacation writing on a story, working on her Spanish book report, and helping vaccinate chickens. On January 1st, after watching the Rose Parade on TV, she wrote in her diary: Horns blow, bells ring, whistles shrill, confetti is thrown, Champaign glasses click, and lovers kiss. This is the way 1959 is being ushered in all over the country. The years seem to be going by quickly, and I don't want them to go by so fast I can't live them. I have the best years of my life ahead of me, and I want to do my part to make them as good as possible. For a New Year's resolution, I want to have a more positive outlook on life, and try harder to be thankful. I did meet a really cute guy over the holidays, and who knows if that will hopefully amount to anything??? Only time will tell. I spent the night at Beth's for New Year's Eve. We watched TV til midnight, and when the New Year came in, we had a champaign toast. (It was the first time I'd tasted it, and I liked all the fizz.) Happy New Year!

Chapter 22

When school began again Monday morning the sky was overcast with thick, dark clouds. Farmers were holding their breaths, hoping and praying for rain. In spite of the cold weather and an even, colder wind, Elaine felt good to be walking to the bus stop. She had fixed her hair in a new style, a French roll and was wearing her Christmas sweater with a black wool skirt. The two weeks off had been fun, even though the vacation had started off on a bad note, with her being on restriction and not being able to talk to Nat on the phone. But everything was looking up now, and she had met a new guy, which was the last thing she had expected. She even found an empty seat on the bus, which made a really good start to the week. When Nat boarded, the girls sat together, and Elaine had a good deal to talk about. Nat didn't have too much to say, since she hadn't even seen Ty during the past two weeks.

The teachers were happy to welcome the students back, and also happy to load them up with homework. Mrs. Jenson was teaching her class about food nutrients, carbohydrates, and vitamins. The girls were separated into groups of four at a table. The sophomores were at the same table, and each group was supposed to plan a good nutritious breakfast. After a few practice breakfasts, Mrs. Jenson told the class that each group could invite a teacher to breakfast. They were all talking at once about which lucky teacher would be invited to eat with them.

Vicki had an inspiration. "Let's invite Coach Carr, and spike his coffee with arsenic."

"What an idea," said Elaine. "And to think she is president of our club."

"You sure hold a grudge for a long time," Megan told Vicki. "Last year in Algebra he bawled you out for something, and you've never forgotten that. You should let it go. Forgive and forget."

"Well, I think he really humiliated me."

"We've all forgotten about it," remarked Megan. "That was a long time ago."

"Well, what teacher should we invite?" Beth asked. After much discussion, they decided on Mr. Dumpke. "I think that will make points with him, and maybe help our Geometry grade," Elaine said.

"If we let Elaine do the cooking, we're all done for anyhow," Vicki pointed out as Elaine playfully slapped at her. Everyone laughed, and Mrs. Jenson called for order.

"My sophomores are noisier than my freshmen today," she said, smiling.

Elaine got her first glimpse of Woody when she walked into Spanish class, and her heart began to flutter a bit. But he was talking to Mary Lou Wright, and did not look up when she came in. Why should I even care, she thought. He is old news, and Jeff is cuter and much nicer anyhow.

In Mr. Sharpe's third period class, he assigned them the worst assignment possible, in Elaine's opinion. Each pupil was to give an oral report on a chapter in their textbook. Elaine's chapter was "Liability and Insurance of the Car Owner." She couldn't think of a duller subject, and she dreaded speaking in front of the class, especially in Sophomore Science in front of Woody, and Mr. Sharpe, who was sure to make a sarcastic remark which wouldn't spare her feelings. They were given two weeks to prepare the reports, and she was determined to make hers a good one.

In PE she relieved her feelings by slamming a badminton shuttlecock across the net. She beat most of her opponents too.

By Friday noon of that same week, the terrible news had leaked out. The beloved Dean Caldwell had been fired by Principal Joe Santini. The school suddenly seemed in an uproar. The girls were at their usual table in the cafeteria. "Everyone knows the principal doesn't really have the authority to fire a teacher," Megan was saying over tuna casserole and peas. "The school board has to do it."

"Well, maybe Principal Santini doesn't know the rules around here," Alma said sarcastically. "If you ask me, he doesn't know too much of anything.

"I don't think any of us have the right to talk against him, unless we know the whole story," retorted Lucy angrily. She, of course, was partial to the principal, since she was going with his son.

"Well, maybe all of this is just a big rumor," Beth pointed out. "We all know how fast rumors and gossip get spread around. Everything travels like wildfire, and we can't believe half of what we hear anymore."

"My mother is on the school board," Karen stated. "She hasn't said much about it to me, but I overheard her on the phone yesterday, and it's something about Mr. Santini just up and firing Dean Caldwell without saying one word of his intentions to the school board. She was upset when she was on the phone, and I guess there has been trouble brewing for a long time between the principal and the teachers. Mr. Santini has even been threatening to fire a couple of other teachers. But he may not be here long enough to do that. I guess this was all supposed to be top secret stuff, but you guys know as well as I do that there are no secrets around here."

"Isn't your dad on the school board too?" Alma asked Natalie.

"He was last year, but now he's out of town too much, so he had to resign."

"What did you mean when you said Mr. Santini may not be here that long?" Lucy was asking.

But Karen did not know enough about the subject to give any more information. Obviously, the students were interested in the problem, since it pertained to them. But there was no one who was willing to disclose any information. In the next class, Geometry, even Mr. Dumpke who usually talked about controversial subjects, said nothing of the matter, and nobody brought it up either.

The students in the library were buzzing like a swarm of excited bees. "It's quite obvious that the teachers won't talk," Marie Frye was saying to her sister and to Elaine. "In this case, no matter what a teacher says, he's going to incriminate himself, and be in favor of either the school board or the principal. Either way, a teacher could be fired. But what is too bad, is that the students don't really have any idea of what's going on. Here we are, almost adults, and yet in many cases we don't know what stand to take because no one tells us anything. Or if we happen to be lucky enough to know someone who gives us information, it's usually a one-sided fanatic who tries to convert us to his way of thinking, never telling us both sides of the story."

Elaine was surprised and impressed by Marie's passionate outburst. She always thought Marie only cared about parties, drinking, and boys. She realized that everyone had a thoughtful side even if they didn't always show it. But in English that day, Mrs. Teague's stern side was showing. She moved briskly and looked very grim. Her class wasn't any too pleasant.

Of course there was a headline in the paper the next day, but the article with it didn't disclose any thing more than general information which everybody already knew.

A few days later the rain finally hit, and it rained hard for about 24 hours. Armedia Valley residents and southern California residents were filled with thankfulness. Of course too much rain too fast was not a good thing, especially where there had been wildfires. There always seemed to be problems in the LA area and around Pacific Coast Highway with flooding and mudslides. But more dark clouds were rolling over the mountains.

Elaine slept fitfully the night before her oral report was due. She had dreamed that she stood in front of the class and gave them the run-down on the Turnabout Dance with Woody, instead of car insurance. If that wasn't bad enough, she'd been giving the report in her baby doll pajamas. She was thrashing around and the bedcovers fell on the floor, just as her mother came in and shook her. "Elaine, why didn't your alarm go off? It's after seven!"

"I stayed up late working on my report, and I guess I forgot to set the clock."

"Well, your dad and I were out packing eggs this morning, since they were too wet last night from all the rain or I would have gotten you up earlier. But you only have a half hour to get ready." In ten minutes she was dressed in her best plaid jumper, and was pulling curlers out of her hair. She wanted to look her best since she would be in front of the class. But her hair was not cooperating, and one side looked good while the other side was too flat. It infuriated her.

Lois called her to come and eat, and she hastily gulped down a glass of tomato juice and a piece of toast, grabbed her books and purse and dashed out into the rain. She was back a minute later, for her report which had been left on her desk, and as she glanced out the window she saw the bus making its way around the corner, about half a block from her house. In her year and a half of high school, she had never missed the bus.

"Mother," she called, feeling suddenly panicky, "the bus just went by, and so you need to take me to the next stop really quick."

"Oh, no, you missed the bus!" Lois exclaimed. "Pam, please watch Timmie while I take Elaine, but don't let him has any more toast and jam. He needs to finish his eggs."

"Mom that bus will be halfway to school, while you're talking about what to feed Timmie. We need to go now!" Lois grabbed the car keys, and they jumped quickly into the station wagon. "I'm glad your father is out feeding chickens and missing all this," Lois said.

The car was cold and took time to start, but at last the motor rumbled and turned over. Lois pulled out of the garage, down the drive, and swung onto the street. As First St. became Main St. they could make out the form of the bus about half a mile away. "Step on it, Mom!" Elaine cried. The speedometer slowly climbed to 60 miles per hour.

"I still can't believe you missed that darned bus," Lois said. "And I could get a ticket for driving this fast through town."

"There are usually no cops around here anyhow," Elaine told her. "And there are plenty of people who drive this fast through town all the time. And I would just as soon skip school today, but I'll get a big fat zero on my report, unless you want to write me an excuse saying that I was sick. Then we wouldn't have to chase the bus at all. Doesn't that sound like a plan?"

"I guess I'd rather speed than lie about you being sick," Lois said.

"I think I do feel a headache coming on, and my stomach doesn't feel too good either."

"Dream on," her mother said. Just as they reached the next stop, the bus began to pull away again. But before it could get off the shoulder, Lois accelerated, and passed it, honking loudly and waving to the driver. Elaine was slinking down into the seat, very embarrassed that her mother was calling attention to them. The bus driver stopped again, and Elaine hopped on. And of course there were no seats left, except way in the back with the group from High Bluffs.

"Ohh, your mommy had to take you to the bus stop today, did she?" one girl asked with a sneer.

"Yeah, it's just one of those days," Elaine mumbled. The rest of that Friday was no picnic. Her report that morning wasn't all that good, Elaine felt. Of course how could you make a report on car insurance really interesting and stimulating? There was just no way. Mr.Sharpe must have felt sorry for her though, because he spared the sarcastic remarks, and gave her a B-.

However, Megan was more critical. "You just need more self-confidence, Elaine. I think you get too worked up when you have to speak in front of a group." They were on their way to the gym.

"I know I get too nervous. I tell myself it doesn't matter that much, but it doesn't help."

"And when I gave my report, my neck broke out into a rash," Vicki said. "I really don't know how to get myself to calm down."

"That might be an idea for one of our club meetings," Megan said. "Maybe we'll get someone to give us pointers on public speaking."

"You're always thinking, and coming up with new ideas, aren't you?" Elaine asked her.

"Her wheels never stop turning," Vicki smiled. "Sometimes I see smoke coming out her ears. I don't think her brain ever shuts down. Sometimes I wish I could just get mine to just pick up the pace a little. Not to change the subject, but tonight's basketball game should be a really good one."

If school spirit had been lacking at the football games, it was overwhelmingly present at the basketball games that winter. The bleachers, which had been long since moved to the gym, were packed at every game. The basketball team had won back the school's loyalty by winning almost every game so far. Tonight's game would prove especially exciting, because they were playing Ralston, their arch-rival. So far, their team was undefeated. It was predicted that Armedia would be slaughtered, and the newspapers had them "doped for the cellar."

"Ralston's won 12 games in a row," Elaine remarked to Lucy that night as they sat in the bleachers with the crowd. "And I can see why. Nearly every player on their team is over six feet tall."

"Ty is really excited about this game tonight," Natalie said. Elaine was so happy that Jackie seemed to be giving Nat more freedom. But that was only when her father was out of town.

The drizzly and windy night did not keep rooters from either team away, and there was scarcely standing room in the gym for latecomers. An aura of excitement filled the room. Elaine had always loved the ruggedness of football on crisp fall nights, but she found the basketball games were much easier to comprehend, and were much quicker. And much warmer of course. In fact it was getting quite warm packed on the bleachers with that many people. Besides, she always liked looking around to see who was in attendance, and a well-lit gym was much better for seeing than dark bleachers on the edge of the football field. It was amusing to watch Mr.Sharpe, the basketball coach, sitting across the room. He never failed to get carried away during the games, and continued to shout, clap his hands, and make sarcastic remarks to the referees. His six year old boy sat beside him, happily engrossed in a bag of popcorn.

As the game started, the team scores stayed within a few points of each other. The two teams seemed to be quite evenly matched. Armedia would score, and then Ralston would score.

"I'm getting dizzy, looking back and forth, back and forth," Vicki laughed.

"It would be so great if we could win this game," Beth said hopefully. "It would really show that snooty school that little old Armedia was better than everyone thought. And to top it off, we could win back our Victory Bell."

"For the first time in two years," Megan added. "It would make up for our horrible loss in football. Oh, get the ball, Willie!" she cried. He was high point man on the team, and Ty was a close second. Woody was up there somewhere too. Elaine cheered wildly for him, as he skillfully intercepted a pass meant for a Ralston player.

"Oh, my brother almost got creamed by the ball," Alma laughed. Her twin, Lenny, was on the sidelines, snapping pictures of the game, since he was assistant photographer on the yearbook staff. At the end of the third quarter the score was 56-55, in favor of Ralston. Their cheerleaders were sitting tauntingly on the Victory Bell, which was placed in front of their rooting section. The bell itself was on a little stand and was painted gold. If Armedia won it back, they would be covering up the gold with red, which was their school color.

"They're so confident they're going to win," muttered Lucy. "I just hope we can destroy them."

"If they do happen to lose. they would probably claim our gym is too small," Vicki predicted, as they went into the fourth quarter. "And I just hate it when they ring that bell every time they make a basket."

The Armedia players seemed more energized as the last quarter began. They ran around the court like greased lightning, dodging the waving arms of their opponents, and passing the ball with precision. The Armedia score climbed ahead by two points. Their fans jumped up and down and screamed as Ty Ramirez shot the basket, which gave them the edge. "We just might win after all," Elaine cried happily. The Ralston team was not so confident now, and that fact was obvious in their playing, since they were making more errors. But the score again became tied somehow. And then Willie made his fifth and last foul, and was sent out of the game. Armedia deeply regretted this loss, but there were only twenty seconds left of the game anyhow. But the Ralston player that was fouled was given two free shots, and he made both of them! Armedia couldn't believe that they were about to lose such a close game by this stroke of bad luck.

The large, lighted scoreboard showed four seconds left, and stopped. Woody had been fouled, and had been given two free shots. Poor Woody, Elaine thought, to be under such pressure. She sat quietly, tightly clenching both fists, willing with all her might for Woody to score. It's only a game, she thought, and we will have forgotten it by next week. The crowd was going crazy. Ralston rooters were screaming like mad to distract Woody, but he seemed calm and unperturbed. He stood still for a minute to catch his breath, and to concentrate on the task at hand, then tossed the ball lightly into the air—and made the first point. By now, every person in the gym was standing up, and was hollering and screaming. On the second shot, Woody took his time as well, bringing the suspense to a new level. Elaine was almost afraid to watch. She was tightly gripping Nat's arm. It will all be over in a second, she told herself. Please, please, Woody, score that point. The ball soared upward, and sunk down through the orange rim, and now there was even more noise in the gym than after his first shot. The fans were beside themselves with excitement. Ralston had captured the rebound, but it had been impossible for them to make a basket in the few remaining seconds. The buzzer went off at the end of the fourth quarter, and the board read 78-78.

"I can't believe this game! We're going into overtime!" Vicki exclaimed, pounding on Megan.

"Poor Willie, he's going to feel bad for missing out on the most exciting part of the game," Megan lamented. "And he's going to be exhausted!"

"So is Woody," Elaine added. "In fact I'm so tired myself, I feel like I've been playing."

A referee held up his hand for silence, which fell startlingly and immediately on the gym. "Due to the scores of the game, and the circumstances, the clock will be set for three more minutes," he said.

When the game began again Ralston made two points almost immediately. Then someone on their team was given a free shot. Armedia was shouting to distract him, while Ralston screamed for the point, and the noise was almost deafening as the player attempted the shot. The ball bounced on the rim of the basket and dropped—outside. Armedia heaved a relieved sigh, as their team caught the rebound. But they didn't shoot for fear of losing the ball. The clock ticked down to 30 seconds. Finally Ty, in desperation, carefully aimed, although he was hindered by a persistent guard. He scored two more points, and the gym resounded with yells and stomps. Then Woody was fouled again, and was given a free shot. "Let's hope he gives a repeat performance," someone muttered.

As the ball sank into the basket, making the final point for the game, there were screams of triumph from the bleachers. The crowd went wild as the buzzer went off, ending the three minutes of overtime. The girls were hugging each other and crying for joy. The boys on the team were hugging each other. And somehow the fans found themselves on the court, hugging the team. The cheerleaders were trying to get everyone quieted down so they could sing the Alma Mater, but that was almost impossible. Everyone was too hoarse, too happy, and too exhausted to utter one syllable of it. Members of the crowd rolled the Victory Bell from Ralston's section over to their own, ringing it loudly. The Ralston students seemed dazed by their defeat. But the expressions of contempt and fury on their faces for Armedia wasn't even noticed by the victors, as Ralston slowly left for the locker room, not wanting to see any more celebrating. The team had lifted Coach Sharpe onto their shoulders, and was carrying him off to the locker room, amid wild cheering. It was definitely a night to remember. The crowd finally cleared out of the gym, so that the frosh, who were sponsoring that night's dance, could take over.

"It didn't take long to transform this place," Karen later remarked. The girls were sitting on the bleachers of a now darkened, definitely quieter gym. The floor had been swept, and a huge, hastily painted sign reading "Victory Dance" had been tacked above the bleachers. A slow song came on and couples started circling the floor. Gradually the girls in Elaine's group were being asked to dance, and then she felt two large hands around her waist, and turned to find Woody's smiling blue eyes and daredevil grin. He steered to the middle of the crowded gym and they began to dance. "How does it feel to be the hero of the game?" she asked him.

"Heck, I was no hero," he answered. "It took the whole entire team working together to win that game. And it sure did feel great to beat those guys."

"But if you hadn't made those free shots, we would have lost," she told him. Woody just smiled and slipped her fingers through his and pulled her very close. They were dancing to the dreamy music of a new song by the Platters, *Smoke Gets In Your Eyes*. Elaine rested her head on Woody's shoulder and closed her eyes. This was really dancing, she thought happily. The day that had started out so badly was having a perfect, romantic ending.

Chapter 23

The following Tuesday morning Armedia High was buzzing with rumors and confusion. Vicki and Karen's usually sunny faces were a grim contrast as they greeted the girls from Ellington when they disembarked from the bus.

"Now what's brewing?" Elaine asked.

"The school board had a meeting last night," Karen began. "It was an open meeting and many parents went to hear about what's been happening. Nobody found out much of anything, except that Principal Santini has been fired."

"Fired!" Lucy exclaimed. "Whatever for?"

"Nobody knows, except the school board," stated Vicki. "My dad went to the meeting, and he said the school board explained that they had good reason to fire him, but they refused to give their reasons as it would incriminate Mr. Santini and keep him from finding another position. Santini is planning to sue the board members."

"Oh, I have to go find Phil," Lucy was saying, and she rushed off in the direction of the cafeteria.

"What a mess! Now we don't have a principal or a dean!" cried Elaine.

"Oh, but Dean Caldwell is returning, since the board appointed him to act as our temporary principal," Karen told them as they reached the Home Ec room, and met Megan at the door, and she had more disturbing news.

"Guess what?" she said. "There is a group of about 30 students who are planning a sit-down strike! They're going to meet out on the front lawn! My sister, Ty, Phil of course, and Lenny Mendoza are some of the ringleaders. Alma is all upset, because she thinks her brother is making a big mistake."

"What exactly is a sit-down strike?" Beth asked.

"Well," Megan said importantly, "it's basically a protest. All the students taking part in it will refuse to go to class, and just sit out front til the board gives a reason for firing Mr. Santini. The strike will probably get a lot of publicity."

"But I really don't think it will solve anything," commented Elaine, as the bell rang.

"It won't," stated Vicki with authority. "It probably sounds good to kids who want to skip class, but I bet they come straggling in after the first bell rings."

"Oops, that's the second bell now," said Karen to Natalie. "We'd better go; we're going to be late to class." There were still students milling around all over the campus, since most people felt that there were bigger problems than getting to class on time.

"I wonder if the parents had anything to do with the strike," Megan said. "My mom was quite disgusted with the school board. After all, the parents voted the board members in, and it doesn't seem like they could just fire someone without a reason. If everyone participating in that strike is really serious, not just goofing off, it might show the public that AHS students take an interest in what is happening to their school. I know you guys probably don't agree with me, but I think I'm going to join them." And she walked down the steps to the front lawn, leaving her friends to recover from her sudden decision.

At the mid-morning break, the entire student body congregated on the circle drive that surrounded the strikers' lawn. Taunts were being thrown back and forth. The majority of the striking students were leading students who seemed to be sure of what they were doing. Elaine and Nat broke away from the other girls and went to talk to some of the ringleaders on the other side of the stone wall.

"I was at the meeting last night," Ty was saying, "and I saw the board fire Mr. Santini just like that! The parents had no voice in the matter! Mr. Santini had no voice in the matter! And of course the students had no voice in the matter! It was just like an old fashioned trial. The prisoner was condemned with no lawyer or chance to defend himself. And this is supposed to be a free country. If this protest goes over, it will show the public that we students have feelings too, and are definitely interested in what goes on in our community."

Then Marie Frye came up to the stone wall holding a petition. It gave an account of the meeting the previous night and concluded that the undersigned students did not consider the meeting as true democratic procedure. Elaine signed, noting that that she was number 136. Nat signed also, and stated that she was joining the strike. Elaine thought hard before making the decision. She knew that maybe Nat and Lucy had ulterior motives for joining. Some of her friends were against the protest, but she did not share their feelings, and felt she should stand up for what was right, regardless of those who tried to influence her otherwise. She had a reputation for being a good high school citizen. Would people think any less of her? What would her parents say? Then she remembered that over the years her parents had told her never to worry about what others thought of her if she felt she was doing the right thing. Without a qualm she stepped over the wall. When she heard the bell ring, ending the morning break, Elaine felt a little apprehensive.

Lenny Mendoza came up to her and said, "If you don't feel right about this, you can always go back, you know. You don't have to stay."

"Oh, I feel right about it," Elaine smiled. It felt very strange, being with the minority of students, sitting in the sunshine on the lawn, knowing that classes were being held. Most of the strikers were upperclassmen.

Marie was counting the strikers and told the rest of the group that they were now 70 strong. "That's a good number," she said. "It's almost one fourth of our school population."

At first the time seemed to pass slowly, but suddenly it was noon time. At first the strikers thought they should stay on the lawn and resist lunch, but decided that would be carrying things a bit too far. Elaine had brought a sack lunch that day. Crossing the student square on her way to her locker, she met a few people she knew.

"I was really surprised when I heard you'd joined the protest," Alma told her. "I thought you had more sense. My brother has no sense whatsoever. The striking seniors might not get their diplomas," she added solemnly.

Greg Okamota and Karen Gillespie were standing near her locker. "You could be expelled and sent to Juvenile Hall," Karen told her, but Greg didn't agree with that.

"Probably the worst that could happen would be that some teachers might give you an F for the day," he said. Greg always seemed to have a lot of common sense, and Elaine hoped he was right.

On the way back to the lawn she met up with DJ and Shawn, who as always, had dire predictions, but, no one ever listened to what they had to say anyhow.

"All you guys will be expelled, never again to darken these hallowed halls of learning," Shawn stated dramatically.

"And your parents will be fined thousands of dollars," added DJ. "They'll probably lose their chicken ranch, and your entire family will all be homeless, because of you."

"Where do you guys come up with this stuff?" she asked, laughing, heading back to the group of rebels, who were eating lunch. The non-strikers tried to make trouble for the others, and there were several fights among the boys. Students were trying to tear down the signs that the strikers had erected, which read, "Reinstate Santini," "Give Students a Voice," and "What Happened to Democracy??"

Dean Caldwell, the acting principal, came down and put a stop to the skirmishes, but he could not urge the strikers to return to their classes. In fact about 20 more students joined the movement during the lunch break. Reporters were showing up now and rapidly taking notes and snapping pictures. Jackie Irby was among them.

Shortly after the reporters arrived, Mr. Santini approached the strikers, along with some of the mothers of the students. He told the group he appreciated their loyalty but he didn't condone the strike, and asked them if they would please return to their classes, and they agreed to do so, but under protest. It was now the latter part of 6th Period, and Elaine and Megan felt sheepish as they walked back into the library, but Mrs. Coyne welcomed them back, and didn't say anything to them about their activities that day. The girls both felt a little relieved that they would be counted as present in English last period, because Mrs. Teague would have given them an F that day for sure.

Elaine explained the day's events to her parents, who were glad she had done what she thought was right, although they reasoned that the strike wouldn't really help matters at all. The front page of the Armedia Appeal the following day featured headlines, a picture, and a detailed article about the strike. Elaine cut out everything for her scrapbook, although she knew she wouldn't forget all the excitement for a long time.

The sit-down strike hadn't made any difference one way or the other, and when the dust settled, the Santini family left the valley for good. Lucy was heartbroken with Phil leaving. The reason for the firing of Joe Santini was never disclosed to the public.

Armedia wasn't the only high school with problems that year. Later that month the Hummer family watched a television documentary titled "The Lost Class of 1959." It portrayed Central High School of Little Rock, Arkansas across the country. Its doors had not opened in

September, or October, or November. Central High, along with other high schools in the area, were still closed. Both white and colored students had acted unfavorably to integration. Their parents liked it even less, and there was so much controversy over the matter that the integrated schools simply shut down, as if that would settle the issue. The students had been stunned when they saw their schools actually closing, and many gave in and declared that they didn't mind integrated schools. But the parents and the school boards had stood firm, and the school doors remained locked. The program told of teen agers previously planning to graduate in June now getting married, or getting jobs, or getting into trouble because there was nothing else to do.

"Probably about a fourth of our school enrollment is a combination of Mexican, Italian, Oriental, or colored students," Elaine remarked. "But we all get along fine, and everybody likes everybody else."

"Of course it must be difficult not to feel prejudiced when you've been brought up to hate another race, and that's all you've heard most of your life," Charles was saying.

"It's a terrible thing that schools here in America are closed for that reason," Lois added. "I'd hate to see our children not graduate because of that," she added soberly.

"I don't know what I'd ever do if Armedia High ever closed," Elaine said with fervor. "It would be the worst thing ever!"

"I know what you can do right now," Charles told her as the program ended. "You can go study for your final exams."

"Well, now I wish the school would close," muttered Elaine.

Report card were issued at the end of January. Elaine received a C in Spanish II and Sophomore Science, B's in Home Ec and English, and A's in PE, Library, and Geometry. The Geometry grade absolutely blew her away, because she had no idea of how that happened. She had come into the classroom the Monday after the final exam, and the grades of the students were posted on the bulletin board. Her name topped the list with a 96%, much to her utter amazement. There must have been a mistake, she decided. Most of her answers on the exam had been guesswork, since she didn't have the faintest idea what a theorem was. It was obvious to the class that Mr.Dumpke knew little about the subject himself. Elaine thought that possibly he hadn't checked the exams very thoroughly. The expression on the faces of Greg, Woody, and Lenny, once they saw that they were below Elaine on the list, made her laugh. It was actually a bit embarrassing, and it was plain to see they didn't believe the tests had been graded correctly either. "Good job, Elaine!" Lenny told her, laughing.

"Congratulations," Greg said to her. "I'll have to enlist your help the next time I'm working on a difficult theorem."

"Are you kidding?" laughed Elaine. "Everyone in this class knows I didn't deserve the highest grade. I feel like writing all your names at the top of the list where they belong."

"Well, you're the one with the top grade, and it's obvious that you know a lot more about Geometry than you're letting on, so in the future we'll be coming to you with our questions," Woody said with a grin. He was another A student in all of his classes.

"Yeah, just ask me whatever you need to know," she joked. "I have all the answers."

*   *   *

After all the excitement at school, life had calmed down a bit. However, there was more bad news early in February, and although it didn't relate directly to the high school, the news was very sobering and saddening for most teen agers across the country. Rock and Roll icon Buddy Holly was killed in a plane crash, along with two other well-known singers, Ritchie Valens, and J.P. Richardson, known by everyone as the Big Bopper. They were on their way to a concert in Fargo, North Dakota, when their chartered plane crashed because of poor weather conditions.

"I absolutely loved Buddy Holly," Lucy was saying. "I have all his records and I play them all the time. It's just hard to believe all three of those singers were killed. What a tragedy!"

"Yes, it is, and they will certainly be missed by everyone," stated Elaine sadly. The girls were homeward bound on the school bus that day, and they were all feeling down, not only about the loss of the singers, but just life in general. They all had a case of the winter blues.

"This is the most boring time of the year," Beth pointed out. "Nothing fun going on at school and too cold for any outside activities. I really don't like winter."

"At least we don't have snow piled up all over the place like they do back east," Elaine reminded her. "Our weather is pretty good compared to theirs."

"Oh, I think it would be great if we had some snow around here," Nat remarked. "There are a lot of good winter activities when you have snow."

"I just want to do something FUN," said Beth. "I can't wait til we can get our drivers licenses. Then maybe we could go somewhere once in a while, instead of always being stuck in Ellington. I have about two months to go til I'm sixteen. And I'll be getting drivers training at school next month."

"School is just no fun without Phil around," Lucy lamented. "And I haven't heard anything from him, not one word. You'd think he could at least write me a lousy letter."

"I know just how you feel, waiting for a letter," Elaine said with sympathy.

"We have a three day weekend coming up soon," Nat reminded them. "Washington's birthday."

"Yeah, maybe we should plan something for that weekend," suggested Elaine.

On Saturday Elaine dropped by Chuck and Cathy's. She needed something to do, and she also wanted to hear anything they might have to say about Jeff.

"Come in, come in," Cathy was saying. "I was going to call you, and now here you are. We had a letter from Jeff yesterday. He's coming for a visit in a couple of weeks, and he is hoping to see you again. I figured you would probably be agreeable to that."

"I'm definitely up for seeing him again. He's so good looking and so much fun."

"Well, he hasn't dated a lot, but I think he's really interested in you, or he wouldn't have mentioned you in his letter. And for all his joking, he is very sincere."

"I've had bad luck with guys in the past," Elaine said.

"Don't let those other fellows give you an inferiority complex," Cathy told her.

"That's right," Chuck said, coming through the front door. "You take my wife's advice, Kiddo." He winked at Elaine. "Actually I think you're too wild for my nephew. I heard about you and that guy from camp, and how you met him secretly behind the cabins every night."

"Where did you hear THAT story?"

"Oh, ministers hear everything."

"So Jeff will be coming here for the long weekend?" Elaine asked of Cathy.

"You bet," Chuck answered. "I was thinking the MYF should plan a trip to the snow on that weekend. There is lots of snow in the mountains right now, and hopefully, they'll get more in the next two weeks. We need an outing anyhow. Maybe you can bring it up at the meeting tomorrow."

"Sounds like a great idea," Elaine said. She stopped at the Hathaway ranch on the way home and found Beth out in the barn grooming her horse, Kirby.

Beth was happy to hear Elaine's news about Jeff and the trip to the snow. "See, now don't keep saying nothing ever works out for you. When I first heard about Jeff, I thought he sounded like your type of guy. Too bad he doesn't have a brother. I wish I could meet some new guys. Last year I went out with Adam, but he only liked me as a friend. I've gone out with Rodney a couple of times, but we're just friends too. Where is the romance? I want someone to sweep me off my feet, the way Ty does with Nat. Hopefully my turn will come one of these days. Until then the only fellow I can trust is my horse. Good old Kirby."

The two weeks passed too slowly for Elaine, but finally Saturday arrived, and everyone who was going, met out in front of the church. Jeff looked cuter than ever, Elaine saw, as he greeted her with a big smile. "If you like, you can ride in Chuck's Ranchero with the three of us," he said.

"That would be fine," she said. "Come on, let me introduce you to everyone."

Adam Irby, home from college for the weekend, was going on the snow trip also, and taking DJ, Beth, Lucy, and Nat. He told Elaine with a wink that they had room for one more, that it would be too crowded with the four of them squeezed in the front seat of Chuck's Ranchero.

"No it won't, it will just be cozy, and I won't mind that at all," Jeff said.

Jack Hathaway, Beth's dad, was also driving, taking some of the younger kids in his station wagon, and the remainder of the group piled into that vehicle. "Looks like the whole town is going on this little expedition," Jeff said, as he opened the door.

"Not really. Our town has a few more people than this."

"Heck, all of Ellington could fit onto our high school campus."

"I don't believe it," Elaine retorted. "Besides, Desert Palms is nothing but sand, cactus, and rattlesnakes!"

"Better not say anything against it. I'm going to show you around there one of these days," he said, squeezing into the front seat. Elaine's heart felt like singing. It was a beautiful Saturday morning and they were headed off for a day of fun in the snow. They went east toward the mountains, which divided the valley from the desert, passing farms settled peacefully in the countryside.

"I'll have to admit there is some beautiful scenery around this valley," Jeff said. The road began to climb gradually, and then steepness led to numerous switchbacks in the highway. Pine trees were beginning to appear, and the air grew cooler.

Elaine and Cathy were quiet, while Chuck and Jeff did most of the talking. Chuck explained that his oldest sister, who was 13 years older than Chuck, was Jeff's mother. But when she got married and had Jeff, she lived in the same neighborhood as Chuck's family, so uncle and nephew were almost like brothers. Chuck had three sisters altogether, two older and one younger. Elaine was fascinated hearing tales of their boyhood. Apparently the sisters were the brunt of much teasing and practical jokes.

"I used to be a terror," Chuck was saying. "I teased my sisters something awful. Remember, Jeff, when I had you find me a scorpion, and I ended up putting it in Judy's bed?"

"Oh, that's terrible," exclaimed Cathy. "They're poisoness!"

"It was a non-poisoness one," Jeff said with finality.

"The worst trick we ever pulled was when my younger sister, Patsy was dating this really jerky guy that we didn't like," Chuck said. "Well, Bob-the Slob, that was our secret name for him, was sitting in the living room one night waiting for Pat, when one of my college buddies, Big Dan, came by for a visit. So we hatched up a little plot. Now, you have to realize that Big Dan is bigger than Jeff and me put together. We were telling Dan what a jerk Patsy was going out with, and how we wished we could get rid of him. So Dan goes in the living room and casually sits down as if waiting for someone. Jeff and I were hiding behind the kitchen door listening to the conversation, which went something like this. Big Dan looks at his watch and says, 'That Pat gets later every time I take her out. I just hope she'll be ready before the second feature starts. After all, she was the one who wanted to see this Elvis movie tonight.'" Chuck stopped to chuckle. "Meanwhile Bob was getting rather ill at ease. He said 'Um, I hope we don't have a date with the same girl. I'm supposed to take Patsy out to dinner tonight. You must have the wrong night.' And with that Big Dan strolled casually over to Bob and said, 'Listen here, Sam, I ought to know when I have a date with Patsy, and I don't get my dates mixed up either. Now, I think you'd better clear out Sam, before there's trouble!' And with that, wimpy Bob made tracks for the door."

"What did Patsy do?" Elaine asked.

"We didn't wait around to find out," said Chuck. "We headed for the hills."

"Pat didn't speak to us for weeks," Jeff added. "But it all turned out okay."

"I hadn't heard that story before," stated Cathy. "What a troublemaker I married!"

"The irony of it all," Chuck finished, "is that Patsy and Big Dan ended up getting married a couple of year later. Now she owes me her undying gratitude."

"What a story! It sounds like your family had a lot of fun together," Elaine told them.

"Looks like we're almost here," Chuck said as they reached a big clearing in the pines. There were several vacation cabins, a lodge, a gas station, and a couple of cafes. A light layer of snow covered the slanted roofs, and the trees looked as though they had been dusted with powder. Chuck pulled over, and they waited for Adam and the other cars. They then turned off onto a very steep side road that led to a big snow park two miles up from the little town, and about 1000 feet higher in elevation. There was about two feet of snow in that area. Everyone piled excitedly out of the vehicles. The young people wasted no time in trying out the snow. Some of the younger group was making snow angels. Adam was throwing snowballs at everyone.

"Your husband certainly didn't waste any time," Elaine told Cathy, noting her snow-covered hair and flushed cheeks.

"It will be your turn next," Jeff said to Elaine. He started pelting her lightly with snowballs and she was returning them. It wasn't long before the entire group was in a free-for-all. When Jeff's back was turned, his attention on snowballing Chuck, Elaine actually managed to hit him for the first time. "Who's the guilty one?" he asked, turning around. "Hummingbird, I know that was you, and I'm out to get you now! I'll wash your face in snow!"

"You'll have to catch me first," she cried, laughing and running away. She hadn't gone very far though, just down the slope and around the bend, when her feet flew out in front of her, and there she lay just as Jeff rounded the corner.

"Ha! Now you're caught, and you'll be sorry!"

"No, no," she cried helplessly, laughing. He leaned over her with handfuls of snow and carried out his threat. She was enjoying every minute of it. "I think I've eaten enough snow to last a long time," she laughed. Jeff was laughing too. Their faces were close together, and they looked into each other's eyes and began laughing again.

"Let's go for a walk," Jeff suggested, helping her up, and brushing off some of the snow on her jacket. He took her hand in his, and they headed over to a stand of fir trees, where there was a narrow path of well packed snow. A thrill went through Elaine as their fingers interlocked. No other guy's touch had ever warmed her like this.

As they climbed the slope, the whole world around them was white, except for a few patches of green just under the trees. It was a silent world with no sound except the crunch of snow and ice under their feet. They didn't exchange words, for words weren't necessary. They reached the top of the slope and stood looking out over the valley, a patchwork of browns, grays, and many shades of green. "Which way is Ellington?" Jeff asked her.

Elaine pointed toward the southwest. "Way over there, among those hills somewhere, about 60 miles away, I'm guessing. Isn't it beautiful, Jeff?"

He nodded. "Let's go back this way," he said, taking her hand again and leading her through a thicket of aspens.

"I am completely lost, mixed up, and turned around," Elaine complained.

"Don't worry, I wouldn't get you lost," Jeff told her. "I know right where I am." The snow was thicker under the trees, and the sky seemed to grow darker. A little unseen bird gave a mournful coo in the dim light. "I think it's going to start snowing again pretty soon," he added. "And guess what? I think we are lost."

"Oh, no!" But she wasn't exactly unhappy about the idea of being lost with Jeff, except she had visions of them freezing to death under the snow. But she figured that Jeff was only teasing anyhow. They came out of the trees and into a clearing. The road was about 50 feet away.

"Know where we are now?" he asked. "We just made a big circle and we'll come to the park several hundred yards down this road."

"I guess you're pretty smart after all," she told him as they started down the road. "Hey look," she said, catching sight of some familiar structures behind them on the left. "There is the camp I went to last summer. See the cabins?"

"You going again this summer?" he asked.

"I don't know," she said. "I really haven't thought much about it." Summer seemed very far away. She didn't even want to think of the future, only of today. Was it only last night that Jeff had comet Ellington? He would be leaving again in two more days? Would she see him again? Her mind was suddenly filled with doubts, and she pushed the negative thoughts from her mind.

They rounded a corner and there was the park. A wonderful aroma of sizzling hamburgers was in the air, and their group was standing around the barbecue grill.

"Better get over here!" Adam yelled. "we're almost out of food."

"Where did you guys disappear to?" Chuck asked. "Got lost somewhere, didn't you? Ah-ha!"

After the burgers and hot dogs had been eaten, some of the group rode sleds down the various slopes. It took some practice to steer the sled right, and to pick out the best and the slipperiest slopes. Elaine tried sledding once, but then went back to stand by the barbecue where the coals were still giving off some heat. Later in the afternoon it began to snow again. The air had grown colder and snowflakes began drifting lightly down. They stayed out in it for a while until everybody was feeling too cold and too tired. Elaine was looking forward to the trip home, and being snuggled up cozily next to Jeff. She was completely exhausted from the day's activities and her hands and feet were numb. The four of them climbed into the car and started the long drive back down the mountain. Jeff's arm was around her and her head was on his shoulder. She tried to think only of the moment, but doubts kept creeping into her mind. Will he want to see me tonight? Will he want to see me tomorrow? Will he come down to Ellington again? Or will he just fade away like Danny did?

It was twilight when they drove up to the Hummer home, and Lois invited Chuck, Cathy, and Jeff to dinner. They came back about an hour later. "You're in for a treat," Chuck told Jeff. "Lois Hummer is a really great cook!"

"Well, thank you. I figured you would be really tired from your trip, and I didn't want Cathy to have to cook tonight," Lois said.

The evening passed pleasantly enough, and only one mishap occurred at dinner when Timmie upset his milk glass. Everyone seemed to enjoy the tamale pie that Lois had made. After the dinner dishes were done, Lois and Charles visited for a bit, and they excused themselves to go pack eggs. Elaine got out a game of Scrabble and they sat at the dining room table and played for a while, but it wasn't long before everyone was yawning, tired from the day's activities.

"I'll pick you up for church tomorrow," Jeff offered, making Elaine's day complete.

Sunday turned out to be just as beautiful a day as the day before. Jeff looked so handsome in his gray suit, and Elaine was proud to be sitting next to him in church. She had always wanted to attend church with a boy she liked. Chuck's sermon was inspiring as always. He always seemed so different, Elaine thought, when he was up in the pulpit, in his black robe, preaching. She was glad that she knew him, not only as a pastor, but as a good friend. All she could think of at the moment was how thankful she was that she had met Jeff and that he liked her. She was full of love and thankfulness for everything that day. She had been attending church ever since her parents had moved to Ellington. How she loved the little white church. It looked so pretty, she thought, with baskets of late chrysanthemums in front, and the candles and Bible on the alter, with the empty cross over it, signifying Christ's resurrection, and the fact that He lived on.

"Shall we stand for the closing hymn," Reverend Graham's voice boomed out," *Are Ye Able.*" It was her favorite hymn, and at that time she felt that she would be able to do anything that Christ wanted her to do.

After church everyone was standing outside greeting each other as they always did. Elaine was introducing Jeff to members of the congregation, elderly ladies and younger couples.

"I would have known you anywhere," Sue Hathaway was saying. "You look so much like our preacher."

"But he sure doesn't act like it," Beth told her mother. "I'm all black and blue from the snowballs he threw yesterday."

"Oh, you poor little thing," Jeff teased.

"Are you going riding today?" Elaine asked Beth.

"Don't I always go riding whenever I get the chance?"

"Do you have a horse?" Jeff asked. "I always liked horses. Can we come over and see it?"

"Of course. Come on over this afternoon. Actually I have two horses."

"Do you want to?" Jeff asked Elaine.

She nodded happily, thinking how sweet it was of him to ask her first.

After a spaghetti dinner at the Graham's, they took the short walk over the Hathaway ranch. No one answered their knock, so they went around the back toward the barn. Jack could be seen on his tractor out in the field, plowing, while Sue was planting some bulbs. Elaine waved and led the way to the barn where Beth's younger siblings were playing in the hay. Beth rode in from the pasture on Kirby and dismounted. "Hi! Anybody for riding?" she asked.

"Uh-oh, my wife is getting that gleam in her eye," said Chuck.

"Well, I was raised in the city, but I spent one summer counseling at camp, and there I really acquired a love for riding," Cathy said.

"Go ahead. Better watch him, though. He's kind of skittish today. He's not used to so many people around." Cathy was up in the saddle in a wink, and was off for a jaunt around the field. Chuck and Jeff were in the next stall talking to Dolly, Beth's chestnut mare.

"Are you having fun this weekend," Beth asked Elaine in low tones. "Seems to me like you are."

"Wonderful. I'm really crazy about Jeff. I didn't want to fall for him until I knew for sure that he liked me, but I couldn't help myself."

"Well, he acts like he really likes you," Beth told her. "And he's really nice and a lot of fun. If you guys start going together, it will be most interesting when Desert Palms plays our school in football this fall. You won't know which side to root for."

"Yeah, I thought of that too," Elaine said. "But that's too far away to worry about."

"Whoa, there, Kirby. Beth, you have a beautiful horse," Cathy said, as she climbed down from the saddle.

"I know. He is a sweetheart," remarked Beth. "Elaine do you want to ride him?"

"I'm not sure. I usually ride Dolly when I'm here. She's more docile."

"Kirby behaved really well for me," Cathy told her.

"Go ahead, take him for a little ride," urged Jeff.

"Might as well," Elaine said. "I haven't been on a horse in ages." She put her left foot into the stirrup, and swung herself into the saddle. She usually felt so high up when she rode. "I'm off," she told them, and nudged Kirby into a brisk walk out of the barn and into the plowed field. It always felt so bouncy being on top of a horse, and she wondered how people could ride for hours at a time. It was a beautiful day, and the sky was so blue with a few cloud wisps scattered across it. Cattle were grazing peacefully in the alfalfa field on the other side of the fence, looking up curiously now and then at Elaine. In the distance, in front of her were the low, coastal hills, just beginning to turn green, and behind her was the higher mountain range topped with white at this time of year, and clearly outlined against the sky.

Kirby wasn't behaving very well. He kept tossing his head and snorting, and going a bit faster than Elaine wanted him to. She was starting to feel apprehensive. They had reached the far end of the field and he turned to go back towards the barn. His brisk walk turned from a trot to a canter to a gallop, which Elaine was totally unprepared for. She planted her feet firmly into the stirrups and pulled on the reins as hard as she was able. But that didn't stop Kirby. He was intent on getting back to the barn, and maybe getting some oats as soon as possible. Elaine had never fallen off a horse yet, and she was determined not to now, especially in front of Jeff and the others. But she could not slow Kirby down. Her feet were sliding out of the stirrups, and before she knew it she was up in the air and Kirby was out from under her, and the next thing she knew, she was flat on her back in the soft soil of the plowed field. Slowly she sat up. She was covered with dirt, but, other than that, she didn't seem to be hurt.

Jeff was hurrying toward her, followed by Chuck, Cathy, Beth, and the younger children.

How embarrassing, Elaine thought, sitting up and brushing off as much dirt as possible. It was in her hair, on her face, on her sweatshirt and jeans. She knew she looked a mess and felt like crying. Jeff reached her first. His usual jovial countenance was one of great concern. "Elaine, are you badly hurt?" he asked. "Gee, I feel as if this were all my fault. I talked you into riding him. I'm so sorry. Are you okay? Say something, Elaine."

She managed a stunned smile. "I guess I'll live." Jeff was helping her up.

"That was quite a spill you took!" Chuck was saying.

"Good thing it was on a plowed field," stated Cathy.

"Kirby hasn't behaved that badly in a long time," Beth told them. "Come on into the house and get cleaned up." Physically Elaine wasn't hurt, except for a few bruises. Her pride was suffering though.

"It's all my fault," Jeff said remorsefully.

"Stop blaming yourself. I wanted to ride Kirby. I usually ride Dolly because she is the older, slower one. But I wanted to try Kirby today, since he's more free spirited. It was my fault, not yours."

After she cleaned up as best she could, Jeff took her back home, where her family had already heard of her misadventure, and they took it in stride.

"How did they know about your fall?" Jeff was asking later, as she got out a beat up game of *Sorry*.

"Nothing ever happens around here, that the rest of the town doesn't hear about five minutes later," Elaine explained to him. "That's just the nature of a small town. Beth's sister probably called my sister. It's just impossible to keep anything secret around here, and that's why I can't wait to get out of this little one-horse town, where no one knows me." She set up the board for the *Sorry* game. Pam and Russ played too, since it was more fun with four players, and Jeff clowned around with the two younger ones. It warmed her heart to see that. He was good with kids.

Jeff had asked her if she wanted to go into Armedia for a hamburger and a movie later, so she went to get a shower and change, while Pam and Russ kept him occupied. While she was in her room changing, Lois knocked on her door to ask her what they had planned for the evening.

"Don't you think you should stay home and take it easy? You've been constantly on the go for the last two days. You two could just stick around here and watch TV or something."

"But, Mom, this will be the first time we're actually going somewhere alone, just the two of us. Don't you like Jeff? You're always wanting me to go out with nice guys, and he's a good, clean-cut Christian guy. And he will be leaving tomorrow morning. This is our last night, and I don't know when he'll be able to come down again."

"I do like him," Lois told her daughter, "and so does your father. We're both glad that you met him, and of course he comes from a good family. I guess you can go tonight. You have all day tomorrow to rest up before school starts again."

The movie *Ben Hur* was playing, and turned out to be very exciting. By the end of the movie, Jeff said he was starving, so they drove over to the malt shop on Armedia's main street, and found a booth in the back. Elaine was hoping someone she knew from school would come in, but the ice cream parlor was fairly quiet that evening. They ordered hamburgers and milkshakes, but Elaine couldn't eat that much. She felt too happy and too full of emotion to eat more than a few bites.

"You don't eat enough to keep a canary alive," Jeff said, as she gave him the rest of her burger to finish. "You're going to melt away to nothing. How about some music?" He fished a coin from his pocket and dropped in into the juke box and told her to choose a song. She picked *Where or When*, since she loved the lyrics. "*It seems that we have met before.*" Where had she met Jeff before? In all her dreams. He was a guy who was everything she always wanted. He was fun to be with, sweet, courteous, kind, intelligent, and handsome. What more could any girl want? Across the table from her was a husky, broad shouldered 16 years old all American boy with blonde hair in a flattop, blue eyes, and a smiling mouth. As she gazed into his eyes, and he gazed back into hers, the rest of the world faded away into oblivion. "*We looked at each other in the same way then, but who knows where or when?*" said the song. Elaine's whole being was filled with love for him.

"I've had so much fun with you the past couple of days," he was saying. "I'm going to hate to go back home tomorrow. But I'll be back down to see you when I can get a weekend off from work, and when I can borrow my dad's car again. Are you going to write to me?"

"Of course," Elaine promised. But her heart ached because she feared that Jeff would be like another guy in her past who had asked the same thing, but forgot all about her once he got back home again. She didn't think she would live if Jeff did not write to her.

"I'm not much for writing letters," Jeff was saying. "But I'll make it a point to write to you every chance I get." It was a promise he had to keep, Elaine thought.

Chapter 24

It was most difficult for Elaine to go back to the routine of school on Tuesday after the exciting and wonderful weekend she had just had. All she could think of was Jeff. She didn't hear much of what was being said in class. She didn't take notes, and she couldn't concentrate on what she was reading. Her back was bothering her and she was a little sore from her fall off the horse. At lunch she hardly ate a thing because she was full of chatter about the last few days.

"Well, Jeff really sounds like a neat guy," Karen commented. "I'm happy for you."

"He and Elaine make a very cute couple," remarked Lucy.

"You get around, Elaine," Vicki pointed out. "Last year it was Warren and Alvin, this year it's been Danny and Woody, and now Jeff."

"Warren and I were just good friends," Elaine scoffed. "And you all know I never gave a hoot for Alvin. Danny was only a summer romance, and Woody was, well, just a little crush. But with Jeff, now that's the real thing."

"Your name suits you," Alma told her. "You're like a hummingbird, flitting around from flower to flower, only in your case, it's from boy to boy."

Everyone laughed at Alma's comparison. "Who will it be six months from now?" Megan asked. "Only time will tell." They all went back to their meatloaf and mashed potatoes.

Elaine was a nervous wreck waiting for a letter from Jeff. She figured that Friday would be the earliest possible time she would get one, and she decided that if she didn't hear from him by the following

Friday she would forget him if it killed her. But she didn't need to worry. Friday afternoon when she walked into the house, there was Jeff's letter waiting on the buffet in the dining room.

"He didn't waste much time in writing you, did he?" Lois asked, coming out of her room where she had been sorting laundry. "Well, what does he have to say, or is it a big secret?"

"Mom, quit teasing!" She pulled the one page letter from the envelope and took it to her room to read: *Dear Elaine, As I told you before, I'm not much for writing letters so if it doesn't make sense, don't mind me. I sure did have a great time with you last weekend. That trip to the snow was a real blast. All I can think of is you and all the fun we had together.*

I sure hope I'll be able to come down and see you again soon. That is if you want me to. I keep busy with my job after school in my stepdad's hardware store. I'm trying to save up for a car. In the meantime, if I come down again, I can probably borrow a car. It's not too long a trip, to Ellington. It probably took me about 2 and a half hours to get home on Monday. Always, Jeff P.S. I Love You.

Elaine couldn't believe her eyes when she came to the last three words. He had only really known her for a few days and he was telling her he loved her! And she knew she could believe someone like Jeff when he said those words. She was already composing a letter in her head to write back to him after her chores were done.

As March crept up, the days gradually began to lengthen and the sun became warmer. The short rainy season which had lasted only a few weeks, seemed to be over. Grass began shooting up all over the valley, and buds began appearing on the trees. The past winter, much in contrast to the previous year, had been exceptionally warm and dry.

Elaine was sorry when basketball season was over. She had enjoyed attending the games, especially when their team had played so well. The varsity team had tied for first place with Ralston, quite an honor for the little school of Armedia. Now that the games were over, there wasn't as much do to. Elaine usually stayed home on both Friday and Saturday nights, and she wasn't too crazy about that. The weekend evenings were spent with Beth or Lucy usually. They watched TV, or made candy, or played Scrabble or cards. Beth had taken her Driver's Ed course at school and had passed with flying colors. "I will be sixteen in two more weeks," she told Elaine. "I'm sure I'll be able to borrow the car until I can get my own, and then we'll have places to go and things to do. We can go to Armedia to the movies every weekend if we want to, or to the skating rink. That's about all there is to do there, anyhow."

"It certainly will beat staying home," Elaine pointed out. "I wish I could get my license, but I haven't driven enough to pass a test. The only driving I've done is down to the store and back, and even then my dad has a fit because I slam on the brake too hard, or don't slow down enough at corners. Of course I've had plenty of practice on the tractor, but it's much easier driving around in a field, even when I'm pulling the trailer or manure spreader. I was told I would be starting Drivers Ed last Monday, but that didn't happen. I'm hoping it will be this coming week."

"Let me tell you, it's no picnic driving with Mr. Gorton. He made me very nervous."

Elaine was soon to find out for herself. She and DJ and Mary Lou Wright started their Drivers' Training course in the school's new 59 Chevy, with Mr. Gorton as their instructor. Since they had already learned the rules of the road in Sophomore Science class, all they now needed was the actual practice, and the applying of the rules. DJ had been driving for months, illegally of course. He casually drove up the the main street that connected Armedia to Lasswood, very calm and collected, Elaine was thinking from the back seat. Then Mr. Gorton had DJ pull over so that Elaine could take the wheel. She hoped he wouldn't be shouting at her and making her more apprehensive, since she was already quite nervous.

She turned on the ignition key, checked the front and rear view mirrors and also looked over her left shoulder before moving out onto the street. Surprisingly the car wouldn't move at first. "It might help if you would release the handbrake," Mr. Gorton said dryly. Mary Lou and DJ were chuckling quietly in the back seat. She drove around for a few blocks on the outskirts of Armedia, and then Mr. Gorton had her drive out to the main road. Very cautiously, she edged out and drove slowly in a northerly direction.

"Elaine, you can go faster than 35 miles per hour, since we are on the main drag. There's not much traffic right now, but people will be honking if you go that slow, say, when there is heavy traffic. Just gradually step on the accelerator and get your speed up." She made it up to 45 miles per hour and felt as if she were going really fast. "Why don't you turn right at the next side street coming up?" Mr. Gorton suggested.

"What side street?" she asked, sailing past it. Mr. Gorton was becoming rather perturbed. "The one right under your nose, that you just passed! Your reaction time is a bit slow for driving," he told her. He had her turn at the next road, and pull over so that Mary Lou could take the wheel for the remainder of the hour. Mary Lou had also had some experience driving. Elaine was so relieved to be in the back seat again.

She began thinking of Jeff as usual. He had been writing faithfully, at least once a week since he had gone back to Desert Palms, and she wrote him a letter just as often. She missed him more than she had thought possible, but she knew how hard it was for him to get time off work. Also a two day weekend went by lickety split, hardly worth the trip to Ellington. He had told her he would try to get some time off during Easter Vacation, which was in April.

The Collette's activities were picking up that spring. The girls were full of enthusiasm for their newly formed organization. The eight charter members, plus three new ones were at the next meeting, held at Alma's home. The girls planned a car wash, a mother's tea, and a money making dance. They were in a talkative mood, which increased the treasury's balance. But everyone had such good suggestions that Vicki forgot the fines. Mary Lou had suggested the dance, which at first brought groans of disapproval.

"Boys don't like dances." "There are too many dances already." "Where could we have it?"

"Hold your fire," Mary Lou said. "There is more to this than meets the eye. How about a Sadie Hawkins Dance, with the girls asking the boys. Look how much better attended the dances are when the girls have to do the asking, and the paying. Besides, it would be informal, with everyone wearing blue jeans and cotton shirts. The guys would like that, since they don't have to dress up."

"I think you just might have a great idea there," said Megan approvingly.

"I don't," Beth moaned. "Just a few months back we had to worry about what boy to ask, and now it's happening all over again."

Alma backed her up. "There aren't any guys in this high school worth asking anyhow."

"Now that wasn't nice," Megan told her.

"Well, it's true," Lucy stated. "Besides the girls chase the guys enough as it is."

"That's just it," Mary Lou pointed out. "Think of all the girls that are waiting for a chance to ask a guy. Our dance will be exactly what they need. We'll probably sell lots of tickets."

"More money for the treasury," Vicki mused. "Where could we hold it?"

"In the high school gym, I guess. We could put bales of hay around the room, have plenty of good snacks there. The guys will all like that.

Maybe even a couple of games." Heads were nodding approvingly, as more of the girls were getting into the spirit of the dance.

"May I make a suggestion?" asked Elaine. "Could we have it on a Saturday night the week before Easter?"

The majority of the group liked the dance idea, and also the date, so they voted in favor of it, and Vicki was assigning committees for publicity, refreshments, games, and set-up. They decided that if they couldn't have it at the high school, the Women's Clubhouse was also a possibility.

April was slow in coming, however, and the last two weeks of March dragged interminably. School seemed especially tiresome these days. Elaine dreaded 6th period each day when she had driver's education. That was so much more stressful that just working in the school library. Her driving was improving, however, on their cruises around the town. They had practiced parallel parking on the baseball field, they had practiced backing up, and they'd practiced stopping on hills. They had practiced signaling, and when they forgot to signal, or signaled incorrectly, they had to stop the car, get out, and stand and signal several feet behind. It was most embarrassing, and after having to stand behind the car and signal, a student never forgot a second time. Elaine was proud of herself when she had mastered the few basic driving skills, although she was not as confident as Mary Lou or DJ, and her reactions were still a bit slow. Finally the day came when the actual driving test was to take place. Mary Lou achieved a fairly high score. DJ made no errors except for speeding in a residential area. When it was Elaine's turn, she started the car and headed out of the school parking lot, very nervous with Mr. Gorton's eagle eye upon her. Out of the corner of her eye, she could see him taking notes, which didn't help put her mind at ease. She drove uphill and downhill and through the back streets of Armedia, and at last came out onto the main road, going north. Then he had her make a left turn and drive around some more. Why is he having me drive around so much, she asked herself. Am I doing something wrong? There was a quiet tension in the car.

"Pull over to the side," Mr. Gorton said abruptly. "You just flunked. You made a left turn from the wrong lane back there, you didn't make a complete stop at the stop sign three blocks back, and you forgot to signal twice. Matter of fact, you turned from the wrong lane on two different occasions. There were a couple more errors too, but I'm just naming the most glaring ones." Elaine was stunned. She had never cried in front of a teacher before, but she could not hold the tears back. Mary Lou was very sympathetic, as they exited the car, and even

DJ refrained from his usual facetious comments. She was filled with a sudden dislike for Mr. Gorton, and was deeply ashamed of her tears, but they would not stop flowing. And she had no time to compose herself, since she had English next, the last class of the day.

To make matters worse, Mrs. Teague sprung a test on them that day, on English grammar and parts of speech. Elaine was so upset she could hardly see the questions. The test only took about 20 minutes, and then the students handed their papers to the student behind them for grading. After Mrs. Teague had collected the papers, and recorded the grades, she handed each test back Elaine was dismayed that she hadn't even made 70%. But apparently entire class had not done well. Holding a ruler,Mrs. Teague stormed furiously about the room. "Sometimes I don't know why I even bother to teach. It's practically impossible to get anything through your thick skulls. All you teen agers care about are parties, clothes, cars, dates, and Heaven knows what else! Most of you don't seem to give a hoot about your studies! America is just now waking up to the fact that schools aren't turning out the students they were 20 years ago! In other countries it is a privilege to go to school, and young people will work hard and study long hours just so they can stay in school and get an education. But American teens don't seem to have much of a sense of values, except how they can make their lives more entertaining." She paused for breath, and 30 students dared not move. The room was as still as the Antarctic. She continued in her deep and powerful voice. "English is one of the most important subjects you take in school, and as your teacher, I'm going to see that you learn it if I have to cram it into those heads of yours. Do you realize that only one tenth of this class passed? Well, those three are not going to be held back by the rest of you morons. Karen, Greg, and Woody will go on to the next chapter, while the rest of you will stay behind. There will be another test on Monday and woe unto those who do not pass! That's all I can say."

On Monday, Mr. Gorton found her in the library. "I'm sorry I lost my temper with you the other day," he said gently. "I guess I was rather harsh on you. You can take the driver's test again, and we'll just take it nice and easy. I'm booked up for the next couple of weeks, but I'll schedule you in around the first part of next month. In the meantime, you can be practicing your driving skills when you're with your parents. How does that sound?" Elaine felt better, hearing those words. Teachers are human, after all, she thought.

She poured out her feelings in her next letter to Jeff, about driving and about school. She also told him about two activities that would take place during his visit in April, the first being the Sadie Hawkins

Dance. Another event was the annual Firemen's Barbecue, a tradition that had been part of Ellington for the past 12 years. She was excited that Jeff would be able to attend both these events with her. Now if she could just get through the next two weeks.

*   *   *

By the end of the month, Beth was the proud owner of her long—awaited driver's license. She celebrated her sixteenth birthday with a trip to the roller skating rink in Armedia, taking Elaine Nat, and Lucy with her. Her parents had more than one car, so they were allowing Beth to drive the 54 Nash Rambler. All four girls were delighted with their new found freedom, although Elaine had received a few warnings from her parents before she left.

"Don't be distracting the driver," Charles told her. "This will be a new experience for Beth, and she'll need to keep her eyes on the road, and her mind on her driving. The way you girls are always talking can be distracting at times."

"I just hope she's a good driver," Lois remarked. "Seems like I'm always reading in the paper about teen agers getting in auto accidents."

"Oh, she'll be fine," Elaine stated. "I've ridden with her before when she was driving, and Jack was in the car. He didn't make her all nervous, like you've made me, Dad, when I've driven. After that fiasco at school, I don't know when I'll ever get my license."

"Don't let that bother you so much," Lois said comfortingly. "You'll get your license when the time is right. You just have to stop worrying about it."

The roller rink was very busy that Friday night. The girls skated for a while and then went over to the snack bar to hang out. Ty was there, since Nat had told him she would be coming. Woody and Lenny were there. Megan was there with Willie.

"This joint is jumping tonight," Woody was saying.

"Yeah, isn't it great?" Elaine asked. "Now that it's getting warmer, I think everyone wanted to get out on a Friday night. Beth drove all of us up here tonight. Now that she has her license, we won't always be stuck out in Ellington so often."

"Yeah, that's cool," Woody said.

"When are you going to get your license?" Lenny asked. Everyone at school had heard about her driver's test. It was most humiliating.

"I have no idea," Elaine said. "Maybe never. I'll just tag along with friends who have theirs."

"Friends who have what?" Lucy asked, joining the group. She opened a bag of Fritos for everyone to share, setting it out on the table.

"Who are those two guys with Beth?" Nat asked, as she and Ty joined them. Elaine squinted and looked across to the other side of the skating rink.

"I think that's Paul Newberry. The other guy looks familiar, but I can't quite make him out."

"That's Duane Kellogg," Woody told them. "He was a senior at school here last year, but he's been out of town for a while. I think he was in Bakersfield."

"Oh, yeah, I remember him now," Elaine said. "Vicki and I were carrying their books around on Initiation Day. We were just scared little Freshmen back then."

"And to think, we'll be Juniors pretty soon. It doesn't seem possible," Lucy remarked. Just then Couples Skating was announced, and Woody pulled Lucy out onto the floor, while Lenny and Elaine skated together. It turned out to be a fun evening.

On the way home, Beth casually remarked that she had a date with Paul Newberry for the next evening. "I'm looking forward to it. He is soo good looking and fun to be around too."

"Well, that's interesting," Nat said. "I remember when he and Vicki were going steady not that long ago."

"I don't think it will matter to her now," Lucy said. "At least I hope not."

"It's just that we have such a small school, there aren't enough guys to go around," Elaine laughed. "No matter who you go out with, it's probably someone who has dated one of your friends before. That's why I'm playing it safe."

"With Jeff, you don't have to worry about that, Elaine. We can all be sure that he hasn't dated any of your friends before," Beth told her, as they pulled into Elaine's driveway. "There, you made it home all safe and sound, and I didn't get us in a wreck, so your parents can rest easy now."

Chapter 25

"This is the first time I've spent the night over at your house in months," Elaine was telling Natalie, as the two girls stood at the sink, washing and drying the dishes. Cheryl, was busily dusting in the living room while their mom was upstairs working in her studio.

"That's true. I think it was before I got busted for going out with Ty to the dance, when I was just supposed to be staying at your house."

"That's right. I guess your folks finally relented, huh?"

"Oh, there's been plenty going on around here," Nat confided. "My dad hasn't been at home hardly at all in the last two or three months. You can't tell anyone this, but I'm thinking he may be seeing another woman."

"Oh, no! I hope not!"

"I don't know for sure, but it's just little bits and pieces of information that I hear when he is home. And my mom seems different somehow. It's like she's making more decisions on her own now. And that is good because she's much more lenient than my dad."

"It does seem that your life has been more normal lately," Elaine told her.

"Oh it has for sure. Everything has been so much better," Nat said emphatically. "In fact I think my mom is even relenting about my going out with Ty. When I asked her about the Sadie Hawkins Dance, and going with Ty, she said she'd think about it. Both Cheryl and I are really trying to help out around the house right now, since I know she's been very upset about what ever's been going on between her and my dad."

They talked and talked long into the night about Ty and Jeff.

Jeff arrived in Ellington promptly at 7:00 on the following Friday. He was proudly driving his father's 58 Ford. He and Elaine spent the evening at Chuck and Cathy's for another round of Monopoly. "I ditched my last two classes at school today," Jeff told her, "so that I could get all ready for this weekend."

"You ditched?" Elaine asked. "I could never get away with something like that. Our school is very strict about ditching or cutting classes."

"Oh, we can get away with anything at school. Of course it helps if you're on the football team," Jeff said proudly. "I ditch every now and then. A bunch of us guys are always taking off and going somewhere."

"Sounds like my high school days," Chuck reminisced. "Always seeing how much I could get away with."

"Did you bring your straw hat for the dance?" Elaine asked.

"You bet. And a pair of old jeans."

"I don't know about this Sadie Hawkins dance," Chuck said. "It's the kind of dance you have to watch out for, Jeff. The girls will be chasing the boys all over the place."

"Oh, he'll be safe with me," Elaine assured him.

"Hey, it sounds like a lot of fun," Cathy remarked. "Oh, to be in high school again."

Elaine was wishing that Jeff went to her high school. She knew he would be very popular with his good looks and his winning personality. And she would be so proud to be his girl. Then they could be together constantly. He would walk her to class, eat lunch with her on the lawn, sit with her on the school bus, or take her to school. They could study together on school nights, and go out every Friday and Saturday night. When he was in Ellington, the weekends went by all too fast, and the weeks were very slow. How she hated the long separations.

"Well, I think we'll call it a night, I'm falling asleep in this game," Chuck said, noticing that it was nearly 11:00. "Shall we all drive Elaine home?"

"I will take her home ALONE, if you don't mind," Jeff said firmly.

"You two behave now," was Chuck's parting shot.

Elaine was wondering if he was going to kiss her that night, since that hadn't happened yet.

"What should we do tomorrow?" Jeff was asking. "How's the beach at this time of year, and how long a drive is it?"

"It should be nice at the beach," she told him. "It's maybe about an hour's drive. The beach would be really nice, but I'll need time to make some sandwiches for the dance when we get back home."

"Okay, we won't stay too long." They sat in the car in silence, and then Jeff opened the door. I'd better get you in," he said, "before your dad comes out here with a shotgun."

"Oh, he likes you," she told him. She felt like telling him that her parents didn't care if she sat out in the car with him for a short while and that she didn't feel like going in just yet. But she slid out of the car and they walked slowly up to the front porch. Jeff squeezed her hand and told her he'd be over at 9:00 for the beach. "Bright and early," he said.

Elaine was puzzled as she walked into the house. His letters were always full of love for her. But why didn't he tell her in person? Why didn't he fold her into his arms and kiss her? He seemed very bashful at times, especially when he was alone with her. She was sure that he wasn't interested in any other girl. He didn't seem to be a "Casanova." He didn't use a smooth, easy line on her that came naturally to some boys, like Danny. His letters weren't the polished letters of guys who made a hobby of corresponding with a number of girls. They were simple and sincere. She decided that Jeff was just bashful and that he would kiss her when he got around to it. She just hoped that wouldn't be too long.

Upon awakening the next morning, Elaine saw that it was a dark, dreary day, and rain was coming down. No trip to the beach today, she thought. Jeff came over at 9:00 anyhow, and together they made sandwiches that she would be taking to the dance. Then they drove on up to Armedia to help with the decorations, and getting the Women's Clubhouse set up for later that night. (They hadn't been able to use the gym at school.) It was fun introducing him to Megan, Vicki, and Karen, who were also helping decorate. Willie was there too, and he and Jeff moved the bales of hay into place, taking orders from Megan.

Later that evening she was dressing with anticipation for the dance. The Sadie Hawkins dance was much easier to get ready for than a semi-formal dance, she thought. She was wearing faded Levis, a red checked shirt, and her straw hat. Her hair was fixed in two pony tails tied with red ribbon. She used eyebrow pencil to add freckles to her face.

"You look really cute," Pam said admiringly. "I want to take a picture of you and Jeff when he gets here, okay?"

"Good idea. He should be here any minute."

"I really like Jeff," Pam stated. He's fun when it comes to games. If you ever get tired of him, just give him to me, okay?"

"All right," Elaine laughed. "Too bad he doesn't have a younger brother."

Lois was just getting off the phone with Sue Hathaway. "This rain may be a problem for getting the meat cooked in the pit for the barbecue tomorrow," she told the girls. "They'll be checking it tomorrow morning, early, and if it's not as done as it should be, they'll divide it up among all of us, and we'll finish cooking it at home. That should be interesting. Right now I've got to get my peppermint chiffon cake made, since I'm on the dessert committee."

The doorbell rang and Jeff was admitted. He was wearing old tennis shoes, Levis, and a sweatshirt with the sleeves cut off and frayed edges.

"Oh, you look neat," Elaine cried in admiration.

"Well, I wouldn't say neat," laughed Lois. "But very cute in that get-up." Russ and Charles looked up from their game of Chinese checkers and laughed at the couple. Pam snapped their picture, and then they were off in high spirits.

"I'm glad all my friends are getting to meet you this weekend," Elaine was saying. "I've told everyone about you." She moved over to the middle of the seat to sit right next to him.

"Well, I hope they aren't disappointed," Jeff said. He put one arm around her, since he could easily drive with just one hand. "I'm anxious for my friends to meet you. They keep asking when I'm going to bring you up to Desert Palms, but I'm afraid they might steal you away from me."

"That would never happen," She felt warm and good inside, all cuddled up close to him.

They reached Armedia and entered the country atmosphere of the dance. The dimly-lit hall had straw on the floor, the bales of hay in the corners, and a couple of old milk cans. Elaine was quite proud of their decorating job. Beth came over and introduced Paul Newberry to Jeff. All the girls in her group were there, and they all had dates. In fact the overall turnout was very good, in spite of the bad weather, and the girls knew the Collette's would have a nice sum to add to their treasury. Enthusiasm and high spirits were displayed by all. Most everyone danced to all the records, even the fast songs. The chaperones were all from Armedia, since the Ellington parents were busy getting ready for their town barbecue.

A group of black teens from the high school had formed a singing group, and they sang a couple of old favorites, *Earth Angel* and *In the Still of the Night.* The group was very good, and the couples all gathered around them listening to the romantic songs.

"Did you have fun tonight?" Elaine asked Jeff, when they pulled into her driveway.

"I always have fun when I'm with you," he answered.

"Me too, with you." she said breathlessly, turning toward him. Their faces were very close, and before they knew it, they were locked into a kiss. His arms were around her, holding her tightly. Elaine decided that the kiss was well worth waiting for.

The next morning was quite busy in Elaine's household. Lois had made her cake the previous night, but now she had beef in the oven that was getting cooked for the barbecue, since it didn't quite get done in the pit. Elaine went to church with her family, except for Charles who stayed at home to keep an eye on the barbecue meat. She met Jeff at church, and then they headed off to the barbecue after that. Everyone in town always showed up for the big event. Ladies in the Garden Club and the PTA made potato salad, baked beans, and coleslaw as side dishes, the 4-H Club sold drinks, and the Boy Scouts always sold desserts and had the flag ceremony. Usually everyone ate outside on long tables, but this year, with the damp weather, they were crowded inside the Fire Hall. Makeshift awnings were in place for the diners that didn't fit inside. People who had lived in Ellington, even for a short time, always came back to the barbecue. It was like a town reunion in some ways. In the afternoon there was a horse show, sponsored by the Ellington Valley Riders Club. The arena was a field that was adjacent to the Fire House. Beth was entered in several events: Trail Horse, Barrel Race and Keyhole Race. Elaine knew most of the kids who were participating.

"This is kind of fun to watch," Jeff said, as they watched the kids go through the paces with their horses. "How come you don't have a horse?"

"We just never have," Elaine told him. "Besides the chickens, my dad has raised calves, pigs, and goats, but we've never had any horses, and that doesn't bother me. As you saw last time you were down here, horses don't like me for some reason. Pam would really love to have one though. She's always asking Dad if we could get a horse, but the answer is always the same."

"I can sympathize with her," Jeff said. "When I was younger I used to bug my folks for a horse, but of course we didn't have a place for one anyhow. Now my goal is getting a car."

"Yeah, our priorities do change as we get older," Elaine noted. "I'm not even thinking about a car yet. I'll just be happy to get a driver's license."

"I don't like your Driver's Ed teacher," Jeff stated. "I think he gave you a complex about your driving. You can practice driving with me, when we leave here, if you want to."

On Monday the weather was clearing up and looking quite nice, but Jeff had to head back home in order be at his job at the hardware store on Tuesday. The rest of Easter Vacation passed quickly, even though Elaine was missing him. On Friday and Saturday there was work to be done at home, since Charles was building two new chicken pens. He usually had Pam and Elaine paint the lumber before he put the pens together. Elaine was painting Jeff's name on the two by fours before she painted over them.

"Dad sure likes this ugly old brown paint," Pam was complaining. "I think a different color would be so much better, don't you? It would make our job more fun too, with brighter colors."

"I agree. I think a bright spring green would be nice," Elaine suggested. "Or how about some pastels? With Easter coming up, a pale pink or a soft yellow would look really nice."

"That would definitely be an improvement. By the way, speaking of Easter, who do you think could have put the Easter eggs in the nests? That was really a kick."

The day before, when they were doing the egg collecting, several of the nests had colored, gaily decorated eggs mixed in with the fresh eggs from the chickens. In the last nest, in the last row of chickens pens was a scribbled note, which read "Not your father, not your mother, not your sister, not your brother, but the EASTER BUNNY!!"

"I have no idea," Elaine told her. "The writing on the note doesn't look familiar at all. I don't think it was Lucy, or Beth or Natalie. Maybe some of your friends?"

"Do you think it could have been DJ," Charles asked, stopping by to see just what the girls had accomplished. "He likes practical jokes, doesn't he?"

"He's a possibility," Elaine said. "I haven't seen him since we found the eggs, but I'm not even going to bring it up to him, because of course he'll deny it. If we don't say anything to anyone, whoever played the trick will have to ask about it at some point."

"That's true," said Pam, "but I've already called a few of my friends about it. And I think they're innocent."

Russ came riding up on the electric feed cart. He and Charles were picking up the painted lumber that was already dry. Russ had his camera with him, and snapped a picture of the girls hard at work. He usually kept his camera close at hand. It was hard for Elaine to believe that he would be entering high school in the fall. He was studying for his Constitution test, which was required for graduation from elementary school. Unlike Elaine, he was not longing to start a new phase of life, although he was glad to be getting out of eighth grade.

Elaine had a hard time understanding her brother though. When she was going into high school, she had that drive to be well-known, to be a participant in many activities. But Russ wasn't going out for any sport, although he had played on some of the grammar school teams. He wasn't planning to play in the band, although he was very good on the clarinet. He was quiet, girl-shy, and calmly sure that he wouldn't be an athlete or be popular in high school. But he didn't mind. He was more interested in photography and stamp collecting. Elaine hoped his attitude would change. She thought her brother was becoming good looking. His freckles were fading out, his hair was cut in the popular flattop, and his glasses gave him a studious look. He was getting taller too, and already towered two inches above Elaine.

Pam will probably be more like me, Elaine thought, except she's much more athletic than I am. She was short for her age, but rugged and wiry. She was the youngest player on the girls softball team, the only sixth grader, and she was one of their top players. She usually pitched. She was also a fast runner, and she excelled when their school had their annual "Play Day," an event where students competed in different athletic games and relays. Like Russ, she was into photography, and had an album full of snapshots.

"Hey, quit daydreaming," Pam said to Elaine. "You're slowing down at your painting. Look, I've got more painted boards in my stack than you do. I bet you're thinking about Jeff."

"No, not really. I've better get busy and catch up to you though."

"Did you know that I have a boyfriend too? It's Billy Hathaway. He has my name written on his baseball glove and he usually sits with me at lunch. But I can run faster than he can. I'll be so glad when school starts up again," Pam continued. "We're playing baseball with High Bluffs, and we're going to beat them so bad."

Elaine wasn't exactly looking forward to school again, but she knew it would come soon enough. And Mr. Gorton, true to his word, had Elaine take the driver's test again. It had helped when she had practiced with Jeff that afternoon after the barbecue. This time she was much calmer and her reactions were much better, and she did well. "Now all you have to do is go to the DMV and take your test, and you'll have your license," Mr. Gorton told her.

"Yes, I'll be sixteen in May, so I'm looking forward to that," Elaine replied.

Spring was definitely in the air. The hills and fields were beginning to turn green, and some of the trees were getting their leaves. The burnt area in the foothills above Armedia was even looking green. Lake Armedia, however was still very low. There just hadn't been enough rain that winter to fill it up. The students were restless because of the warm Spring days. Romance blossomed in the classrooms, in the halls, and on the front lawn. Absences from school were more frequent, since the southern California beaches were very pleasant and warm in April, and much more exciting than the monotony of the classroom.

The sophomore class rings had arrived, and that was an exciting time. The rings were of ten carat gold and were very handsome. The class numeral, 1961, was on one side, and the initials of each individual were on the other side, and the school initials, AHS, were in the middle. Elaine had had to save her allowance for a six weeks to buy the ring, (it was the hefty price of 15.00) and she wore it proudly.

Mrs. Teague had planned a field trip for her English classes to the Huntington Library and Museum in the Pasadena area. Besides being educational, the trip would be an unforgettable experience for the students to see the authentic letters of George Washington, Abraham Lincoln and others. They would also be seeing many original paintings. The rest of the school looked on with envy as the group boarded the buses one sunny morning. The drive would take about two hours.

By 11:00 they were reaching the outskirts of their destination and everyone begin to dig into their sack lunches that they were advised to bring. Elaine was happy that she'd thought ahead and brought a can of soda and even remembered the little opener, or the "church key" which was slang for the opener. The coke, even a bit on the warm side, would taste good with her bologna and cheese sandwich. But when she opened it she got a big surprise. It must have been shaken up for it exploded in a huge spray, hitting the bus ceiling, and raining back down on her, making everything a big sticky mess. Of course the exploding coke caused an explosion of laughter from her peers. "Oh, my gosh!" cried Lucy, who was sitting next to her, but trying to move away. "What did you do?" Sticky soda was dripping everywhere.

"Bombs away!" called Lenny, from across the aisle.

"Hey, it's raining soda," Greg remarked. "Watch out for Elaine, she's dangerous."

Elaine didn't have much to say. She was too mad, and feeling too sticky. She couldn't very well clean everything up with her one little napkin, and she knew her hair and her clothes would feel sticky for the rest of the day. She was glad Mrs.Teague and Mrs.Coyne were sitting up at the front of the bus, since she was close to the back. Now her sandwich would be really dry without anything to drink. Why did she always have to suffer so much humiliation?

The bus had reached San Marino, the city where the museum was located, and the students were amazed at the beauty and the austerity of the large homes and estates on either side of them. The huge lawns, stately trees, and trimmed hedges surrounding the mansions, were manicured to perfection, and made the occupants of the bus feel rather underprivileged.

The bus reached the grounds of the Huntington Library, and the group kept their dignity in getting off. They planned to remain calm, cool, and collected during their day, knowing they couldn't possibly be their usual silly and undignified selves in a place like this. Besides Mrs. Teague would have their hides if they got out of line. Two elaborate white buildings of wood and marble looked very impressive set in the midst of beautiful gardens. The gardens were complete with hedges, sycamore and fir trees, roses, lilies and trumpet vines. Magnificent iron statues of Diana and Apollo looked down upon the group as they entered the quiet building.

A guard (guards were watching them constantly) showed them into a large room filled with letters, manuscripts, and books in glass cases. Original paintings of Washington, Jefferson, Franklin, and others adorned the walls. There was a huge Gutenberg Bible written in Latin, the original King James Bible, a first edition written in 1611, and John Eliot's Indian Bible. There was a letter written by Columbus' secretary, with notes in the handwriting of Christopher Columbus, listing the privileges the king and queen of Spain had given him for his discoveries. Another letter was written by King George III explaining that he was not responsible for granting independence to the American Colonies. There were manuscripts of two of Elaine's favorite authors, Robert Burns and Edgar Allan Poe. She stood gazing at the neat handwriting of Poe's *Annabelle Lee*, thinking how romantic the verse sounded: *It was many and many a year ago in a Kingdom by the sea.*

"Wake up, Dreamer," Natalie whispered loudly. "Maybe someday your poetry will be treasured here, in one of these glass cases you just never know." They both laughed, forget-ting the rule to keep quiet, and went on to the next room, which was devoted to writings and pictures of Abraham Lincoln. Other rooms held exquisitely carved statues of stone and marble, and cedar chests which held the dowries of long-ago maidens. Some of the rooms displayed beautiful tapestries, dating back to the 1700's.

They left the library and crossed a velvety lawn and a huge patio to the Huntington House which, in the girls' opinion, proved to be even more fabulous than the museum. Mrs.Teague had explained to the class how the late Henry Huntington and his wife had started the collection of authentic manuscripts, letters, and paintings in the early 1900's. The living room of the house was filled with 18th century furniture, Chippendale and Sheraton. There was also a drawing room and a library with over 1,000 books. Sets of old China and porcelain dishes featuring exquisite and colorful designs were in glass cases.

"Just think how carefully these designs were hand painted on," one tourist lady exclaimed. "Now some machine puts designs on all our dishes."

The girls climbed a very wide, carpeted staircase to the gallery where the paintings were hung. Hanging over the staircase rail were gorgeous, colorful tapestries. The painting gallery featured Thomas Gainsborough's *Blue Boy*, Sir Thomas Lawrence's *Pinkie*, the beautiful little Miss Sarah Moulten-Barret posing. *The Tragic Muse* fascinated the girls, although they couldn't figure out why. *The Duke of Ellington* also held their interest. His eyes seemed to follow them about the room.

Their tour of the house completed, the girls sat down to rest on the carpeted stairway.

"How would you like to live in a place like this?" Elaine asked.

"I can just see myself floating down this stairway in a billowing gown," Megan said dreamily.

"And then there's my goofy brother waiting for you at the bottom of the stairs in his old jeans and t-shirt, his pack of cigarettes rolled up in the sleeve," laughed Vicki.

They got up and went outside to tour the three gardens, a Japanese Garden, a Cactus Garden, and a Rose Garden. They went to the Japanese Garden first. The garden, which was once an unattractive canyon with a dam for irrigation, covered five acres. The girls walked down a narrow path which wound between huge vines, to a tiny Oriental building holding a huge gong which made an eerie sound when rung. An orange moon bridge overhung with willow trees crossed a small stream. At the Oriental House and Shrine they met Woody, DJ, and Lenny examining the stone lanterns.

"Careful, don't touch anything," Beth laughingly warned.

"This is the first thing I've been able to touch all day," stated Woody. "I haven't seen any guards for five whole minutes. They're probably hiding in the trees and bushes, and I wouldn't be at all surprised if one jumped out at any time."

They had just enough time to tour the other two gardens, before they had to go back to the bus. They were full of talk and laughter, and some clowning around on the ride home, after their model behavior at the museum. The most talked about subject was the school elections, which would be taking place in the next few weeks.

Chapter 26

The Student Council Nomination Assembly was held the first Monday in May. Almost all of Elaine's friends were running for something. Vicki and Megan were trying out for a varsity cheerleading position, and Alma and Karen were hoping to be part of the Song Leader group. Both Lucy and Mary Lou Wright were running for Student Council Secretary. Greg was running for Student Council VP, and Lenny was running for Junior Class President. The Nomination Assembly was long and drawn out, as many students were nominated, some from petitions and some from the floor.

Later that day in the Library, Elaine asked Megan about the office of yearbook editor. "That's what I'm most interested in," she told Megan, "but I didn't hear anything about it at the assembly."

"That's not an elected office," Megan explained. "If you want to run, you have to sign up, and then give a speech to the Student Council. They choose from the applicants, and then that person becomes assistant editor for their junior year, and becomes editor in their senior year. I'm planning to run for that, and so is Mary Lou Wright. But you should run too, if you're interested."

"I think I just might do that," Elaine said. "But you know how I am about speeches." During her quiet time in the library, Elaine picked up her pen and wrote a full page speech about a school yearbook. She was full of ideas, and she knew her talent for writing would be an asset to the editor's job. But the more she thought about, the more she talked herself out of it, since the idea of a speech was just too overwhelming. With resignation, she stuck her speech into the back of her notebook, and began to work on campaign posters. She had promised her cousin Scott that she would be his campaign manager, since he was running for Sophomore Class VP.

By the middle of the week school buildings were almost covered with campaign posters, large and colorful. Each campaign manager tried to outdo the other on the originality of the posters. Some were 20 feet long, stretching across a big section of the building. Others had been placed on the side of the three-story main building, above the third story windows, leaving people to wonder how someone had possibly managed to get them up that high. The gym walls were almost completely covered, and the cafeteria had its share too. Some of the candidates got very original and handed out homemade campaign buttons.

Later that day Elaine was sitting in English class, when suddenly Mrs. Teague's words hit her. The teacher had been reading from a book of quotations: *You may be disappointed if you fail, but you are doomed if you don't try.* What a dope I've been, Elaine thought. I've been so afraid of failure, that I haven't been willing to give anything a try. Maybe I'm not good at speeches, but I could at least try for the yearbook position.

The next day at her first opportunity, she sought out the current annual editor to sign up for tryouts. She wrote Elaine's name down with the other applicants and said "You made it just in time because try-outs are today in the Student Council Room at 2:00."

"But I thought they were a week from today. My speech isn't ready."

"The older girl laughed. "It seems that everybody got the dates mixed up. Don't worry about giving a long, memorized speech. Just tell in a few words why you want to be assistant annual editor. See you there."

Elaine went to tell her friends, who were outside the cafeteria at the mid-morning break.

"Oh, no, I don't know where I heard that it was next week," Mary Lou groaned. "My speech isn't ready."

"Did you know my brother is running too?" Alma asked them.

"Noo!" said Megan. "With his straight A average and all his talent for photography, he'll be a shoo-in. The rest of us might as well bow out."

The hours seemed to crawl by that day. Every time Elaine thought about giving her speech, her knees began to shake in the old familiar way. She couldn't eat lunch because of the butterflies in her stomach. "She must be nervous," Lucy exclaimed at lunch. "I never thought I'd see the day when Elaine went without a meal!"

At last 2:00 rolled around. The contestants were sitting nervously in the Student Council room, waiting for the council to finish their discussion of the merits of a life-time pass to all the school sporting events for a deserving person in the community. Finally the president cleared his throat, stood up, and announced that they would be choosing an assistant annual editor for the next year. "We'd like to hear from each applicant on why they want this position," he said. Since Mary Lou was sitting on the end, he suggested that she go first.

The talks went quickly and soon Elaine found herself, with clammy hands and shaky knees, at the front of the room. Her mouth was dry and she was afraid she wouldn't be able to open it to say a word. But at last she started in a clear and sincere voice with "The word, 'annual' means a literary work published once a year. To me, and to the school, this word should have much more meaning. An annual is the personality of a school." She went on, talking about school spirit, and concluded with . . . . "And that is why I want to be the editor of our school yearbook someday in the future. I want to be able to help create something that will show everyone the personality of our school, a book of memories that will be something the students of AHS can treasure for years to come!" She sat down with a relieved sigh. She was positive she had failed to get her point across, but she had a feeling of confidence that the right person would be chosen. The last contestant finished, and the six left the room while the council voted.

"Well, I am so glad that's over," Lenny remarked to the quiet group. "Giving speeches is not a fun thing to do." Elaine was surprised to hear him say that. He always seemed so confident and full of poise.

"But you're running for our class president for next year," she told him. "If you're president, you'll have to speak all the time."

"Oh, yeah, I know, but that won't be so bad, and I'll get used to it over time."

A few moments later, they were summoned back into the room. Not a word was spoken as they entered. Suddenly the council president said without preamble, "Our next year's annual assistant is Elaine Hummer." Her mouth dropped open and her heart seemed to suddenly stop. She was sure she had misunderstood. But everyone was looking at her and smiling their congratulations. Megan was saying, "Way to go, Elaine! I'm so happy you got it. Well, say something, Elaine!"

For Elaine, near tears, was temporarily tongue-tied. SHE was assistant annual editor. She smiled a quick thank you to the group, and they were dismissed to go back to their classes. As they left the room, she told the other five that they should all be on the yearbook staff together, and that they would be putting out the best yearbook ever.

"Your speech was really good, Elaine," Megan told her later. "You didn't seem nervous at all. And you sounded so sincere. I know you'll do a wonderful job. I hope you'll let me be your business manager."

"That job is yours," Elaine promised.

Elaine's sixteenth birthday was in the middle of May. If Jeff had been able to be with her, the occasion would have been perfect. However, he sent her a gift that made her very happy, a pearl on a ten carat gold chain with a card that said, "To Elaine, the girl I will always love." What more could she ask for? To celebrate, she went to the movies with Lucy, who had just obtained her license. She was on Cloud Nine that weekend, in love, and thrilled with her upcoming job at school.

School elections were held the following Tuesday. The next day was filled with suspense, and at last the students filed excitedly out to the bleachers to hear the results. Elaine was happy that most of her friends had won their nominations. Megan had been made head cheerleader, to no one's surprise. Woody had run against Alvin Minegar for Boys Representative, and had won with ease, even though he didn't have near the amount of publicity signs that Alvin had put out. Mary Lou had won over Lucy for Student Council Secretary. Elaine was very happy for Scottie for winning the VP spot for the Sophomore class for next year. She wouldn't have traded places with anyone though. She was daydreaming again, thinking of the wonderful annual she would be editing in their senior year.

So engrossed was Elaine that she almost missed the question that Mrs. Jenson was asking in Home Ec class. They had been studying boy-girl relationships, which was a most interesting subject. Their teacher had asked each girl to write ten questions concerning the subject, and then the questions would be discussed in class. Mrs. Jenson smiled slyly as she put the next question out to the glass. "How does one know if it's really love? Very good question and one that has been plaguing people for years. Does anyone want to attempt to answer that one?"

Without thinking, Elaine raised her hand. "Well, I would say that love only takes place after quite a long time period of liking someone. It shouldn't have anything to do with looks, or popularity, or money. It's caring for someone because of their personality, or the type of person they are. It's loving him regardless of obstacles that come along, such as being at different schools and having to deal with long separations . . . ." She stopped suddenly as Megan started giggling. So did Vicki and Beth. Elaine was embarrassed, realizing that she had put her feelings for Jeff into words. But she laughed too, and even Mrs. Jenson was chuckling.

"That's a very astute answer," she commended Elaine. "However, I think in high school, most of you are attracted right away because of a person's looks, or maybe their status in school. In many cases it seems to be love at first sight, and that usually doesn't work out into a long term relationship. There are so many other things that factor in."

"Well, I definitely fell for Willie at first sight," Megan spoke up. "And we're still together two years later." After that, everyone in the class had something to say, and a long discussion followed.

Spanish class was calmer. The students were putting on plays in Spanish and recording them. It was interesting to hear someone's voice on tape, but Elaine didn't like hearing the sound of her own.

Sophomore Science class was fun for a change. They were studying First Aid and having each pupil demonstrate artificial respiration. Elaine felt sorry for DJ, the guinea pig. Since the semester was coming to a close, Mr. Sharpe announced another oral report assignment, much to everyone's dismay. Elaine figured, however, if she could give a good enough speech to make assistant annual editor, she could manage an oral report.

PE was enjoyable because they were doing dancing: folk dancing, modern dancing, and the contemporary dances like the Bop, Chicken, Cha-Cha-Cha, Calypso, and Stroll. It seemed that every girl in school enjoyed dancing.

Elaine saw Jeff one more time before school let out. He came to Ellington on Memorial Day weekend, and they made plans to go to the beach on Saturday. This time Jeff was the proud owner of a new car. "Well, it's new to me, anyhow," he explained to Elaine who was excited about it.

"It's a 1952 Studebaker sport coupe," Jeff said proudly. "It's got a good radio, and heater, and a 281 cubic inch engine with valve covers, and an intake manifold which houses a four-barrel carburetor."

"That sounds really great," Elaine told him, having no clue about the engine and the manifold. However, there was a problem under the hood the next day, and Jeff and Chuck worked on the car for two hours before they could leave for the beach. Chuck and Cathy had other plans for the day, so it was just Jeff and Elaine. Neither one could think of much to say, except for comments on the scenery and the songs on the radio. Elaine realized how quiet they always were with each other when no one else was along. The long silences bothered her. Sometimes she felt that she didn't know Jeff at all. What he was like when he was at school, she wondered. What is he really like?

Although the sun had shone brightly in Ellington, they found the beach cool and cloudy. They spread out a blanket, towels and suntan lotion on the sand. Jeff headed toward the water, but Elaine settled herself on the blanket, explaining that it was too cold for her. Another reason was that she didn't want to remove her beach jacket, since her last year's bathing suit was faded and out of shape. A cool breeze began to tangle her hair, and she wondered why they'd decided on the beach trip in the first place. There were lots of people around because of the holiday weekend, but not too many were in the water. Elaine noticed a few surfers in wetsuits, with their boards, down at one end of the beach.

Jeff came back shortly, dripping water all over her, and threatening to throw her in. "It's cold out there in that ocean!" he said. "I'm turning blue!" They lay on the beach for a while and then took a walk out to the end of the pier. The smell of the refreshing salt air mingled with French fries and hamburgers from the various snack bars, and with fish that were being hauled in out of the water by fishermen. The pier was fairly busy. Fishermen had lines thrown out into the ocean, their bait buckets surrounding them, and little kids, teen agers, and older people were milling around. It was interesting just to enjoy the sights and sounds and smells. After a greasy, but tasty lunch of hamburgers and fries, they got ready to leave. Since the weather was too cold for swimming, there wasn't that much to do.

"Let's go home a different way," suggested Jeff, turning north on Highway 1. To the south was Carlsbad, and San Diego, but they were headed towards the north beach cities, San Clemente, San Juan Capistrano, Newport Beach, Huntington Beach, Santa Monica, and Malibu. Of course they wouldn't be going that far. There was a turnoff at San Juan Capistrano, Highway 74 that took them over the mountains in the general direction of Armedia.

They started across the paved mountain highway which led through miles of dry brush, and then through blackened land. Elaine was telling Jeff about the fire in December. Scars from that horrible fire were prominent now, charcoaled trees and stumps, and piles of black debris. It looked like a gray moonscape. However, new life was trying to make an appearance. Green shoots of grass were pushing through the soot covered soil, and there were tiny leaves on some of the bushes that the fire had somehow missed.

"From the looks of the landscape, it must have been a really bad fire," Jeff noted. "Out in the desert, there's really nothing to burn, so we don't have to worry about fires."

Jeff was able to stay until Monday morning, and then he again had to make his way back to Desert Palms. And again Elaine was filled with sadness when he left. But this time she was excited about the coming of summer, and school getting out. She planned to keep busy with her writing, and was hoping to do some sewing also. Beth had said Elaine could bring her sewing over to her house any time, since she had a much more modern sewing machine with all the latest attachments.

Today it was warm out on the lawn with only a light breeze blowing. There were the combined scents of the pepper trees, orange blossoms, and the not-too-pleasant smell of the drying lakebed. A bee buzzed lazily around them. The lunches had long been disposed of, but the girls didn't have much energy for anything except talking.

"I can't believe how fast this year has zipped by," Karen remarked. "Seems like school just got started, then football games, dances, ..."

"Vicki's slumber party where we all got scared silly, the organizing of the Collette's, and the Turnabout Dance," added Elaine.

"That great basketball game where we beat Ralston and got our Victory Bell back, the sit-down strike, the Sadie Hawkins Dance, student elections, and now here we are with only a few days of school left," Beth finished off. Each girl sat daydreaming as they got quiet for a moment, listening to the slow, but stirring music of *Pomp and Circumstance*. The seniors were practicing their graduation march out by the bleachers on the football field.

"We're nearly halfway through high school," Karen stated. "In only two more years, we'll be marching up onto that platform ourselves."

"That's just hard to imagine," said Lucy. "The boys in our grade have a lot of growing up to do first. But I guess we all do though."

"I get so sad when I think of Ty graduating and leaving school," a tearful Natalie remarked.

"I know just how you feel," Megan added soberly. "It's breaking my heart."

"Well, both of you would feel much worse, if they'd flunked or something," Alma told them. But no one laughed at her attempt to lighten the mood.

"It's just sad to think of everybody going their own separate ways," Elaine mused, wiping her eyes. "We're all together as a class for a few years, we get very close, and then it's all over after graduation. I don't think I'll be dying to graduate and get out on my own like most seniors. I like high school too well."

"Hey, hey, no tears now," Vicki said, playfully punching her arm. "This group is getting way too somber! We've still got two years to go, and they're going to be the greatest yet! We definitely have to make the most of them!"

Report cards were issued the next day. To her great joy, Elaine received two A's and four B's. It was almost good enough to make the California Scholarship Federation. Almost, but not quite, and there is always next year, she thought.

The ninety plus seniors received their diplomas later that week on the outdoor stage that had been set up on the football field in front of the bleachers. After the speeches, awards were presented. Elaine had been proud of her senior friends. Ty Ramirez had received the award for Outstanding Athlete. Nat was elated. And no one was surprised when Willie Bannister got the award for Outstanding Senior Boy. Deserving students were the recipients of scholarships. The Alma Mater was sung by the seniors for the last time, and then their caps were thrown into the air with gusto.

The day after graduation was the last day of school forever for about half the class who weren't planning on attending college. Several of the senior girls were planning June weddings. The traditional Awards Assembly was drawn out as usual, since letters were given to every person who had gone out for any sport, awards were given to outstanding drama students (it seemed like all the drama students), etc. Elaine was proud of Woody when he received his varsity football letter. The CSF awards were given, and no one had any doubt as to who would receive the award in the sophomore class. Dean Caldwell smiled as he called both Greg Okamota and Woody Stuart to come forward for the honor. As he presented the award he said, "Both Greg and Woody have maintained an A average both the years that they've been here, and I'm proud to be presenting them with this award. I have a feeling that they will continue to keep their A average in their Junior and Senior years." Greg walked back to his place next to Karen, looking a bit self-conscious, but very happy, and Woody had a huge smile on his face. How they do it, Elaine wondered.

After the solemn ceremony was over, where each class moved up a section, the assembly was over, school was out, and students dashed to their lockers, to the parking lot, and to the buses.

Elaine was glad the Collette's had decided to have a beach party for the remainder of the day. The girls would be taking the trip over the mountains in the back of Willie's pick up. (Megan had had to do a good deal of sweet talking to get him to agree to that). The girls had changed into Bermuda shorts and tee shirts, and hurried out to the parking lot to pile into Willie's pick up. They were all talking at once, as usual. "Just think, we're Juniors now!" "We're upperclassmen!" "We'll be running the concession stand." "And putting on the Prom."

The girls spread blankets across the bottom of the pickup for comfort. Before taking off, Willie warned them not to stand up, or too make too much noise. "Though that may be impossible for you six," he added. "But the road over the mountain is full of switchbacks, and I certainly don't want to lose anyone," he joked. "And I promise I won't go faster than eighty miles per hour."

"I'll see that he doesn't go over fifty-five," Megan assured them, climbing into the front seat.

"Boy, am I henpecked or what?" Willie teased her. "And you'll have to do your best, Megan, to keep me awake, since I am kind of worn out from all the partying last night. But I can always nap when we get there."

Two of their group wasn't riding with them. Nat was going to the beach with Ty, and Karen was riding with Greg. But six was a good number for the pickup bed, since they weren't too crowded that way. "I was on this road with Jeff a couple of weeks ago," Elaine told her friends. "Except we were coming from the other way." As they climbed, they looked back at the panorama below them, the outline of the drying lake bed, the the darker brown of the olive and orange groves, and the lighter green of the various fields.

"That dry lake sticks out like a sore thumb," stated Mary Lou.

"It certainly does," Beth added. "Last year it was so nice and full and beautiful. Quite a view from here, though. We can see almost halfway to Ellington in one direction, and partway to Lasswood in the other."

"There's the lookout point where all the couples park," Vicki pointed out.

"Oh, so you've been up here lately to watch the submarine races?" Alma asked her.

"Not me," Vicki said innocently. "But do you know what I heard about last night, after the big Senior party?" And she went on to tell everyone the latest gossip.

"Is that right?" "That sounded pretty wild!" "Where did you hear all this?"

"From Willie. It's all over town by now. A big scandal," she added, proud to be the one to spread such a delectable tidbit of news.

After more gossip, the girls began singing school songs, their Alma Mater, and then gave their newly acquired Junior chant. Soon the salt smell of the ocean was in the air. Willie turned off the mountain highway onto Interstate 5, and went south toward San Clemente Beach. The landscape on the girls' left featured flower covered slopes going down to the sand. But soon their view was hidden by houses so close together that if one reached out his window, he could almost touch the stucco wall of the house next door. But being within spitting distance of the neighbors' house would be well worth living right next to the beach, the girls concluded. It took some time to find a parking spot, because many schools were getting out, and many teens had the same idea. The weather was warm and beautiful, unlike the last time Elaine had been at the beach. They had to walk a way to get down to the sand, and then there it was, the long line of Pacific Ocean stretched out endlessly before them.

The girls were carrying their beach bags, cameras, transistor radios, towels, blankets, and wearing straw hats. Armedia students seemed to be everywhere. Elaine saw Adam Irby with a girl she didn't know. DJ, Shawn, and Woody were body surfing, riding in the waves. Several seniors, exhausted from the previous night's activities, lay tiredly on the sand.

The Collette's found a spot for their beach towels and took off their shorts and shirts to reveal brightly colored swimsuits. They smeared on suntan lotion, since they were all hoping to get as much of a tan as possible in one day. The latest form of tanning lotion was baby oil mixed with iodine. They stretched out to bask in the warm sun and listen to their radios before going into the water. KFWB, a Los Angeles station, was always great for the latest songs. Sometimes they could get the station at home, but not always.

Vicki and Elaine went in the water after they had baked awhile in the sun. They found some seaweed and tied it around their waists, and added sprigs to their hair.

"Look, we have Seaweed Girls among us," said Woody and DJ, who were still riding the waves in.

"Let's take it off them," suggested Shawn. That started a scuffle that was rather fun, and they didn't notice a large breaker coming in, and were all momentarily dragged under. "Help, I'm half drowned," Vicki cried, squeezing saltwater from her bedraggled pony tail.

"That won't do you any good," DJ told her, ducking her under the wave. Then they all went out into the water as deep as they dared and rode the waves in. The girls were enjoying themselves when the three boys shared their rafts with them, but after an hour of saltwater, they felt like drowned rats and returned to the warm sand and their towels for snacks and a rest.

Elaine daydreamed as she lay in the sun. The breakers made a monotonous roar, almost lulling her to sleep. What a year it had been, with plenty of excitement, activity, flirting, love, and just plain fun. She decided that it would be good to slow down and kick back, and just take it easy this summer, before gearing up for her third year of high school.

Part III

Chapter 27

Bright moonlight shone into Elaine's bedroom that night in late June. She hadn't been sleeping very well anyhow. She had been extremely restless, tossing and turning. She shined the little flashlight that she kept by her bed onto the clock, which read 2:30 am. In the moonlight she could barely make out the familiar furniture. She got up quietly to close the blinds and block out the light that was coming into the room. But it wasn't just that light that was keeping her from sleeping. A lonely cow in Mr. Hobbs field across the street mooed dismally, and several dogs in the area howled at the moon. Elaine's thoughts, more than anything else, were keeping her up. She kicked off her solitary sheet and wiped her perspiring forehead, and walked silently out to the kitchen for a glass of water. She thought back to the dinner conversation with her family that evening.

Charles was explaining to the rest of the family that they probably wouldn't be taking a vacation that summer, since the family finances were a little short. He also told them that the water pressure and output from the well wasn't enough, and that their well would have to be deepened at some point in the coming months, and that would be an unexpected expense. Elaine didn't especially mind not going on a family vacation, but she got a bit worried when her father started talking about money. She was also thinking that it might be a very dull summer. She had missed the deadline for sending paperwork in for MYF camp, but that didn't bother her too much either. She hadn't really saved any money for it, since she had bought her class ring instead, and also had to have a new bathing suit. Camp was already over, and Scottie had attended, along with a few others from their

youth group, but Beth and Lucy hadn't gone either. Scottie told her
that he'd had a wonderful time. He'd also mentioned that Danny
had asked about her, but then he'd had another girlfriend during the
week of camp. Her three cabin mates from last year, Dottie, Sandy,
and Moe, were there again, and Elaine was sorry to have missed them.
Scott had told her that Dottie was just as crazy as ever.

Another thought running through her mind was that Chuck and
Cathy were holding a Family Reunion that weekend for the Graham
family, so she would be seeing Jeff. She was excited about seeing Jeff,
but nervous about meeting the rest of his family. From what she was
hearing, they had quite a large family and they could be really loud,
but very enjoyable. She had spent the day over at the parsonage
helping Cathy make potato and macaroni salad, and also helped
with the vacuuming and dusting. Cathy was so involved with church
activities, like the MYF group, the choir, and the Ladies Aid Society,
that she didn't always have much time to keep the house tidy. Elaine
finally fell back asleep, dreaming that the Graham reunion was held at
the Hummer chicken ranch, and that together, they'd all helped dig a
new well right in the middle of the living room.

Elaine was ready when Jeff arrived at her house the next morning.
She was wearing a pair of new green print pedal pushers she had made
(with Beth's help) just the week before, and a plain green top. "Well
are you prepared to meet my crazy family?" Jeff asked her as she slid
into the car, carrying one of her mother's peppermint chiffon cakes.

"I hope so. Between you and Chuck and Cathy, I've heard enough
about them. I'm not good about remembering names, though."

"That's okay. You can just say 'hey you.' One of the sayings in
our family is, call me whatever you want, just don't call me late to
dinner."

"Oh, that's a good one," Elaine laughed. "You're driving a different
car? Where is your Studebaker?"

"Oh, we all came down here in the family car," he stated. "My car
needs some work done on it, and also new tires before I drive it down
here again. I rode down here with my mom and stepdad, and I'll ride
back with my dad and stepmom. Keep everyone happy that way."

"I'm surprised that both your mom and your dad will be at this
reunion," Elaine told him. "And they've both remarried, and everyone
gets along okay?"

"They seem to," Jeff answered. "which is lucky for me. My mom and
stepdad, have a boy and girl, so I have a half brother and sister, and
my dad and Louise have one boy, so I have another halfbrother there.
Well, here we are." he added, pulling up behind a few other cars.

Since it was still early in the day, everyone hadn't arrived yet, but it already seemed to Elaine like a very large group, much larger than her family get-togethers at Christmas. During the next couple of hours she met Ellie and Roger, Jeff's mom and stepdad, and their two younger children, Dougie and Dani, and Kenny and Louise, Jeff's dad and stepmom. Jeff's grandparents (Chuck's parents) were there also, Windy and Beryl. "Windy's not his real name," Jeff explained to her, "but he talks a lot, so that's why the nickname." Then there were Chuck's two sisters, (Jeff's aunts) Judy and Patsy. There was also a large assortment of youngsters, playing tag. Elaine thought Jeff's little six year old freckle faced sister was adorable. "My real name is Danielle, and my older brother's name is Douglas," she explained very seriously to Elaine, "and you can call me Dani. But you have to call my brother Doug, 'cause he thinks Dougie is a baby name, now that he's ten, and he really doesn't like to be called Douglas either."

"I'll try to remember that," Elaine told her solemnly, as Dani, shrieking delightedly, ran off from a boy who seemed to be chasing her.

There were a few in the family who really stood out. One was Jeff's great grandmother, who was a delightful little lady, very spry, spunky, and friendly. She gave Elaine a huge hug when introduced, and had plenty to say to her, which made Elaine feel quite welcome. "Why, you're just as cute as you can be," she stated. "I am so glad that Jeff has met you, and he's told me so much about you. He said that you're a farm girl. I was raised on a farm too, only it was back in Georgia. I spent most of my life back there. It was a big change when I came out here to live, out in the desert." Her smile warmed Elaine's heart.

"Othermama is a very special lady," Jeff told her.

"What do you call her?" Elaine asked.

"My real name is Pearl, but the little ones have been calling me Othermama for years now."

"She has a boyfriend with a Harley motorcycle," Jeff told Elaine, "and she goes riding around our town on the back of it, hanging on for dear life. She has a wild side to her."

"Now, Honey, you're telling all my secrets," Othermama chided. "Wait till I get to know this young lady a bit better, before you go telling her everything."

"I see you're getting to know my grandma," Chuck said to Elaine as he walked by carrying a large platter of hamburger patties. "I'm going to get these on the grill, and with Uncle Fred doing the barbecuing, we should be eating pretty soon."

The June day was beautiful, warm and balmy with just a slight breeze. Long tables from the church social hall had been set up in the back yard of the parsonage. Jeff and Elaine began setting folding chairs around the tables. The burgers were ready shortly, and everyone gathered around for the blessing, and then began digging into the food. There were side dishes of baked beans, coleslaw, ambrosia salad, carrot and raisin salad, three bean salad, just to mention a few. Othermama insisted that Elaine try some pickled okra. "They grow okra back in the south," she explained. "We pickle it and can it, and I got this when I was back there visiting my sister, Opal."

Elaine wasn't sure she liked the green vegetable, but she wasn't about to say anything of course. She was sure she had never seen so much food all in one place. A picnic table on the side of the house was laden down with all the desserts, but Elaine was way too full to even think about dessert.

"Who made all those great big layer cakes?" she asked Jeff.

"Othermama makes those every year," Jeff told her. "They're German chocolate cakes, and she makes four of them, and they are my favorite."

"I don't think I've ever had that kind of cake before," Elaine said. "But why so many?"

"They are everyone's favorite. And also we have a custom in this family. She makes three for us to eat here, and one for someone to steal. Every year, someone sneaks the cake away, and hides it somewhere til time to leave. Last year my Aunt Patsy and Uncle Dan had it hidden in their car, but they didn't lock the car, so someone else stole it from them. I forgot who ended up with it. It gets really crazy sometimes. They're cutting it now, and I'll go get us a piece." Even though she didn't think she could eat another bite, Elaine tried the cake and found it absolutely delicious. The coconut frosting was spread thickly between each layer.

After the meal, there was volleyball for the younger, more energetic members of the family, and cards or board games for those wanting a quieter activity. Charles and Lois came by for a little while, since they wanted to meet members of Chuck's family. After the volleyball game, Uncle Fred was trying to get some teams together to play horseshoes, but the consensus was to wait till the weather cooled off a bit. Elaine was enjoying just sitting in the cool shade of the umbrella trees. "Your Uncle Fred seems like a real character," she told Jeff.

"He is definitely that, and he can be quite a practical joker too. When I was about six, he came over to visit us, and he always took us kids out for ice cream. He asked me if I had a girlfriend, and I said I did. Well, he asked where she lived, and I told him, and he drove to her house and pulled up in the driveway, and told me to go knock on the door and ask her to go with us. I mean, I was only six, and I liked this girl, but, heck, she didn't know that. I was all worried about it, and was so relieved when no one was at home. I could go on and on telling you stories about him. He's my favorite uncle, besides Chuck of course."

"Your uncle likes his beer," Elaine said, noticing that Uncle Fred always had a bottle in his hand. "Does that bother Chuck, being a minister, to have people here drinking?"

"I don't think so," Jeff told her. "Chuck doesn't drink, but I don't think he cares if others here do, unless everyone got really rowdy. Of course, there are plenty of rowdy people here, who don't even drink. That's just my family."

"Well, they're a pretty friendly, fun family," Elaine told him with approval. "In comparison, my relatives seem fairly quiet."

On Sunday afternoon, when Jeff left, he told Elaine he didn't know when he would be coming down again, since his car needed work, and now that school was out, he would be working longer hours in the hardware store. "Of course longer hours are good because that means more money, and the sooner I can get what I need for the car," he stated.

"That's okay. I know you'll be down here again whenever you can," she said, as they kissed goodbye. It wasn't easy watching him drive down the driveway.

When Elaine went back into her house, Lois reminded her that she had a dentist appoint-mint in Armedia on Monday. "Oh, Mom, I hate going to the dentist. And getting a cavity filled really hurts. That Dr. Andrews never uses Novocain, and it's very painful. It's so unfair because I brush my teeth all the time, and Pam doesn't, and she never has to get fillings."

"I just have really top quality teeth," Pam announced, coming into the kitchen and showing off her teeth in kind of a strange smile. "You should be so lucky."

"Now, Pam, don't be such a show-off," Lois told her. "We'll have to leave about 9:00 tomorrow. Pam, I need you to babysit Timmie. Russ has to get a filling too, so I'll drop you both off while I do some errands. I do have some good news about the dentist though. Dr. Andrews retired, and a new guy bought his practice, Dr. Colson, or Colman, something like that. He's a much younger guy, so you'll probably like him better. And we'll hope that he uses Novocain."

Her appointment did turn out to be much better than previous ones. Dr. Coulter was very friendly, and put her at ease, and he did use Novocain. After finding out what grade Elaine was in, he told her that he had a son and daughter of high school age. "My daughter's name is Christy," he told her, "and she's worried about going to a new school this fall. We just moved here from Oregon," he said. "And it's been kind of hard on the kids."

"Our high school is very friendly," Elaine told him. "I don't think they'll have a problem at all making new friends."

The month of July ushered in a heat wave, the likes of which Ellington hadn't seen in a very long time. Also that month, Jack Hathaway brought his rig over to the Hummer property to begin the digging of a new well. In the meantime, the family had to take quick showers, since there wasn't much water pressure, or water. Digging the well was a slow process. It took about three weeks to dig down 200 feet, and still no water. One July day the temperature got up to 114 degrees and there wasn't enough water pressure to spray the chickens adequately to keep them cool.

"We lost 180 laying hens yesterday," Charles said grimly at dinner. "Russ, I'll need your help in digging a big hole for burying them, and I want to start about 6:00 tomorrow morning, while it's still cool. And Elaine, we'll need you to help your mother with egg packing in the morning."

"Sure, Dad."

"And I know, you'll need me to watch Timmie, and get his breakfast," Pam stated.

"Hey, you're pretty good, you actually read my mind," Charles told her.

"I can help dig the hole," said Timmie. "I'm strong, and I have a very good little shovel."

"Well, maybe Pam will bring you out back to help us," Charles said, chuckling. "And be sure and bring that little shovel."

Elaine rode to Armedia with Beth, Lucy, and Natalie the following day after she had helped with the eggs. She and Beth were going shopping for fabric, but the other two were just going along for something to do.

"It's good to be out of the house," Elaine was saying to her friends. "We have to worry constantly about how much water we're using, and we've lost a lot of chickens in this heat."

"Yeah, and my dad says that digging that well is turning out to be a kind of a problem," Beth said. "Sounds like the WELL isn't going very well." They all laughed at her attempt at humor.

"Not to change the subject, but I have something to tell you," Lucy announced.

"Okay, girl, let's have it," Natalie told her.

"I may be gone for a few months," Lucy stated. "My mother is talking about going back to visit her mother in Alabama for a long period of time, and I would be going with her."

"Back to Alabama! Oh, what a change that will be for you!" exclaimed Elaine.

"That's really far away!" Beth added.

"Why is she visiting your grandma all of a sudden?" Nat asked. "And why would you both be staying so long?"

"She and my grandma have never been very close," Lucy explained. "And now Grandma is sick. I guess she has some kind of cancer. So my mom wants to spend some time with her. At first I was just going to stay here with Dad. But after thinking about it, Mom and I both thought I should go too. I've only met my grandma once, and I was too little to remember. She's been writing to Mom lately, and really wants me to go back there too. Of course Dad will be awfully lonely. He'll be rattling around in that house all by himself."

"So you would be going to school while you're there?" asked Elaine.

"Yeah, that's the plan. At first I was quite worried about that. But now I'm thinking it sounds kind of like an adventure, living in a different part of the country for a while, trying out a new school. It might be fun. I can't remember ever living anywhere else except here in Ellington, and sometimes this town can be pretty boring. I guess I'm just ready for a change, if only for a few months."

"But those people back there think way differently than we do," Nat pointed out. "I mean, look at all the problems they've had recently with trying to integrate the schools."

"I think you'll get the change you're looking for all right," remarked Beth. "When would you be leaving?"

"We're not sure yet, but I'll keep you guys posted of course."

They had reached Sprouse-Reitz in Armedia, and went in to look at patterns, thread, and cotton fabric. Both girls were in the process of making sheath dresses for school. They did some window shopping also. "Skirts are getting shorter," Lucy observed, as they looked in the window of MODE O'DAY.

"And lavender seems to be the color this year," added Nat.

Before leaving Armedia, they had to make a stop at Micki's Malt Shop, not only for sodas, but just to see if anyone important was there. But the place was fairly quiet on that Wednesday morning. The girls sat around talking long after they had finished their drinks. As they were getting up to leave, they ran into a tall, good looking man with two teen agers. Elaine kept thinking there was something familiar about him. Once he said hello to her, she remembered him as the dentist she had seen not too long ago. Introductions were made, and he invited the girls to stay a bit longer and have lunch with them.

His daughter, Christy was very pretty, tall and slim with big blue eyes and pale blonde hair, and a sweet personality. Alan was tall and dark like his father. The girls enjoyed their visit with them, and were glad to answer all their questions about school. Christy would be a junior, and Alan a senior, and the two seemed very glad to be meeting some new friends.

On the ride home, the girls decided that Christy would make a good addition to the Collette's group, and that Alan would be very popular with all the girls. "He kind of reminds me of Phil Santini," Lucy said sadly. "I could be interested in Alan if I weren't leaving town."

The rest of the summer passed by quickly as usual, even though there wasn't a whole lot going on. Elaine did some babysitting on a regular basis for a neighbor lady. Work continued on the well. A third shot of dynamite was put into it, and that seemed to speed up progress a little. But another heat wave hit the area, and this time about 120 chickens were lost, even though Charles was out working with the chickens for most of the day. Jack Hathaway was ready to put the casing down in the well, and that turned out to be a challenge.

"Everything about that well seems to be a problem." Elaine mentioned to Lois as they were packing eggs that morning, while Charles and Russ were burying chickens again.

"Yes, it seems to be very slow process," Lois agreed. "This had been a rough summer, but God will see us through. And the well is making progress. We've ordered a new submersible pump from a company in Oklahoma. But I've been doing a good deal of praying these last few weeks. More than usual in fact. That's what keeps me from doing too much worrying, just turning all the problems over to the Lord."

At last the well was finished. The pump was installed, the wiring done, and two pressure tanks set up. It was wonderful having all the needed water pressure again, and Elaine and Pam enjoyed their long showers that evening, vowing never again to take running water for granted.

*   *   *

Lucy told her friends that she and her mom would be leaving the last week of August, so Beth decided to have a going away party for her. She told Elaine that she wanted to keep it small, and hoped that the usual group of party crashers wouldn't be coming.

"I think I'll just mostly invite the kids from here in Ellington," she told Elaine. "It's warm enough to have either it out on our back patio, or the screened-in porch."

"I think you can keep it small because its summer and the news won't be able to get out on the school grapevine," Elaine said. "What guys are you planning to invite, besides Paul of course."

Beth had been going out with Paul Newberry off and on for the last few months. "Well, Paul's buddy, Duane Kellogg, and Ty Ramirez for Natalie, and probably DJ. He's known Lucy for all these years, and he's usually a fun addition to a party. At least he's not as goofy as he used to be. And what do you think of having banana splits, since it's summer time? That would be something different."

"That's a great idea. We can set out the nuts, and chocolate syrup, and bananas, and everyone can fix their own, and put on whatever toppings they want."

"You can be the co-host," Beth told her, "and we'll have chips and dip too, of course."

The party turned out to be pretty good, and it stayed small. Beth had run into Vicki, Lenny, and Woody the night before at the Skating Rink, so she'd invited them at the last minute. Another last minute addition was Adam Irby, who was home from college. It was a balmy summer evening, and the party was nice and relaxing. Lucy was telling everyone about her new adventure. Woody and Lenny were dancing with all the girls. Vicki and DJ seemed to be spending a lot of time together. The only thing Elaine didn't like was all the smoke floating around. It seemed that many of the boys were smokers.

Elaine had a good visit with Adam, who said that he was enjoying college, even though it was a great deal of work. "Of course there are plenty of fun activities along with all the studying," he told her. "There's dorm raids, pep rallies, exciting football games, interesting clubs, fraternities, you name it, we've got it."

"Did you join a fraternity?" she asked him.

"I haven't so far," Adam said. "And I don't know if I'll go out for football, even though I played in high school. At Armedia High, you're a big frog in a little pond, but at college, you're just a little frog in a big pond. Way more students, and way more competition for everything."

"What are you majoring in?"

"Well, I started out majoring in business because that's what my dad wanted me to do, but I'm thinking of changing to Education, since I enjoy being around kids, and the thought of teaching appeals to me."

"I think you'd be good at that," Elaine told him. "Excuse me, I need to refill the chip bowl, since I am co-host of this shindig, and I see that we're out." She started back through the screened porch with the empty bowl, but Duane Kellogg was blocking the doorway. He was big and tall, with dark wavy hair, and brown eyes.

"Sorry, Hummer, but this is a tollbooth, and I can't let you through without payment," he said.

"Just put it on my account, on account of I ain't got no money," Elaine said, laughing.

"Who said anything about money? I meant a kiss." He smiled impishly. A slow song came on the record player just then and Elaine said, "How about a dance instead?" as she grabbed his hand.

"I guess that'll have to do," he grumbled. "So where have you been keeping yourself lately?"

"Oh, I get around. You've seen me at the Skating Rink, probably. Heck, I can remember the very first time I met you."

"Is that right?" he seemed impressed. "And just when was that?"

"It was the very first day of school, our freshman year, and Vicki Bannister and I couldn't find our classroom, and we asked you and Paul for directions, and you guys were no help at all."

"Well, I'm sorry to hear that. It probably gave you a really bad first impression of us."

"It did. And our next encounter with you and Paul was on Initiation Day, when you had me and Vicki lugging books around for you, and hand feeding lunch to you guys out on the lawn."

"Gee, you remember all that? I only vaguely remember two bedraggled looking girls feeding us our burgers! That was a long time ago. And how you've changed from that weird looking girl with her hair all in pigtails to one sharp looking chick."

Elaine was enjoying their flirty conversation. "I had a crush on you back then," she told him. "But you were just a big shot senior and paid no attention to little old me."

"Well that was a big mistake on my part," he stated.

"I know you and Paul are buddies, and hang around together," she said. "But weren't you out of town for a while? 'Cause I'd see Paul every so often, but didn't see you."

"After graduation, I moved to Bakersfield, since I have family there. My folks are divorced, my dad lives in High Bluffs, and my mom is in Bakersfield. But I'm back here to stay now. My brother will be moving here too. He's 16, and is a real hell-raiser. He's moving back right before school starts."

The music ended, and Elaine told him she had to refill the chips, but he kept holding onto her hand. "Are you dating anyone?" he asked.

"Yes, I have a boyfriend, but he lives out of town, or else he'd be here tonight."

"Wouldn't you know it, just my luck," Duane sighed disgustedly.

Chapter 28

"I am really excited about this trip, but I will miss you both sooo much," Lucy told Beth and Elaine, who had come to see her off on a bright Monday morning.

"You girls will have to stop by the house from time to time to say hello," Marvin Snowball said to Beth and Elaine. "Because I'm going to be awfully lonely without my Lucy and my Dorothy around here. I'll probably live at the post office." He was the postmaster for the little Ellington post office.

"You be sure and write to me," Lucy told Elaine as they hugged. "You have to keep me filled in on all the news from around here and everything going on at school, all the latest gossip."

"I promise," Elaine said solemnly. "And I want to hear all about your adventures, once you get settled back there. I'll share the letters with Beth and the other girls."

"I'm not good at writing, you know that," Beth told Lucy. "But Elaine can tell you my news."

Lucy climbed into the front seat with her mother, as the car started, and pulled out onto the street. She turned around to watch a waving Elaine and Beth as they grew smaller and smaller, until they gradually disappeared.

"Well, I can't believe that we're finally off," Dorothy said. "And I have to say I never thought we'd get everything to fit in the car. Didn't realize that we were taking so much stuff. Your father is a good packer."

"Well, our trunk is pretty roomy, and we also have the back seat," remarked Lucy. The car was a 1958 Impala with a blue and white paint job, and was clean and shiny, ready for the long trip. "I see you have plenty of maps, so we shouldn't get lost."

"Yes, and you can be the navigator," Dorothy told her. "Of course, we'll be on the same road almost all the way. We'll be going east on Interstate 10, and we'll go through Palm Springs, Indio, and then Blythe. By tonight we'll be somewhere in Arizona and we'll stop either in Phoenix or Tucson. When I get tired, I'll pull over and let you drive. But I do want to stop at night, so we can get a good night's sleep and a shower. No point in pushing ourselves. And I'm sure we'll be running into hot weather, since the first part of the trip will be nothing but desert."

"But this car has air conditioning," Lucy reminded her.

"Yes, but we can't use it when we're climbing hills, or the engine will heat up too much. So we'll have to be aware of that, since we certainly don't want any car trouble on this trip."

"How many miles til we get to Middleburg?" Lucy asked.

"It's probably around 2,000 miles. So I figure if we drive about 500 miles a day, or around eight hours, we should be there in about four days."

"It's the longest trip I've ever been on," Lucy remarked, turning on the car radio.

"Yes, we have many miles to cover, so put on a good station, and get comfortable," her mother told her. "We'll be losing our radio stations once we get out to the desert, so enjoy it while you can. Or sleep if you want to. I'll have you drive later on this afternoon."

Lucy grabbed a small pillow from the backseat and leaned back. But she was too excited to sleep. The miles rolled by, and soon they were in the desert, surrounded by yucca plants, Joshua trees, creosote and mesquite bushes, and California junipers. The desert scenery went on for miles and miles. They stopped for lunch in Blythe. Lucy had packed a lunch of tuna sandwiches and fruit. They'd pulled into a little roadside rest stop near the Colorado River.

"You said I could drive in the afternoon," Lucy reminded Dorothy, as she pulled sandwiches from the ice chest.

"I would be most happy if you drove, and I will get a little nap. I can't believe how hot it is here," Dorothy said, wiping her forehead. They ate quickly and climbed back into the car.

Lucy felt wild and free as she traveled along the interstate, going the speed limit, which was 55 mph. It was a nice easy drive, but she wished they'd been able to get a radio station. At least they were getting the benefits of the car's air conditioning, since they weren't doing much climbing. Dorothy awoke after a while and began studying the Arizona map.

"We're making good time today," she remarked. "I think we can make it into Tucson before we stop for the night. But we're not going to go all the way into Phoenix. It's a nice city, but it's very spread out, and the roads tend to get congested. Let's take Highway 85 south, which will run into Interstate 8, and then back into the 10. That should save us some time. Just watch for signs that say Buckeye and Gila Bend."

"Okay, that sounds like a plan, but then I won't get to practice driving in the city if we don't go into Phoenix."

"Oh, believe me, I don't think you'll mind missing out on driving around Phoenix. There's always a lot of road construction and delays there." Lucy got tired after two more hours of driving anyhow, and she pulled over so they could trade places again. They finally reached the turnoff for Highway 85, and started south. Lucy spotted some Burma Shave signs, and pointed them out to Dorothy. The little rhymes that were spread out over six small red signs were always fun to read. They were usually advertising their shaving cream, but some of the signs had verses that pertained to safe driving.

Lucy read them aloud to her mother: "To kiss . . . . A mug . . . . That's like a cactus . . . . Takes more nerve . . . . Than it does practice . . . . Burma Shave

"Those little signs have been around for years," said Dorothy smiling. "They're just part of a trip, except we probably won't see them along the Interstate. And to tell the truth, sometimes it's nice to get off the Interstate, and just drive on a smaller highway like we're doing now."

They made it into Tucson about 6:00 that evening and found a motel. It was bright pink, surrounded by cactus plants. They were both hungry by then, so they made a quick stop at a little cafe next to the motel, before settling in for the night.

Both Dorothy and Lucy felt stiff and sore the next morning. "I don't know whether it was the long drive or that mattress we slept on," Dorothy stated, "but my back is hurting."

"Well, that bed wasn't too comfortable," Lucy stated. They weren't that hungry, so they made the decision to just drive for a while. "How many years has it been since you've seen Grandma?" Lucy wanted to know.

"It has been about 12 years," Dorothy told her. "I think you were around four at the time. I know that was a really long time ago. It's just that my mother and I never got along very well at all. We argued with each other the entire time I was growing up. I could never do anything to please her, and she criticized me constantly. She definitely favored my younger brother, Elmo."

"Yes, I've heard you talk about Uncle Elmo," Lucy said.

"Elmo and I always got along okay, but Mother did spoil him as a child. And he's only a couple of years younger than I am, but he still lives at home with Grandma. I mean she lives in a big old house with plenty of room, but you'd think he would have gotten out on his own, or found a girl and gotten married after all these years."

"Does he have a job?" Lucy asked.

"Yes, if you want to call it that. He's been best friends with this guy named Clem, who owns bait and tackle shop on the outskirts of town. Clem is also a bachelor. His family had money, and bought him the shop years ago. Well, Elmo works in the shop with Clem, and I think he gets paid pretty well for the little work he does there. Clem even put his name on the sign, so it reads 'Clem and Elmo's Bait and Tackle.' They mostly sit out on the front porch and talk to everyone who comes in, but I guess they get enough business to make a go of it. There's a small lake not too far away. Wait till you see all the lakes and rivers back there. You'll be amazed at how green everything looks."

"Yeah, it will be nice to be in a place where there is plenty of water," Lucy said. "So you and Daddy went back to visit Grandma when I was four."

"Yes, we did, but the visit didn't go very well. You see, my mother always wanted me to marry a southern boy and settle down right there in Middleburg. Your dad was stationed at a naval air station at Pensacola, Florida when we met. I went with some of my college friends to a club in Pensacola, and that's where I met Marvin. When we saw each other, it was love at first sight. Of course he was born and raised in Orange County, so my mother considered him a Yankee."

"Yes, I've heard before how you met Daddy. But that's just weird that Grandma didn't like him simply because he was from a different part of the country. It's still the USA, and it's not like it's back in the Civil War days."

"I know, but some people in the South are just plain old fashioned and set in their ways, and Grandma is definitely one of them, sorry to say."

"You told me that she has cancer. What kind of cancer?'

"It's breast cancer, but she doesn't want anyone to know, so once you get to meet some of the people in town, just say she is sick. People don't want to hear about cancer, especially that kind."

Lucy became silent as she wondered what kind of strange town she would be living in for the next few months.

After stopping in Wilcox for breakfast, they drove on and crossed into New Mexico. They covered many more miles before they came to Las Cruces, and crossed the Rio Grande. Lucy had heard about the Rio Grande before, but the river was quite small, despite the Spanish name of "Big River." In Las Cruces, the I-10 veered to the south into El Paso, Texas. The buildings in El Paso, at least the ones near the freeway, were old and run down.

"Mexico is just across the river," Dorothy pointed out.

"Oh, can we go over there?" asked Lucy. "I've only been to Mexico once, that time I went to Tia Juana with the MYF group. We went to a mission there in the middle of the city. We had a good time, and got lots of souvenirs pretty cheap. I still have some earrings I got from a street vendor. We could do some shopping."

"No, Sweetheart, I really don't want to drive into Mexico. I wouldn't know where I'd be going, and if I even got in the slightest little fender bender, it would mean big problems. We have to pass on that."

Lucy was disappointed, as they turned east. There was not so much to see any more. The vast Texas landscape was nothing but railroad tracks and windmills, and miles upon miles of nothingness. Lucy pulled a book from the backseat to keep herself occupied. That day the trip seemed endless. After nearly nine hours on the road, they stopped in Fort Stockton, Texas to spend the night. The bed at that motel must have been more comfortable since they both felt very rested the next morning.

"Well, I wonder how Daddy is doing by now," Lucy remarked as they started out again on the new day. "I bet he is missing us in a big way."

"I'm sure he is. I need to call him as soon as we get into Middleburg because he'll want to know if we made the trip okay. I almost called him last night from the pay phone at the motel, but long distance is so expensive."

"I know Texas is our biggest state," Lucy said, "but I am already so sick of this boring, never ending landscape that seems to roll on forever, with no mountains or trees, or anything interesting to look at. And I see from the map, that we'll probably be here all day today."

"You got that right, Kiddo," her mother told her. "But with any luck, maybe we'll make it as far as Houston today. We're about 500 miles from there, and once we get there, it's not that far into Louisiana."

However, as they got into the outskirts of San Antonio, they both felt that they needed a break from riding in the car. Lucy came up with the idea that they should stop and visit the Alamo. "It was only a few years ago that Davy Crockett was so popular with all the kids," she said. "There were lots of TV shows about him, and about the battle of the Alamo."

"Yes, I remember all the boys were wearing coonskin caps at the time," Dorothy added. "We need to stop for gas anyhow, so I'll get some directions for the Alamo."

It wasn't as easy as they thought it would be, to reach their destination. San Antonio was a good sized city, with many one-way streets, and the city map really wasn't that helpful. After driving around for what seemed like a long time, they finally found the Alamo smack dab in the middle of the city.

"Well, the building looks the same as pictures I've seen, but I figured there would be some acreage around it," Dorothy said.

"Yeah, it looks funny with all the city buildings completely surrounding it," Lucy added. She was busy snapping photos. Before they realized it, two hours had passed while they looked at the various exhibits, and spent time walking around the area.

"Well, we needed this break," Dorothy said. "It felt really good to get out and walk around for a while. But now it's getting late, so we'll just find a motel here in San Antonio. Once we get settled though, I do want to call Marvin."

Lucy had been writing a little each day in a letter to Elaine, so she added some more that evening. "*I think by this time tomorrow night, we will finally leave Texas behind us. It has the honor of bring our biggest state, but also the most boring (if one is driving through it.) The most interesting sight we saw was the Alamo, and we had a hard time finding that. I just feel like Mom and I are so alone right now, and so far away from everything. But I wanted to have adventure, so I'm in the middle of it right now. Will wrote more tomorrow.*"

They both felt refreshed on the morning of the fourth day, and got an early start. Lucy noticed that the landscape east of San Antonio had much more to offer. They crossed over two rivers, the San Antonio, and the Guadalupe, and the area was becoming much greener. There were some weathered farmhouses, picturesque windmills, and a few faded wildflowers.

"Last time we went on this trip," Dorothy told her "it was in the Spring, and there were wildflowers everywhere in this area. The Texas state flower is the bluebonnet, and there happened to be fields of them all over the place, as far as the eye could see. Of course at this time of year, most all the wildflowers are long gone."

"It's cooler here, too," Lucy remarked, sticking her arm out the window. "Feels a bit humid." After a few hours, they went through Houston, and were on their way to Beaumont.

"Looks like some clouds are building up ahead," Dorothy commented, squinting at the horizon. "We may be in for a thunderstorm."

"Well, that should make things interesting. We don't get too many of those at home."

After another hour of driving, the sky grew very dark, and they could see the rain coming down about a half mile ahead, along with thunder that seemed to rock the car, followed by blinding flashes of lightning.

"The thunder and lightning at home are nothing compared to this," observed Lucy. "And it's weird, that you can see where the rain starts."

"You'll see that the storms in this part of the country are way different than storms at home."

All of a sudden they were in a downpour. Dorothy turned the wipers on at full speed, but could hardly see the road ahead of them. The noise from the rain was deafening, and there seemed to be some hail mixed in with it. "I'm going to pull off the freeway!" she shouted to Lucy. "It's just about lunchtime anyhow, and we'll find a place to eat, while we sit out the storm!" But once they pulled off the main highway, there didn't seem to be any place to stop. Finally they turned off at a sign on a side road that advertised Claude's Cafe. They had gone two miles on the side road, and were about to give up when they came across a small run-down building with the paint and stucco peeling off the outside. But the interior looked clean enough. There were only six tables inside, and one was occupied with two older, bearded men playing a game of checkers. The heavy set man running the establishment looked like he was the chief cook and bottle washer. "What can I get for you ladies today?" he asked.

"Do you have a menu?" asked Lucy.

"No Ma'am, sorry we don't. There are only a few choices. We have hamburgers and fries, some of our hot Texas chili, and meatloaf with mashed potatoes. And our special today is possum stew." He was grinning at Lucy, who got a bit pale at the mention of the special.

"I'll have a hamburger and fries please," she said. Mrs. Snowball ordered the meatloaf.

"Mom, I've not even sure we should be eating here. Now I'm going to wonder what's in the meat. We could get food poisoning or something," Lucy whispered.

"Oh, I think we'll be okay. He was probably kidding about the possum stew, having a little fun at our expense. And this is the only cafe around here, and it does look fairly clean. Besides we have to sit out the storm anyhow."

"But this place is weird. And those guys playing checkers are staring at us." Lucy was feeling uncomfortable. Looking around the cafe, she saw an interesting looking animal mounted in a glass case at the end of the bar. It looked like a big rabbit, but it had antlers on it. "What type of animal is that in the glass case?" she asked, as her hamburger was placed in front of her.

"Oh, that there is a jackalope, Missy" the big man told her. "Once you git out on the road again, you keep an eye out for them, since them critters are runnin' around all over the place. They multiply like jackrabbits."

"Okay," Lucy said, taking a bite out of her burger. It tasted delicious. She hadn't realized how hungry she was. They took their time eating, and by the time they had finished, the rain had slowed considerably, and they were ready to hit the road again. "Y'all come back now," the proprietor called to them.

"Well, after that experience, I am finally starting to feel like I am in the South," Dorothy said. "And, for future reference, there are no jackalopes. That's a joke in Texas, for the benefit of unsuspecting tourists. Again, he was just feeding you a line."

"I guess they can see me coming a mile away," Lucy remarked, getting into the driver's seat. They made their way back to the freeway. As they got closer to Beaumont, the scenery was getting prettier all the time. There were a few green hills, and other areas where the land was flat and marshy. There were small stands of woods, with mixed pine and sweet gum trees, and there were big areas of grasslands. Her mother was reading the guidebook while Lucy did the driving. "We're almost to Beaumont," Dorothy stated. "And once we leave there, it will only be a half hour or so, and we'll be in Louisiana. I think we can make it as far as Lafayette before stopping for the night."

"That sounds really good," said Lucy happily. 'I can't wait. I'll have lots to say in my letter to Elaine tonight. That little cafe was strange. Possum stew! Jackalopes! Unbelievable!"

They were soon crossing the Sabine River, which was the border between Texas and Louisiana. The further they traveled into Louisiana, the greener the landscape. Small stands of trees dotted the land. There were longleaf pine, cypress, hickory, and southern white cedar. When they reached Lafayette that evening, and stopped for the night, they were exhilarated that there was only one more day of travel for them. Five days on the road was long enough.

The following day, though, seemed very long. Lucy was amazed when they crossed the huge Mississippi River in the Baton Rouge area, since she had never seen a river anywhere close to that size with that many types of boats traveling up and down on it. After Baton Rouge, they turned off the interstate and headed north. "If we'd kept on the same way we'd wind up in New Orleans," Dorothy told her daughter. "That is an amazing city, but it would slow us down to go that way. Maybe we can stop there on our drive back."

"That's fine with me," Lucy responded. "I'm getting tired of riding. It will be good just to get there and settle in for a while. Every so many miles I see a sign that says parish. We just passed one that said Tangipahoa Parish. What exactly is a parish?"

"Parish is just another word for county," Dorothy explained. "I think Louisiana is the only state that has them."

Just before crossing the border into Mississippi, they were back on Interstate 10 again. Now there were waterways everywhere. If there wasn't a river, there was a low, swampy area or a pond, or an inlet from the ocean. Most of the little houses in the area were on stilts.

"Why are all these houses so far up off the ground?" Lucy asked.

"With all this water around, an area can get flooded very quickly," Dorothy told her. "And also they get hurricanes around here, so the houses have to be up high so they don't flood."

"There is just so much water around here! We could sure use some of it around Ellington," Lucy said. "Ohh, look at all those birds! Aren't they pretty?"

"They're beautiful. The white ones with the long legs are egrets. Keep looking, because with all these lakes and ponds, you'll probably spot some pelicans and herons too."

They passed a big park honoring Civil War heroes. Across the Mobile Bay and the river were huge factories right at the river's edge. The rivers and waterways seemed to be the center of great activity. As they journeyed further into the Deep South, Lucy was noticing all the cypress trees, hung with Spanish moss, and the sight of them made her feels as if she were on a different planet. "Oh, I love those trees, they look so interesting," exclaimed Lucy. "Aren't they beautiful, Mom?"

"Very picturesque," Dorothy agreed. "I'm so glad you decided to come on this trip. It's much more enjoyable for me to share all this with you. And it is definitely beneficial for you to experience a different part of the country. It's such a contrast to southern California."

"It seems like an entirely different world down here in the south," Lucy remarked dreamily.

"Oh, you haven't seen anything yet," her mother told her.

Chapter 29

Elaine had her brother to walk with her to the bus stop on that first day of school. Russ was acting very calm, but Elaine could tell that he was a bit nervous. But once he got to the bus stop and saw a couple of other freshmen friends, he felt better.

Beth was already there waiting. "It seems strange without Lucy here," she said. "We're going to miss her. Have you heard from her yet?"

"Just got a letter yesterday and it's in my purse. You can read it on the bus, since it's kind of long. She's telling all about her trip driving back there."

"I will probably be taking the car to school some of the time," Beth told Elaine, as they took seats on the bus. "So we won't have to put up with this bus ride every day."

"That sounds really good. I think I'll like that."

Once the girls were at school, they went to the student square hoping to find their group of friends. They saw Karen Gillespie first. The petite auburn haired girl ran up to greet them. Alma and Megan weren't far behind her.

Elaine saw Christy Coulter standing by herself looking lonely, and called to her to join their group, and she seemed very grateful. The girls were all talking at once, as they were trying to catch up on all the news that had taken place during the summer months. Elaine and Nat were telling them about Lucy, Karen was saying that she had broken up with Greg, and Megan was telling them about the new high school principal. Alma was asking if anyone had met Dennis Kellogg, the new boy in their class.

"No, but I talked to his brother not too long ago, and he said Dennis was moving here from Bakersfield," Elaine told her.

"I think he is so cute," Alma stated. "I could go for him in a big way."

Following the traditional Beginning of School Assembly, the girls got their class schedules, and scattered off in different directions. Elaine, Alma, and Christy were the only ones who had U.S. History first. Mrs. Gimple was their teacher. Elaine had been in her Freshman Geography class. She was nice enough but had a very quiet voice, which didn't always work too well with a noisy, fidgety class. Of course, at that early hour, the students were still fairly quiet for the most part.

Second Period was Biology, with a new teacher, Mr. Nichols. He seemed as if he would be interesting, and he had a good sense of humor. Several of Elaine's close friends were in this class, along with Woody and DJ, and Alvin Minegar. She hoped Alvin wouldn't be too much of a pest like he had sometimes been in the past. Mr. Nichols explained that they would be studying plant life one semester, and animal life for the second semester, and that they would have to dissect a frog. Elaine didn't think that sounded like much fun.

After the mid-morning break, Elaine went on to English class, again, with Mrs. Teague. She was just glad she didn't have English last period as she had last year. Sometimes a person could get very tired by the end of a busy school day, especially when there were seven periods in a day. This year they would be going back to just six classes a day, with no Study Hall. That had seemed like a waste to some of the students, who just used the class as a time to goof off. Mrs. Teague announced that they would be studying American Literature this year.

Elaine had Typing as her Fourth Period class. She figured that would be an important class to take if she was going to get serious about her writing. Mr. Barber was the teacher.

At lunchtime the girls assembled in their favorite spot out on the lawn. Christy had been invited to join them. "Well, here we all are again," Vicki was saying. "Ready to embark on another wonderful journey at good old Armedia High. Yeah, right."

"I hope we can win a few football games this season," Elaine said. "We didn't do too well last year."

"The players are more experienced this year," Megan pointed out. "Several of them have played as sophomores, and now they're juniors. And we have a lot of seniors on the team too. Hopefully that will make a difference."

"Does it seem strange at school without Willie around?" Natalie asked her.

"It does, and you're probably feeling the difference now that Ty is gone too," Megan pointed out. "We're just going to have to be independent women this year."

"You're brother seems really nice," Karen was telling Christy. "He's in my Spanish class."

"As brothers go, he's not too bad," Christy remarked. "We get along pretty well. He didn't like changing schools in his senior year, but my folks really wanted to move down this way."

"You're from Oregon, right?" Beth asked her. "It's so beautiful and green up there."

"Yes, but we pay a price for that because it rains so much. Also we have lots of family living down this way, and my folks wanted to make a change. It just seems so dry around here, though. I see riverbeds when we're driving around, but they're all dried up, just sand."

"That is so true. Welcome to southern California," Alma laughed.

The last two classes of the day for Elaine were PE and Journalism/ Yearbook. She was happy about that. After her first three classes were over, the rest of the day would be a breeze. Miss Lippert, the art teacher, also taught Journalism. She was in charge of the annual staff and the school newspaper staff. As assistant annual editor, Elaine could hardly wait to get started. Lenny Mendoza and Shawn O'Dell were on the yearbook staff. Lenny was the photographer for the school, and Shawn would be doing art work. Elaine was surprised when her cousin Scottie came into the class with paperwork for Miss Lippert.

"Hey, Scott, are you joining the yearbook staff?" she asked.

"Yes, it's a last minute change. I'll be the assistant photographer, helping Lenny."

"I think that's great," Elaine told him. "Lenny, did you know that Scotty is my cousin?"

"I did not know that," Lenny said. "I have a few cousins at this school, but they usually pretend they don't know me," he added jokingly.

"I think I knew Alma for several months before I knew you were her twin," Elaine said.

"See what I mean. She doesn't like to claim me," he laughed. "Hey, there's Big B. How're you doing, man?"

Big B was on the annual staff as the Sports Editor. His real name was Bobby Jackson, and he was literally a big man on campus. He was Senior Class president, a big black guy well over six feet tall, and weighing around 225 pounds. His size was a real asset to the football team where he mostly played tackle or guard. He was also on the wrestling team. His great sense of humor made him popular with everyone. Affectionately known as Big B, he had nicknames for people too. His name for Elaine was Humbug, while other people called her Hummingbird.

At dinner that evening, much of the talk at the table was about high school, and Russ had plenty to say about it. He had several of the same classes and teachers that Elaine had two years ago. "I think I'll like Mr.Carr," Russ was saying. "He seems like he'll be a good Algebra teacher."

"He might if he sticks to Algebra and avoids all the talk about football," Charles stated. "Sometimes I wonder where they get these teachers. And I don't know about that Mr.Dumpke. Last year I ran into him at Armedia Lumber, and asked him what I could do to help Elaine raise her grade in Geometry, and he didn't really have an answer, he just hemmed and hawed around."

"Maybe that's why I got an A in that class," Elaine told him.

"And you don't know a thing about Geometry," remarked Charles. "I'll never know why he gave you A's. You and I both know you didn't deserve it."

"She must have been the teacher's pet," Pam giggled.

"Well, anyhow, I think high school will be okay," stated Russ. "Or it will be once we get past Slave Day. I'm not looking forward to that."

"You'll have it much easier than we did two years ago," Elaine told him.

The assembly at school, or the "Slave Auction" was held a few days later, and the incoming freshmen were auctioned off to to those who wanted to participate. Since the auctioning was done by number, no one knew who they were getting. The proceeds of the auction went to the buyer's class. As they had the previous year, the three Ellington girls went together to buy a slave, and they were happily making plans for the unfortunate freshman.

"They have to wear just about anything we tell them to," Nat was saying, "within reason of course. What about diapers, maybe over shorts?"

"That sounds like a plan. We'll make them work like a dog too, carry all our books around, and really kow tow to us," added Beth. Elaine was busy writing down the dress code, and other requirements.

As the auction began, the girls could not make themselves heard, so Woody offered to bid for their slave. Once he was paid for, he was asked to stand, and the girls turned to the freshmen section to get a look at their purchase. He was a tall, dark-haired fellow with a defiant look about him.

"Oh, that's Karen's brother, Wayne," Vicki exclaimed.

"We'll break his spirit, but good!" said Elaine.

Friday morning, during the break Wayne's dignity was forgotten as he walked in front of his masters. He was wearing a T shirt and bib with the words "I Eat Gerber's" written on it. On his back was a sign saying "Juniors are the Greatest." One foot wore a beach thong, while the other featured a lady's slipper. And of course the diapers over the shorts finished off his look. He carried a baby bottle, along with a pile of books.

"My purse is starting to feel awfully heavy," Beth was saying, "so I'm going to have you carry it temporarily. How about you girls?"

"Yes, you can carry mine too," Elaine added. "And also my lunchbox."

"You know, I only have two hands," he griped, as they handed him more stuff.

"Well, use your head, Slave," Nat told him. "The purses all have straps, so put them over your shoulder, and stuff the baby bottle in your pocket."

"What will you girls think of next?" Wayne groaned. "All this hard work is bad for my heart."

"Oh, quit complaining," Elaine told him. "Your day is just beginning. Enjoy it! In the years to come, this day will be a fond memory for you."

"Like heck it will!"

"I've never seen my little brother work so hard," asserted Karen, joining them on the Student Square. "I wish I had my camera. My parents will never believe this!"

"Find Lenny, he's somewhere around here snapping pictures," Elaine told her. "And I want him to get a picture of Russ too."

Russ was standing in the cafeteria line for a couple of guys. He was wearing a short skirt that belonged to Pam, with nylon stockings and a garter. He had some old high heels that Elaine had found at the Goodwill Store, and a blouse that belonged to his mother. Elaine had enjoyed putting on all his makeup that morning. He also had on several necklaces and a pair of earrings. Pam had taken his picture before he had left for school that morning.

"Russ, you look absolutely fetching!" she called to him, as he gave her a dirty look in return.

"Elaine, my friend, I'm wondering if you can do me a big favor tonight?" Beth asked.

"Well, now Buddy, that all depends on what it is," she responded.

"You know how I was planning to drive us girls to the Freshman Welcome Dance tonight?"

"Yes, that's been the plan."

"Well, now Paul wants me to go with him to the dance, and Duane wants to go too, but he won't be able to get in unless he has a guest pass, which means he needs to be dating someone in school, and I thought of you. Of course it wouldn't be a real date, but it would just look that way til we get into the dance."

"But what about Nat? She was planning to go with us too."

"I really don't care that much about going," stated Nat. "I can be just as happy staying home and writing Ty a letter."

"I could never be like that," Elaine remarked. "I have to be going places and doing things, and keeping busy. So, yeah, I'll go with you guys tonight."

"That's great. I'll give Paul a call when I get home. Be over at my house around 7:00 this evening, and we'll leave from there."

"That's probably best, because my family really likes Jeff, and they'd probably get the wrong idea and think I was going out with someone else."

Elaine was thinking about Jeff on the way to her next class. He was great as a boyfriend, always courteous, and sweet and thoughtful, but it sure was hard being separated all the time. In his last letter, he told her that he had changed jobs, and was now working in a restaurant, but still needed to save money for car repairs before he could come to Ellington again. But did that mean she was supposed to just stay at home not having any fun?

Paul and Duane arrived at Beth's in Paul's white 55 Chevy. Beth was sitting next to Paul in the middle of the front seat, while Elaine stayed on the far side of the back seat next to the window. "Hey, you can sit next to me, I don't bite," Duane said, smiling. He was looking very dapper in cords and a button-down shirt, and he had on some good smelling cologne.

"This date is for appearances only," Elaine told him, scooting over next to him. He put his arm around her, and said emphatically that he was total in agreement with that. But Elaine had a feeling that the evening really wouldn't play out that way.

Chapter 30

Two thousand miles away in a small Alabama town, another high school year was beginning that week, and Lucy was very nervous as she walked up to the big square brick building, with the only two friends she had made so far, Clydean and Jimmy Lee.

She and her mother had arrived just ten days ago, and Lucy knew that there were many differences to which she would have to become accustomed. On the day of their arrival, they had pulled up in front of a large, two story white house, surrounded by a picket fence. There were several magnolia trees in the front yard. The fence was broken in some places, the shrubs in the yard were growing out of control, and the wide front porch sagged at one end. Dorothy was thinking that if her brother was living there too, why wasn't he taking care of the needed repairs? Or doing any yard work? Lucy followed her mother up onto the porch, wiping the perspiration from her forehead. It was about 4:00 in the afternoon, and the heat and the humidity were intense.

The front door opened, and there was her mother, Edith, with a wide smile on her face. She threw her arms around Dorothy. "Oh, you're here, finally. It's so wonderful to see you. I can't believe you're really here! And Lucy, you're a sight for sore eyes. Why, Honey, the last time I laid eyes on you, you were just a little bitty thing, and look at you now, all grown up!" Lucy was enveloped in a huge hug. Her grandma was shorter than she was, and was wearing a big, flowing gown, similar to a muu muu, but dressier. She had on a great deal of makeup. "Come in, come in, out of this humidity. We've been having a real heat wave the last few days, but it should be letting up soon. Now that September is here, things will start to cool off a bit. I've got all the fans going inside."

The entry way and living room were dark, with the draperies pulled. Two large fans were going at full blast, but it only felt slightly cooler inside to Dorothy and Lucy. "Y'all have a seat and I'll bring you something cold to drink," Edith told them.

"After that long, long drive, it's hard to believe we're finally here," said Lucy.

"Yes, it will feel good to be staying in one place again," Dorothy remarked.

Edith came back into the room with large glasses of ice tea. Lucy found it very, very sweet, but cold and refreshing. The rest of the afternoon passed quickly, as they visited, and settled into their rooms. Lucy and her mother each had their own rooms. Lucy's room, at the top of the stairs, was small, but clean and neat. She liked the big antique dresser and bed. The view from the window showed a large vegetable garden out in the back. The only drawback to the room was the incredible heat. She pulled down the dusty shades that were on the two windows to keep out the blinding rays of the sun. It felt so strange to her to be so far away from her home and friends. She wondered how long it would take her to make any new friends. She'd asked her grandmother if there were any young people living on the street, but was told that it was an older neighborhood, and most of the neighbors had lived there for years, so their kids were grown. Lucy figured she probably wouldn't be meeting any new friends until school started, and that was more than a week away.

Lucy slept in the next morning. She figured that she was still on Pacific Daylight Time. She dressed quickly in shorts, a cotton sleeveless blouse, and sandals, and went downstairs to find Edith cooking up a storm. There were fried potatoes, and also hash browns, fried eggs, bacon and sausage, and something that looked like cream of wheat. There were also two kinds of sweet rolls. Lucy was thinking that even when they had company at home, they didn't have that much food at breakfast. She was introduced to her Uncle Elmo, who gave her a big bear hug. He didn't look anything like her mother. He was short and stout with a receding hairline, and wearing bib overalls. His teeth were slightly discolored, but he did have a nice smile and twinkling blue eyes. "Oh, Lucy-Girl," he exclaimed. "It's just great to see you-all again, after all these years! Last time I saw you, you were just knee-high to a grasshopper. Sorry I got in too late last night to see you and Dorothy, but Clem and I were doing some fishing."

"Honey, we need to get some meat on your bones," Edith stated, setting a large plate in front of her. It was about four times the size of the breakfast she usually had, and Lucy really had her doubts that she would be able to clean her plate.

"Those are grits," Dorothy told her, indicating the white blob on the plate that looked like cream of wheat. "That is a breakfast staple here in the south. You can have it with butter, or gravy, or milk and sugar, whatever you feel like."

"I'll try it with butter," said Lucy. She found that the grits didn't have a lot of taste, but they were okay.

The breakfast conversation wasn't that interesting to Lucy, since they were all talking about people she didn't know, and events that had taken place in town umpteen years ago. She finished her breakfast as best she could, and took her plate to the sink. "Would it be okay if I took a walk?" she asked. "I'd like to check out the town, and it's cooler now, so I thought it would be a good time." The town of Middleburg was about the same size as Armedia, but it wasn't nearly as spread out. Edith had told Lucy that they were only a few blocks from downtown.

"Of course Honey," Edith told her. "Just make a left turn in front of the house, and go for two blocks, then turn right for about three more blocks, and you'll be downtown." Lucy was glad to be outside, even though she felt as if she had just stepped out of the shower. The air was already very warm and heavy, and she could smell a strange, musty odor. The neighborhood was definitely an older one with large, but run-down homes with expansive lawns, and mature shrubs and trees. Most of the yards were lush and green with vines creeping all over the place, and colorful flowers that seemed to pop up everywhere. Many of the tree trunks were covered with vines. A large culvert running along the edge of the sidewalk was half full of water, and at the corner she noticed an old colored man fishing from the culvert. What a strange place this is, she thought. It didn't take long to reach the downtown area. Most of the little towns she had seen in the south were set up the same way and Middleburg was no exception. The brick courthouse was in the middle of town, and there was a big town square across from it. Also on the same street were a small cafe, a clothing store, a five and dime, a hardware store, and a mom and pop grocery store. Two blocks on the other side of the courthouse was an old movie theater. In spite of the theater looking old and run down, the movies playing there had just come out that same year, and Lucy thought she might take in a movie before school started. Two blocks past the theater, was the square brick high school. She wondered how different school would be, compared to Armedia High School. She wondered how many weeks or months they would be staying there in Middleburg. Her grandmother didn't look sick at all and didn't act sick either. But she knew any type of cancer was really serious, and that a person usually didn't recover from it. This might be the last chance her mother would have to be with her grandmother.

So deep in thought was she, gazing at the high school, she didn't see the bicycle rider until the last minute, and barely had time to jump out of the way. But as she jumped, her feet slipped, and she fell down on the graveled parking lot in front of the school.

"Oh, I am so sorry, Miss," the young bicycle rider was saying, as he quickly braked, and leaned the bike up against the fence. "I didn't see you. Are you all right?" He quickly offered his hand to Lucy, who felt more embarrassed that anything else. Her knee was scraped a bit, but other than that, she was unhurt. She noticed the rider was a very good looking dark haired boy who looked to be around her age. She stood up, with his help, and brushed herself off, chagrined by his scrutiny.

"I don't believe I've seen you around here before," he was saying, "And I surely would have noticed someone as pretty as you."

Lucy blushed at his compliment. Maybe she would find these southern boys to her liking. "I just got into town yesterday," she explained. "And I'm just learning my way around here, and finding out where things are. You guys have a nice little town here."

"You guys?" he asked, laughing. "What's with the 'you guys'? I can tell from your speech that you're not from around here. Let me guess, you're from somewhere out west. By the way, my name's Jimmy Lee Thompson."

"Lucy Snowball. And I'm from a long way from here, southern California," she told him. She had a few questions for him about school, and he was interested in hearing about her home town. She found out that he was a sophomore, and that he had a sister who was a junior. They seemed to have a lot to say to each other, and when Lucy checked her watch, it was almost noontime. "Oh, I should get going," she said. "I didn't realize it was so late. Everybody will be wondering about me."

She was surprised when Jimmy Lee asked for her phone number. "I don't even know it yet," she told him. "My mom and I are staying at my grandmother's for now."

"Well, what's your address," he persisted. "Maybe my sister and I will drop by to see you this next week, before school starts."

Lucy was more than happy to give him her address. "It's 614 Azalea Lane." She felt so much better as she headed back to her temporary home. It would be wonderful to have a couple of friends at least before school started.

The following day was Sunday. Lucy was sure that would turn out to be a long day, but at her grandma's insistence, they would be going to church. She was a member of the Oak Street Baptist Church. Lucy was glad that she had packed some nylons and high heels and gloves. "All good southerners belong to a church," Edith had told her. "After all, you are in the Bible Belt now." Even Uncle Elmo was dressed up, with his good slacks, a long sleeved short, and a tie. And he wasn't chewing on his customary wad of tobacco. He kept wiping his forehead with his handkerchief, as he drove them to the church. Lucy had thought they would be walking, since it was only a short distance away, but she discovered that, with the heat and humidity, it was just easier and more comfortable to drive. As they drove to the church, she finally asked about the strange smell she noticed every time she went out.

"What smell?" Uncle Elmo asked, but after he thought for a minute, he said, "Why, Honey, that's from them two lumber mills in town. You won't even notice it after you've been here for a while."

As they sat in church, she thought about the little Methodist Church back in Ellington, and was comparing the preacher's hellfire and brimstone sermon to the more gentle sermons that pastor Chuck Graham gave back home. Everyone at church here seemed very dressed up, and many of the congregation had their little cardboard fans, and were trying to keep cool. After church, she met some of her grandma's friends. One of Edith's younger friends had two teen age daughters, Hattie Sue and Tessa Brubaker, and Lucy had a chance to chat with them for a bit. They seemed a bit opinionated, and Lucy wasn't sure if she liked them or not.

That afternoon, Lucy had been planning to go to the movie theater, but when she mentioned it, Edith told her that the theater was closed on Sundays. She had asked Dorothy if they could go to the little clothing store she had seen in town, but was told that it was closed also. "Everything around here closes on Sundays since it's the Lord's Day. I think the only store open is the Piggly Wiggly Market out by the interstate," Edith remarked. Lucy didn't like the idea of spending all afternoon in the dark, depressing house, but it was too hot for walking. She got out writing paper to write another letter. At this rate, Elaine will be getting lots of letters from me, she thought.

Finally, on Monday afternoon, she went to the movie theater. It was strange going by herself, something she had never done at home. But two good movies she hadn't seen before were playing: *Some Like It Hot,* with Marilyn Monroe, Tony Curtis, and Jack Lemmon, and

Sleeping Beauty, an animated film. There was a long line in front of the ticket booth, but around the corner was a much shorter line. She didn't know why there were two lines, but she picked the shorter one, where there were only three people ahead of her.

"What'dya think your doin' in dis heah line, chile?" asked the colored lady at the ticket booth. "You know that dis line is fo' de coloreds only. Yo' all ain't got no business heah in dis line!"

"What do you mean?" Lucy asked, full of confusion. "I have no idea what you're talking about."

"Well, I can see dat yo'all ain't from around heah," was the reply. "But they's a line fo de whites and another line fo de coloreds, and you need to go stand in de line for de whites." Lucy had never heard of anything so ridiculous, but she went around, back to the longer line.

When she finally got up to the booth and bought her ticket, she told the man in the booth about her mistake. He laughed and said, "Another thing you should know is that the coloreds all sit up in the balcony, so don't sit right under it, because sometimes they throw trash down, or spill coke or popcorn. Sit back under the balcony, or way out in front of it." This is crazy, she thought. But it was a few hours of good entertainment, and she did enjoy both movies.

That first day of school Lucy was mulling over everything that she had experienced, as she sat in what they called the Home Room class. The teacher was taking roll, and then they would be getting their class schedules. One thing about this school, she thought, is all the classes were in the same building, and not spread out all over, as they were at home. So I won't be getting lost, she thought. When she had pre-registered a few days ago, she had signed up for Civics, Home Economics II, English Lit, Shorthand, Biology, and PE. She hoped it wouldn't take long to get over feeling like an outsider. She already noticed that the girls seemed a little behind the times here. They were still wearing the full skirts, with starched petticoats underneath. Girls at home hadn't been wearing that style for at least a year now. Lucy was wearing one of her sheath dresses. But she was happy since she was meeting Jimmy Lee for lunch by the first group of picnic tables out behind the school. There was nothing worse than eating lunch by oneself, she thought.

At noon time everyone was congregating at the picnic tables, and sure enough, Jimmy Lee was there just as he said he would be. His sister, Clydean was also there, and Lucy met a few more girls, Verlin, Emma, and LaDonna. There were so many people and names; she didn't think she would ever get them all straight. And about half the people she met seemed to have two names, which made it twice as difficult to remember. She did find, however, something she had in common with all the new people she was meeting. The music was the same, and Frankie Avalon, Paul Anka, and the Everly Brothers were just as popular with teens in the south as they were at home. Football was another thing both schools had in common. The talk of the group centered around Middleburg High's football team. They'd had a great year last year, but some of the best players were seniors, who were no longer there of course. When the bell rang, Jimmy Lee walked her to her Shorthand class, since his class was just down the hall.

After school was out, she was in her room relaxing, when Dorothy came in to ask about her day. It was still hot in both upstairs bedrooms, and both Dorothy and Lucy were doing their best to get used to the heat and humidity.

"So, how'd everything go today?"

"Okay, I guess. I met a lot of people, and it will take me awhile to remember who is who. My classes seem all right, and I have some really nice teachers. And Jimmy Lee has been a very good friend to me, showing me around and introducing me to people."

"Yes, he and Clydean both seem to be good, responsible kids," Dorothy added. "I'm glad they came over the other day, so I could meet them. Grandma said their aunt goes to her church."

"How is Grandma doing anyhow?" Lucy asked. "She doesn't really seem to be all that sick."

"Well, she's going to have surgery this week," Dorothy told her. "She's going to have a mastectomy, and after that she will have to go through chemotherapy and radiation treatments, which are really hard on a person. Her doctor wanted her to have the surgery several weeks ago. But she is such a stubborn lady. She was waiting for me to get back here. So I'll be running back and forth between here and the hospital for a while. You might be on your own around here for a few days, Kiddo, since I want to spend as much time as possible with her."

"Oh, that's not a problem. I mean that's why we came all this way, to be support for Grandma. And you seem to be getting along okay with her."

"Yes, she seems to have softened up quite a bit. She doesn't criticize me near as much as she has in the past, and we're enjoying each other's company now. But it's just sad that her getting cancer is what it took for her to change," Dorothy added, wiping her eyes. "Seems like we've wasted a lot of years."

"Well, you're here for her now," Lucy told her mother, as she hugged her. "We both are."

Later that night, Lucy was having trouble falling asleep. The weather had cooled off a bit, and a light breeze was blowing in through the window, and for the first time she wasn't too warm But Lucy wasn't thinking of the weather, or her grandma, or of school that night, she was thinking about bugs. She knew when she was sleeping, little waterbugs would be running around on her walls because the night before she'd had to turn on her light. The entire wall seemed to come alive! And the cockroaches here were enormous! They had them at home in southern California, of course, but they were quite small compared to what they had in Alabama. Lucy had gone into the bathroom the other evening to find one that looked big enough to carry her off. Uncle Elmo came upstairs when he heard her cry of alarm. "It's just a little ole' roach," he told her. "They don't bite."

"I know that, but they still scare me, and that one certainly wasn't little," she told him. He went to a closet and found a spray can of insect repellent. "Here, you can use this when you need to," he told her. "Spray all the cracks too, 'cause that's where they hide. The city of Middleburg hires some outfit to spray around town about once a month, and I think they're about due to spray again. Helps keep them down a little. But we have all this water around, in the culverts and the bayous, and them roaches and water bugs are attracted to water. The drain water from everyone's washing machines and sinks runs out to the culverts, so they stayed filled pretty much."

Lucy was horrified. "You mean all the sewer water just drains outside?"

"No, not sewer water. That all drains into septic tanks. It's just water from bathtubs and washin' machines and dishwashers. At some point the city will lay pipe, and install a regular city sewer system, but most people are against that because it will raise the taxes around here. Of course nobody wants that, even though it would help with the water bug and roach problem."

Lucy was thinking that she should be spraying her room every night, but then the odor of the insecticide was not very pleasant. She fervently hoped that the city would be doing their spraying soon.

*   *   *

Later that week, on Saturday, Lucy was getting ready to go to the lake with Jimmy Lee, Clydean, and some of their friends. It was Lucy's first real date, and she was excited. She thought Jimmy Lee was really cute, tall and slim with his dark good looks. At home, she never would date a boy that was younger than she was, but it didn't seem to matter to her now. And he drove a car, even though he was only fifteen. She didn't know if the law was different in Alabama or not, but she wasn't worried about that either. She put some suntan lotion in her beach bag along with her bathing suit, towel, and sunglasses. She got her package of hot dogs from the refrige. They would be barbecuing "along about suppertime" Jimmy Lee had told her, and everyone was bringing some food. The house was very quiet. Uncle Elmo was at work, and her grandmother was still in the hospital recuperating. The surgery had gone okay, and her mother was spending most of the day there too.

"Well, I'll be, if you don't look as sweet as cotton candy," Jimmy Lee told her when he picked her up. She was wearing pink plaid Bermuda shorts, and a pink seersucker sleeveless top.

"Well, thank you, and you're looking pretty good yourself," she responded. "So where is this lake we're going to?"

"Oh, it's over yonder a bit. Take us about an hour to get there. But you need to go back and change your sandals, and put on tennis shoes instead. Sorry I didn't tell you that before." She changed her shoes, came back, and climbed into the front seat next to him. Clydean and her date, George, were in the back seat, along with Verlin and a guy named Tommy. They were asking her questions about California. Somehow they had the mistaken impression that most California teen agers were very fast and wild. They drove through miles of pine trees, and then turned off onto a side road. Lucy was telling everyone that she thought there would be palm trees, not pine trees in southern Alabama.

"It's strange isn't it, how we get such different impressions of other parts of the country," Clydean was saying. "Most of us have someone in our family who work the lumber mills around here, either as truck drivers or actually work at the mill. And these pine woods are full of deer and squirrel, which provide a lot of people with food."

"Well mostly it's the poorer people who hunt squirrel," Jimmy Lee pointed out.

"But deer hunting season will be here soon," George said from the back seat. "I've got to start getting ready for that."

"So some people actually eat squirrel?" Lucy asked. "And what about possum?" She was told yes, those critters were a source of food for some of the people around there. The two couples in the back seat were chattering away, but Lucy was taking in the strange sights they were passing. The winding road had left the pines for the most part, but was now passing an ancient church and graveyard. The windows of the church were broken out, and the old graveyard looked very unkempt, with crumbling tombstones and shrubs growing over everything. The trees became denser, turning into thick jungle, which kept out the sunlight. Thick green vines were snaking their way around everything in its path. Jimmy Lee slowed the car in order to cross a rickety, narrow, wooden bridge, which was covered by hanging vines and Spanish moss. Swamp water that looked like thick green pea soup appeared on either side of the old bridge.

"That vine covers just about everything," said Lucy. "What's the name of it?"

"It's called kudzu," Jimmy Lee told her. "It grows like crazy around here, and everyone hates it because it takes over trees and other plants, and even buildings, and you can't get rid of it no matter what you do."

"Even if you burn it, the stuff seems to come back," remarked Verlin.

"We're pert'near there," Jimmy Lee announced. "It's called Deadman's Lake," he told Lucy.

"Catchy name," Lucy remarked. "I bet there's a story behind that."

"I'm not sure where it got that name," mused Jimmy Lee, "but a lot of the school kids come out here to party."

At last they pulled up in a little clearing and parked the car. Lucy had pictured a clear and sparkling lake, so she was disappointed to see a very marshy looking brown lake, which was almost swamp like in appearance. There were a few stumps sticking out here and there, and grass and reeds. Cypress trees lined the edge of the body of water. It had a weird look to it, and she could see why it had earned its name. Lucy was surprised that there were no little cafes or gas stations nearby, since most of the lakes in California were more commercialized.

She wondered if there were any restrooms nearby, but when she mentioned that, Verlin said, "No restrooms, but plenty of trees for cover. But you do have to watch out for snakes, since there are several poisoness varieties around here."

"I also thought we would be going swimming," she said to the other girls, "but the water doesn't look very inviting for swimming."

"Oh no, you don't want to swim in that lake," Clydean told her. "It's full of gators and water moccasins. We came here once with someone who brought their dog, and it went out into the water, and was eaten by a gator."

"Ohh, how sad! Do you think we'll see a gator?" Lucy asked.

"Probably not, since they stay in the water. Sometimes at night, though, when you shine a light toward lakes or rivers, you can see their eyes, glowing red, just above the water line."

"We probably should have brought our fishing poles," the boy named Tommy was saying. "You know there's bound to be some big catfish out there."

Three more carloads of teen agers drove up. Lucy wondered what they would be doing for the afternoon, if they weren't going to be swimming, but the time passed quicky enough. Some people had brought decks of cards, some brought transistor radios, but most of the music was supplied by the car radios, all on the same station. It was hot though, and muggy too. The gigantic mosquitoes were thick, and Lucy was glad Clydean loaned her some repellent. There was already a big fire ring there, and they lit a fire later on to barbecue the hotdogs. The smoke helped to chase away the mosquitoes. Most of the boys, and even some of the girls, were drinking, but Jimmy Lee wasn't, and Lucy was thankful for that. As the evening wore on, people were getting louder and rowdier, and two of the boys almost got into a fight. Lucy and Jimmy Lee were sitting on the tailgate of a friend's pick up, and he was holding her hand. "So are you having a good time?" he asked.

"You bet," she told him. "This lake is way different than any lake I've ever seen before. And we can make all the noise we want, and there is no one around to care. We have nothing like this back home. And I just love those cute little fireflies that are flitting around, but the rest of the insects, not so much," she added, swatting at a mosquito. "They won't leave me alone."

"They just like you 'cause you taste so sweet," Jimmy Lee whispered, as he pulled her close to him for a kiss.

Chapter 31

Mrs. Gimple was speaking to the first period U.S. History class, and was droning on and on in a monotone, and Elaine was trying hard to follow what she was saying. Her desk was toward the back of the room, and she could tell that most of the class wasn't really paying much attention. Elaine was thinking about her "non-date" with Duane, at the dance the other night. It had certainly turned out to be way more fun than she had expected. Duane and Paul together, had been cracking jokes the entire time, and then Duane had been very attentive at the dance. Some of her friends had been surprised to see them together, but she explained it was just a temporary, onetime thing.

"I'm glad to hear that," Karen had said, "because Duane just doesn't seem like your type."

"What exactly is my type?" Elaine wanted to know.

"Oh, I don't know. Someone like Jeff, I guess. Duane is kind of wild, or so I've heard."

Duane's younger brother, Dennis, had been dancing with Megan for most of the dance, and Megan seemed to be enjoying herself, even though she was still going steady with Willie. But of course he was away at school. Mrs. Gimple interrupted her thoughts.

"Okay, class, I'm going to open this up to discussion now," Mrs. Gimple was saying. "Shawn O'Dell, can you name some of the problems pertaining to the First Continental Congress?"

Elaine was very glad she hadn't been called on, but Shawn, just across the aisle from her, usually looking like he was asleep, or comatose, always got singled out. It never failed.

He cleared his throat and said, "Yes, they were concerned with building bomb shelters for everybody and they were also trying to beat the Russians to the moon. And they all had mental problems, and there weren't enough psychiatrists to go around." The class was roaring with laughter at his ridiculous answer. He always has to be a clown, Elaine thought, but then his answers never failed to perk up a dull class.

"Mr. O'Dell, that will be enough. Another outburst like that, and you can leave the room!"

"Is that a promise?" Elaine heard him mutter under his breath. In spite of her dry lecturing and slow pace, Mrs. Gimple's exams were stiff, and Elaine was dreading the first test of the year.

She wasn't faring much better in Biology. The class was studying the plant kingdom. The two phyla were angiosperms and gymnosperms, and under them were many classifications, which all had to be memorized.

"I don't know why we have to learn these silly names and classifications" Vicki grumbled to Elaine. They were at a lab table drawing a cross section of a monocot leaf.

"Me either," agreed Elaine. "When I see a plant in the ground, I really don't care if it has a vascular root system or has xylem or phloem in it."

"Girls, how about less talk and more work?" Mr. Nichols said, as he checked on their drawings.

Once he had passed them, Elaine whispered, "So what's the deal with you and DJ? You seemed to be spending a lot of time with him at the dance the other night?"

"You know, I actually think DJ is kind of cute. I think he's gotten taller over the summer, and he has the dreamiest brown eyes," was Vicki's answer. "And he seems more serious, lately, not the goofball that he used to be."

Elaine was quite surprised to hear Vicki's assessment of DJ. But before she could answer, Mr. Nichols interrupted their conversation. "Are you girls discussing Biology?" he asked. "And if so, I think the entire class needs to hear what you're saying."

"Definitely," Vicki replied seriously. "Mr. Nichols, how will it help us in life to know whether a plant is a monocot or a dicot." That was fast thinking, Elaine thought. Vicki could always think on her feet. She was much bolder in class this year, and she liked to pester Mr. Nichols with questions.

"Oh, it will help you in many ways," Mr. Nichols said. His eyes twinkled behind his glasses. "Next time you go to a dance, and your date gives you a corsage, you'll be able to figure out which class the flower belongs to, and that is something important that you'd need to know." His answer had everyone laughing.

In English the class was studying Thornton Wilder's play, *Our Town*. The simple, peaceful way the story about the little town was written reminded Elaine of Ellington. The drama class had performed the play the previous year, and everyone had done an outstanding job.

Typing class was a breeze for her, almost boring. She had already mastered the touch system typing on her mother's old typewriter at home, but she was taking the course to get her speed up. But the rest of the class was just beginning to learn the position of the letters.

"Fingers on the keyboard," Mr. Barber was saying. "Now, left hand, R-E, R-E, R-E," he chanted. "Now change to the right hand, U-I, U-I, U-I."

"This is silly, this is silly," Elaine typed. "I am bored, I am bored."

The Fifth Period P.E. girls had volley ball sessions at the end of the football field every day. They liked this outdoor sport since the Fifth Period boys gym class was also out on the field. They enjoyed being whistled at in their gym clothes, and enjoyed watching football scrimmages.

"Girls, girls," Frankie, the gym teacher would remind them, "keep your mind on the volleyball game, not on the football players." Football always reminded Elaine of Jeff, since he played the game and loved it. She wished she could see him play in a game. The Armedia-Desert Palms game was scheduled for later in the season, and it was an away game. If only he went to Armedia High, everything would be so perfect.

"Elaine—the ball!" someone cried. But it was too late to hit the ball, and she slipped on the grass in her effort to do so. Everyone laughed, and she wished she could put boys out of her mind for good.

Sixth Period was her favorite. The yearbook staff was scheduling class pictures, but until they were taken, there wasn't a great deal to do. Page layouts couldn't be drawn up until the number and the sizes of the pictures were known, and that applied to the write-ups also. Aside from getting organized, there was not much to do. So the time was used as a study period. But like in last year's Study Hall, it was hard to do any actual studying because listening to everyone's conversations was much more interesting.

Barbara Larson, the annual editor, was a popular senior. Her parents were wealthy, and she was always talking about some new possession she had acquired, the latest being a '58 Chevy Impala. Megan always had some astounding bit of news to contribute, and the fellows in the group spiced up conversations with witty comments. Even Miss Lippert seemed more humorous than usual. Today Elaine was using the time to write to Jeff. His letters were always so sweet, and Elaine knew hers were growing cooler and cooler. She was pondering what to say, when she heard a deep voice over her shoulder saying dramatically, *Dearest Jeff, Here I am in my last class of the day, and—*"

"Shawn O'Dell, quit being so nosy," she told him, hiding the letter under her notebook.

"But it looked so interesting, so passionate," he said, pulling a chair up beside her. "And who is this mysterious person you're writing to?"

"Well, it's like this," she explained. "I've been going with Jeff for about seven months now, and I've only seen him about five times. He lives so far away that he never gets enough time off his job to come and see me or to take me to any of the high school events. He's a really great guy, but it's just hard being so far apart all the time."

"Tsk, Tsk, what a shame!" Shawn said dramatically. "Two star-crossed lovers separated by time and distance and fate!"

"Oh, Shawn, do be serious, for once."

"But didn't I see you at the dance the other night with Duane Kellogg?"

"Oh, that wasn't a real date," she told him. "That was just so he could get into the dance."

"Well, from a bystander's point of view, it certainly looked like a real date."

It did seem to Elaine that Duane was becoming more interested in her, and it was rather flattering, since he was darkly attractive, interesting, and fun. Elaine and Beth attended the Friday night football game, and were sitting in the bleachers, when the two older boys came and sat with them. They persuaded the girls to go on a drive with them, instead of going to the dance. Since Beth had driven her car to Armedia, she and Paul headed down toward Ellington in her car, and Elaine went with Duane in his '52 Olds hardtop.

"So how is school going so far?" Duane asked her.

"It's going pretty good," she answered. "And that football game tonight was great. I can't believe that we won for a change. Last year was such a bad season."

"Yeah, that was a good game," agreed Duane. He began talking about when he had played on the team. "I never thought I'd say this, but there are times when I actually do miss my high school days," he added.

They reached the Hathaway house, where Beth parked her car, and then she and Paul got into the back seat of Duane's Olds. The Hathaway's seemed to be so easy-going compared to Elaine's parents. If they'd known she was going out cruising around, they probably would have had a fit. As it was, she needed to be home by 11:30 that evening. Sometimes her mother was asleep, but not always. And of course Elaine had thought she would be at the dance, and that is what she had told her parents earlier that day.

"Well, where to, everyone?" Duane asked.

"Let's take a drive down to High Bluffs," suggested Paul. It was a lovely, warm September evening, almost balmy, and there was a full moon in the sky. They decided to stop at Deb's Diner in Ellington before heading on down to High Bluffs. The diner seemed unusually busy for Ellington, and after they'd finished their burgers and fries, and went out to the parking lot, Paul and Duane were talking to some friends the girls didn't know, so they just waited in the car.

"They must be some guys from High Bluffs," Beth remarked, as they sat in the car waiting.

"Or maybe it's some guys they work with," added Elaine. Both boys worked at a small foundry in High Bluffs. She rolled the window down, since it was getting warm in the car. The boys came back to the car, and Duane peeled rubber, and headed east out to the freeway. Elaine felt a little nervous, since he was driving so fast.

"What's your big hurry?" she asked. "I thought this was supposed to be a nice leisurely cruise."

"Oops, sorry, sometimes I get a lead foot."

"Yeah, slow it down, man," Paul called from the back seat. "I get very nervous when you go too fast," he added in a high pitched voice, making them all laugh.

"You're a speed demon too," Beth told him.

"Hey, this would be a good night for the Wolfman to be out," Paul remarked. "Full moon and all." That led to a discussion of scary movies, and each person had a favorite one. *The Blob, The Fly, Return of the Fly, Dracula*, and *House on Haunted Hill* were all mentioned.

"*House of Wax* was the scariest movie I've ever seen," Elaine remarked. "It came out several years ago, but I had nightmares for months after I saw that one. Lucy's mom took us and dropped us off at the theater. I don't think she was paying attention to what movie was playing," she told Beth.

"I remember that one," Duane said. "with Vincent Price. His movies are guaranteed to be scary."

As they approached High Bluffs, Duane took a left turn which led out of town on a narrow country road. They passed some alfalfa fields and then empty fields on either side of the road. "Hey, just where are you heading, Kellogg?" Paul asked him. "Isn't this the road that goes out to the old silica mine?"

"I believe it is, but we're not going way out there. I'm just taking us on a drive in the country on a nice night. Is there anything wrong with that?"

"We have to watch the time, since I need to be home by 11:30," Elaine reminded him. "We still have about forty five minutes."

Duane pulled off the road about two miles later at a small grocery store, which was closed for the night. There was a picnic table next to it, in front of a row of tamarack trees. "This looks like a good place to stop," Duane said. "Everybody okay with this?"

"I don't know, it's kind of lonely way out here," complained Beth. They walked over to the picnic table and sat down on the top of it. Elaine was reminded of Lucy's last letter, and she told the rest of the group about the strange lake, way back in the swamps, and how it was a popular spot for parties for the Alabama teens.

"Well, this is way better than some old swamp," Paul remarked. "And with that full moon we have plenty of light."

"Good night for the Wolfman to be prowling around," Duane said.

"Oh, you brought that up earlier, and then you started in on the scary movies," remarked Elaine. "But we don't scare that easily."

"Good to know," Paul said. "I wish that store was open, 'cause I could sure use a beer right now."

"I might have part of a six pack left in the trunk," Duane said, "That is if you don't mind it being a little warm." They walked back toward the car.

"Oh, great, now they're going to be drinking," Beth said to Elaine.

"Maybe I should tell them that we need to get going now. Shhh," she added suddenly. "Did you hear something over in those bushes? I thought I saw something moving too!" She grabbed Beth's arm.

"There is something over there!" Beth exclaimed, jumping off the picnic table. Duane and Paul were standing behind the car talking and laughing "Hey, guys, get over here! Hurry!" she called to them, as the girls watched a short, stocky man come from behind the bushes. He had a nylon stocking pulled over his face, so his features were all scrunched up, and he looked very scary. He was wearing baggy pants and an overcoat. He didn't say anything, but grunted a couple of times, as he headed toward the picnic table. The girls didn't waste any time, as they left the table and hurried toward the car. "There's some crazy guy out there!" Beth cried.

"Well, what do we have here? Some kind of a nut running around?" Duane said. "You girls get in the car and lock the doors behind you!" Elaine climbed in on the right side, and slid over in front of the steering wheel and Beth was right behind her. They were both hastily rolling up the car windows and pushing down the lock buttons.

"My heart's just pounding!" Elaine cried. "What kind of weirdo would be running around out here in the middle of nowhere with a stocking over his face?"

"Who knows? My hands are shaking, and my knees are like rubber. What are they doing?" Beth asked as she watched Paul and Duane striding purposefully over to the strange man.

"They're probably telling him to get out of here," Elaine said. "You would think he'd be scared of Paul and Duane, since they're both pretty big guys."

"Did I leave my purse out on the table?" Beth was asking. "Oh good, I do have it right here, hanging on my shoulder."

"Beth, look, he's coming right over here to the car!" Elaine cried. She didn't see Paul and Duane, but the scary face was suddenly pressing right up against her window. She was glad the door was locked. She turned toward Beth, and was about to say something, when suddenly the car door swung open, and he was right there next to her! Elaine had never moved so fast in her entire life. Somehow she crawled to the other side of the car, right over Beth, and she was out the right side of the car before Beth could even move. The man quickly circled the car and was right behind her! She started running down the road, wondering where Paul and Duane were. This was not good, she thought, since was getting farther away from the car. But she was surprised at how fast she was moving. She was normally a pretty good runner, and now adrenalin had kicked in, and she was even faster than usual. She suddenly swung around in the middle of the road, and ran back toward the car. She reached it in a couple of minutes, and ran right up to Duane, and grabbed him and hung on for dear life. Duane and Paul were both laughing.

"It's all a big hoax," Beth said to Elaine, who couldn't say much since she was completely out of breath. The weird guy (who was also out of breath) walked slowly over towards the four of them, pulling the nylon stocking from his face. It was Duane's brother, Dennis! Elaine could hardly believe her eyes. She just kept staring at him with her mouth open.

"Boy, that nylon stocking really distorted your face," Beth was saying. "I just had no idea it was you. And since you were all stooped over, like a hunchback, you looked so much shorter." Dennis, who was huffing and puffing, was pulling off two bulky sweatshirts.

"You can really run," he told Elaine, between breaths. "Maybe that was a good thing, because I didn't know what I would do once I caught you!"

Duane and Paul were still laughing. "We gave Dennis the car keys, so he could open up your door, Elaine," Duane said

"I couldn't believe my eyes, when you came out the other side, ahead of Beth! Didn't know you could move so fast! That was a riot!" Paul told her, slapping the car. "Funniest thing I've ever seen!"

"It really wasn't all that funny," Beth told him. "You guys had it all planned out, didn't you?"

"We could have had a heart attack or something," Elaine said, finally able to talk again. "'I was almost going to swing my purse around and hit you with it, Dennis. Now I wish I had hit you. And just when did you guys put this little practical joke together? It was actually kind of mean."

"We pulled this on some girls when we lived in Bakersfield," Duane said. "It works every time."

"Well, we've had our fun for the night, and I think we'd better be heading home now," Elaine told them. As she and Beth walked around to their side of the car, she whispered, "I have a trick of my own, so just play along with me." She took a couple of steps toward the car, and then fell down onto the ground, in a dead faint.

"Oh no, it must have been too much for her!" Paul said anxiously.

"Oh, my gosh, now look what you've done!" Beth told them

"She must have been really scared," stated Duane. "Do you think she just fainted, or maybe she could have had a heart attack?" He bent down to look at her. "Well, come on, help me get her into the car. We might have to drive her to a hospital, and I don't even know where the nearest one would be!"

"Does anybody know, what is it, CRP, or CPR? Whatever it is, it's mouth to mouth," Dennis was saying. Elaine could no longer keep a straight face, and started laughing as they began to pick her up. Her plan had worked like a charm, since it sounded like they were all scared.

Duane looked at Paul and Dennis. "Looks like we got paid back, so we're even now," he stated.

"When I was younger, I thought I wanted to be a movie star," she explained, climbing into the car. "And I used to practice falling down like that all the time, since I thought movie stars needed to know how to either faint or drop dead. I never actually thought it would come in handy some day."

"Well, it looked very realistic," Beth told her. "You did a great job of fainting."

"Yes you did. It had me scared," Duane added. "I thought for a minute, maybe we'd killed you, and I certainly wouldn't want that on my conscience. You're too young for a heart attack though."

"You never know," she told him. "What if I'd had a weak heart and it just gave out from all that excitement? You'd have to live with the guilt the rest of your life!"

"Let me check your pulse," Duane said, grabbing her wrist. "Feels good and strong to me. I think you're pretty healthy. However, I was about to give you mouth to mouth, and I was really looking forward to that," he added with a grin. "It was actually kind of disappointing when you opened your eyes." Elaine reached over and gave Duane a playful slap. She was thinking about what he had said, and it sounded rather appealing.

Later, when they dropped her off at home, it was about a half hour past her curfew. Elaine tiptoed softly into the house, and luckily for her, everyone was asleep, even the cat who was snuggled up cozily on her pillow.

Chapter 32

October, as always was a hectic month. Elaine was busy at home, as well as at school. Her father was building more chicken pens, and she and Pam were delegated to paint the lumber again before the pens were constructed. There were also chickens to be vaccinated and debeaked. Lois was on the planning committee for the PTA Halloween carnival, and was helping work on an Evangelistic Crusade for the church. She was good at multi-tasking, and Elaine always wondered how her mother managed to accomplish so much with all that she had going on in her life.

At school, there were the usual football games and other fall activities. The Collette's had their first meeting of the year at Megan's home in Armedia. They made plans for a formal installation of new officers in the middle of November, and they planned an Initiation party for incoming members. They also decided to collect used toys to refurbish for needy children at Christmas, and they planned a rummage sale. After the meeting, they all discussed Armedia boys as usual.

They felt that the boys were finally growing up somewhat, and were at last getting interested in dating. DJ and Vicki had been going out. Vicki was telling them that he had finally acquired a car of his own.

"He is just so stoked about his car. It's a '50 Chevy, black with white-wall tires, and red and white tuck and roll upholstery. And a dual-exhaust with 30 inch mufflers. Of course that last part is a quote from DJ, since I really don't know, or care to know about all that."

Woody was dating Christy, and everyone agreed they made a cute couple. Alma was seeing a senior football player, and Karen was dating Christy's brother, Alan.

Megan had broken up with Willie and was dating Dennis Kellogg. She was so surprised to hear about his part in the practical joke on Beth and Elaine. "That just doesn't sound like something Dennis would do," she told them.

"I wish I'd had a camera that night," Elaine said. "He didn't look like himself at all. He could use that get-up for a Halloween costume."

"Well, are you going out with Duane now," Alma asked her. "What about Jeff?"

"I've gone out with Duane a couple of times," Elaine told her. "Jeff and I have never discussed just being exclusive, and Duane and I aren't serious. We've never even kissed or anything. We're just friends." She knew that Paul and Beth were getting serious, because they were now going steady.

Megan told them that the Turnabout Dance had been scheduled for the first weekend in December, later than it had been in the past. "All of us should try to go," she added. "As one of the best off-campus clubs in school, we should be well-represented there." Elaine wasn't happy about the new date, since Jeff would be more likely to come for a visit around Thanksgiving, because there was a break from school. She'd have to figure out what to do.

When she got home that Saturday afternoon and walked into the house, Charles and Lois were in the living room, slow dancing to *Chances Are*, a romantic Johnny Mathis song. She was so surprised to see that, since she felt that his songs were just for her generation. And here were her parents dancing together in the middle of the afternoon!

"I'm just taking a break from the farm work to dance with my best gal," Charles told her.

"Your father is a wonderful dancer," Lois added. "I think that's what attracted me to him in the first place."

"Don't mind me," Elaine said. "I need to get out and gather eggs anyhow."

"Oh, by the way, you have two letters on the buffet," her mother was saying.

Oh good, two letters, Elaine thought. Letters came before chores, and she tore Jeff's letter open with haste.

> *Dear Elaine, I'm sorry I haven't written for awhile, but I've been really busy with school, football, my job, and working on my car. How are things going with you? I realize that we are far apart*

and that it has been a long time since I've been down to see you. It's not because I haven't wanted to, but everything keeps getting in the way. But I do think about you all the time, and my love for you grows every day. And I hope you're feeling the same way about me.

I'm working out a plan here, for us to see each other. Chuck and Linda are coming out here for Thanksgiving, and I was hoping that you could come with them. Then on Friday, after Thanksgiving, I will drive us back to Ellington, and stay there til Sunday. Doesn't that sound like a great plan? I know it's over a month away, and by then my car should be ready for a long trip. It would be so wonderful to see you again. Write soon and let me know if this will work out for you. Love always, Jeff

That sounded like a good plan to Elaine, but she wasn't sure her folks would let her go, since they would probably want her around for Thanksgiving. She would have to discuss that with them. The second letter was from Lucy.

Hi, Elaine (and Beth and Natalie), How is everything in your part of the US? I just feel so far away from everything, and yet some things are so familiar. I've been going to the football games here at Middleburg High. Boy, the entire town shows up for them. It's really a big deal back here, with huge crowds cheering on the home team. Our school could use some of that enthusiasm. I'm still with Jimmy Lee, and he is a great guy, although I'm not near as crazy about him like I was with Phil. (Well, part of the reason for that is our stay here is only temporary.)

My grandma is going through some cancer treatments called chemotherapy and radiation, but they are really hard on her. She is very tired and sick all the time, and Mom and I and my uncle are helping her with everything we possibly can. She has lost all of her hair because of the treatments, and she doesn't go anywhere anymore, not even to church. It's very sad.

On a happier note, Jimmy Lee took me to the beach last weekend, since it's still nice weather around here. We went to Pensacola Beach, and it was a lot of fun. The Florida beaches have very white sand, way prettier than our southern Calif. beaches. The water is much warmer too in the Gulf. I miss you guys, I mean I miss y'all. Love, Lucy

Upon arriving at school Monday morning, everyone noticed a terrible stench in the air. It smelled like something very rotten or decayed. There had been times in the past, when the drying lake bed, which was in close proximity to the school, had smelled pretty bad from the rotting carp, but this odor, whatever it was, seemed to be much stronger and more offensive.

"Well, I hope we don't have to put up with that smell all day," Nat was saying, as they walked up to the student square.

"It's enough to gag a maggot," added Beth. "It must be something that died out on the lake bed and the wind is blowing it this way."

Once they reached the group of students on the square, everyone was talking about the same thing. That coming Friday night was the football game with their arch rival, Ralston High. Apparently, last week, someone had blown off Ralston's "R," which was on the hill above the desert town, and Ralston was putting the blame on Armedia's football team. Of course the football team was claiming to know nothing about that. But in retaliation, Ralston had dumped dead jack rabbits all over the school lawn, on the walkways between the classrooms, and everywhere else they could think of. The rabbits had been disposed of, but the foul odor was lingering.

"With this breeze, the smell will dissipate soon enough," Mr. Nichols said later in Biology class. "Too bad the custodians didn't leave us a rabbit to dissect as a class project."

"Ohh, leave it to you to think of something like that?" Vicki told him. "Yuck!"

On Friday night when the rooters were sitting in the bleachers, waiting for the game to start, they heard that someone from Ralston had somehow gotten into the locker room before the game, and all Armedia's team uniforms had been thrown into the showers. There was no time to dry them, so they were all playing in wet uniforms on a crisp October night. It was the night of the Homecoming Game, which came earlier than usual that year.

"They're still mad about losing that basketball game to us last year," said Elaine. Their little group in the bleachers was smaller, since Megan and Vicki were cheerleaders, and Alma and Karen were song leaders. Elaine, Beth, Natalie, Mary Lou Wright, and Christy Coulter were sitting together. Christy's brother, Alan was sitting with them. Woody Stuart, of course was playing on the team, as were Greg and Lenny. Duane and Paul weren't at that game, and Beth wasn't sure where they were that night.

Elaine was telling Christy that the Ralston Riffian's team was their big rival, in both football and basketball, and she also mentioned the Victory Bell that went back and forth between the two schools.

"So that's why they threw the rabbits around, and why they soaked all the uniforms?" Christy was asking.

"They're still upset about losing to us in basketball last winter," Mary Lou explained, "and they will do whatever it takes to get even. This should be a good game."

Armedia's receiver returned the opening kickoff 38 yards. On the first play from scrimmage, it was carried another 18 yards. Finally Greg Okamota bullied his way into the end zone for the remaining eight yards. The Riffians had no chance to move the ball after kickoff as Lenny Mendoza pounced on a Ralston fumble, and the Armedia Leopards were again in scoring position. Armedia's quarterback accounted for the touchdown with a twelve yard keeper around the left end, so just fifteen minutes into the first quarter, the score was already 14-0.

"Wow, we are on a roll tonight!" exclaimed Beth. "They are looking GOOD!"

"Let's hope they can keep the momentum going," Natalie remarked. "We definitely want to hang onto our Victory Bell."

"We're from Armedia, couldn't be prouder, and if you can't hear us, we'll yell a little louder!" chanted the cheerleaders.

As the second quarter began, Ralston was pushed back to its eighth by another series of penalties. But they fought back with new energy and impressive drives, and finally advanced the ball to Armedia's tenth yard line. It didn't take long after that for them to get into the end zone and make a touchdown, along with the extra point.

At half time, there were the homecoming festivities, and the homecoming king and queen were crowned, and the crowd's enthusiasm was at a new high for their team and their school.

In the third quarter Armedia kicked off, and Ralston's receiver caught the ball on the 10 yard line, and ran the ball back to the 25 where he was tackled. In the next play Ralston's quarterback was sacked by Bobby Jackson on the 15 yard line. After that the quarterback attempted a pass, and Armedia's defensive back intercepted it, so the opposing team was thwarted again. Three plays later Greg broke through the line, and went all the way for a touchdown.

"This is such a great game. I can't believe how well they're playing tonight!" Elaine cried happily. "And it's so perfect for Homecoming."

"I'm really proud of Woody!" exclaimed Christy. "He looks great out there!"

Armedia's final touchdown came midway through the fourth quarter. Greg's continual running set up the tally as the Leopards drove from their 40th to the Ralston Riffian's two, and Lenny plunged over to make the final score 28-7. It was a sweet victory for the Leopards, especially after last year's dismal season.

Two weeks later, in early November, Armedia played Desert Palms High School. The girls were all on the rooter's bus on the long drive out to the desert town.

"Well, Elaine, this will be a very challenging game for you, since you want Jeff to do well in the game, and yet you'll have to be rooting for our team," Vicki remarked on the bus ride.

"I know. I'm just going to cheer both teams on," replied Elaine. "Jeff is playing tackle, and is Number 75, so you guys have to cheer for him too."

"Will you get to actually see him and talk to him tonight?" Christy asked.

"Not for long. I'll walk down to the field after the game, before he goes to the locker room, and we'll have a few minutes. But at least I'll get to see him play."

"I'll go with you after the game, since I'll need to find Woody," Christy told her.

That game didn't go nearly as well as the game with Ralston. Year after year, Armedia had lost to Desert Palms. Their players were bigger and always seemed to get the all the breaks in the game. And throughout this game, Armedia was plagued with injuries. Two players were already sitting out the game. Then Woody had been hurt while trying to pass. The crowd in the bleachers also felt that the referees were in favor of Desert Palms.

"They just seemed so prejudiced against our team," Elaine complained. "They could give us a break once in a while."

"Your Jeff is doing a good job," Christy told her. "And so was Woody of course, until he got injured."

"It just seems to me, that their players have ours psyched out, as they do every year," Beth observed. "Most of their guys seem about the size of Bobby Jackson, so it's intimidating to our team." However, during the final quarter, the Armedia Leopards fought hard and gave their all until the gun sounded, ending the game. But there had been too many obstacles in their way. Desert Palms overwhelmed Armedia with a final score of 45-14.

As soon as the buzzer went off, signaling the end of the game, Elaine and Christy made their way hastily down the bleachers and onto the field to look for their football players. It felt strange to Elaine to be walking over toward the opposing team, in their blue and gold uniforms, but Jeff spotted her, and ran up to her, enveloping her in a big hug.

"You played a great game," she told him. "You looked so good out there tonight."

"Oh, it was just another game," he said modestly. "We only have one more game this season, and then it's all over."

"Yeah, this is your last year of school," Elaine said sadly.

"Oh, that doesn't bother me. It will good to be out of school and get on my own." They talked for a few more minutes. Elaine was telling him that her parents were having a big family get together for Thanksgiving, and wanted Elaine to be at home for the occasion, so she wouldn't be able to go with Chuck and Cathy to his family Thanksgiving in Desert Palms.

"But will you still be able to come on Friday?" she asked him.

"I don't see why not. Heck, I'll try to drive to Ellington on Thursday morning," he said. "That is if I'm invited to your Thanksgiving dinner."

"Of course," Elaine told him. "That would be wonderful."

The Collette's held their formal Installation of Officers at the Women's Clubhouse in November, and it was a very nice affair. They had sent out engraved invitations to parents and friends. The next day an initiation party was hosted by Mary Lou Wright, and four new members were added to the club. Christy Coulter had joined the club. Her sweetness and friendliness had made her popular with everyone.

The evening before Thanksgiving was a busy time at Elaine's home. She and Russ put the extra leaves in the dining room table, and then set up two card tables. They had borrowed some folding chairs from the church. There would be 18 people coming the next day. The turkey was thawing out, and Lois was busy making pumpkin and mincemeat pie. Grandma Grace was there too, sitting on a stool at one end of the counter peeling potatoes. Scottie and Pam were helping with the egg packing and sorting. Timmie was in his room, and he was supposed to be putting his toys away. Everyone had a job to do. Their Thanksgiving dinners were usually smaller, but as Lois had said to Charles a few weeks earlier, "Your mother always hosts the Christmas dinner, and does all that work to get everything ready, and I think the least we can do is to host Thanksgiving this year." A year ago, Elaine thought, she would have been at the Turnabout Dance, but it had been rescheduled, and was still two weeks away. And she didn't know what she was going to do about that. She was sure that Jeff wouldn't be able to come down again, just for the weekend, and yet she really wanted to go. Beth had told her that Duane was interested in her, and she could probably ask him. But what would Jeff think about that? It was a dilemma all right.

"Hey, quit daydreaming," Russ told her, handing her two tablecloths. "You need to put these on. I'm going out to the packing room, and change places with Pam. This is woman's work!"

Jeff arrived the next day, just in time for the big feast. He told Elaine that he'd seen Chuck and Cathy last night when they'd arrived in Desert Palms for a short time, and that they would be back in Ellington on Friday. "And I will be able to crash at their house tonight. They always leave their door unlocked." Elaine was busy introducing him to her relatives. Once dinner and cleanup was over, the kids went outside, since the weather was fairly decent, and Jeff had most of them playing a game of touch football on the lawn.

The weekend went by quickly as it usually did when Jeff was visiting. They took in a movie on Friday evening, hung around with Chuck and Cathy on Saturday, playing Monopoly again, and went to church on Sunday. Elaine still didn't know what she was going to say about the dance, but she finally made the plunge, knowing that he would be leaving shortly. They were sitting in Jeff's car, in the parking lot of Deb's Diner, following a quick lunch there.

"There's a dance coming up at school about two weekends from now," she said. "It's a pretty important dance, and I don't suppose you could come down again then?"

"I doubt it," Jeff said. "I quit my job at the restaurant because they wanted me to work on Thanksgiving, but I have another job lined up when I get back home. My Uncle Fred is the manager of a lumberyard, and I'll be going to work there, but I probably won't be able to get any time off for a while. I'll most likely be working every day after school, now that football is over, and also on Saturdays."

"I know it's hard for you go come down here," she told him. "What if I went to the dance with another guy, just as a friend?"

Jeff turned to her with a worried look on his face. "How good a friend is this guy?"

"Oh, he's just a friend. I've known him since I started high school."

"I guess that would be okay. But don't you go getting interested in someone else now, since you know how I feel about you. You mean everything to me." He took her in his arms and they exchanged some long goodbye kisses before he had to head back out of town.

Chapter 33

Elaine and Beth were out on the screened porch at Beth's. They were sitting in the lawn swing and were waiting for Paul and Duane to drop by. "They're always so unpredictable about when they'll get here," Beth grumbled. "They like to keep us guessing."

"I think I hear Paul's car now," Elaine said.

"It's about time you got here," Beth said to Paul, as the two guys strode into the back yard.

"Sorry about the delay," said Duane. His brown eyes twinkled mischievously. "But we got to talking to some good-looking chicks in High Bluffs and sort of lost track of the time."

"Is that so?" Elaine asked.

"Not really. Don't believe everything I tell you." Duane said. "I just like to tease you because you take everything so seriously." The two couples made their way out to the driveway and got into Paul's car. They were driving up to the Armedia roller rink for the evening. Football was over for the year, and the basketball games hadn't started yet, so that left the roller rink or the movie theater for entertainment.

"You're looking very cute tonight," Duane complimented. "And by the way, I hear you have a question for me." She was thinking that Duane looked very handsome in a plaid cotton shirt and Levis, and he was smiling at her in a very engaging way.

He isn't wasting any time, getting right to the point, Elaine thought. "You probably already know what I want to ask you about," she said. "I'm sure Paul told you."

"Yes, he did, but I want to hear it from you."

"Okay, as you know the Turnabout Dance is a week from tonight, and I was wondering if you would go with me?"

"Now, that all depends. Am I going just as your friend, or something more than a friend, like a real date?"

Elaine was really stumped at his question. If she was going to be honest with Jeff, she should tell Duane she just wanted to go as friends, but she was starting to have feelings for Duane too. He was very good looking, and was a lot of fun, and he lived right here in the area. She didn't have to wait for weeks to see him.

"Well, cat got your tongue?" he asked. "Is that such a hard question to answer, Elaine?"

"I'm just trying to be as honest as possible," she explained. "I told Jeff that I wanted to ask you, but just as a friend, but now I'm starting to think it's more than just friendship between us."

"I like that you're being truthful with me, and I'll do the same with you. I want more than friendship from you, and if I take you to this dance, I'm going to expect something in return." Elaine was quiet, thinking about what he said. She wasn't sure exactly what he meant.

"Hey, you're all quiet again. But I need to know, is it too much to want some hugging and kissing after the dance? I mean I'll have to dress up in a monkey suit, and a tie, and I'm just not a dress-up kind of guy. But I'd do it to make you happy."

"Thanks, Duane, I think we'll have a fun time," she answered, reaching for his hand.

"Good. We'll seal the deal with a kiss," he said, leaning toward her. The French kiss was long, lingering, and exciting, and she thought back to when she had first met him in her Freshman year, never dreaming that they would be sharing a moment like this. She was feeling tingly and lightheaded.

As soon as they got there, they found a table in the snack bar area, and the guys went to buy sodas for the group. "He's going to go with me," she told Beth, "but he definitely wants to be more than friends. What am I going to do? I really care for Jeff, and I thought I loved him at one time, but I don't feel as strongly about that as I used to. I am thinking I could really go for Duane. But I can't be dishonest with Jeff! He is such a great guy, and I'm not going to feel right if I start dating Duane.

"Things can't ever be just simple and easy, huh?" Beth asked. "I guess you need to give yourself some time to think about this. Give it a couple of weeks. If you really like being with Duane, and you think you're falling for him, you'll have to break up with Jeff. Or if you go out with Duane a few times, and he's not measuring up, then tell him it's not working out. At some point you'll have to make a decision though, and I know that will be difficult."

Later that weekend, when Lois heard of her daughter's plans, involving Duane, she was not at all happy. "What do you mean, you're going to the dance with Duane Kellogg?" she asked. "Did you and Jeff have a falling out? What's going on?"

"No, nothing happened between me and Jeff," she told Lois. "In fact I did ask Jeff if it was okay if I went to the dance with someone else, as a friend, and he was okay with that."

"Well, I don't think I'm okay with it," Lois replied. "It just doesn't seem like the smartest thing to do. And we don't know anything about this Duane guy."

"Sue Hathaway knows him, so you could ask her. And he and I would be double dating with Beth, and Paul Newberry. They've been going together for a while."

"I do know Paul's mother. She works at the five and dime in Armedia. Still, I don't see why you have to go to this dance. Couldn't you just stay home? In my opinion, if you really cared for Jeff, you'd be content to miss out on the dance."

"Every girl in the Collette's is going."

"Well, heaven forbid, the entire club would disintegrate if you were the oddball, and didn't go! I know the girls in that group are very nice girls, and you had a lovely installation ceremony, but you don't have to do everything that everyone else does. I'm sure they would all like you just as much if you didn't make an appearance."

"Oh, Mother, you don't understand," Elaine said, retreating to her room. She took the phone with her. The long cord just barely reached. When she'd told her mother that all the girls in her club were going, it wasn't exactly the truth. Nat wasn't going. She and Ty were still going steady even though he was away at college. He had gotten a football scholarship to Arizona State, and Nat hadn't seen him since he had left in September. She remembered all the fun they had had double dating at the Turnabout last year. Life had seemed so simple back then, and now everything was getting complicated.

"Nat, I just don't know how you do it," she told her friend on the phone. "You're so faithful to Ty, and so good about staying home, and waiting until he gets a break from school. How do you manage to do that?"

"I guess I'm just so madly in love with him, that I don't mind missing out on stuff," Nat told her. "But he's coming home in three more weeks for Christmas vacation, and I'm really excited about that. And now that I'm allowed to date, I still have a problem, because my dad is such a racist, he won't like Ty, I'm sure. I'll probably have to sneak out to see him."

Elaine told her about her dilemma, and that she might have to make a choice between Jeff and Duane. "How do I get in these predicaments?" she asked mournfully.

"Isn't that the way it always is?" Nat asked. "For your first year and a half of school, you didn't really have anyone in your life, and now there are two guys at the same time. But I think if you were really madly in love with Jeff, you wouldn't be so attracted to Duane. Did you ever think about it that way?"

"I suppose that's possible. And I'm only 16, and I don't really know my own mind, and I'm just not ready to settle down to one guy. I have to finish the rest of high school, and then college. By the time I graduate from college, there will probably be lots of guys.'

The night of the dance Elaine waited on pins and needles until her friends came to pick her up. Her entire family had been very verbal about the fact that they liked Jeff much better, and how could she be dating someone else? Her parents hadn't met either Paul or Duane, and she had told Beth to be sure and bring them into the house before they left. Duane wasn't wearing a suit, but he did have on a sport jacket and slacks, a dress shirt and tie. He looked nervous as Elaine made the introductions. Everyone made small talk for a few minutes and then they were off. "Boy, you dad must have been a drill sergeant in his earlier life," Duane said, as they slid into the back seat of Paul's car.

"Oh, he wasn't that bad. He was just trying to get to know you a little bit."

This year's theme for the dance was "White Christmas" and there were fake, flocked trees everywhere, and big snowflakes hanging from the ceiling and the basketball rims. Paul led them to a table way back in the corner. "Suppose you girls will be expecting us to do a lot of dancing," he said to Beth. "And I don't know if that's going to happen, because my dress shoes are killing me."

"Well, just kick 'em off," Duane suggested jokingly. "That's what the girls do with their high heels."

Paul playfully elbowed Duane, and they began arguing with each other good naturedly. The first couple of hours of the dance went by quickly, and even though Elaine was having a good time, she felt very guilty about Jeff. The boys wanted to leave early, so they didn't get to see the crowning of the football king and queen. It didn't matter anyhow, Elaine thought, since the same people were usually chosen for honors like that. They cruised around Armedia for a while, and then Paul drove around to the west side of the dry lake, and continued on up the highway that crossed over to the mountains. At the lookout point he pulled the car over and parked.

"Good place to watch the submarine races," said Paul. It was quiet in the car, and before she had time to think too much about it, Duane was holding her and kissing her, and caressing her, and whispering all kinds of sweet nothings. "I've waited a long time for this," he told her.

The following morning Elaine was sitting in church, but she wasn't listening to Chuck's sermon at all, she was busy reliving the events of the night before. The dance had been fun, and parking later and making out with Duane had been exciting, but she'd had to ask him to slow things down a couple of times. He wasn't really content to stop with just kissing. Maybe he was too old for her, or too wild, she thought. Even though she'd had a great time, she was really feeling guilty. She had a feeling, deep down, that Jeff had a great deal more respect for her than Duane did. But Duane lived right here in the area, and if they kept on dating, she wouldn't have to worry about any activity that came along, he would always be there. But what about Jeff? And what would Chuck and Cathy think? They would probably be really upset with her if she were to break up with Jeff. What a dilemma! And the way her mother'd had a hissy fit with her, over just one date with Duane, why she would probably have a heart attack if Elaine continued to go out with him.

Sunday afternoon she and Beth were driving around collecting used toys for the Collette's toy drive. They decided to stop at Chuck and Cathy's just for fun.

"Of course, we've got lots of toys," Cathy answered, "with our 29 children, what do you expect?" She invited them in. "Chuck and I were just planning a Christmas schedule for the church. It is surprising the number of activities that one small town has around Christmas. The grammar school program is on Friday night, 4-H party on Saturday afternoon, the MYF party is on Sunday night."

"And then the church program is on Tuesday night, and on Wednesday the church youth will be going Christmas caroling," Chuck added.

"And coming over to our house for hot chocolate and goodies afterwards," Elaine added.

"You bet," said Chuck. "Then Thursday night we're having a Christmas Eve candlelight service at the church."

"After all that activity, I hope you're not too tired to enjoy Christmas Day," Beth told them.

"I'm already tired just thinking about so much going on," Cathy said. "If you girls could fit it in, I could sure use some help, especially with the 1st and 2nd Grade Sunday School class in the Christmas program."

"We'll be glad to," Elaine said, feeling guilty about her inactivity at church. She, Beth, and Lucy had all dropped out of MYF more than a year ago. Scottie and Russ still attended, and there were eight to ten other kids who did also. But Elaine always seemed busy with something on Sunday evenings. And the group they had now seemed so much younger.

A few days later she received another letter from Lucy. She'd hadn't heard from her in about a month.

> *Dear Elaine, How is everyone doing? This has been a very sad time for us. After going downhill steadily, Grandma died yesterday. She'd been in the hospital for the last two weeks, and both Mom and I had a feeling that she wouldn't be around for much longer. But it was good that we were able to spend these last few months with her. Mom and Uncle Elmo are making arrangements, and after the funeral, we will start that long, long drive home. It will be so good to see everyone again, and I'm excited that we'll be home for Christmas. Love, Lucy*

Elaine, glanced at the postmark, and figured that she would be back in a few more days, and that was good news. She was really looking forward to seeing Lucy again.

Lois also had some good news. "I got a call from Aunt Sandi today, and she was wondering if you and Pam would like to spend the week after Christmas with them in Huntington Beach. We talked about it some when they were here for Thanksgiving. I know you girls always have a good time with your cousins."

"I think I'd enjoy that, Mom," she said. "Lynne is always fun to be around, and Pam will like spending time with Annette too." Elaine knew she would enjoy getting out of town for a few days. "Besides, by then all the Christmas activities around town will be over with anyhow."

Lucy was home by the weekend, and she had Elaine and Beth spend the night on Friday, and the girls all had much to catch up on.

"I can't tell you how good it is to be home," Lucy said. "I've always thought this small one-horse town was for the birds, but I think I'll appreciate it more now."

"Now that you're a worldwide traveler," Elaine told her.

"It's like an entirely different world back there, and I think they're about ten years behind southern California. And they grow bugs that are big enough to carry you off!"

"No place like home, huh?" Beth added.

"That's right. And now I want to hear all the latest gossip, and all your news, and about everyone's love life," Lucy said. "I know I have a lot to catch up on."

Fortunately, Elaine was caught up on all the busyness of Christmas the next two weeks, and she didn't see Duane and she didn't hear from Jeff during that time, and that was just as well. She enjoyed helping with the Primary aged Sunday School class. The little ones that age were so cute. There was last minute Christmas shopping to do, and cookies to be baked at home. Lots of cookies were needed for the get-together after caroling. Christmas caroling was always enjoyable, although it was cold. The kids were riding in the back of pick-up trucks, bundled up in heavy jackets, caps, gloves, and scarves.

Pam and Elaine had their suitcases packed before Christmas, since they would be leaving with their aunt and uncle after the annual Hummer Family Reunion in Redlands. Russ would be doing their chores, and Scottie would be helping also. "We've got it covered," Charles had said.

When Uncle Bob and Aunt Sandi left the family gathering on Christmas afternoon, four chattering girls were in the back seat of their Cadillac, headed for Huntington Beach. "Now you understand that there will be no talking on the way home," joked Uncle Bob.

"Oh, Daddy, you're just plain silly," his younger daughter, Annette told him.

"That would be like holding the ocean back, to expect you girls to be quiet, huh?"

Lynne and Elaine were comparing high schools (Lynne was a Sophomore.) Annette was in 7th Grade in Junior High, but of course Ellington didn't have a Junior High. Pam was telling Annette about all her athletic accomplishments. Uncle Bob was Charles' younger brother, and he was an engineer for a large company. They had a lovely home in Huntington Beach. Elaine was feeling a little envious, as they entered a large foyer. The thick, white carpeting made the house look so open, and the sunken living room was decorated beautifully. The furniture was all very formal. Elaine and Pam followed the girls upstairs to their rooms, which were also decorated beautifully, with nothing out of place.

"Oh. your room is just gorgeous, and I love all your pink," Elaine said. "And you are so, so lucky to have a room all to yourself. I don't know how you do it, with everything in its place like this. Even if I had my own room, it wouldn't be anywhere near this neat."

"Oh, it can get messy. In fact, watch this," she laughed, knocking the large assortment of stuffed animals off her bed, and sending them flying all over the room. She followed up by jumping on the bed, wrinkling the pink quilted bedspread.

"I think I have one crazy cousin," Elaine giggled.

"This should be a great week. Some of my friends are having a party tomorrow night and lots of cute guys will be there. My dad is taking us all out to dinner to a really fancy restaurant later in the week. And Mom and Dad are talking about us all going to Pasadena to the Rose Parade for New Year's Day!"

"Oh, that sounds wonderful. We watch that on TV every year, and I always wondered what it would be like to actually be there and see it in person."

"And I have some new phone tricks to play on people, and you can help me with that since they won't know your voice."

"Sounds like we'll have plenty to keep us busy."

The fun filled week went by very quickly. The party, given by the older brother of Lynne's best friend was good, not that much different from parties in Armedia, except that everyone in Lynne's circle had money. The boys around here drove shiny new cars, nothing like the jalopies and hot rods driven by Elaine's friends. There were the teens that still had to drink at the party, and Elaine noticed the host's mom keeping an eye on the punchbowl. Lynne was drinking wine (she said she drank a little at home sometimes) and Elaine had to try some. Her parents never had any alcohol in the house, and for some reason she always thought that wine would taste really wonderful. But she was disappointed when she tried it. "I think it's something you have to acquire a taste for," Lynne told her. "I don't like it that well myself, but I drink a little from time to time. My folks drink it a lot at home."

The dinner at Antoine's French Restaurant was a new experience for the unsophisticated country girls. The menus were in French, and the prices weren't even on the menu, but Uncle Bob wasn't concerned with the price anyhow. He helped the girls order, since they didn't have any idea what they wanted. Elaine told him she definitely didn't want anything that had chicken in it.

"Oh, but I thought that you loved chicken," Uncle Bob quipped, "since that's probably a dish you never get at home!" She ended up having crab quiche and salad with a new kind of dressing, and chocolate mousse for dessert. It looked like chocolate pudding to her, but tasted way better. The restaurant experience was really wonderful.

"We only have one place to eat in Ellington, and it's just a little diner," Elaine told Lynne later. "And here you have all these choices about where to eat. Our family very rarely goes out for dinner. I think I'm liking city life better and better. No end of places to go and things to do."

"Yeah, I can't imagine what it would be like living out in the country," Lynne said. "I guess you have to make your own fun, like when those guys cooked up that boogeyman scare."

The trip to the Rose Parade was the highlight of the visit. They had to get up at 4:00 am to make the drive from Huntington Beach to Pasadena. Ordinarily it wouldn't take that long, but they had to allow for all the traffic, and the time to find a parking spot. They were walking around the parade route at 7:00 am, and it seemed so strange to see the people on the sidewalks in their sleeping bags, having arrived there the night before. They must have really wanted to see that parade, since they braved the forty degree weather during the night. And if you wanted to get breakfast, there was an hour's wait at most of the restaurants and cafes in the area. It was the same situation for the restrooms. There were just huge crowds everywhere, all milling around Colorado Boulevard waiting for the parade to start. Uncle Bob had bought donuts, coffee, and hot chocolate when they first left the house, so they didn't have to worry about breakfast. And they had a place to sit too, since Aunt Sandi knew someone on the parade route, who had planned for them ahead of time. She had put lawn chairs out for them on the sidewalk. It was perfect.

At last the parade started. It was a bright, sunny morning, and the temperature was supposed to get up into the low 60's. The parade was in its 70th year, having been started by the Pasadena Valley Hunt Club back in 1890. The floats, all made of flowers, were absolutely gorgeous, and the ideas that the float designers came up with were so original. There were also top marching bands from across the country in the parade, and there were equestrian groups riding beautiful horses. The entire parade was an amazing, indescribable experience.

Two days later, on Sunday, Uncle Bob was driving the girls back to Ellington. Vacation was nearly over, a new year, 1960, was just beginning, and school would be starting the following day. Elaine wasn't especially looking forward to getting back in the grind and facing her problems, but she knew it wouldn't do much good to just ignore them either.

Chapter 34

After the fun filled Christmas vacation, it wasn't easy getting back into the school mode. Elaine had so enjoyed sleeping in every morning, and doing whatever she felt like doing during the day, and now she was back to hearing the shrill ring of the alarm clock every morning at 6:00. She hadn't made any formal New Year's resolutions, but she had some in the back of her head. She wanted to become more active in church again, and also to spend more time studying. (She had made that one before though, and it was a hard one to keep.)

School seemed fairly quiet after the holidays. Surprisingly enough, the students seemed ready to take up their studies again and were prepared for the heavy homework loads the teachers assigned them. There were Civil War battles and dates to learn in US History, types of algae to be memorized in Biology, a novel by an American author to be read in English class, basketball rules to study in PE, business letter forms to be typed in Typing Class, and new layouts and deadlines in the Yearbook Class. The month of January was passing slowly. There were no parties, no one seemed to be dating much, and even the Collette's had run out of entertaining ideas. On the weekends were basketball games, and if the game was a home game, it was followed by the customary dance in the gym. Beth was still going steady with Paul; Megan and Dennis were still together, as were Christy and Woody. But the other girls were kind of at loose ends. At least they all had driver's licenses now. Even Elaine had finally given in and gotten hers, but since her family only had the one vehicle, she rarely had a chance to drive it.

One Saturday evening, the girls were cruising the streets of Armedia with Vicki at the wheel of her parents' station wagon. They made the rounds of the pizza place and the malt shop and the skating rink. Cruising was becoming a popular pastime for the small town teens. Sometimes they would be on the lookout for the cars belonging to certain guys, and other times they would just cruise for the sheer fun of it. Tonight Megan was with them, having told Dennis that she just wanted to spend time with her girlfriends.

Megan was informing the rest of the group that Dennis was having a big party around the end of the month. It would be held at the home of his dad and stepmom in High Bluffs. "I'll be helping to host it, and if I have my way, we'll make it a beatnik party. It should be fun for everyone to dress up like that. And hopefully, things won't get too wild and crazy, the way some parties do."

"Well, what about all the party crashers that usually show up?" Lucy asked. "They're the ones that create problems and do all the drinking."

"Maybe that won't be as much of a problem, since it's not right here in Armedia," Megan said. "Hey, Vicki, why don't we pull in at Tony's Pizza? It looks like that's where everyone is tonight." More than a few cars were in the parking lot, and fairly large groups of people were standing around, even though it was a cold night. On their way into the pizza parlor, they stopped and talked to DJ, Shawn, and some other boys. Elaine saw Duane standing over by his car smoking a cigarette, and walked over to say hi to him.

"Hey, Hummingbird, how have you been?" he asked. "It's been awhile since I've seen you."

"Yes, it has. I was out of town for a week over Christmas Vacation," she told him.

"I know. You were at your cousin's at the beach. Believe me, I keep tabs on what you're doing."

"And just what have you been up to lately?" she asked him.

"Oh, this and that. I've been staying at home more lately." He and Paul were renting a small house in High Bluffs. "I'm trying to save some money, since my car needs work done on it."

That sounded familiar to Elaine. These cars, she thought, are such a drain on everyone's wallet. He asked her out for next Friday night. "Maybe we'll go to the basketball game, or maybe we'll go to the movies," he said. "We'll probably double with Paul and Beth."

By Sunday evening she had composed a letter to Jeff. She wrote the letter several times before she really figured what she wanted to say to him, and no matter how it was worded, it came down to the same thing. She was breaking up with him. She was glad that Pam was gone for the afternoon, and that her parents were out visiting friends because she was crying the entire time she was working on the letter. All his letters to her were so sweet. He's going to hate me after he gets this letter, she thought, and so will Chuck and Cathy. But I want a boyfriend who lives around here, one that I can see all the time, not someone who lives more than 100 miles away. He doesn't do me much good way out there in Desert Palms when it comes to taking me to parties and events around here. She carefully copied the final draft on her best stationary. *Dear Jeff, It's going to be most difficult to write this letter, but I'm trying my best to be truthful with you. I just don't feel the same way about you that I once did. I'm not really sure what happened and it wasn't anything that you did. I guess it's just the time and distance between us that has changed my feelings. Please forgive me, Jeff. What we had was really wonderful while it lasted, and I am just so sorry that it had to end this way. Sincerely, Elaine*

She stuck her four—cent stamp on it and walked down the street to the post office and put it into the mail box out in front before she chickened out and changed her mind. On the way back she passed Beth's house, and thought about stopping to tell her, but then decided against it. She decided that for once, she wouldn't tell anyone until a few days had passed. She knew her parents wouldn't be too happy about what she had done, especially her mom. And she didn't want Chuck and Cathy to hear about it from someone else. She would have to tell them in a few days.

But as the week slowly passed, she knew she would have to tell Lois, since she had that date with Duane on Friday night. And the conversation did not go too well, just as she had expected. She and Pam and Lois were cleaning up the kitchen after dinner when she broke the news.

"I cannot believe what I am hearing!" Lois exclaimed. "I think you've taken leave of your senses!"

"I always thought Jeff was a really fun guy," said Pam, wiping the table off. "It makes me sad that you broke up with him."

"But he just lives so far away, and we did not get that much time together," Elaine protested.

"Well then, why couldn't you just see him when he came to visit, and date other boys in the meantime?" Lois asked. "Why does it have to be one boy at a time? Can't you play the field?"

"No, Mom. I honestly don't think that would work. Maybe some girls like Megan Frye could do it, but I can't. It doesn't work for me like that."

"Well, Honey, I think you made a poor decision this time choosing someone else over a nice guy like Jeff. I've only met Duane that one time when he took you to the dance, and I think he's too old for you. And just exactly what is so great about Duane?"

"He happens to be a lot of fun. We always have good times together when the four of us are together. And he's only two years older than Jeff."

"I just hope you know what you're doing, and you don't end up being sorry later," were Lois' final words as she took off her apron and stalked out of the kitchen.

After the basketball game, Paul, Beth, Elaine and Duane cruised around Armedia, seeing who was out on the town that night and ran into most everyone at Tony's Pizza. Megan and Vicki were there with Dennis and DJ. Dennis was talking about the big bash he was throwing the following weekend.

"Yeah, my dad and stepmom will be in Vegas for the weekend, so I have the house to myself," he was bragging. "It will probably end up being a free-for-all, an orgy."

"But you need to quit broadcasting it all over," Megan told him. "That's when you'll get all the party crashers, and you want the house to still be in good shape when your folks get home."

"Oh, you just worry too much," Dennis told her. "It will work out fine. It's supposed to be a beatnik party so everyone can wear their old clothes and look sloppy."

Before the party, there were semester finals to get through, and it turned out to be a long week. But exams were finally over, leaving the students feeling high spirited and free. Elaine knew that she had done fairly well on most of the tests. But just the same, it took some work on her part to convince her parents that she should be allowed to attend the party.

"We've never met Dennis Kellogg," Charles was saying. "We know he's Duane's younger brother, but we don't know anything about their parents, or what kind of party they would allow their son to have. Usually when someone has a party, there's always drinking and driving."

"Is it just a small party, or one of those where half the school shows up?" asked Lois.

"Megan is helping plan it," Elaine pointed out, "and she's trying her best to keep it small and low key. No one likes those great big parties anyhow."

"How are you planning on getting there?" Charles wanted to know.

"Lucy will be driving me and Natalie, and she is really a good driver." Elaine had a date with Duane that night, but she was meeting him at the party.

"I'm sure she is, but that's not what I worry about," said Charles. "I'm always worrying about the other drivers on the road."

"And remember you have church the next morning," Lois reminded her.

"I am planning on going, and also Cathy's counting on me to help out with her Sunday School class."

At last Charles gave his reluctant permission, but added a final word of advice. "I just hope you girls are really careful when you're out driving on a Saturday night. You need to go right to the party, and when it's time to leave, you head right back home again. No cruising around."

"It's no wonder I'm getting gray hair," Elaine heard her dad say as he went out the back door. Parents, she thought with exasperation. They always have to make such a big deal out of everything. She certainly hoped word wouldn't get back to them that there would be no adult supervision.

Saturday night Elaine, Lucy, and Nat felt very conspicuous as they entered the Kellogg home wearing tights, or leotards, with long tunic tops. They had heavy eye makeup on, but no lipstick. They found their way through the lovely home to the recreation room at the back of the house. All the furniture had been moved way to the back of the room, and everyone was sitting on the floor or on pillows. The dim light was made by a few fat candles.

"Hi," Megan greeted them, looking adorable in a print tunic with black tights. "How do you like the decorating Dennis and I did on the place?" She gestured to the posters on the walls and the tiki masks placed around the room. "I'm afraid the refreshments are the same old punch, chips and dips. Better have some punch now before someone spikes it. I'm doing my best to keep an eye on it." She led the way to the bar. "It's good to see you here, Natalie," she added. "It's been awhile since I've seen you, except at school."

"Yeah, I'm thinking that I need to get out more. It gets old staying at home all the time."

There wasn't much activity during the first half hour, but gradually more and more people started to show up. Duane came in with Beth and Paul, but Elaine was disappointed that he was dressed in his usual attire, jeans and a button-down cotton shirt, and so was Paul.

"Hey, this is a theme party," she told him, "and here you show up looking the same as always."

"Well, I only have one big baggy sweatshirt, and I wear it at work," he said. "We just wanted you girls to dress up anyhow. All these tights on the girls are great to look at." She slapped him playfully, as she was checking out the group who had just come in. DJ and Vicki were there, and Shawn had come with them. Woody and Christy, and Alan and Karen were there. Mary Lou and Alma had come together. Couples were starting to dance, and still more people were showing up. Willie Bannister, who was supposed to be away at college, staggered into the house with a few of his friends who had graduated last year. It only took one look to tell that he'd had way too much to drink, and that he might start trouble.

"All right, where's the little punk who is throwing this shindig?" he asked, slurring his words. "He didn't get my permission to do it, did he?" It had been rumored that Willie had not taken it well when he and Megan broke up for the last time. The group grew suddenly quiet, wondering if there was going to be a fight. Fortunately, Dennis, who was smaller than Willie, was out of the room at the time. Megan stood silently at the back of the room, trying to be inconspicuous. Duane stepped forward and said, "You know damn good and well, it's my brother who is throwing this party, and you may have issues with him, but this isn't the time or the place, so I suggest that you and your buddies get back in your vehicle, and leave right now!" Elaine noticed that Paul was standing behind Duane. If there was a fight, she figured Duane and Paul would come out on top. They were big muscular guys, and had been on the wrestling team at school. Besides, Willie and his cronies were all too intoxicated.

"Hey, man, didn't mean no harm," Willie said, backing away. "We don't want problems with you. Got another party to go to anyhow," he added, as the group walked out the back door. A new record came on and dancing was resuming.

"Well, you handled that pretty well," Elaine said, as she and Duane swayed to the music. "I would hate to see a fight get started in your folks' house. That would be awful."

"Yeah, that would be kind of hard to explain," he said. "It certainly could have turned ugly. And while High Bluffs is a good place to have a party, since there are no cops around here, the other side of the coin is, if there had been a big ruckus around here tonight, they wouldn't be here to stop it either." As the dance ended, Duane reached into the small refrigerator under the bar, and pulled out a beer. "I need a cold one after all that. And don't be frowning, Elaine. It's only my second one tonight. I'm a big boy, and I can handle it."

As the evening wore on the party got crazier, there were still more new arrivals, and many of the guys were drinking. As usual, most of them were at least doing the drinking outside.

"I give up," Megan was saying. "All the same people, the party crashers and the drunks are all here. There's just no way to have a nice, fun party. And this cigarette smoke is getting to me."

Vicki wasn't too happy either. "I came with DJ and Shawn, and they're both drinking. And there are so many people in this house, there's not much room to move around."

Lucy and Nat were ready to leave, so Elaine told Duane she was going.

"Can't you stick around a little longer?" he asked. "I'll be glad to drive you home when this starts winding down."

"No, I should get going now," she told him.

The girls left the party and were heading back out to the main road going to Ellington. They were about three miles north of High Bluffs and halfway to Ellington when the traffic seemed to come to a standstill, and then it was diverted into the left-hand lane. There were orange cones all over the place. They could hear sirens in the distance.

"Well, that means there's been an accident up ahead," Lucy stated. "We might as well get used to the idea of being delayed."

"That's just great," Elaine remarked. "You know how my parents are always worrying about wrecks and this won't help my situation at all if they read about it in the paper."

"You're just thinking about yourself," Nat told her. "What if it's someone we know? I think almost all of our friends were at that party."

"You're right, that was kind of a dumb statement."

They edged closer to the accident. Three Armedia police cars were there, blocking off the area, and it looked as if two cars had collided. "Oh, no," Lucy breathed. "That gray Volkswagen certainly looks like Woody Stuart's!"

"I don't know anyone else with that make and model of car," Nat added grimly. "I didn't notice when Woody and Christy left the party."

Elaine's heart was pounding and her hands were shaking. It couldn't be Woody's car, she thought. Woody was always such a good driver, and he hadn't been drinking, at least she didn't think he had. And he had always seemed more focused than some of his peers. As they drove slowly by, they saw that the police were questioning three fellows.

They dropped Elaine off at her house, and the girls made a pact that the first one of them to get any information about the accident would let the others know. As Elaine slipped into bed that night, she said a prayer for the victims of the accident, whoever it was. But she wasn't able to fall asleep for a long time.

There was nothing in the Sunday morning paper, but then the little paper sometimes took a couple of days to get pertinent news. While Elaine was getting ready for church, Natalie called her. "My mom has connections, since she works for the paper, as you know. The news is really bad. It was Woody and Christy who were in the wreck. Apparently they were driving home from the party, and this other car ran over the line, right into oncoming traffic, so there was a head-on collision. The guys who hit Woody's car were drunk. Woody wasn't hurt that bad, but Christy was. She's in the hospital and is in a coma!"

"Oh, that's so horrible! I just can't believe it!" Elaine cried. "When I get to church this morning, I will tell Chuck, so he can have everyone pray for Christy." She was crying on the way to church, as she told her family what had happened. At least her parents refrained from saying "I told you so."

As she and Cathy were helping the 1st and 2nd graders with their Sunday School crafts, she told Cathy about the wreck, and Cathy said she'd get the word to Chuck before the church service started. But she completely forgot to tell her about her break up with Jeff. That had been dismissed to the back of her mind.

Stunned and sober Armedia High students went back to school that Monday morning with little on their minds except the terrible accident. That's all anyone was talking about. Elaine and her friends were in the student square all talking at once. Karen had gone to the hospital with Alan the day before, and she was saying that Christy had massive head injuries, and that the prognosis didn't look good. "I just feel so bad for her family," she kept saying.

"It never would have happened if Dennis hadn't had that drunken brawl," Mary Lou stated.

"Well, it wasn't Dennis' fault," Karen reminded her. "Any of us could have had a party, and it could have turned out like that. So many of the guys just have to drink, that's the problem!"

"'What happened with Woody?" Alma asked.

"He has a broken arm, and he got some cuts and bruises also," Karen told her. "He's not at school today. His car was totaled too, although that's nothing compared to what happened to Chris."

"Did you and Dennis get his folks' house back in order?" Nat asked Megan.

"Yes, finally. You guys left before the last hour, and it was good you did. It was getting to be pretty wild, and the place smelled like a brewery. Someone got sick all over the living room carpet. It was so disgusting! Beth, I want to thank you again for cleaning that up. Paul and Duane were a big help too, picking up bottles, and putting stuff away. Everything turned out to be such a nightmare!"

"Who were the guys who hit Woody's car?" Elaine asked. "And did they get hurt?"

"It was in the paper this morning," Vicki remarked. She named some names that Elaine barely recognized. "I think they graduated about two years ago. Willie said he knew them. That's another thing that gives me the chills. Willie and his friends were drunk, and they could have been in a wreck themselves, or caused one. And, no, the guys who hit Woody's car weren't hurt at all. That's what is so frustrating! They were probably too drunk to get hurt!"

A week later the heartbreaking news was out: Christy had succumbed to her injuries, and the funeral was to be on Friday. Everyone had grown to love the sweet and friendly girl during the few short months she had been at Armedia High. Elaine, on her way to school on Friday, was trying to recall the few brief conversations she'd had with her. She remembered that Chris never seemed to have a bad word to say about anyone. She wondered how poor Woody must be feeling. Knowing how sensitive a person he was, she was sure he would blame himself for the accident, although it was not his fault. What if she and Natalie and Lucy had been the ones driving down the road at that time? Why couldn't Woody and Chris have been there one minute earlier or one minute later? How could Christy really be dead? Why had everything happened the way it had? Was Christy's untimely death meant to be? Just hours before the fatal accident Elaine had talked with her and joked with her. Then she had been healthy and alive, never dreaming that she had only a few hours left on this earth. But now her young, broken body was lying cold and lifeless at the funeral home in Armedia.

Elaine bit her lip hard to keep back the tears. How could such a cruel and unfamiliar thing as death strike so suddenly at such an early age to one so good and lovely? Was that part of God's plan for Christy all along, Elaine wondered. Or had she just been in the wrong place at the wrong time? Now Chris would never graduate from high school, or go to college, or marry and raise a family. But she was in a much better place, Elaine thought. She would be with Jesus now. Elaine could not stop the tears from falling. It had all been so sudden. And it could have happened to any one of us driving around on Saturday night.

She shivered, realizing how quickly a life could suddenly be snuffed out forever. And the lives of Christy's family would be tragically altered by this terrible event. That nice dentist she had met before school had started would be eternally heartbroken, missing his only daughter for the rest of his life. And poor Alan. He and his sister had seemed fairly close. How was he handling all this?

The bus pulled up in front of the school, and Elaine numbly headed toward her locker, with her friends at her side. In the warm February sun, the tragedy seemed even more unreal to the girls. Everyone knew what was on everyone else's mind, and no one was saying very much.

"The funeral is on Friday at 11:00," Megan informed the group. It's being held at the Baptist Church, and I think it would be a good idea if the Collette's sent a wreath or some flowers. I'll be glad to call the florist and make the arrangements." Everyone was in agreement with that.

"I stopped by Karen's yesterday," said Alma. "She's really broken up, naturally, not only being close to Chris, but close to their whole family. She said Alan was the last one to see her before she died at the hospital. Her folks had hardly left her side at all, but finally went to get something to eat. Well, he said Chris came to for a little bit, and was calling for her mother. And Alan was holding her hand, and was excited that she had come out of the coma. He kept saying, 'Oh, you're back, you're back with us.' He said she was mumbling and hard to understand, but she said he should tell them goodbye for her, that it was her time to go now, and her face, even with all the scrapes and bruises, looked very peaceful and happy. And then she just closed her eyes and was gone. I can't believe this really happened to one of our friends," sobbed Alma. All the girls were crying by now.

"I wish I'd stayed home today like Karen," Vicki cried. "It's just so terrible to think we'll never see her walking down these halls again!" Fresh sobs broke out, and the bell rang, sending the girls to their classes. Elaine walked to the US History class with Alma, both of them only too aware that Christy had been in the same class. The teachers were all sympathetic. Mrs. Gimple gave her class a study period, realizing that no one would be listening to her lecturing anyhow. In Biology, Mr. Nichols had them read a chapter from their book. Mrs. Teague talked a little about the tragedy saying, "I know that everyone's mind is on Christy Coulter today, and my sympathies go out to all of you who knew her. It really hits hard when a small school such as ours has to deal with a tragedy of this magnitude. Your assignment for today is to write about what you're feeling right now. You can write about Christy, or about the wreck, or how you hate the reason for the accident. It can be very cathartic to put our thoughts and feelings down on paper. Don't worry about punctuation, or spelling, or sentence structure, but just write about what you are feeling." At the end of the period she collected the papers. "I'm not even going to be reading them for now," she told the class.

Elaine couldn't keep her mind on anything that week. She just felt that she was a robot, moving automatically around school. She retreated into the shell she sometimes pulled around her, and was very quiet. Her parents understood, and they didn't nag her about her farm chores or homework. They could not resist reminding her, however, of their constant concern about teen age drinking, and driving.

On the day of the funeral, students were excused at the morning break. The girls, wearing their best dresses, and gloves and high heels, rode to the church together. Once at the church, they met up with their families, since most of the parents were going also. Dr. Coulter was Armedia's only dentist, and everyone seemed to know him, even though he'd only been practicing there for a short while. The silent, flower-filled church was full of mourners on that bright, sunny Friday morning. An organist began to play softly in the background, and the sweet, perfumed fragrance of the flowers filled the air. The girls had contributed a heart shaped wreath of roses, which was on a stand near the casket.

A soloist sang a song, *In the Garden,* followed by a message from the minister summarizing Christy's short life and trying to offer words of comfort to her bereaved family and friends. His message concluded with the scripture from the 14th Chapter of John, verses 1 through 4: *Let not your heart be troubled; you believe in God, believe also in Me. In My Father's house are many mansions: if it were not so I would have told you. I go to prepare a place for you. And if I go and prepare a place for you, I will come again and receive you to myself; that where I am, there you may be also. And where I go you know, and the way you know.* After the singing of the hymn *Amazing Grace,* the casket was opened and the mourners filed slowly up the aisle to take one last look at their beloved Christy. She looked very pretty, Elaine thought, but not quite herself because of the heavy makeup that had been applied to her skin. Her long, pale blonde hair framed her tranquil face. Elaine, choked with sobs, hurried out to the front lawn of the church, where most all her friends were, all crying. It was only a little more than two weeks ago that she and Chris were madly studying for their US History final together. What a difference two weeks made.

Chapter 35

Tragedy always brings emptiness into the lives and activities of those left behind. The Collette's did not meet again for a while. The high school students seemed calmer to some extent, but much of life went on in the same old way. The weekly basketball games were going on. Tall, thin Alan Coulter was a real asset to the team, and it was probably good for him to get involved in the game to keep his mind off the loss of his sister. Woody was out for the remainder of the season because of his broken arm. But the coach kept him busy, helping with the team in different ways.

Elaine stopped by Chuck and Cathy's house on a Saturday morning. She hadn't really had a chance to visit with them, and she'd never told them of her break up with Jeff. She figured that they had already heard about it by now. They had just finished a late breakfast, and offered Elaine a cup of coffee.

Elaine thought she'd better get her news off her chest as quickly as possible. "I was planning to tell you about this much earlier, but then with everything that's been happening around here, I actually forgot, but I broke up with Jeff a few weeks back."

"Yeah, that's what we heard," Chuck answered. "I talked to my sister on the phone last week, and she told me. So what exactly happened?"

"It wasn't anything that Jeff did," Elaine explained. "My feelings just gradually changed, and I realized that I didn't want to be tied down to just one guy, so I wrote to him. I felt really badly about it, but I just thought we were getting too serious. I'm sorry. I know what I did was hurtful. I'm kind of seeing someone else, but it's not serious." She stopped talking because she was getting teary again. Lately she felt like crying every time she turned around.

"Well, I think you're both too young to get too serious anyhow," Chuck said. "If you felt that way, what happened was probably for the best in the long run, even though it's rough at the time."

"I know break ups can be really difficult," added Cathy. "But how do you know what kind of guy you want, unless you play the field, and date different types of guys? And living so far apart turned out to be a challenge for both you and Jeff."

"So what else has been going on with you?" Chuck asked. "And who's this guy that you are dating?"

"It's Duane Kellogg. He and Paul Newberry are close friends, and Beth is dating Paul, so the four of us get together. We have some laughs, that's all. But not much is happening at school. Things have been pretty quiet since the accident."

"A tragedy like that usually brings a calm in the storm," Chuck observed. "It will make people stop and think for a while, and then they will go on about their merry way, living just as before. Of course it's usually the innocent who get hurt, like your friends in the wreck. They hadn't been drinking, had they?"

"Not at all. Christy was pretty religious, active in the Baptist Church. She wouldn't have been with Woody if he had been drinking. I keep thinking that it could have happened to any one of us who were driving around that night after that party."

"When someone loses their life so quickly that way, it makes all of us stop and think that we could go at any time," Cathy said soberly.

"I guess we do tend to take life for granted," mused Elaine. "There are so many things I want to do in life before I die—go to college, get married, have a family, travel, find out the answers to a lot of questions."

"Such as?" Chuck prompted.

"Oh, like what purpose God has for me on earth, what life is all about. Sometimes I feel I have a split personality. One side wants to be wild and live it up, and just think of the present, and how much fun I can have. But at other times I feel that I'm supposed to have more of a purpose and should be working towards some goals, although I don't know exactly what they would be."

"We had the same feelings when we were younger," Chuck told her. "The conflict between good and evil is in the heart of all human beings. God gave us the choice, free will. At your age a person is more aware of that choice because this is the time you have to decide whether to follow the crowd, or your convictions. You also have to decide on a vocation, and a life's mate. Of course a person can be a Christian in any vocation, from a ditch digger, to a secretary, to a missionary. Also at your age there are more temptations to be met-to drink or not to drink, to be promiscuous or not, to be a good influence to those around us, or to just have a good time, and not worry about tomorrow. I wouldn't worry too much about it, Elaine. By the time a person is your age, the dye is pretty well cast, so to speak, depending on one's upbringing, what standards and codes they have been given to live by, and what kinds of examples they have to follow. I know that your parents have brought you up with high ideals, and I don't think you need to worry about what sort of adult you'll turn out to be, if you'll just follow your heart, or your conscience, as the case may be."

"I hope you're right," Elaine said. "Sometimes I think my conscience falls asleep, though. Or I feel as if I just don't care. I can't understand why some things happen the way they do, why God allows it. Take the wreck, for instance. Why couldn't those guys who ran into Woody and Chris have been hurt or killed instead? They were the ones in the wrong. And sometimes it seems like there is so much evil and wrongdoing in the world. Every day you read in the paper about racial violence, and the cold war, and men going crazy, killing their wives and kids, stuff like that. It makes me feel like saying 'Stop the world, I want to get off.' It makes me feel like I don't have faith in anything."

"Those futile feelings are felt by all of us at times," Chuck explained. "We all wonder why there is so much hatred and bitterness, and lack of love in the world. Philosophers and social scientists ponder the progress of the modern world, and compare it to the days when Rome was at the height of its glory. And when you compare today's people with the world civilization center of 2000 years ago, it is obvious how much love and humanity has spread throughout the world since Christ came into it. But of course mankind still has a long way to go. We still have a very imperfect world. And as I said before, God gave man the choice between right and wrong. The innocent and righteous sometimes have to suffer along with the wrongdoers. But we know that the followers of Christ won't suffer in Heaven."

Elaine was dubious. "I think I see what you mean," she remarked shortly. "And I know that Christy is in Heaven and is happy. But when I think of all the prayers that everyone was praying that week before she died, it's just hard to have faith, because those prayers weren't answered."

"They weren't answered in the way we thought they should be answered," Cathy interjected. "But they were answered. Christy was healed, but just not in the way we hoped she would be. God created this earth, and He cannot go against the laws of nature and stop two cars from colliding, or maybe He cannot heal the body of someone to whom too much damage has been done. I do believe He can still work miracles, however. I know when I used to get feeling downhearted and doubting God's love for me as an individual, I would take a look at the world around me. Think about the glory of a sunset, or the soft petals of a rose, or a newborn baby's tiny, perfect body, or the waves of the ocean rolling up on the beach, or the love between a man and wife. It's the everyday things like that which make you realize the miracles God can work, and the love with which He created this earth. We have to be constantly on the lookout for miracles, and we have to constantly be in a state of thankfulness, even when things don't go our way."

"Okay, that does make some sense, especially when you said that God healed Christy, but just not in the way we were expecting it," replied Elaine. "Gee, I didn't realize what a serious discussion this would turn out to be."

"Now you can skip church tomorrow," Chuck teased. "You've had your sermon for the week, two of them in fact." He turned to Cathy and said fondly, "Sweetheart, you should be in the pulpit instead of me."

Elaine did not miss the radiant look of love that passed between the young couple that she so admired. How she hoped that someday she could share a love such as theirs with some special someone. Maybe it could have been with Jeff, she thought sadly. But something went wrong with my feelings, I guess. Maybe I made a big mistake in breaking it off with him, but it's way too late to worry about that now.

Chapter 36

"That Mr. Nichols is unbelievable," Vicki was muttering as they left the Biology classroom. "Not only do we have to dissect frogs in there, but now he's assigning another yucky project."

"I can't really think of anything worse than a bug collection," agreed Elaine.

"I hate the thought of even looking at an insect," sighed Lucy. "And now we have to kill them, stick pins through them, and put them in little boxes, and classify them. I could have found some really huge ones when I was back in Alabama."

"Maybe we could get some of the boys to help us catch some," Elaine suggested.

"That's an idea," said Vicki. "Of course we have plenty of time. The project's not due until the Monday before Easter Vacation. We have more than a month to get them done."

"Right now, there aren't that many bugs out anyhow," Lucy said. "It's still too cold." The days were getting longer, now that they were into March, but the cold, damp winter weather was lingering.

That weekend was a busy one for Elaine. Natalie asked her to spend the night on Friday night. They hadn't gotten together for quite a while, and didn't even make their nightly phone calls as much as they used to. Elaine sometimes sensed that Nat was pulling away from her a bit.

"Oh, you changed your room around since I was here last," Elaine noticed.

"Yeah, I think this way gives me more space," said Nat. "We haven't really had a chance to talk for a while, but there is a lot going on with me right now."

'Well tell me, I'm all ears."

"Well, my parents are splitting up for good. Dad moved out about two weeks ago. I guess he is somewhere down near the LA area, and I think it's for the best."

"Oh, Nat, I am so sorry to hear that. It's got to be pretty hard on your whole family though."

"I don't know what the issues were between my folks. I thought for a while that my dad was cheating on Mom, but now I just don't know, and all Mom is saying is that they can't get along, or agree on anything. She is working more hours these days though, although she keeps telling me not to worry about money. But at least I feel like I have a little more freedom now. I mean, let's face it, my dad was really unreasonable most of the time."

"And your mom likes Ty, doesn't she?"

"She didn't at first, but now she's okay with him. Although we haven't seen too much of each other this past year. But that's probably just as well. After he went back to college in January, I had a big scare. I thought I was pregnant for a while, but I'm not."

"Oh, my gosh, Nat!" cried Elaine. "So you and Ty went all the way."

"We've done it a few times," Nat confessed.

"Was it really wonderful?"

"Well, to be honest, we were always in the car, and it wasn't really that comfortable for me," Nat said. "I think everything leading up to it was actually better. Now what I've told you is in the strictest confidence, of course."

"Oh, that goes without saying. I have always kept your secrets," Elaine said.

"I just have to be more careful when I'm with him," Nat remarked. "That was a very, very scary, worrisome time for me, and I never told Ty that I thought I might be pregnant, because that kind of news is, well, you just can't say it in a letter. Of course I wrote all about it in my diary. I changed the hiding place for my diary about three times, since Dad was still living here at that time, and if he'd ever found it, well, my life would be over. Ty will be coming home for Easter Vacation, and then I'm going to tell him everything I went through 'cause it's just too hard to keep to myself. And now you know, of course."

"Oh, I'm sure that was a terribly hard time for you," Elaine said softly.

"Enough of all this serious talk. Let's go downstairs and get some ice cream."

The following night she went out with Duane. The four of them, in two separate cars, were going to the drive in movie theater north of Armedia, near Lasswood. They all wanted to see the Alfred Hitchcock movie, *Psycho,* and it certainly lived up to all the hype. It was a very good, very scary movie. The second feature didn't hold their interest, and Paul tapped on the car window.

"We're going to the Snack Bar. You guys want anything?"

They declined the offer. "That Hitchcock is a genius," Duane concluded. "He's the best when it comes to making creepy, scary movies. It's enough to give a person nightmares."

"Now, every time I'm in the shower, I'll think of that movie," remarked Elaine.

"Ohh, that's a good thought, thinking about you in the shower," Duane said to her, pulling her closer to him. He was wanting to make out, and Elaine was trying to discourage him. She really didn't want to sit through the second movie necking with him, and yet trying to keep him from getting carried away. He was breathing hard as he was kissing her neck, and his hands were everywhere. Elaine kept thinking about what Nat had disclosed to her the previous night.

"I think we should cool it a little bit," she said, pulling away, and moving over to her side of the car.

"Oh, come on, you know you like this," he said. "I think we should take things to the next level. I want more with you than just kissing, and I think you want it too. You're just trying to act bashful, and coy, and play hard to get with me."

"No, I'm not, I really mean it. I love kissing you and cuddling, but it needs to stop there."

"You're kind of being a little tease, aren't you? I bet most all your friends give in to their boyfriends. I bet you gave in to that other guy, that Jeff, didn't you?" He reached across and caressed her neck. "Looks like I already gave you a hickey."

"Well, I hope I can hide that from my folks. And no, Jeff didn't try anything with me. He was a gentleman and respected me, which is more than I can say for you. You know, I'm sorry, but I'm just not ready to take things to the next level," she told him firmly. "Maybe some girls are, but that's just not me."

"You're saying one thing, but your body language is telling me differently," Duane said, trying a different tactic. "Come on, Baby, aren't things good between us? Kissing you is really great, but I'm a guy and I have needs. And, believe me, I need more from you than just kissing."

Elaine just shook her head at him, and stayed on her side of the car. It might turn out to be a really long night, she thought. She wondered how long before the movie would be over. She'd never had this problem with Jeff. Duane reached into his pocket and pulled out his pack of cigarettes and lit one. He didn't even crack his window to let out the smoke, but sat silently in his corner and pouted during the remainder of the movie.

But on Sunday evening Duane called her from Beth's, wanting her to come over for a little while. He and Paul were sitting on the porch swing at Beth's, laughing and joking. Duane walked her out to the end of the lawn and apologized for his behavior the previous night. "Sorry, Babe, I guess I was just in a bad mood last night. I don't know what got into me. Can you forgive me?"

"You know I will." She did of course, but she still had had misgivings. Would there be a repeat performance of the drive in date the next time they went out?

Duane slipped his class ring from his finger saying softly, "I've been thinking that I would really like you to wear my class ring, and be my girl."

"Oh, Duane, this is a surprise," she responded. "You're asking me to go steady."

"Just say yes. That would make me very happy."

"Okay, my answer is yes." He placed the ring on her finger. Elaine gazed happily at the gold initials and the numeral on each side, the ruby in the middle with AHS beneath. "It's too big for my finger, but I can put it on a chain," she said happily. She was floating on Cloud Nine.

A few minutes later, Dennis stopped by Beth's. He came in through the back door of the screened porch minus his usual jovial expression. "I just came from Armedia," he said, "and there's going to be trouble with Willie Bannister and some of his friends. They are looking for a fight in the worst way, and they're looking for me. They've all been drinking and they're hanging out behind the pizza parlor, bragging about how tough they are. Shawn O'Dell heard about it somewhere, so he wanted to let me know. So I need you guys to come back me up," he concluded to Duane and Paul.

"That Willie is an idiot," Duane stated grimly, getting up off the swing, "and he's going to get his clock cleaned. You ready to go kick some ass, Newberry?" he asked of his best friend.

"That whole group is waiting to get their asses kicked, and we're just the ones to do it," Paul stated firmly, as he followed Duane out to the car. The two girls were right behind.

"You guys need to be careful," Beth told them worriedly. "It will be just you three against them, and they have a whole big group."

"Do you have to do this?" Elaine asked. "I hate to see all of you get in a big brawl, and someone could get hurt. Why don't all of you just stick around here, and those guys will forget about it later? You know how they like to drink and shoot off their mouths and act really tough."

"Because it's a matter of honor," Dennis said. "We have to show up or I can't show my face in school or anywhere else around Armedia. I can't be the one to back down."

After they had left, Beth and Elaine discussed the situation. "I don't know exactly when all this started," Elaine said, "but the mess was kind of created by Megan. She was Wilie's girlfriend for so long, and she finally broke it off for good to be with Dennis."

"And it's too bad that Willie ended up quitting college and came back to town," added Beth. "He's just kind of been going downhill ever since then. In school, he was a star football player and a really popular guy. But lately, he's been acting like a jerk. He needs to get his life back on track. Do you think maybe we should go up to Armedia?"

"No, I guess not. Actually, I told Mom I wouldn't be gone too long, and I do have homework. Seems like I always put it off until the last minute. But before I go, what do you think of this?" she asked, holding up her hand which was proudly wearing Duane's ring.

Beth's answer was a squeal of delight. "I think that is just great. I'm so happy for you! I really enjoy it when the four of us get together, 'cause we always have so much fun."

"We do," Elaine agreed. "I don't think I'll tell my folks that I'm going steady, though. They aren't exactly crazy about Duane, so don't say anything about it to your mom, since it might get back to mine through the town grapevine. You know how that goes."

Later Beth called to tell her that things had blown over with the boys. After Paul, Duane, and Dennis had gone to confront the other guys, both sides had made some threats, but their bravado had diminished and there were no punches thrown, and Willie and his group had backed down.

"All those guys just like to talk and act tough," Beth concluded, "but then they end up doing nothing, which is for the best of course.

The drama with Duane continued however. The following weekend Elaine and Beth were going to the roller rink with their guys and then to the movie theater. She was ready and waiting for them, dressed in a blue flowered blouse with plain light blue Capri pants. They were late again as usual.

"They are always so unpredictable about when they will get here," she muttered, pacing the living room floor. She always hated waiting for a date to show up. The rest of her family was engrossed in watching *Rawhide* on TV.

"Are you still here?" asked Russ. "When are those guys coming?"

"They certainly like to keep you waiting," Lois remarked, looking up from darning socks.

"I would tell them to get lost," Pam said. "Jeff was always on time."

"It's not Duane's fault. He usually rides with Paul, and I'm sure they have a good reason."

"Too bad you can't just stay home and watch TV with us," Charles teased. "I guess the family is just no fun for you anymore."

"I hear Paul's car now," Elaine said, going to the back door.

Elaine was in a good mood, happy to have something going on every weekend. Duane handed her a can of soda when she got into the car, but she wasn't happy to see that he was holding a can of beer. "Can't you at least wait til we get to Armedia to have your beer?" she asked him. "If the cops pull you guys over, you'll get a ticket."

"Are you trying to boss poor Duane around already?" Paul asked from the front seat. "Beth don't care if I have a beer."

"That's what you think." said Beth. "You know I don't like it either, not when you're driving."

"You girls are just big worry warts," Duane told them. "The cops usually don't bother to patrol down here in Ellington, and even if they do, we know both of them. They would just give us a warning." The four of them were unusually quiet as they drove up to Armedia.

"If you girls are going to be such bad sports about this," Paul said, serious now, "I think Duane and me will go have another one."

"How do you like them apples?" asked Duane.

"We don't like it," Beth stated. "You know that ever since that wreck, we always think about the problems with drinking and driving. The outcome of that was a terrible tragedy."

"Well, you're in some kind of mood," Paul told her. "Let me tell you right now, I don't ever like anybody else telling me what I can and can't do."

"That goes for me too," added Duane. "and you know that if we only have a couple of beers, it's not going to affect our driving. Those guys who caused the wreck were really wasted."

They arrived at the roller rink and got out of the car. The rink was an outdoor one surrounded by chain link fence. Beth and Elaine went to one end of the fence, while the guys went to the other.

"Ohh, that Paul makes me so mad," said Beth furiously. "At times he can be so sweet, but at other times he can be the most stubborn guy I've ever come across."

"And Duane is a carbon copy of Paul," Elaine agreed. "I mean it's not like we're asking them to give up their drinking, but we just don't want them doing it around us, or when they're driving." They watched the two guys, down at the other end of the rink, smoking, and laughing and joking with some girls. Once they were all back in the car, on the way to the movie theater, Elaine said to Duane, "I saw you flirting with those girls. I hope you're happy."

"Oh, do I detect a little jealousy there?" he asked. "They don't even hold a candle to you. I wouldn't trade you for all the girls in this valley. You don't need to be jealous, Honey," he added, kissing her.

All of Elaine's anger faded, and she smiled at him. "I hope you really mean that," she said.

"Scout's honor. And I won't drink any more when I'm with you," he promised. Paul and Beth had made up too, and the remainder of the evening and the weekend passed pleasantly enough. On Sunday afternoon they drove up into the foothills of Ellington. From the top of the grade, Ellington was laid out flatly before them. The fields, green, brown and golden made the landscape look like a checkerboard. Elaine thought it was particularly beautiful in the late afternoon sun. Life was good.

Chapter 37

Elaine, Lucy, and Vicki were sitting in the back booth of Micki's Malt Shop in Armedia looking as if the world was coming to an end. "What is the matter with us?" Vicki muttered, stirring her soda with her straw. Their gloomy faces seemed to be in contrast with a sunny Friday afternoon, when most teens were in an exuberant mood, gearing up for the weekend.

"What were we thinking?" Lucy remarked with remorse.

"We all knew those bug collections were due the Monday before Easter Vacation," Elaine stated. "Yet we kept putting it off, and putting it off, and now we have only this weekend to get it done."

"The only bugs I have are a fly and some type of beetle that I saved when I first heard about the insect collection," moaned Lucy.

"I didn't realize how much work was involved in those collections until I got a look at Greg's and Lenny's, and Mary Lou's," Vicki said glumly. "They've got everything neatly labeled, and the smaller insects are so carefully mounted."

"They'll get A's for sure," Elaine said. "But I guess that's why they're A students and we aren't."

"I don't know where to begin looking for 25 different insects," sighed Vicki. "We should have started long before this. I think our goose is cooked."

"Oh, don't give up so easily," Elaine told her. "There are lots of insects around our farm." She looked up from her soda. "Hey, I've got an idea. Why don't the two of you spend the night with me tonight? We can look for bugs this afternoon, and get started. Then we can get out early tomorrow and look out in the hills behind town. We should be able to find plenty there. I don't think the streams have dried up yet, and we should be able to find some water bugs there. By tomorrow at this time we'll probably have a lot of insects, and if we have to, we'll stay up all night on Saturday night, mounting them and labeling them. What do you think?"

Lucy brightened. "Maybe that would work," she said. "But the afternoon is half over. We'd better get busy. I have the car today, so we'll stop by your place, Vicki, so you can check with your mom if it's okay, and Elaine, you need to call your mom from there, to let her know of our plan."

Now, full of eagerness for their plan, the girls set things into action. "We'll need to stop at the store for some cigar boxes," Lucy said. "That's what everyone is using. We'll each need about two."

"What's poor Duane going to do without you this weekend?" Vicki asked, getting into the car.

"I'm sure he'll manage to survive somehow."

Vicki got her mother's permission, and they scrounged up three cigar boxes, but it was about five o'clock by the time they'd reached Ellington and changed into their old clothes. Their class project turned out to be a family project. Russ knew where there were some black beetles. Pam offered to catch some horseflies. Charles jokingly suggested that they might find some lice on the chickens. Timmie offered them up two dead, dried up moths that he had found. Boomer, the cat followed the insect hunters around, and even his appearance suggested that he be searched for fleas. Lois had offered to ask for more cigar boxes when she went to the market the following day. Elaine had to gather eggs first, which she did in record time. Her friends were walking out around the chicken pens, looking on the ground. They finally came in once it was too dark to see anything. Lois had saved each of them a plate of dinner.

"Why didn't you start on this project sooner?" Charles asked them. "Planning ahead would have been so much better, and then you girls wouldn't have all this last minute worry."

"You are so right," stated Lucy. After they had eaten, they retreated to Elaine's room to make labels, and look up the classifications. Russ, who had agreed to pin the insects, suddenly became very popular. Russ also suggested that he and Scottie go with the girls the following day, and they were delighted with the idea.

"The more of us that go, the more bugs we can find," he pointed out. "And I know Scott will be glad to help. He's always ready for an outdoor project. It's just what he likes. I'll give him a call right now."

"Your brother is so sweet to help us like this, especially with pinning them, since I can't stand to touch the crawly old things," Vicki shuddered.

Lucy was putting carbon tetrachloride onto cotton balls, which went into the jars. "They sure die fast with just a few drops of this stuff," she said. "I used alcohol on that one beetle I had, and he didn't die for a week." By midnight each girl had five insects neatly pinned and labeled in their cigar boxes.

"Now we only need 60 between us," Elaine sighed, plopping wearily on the bed. "I hope we're lucky tomorrow, but I don't see how we're going to find so many in such a hurry."

"Classifying them is what's hard," remarked Lucy. "It's taken us all this time just to do the few that we have here."

"Why don't you turn on your porch light?" Vicki suggested. "That might attract some moths and some flying insects. It's kind of early in the season for night bugs though. If it were in the middle of summer we would have no problem at all."

Elaine, laughing, threw a pillow at her. "No we sure wouldn't, 'cause school would be out anyhow! We'd be doing something really fun instead of this!"

"You know what I mean!" They went out to the porch with their jars, and got a few more specimens. But they were all really tired by then, and settled down for the night to get a few hours' sleep.

They were up by 7:30 on Saturday morning, getting their gear together for their expedition. They had some insect classifying books, a couple of butterfly nets, several jars, and the bottle of carbon tetrachloride. Elaine and Lucy were making sandwiches for a picnic lunch for five. Charles came in and handed them two pairs of work gloves. "You will probably need these if you catch any bees," he suggested. "We don't want anybody to get stung, especially if you're allergic to bees, like Elaine."

"Thanks, Dad," she said. "I hadn't even thought about that."

Timmie came into the house with a plastic dish. He had found a dead grasshopper, four pill bugs, and a fat garden spider, and he was very proud of himself. "I've been out looking for bugs for you guys," he said, handing over the dish. "I bet I'll find some more today, and I'll save them for you."

"Thanks, Timmie, you're really a big help," Elaine said, giving him a hug. He looked embarrassed as the other girls hugged him too. "But you can set the spider free, since we can't use it," she added.

"Oh, right, I forgot. It has too many legs," he said.

"Your little brother is so smart," smiled Vicki.

Scottie arrived at that moment, and the five of them were off. They drove up Oak Street and parked at the end of the narrow dirt road, where they would be going the rest of the way on foot. The girls were thankful the day was sunny, for they would have had trouble finding insects in rain or fog. Once they reached the brush covered hills, there seemed to be an abundance of insects from various types of ants, to grasshoppers, to brightly colored beetles.

"Dibs on that bumble bee," shouted Elaine, waving her net in the air.

"If you can catch him, you can have him," replied Vicki. "But use the gloves when you put him in the jar." She was on her hands and knees by a small stream scooping out water bugs with a plastic dish. "Ohh, these guys are fast. They really don't want to be caught!"

"I see a Coleoptera," Lucy cried. "Let me at him." Russ and Scottie were quieter, scouting around and through the manzanita bushes and bunchgrass. The bumblebee was caught although Elaine had difficulty transferring the furiously buzzing bee from the net to a jar. The day wore on and the sun climbed higher in the sky.

"I'd like to catch a bunch of these gnats that keep flying around," Lucy stated, wiping her brow. "Well, we have quite a mess of insects now. Our jars are filling up."

"It still isn't enough," Vicki pointed out. "And even when we get enough, we'll probably need extras, in case some of them get damaged while they're being pinned."

"There should be some butterflies around here somewhere," remarked Elaine. "Only they're so pretty I hate to kill them."

"Well, Nichols will kill us if we don't turn in a good collection," stated Lucy. "Where'd the boys go? I haven't seen them in a while."

"They should be back soon. It's getting close to lunchtime." The boys did return soon with an assortment of beetles and they received plenty of praise from the girls for their efforts.

"I never thought I would be this elated over a bunch of beetles," Vicki said smiling. "You boys are just the greatest!"

"All in a day's work," Scottie told her. "We aim to please."

"And we know the best places to look," Russ pointed out.

After a quick lunch of bologna sandwiches and Fritos, their search continued. By afternoon the girls were exhausted and much the worse for wear. Elaine had a big blister on one foot, Vicki had tripped and tumbled into the stream, and Lucy'd been stung by a wasp she was trying to catch. The boys seemed to be doing okay, no mishaps with them.

"I guess we should call it a day," Elaine suggested. "Once we get home, we'll have to divide everything between the three of us, and see what we still need, if anything."

Once they were back at the house, Timmie came running up to the girls, and handed Elaine a plastic dish. "I have a surprise for you," he said proudly, grinning from ear to ear.

"Oh, you found some more bugs?" she asked. She pulled the lid off, then screamed and almost dropped the dish. Inside was one of the ugliest bugs she had ever seen. "Ohhh, a potato bug!" she cried. "Oh, they're so creepy looking. That gave me a real scare, Timmie! Are you trying to give your big sister a heart attack? Pam, I bet you had something to do with this too!" Pam was standing next to her little brother, her Brownie camera in hand.

Timmie was laughing heartily, and so was Pam, who was right behind him. "I hope that photo turns out," she said. "That expression on your face was priceless!"

"He's been waiting all day to scare you with that," Charles said, coming up onto the back porch. "That is a Jerusalem cricket, although some refer to it as a potato bug," he told them. "They are rather ugly. What else do you girls have here?" he asked as they set their jars down on the patio table. "Looks like you found a fairly good assortment."

Just then Timmie handed Elaine another plastic dish, and he started laughing when she refused to open it. "I'm not falling for that again," she told him. "No telling what you've got in there."

He took his time, pulling the lid off very slowly and dramatically, revealing three shiny green beetles. "Ta Da! June bugs. They were out by the fig tree."

"They're also known as green fig beetles," Charles told them. "And they're out really early, since they usually start showing up in June. I'm surprised that Timmie was able to find them."

After dinner, the table was cleared, and covered with an old sheet, and the work began in earnest, with Russ and Scottie pinning the insects, the girls mounting the smaller ones, and looking through the book for the classifications. Elaine, who had the best printing, was making labels. The boys had their job done in a couple of hours, and when they left to go back to Scottie's, the girls promised them a trip to the movies during Easter vacation, since they had been such a help. The girls kept at it, and by midnight, their eyes were getting heavy, and they were also getting sillier, but they weren't about to stop. Finally, around 2:30 a.m. each of the girls had their 25 insects neatly pinned and labeled in their cigar boxes, but they had done it the hard way, and they were exhausted. They decided that never again would they wait until the last minute to complete a big project for school.

Chapter 38

Easter Vacation was just around the corner, and everyone had spring fever. It was hard to be in school on that long Friday. Mrs.Gimple gave her History Class a test covering the aftermath of the Civil War, knowing that tests were the best way to keep the class quiet. Loud whispers of "carpetbaggers" and "reconstruction" were heard from the back of the room for the benefit of those who needed certain answers. Elaine had studied for the test, and she was fairly confident of her answers. It also helped that she liked to read historical fiction about the Civil War. *Gone With the Wind* was one of her favorite books.

They were still studying insects in Biology Class. The girls had turned in their collections on time, but Mr. Nichols told the class it would take him awhile to get them all graded. He reminded them that after Easter Break, they would each pair up with a lab partner, and would be doing some dissecting. The girls were not too thrilled to hear that. "Hopefully, we'll get a boy to be our lab partner," Vicki whispered. "And they'll probably do most of the work."

In English the Juniors were deep in the study of Nathaniel Hawthorne's short stories: *The Minister's Black Veil, Rappuccini's Daughter,* and *the Ambitious Guest.* Mrs. Teague was very fond of Hawthorne and probed into the depths of the *Tanglewood Tales,* hoping that maybe a few of her students would realize the greatness of the author. But the majority of the class was smitten with spring fever, dreaming of the carefree days the following week would bring, and planning on how to fill those precious hours.

The Fourth Period. P.E. girls were involved in softball now, a sport that Elaine disliked. She always volunteered for a position in the outfield, since few of the girls were heavy hitters, and all she had to do was stand in the sun and look alert. She figured that Pam would be in seventh heaven. (If she were in Elaine's shoes, and would probably be on the pitcher's mound.) Today Beth was center fielder, and the two girls were trying to carry on a conversation about Paul and Duane.

Students in Typing Class were learning business letter forms, telegrams, and night letters. Elaine always finished the assigned work with ease, and had time left to write letters or do homework. Since she wasn't writing to Jeff any more, and Lucy was back home, she really wasn't writing to anyone. She wondered how Jeff was doing. Chuck and Cathy had told her back in February that he had wanted to quit school and join the Navy, but his family had talked him out of doing that. Elaine was glad he hadn't followed up on it, since it would have crazy to quit school just a few months before graduation.

In her Sixth Period Class there were deadlines to meet for the yearbook. They were all working hard on cropping photos, doing layout pages, typing copy, proof reading the copy, and putting finishing touches to the art work. Everyone had a job, and was taking it seriously. There was no daydreaming in that class. The work had to be in by the first of May, and there wasn't much time left. Elaine knew that seeing the completed yearbook, which would reflect all their hard work during the year, would be pretty exciting.

At last the final bell rang, and the exuberant students hurried outside, to the parking lot, and to the buses. Elaine found a seat next to Lucy who was chattering eagerly about vacation plans. "We girls need to get together and go the beach one day this week," she said. "We could spend the entire day relaxing in the sun, taking life easy, and forgetting our problems."

"I need to work on getting a tan," Elaine remarked.

"Well, with my red hair and fair skin, I would just burn, so that's no good for me. But I need to get away from the rat race for a while. Let's plan on Tuesday for the beach, that is, if I can get the car."

"I'll talk to Beth and Natalie," Elaine said. They weren't on the bus that day, but Elaine knew she would be seeing Beth that evening on their usual Friday night double date.

When they stopped to pick her up, she was surprised to see that Duane was driving a different car. "Well, what you think of my new wheels?" he asked her.

"Wow! It's a cool looking car! When did you get this?"

"Earlier this week," he said. "There were too many problems with the old Oldsmobile. I happened to be in the right place in the right time, and bought this from a guy at work. It's a 58 Chevy Impala with a stock 348 inch engine and a turbo glide transmission. And it will do approximately 90 M.P.H. in a quarter mile. Listen to that engine purr," he said, as he turned on the ignition.

"This is really great," Elaine said admiringly.

"Pretty comfortable in the back seat too," added Paul. "And it has a nice smooth ride."

As they sat in the Armedia movie theater later that evening, Duane and Paul were in a talkative mood, but the girls were trying to watch the movie which was *Oceans Eleven*, a story about a Las Vegas casino robbery with Frank Sinatra, Dean Martin, and other members of the Rat Pack. It was quite entertaining. They didn't stay for the second feature, but stopped at Tony's Pizza instead.

After filling up on pepperoni pizza, and going back out, they ran into Willie Bannister and some of his friends. Elaine and Beth were already in the car, but the guys were all conversing. Elaine could tell from their gesturing, that they were all talking about Duane's new purchase.

"I guess they're all friends now," Beth observed. "So that's good news. And it also helps that our guys weren't drinking tonight."

"Yeah, they always act like they're so tough when they've had a few drinks," added Elaine.

Duane and Paul got into the car, and Duane peeled rubber as he quickly pulled out of the parking lot. He turned left, and headed west, toward the other side of town.

"Hey, what's the big hurry?" Elaine asked. "Aren't we going back to Ellington?"

"Not just yet. I have to prove something to those guys first."

"Willie thinks his truck's faster, so we're headed out to Old Sitzler road right now. This won't take long," Paul explained. Elaine and Beth exchanged worried glances. Duane's foot was heavy on the accelerator, as he sped toward the outskirts of town. Elaine was hanging onto the edge of the seat. It didn't feel like a nice smooth ride now, and she was sliding back and forth every time he made a turn. She grabbed for the handgrip above her and hung on tightly. They reached their destination a few miles out of town. Willie's truck was behind them, followed by a few more cars. The road had very little traffic, and was considered a great place for drag racing by Armedia's teen age males.

"Are you going to let us out?" she asked Duane.

"No, you girls will be fine," was his reply. "You know I'm a good driver. Just hang on." Willie's truck was pulling up next to them on the left side of Duane's car.

"But what if another car comes from the other way?" Elaine was asking, raising her voice because the window was down, and the engines on both vehicles were racing.

She didn't get an answer, as both cars leaped forward. The scary feeling in the pit of her stomach seemed to grow, and her heart was pounding fast as both cars gradually picked up speed. She had her eyes closed part of the time, but then she'd open them again to sneak a peek at the speedometer. It went quickly from 50 to 60. She closed her eyes again, and said a quick prayer. Armedia Valley did not need another auto accident.

"He's gaining on us," Paul hollered from the back seat. "You'd better floor it, man!"

Elaine opened her eyes, to see the landscape speeding by very quickly in the moonlight. The speedometer was reading 75 and was on its way up. They heard a thump coming from under the car's tires. Paul was laughing. "Hey, I think you just nailed a rabbit!"

"No, it's a damn skunk!" Paul answered, as they all noticed the odor. The speedometer was now 85 and was still climbing. But as they looked back, they could see Willie's truck was now several car lengths behind them. The needle on the speedometer had hit 93, and Duane was finally slowing down, and Elaine's heart rate was slowing down also. Her knuckles were white from hanging on.

Duane opened his window and stuck his hand out, flipping the bird to the car that was behind them, yelling "Eat my dust, Bannister!" as he continued south, but at a slower speed.

"That was great, man, you did it!" Paul was exclaiming. "Now you know for sure how fast she is!"

"Well, I certainly didn't know we were going to be in a drag race tonight," Beth said.

"Neither did I, but that was cool," remarked Duane. "We told you this wouldn't take long, and we sure showed those guys. Are you girls okay?"

"Yeah, but that scared about ten year's growth out of me," Elaine told him.

"Well, there's never a dull moment when you go out with us," Paul stated. "It's always exciting."

"That's for sure, we just never know what's going to happen when we're with you guys," added Elaine. They had reached Ellington now, but Duane wasn't traveling in the direction of either of their homes. He headed up Oak Street, past the cemetery, and parked at the end of the winding dirt road. Elaine knew what he had in mind, and she was getting a little nervous. It wasn't that she didn't enjoy the kissing and hugging, but Duane never wanted things to stop there. And after a while, just as she expected, they got into another argument, when she kept pushing his hands away.

"You're my girl, you know," Duane whispered softly, showering her with kisses. "And you're so beautiful, and you know how much I love you, and I just want to give you all my love. I know you feel the same way about me, so what's wrong with us sharing that love with each other?"

"I'm sorry, but I am just not ready for that yet," she told him. "For one thing, I had a friend, who had a big scare when she thought she might be pregnant, and nobody wants to go through that."

"There are ways to prevent that, you know," he answered.

"That may be true, but my answer still has to be no," she stated emphatically.

"That's just great!" he exclaimed, pulling away from her. "Hey guys, I think it's time we headed home now," he said to Beth and Paul, who were tangled up in each other's arms. They were only a few minutes from Elaine's house, and when he pulled up into the driveway, he didn't even get out to walk her to the door. She slammed the car door hard, then quietly tiptoed into the house, not wanting to disturb her sleeping family. She pulled his class ring and chain over her head, dropping them onto her dresser with a thud, wishing she'd thrown them at him while she was still in the car.

*   *   *

The girls didn't go the beach on Tuesday because the unpredictable April weather wasn't cooperating. Monday and Tuesday were cloudy and cold. Elaine and Lucy kept their promise to Russ and Scott for their help with the insects, and took them to the movies on Tuesday night. *The Time Machine,* from H.G. Wells' book of the same name, was playing, and they all thoroughly enjoyed it.

By Thursday the clouds were clearing up, and Friday morning dawned sunny and warm, so the girls quickly made plans to drive to Oceanside Beach that day. It was always so exhilarating when they first smelled the salt air of the ocean, and saw the sparkling water, and they felt good to be alive. The girls spread out a blanket and settled down, noting that the beach was quite crowded with young people and families.

Natalie was saying that she was having a fun week, with Ty being home from college. "Today was perfect for me to get together with you guys," she said, "because he has a bunch of errands to do. And then he'll be leaving on tomorrow night to drive back to Flagstaff. But summer is not too far off, thank goodness."

Elaine was telling her friends that she was upset with Duane, and she felt like he didn't really respect her, and she didn't like the way he was racing his car the other night.

"I just don't know how much longer we're going to be together," she said.

"I know you're upset with him, but the prom is coming up next month," Beth pointed out. "It would be very bad timing to break up with him right now," she added.

"Well, you have a point there. But both Paul and Duane hate dressing up anyhow, so they'll be griping about that."

"Well, I don't know of one guy who does like to get all decked out," Nat remarked. "That's something we girls enjoy a whole lot, but not guys." As the conversation went on, Elaine was noticing three fellows in the sand several yards away from them. One was playing solitaire, another, with a straw hat at a rakish angle on his reddish hair, was plucking the strings of his guitar, and the third was lying on his stomach staring moodily out at the ocean rolling in. He was very attractive, Elaine decided, with a tanned, muscular body and brown hair in a Napoleon style haircut. He turned, and his eyes glanced in her direction, so she quickly looked away.

"Elaine, quit making eyes at those boys over there," Lucy told her. "You know that men are the root of all evil. However, I do think the one playing the guitar is kind of cute."

The morning passed quickly and the girls were too intent upon getting a tan to venture out into the water. When the sun was high in the sky they headed to the nearest hamburger stand. Elaine and Lucy noticed that the guys were watching them as they walked past.

After lunch, they lay on the blanket until the sun got too warm, and then decided to try the water. They edged cautiously out to the breakers. They watched the waves roll in as they went out into deeper water. "Too bad we don't know how to surf," Lucy said. "That would be a lot of fun."

"Shame on you, Elaine!" Beth nudged her, noticing that the three fellows were walking down toward the water. "Those guys followed us out here because you kept staring at them!"

"So was Lucy," Elaine giggled.

"You bet I was, and I got dibs on the tall one with the reddish hair," said Lucy.

"Well, just for that, you can have them all," stated Nat. "Come on, Beth, let's go back up on the beach and see what happens." They headed back toward the sand. Lucy and Elaine followed, but more slowly, timing their walk so that the guys would meet them at the water's edge.

"You girls going in all ready?" The red headed one asked.

"The water's kind of cold," Lucy responded.

"Oh, it can't be that bad. Besides you've been here all day, and haven't really been swimming yet," stated the brown haired one.

"Well, we've been trying to get a tan," the girls explained. The boys persuaded them to stay in the water a bit longer. Elaine decided that the fellow was even more attractive up close. He had clean cut features, the prettiest blue eyes with long eyelashes, and a well-toned physique. His two friends were talking to Lucy.

"Want to go out a little farther, and ride in some of the waves?" he asked her.

"Well, I'm not a really good swimmer, especially in all those waves."

"I won't let you drown," he told her. They walked side by side out into deeper water. "Are you from around here?" he asked.

When she told him, he had never heard of Ellington. "You've never heard of it? It's a hick town out in the sticks, but it's only 45 miles from here. I'm surprised you haven't heard of it. Where are you from?"

"I'm from a long way from here, Lafayette, Louisiana, and I bet you haven't heard of it either."

"Actually, I have because my friend over there just made a trip back to the south a few months back, and she spoke of driving through there. Now that you mention it, you do have a slight southern accent. Why are you so far from home? Are you on vacation?"

"I wish," he answered, grinning. "No, I'm definitely not on a vacation. I'm in the Marines, stationed at Camp Pendleton. And so is my buddy, Red, over there with your friend. He's from Mississippi."

A Marine, thought Elaine. What would Beth and Nat say to that? He seemed very nice.

"Well, how do you like California?" she asked him.

"It's a great state. I've been out here almost a year, and I don't have any complaints."

"Yeah, I like it pretty well myself. I've course I've never lived anywhere else, so I can't really judge. Ohh, big wave coming!"

They were waist deep in the water when suddenly a large, unexpected wave towered over them. He grabbed Elaine's hand and they both went under together and washed up closer toward the shore. They were both sputtering and wiping their eyes.

"There—I saved your life already," he said laughing, "and I don't even know your name." She told him, and he said that his name was Mike Kowalski, but that his friends just called him Ski.

"How long have you been in the Marines?"

"Two years and eight months. I'm a short timer now, only 14 more months to go. "I'll get out in June of 1961."

"You sound anxious to get back to civilian life."

"Yeah, a lot of us are that way."

They rode the waves for a while until Elaine got tired and wanted to go back to the sand. She noted, as they walked up on the beach that Ski's buddies had made themselves at home on the girls' blanket, and seemed to be in deep conversation with them.

"We might as well go sit on my towel," remarked Ski. "There doesn't seem to be much room left on yours."

Elaine threw a triumphant smile at her girlfriends and sat down next to Ski on the towel, as he picked up the guitar and moved it.

"Do you play the guitar?"

"No, that's in Red's department. He's good at it. Sings too."

"What's the other guy's name? With the blonde hair?"

"Wyatt. His first name is Julian, but he'll hit anybody who calls him that."

"Yes, I've heard that Marines have a reputation for fighting," Elaine smiled.

"Oh, we're the roughest and toughest branch of the service," Ski grinned. "But actually the Marines are given credit for being much wilder and meaner than we really are. There are guys who give us all a bad name by getting drunk all the time, and getting into plenty of fights. I bet if you tell your mother you met a Marine today, she'd say 'Heaven forbid-a Marine!'"

Elaine laughed. "That's exactly what she would say, and I kid you not."

Ski lit a cigarette and offered her one.

"No, thanks, I don't smoke."

"I'm glad to hear that. I don't like to see a girl with a cigarette hanging out of her mouth. The fact that you don't smoke tells me a lot about you."

"What do you mean?"

"Well, you probably don't drink, or swear either, and I bet you go to church on Sundays."

"You're pretty smart at figuring people out," she said. "So much for my trying to be mysterious. You know a lot about me now, and I know very little about you."

"Not much to tell," he said modestly. "I was born and raised in Lafayette, graduated from high school in 1957, turned eighteen, and joined the Marines after graduation. I've been overseas once, and I'm going again the middle of next month. I have one older brother and one younger. My life story in a nutshell."

"It's much more exciting than mine," Elaine said. "I was born in Long Beach, and my parents moved out to Ellington when I was just three. I've lived there ever since, and my dad raises chickens."

"How old are you? Wait—let me guess. Hmmm—" His blue eyes squinted at her. "Eighteen."

"Oh, you're flattering me. I'll be seventeen next month"

They sat and talked and played cards for another hour. Elaine noticed that the sun was getting lower in the sky, and knew that they would have to be leaving soon. Beth called to her shortly and suggested that she start gathering up her belongings. She was thinking how pleasantly the day had turned out, and what a nice guy Ski seemed to be. She hadn't thought of Duane all day, or how frustrated she was with him. Ski, Red, and Wyatt walked the girls to the car.

"We just might have to make a trip over to Ellington and check the place out," was Ski's parting comment.

Lucy seemed to be in a good mood on the way home, and confided to the other girls that Red had asked for her phone number and sounded serious about making a date in the near future. "And that would be great because he's the first guy that I've been remotely interested in since I was back in Alabama."

Chapter 39

In the blink of an eye, Spring Break had passed, and before they knew it school had resumed again. As they stood in the lunch line on Monday, Beth was explaining to Elaine something that Paul had told her. "He said that Duane said he was going to cool it with you for a while, whatever that means."

"Well, that's just fine with me," Elaine stated crossly. "He can come and get his ring back if he wants. He just acts so childish when he doesn't get his way, and I'm tired of it."

"Oh, you don't mean that. The four of us always have so much fun when we go out. I hope you two can get things worked out between you. I think both Paul and Duane are planning on being at the barbecue on Sunday, so maybe you'll get a chance to talk to him then. I mean the Prom is just a few weeks away, and then school is out after that and summer is always a fun time to be dating."

The annual Fireman's Barbecue was scheduled for the last Sunday in April. The day dawned bright and sunny, unlike last year's rain and gloom. Elaine and Beth both helped this year, dishing up salads as the long line filed past. Later on, Beth participated in the horse show, and Elaine watched it with Lucy and Nat. Lucy confided that Red had called her, and was driving out to see her in a couple of weeks.

"That's great, but what will your folks think about you dating a Marine?" Elaine asked her. "My parents would probably have a cow."

"Well, Mom and Dad will talk to him and get to know him a little when he comes over," Lucy said. "I think they'll be okay with it. I'm almost seventeen now, and they trust my judgment. It's funny how well Red and I hit it off, just meeting him for that one day at the beach. That time I spent back in Alabama really helped, because I could relate to him about what life was like back in the south."

Elaine went over to Beth's after the barbecue was over. She was beginning to feel sad instead of mad that she and Duane weren't getting along, and she was starting to miss him. He was so good looking, and had been one of the most popular guys in school. If he could just see things her way. She and Beth sat rocking on the porch swing, and they heard a car in the drive.

"That sounds like Paul's car," Elaine said, and her heart began to flutter in excitement. But as the car pulled up, she could see that there was a girl sitting between Paul and Duane. When they got out, Elaine saw that the girl was Bonnie Carson, a senior who lived in High Bluffs. She was tall with thick brown hair, absolutely straight, hanging past her shoulders. She wore no lipstick, but had on heavy eye makeup. She looks like a beatnik, Elaine decided, but she couldn't help liking Bonnie because of her amusing personality and cynical sense of humor.

"Ellington's not a bad town," she remarked, lighting a cigarette. "But what to you do after dark?"

"Oh, we can get very creative," Beth said.

"At least in High Bluffs we have a few restaurants and a few bars," Bonnie remarked. "But it's still a dead town, even though Duane and Paul may disagree. I hate it, and you can bet that I'll be out of there the minute I turn eighteen."

Duane laughed. "You won't ever leave High Bluffs. You've lived there most of your life."

"Rotten luck," she said. "My old man left my mom when I was little, and then we moved to that crummy pad in High Bluffs. The town's been better since those two came." She indicated Paul and Duane. "They're always managing to scare up some excitement."

Elaine felt sorry for Bonnie. She didn't seem very happy. All her remarks were full of sarcasm, and even her laughter sounded bitter. Her eyes were lit with adoration and love every time she looked over at Duane. She wondered why Bonnie was with the boys tonight. Was she just a friend, or was she Duane's date? Elaine knew that he had dated her in the past.

Two weeks passed, and Elaine still hadn't heard from Duane. She figured that whatever she and Duane had together was now over. But she still felt like she needed to see him one last time and give him back his class ring, and say their good-byes. She missed the fun the four of them had had together, and she missed making out with him too. She tried not to think too much about him, but to concentrate on school work instead.

Mr. Nichols had half the class draw names for lab partners, and Elaine got Alvin Minegar's name. She was okay with that, however, because he didn't pester her for dates anymore, and she'd seen him with a sophomore girl a few times. So she was happy for him. And he was a good lab partner when it came to dissecting the frog.

"So are you still going steady with Kellogg?" he asked.

"Yes, we're still together," she said. (She wasn't about to explain the crazy soap opera scenario to him.) He then told her about his girlfriend. He also mentioned that he'd been accepted by Cal Poly, and would be majoring in Agriculture there.

"It's hard to believe that graduation is just around the corner," he said. "By the way, how'd your insect collection turn out? I heard you girls were scrambling like mad at the last minute."

"Yeah, that was rather crazy, and stupid of us to wait so long. But we all got B's, so it all worked okay in the end."

The Yearbook Class was much more relaxed now that all their work had been sent in for publication. The last few days of April had been hectic. Lenny and Scottie had been in the school's darkroom, developing pictures of the school's most recent activities. Shawn O'Dell was busy with last minute artwork. Most of the girls had been typing copy. Elaine had been trying to read Big B's handwriting on descriptions for the baseball and track photos, and he was joking with her, saying, "Are you blind, Humbug? Anyone could read that. I think you need glasses!" But then he'd look at what he'd written, and even he had problems deciphering it.

"We're going to miss you around here next year," she told Big B. "This yearbook staff won't be the same without you. Of course neither will a lot of other things, like the football and wrestling teams."

"Yeah, I'm going to miss all that," he said soberly. "All good things have to end.

Lucy called with some news about Red and Ski. "I don't know how you feel about this, Elaine," she said. "But Red wants to come to Ellington this coming weekend, and Ski wants to come with him, that is if you would go out with him. I told Red that I wasn't sure if you were still with Duane or not. But I did give him your phone number and I hope that's okay with you."

"I'm not really sure where Duane and I are at right now," Elaine said. "But with the way he's been acting toward me lately, I would be glad to go out with Ski. He seems like a really nice guy, but he won't be around much longer, since they're sending him overseas pretty soon."

"Well, I'll get off the phone since he'll be trying to call you," Lucy said. "If you go out with him, it will show Duane that you're not just sitting around waiting for him. Besides he was with that Bonnie on the day of the barbecue, whatever that was all about." Elaine had no sooner gotten off the phone with her when Ski called and they talked for a few minutes. Ski told her they would let the girls decide what they wanted to do on Friday night.

Of course Elaine had to tell her parents about what was being planned, and they reacted about the way she figured they would. "I don't know if I like the idea of you going out with a fellow you just met at the beach-especially a Marine," said Lois.

"Marines are known for their wild reputations," said her father. He was at the dining room table helping Russ with his Algebra. "I bet this guy has girls in every port. And he probably feeds them all a big line of malarkey."

"Yeah," Russ added in order to get into the conversation. "Marines are nothing but jarheads anyhow."

"I'm on your side, Elaine," her little sister called.

"I am glad that somebody is. For your information," she told her parents, "he and I would be double dating with Lucy and Red, the guy that she met. And probably this weekend will be the last time that I'll see Ski, because he is scheduled to go overseas very soon."

"Well, I guess that sounds okay," stated Lois. "By the way, did you and Duane break up?"

"We are taking a little break from seeing each other."

"I'm happy to hear that, and I wouldn't care if you broke up permanently with him," Lois said. "I don't know why, but I've just never cared too much for him," she added.

That Friday Ski and Red came and talked with her parents for a short time before they left and Elaine could tell that the brief visit went well. After they left, Lucy had them driving around Ellington, showing them the old grammar school, Deb's Diner, the grain elevator and other points of interest, which were few. "This is it?" Ski asked.

"How did you girls grow up in such a small place?" Red asked. "You could sneeze and miss it while driving by. We were planning to stay at a motel while we are here, but I didn't see any."

"There are motels in Armedia," Lucy told them.

"Do you girls have something planned for us to do while we're here?" Red asked.

"Of course we do," Elaine told him. "Tonight we're going to the Lettermen's Club Talent Show at our high school, and tomorrow night we'll just go the movies. We do have a local theater."

The May night held all the ingredients of a perfect date. The smell of orange blossoms filled the air of the spring evening as they drove to Armedia in high spirits. A full moon smiled merrily down upon them from the star filled sky.

"Ellington reminds me of some of the small towns we have in the south," Ski told her. "Back there are different farming towns about every few miles. But here in California, I notice that everything is cities, with suburbs that kind of run together, mostly all urban."

"You're right, and I think Ellington is one of the few hick towns left around here," she remarked.

The talent show, which was held in the high school gym, turned out to be riotously funny, and everyone was laughing at the husky athletes who were dressed as chorus girls, nursery rhyme characters, and ballerinas. The two acts which brought down the house were when Mr. Sharpe, the basketball coach, complete with wig and guitar, pantomimed an Elvis song, and Big B, Woody, and Greg dressed in pink tutus, were prancing around the stage to the Dance of the Sugar Plum Fairy. Of course the show was much more enjoyable for the girls, since they knew the performers. Both Ski and Red were surprised to hear that Big B, a black athlete, was one of the most popular boys at school. Of course, being in the Marines, they had black friends, and were less prejudiced than some of their friends back home. "Well, maybe some day our schools back there will be integrated, but who knows when that will happen?" Ski said.

Lucy then told them about her experience about the movie theater back in Alabama with two separate lines, one for the whites and one for the blacks. "Oh, yeah, you see that all over back home," Red remarked.

After the show they drove over to Tony's Pizza. Of course there were lots of teen agers there, since many had the same idea. Elaine was so thankful that Beth, Paul, Duane, and Dennis had gone out of town to some drag races that evening. She didn't think it would be good for them to meet up with the two Marines, since there would probably be trouble. She knew, without a doubt that Duane would eventually hear about her date with Ski, since they were seen together by half the high school. Of course Beth knew, but she was sworn to secrecy.

The following evening the four of them went to the movies, and came back to Deb's Diner afterwards, where things were quieter. Red was telling Lucy that he would try to get a pass again in two weeks so that he could take her to the Junior Senior Prom. Elaine felt that would be great for her friend, since she hadn't been dating much that year, not since she'd returned from Alabama. But at the same time, she was feeling sorry for herself, since she knew she wouldn't be going. If only Ski didn't have to leave. But there was nothing anyone could do about that. Ski wasn't happy about it either. "It's really sad that I have to leave right when I've met a girl I really like," he told her.

"I bet you say that to all the girls," she said teasingly, and then added, "It is bad timing, just when we're getting to know each other."

"Will you write to me?" he asked.

"Of course I will if you want me to. But how can you get letters when you'll be moving around on a ship, and going into different ports? You said yourself that they haven't told you guys exactly where you'll be going."

"You would be writing to me in care of the FPO in San Francisco. There are ways we get our mail. Helicopters come out to the ship. Other times our mail comes into the port. Sometimes it takes a while for us to get the letters, but we do eventually." He took a napkin and wrote out a long address with lots of numbers, and Elaine also gave him hers. The next morning the guys checked out of their motel, and they spent a few hours at Lucy's, playing cards before they had to leave. It was bittersweet as they kissed goodbye. They had to get back to the base for an inspection, and Ski had to be out at the ship later that week. Elaine had a feeling that she wouldn't ever see him again, because it would be six to eight months before he would be back at Camp Pendleton, and a lot could happen between now and then.

The Junior Senior Prom took place next Saturday night. Natalie had her mom's car, and the girls went to the movies to keep themselves occupied. All their friends had dates for the Prom, so they were feeling kind of low.

"Of course I knew I wouldn't be going," Nat was saying, as they settled into the theater seats, carrying their popcorn. "But you were planning on going with Duane, so I can understand why you're feeling really let down."

"But I've seen this coming for about a month now," Elaine remarked, "and it's probably for the best. Summer will be here soon, and you'll be with Ty, Beth has Paul, and Lucy is starting to date Red, and I won't have anyone. I think it's going to be a long and lonesome summer," she added soberly. The movie turned out to have a sad ending, which didn't help Elaine's mood. She was fighting tears all the way home. This was also the time of year that she always felt a little blue. Even though summer was almost here, and she loved summer, she always felt sentimental as the school year came to a close.

One of the big year end activities was the school play. The drama department was giving the performance of *Little Women*, the story of

Meg, Jo, Beth, and Amy, based on Louisa May Alcott's beloved classic of four sisters during the Civil War era. Elaine had tried out for the part of Beth, but lost out to someone else. So she settled for working on the production crew and helping with the costumes. The costumes were loaned out to the school from a collector, and were very valuable. Four of the costumes were over 100 years old, and the costume worn by Beth was 125 years old, and was valued at fifteen hundred dollars. So utmost care was given in the handling of the beautiful antique dresses of silk and satin. It was interesting and fun working on the production crew, but extremely time consuming. The set and stage props were built by Lenny Mendoza and Bobby Jackson. There were students who did the lighting, and students who worked on sound effects and special effects. Miss Lippert's Art Class was involved in painting backdrops. Elaine was staying after school and riding the late bus home for most of the month. Her weekly allowance was diminished quite a bit, since she was paying Russ and Pam to do her share of the chores. But she was enjoying helping out behind the scenes, and she felt as if she were a part of something really important. There were two evening performances at the end of May and one matinee, and together the actors and all the others had a wonderful feeling of accomplishment when the curtain fell on the last performance.

The final day of school had arrived at last. The graduation ceremony the night before had been sad for some of the Junior girls who had seniors for boyfriends. Karen looked tearful as she and Mary Lou, chosen for the Honor Guard, held up a flower covered arch for the seniors to walk under as they made their way up to the outdoor stage. Elaine was sitting next to Megan and the rest of her friends in the bleachers. Megan was looking distressed, as she kept telling Dennis to lower his voice. (He had continually commented on how he wished he was a senior, and how everyone would be getting drunk at the all-night party following graduation.)

But today, at the last assembly of the 1959-1960 school year, most of the seniors were serious and sober sitting in their section for the last time. Every last award, athletic letter, and certificate had been presented, and every last speech had been made. Now was the time for the traditional ceremony ending the school year. The student body president dismissed the seniors from the assembly, and the juniors moved up to the senior section, and the sophomores to the junior section.

"Well, we finally made it," DJ said. "I thought this day would never get here. Go Seniors!"

"This school won't be the same with us running things," Vicki told him

"I can't believe we're really seniors!" Beth exclaimed.

The weekend that school let out, Lucy hosted a Collette's slumber party. It was the first time in many weeks that the girls had all been together. They sat on the living room floor discussing the past year. "It's been hectic," Mary Lou sighed happily. "There have been so many activities to keep us busy. And the boy situation has certainly improved for all of us." She was dating Lenny at the time. The atmosphere was just right for a slumber party. There was much chatter and laughter. Elvis songs were on the record player, making for good background music. The iconic singer had been recently released from his stint in the Army, and all the teens were glad to have him back on U.S. soil. His songs were more popular than ever.

"This is the first time we have gotten together as a club in ages," Alma remarked. "What is happening with the Collette's anyhow?"

"I think we formed the club when none of us went out much," stated Vicki. "Now we all have boyfriends to keep us busy, so we don't need the club activities."

"Yes, the Collette's did serve its purpose when we needed it," Karen declared. "If decide to disband, we'll have to save our charter and constitution for posterity."

"We still have about 35.00 left in the treasury," announced Elaine. "If we disband, we need to figure out how to spend that money."

"I have an idea if anyone wants to hear it," Megan said. "We could contribute it as a memorial to Christy. Her parents are having a stained glass window put in the Baptist Church in her memory." The room grew quiet, as they thought of their friend who had been lost to them so recently. Of course everyone was in favor of Megan's idea.

"Well, only one more year until graduation," Lucy said somberly. "Kind of exciting though, thinking about being out on our own."

"Don't mention it," Elaine told her. "You know I don't even like to think about all of us being scattered to the four corners of the earth."

"I don't even know what I'm going to do after graduation, or where I'll go to college," Alma said. "And I get frustrated just thinking about it." Mary Lou and Megan were the only girls in the group who had chosen certain colleges as possibilities.

"College is still too far in the future for me to think about," remarked Vicki, never serious. "I only like to think about the present. It is interesting to wonder, though, what all of us will be dong ten years from now."

Megan smiled wisely. "We'll be busy changing diapers, making cookies, and going to PTA meetings." The girls all laughed, and the discussion turned to what they were going to do over the summer.

Later, as the sun was sinking low in the sky, they took a walk around the town. It seemed that most of the town's residents were outside also, enjoying the pleasant summer evening. People were sitting out on their front porches, and boys were cruising on their bikes up and down Main Street. Beth's younger sister was on the sidewalk in front of her house, and she and Pam were involved in a game of Hopscotch. They could hear the calls of some youngsters playing Red Rover in the vacant lot out behind the gas station. The chorus of crickets had begun their evening serenade. The teens decided to make their way down to Ellington's dry river bed, which was a few short blocks from Lucy's home. It was warm for early June, and the girls, in high spirits, and feeling daring and adventurous, removed their shirts and shorts, and walked down the sandy river bed clad in only their bras and panties, and their tennis shoes. The river banks on both sides of them were fairly tall, and they weren't near the town's one and only bridge, so it was a safe bet that no one would see them. Their little escapade gave them a real sense of freedom, and, looking back on that memory, they never recalled whose idea it had been in the first place, but it had been tons of fun.

Part IV

Chapter 40

As the Greyhound bus pulled into the bustling harbor city of San Diego, Elaine knew the ride wouldn't be much longer, and she could hardly wait to get off. She had boarded at the bus stop in Ellington and ridden the 85 miles down to California's southernmost city. She was there at Natalie's invitation. Elaine reflected on how quickly things could change, and what had taken place with Natalie. Shortly after school was dismissed for the summer, Nat had gotten a letter from Ty, and he was basically breaking up with her after a long year of mostly separation for the two of them. He had found a summer job in Flagstaff, a good job, he'd told her, so he wouldn't be coming home as he had planned earlier. He'd said in the letter that it was better that they go their own separate ways, and Nat's heart had been broken. Elaine felt badly for her. Of all her friends, she seemed to be the one who had really been in love, and had missed out on many school activities during the past year, just being content to write to Ty, and to wait for him. Seeing how depressed her daughter was, Jackie had sent her to San Diego for a few weeks, hoping a change of scenery would be good for her. Nat was staying with her aunt and uncle, and she'd invited Elaine to come and spend a couple of weeks with her

Finally the bus reached its destination, and the passengers began getting off. Nat was waiting inside the depot as Elaine struggled with her heavy suitcase. She found her friend looking prettier than ever. Her skin was deeply tanned from her days at the beach, and her sun-bleached blonde hair was hanging past her shoulders. She was the only girl Elaine knew whose hair looked good perfectly straight.

"You look really good," Elaine told her. "I think San Diego agrees with you."

"Well, straight hair is coming in style," she told Elaine. "Around here all the girls bleach their hair and wear it straight. Some of the guys are bleaching their hair too. All day long the kids hang out at the beaches and ride the waves on surfboards. It's really a blast. They call themselves surfers, and it's a huge craze at the beaches here, and all up and down the west coast. In fact, surfing is just about all anyone talks about in this town. I'm having a good time here, and it's nice to be in a different place for a change. In fact, it's great to be anywhere besides Ellington. I am so sick of that town. But it's going to take me a long time to forget about Ty. I don't even know if I can forget about him, but I have to try. Aunt Jeannie and Uncle Hank have been really swell. They only live a few blocks from the beach, and so many things are within walking distance, I can go a lot of places on my own. Today, I borrowed my aunt's Corvair, but I had to park a couple blocks away." She paused a minute to take a breath. "Here, I'll carry your suitcase for a while," she added, grabbing the handle. "You must have put rocks in here. It weighs a ton! They need to put wheels on these things."

"Well, you said to bring clothes for different occasions," Elaine laughed. "And you also told me that the evenings can be chilly, so I brought two or three sweaters. I just followed orders. So what else have you been doing, besides going to the beach?"

"I've gone to a few parties. I went out with a college guy, a sailor, and a couple of surfers. I think I could stay here permanently. It'll be very boring when I get back home. So what's going on with you? Have you heard from Ski?"

"Yes, I did get a letter from Ski, a really sweet one. His ship is over somewhere near Japan, I guess, and it will be out for about six or eight months. You know, I hadn't really thought about it much until lately, but do you realize that the guys in our class that will be turning eighteen in this next year will have to register for the draft?"

"I know. Ty doesn't have to worry as long as he's in college, but if he quits, he might have to go."

"Well, not everybody gets drafted. Paul and Duane haven't been. Oh, speaking of Duane, we went out the other night, first time since that night we had that crazy drag race with Willie. And we had a good time. It was just us, not Paul and Beth. We got pizza at Tony's, and then went to the roller rink, and just did a lot of talking. I like him much better when he's not around Paul. But I did give him back his ring. His whole attitude was too possessive when we were going steady.

Plus, I never told anyone in my family, except Pam. My folks would have had a cow if they'd known about that."

"Well I'm glad to hear that you're not going steady because I'm fixing you up with a couple of guys. What do you think about that?"

Elaine and Nat kept very busy for the two week visit. The girls went shopping together, saw the San Diego Zoo, made trips to Point Loma and Mission Beach, rode a ferry boat, and rode the glass elevator in the El Cortez Hotel. Some of their activities included Nat's aunt and uncle. The girls went to a beach party with a surfer, and to the Del Mar fair with Nat's cousin. Later she and Nat went to a folk singing concert, called a Hootenanny, with two college guys that Natalie had met earlier that summer. Folk singing was starting to become very popular that year.

They went to the 4th of July celebration while they were there. The girls sat on the beach with Nat's cousin, and they watched the fireworks explode over the ocean. There was a huge crowd at the beach, but it was worth all the crowding to witness the spectacular display. The fireworks became very impressive as the colors formed a continuous kaleidoscope of gorgeous brilliance. It was fun to see the bright reds, greens, blues, and yellows brighten the dark sky, only to immediately fade into small puffs of smoke. The spectacle was terminated when a huge American flag cast its reddish glow across the water from the far end of the pier.

As the days passed, Elaine felt that she was having so much fun, that she hated the thought of going back home. And then two days before she was to leave for home, Adam showed up. Nat hadn't seen her older brother for quite some time, and she was glad to see him. The two siblings had always been close. Elaine was happy to see him too.

"Don't think I've seen you since that get-together Beth had at her house last summer," she told him. "How are things going with you?"

"Good. I had a little free time, so thought I'd go back to Ellington, and found out that my sister was down here. I start a new job next week right on the UCLA campus and I'm looking forward to that. I also want to try and see Warren while I'm down here. I'll have to give him a call. If he's free, maybe we could all spend the day at the beach."

The day turned out to be a lot of fun. It was great to see Warren again. He was taller than ever and very tan and muscular. Elaine remembered when she used to have a big crush on him back when she was a freshman. Now that was ancient history. He and Elaine had lots to talk about though. "It's been a long time," he said to Elaine, sweeping her into a hug. "Great to see you!"

They set some beach chairs out on the sand. "Do your folks still like their church down here?" she asked him.

"They like it real well, but the church in Ellington was just something special for them," he said. "And because it was a small town, they really got to know everyone and their problems. I know they have some very fond memories of their years in Ellington."

"That's funny since Nat and I were just talking about how much more there is to do in San Diego," Elaine told him. "We haven't had a dull moment since I've been here. I love city life."

"I have to agree," said Warren. "I've enjoyed the high school here, and it had much more to offer than Armedia High. Now I'm really looking forward to starting at San Diego State this fall."

"The time has just flown by. Seems like I was just a freshman not that long ago, and Adam was a senior, and now he's halfway through college."

"Remember that crazy time at MYF Camp?" Warren asked. "That was silly and fun, but you know, looking back on that experience, everything just seemed so juvenile."

"Yeah, I agree. I don't even go to the MYF meetings anymore. They still have a good group, but it's a younger crowd there now. Russ enjoys going," remarked Elaine. She noticed that Nat and Adam were deep in conversation. "I'm glad Adam came down. He's good for Natalie. She's going through a hard time this summer, since she and Ty broke up after almost two years of going together."

"I'm glad he's here for Nat," Warren stated. "From what Adam tells me, he does a lot of worrying about his kid sister. Well, it's getting hot here on the sand. I'm going to hit the waves." The boys went body surfing while Nat and Elaine read some *True Romance* magazines.

"These magazines always have good stories," commented Elaine, "but my mom doesn't really like me reading them."

"Aunt Jeannie has a whole stack of them."

Elaine read for a short time, but it was more fun just relaxing and taking in the sights and sounds of the beach scene, dozing in the beach chair, and listening to the endless rhythm of the waves as they rolled up onto the sand. She had loved her visit to San Diego. It was so awesome to spend time at the beach every single day. Nothing was more relaxing than lying on the sand, getting tanned, or more invigorating than a swim in the ocean. It was also fun to watch the surfers with their boards catching the waves and riding them in. After being around the surfers, she had learned phrases such as "shoot the curl" and "wipeout" and "hotdogging." Oh, if only she lived here in this paradise, she thought. It would be such fun to go to the beach every day, and learn to surf, and meet new people all the time. She and Natalie were heading back to boring old Ellington the following day. At least they didn't have to ride the bus back, since Adam was driving that way anyhow. Once she got back home, the weather would be relentlessly hot, and there wouldn't be much to do. She'd received a letter from her mother just the other day, and her family had vacationed at Whitney Portal during the two weeks she'd been in San Diego. Of course they would be back by the time she got home. They had wanted her go with them, but between going camping with her family or going to the beach with Nat, it was no contest. The beach had won hands down.

Chapter 41

Everything in Ellington was just what Elaine had expected it to be once she was home again. The mid July temperature had hit the three digit mark. The hills on the west side of town, which had been nice and green during the spring, were already looking brown and dried out. Once again the hot temperatures were a problem for her family. At least this summer, with their new well, water was plentiful. Last summer they had lost quite a few chickens before the new well was finished. Even though there were sprinkler systems in each chicken pen, the hens piled together in the corners, and some of them would suffocate in the heat. Members of the family took turns walking around the rows of pens with the garden hose, spraying them off, and shooing them out of the corners. Keeping the egg layers cool was a tedious job, but it had to be done.

"I'm just glad this heat wave didn't hit until we got home," Charles was saying at dinner that evening over chicken and dumplings.

"Yes, the timing was perfect," added Lois.

Charles and Russ were talking about their backpacking trip up to the top of Mt. Whitney, and how much they had enjoyed the gorgeous scenery, and the fact that they had made all the way to the top. They'd had the bear experience too. At night they had to hang their food on a line strung between the trees, so a bear couldn't get into their supplies.

"A bear sniffing around your camp sounds kind of scary to me," Elaine remarked.

"It did make us both a bit nervous with that old brown bear shuffling around," Charles said. "But when he realized there was no food he could get into, he went on his way."

"What did you do in camp while they were gone?" Elaine asked her mother.

"The usual. We took some walks, I got caught up on some reading, I wrote some letters, and just relaxed."

"And Timmie fell into the creek," stated Pam.

"I didn't fall in. I wanted to cool off, and also I was trying to catch a fish with my hands," he said.

"No, you fell in," Pam told him, which started an argument. Pam was rather wound up. A new family had moved to Ellington that summer. They had two girls, one who was Pam's age. They had met at Sunday school, and Pam and Missy were instant friends. Missy was kind of a tomboy, and also liked playing baseball, so she and Pam had hit it off. Elaine was happy for her sister, since Dodie Fawcett, who had been her closest friend, had moved to San Diego two summers ago.

After Elaine and Pam had finished with the dishes, they sat outside on the back patio. "I can hardly believe I'll be in 8th Grade this year," Pam was saying, "It just sounds so old."

"Wail til you're a senior, then you'll really feel old," Elaine told her. "Watch out, Timmie, you nearly ran over my foot!" Timmie was riding his tricycle around and around on the patio. Russ had lowered the back end for him, and it actually looked like a souped up tricycle.

"He's only five, and he's already a hot-rodder," laughed Pam.

A car turned into the drive, and Elaine could tell by the headlights, that it was Duane's car, and her heart began to pound with excitement. In spite of their differences, she enjoyed spending time with him. Beth and Paul were with him also. They sat outside on the back porch for a while, discussing what they wanted to do for the evening. Paul and Duane were always teasing Pam, saying that she would be the first female to be in major league baseball, and Pam enjoyed the attention. Timmie, who was feeling left out said, "Do you guys know I have a hot rod?"

"You do?" asked Duane. "Well, let's see you drive it."

"Okay. It's a real fast one too," he added, climbing onto his tricycle and pedaling in circles around the patio. Lois came out shortly to greet everyone, and to get her young son in for his bath. Elaine knew her mother was only putting on a friendly act toward Paul and Duane, since they were not her favorite people. Lois disappeared into the house with Timmie and Pam.

"Elaine, you got a good tan while you were at the beach," Beth said. "I feel pale in comparison."

"I didn't even notice you were gone," Duane told her. "There were plenty of other girls around to keep me entertained." But the kiss he gave her told her that he had missed her. "So what do we want to do tonight?" After a discussion, it was decided that they would cruise around for a while, and then go to the movies. They cruised the pizza parlor, the skating rink, the malt shop, and went by the movie theater, but neither movie sounded too good, so they went south, back to Ellington, then on down into High Bluffs, and beyond. "Just keep going, and we'll be in San Diego," Elaine said. She was telling the rest of them about the parties and the surfing scene, and all the fun they'd had. Duane was getting a little jealous, she could tell. They finally turned around and went back to Beth's. Her big back yard had plenty of comfortable lawn chairs. Duane led her to a dark, shadowy corner of the yard, away from the house.

"So how were the guys down there?" Duane asked suddenly. "And don't tell me you didn't meet any, since there are always plenty of guys at the beach, and also sailors all over the place."

"I did meet some guys, and they were okay, but I didn't really get to know any of them that well."

"Good. I'm glad to hear that. You're my girl, even though you gave back my class ring. You know, Paul is thinking of asking Beth to marry him, probably after high school graduation. What would you think of us getting married?"

Elaine was quite surprised at his question. "Well, I haven't really given it any thought because I'm planning on going to college, and I will turn eighteen right before graduation, and I think that's too young to get married anyhow. Maybe not for Beth, but it would be for me."

They were lying down on the grass, just talking, but then all of a sudden they were drawn together with hugging and passionate kissing, and more. She felt like just melting in his arms, and she was aware of strange, arousing sensations surging through her body. It was a beautiful, balmy summer evening, and the stars seemed to be really bright that night, and the radio was playing romantic songs. Elaine felt that, over time, Duane was gradually wearing down her resolve, little by little and bit by bit. He kept whispering sweet nothings, and saying that he loved her, and telling her that one of these days, she was going to prove her love to him.

The next morning was Sunday, and Elaine was helping with the 1st and 2nd Grade Sunday School class, and feeling guilty about the night before. She felt that things were getting out of hand with Duane, and that maybe her life was spinning a little out of control. She tried to concentrate on the task at hand, which was helping a little first grader on his craft project. Later, as church was let out, Cathy asked Elaine if she could drop by their house that afternoon.

She told her parents she would walk home that day, since it was not too hot. But when she got home, there was a discussion going on, and seemed that Pam was in some trouble.

"I can't believe that you would do something like that," Charles was saying to his youngest daughter. "This is just so out of character for you."

They were in the living room talking, but Elaine could easily hear the conversation from the utility porch. Usually she was the one who was getting in trouble, so it seemed strange that it was Pam this time. She knew she shouldn't be eavesdropping, but she stood there quietly anyhow, listening.

"It was Missy's idea," said Pam meekly.

"But you should have had the good sense to know better," Lois told her. "And you girls were in that old barn, and could have started a fire. That was just very reckless!"

"Where did you get the cigarettes?" Charles asked.

"Missy had them with her, but I don't know where she got them."

"Well, we're going to have to talk to her parents," Charles said. "And you're going to be on restriction for this coming week. I also want you to write me a little essay on why what you two girls did was wrong. It needs to be three pages long. You can go to your room right now and get started on it."

Elaine was sitting on her bed when Pam came into the room, in tears. "What was all that about?" she asked. "I just came in and heard the tail end of it."

"On, Missy had a couple of cigarettes, so we wanted to try smoking, just to see what it was like," Pam sniffed. "And we were in that old barn that is catty-corner from our house that no one ever uses."

"That barn's been empty for years. DJ and I went in there once, a long time ago. The big front door was locked, but there was a little door in the back that wasn't locked."

"That's how we got in, through that little door. But I guess Mr. Hobbs saw us going in there, so he came nosing around and caught us smoking, and of course he told Mom and Dad at church today. So now I'm in really big trouble."

"That Mr. Hobbs is such a busybody," Elaine remarked. "Years ago, when I was in first grade, I took my shoes off on the way to school, 'cause I wanted to go barefooted. Well, he must have seen me doing that, because he told on me too, and I got in trouble. I know you've been having fun with Missy, ever since her family moved here, but just don't go along with her when she gets a crazy idea. Seems like she's always getting into something. But I've met her folks at church, and they seem really nice."

"They are nice, but they're kind of strict, and Missy likes to get into mischief. Her name should be Mischief, not Missy," Pam giggled. "Well, I'd better get busy and write this paper for Daddy."

After Sunday dinner, Elaine headed over to the Graham house, where Chuck and Cathy were sitting out on their front porch.

"There she is!" Chuck said, as Elaine came up onto the porch. "How are you doing, Young Lady? We haven't seen you for a while."

"I just got back from San Diego a few days ago. It was so great down there at the beach."

"I bet it was," Cathy said. "We want to hear all about it."

After Elaine had told them about her out of town adventures, Chuck asked her if she would like a temporary job. It seemed that the church secretary would be having some surgery, which would require a month's recuperation. "The job is mostly answering phones, doing some typing, getting out the church bulletin and the newsletter, which is done on the mimeograph machine. I think you should be able to handle all that. The church board gave me the go ahead to hire someone temporary for the job. So Cathy and I thought of you. The church office is only open during the mornings, so it wouldn't interfere with your job at home."

"Well, thanks for thinking of me," she said. "That sounds like it would be an interesting job, but I'd probably need a little help with the mimeograph machine. The timing is perfect though, since school won't start for more than a month."

"Oh, I can show you how to cut a stencil and run that machine," Cathy said. "It's old and sometimes tempermental, but it's not really that difficult. The hours are from 9:00 to noon on weekdays."

"And the pay is a dollar an hour," Chuck added.

"That's way better than my egg money," Elaine laughed. "And the work will be much more fun too."

"Well, that's why it's good that the job is in the morning," stated Chuck. "That way you still can do your other job. I don't want your folks thinking I'm trying to lure you away from working for them."

"Oh, no. I'll be doing that job until I leave home," Elaine said. "I get so tired of collecting eggs every day." Cathy left the room to get ice tea for everyone, as Elaine asked how Jeff was doing.

"Oh, he stuck it out til graduation, and then he and a buddy enlisted in the Navy. They'll be in for four years. He'll be going to boot camp in San Diego any day now."

"Well, I wish him all the best," Elaine said softly, feeling an unexpected sadness.

"How are things with you and Duane?" Chuck asked suddenly.

She was surprised at his question, since she had never said much about Duane to Chuck or Cathy, and still felt somewhat guilty over breaking up with Jeff. "Oh, things are fine with us, I guess."

"I only met him once," stated Chuck. "And he just strikes me as a playboy type, and I don't think he's good enough for you. But I guess you're old enough to know your own mind and make your own choices. If you ever want to talk anything over, Cathy and I are here for you."

"Thanks, that's good to know. But, Duane really is a good guy, once you get to know him."

The summer days were going by quickly now that Elaine was working. She liked her new job, and it didn't take long for her to learn how to use the mimeograph machine. Chuck was fun to work for, and she liked every aspect of the job. It was interesting answering the phones, and she knew most everyone who called. Chuck explained to her that there were certain situations that had to be kept confidential in that line of work, and she could understand that. She was always surprised when anything in the small town was kept quiet, though, because there were constant rumors and gossip. She certainly had had some of her secrets exposed in the past, but mostly innocent ones.

*   *   *

August of 1960 was well on its way. The summer had been extremely hot and dry, with long sunny days, and warm nights. To the teenagers, this season was the best time of the year. Their days were filled with various jobs, various hobbies, and various ways of having fun. As a result of the jobs, everyone seemed to have more money at this time of year, or at least they had the time to spend it. Their parents were more lenient, and there was rarely a curfew, since there was no school to worry about. The younger kids roamed the streets of Ellington and Armedia, while the older ones cruised everywhere in their cars. The evenings were long, warm and fun-filled.

One late afternoon the Ellington girls, with the exception of Beth, who was on vacation with her family, took a drive up to Armedia, just for something to do. They cruised around the town to see if anything of interest was going on. Nothing was stirring. Armedia High, under the pepper trees looked lonely and deserted. So did Tony's Pizza. And it was too early in the evening for the usual crowd at the roller rink. The sun, which was low in the western sky, was drenching the town in heat waves, so the girls deciding that chocolate shakes would taste good, made a stop at Micki's Malt Shop.

"So how are things with you and Red?" Natalie asked Lucy.

"Really great. He's just a lot of fun, and he's thoughtful and considerate, and caring. A perfect southern gentleman. I was in the right place at the right time when I met him at the beach that day. You know, he's asked me if I had any unattached friends. Maybe we could set you up with a blind date sometime."

"Oh, I don't know," Nat said. "A blind date? I'll have to think about that—Okay, I've thought about it, and it sounds good to me. He has to be very cute, though, and have dark hair, since I'm partial to that." They all laughed.

"Well. who do we have here?" said a male voice, interrupting the conversation and laughter. "Looks like all the Ellington chicks are out on the town today." It was DJ's voice, and he was with Shawn O'Dell and Dennis Kellogg.

"Greetings and salutations," Shawn's deep voice called to them.

"May we join you lovely ladies?" Dennis asked. Of course the girls agreed. and moved over in their booth, so the boys could sit down too.

"So what are you girls doing so far from home?" Shawn asked. "I know, you're getting tired of Ellington, and you're looking for more excitement here. Except I don't think that's going to happen. This place is deader than a doornail."

"Did you hitchhike up here?" DJ asked. "Or come on your brooms?"

"That was a mean thing to say!" Elaine told him, giving him a shove.

"We came in MY car," Lucy stated. "It's only a '53 Buick, but it's a good running vehicle," she added proudly.

"You have a car?" asked Dennis. "Oh no! That means another woman driver on the road that us guys have to watch out for!"

"Omigosh!" Shawn exclaimed. "I just backed into a Buick in the parking lot. Tore it up completely. It sure was an ugly old heap, and I mean WAS-past tense. Now it's just a pile of nuts and bolts. So sorry, Lucy. If I'd known it was yours, I would have been more careful."

"He talks too much," Dennis said to Lucy, who was turning pale. "O'Dell, you should be ashamed of yourself for scaring the poor girl.

We came in my car anyhow. Besides you can't talk, Shawn. You're lucky to get that old heap of yours to roll out your driveway."

"Please, Dennis. That car is my great pride and joy," Shawn stated in mock sadness. "It breaks my heart to hear you cut her down."

"What kind of car do you have?" Elaine asked him.

"It's a '49 Chevy convertible. The interior of it features ratty blue seat covers, threadbare carpets, and a dinged, dusty dashboard. The exterior has a dirty green paint job, and under the hood there's a rusty radiator, a nearly-dead battery, one faulty carburetor, and some extremely dirty spark plugs. Oh, and an engine!" They were all laughing at his description of his car, but Shawn was on a roll. "And you can't forget the four tires, smooth as a baby's bottom, and set off by dirty whitewalls, and three dented hubcaps!"

"Well, Shawn, it sounds like you have your work cut out for you," stated Natalie.

"I'm not finished yet," he said. "The customizing includes a crumpled right front fender, compliments of Bobby Jackson, and also one pair of rusty pipes. But I'll have her up and running in no time at all, maybe in just two or three years."

"You crack me up, Shawn," Elaine told him, laughing.

"So you girls are out on the town all by yourselves tonight?" DJ asked. "Everyone had better watch out! Where are your guys?"

"Red comes to see me when he can get leave from the base," Lucy said.

"I don't know where Duane is tonight," remarked Elaine. "I usually only see him on weekends."

"And Ty and I are no longer together," Nat told them. "I'm playing the field now."

"Uh-oh, another female on the prowl," said Dennis.

Three more weeks went by, and school was starting on Monday. Elaine's job at the church was over with, and she was getting ready for school. She was at the clothesline on that bright summer morning in early September. She was hanging out a load of her own washing, and had volunteered to help out her mom by hanging up the family's laundry also. She was daydreaming about what a carefree summer it had been, with lots of dates, and plenty of laughs with Duane and Paul. School would be great too, that year, with the football games and dances coming up. Best of all was her job as the yearbook editor. The 1961 annual would be awesome. And her senior year at school would be the best ever!

She was nearly done with the clothes, just a few tee shirts left in the laundry basket, when she noticed Beth walking up the driveway.

"Want to go for a walk?" asked Beth.

"That sounds good. I'm almost done with the clothes," she said.

""You don't look happy," she said to Beth, as they started back down the driveway. "What's up?"

"This is going to be really hard to tell you," she said. "But I'm afraid I have some bad news."

"Oh no! About Duane? Don't tell me he got in a wreck! He loves to hot rod that car of his!"

"It's about Duane, but he didn't get into a wreck." Beth stopped walking. "Duane and Bonnie Carson went to Las Vegas earlier this week, and they got married. I am so sorry. I know what a shock this is for you! It was for me too."

"No! I don't believe it. All four of us went out last weekend, and everything was fine between Duane and me. It was one of our better dates, and we didn't even argue about anything! Are you sure he got married? I bet it's a joke. You know how he and Paul like practical jokes." Elaine's hands were shaking, and her knees felt weak. This could not be true!

"When Paul told me last night, I said the same thing to him, that I thought Duane was just trying to pull something funny. Paul said that he and Dennis went to Vegas with them, and were like witnesses at the wedding. It was at one of those little wedding chapels they have there. I asked him if Bonnie was possibly pregnant, since it was all so sudden. He said he didn't think so."

"Oh, my gosh, this is so unbelievable," Elaine cried, covering her face. "It's too much! How could he do this to me? If he wanted to break up, he should have told me! Just running off and marrying someone else is unreal! I bet she's pregnant. She's always had a reputation! What a slut! I really hate her! Oh, Beth, what am I going to do? This is terrible! Here I was all happy, thinking about this coming year, and now everything is just one big huge mess!" They'd almost reached Beth's house by now, and Elaine was crying.

"Come on in the house," Beth suggested. "My mom took the kids shopping for school clothes, and no one is home right now. You've just had a big shock, and you need to come in and wash your face."

"I can't let my parents see how upset I am," Elaine said between sobs. "They'll just say 'I told you so.' It's better that I'm here at your house for now."

"I know. This is just really horrible for you," Beth said comfortingly. "How could that ratfink Duane go and do something like that without even saying one word to you about it! What a bum! Paul better not bring him over to my house ever again!"

"But he was always telling me how much he loved me, and saying such sweet things. He didn't mean any of it, I guess. I really hate him, and her too! You called him a bum, but I can think of a few choice words that are much worse than that. I'll never be able to get past this! My life is over!" She sank down on Beth's couch, and the tears came.

Chapter 42

As Elaine got up the morning of the first day of school, her heart felt very heavy, and she was completely lacking in her usual enthusiasm she'd always had at the beginning of a school year. It had been four days since Beth had told her the news about Duane, and she had cried herself to sleep every night. She told her family very little about what was going on, just saying that she and Duane had broken up for good this time.

"Honestly, Sweetheart, I can't say that I'm sorry to hear that," Lois had told her. "If you're feeling bad about it right now, then know that I feel bad for you too. But he just wasn't the right guy for you. And, believe me when I say that there will be plenty of other guys in your life."

She had spent a good deal of time on the phone with Nat, who basically told her the same thing. "Listen, Elaine, I don't think you were really in love with him. Remember when you were broken up with him a few months back, and we girls all went to the beach, and you met Ski? You had a good time with Ski, and you weren't missing Duane at all. I think you liked the idea of being in love with Duane, but it wasn't really love. You just liked having someone to go out with. But after my break up with Ty, I can certainly relate to what you're going through. It's extremely difficult. You just have to think about something else, and stay busy with other things. Oh, by the way, I went out with a new guy just this past weekend. It was a blind date. Red brought a buddy with him when he came to see Lucy, so she set it up. His name's Gary. We went to the roller rink, and it turned out to be fun."

"Oh, Nat, that's good. I'm glad to hear it 'cause it's time you find someone else. Is he cute?"

"Very good looking with dark hair and brown eyes, my favorite look in a guy. Hey, I've gotta run. Mom needs the phone. Just remember what I said, about keeping your mind on other things."

"I will try hard to do that," Elaine told her. Of course that was much easier said than done. Every time she listened to the radio and heard Elvis sing *It's Now or Never* or the Drifters song, *Save the Last Dance for Me,* she nearly lost it. She would probably be better off not even turning on the radio, but she loved hearing the KFWB's Fabulous Forty Survey on the radio, and the station came in really well even though it was clear over in Los Angeles. KFXM was a good station too, and that one was even closer.

Lucy, who was driving the girls to school Monday morning, turned into the high school parking lot, and the girls strolled up the hill to the student square to find their Armedia friends. It didn't take them long to locate Vicki, who was bubbling over as usual, Alma with her dry sense of humor, and auburn haired, petite Karen. The girls exchanged greetings and talked over their past experiences and summer escapades until the bell rang loudly and clearly across the campus. The students headed toward the gym for the traditional Beginning of the Year Assembly. Vicki was walking beside Elaine. "Dennis told Megan and me that his brother got just married last week to Bonnie Carson. I was really surprised of course," she said, "since I thought you and Duane were going together. That sure happened all of a sudden."

"We kind of broke up right before that," Elaine said, fudging on the truth, "So I guess he just married Bonnie on the rebound. Weird, huh? But there's other fish in the sea, and I'm not planning on losing any sleep over him."

"That's the spirit," Vicki applauded. "Good riddance to bad rubbish!"

They found their seats at the assembly. It seemed strange to be sitting in the long anticipated senior section, and their senior class yell rang out loudly, filling the gym. Elaine looked around and saw DJ, Shawn, and Dennis, sitting in the last row of their section. DJ was wearing his customary devilish grin, Shawn was in the act of throwing a paper airplane at the freshmen girls across the aisle, and Dennis was busy folding up another paper airplane. Megan had joined her friends. "You know Dennis, he has to sit with his buddies so they can all goof off," she told the girls.

"Well, they certainly aren't acting like seniors," observed Karen.

"But seniors always act crazy, that's part of the fun of it," Natalie stated.

The principal gave a short, welcoming address, which was followed by the speech of the student body president, Greg Okamota. After various introductions, class schedule cards were passed out, and the students were dismissed. Elaine's first class was English. It was a small class, consisting mainly of higher achieving students. Mary Lou, Karen, Lenny, Greg, Shawn, and Woody were also in the class. The brisk tapping of Mrs. Teague's high heels on the wooden floor was heard, and the students suddenly ceased their laughing and talking. Mrs. Teague was the shortest teacher at school, but she had no discipline problems whatsoever. Her classes were ruled with an iron hand, but the students sincerely liked and respected her. She had warm sense of humor and an endearing smile.

"So this is the group that makes up my first period class," she was saying. "My senior classes are always my favorite, and I'm glad I have you first thing in the morning. It will start my day off nicely. Did everyone have a wonderful summer? I certainly did. Mr. Teague and I vacationed in northern California. We spent time at Yosemite, Lake Tahoe, and Lake Almanor. The fishing there was fantastic. You should have seen some of the whoppers we caught!" The class laughed. Mrs. Teague's favorite pastime was fishing, and she never hesitated to talk about it when she was in the mood. Elaine had always enjoyed her classes because of her sparkling personality. Her line of conversation was fascinating because it was filled with colorful adjectives, metaphors, and similes. She was never at a loss for descriptive words.

"Well, Seniors, you finally made it. I suppose some of you have already counted the number of days until graduation."

Greg waved his hand in the air. "One hundred and seventy-seven days," he stated, grinning triumphantly. The class laughed. So did Mrs.Teague.

"Greg always has all the answers," she said. "How many of you did I have last year? Hands please. Thank you. Yes, I remember some of you struggling through Junior English. Well, now you're seniors and everything will be much clearer to you. Because seniors know EVERYTHING, don't they? We have wonderful new literature books this semester. I'm going to need some husky boys to pass them out. How about Lenny and Woody?"

"They look awfully thick," Woody said. "I don't know if we'll be able to carry them."

Mrs. Teague laughed. "You're as obnoxious as ever, Woody."

When the bell rang, the girls headed over to the Home Economics classroom. They were all looking forward to taking Senior Homemaking. Mrs. Jenson had been teaching it for three years now. She was young and attractive, and seemed eager to please everyone. "There are many different subjects we can cover in this class," she said in her clear, soft voice. "Besides sewing and cooking, there is interior decorating, marriage and family—"

"That's the subject for me, "someone was heard muttering. The girls all laughed. Mrs. Jenson passed out preference sheets to everyone.

Elaine was headed to gym class with Mrs. Franklin, or Frankie, as everyone called her. There was nothing to it the first day, and they just listened to Frankie speak about the required gym clothes, and class participation. She was sitting with Karen, and they were busy catching up on each other's summer activities. Elaine told Karen what she had told Vicki about Duane that they'd broken up and then he went off and got married. To her, that sounded better. "Are you still going with Alan Coulter?" she asked.

"Yes, and he didn't go that far to college. He was planning to go to Oregon State, but after Christy died, I think he wanted to be closer to home, and his folks wanted him closer too, of course. So he's just going to City College, only 45 minutes away, which works out really well. No long distance relationship for us. And we both went to Baptist Youth Camp this summer, and it was a life changing experience."

"Really. What do you mean," Elaine wanted to know.

"Well, I feel like a new person. All through high school, I've been interested mainly in guys. They came first—before my schoolwork, before my family, and before church. My main concern was going out and having fun, and having a date for all the big social events. Most all the girls are that way, I know. But camp made me see things differently. Now I feel that in order to be really happy and content, I have to put Christ first in my life."

"But Karen, I always thought you were a good Christian already."

"Oh, I went to church, and to Baptist Youth Group, and didn't smoke or drink, but there's more to it than that. I didn't really witness for Christ, or read the Bible, or be a true example of what a Christian should be. I'd go out with boys and we'd make out. I know most kids do that. But I never stopped to think of whether or not I was behaving like a Christian, or that too much kissing could lead to trouble."

Elaine wasn't sure if she was going to like the reformed Karen as well as the old one. Her friend's new zest for the Lord made Elaine feel a little guilty.

The fourth period class was Senior Problems, a required subject for all seniors. The new teacher was a solemn looking young man who surveyed the class with interest. Elaine's first impression of him was that he was stern and unfriendly, but she soon changed her mind.

"My name is Thomas Mauldin," he announced with a southern drawl. "I graduated from the University of Texas in June, and this is my first teaching job, so I hope that you all will go easy on me." The class laughed. "I guess anyone can tell where I'm from by my accent. I'm sure all of you know that Texas is the best state in the union. Have you heard about the old Texas cowboy who decided to—. Never mind, I guess I'll save the jokes until the class gets too dull," he laughed. "This first semester we'll be studying civics and government naturally. Maybe we can take up Psychology the second semester. Psychology is my favorite subject. Now that I've told you all about myself, I'd like to hear about each one of you. Your names please what town you're from, and what you did this summer." He indicated Mary Lou Wright in the first row.

"Mary Lou Wright from right here in town. I went to Oregon this summer."

"Nice state, but it can't beat Texas," Mr. Mauldin said. "Next."

"Megan Frye from Armedia. I did some babysitting this summer, and also went waterskiing."

"Hope you didn't do both at the same time. Next."

"I'm Elaine Hummer, and I spent some time at the beach in San Diego. Oh, and I'm from Ellington, out in the sticks."

"Ellington's a nice little country town. I just took a drive down there just last week. Next."

"Woody Stuart from Armedia. I spent the summer working with my uncle in construction."

They went on down the row until they came to Shawn, who was in his customary spot in the back of the room. Elaine figured his answer would be unique, and he didn't disappoint. "You're looking at Shawn Worthington Xavier O'Dell the Third from the south side of the lake, and I goofed off all summer. I didn't do a cotton pickin' thing! You can ask anybody!" Of course his comment was met with the usual outburst of laughter.

"Well, you can't complain about a summer like that now, can you?" Mr. Mauldin said mildly. Elaine had a feeling that this would be a very pleasant class.

At the lunch break the girls all met at their favorite spot out on the lawn under the pepper trees. They usually brought their lunch from home in nice weather. That September day was extremely warm and dry.

"That Senior Problems class seems like it will be fun," remarked Mary Lou. "Mr. Mauldin will be a fun teacher, I think."

"It's too early to tell about that," Elaine told her. "The first day in Mr. Dumpke's Geometry class, I thought he would be really strict, and that turned out to be one of the easiest classes I ever had."

"This is great, all of us together again in our usual spot," Karen said.

"We've been sitting right her since we were freshmen," Alma stated. "They should engrave our names in that tree for posterity after we're gone. No, I can't talk about that or Elaine will get upset."

"Oh, that's okay, I am past that now," Elaine told her. "Talk about us graduating all you want."

"You're not eating lunch with Dennis?" Beth asked Megan.

"No, he has to have his time with his buddies, and I'm okay with that," stated Megan. "Dennis, Shawn, DJ, and a couple of other guys have their little group. Even Woody is running around with them now sometimes. I think they're calling themselves the Uncatchables this year."

"Oh, that cracks me up!" Elaine said. "Like they think all the girls want to chase them! How funny!"

"One thing that's not so funny is that last year most of us had boyfriends, but not this year," Alma pointed out. "Now it looks like some of us are part of the old maids circle. We're going to have to get busy. Those cute frosh and soph girls are going to give us competition."

"But the year is just getting started. Give us time," laughed Mary Lou. "But we're not interested in those Uncatchables. I think their name should be the Misfits, not the Uncatchables."

"I can think of one that's not uncatchable," Megan said, spotting Dennis on the circle drive. "Excuse me, girls." She got up and headed over to him.

The lunch period was nearly over, and the girls slowly started back up toward their lockers. "I think Megan treats Dennis just about as badly as he treats her," scoffed Natalie. "Last year it was disgusting how she bounced back and forth between Dennis and Willie, causing all those problems. They were suckers to take it from her. I wish, just once, that she would get dumped."

"I really like Megan, but I know what you mean," Elaine whispered, since they weren't that far away from the other girls. "But even if Dennis broke up with her, she'd just find another guy. She's one of those females who leads a charmed life, and always has a date for everything."

Mary Lou Wright caught up with them. "I heard some bad news," she said. "And I got it from Greg, who should know the truth, since he's our ASB president. There will be no Slave Day this year. Nothing! We had to go through that really bad initiation, and they toned that down the last two years, made it into a Slave Day, and now there's nothing in our senior year! Just our luck!"

"Oh, that's horrible news!" Elaine cried. "Wouldn't you know it would be stopped in our Senior year? That's just frustrating!"

"Another one of those unfair things about life," stated Natalie. They went their separate ways at their lockers, since they all had different classes.

In Fifth Period Elaine met up with Vicki in Mr. Carr's classroom for World History. "Well, this is new for Mr. Carr," Elaine said to Vicki, as they entered the room. "He usually teaches Algebra or PE. I know he's not exactly your favorite teacher. Are you going to be okay with him?"

"Oh, I think I can rise above that," Vicki told her. "I can handle this, no problem." Elaine felt like this would be an interesting class, and she hoped Mr.Carr would stick to the subject, and not spend too much time on football. She liked the books with their chapter headings of the Christians at the coliseum in Rome, the Crusades, and the Roman Empire.

Mr. Carr was explaining to the class that teaching the World History class would be a change for him, and that he hoped the group would bear with him. He did admit that the subject was a favorite of his, and that he hoped to impart some of his enthusiasm to the class.

The sixth period, as in her junior year, was the Yearbook Class, which would be her favorite of course. She was glad to be back in the Crafts Building, working with Miss Lippert again, who was the advisor for both the yearbook and the school newspaper. Elaine looked lovingly at the members of the staff, optimistic that the group would produce the best yearbook Armedia High ever had. Mary Lou was the business manager, and Elaine knew that her friend would be very capable at balancing the books. Lenny and Scottie were the photographers, and Lenny would also be doing some of the artwork. Woody was Sports Editor, and Shawn was Senior Section Editor, and also did artwork. Megan was Section Editor for the other three classes, and Karen was Advertising Editor. Elaine was meeting the Assistant Annual Editor for the first time, a Junior girl named Louise Flynt. There were a few others in the group that Miss Lippert had chosen to be on the staff.

The teacher was explaining to the group that there was not much to be done until they had pictures to work with. She called a small meeting with Elaine and a few others to do some preliminary planning, but that only took about half the period. Elaine found herself sitting by Shawn at the back table, and she was thinking of moving up by Megan and Karen, when Shawn began talking to her.

"So what happened between you and Kellogg? What terrible, shocking thing did you do to that guy to suddenly drive him away like that into the arms of someone else?" Shawn joked. "You must be an awful, horrible person!"

"Oh, Shawn, it was really so strange," Elaine said, all serious. "The last time we were together, we were just getting along fine, better than usual in fact. And then just a few days later, I find out that he went to Vegas and got married. No explanation, no nothing."

"He and that Bonnie, well, they deserve each other. There was a lot of talk about her last year around school, among the guys, and it wasn't very nice, if you know what I mean. And you were always way too good for Duane, you know that, don't you?"

"Why, Shawn, that's sweet of you to say." Elaine could tell that he was serious for once, and she was really touched. She was surprised that she'd opened up to him as much as she had, since, until now only Beth and Nat knew the exact truth of what had really happened. "Just don't tell anyone else what I told you, okay?"

"My lips are sealed," he said.

Chapter 43

As the September days passed, Elaine found that she thought less and less about Duane, and the world looked a bit brighter. She saw that life was still going on somehow, and maybe everything wasn't as world shaking as she had felt on that terrible day when she'd first heard the news. Her mind and heart were letting school take over, just as it should be. Each school activity that she became involved with that year made her more aware that she was doing it for the last time. She wanted to do as much as possible, but it wasn't easy to combine school activities, homework, and have a social life too. Her parents were constantly reminding her that her grades had better be good in order to get into a college. But she wasn't really ready to think about college yet. She had no idea where she wanted to go, or what she would pursue as her major. She wasn't even one hundred per cent sure that she wanted to go to college. She only wanted to think about the present.

The Senior class held their first meeting to discuss what they would be doing for fund raisers for the year, and get some ideas for their Senior Ditch Day and Grad night, even though those events were still months away. Three of Elaine's friends were class officers. Woody was the class president, Megan was VP, and Karen was the class secretary.

The first pep assembly was held, under the guidance of Alma Mendoza, who had been elected as Rally Commissioner. The cheerleaders were their peppiest in their red and white sweaters and skirts, and the songleaders were gay and enthusiastic. Natalie's younger sister, Cheryl, was one of the songleaders, and she was doing a good job. This year's football team ambled onto the stage at the cheerleaders' request. Of course Lenny, Woody, Dennis, and Greg were on the team, but more juniors and sophomores made up the rest of it.

"Nice looking group," Nat said to Elaine. "Now if we can just win a few games this year, it will be great. Oh, for the days that Ty was on the team. That was so much fun!"

The first football game and the Frosh Sock hop were that Friday night, and Elaine, Nat, and Lucy went together. Red wasn't able to get leave from the Marine base every weekend, so Lucy was free. The football game ended well, since Armedia won. And the dance turned out to be fun. Beth and Paul were there for a little while. Elaine hadn't seen Paul since the last time she'd gone out with Duane, which was about three weeks ago. She sat on the indoor bleachers talking to him.

"You know, I really don't know what got into Duane, or why he married Bonnie so sudden like that" Paul stated. "I thought I knew the guy. We've been good friends for years. But I have to say what he did to you was pretty low down."

"Well, he's nothing but a dirty, rotten two-timer! I think he was seeing Bonnie behind my back all along," Elaine said. "He has no conscience, no sense of what's right or wrong."

"The only time I see him any more is at work at the foundry, and we don't really get a chance to talk much. He and I were renting a place together, but now he and Bonnie are in that little trailer park out past the foundry on the edge of town."

"Well, I think they deserve each other, and I'm just glad that I didn't end up with him," were Elaine's parting words, as Woody came up and asked her for a dance.

The Collettes group started up again, and they had their first meeting. They had almost disbanded at the end of last year, but then they decided to keep going in their last year of school. Since the majority of the girls were seniors, they figured the club would naturally die out after graduation. Of course one of the first orders of business was to plan a party. Alma volunteered her home for a party.

"My brother's been wanting to host a party. So Lenny will help with it, and he'll invite a few of his friends, and all of you will be coming, and we'll just try to keep it low key, so things won't get out of hand, and there won't be a bunch of crashers and drinking. How does that sound to everyone?"

"Sounds like a good plan to me," said Mary Lou, the newly elected president. "When do you want to have it? Halloween will be coming up pretty soon."

That question was followed by a discussion, which went on for awhile, of whether or not a costume party was the best idea. They voted, and made the decision just to have a beatnik party.

"And I want to have some games this time," Alma stated firmly.

The party was held on the second Saturday in October, in the rec room of Alma and Lenny's parents home. Of course Elaine got the usual lecture from her folks about cars and cruising. But then Vicki asked her to spend the night, which solved the transportation problem for Elaine, since her Ellington friends all had dates. She and Vicki arrived at the party wearing the big tunic tops and tights, and lots of eye make up. The boys were all wearing sweatshirts, just like the last time.

One of the games Alma was insistent on playing was Pass the Apple, which turned out to be hilarious. Everyone made a line which alternated boy, girl, boy, girl. Alma explained that each person had to hold the apple beneath their chin, and couldn't touch it with their hands, and that's how it had to be passed on to the next person. Of course there was much hugging and closeness in the game. Elaine was between Woody and Dennis. She once thought she had a crush on Woody, a big blonde footballl player, but now she just liked him as a friend. But she enjoyed him passing the apple to her, and everyone was laughing at the awkward positions the game demanded if you were to pass the apple correctly. She then had to pass to Dennis. Even though he was dressed in an old sweatshirt, he had on some very good smelling cologne.

After a couple of games, there was refreshments and dancing, and the party seemed to be in full swing with everyone enjoying themselves. Scottie, had become friends with Lenny, since they were both photographers for the school, and he was there. He was becoming very popular at school, and had even been elected president of his junior class. He'd come with one of his junior friends. Elaine was so glad to see her cousin having a good time. He was just such a positive person, and had a great sense of humor. As the next record came on, Elaine headed into the kitchen carrying some empty pop bottles. To her surprise, there was Shawn O'Dell sitting at the kitchen table, feeding pizza scraps to Alma's little cocker spaniel.

"Hey, the party's in the other room," she told him.

"Oh, it just got too wild and crazy for me, so I had to retreat in here," he said in his deep voice.

"Too wild and crazy?" she asked. "I don't think so. Everybody's out there having fun, and you'd better go get in on it."

His green eyes looked into hers. "Come here for a minute, and I'll tell you a deep, dark secret." She suddenly felt bashful with him. Sometimes Shawn seemed so mysterious and so different from the other boys. However, she liked men of mystery.

"Okay, what's the secret?"

"Promise not to tell a soul?"

"Well I told you a secret in class not too long ago, so now any secret that you have is safe with me. Cross my heart and hope to die."

"I can't dance," he stated, getting out of his chair to pick up some pizza scraps off the floor.

"Oh, is that all? That's no problem. All you have to do is stand on first one foot and then the other in time to the music," she told him, quite surprised that he seemed concerned over not being able to dance."

"Besides that," Shawn continued, "when I left the house with the guys tonight, I didn't know we'd be going to a party, and I'm not exactly dressed for it." He had on Levis and an old sweatshirt with a grotesque face on the back and the slogan "Pray for Surf" on the front. Elaine's mouth dropped open. She was most surprised that he cared how he was dressed, and he was just right for that type of party, and that's what she told him.

"It's a surfer's sweatshirt," he explained. "I stole it off some surfer at Balboa Beach, but I think I'll change the wording around though, and write 'Pray for Sex' on it."

"Shame on you," Elaine said blushing. She just never knew what Shawn would come up with next. Maybe that was one reason she enjoyed being around him-he was always full of surprises.

"This is supposed to be a beatnik party, so what you're wearing is perfect. I guess you guys don't talk about theme parties or worry about what to wear," she laughed.

"Oh, but of course we do. We have to check out our clothes every time there's a dance or party, to find exactly the right outfit to wear, because there would be such an outrage if our colors clashed, or if we didn't have the right pair of pants. Why, we would be ostracized at school, and it would be the end of our lives as we know it." He was getting wound up again.

Elaine was laughing at his usual dramatics. At the same time she was surprised that he even cared how he was dressed. She was wondering if she should go back into the rec room or stay in the kitchen with Shawn. He seemed lonesome and she always enjoyed talking to him.

He was so witty, and was always making her laugh. Then she had an idea. "You know what? I could teach you to dance," she offered shyly.

"What? A clod like me with two left feet, dance with you? I couldn't, I couldn't," he exclaimed.

"Come on, it's not that difficult," Elaine told him.

"Well, if you would teach me, it would be greatly appreciated," he said. They could hear the music from the other room. A slow song came on and they started dancing. Shawn reached out and switched off the kitchen light. "I can't learn to dance in all this light," he said. She felt comfortable dancing with him, and he was a good pupil and seemed to catch on fast. She was surprised that he was a little taller than she was.

"Whatever happened with that guy from out of town that you were going with last year?" he asked her. "The boyfriend that was before Duane-the—Jerk?"

"What a memory you have," she told him. "That was Jeff. It was hard on us since we lived too far apart to get together that much. He lived in Desert Palms, so it was kind of far away."

"Love makes time pass, or time makes love pass," he quoted.

"Hey, that's beautiful," Elaine cried, surprised that Shawn could quote something so lovely. "Where did you get that?"

"Oh, I don't know. Must have read it somewhere," he muttered, acting as if he was ashamed he'd said it. "Hey, I'll have my sheen on the road pretty soon now," he told her, changing the subject.

"Your what? Oh, your car," Elaine laughed. "Hey, that's really good news. I'm glad to hear that."

"I just bought two tires, and I'm getting the spark plugs cleaned, and I'll probably have to buy a new carbuerator, but it's getting there little by little, piece by piece," he said.

The record changed, but they kept on dancing. Elaine told Shawn that he danced as well as any of the other guys in school, but he didn't suggest going back into the rec room, and she didn't mind, since she was thoroughly enjoying herself. "You know, I think you were putting me on about not knowing how to dance," she told him. "Now that I think about it, we have danced together a time or two, probably at the school dances. You tried to trick me."

"Oh, you caught me," he grinned. "I'm in big, big trouble now." At that moment the kitchen door swung open, and Megan and Dennis appeared.

"Do my eyes deceive me, O'Dell?" Dennis asked. "You and Hummingbird out here all alone, dancing in the dark, and having your own little private party. Very interesting!"

Megan just flashed her a knowing smile. Dennis and Shawn excused themselves and went out the back door. "You two looked kind of cute together," Megan was saying.

"There was nothing to it, Megan. I was just teaching him how to dance." But Megan gave her a look to say that she knew better.

"Where did they go?" Elaine asked.

"One guess. Outside for a beer. I don't know why they have to drink," she complained, picking up dishes from the counter. "However, this party has been better than most. There are no crashers here, for a change, and not too much drinking either." Elaine helped straighten up in the kitchen til the boys came back.

She and Shawn, hand in hand, walked back into the rec room where some of the group were practicing some new dance moves to a song called *The Twist* by Chubby Checker. It was the latest dance craze, and was very popular. "I haven't learned that one just yet," Elaine said. They decided to observe for the time being.

"Looks like all it is is moving your hips back and forth, and acting like you're drying your butt with a towel," noted Shawn. "But I'd need another beer before I'd even attempt it."

Elaine was with Shawn for the remainder of the party. They danced all the slow dances together, and sat in the corner and talked when they weren't dancing. Elaine noticed that Scottie was with Cheryl Irby, and Vicki and DJ were together. They had dated some in their junior year, but then Vicki felt that he was just too immature. And Mary Lou was with Woody. Elaine knew tht Mary Lou had been interested in Woody the year before, but after Christy had died last January, Woody seemed to withdraw from the dating scene. But now, he was finally getting back to normal, Elaine figured.

Her spirits were high that night. Shawn was cute, she thought, and he had a good personality. He made her laugh, with his wisecracks, and the unexpected sayings that he came up with. Being with Shawn at the party made Elaine feel happy and content, for the first time in weeks.

Chapter 44

The girls were out on the school lawn at lunchtime reading the school newspaper, which had just been distributed. For once Elaine was happy with a gossip column article, which read: "What were E.H. and S.O. doing out in the kitchen for so long at A. M's party last Saturday night? Having their own private party? Could this be the start of a new romance?"

Ever since the night of the party, Elaine had wanted to go out with Shawn O'Dell. She wanted to know what was behind his thoughtful green eyes, and what made him tick. She couldn't explain to anyone why he was so intriguing to her. He flirted with her constantly during their 6th period class, but did not ask her out. Elaine was remembering how disgusted she and her friends were earlier on in school, when they felt that the boys just didn't date, and that they were so immature. But that was gradually changing. The girls were changing too. The members of the Collettes mostly all had good reputations. They didn't smoke and they didn't drink. But they tolerated the smoking and drinking at their parties. And they all did their share of parking and making out with the boys. Except for Karen, Elaine remembered, thinking back to their conversation at the beginning of school.

The month of October was flying by. Elaine was not spending much time with her family at all, since she was mostly busy with school activities and friends. She knew she needed to pull back from her social life and do more studying since report cards would come out in November. Her grades, as always, needed to improve, especially since she would be applying for college admission in the spring.

All her classes seemed interesting this year. Mrs. Teague's senior English class was studying and analyzing Shakespeare's *Twelfth Night* and *As You Like It.* Shakespeare wasn't easy to interpret, she decided, but she liked it because she'd always heard so much about the famous author of 16th century England, and also was enjoying finding his well-known quotations in his works. Later Mrs. Teague had them digging deep into his tragedies, *Hamlet* and *McBeth.* The class acted out *Hamlet.* Elaine, Mary Lou, and Karen were assigned to be the three witches. Mary Lou had perfected a great witch cackle, and the girls went around quoting "Bubble, bubble, toil and trouble."

Senior Homemaking was studying a favorite subject of the senior girls: Marriage. There were interesting discussions on how long couples should date before before tying the knot, and also interracial marriage was discussed. Most of the girls were in favor of it. Elaine wished that Natalie could have been in the class because she would have liked what was said. Mrs. Jenson also had the girls planning weddings on given budgets. Another assignment was planning a budget for a family whose monthly income was $350.00, which was about average. That was quite interesting because most of the girls had no idea how much utilities were, or rent, or house payments. They did know that a gallon of gas was about thirty-one cents, that hamburgers were anywhere from fifteen to twenty five cents, and the cost of a coke was a dime.

"Red and I already have a budget planned out if we get married while he is still in the service," Lucy whispered to Elaine.

"Sounds like you two are getting quite serious," she answered. "Are you really positive that he's The One for you, Lucy? Marriage is forever. How can you be so sure?"

"I just know," Lucy answered.

"Well, I wish I knew what I wanted," Elaine answered.

"Girls, are you talking AGAIN?" Mrs. Jenson asked.

"But it's on the subject we're studying," Elaine answered truthfully. The conversation stopped, and each went back to work on the composition assigned to them, "Qualities I Want in a Husband." No one had too much trouble writing about that subject. When Elaine finished hers, she found it to be a mixture of Shawn and Jeff.

In Girls PE, Mrs. Franklin had them doing Modern Dance, and most of the girls were enjoying that immensely. They also practiced some of their own dances that were popular at that time, like the Twist, quickly gaining in popularity, and the Bop, which had been around for several years. After school, the girls always enjoyed watching the dances that were done on Dick Clark's American Bandstand. That television show usually set the trend for whatever songs and dances became popular with the teen set.

Senior Problems was a most enjoyable class, even though one wouldn't think a class about politics would be that interesting. Each day Mr. Mauldin started a discussion in politics and government, but after about ten minutes, he would get switched over to another subject, and forget all about politics. The students learned early on, that it was easy to get him off onto just about any subject they wanted to discuss.

"Mr. Mauldin, are you a Republican or a Democrat?" Dennis would ask him.

"Well, now," the young teacher drawled, "since I'm a teacher, I'm not really supposed to let you all know either way, but I'll tell you a little secret. I definitely favor Kennedy in the upcoming election. You know, class, Election Day is just around the corner, and I think it would be most interesting to have a political debate right here in class. Why, back in Texas we used to debate all the time. I love to argue. We also need to have our own presidential election in this class. That would be most interesting." Even though her parents were Republicans, Elaine liked the handsome, young, charismatic, presidential nominee, and voted for Kennedy in class, instead of Nixon.

Mr. Mauldin continued involving his class in discussions on a wide variety of subjects. One of his favorite subjects was country singer, Johnny Cash. He could talk for 20 minutes on the upcoming young singer. Football was another favorite subject of his. He'd say, "I could start an argument right now by saying that I think that Ralston's gonna beat you all in the football game tomorrow night. Now that's my honest opinion. Anybody want to lay odds on that?" And that was how the Senior Problems class went.

World History, for Fifth Period, turned out to be rather difficult. Mr. Carr stuck to his subject this time. Elaine liked the content of the class, but the test questions were not easy. Mr. Carr didn't ask easy questions like dates, or heads of state, but wanted essay questions from the class, such as comparing Mesopotamia and Egypt, and writing about the role the rivers played in developing civilizations. This was not a class she would be able to just breeze through, she decided. There was already much time consuming studying involved. But Mr. Carr told them that he was preparing them for the college, and wanted to make them think.

Last, but certainly not least, was the yearbook class, which Elaine, of course, loved. Being editor was way better than being assistant editor, but then the job had more responsibility too. Sometimes she felt bogged down by the weight of her responsibility. She had to keep continually nagging at her staff to meet certain deadlines. She had to see that the work turned in was done correctly, since a yearbook couldn't be sloppily done. She now understood why Barbara Larson, last year's editor, had been so irritated with Shawn at times. And even some of her best friends didn't do as good a job they were capable of doing. Megan, who usually did such good work, hadn't planned the class sections in accordance with the book's theme. Woody was behind on his football write ups, and Lenny, usually a perfectionist, had turned in some photos that didn't seem up to par. Karen was falling behind in solicitation the advertisements for the book.

When Elaine walked into the classroom that day in early November, Shawn said to her, "Better watch out. Lippie is on the warpath today!" And that proved to be true.

"Students, if you want a really good yearbook, you had better get busy," she was saying to them. "So far, I am not thrilled about the work that has been turned in. A yearbook is something that you'll be keeping for many years to come, and I know you want it to be the best it can be. Lenny, what do you mean by turning in photos like these?" she said, indicating some classroom shots.

"I'll take some more pictures," he said meekly.

"You do that. Remember to blow up one classroom picture for a section page. We need it ASAP so we can get the classroom sections drawn up. Karen, how many ads have we sold at this point?"

"About ten or twelve, I think."

"Well, you're going to need a lot more than that," Miss Lippert said firmly. "Your assignment is to triple that number by the end of next week. And class, all of you can work on getting ads. Some of you live in different towns, so work the areas where you live. Talk it up. It's not Karen's job alone to be responsible for the advertisements. We should have a total of about 60 ads at least, to help pay for this book. So Karen, you can assign some people to help you."

"Okay, I'll take care of that."

Miss Lippert continued. "Woody, we need those football write ups, even if it means you have to stay home one night to write them. I know how you must hate to miss out on a night with your buddies, but the annual comes first." Everyone laughed. Elaine always wondered how Miss Lippert knew so much about her students

Megan was told to draw up another section. "But Miss Lippert," she protested, "Why couldn't we fit my idea—"

"No buts about it," their advisor said. "You can work out another idea. Elaine, it's your responsibility to see that this staff meets the deadlines, and turns in superior work. You can't just accept something that's mediocre. You aren't being firm enough."

"But we have lots of time until our first deadline," Elaine protested.

"My dear young lady, do you remember the mad scramble we had last year just before Christmas to get the class sections and the football sections turned in? I was on tranquilizers for the last two weeks before vacation. I don't want a repeat of that this year. Now be firm!"

Elaine turned to her staff. "Well, what are you all standing around for?" she asked, slapping her palm on the table. "It's time to get to work, Staff. Everyone needs to keep busy, no goofing off, and no talking, unless it's about the job you're doing!" Miss Lippert smiled and gave her the thumbs up sign.

Miss Lippert made arrangements for ten members of the staff to go to a yearbook workshop held at the University of Redlands. It was very interesting and informative, with classes on Photography, Selling Advertisements, Layout, Covers and Bindings. After a day of attending the different classes, everyone was quite enthused about their work on the annual.

After school one fall day, Elaine, Mary Lou, and Karen, in Karen's parent's car, set out to solicit ads for the yearbook. The sun shone down warmly on the November afternoon, and the leaves, which were changing colors, fluttered gently in the light breeze. "Where should we begin?" asked Karen. "The few ads I've sold so far have been to Armedia merchants. Want to drive down to High Bluffs?"

"Might as well," said Elaine. "No one on the staff lives down that way, so I guess it's up to us to solicit the ads. There are some bar owners who usually buy ads.

"In the past, the clay mining plant has had a full page spread," Karen said. "And the foundry too."

"Scottie and I talked about selling ads to the Ellington merchants in the next few days," Elaine told them. "There's Barney's General Store, Bub's Place, and Deb's Diner, to name a few. And the gas station, and maybe even the grain elevator too," she added.

Selling ads wasn't as easy as Elaine had imagined. Some of the owners or managers weren't at the business establishments at the time, and the girls were told to come back later. Other merchants weren't interested. One woman even told the girls to get out of her cafe. "Why should I buy an ad for your yearbook?" she snorted. "High school kids don't even patronize my restaurant, so I certainly don't feel obligated to help them out? Hmmph! Only time I ever hear from them young punks is on Halloween when they try to mess up the joint.

Why, just this past Halloween, they left a real mess out in front, and soaped my windows!"

"Don't be so hard on them, Babs," said a customer seated at the bar. He turned toward the girls with a big smile. "You just caught her in a bad mood today. You pretty ladies can come sell me an ad if you like." He was obviously drunk, and the girls retreated quickly.

"We didn't hear anything at the yearbook workshop on how to handle that," quipped Mary Lou.

"I'm not crazy about this town," remarked Karen. "I never come down here unless I have to. Alan hasn't been here since Christy was killed. He still feels that he was responsible for her death, since she and Woody weren't planning on going to that party, and then he talked them into it."

"That must be an awful feeling," said Mary Lou soberly, as they walked down the street to the next place. "But of course there was no way he could have known what was going to happen."

"She was just in the wrong place at the wrong time," Elaine added.

"My dad is always saying that when your time is up, it's up, no matter where you are," Mary Lou said. "Which means that even if she wasn't at that place at that moment, something else would have happened to her."

"Well, yeah, God knows when our time is up, but does that mean we can do reckless things, and not worry about it because it's not our time to go yet yet? I don't think so," stated Karen.

"Girls, there is no end to this discussion," Elaine said. "We could just go round and round on it, and not come up with an answer, so we might as well drop it."

They were able to sell some ads at the next two places, and then got their full page ad from the clay mining outfit. They hurried over to the foundry at the south end of town, since the sun had sunk behind the mountains, and it was almost quitting time. "Let's hope the boss didn't leave early today," Mary Lou said. Elaine wasn't worried about the ad. She was mainly hoping that they didn't bump into Duane, who would probably be getting off work there any time now. But they were able to get their half page ad, and were out back in the car before the five o'clock whistle blew.

Election Day came and went, and as a result, John F. Kennedy, the young senator from the state of Massachusetts, was elected president. It had been a close contest, however. Judging from the reaction in the Senior Problems class, many of the students thought he would make a good president.

Later that week Elaine wore her prettiest cotton sheath dress and combed her hair into a smooth page boy. She drifted through all her classes that day, waiting for Sixth Period. Today, she had decided, she was going to ask Shawn to the Turnabout Dance. It was still about three weeks away, but everyone was beginning to talk about it. She hoped she wouldn't be putting Shawn on the spot, since she knew he didn't have much money. Everything he earned at the market where he worked went into parts for his car. Of course, she would be buying the tickets for the dance, but he would be obligated to get her a corsage. And they would probably stop somewhere after the dance for food. She knew that even if his car wasn't drivable yet, they could double with DJ or Dennis. She decided not to tell anyone about her plan, hoping to surprise her friends later with the news that he would be her date for the dance.

Her thoughts went back to previous years. Her freshman year, she had such a crush on Warren, and had wanted to ask him, but his family had gone out of town the same weekend. And then she had liked Woody as a sophomore, and they went together and had a good time. But he never did ask me out after that, the big fink, she thought. Of course last year she had gone with Duane, and that was the beginning of her relationship with him. No, she didn't even want to go there.

The clock above the chalkboard in the World History class showed ten minutes until Sixth Period. They had a substitute teacher that day, who just gave them a reading assignment. Elaine was doodling Shawn's name on some scratch paper. Shawn was a beautiful name, she thought, so different. She wondered if he was Irish. He doesn't look it. I'll have to ask him some time. The clock ticked off five more minutes.

"Ohh," cried Lenny, coming up the aisle. "Whose name do I see on your papers? I'll have to tell O'Dell to watch out!"

"You'd better not!" she cried, crumpling up the paper.

"All right, class, you can put everything away now," the teacher told them. The familiar rustling and scraping of chairs was heard, and at last the shrill sound of the bell. Elaine dashed out to the art room, slowing her pace as she walked casually through the door. But Shawn wasn't in his usual spot at the back table.

"Oh, Elaine, I need to go over these layout pages with you," said Miss Lippert. She leafed through numerous notes and was deep in conversation with Elaine when Shawn ambled into the room. She was afraid she wouldn't get a chance to talk to him with the other students around. Her teacher gave her new instructions, and ordered Shawn to the back table with Elaine to work on layout pages. The members of the group began going about their work. Outside a steady drizzle was coming down, one of southern California's infrequent rains.

"My God, Miss Lippert," Shawn was saying loudly, "do you mean I have to draw up all these pages again?"

"That's exactly right, Shawn. And I don't want to hear that kind of talk in the classroom."

"Miss Lippert, are you an atheist?" asked the irrepressible Shawn. Everybody in the group laughed, and even Miss Lippert had to suppress a smile.

"Shawn, you aren't afraid of any of the teachers, are you?" Elaine asked.

"Nope. All they can do is kick me out of class," he replied. "And that has happened a few times."

"But don't you care about your grades?"

"My grades can't go down much lower. Oh, I care, I guess. I'm not sure why I say the things I do sometimes. I think of something, and then I say it, just for laughs. I'm convinced I like to hear the sound of my own voice."

Elaine laughed. "Are you planning on being a politician?" she asked. "They like to hear the sound of their own voice. Or how about a singer or an actor?"

"No, none of that appeals to me. But I wouldn't mind being a disc jockey. They have to do a lot of talking, which I could do. They also play records and tell dirty jokes. I have quite a collection of them. Want to hear some?"

"Records or dirty jokes?" Elaine asked smiling.

"The jokes of course—no I couldn't tell you. You're too sweet to hear them, too much of a lady."

"Why, thank you, Shawn."

Elaine worked for a while on her write up for the freshman class, then decided now was her chance to ask him the question that had been on her mind all day. And he said yes.

"With a little luck, my car just might be ready to go by then," he said. "If not, I'm sure we can double with someone else." Elaine was feeling euphoric and in love again. She hoped, however, that Shawn would ask her out before the dance, just to prove that he had some interest in her beyond classroom flirtations.

The following week promised to be exciting because of the Homecoming Festivities. The classes were working feverishly to complete their floats for Friday's parade, and were voting on class princesses and the Homecoming queen. Elaine had hoped that Shawn would ask her to the Homecoming game and dance, but that didn't look as if it that would happen. The Rooter's Bonfire Rally was held on Wednesday night. It was all set up in the dirt area near the shop classes. The four senior boys, Dennis, Shawn, JD, and Woody came in a group, wearing silly hats and old clothes.

"I wonder what they're up to." Vicki was saying.

"No good, as usual," said Mary Lou.

"I heard Shawn saying that they were planning to scatter sulfur around the bonfire," Elaine offered. "That would make a nice mess."

"Those guys think they are so cute," Vicki added scornfully. "But they really are," she added with a smile. "However, their name is just too much. They think it's a challenge for us girls to throw ourselves at them."

"Well, I'm calling them the Misfits," stated Mary Lou firmly. "That's much better suited to them."

The bonfire was lit, and blazed high. The song leaders and the cheerleaders were doing their job, keeping the crowd busy with yells. The crowd grew louder and more enthusiastic as the evening progressed.

Friday afternoon was the parade, and Elaine was happy because Shawn had asked her to help decorate DJ's car, and ride in the parade. She and Vicki were busy making red and white pom poms to go on the old black 50 Chevy. Since the girls were doing most of the decorating, Shawn and DJ were busy cleaning out the inside of the car. They were pulling out hamburger wrappers, coke and beer cans, and all sorts of papers. "Oh, here's that homework for Senior Problems that I couldn't find awhile back, and had to take an F from old lady Gimple," DJ was saying, crumpling it into a ball.

"DJ, you are sooo disorganized," Vicki told him. "I don't know how you ever made it to a senior."

"Is your car like this too?" Elaine asked Shawn.

"It certainly is not," he stated emphatically. "It's clean as a whistle inside. Of course that's because I haven't been able to drive it anywhere yet. But it won't be too much longer now."

Three couples and Dennis were squeezed into DJ's car. Dennis was by himself because Megan was riding on the big float, since she was Homecoming Queen. Elaine didn't mind being squeezed in next to Shawn. He is so cute, she thought, sitting next to him in the back seat. A curl of his brown hair hung over his forehead, and his green eyes looked mischievous. He wasn't big and husky like Duane, or Jeff, or Woody, but he was taller than Elaine, which was all that really mattered. He was, however, the first boy she liked who wasn't an athlete. Once she had asked him why he didn't play football, and he had said, "Stomach trouble, no guts." He was the most honest boy Elaine had ever known, always seeming able to face up to the truth about himself.

Elaine and Vicki were disappointed with the game and dance. Their guys hadn't shown up for the game. Elaine had spent most of the time looking around for Shawn instead of watching the game. Armedia's loss of the game was little consequence to her however, compared to the fact that Shawn was nowhere around. He did appear at the dance later with DJ and Woody.

"I guess those guys can't make up their minds about how to treat us, Vicki said. "They sure like to play hard to get."

"Well, at least they're not dancing with anyone else," Elaine noted.

"I wish we could play hard to get," Mary Lou remarked. "But it's rather difficult without another guy handy to claim our attention." The girls were disappointed in the Homecoming Dance, but decided to be positive, and hope that the next school activity would be better and more fun for them.

Chapter 45

Even though Elaine had been In the Girls Athletic Association all four years of school, she had never been on the decorating committee for the Turnabout Dance until this year. They had decided to go with the theme "Tropical Paradise". They had borrowed small palm trees, potted ferns, and a variety of other plants from the local nursery, and placed them around the edge of the gym. (They were fortunate that one girl on the committee had parents who owned a nursery.) At one end of the room they had placed a child's wading pool, which they had turned into a little fish pond. But a near disaster had occurred when the pond, filled with water and fish, had sprung a leak that Friday afternoon. Girls were scrambling madly to recover the floundering goldfish, and mopping up the water. They were able to finding another wading pool however. By Saturday morning the decorations were all in place, and the girls went home to rest up and get ready for their big dance.

Elaine dressed with great care that Saturday evening. She had been in a bad mood for the last two weeks, since she felt that Shawn was ignoring her. She just had a feeling that the dance would not be much fun, that Shawn was not really interested in her, and that life was one big series of ups and downs, mostly downs. But once she had on her new dress, and had her hair fixed in a fancy French roll, she felt a little better. Her mother had made her dress of lavender taffeta, with elbow length sleeves, and empire waist, and a scoop neck. The bodice and sleeves were trimmed with lace. Her shoes had been dyed-to-match the dress, but were flats, not heels, so she'd be sure to be shorter than

Shawn. He had asked her in class that day if his gray suit would match her dress, and she had thought his concern very sweet.

She slipped a gold chain with a pearl on it around her neck, but suddenly felt guilty, because the necklace had been Jeff's birthday gift to her when she turned sixteen. That had seemed so long ago. The doorbell rang, and she sat down nervously on the bed. She wondered what kind of corsage he would bring her. This was their first real date. Would it be their last date too? She heard Pam answering the door, and her father politely asking Shawn, DJ, and Vicki to come in. Of course her parents already knew DJ and Vicki, but they were introducing Shawn to them. Pam entered the room. "Hey, he's kind of cute," she said. "I like his deep voice. And he's funny too. The first thing he said is 'This collar is killing me, I am slowly choking to death.'"

"Yeah, he really is a nut. You just never know what he's going to say next," Elaine laughed, picking up her evening purse and a boutonniere for Shawn, and going out to join the group.

Shawn's eyes lit up, when she walked out into the living room. "Greetings and salutations. Your carriage awaits, m'lady." Of course the group had to pose for the customary pictures that Charles and Pam wanted to take.

"Have fun," her parents called, as she picked up her wrap.

"I can't say when I'll have her back," Shawn told them. "If DJ's car breaks down on the way home, it could be hours from now." Everyone laughed as they walked out into the cold December evening.

"I'm really sorry that I didn't get you a corsage," Shawn was saying, as they climbed into the back seat, "but my money situation isn't too good right now."

"That's all right," Elaine told him softly, as she unwrapped the boutonnière and pinned it to his lapel.

"Hey, don't be throwing that wrapper down in this car," DJ said. "I'm trying to keep it clean!"

"Oh, we saw all the trash that came out of here the last time you cleaned it," stated Vicki.

There was much talking and laughing as they drove on up to Armedia. DJ was commenting on how they'd had to clean out the interior of his car again, and the mess had been even worse than the last time, and how he'd found some guy's underwear in there and it wasn't even his.

"I don't think I'd be broadcasting that around if I were you," Shawn told him.

"Well, it makes me wonder who has been in my car, and what they've been doing in it."

"Well, I'm just glad you didn't find some girl's lingerie in it," Vicki told him.

"Well, maybe I found that too, and I'm just not telling," he answered.

Elaine told everyone about the fishpond fiasco from the day before. They arrived at the gym in high spirits. The high school dance band was seated up on the stage, playing *Georgia On My Mind*, a song Ray Charles had made popular. Elaine waved at Lucy and Nat, sitting near the entrance with their Marine boyfriends. She knew that Beth and Paul were around somewhere too. Shawn had been very polite and gentleman like, which was quite a change from his usual irrepressible demeanor. They danced to most of the slow songs, and even made an attempt at doing the Twist.

"You looked good out there doing the Twist," Elaine said to him. "You were really moving, and you didn't even need a beer."

"Maybe so, but it's a good thing I loosened this collar, or I probably would have keeled over."

The black group that had been singing for the last two years performed with several songs. They were getting quite good, and everyone enjoyed them. They were calling themselves the Chantells. They sang *A Million to One* and *Tonight's the Night*.

DJ and Shawn made plans, once the dance was over, to meet Dennis and Megan, and Woody and Mary Lou at the pizza parlor. Of course it was packed since everyone else had the same idea. And DJ took the long way to Armedia, going around the dry lake bed. Shawn pointed out to Elaine the street where his family lived on the south side of the lake, but it was too dark to see much. Elaine figured out that DJ would be driving around a lot that night, since after he dropped her off, he would go back to Armedia to take Shawn home, and then Vicki, and would again come back to his home in Ellington. DJ mentioned that his car was getting low on gas, so between the four of them, they came up with almost a dollar in change, and he pulled up to the one and only gas station in Ellington, and gave the attendant the change. "That'll get me about three more gallons," he remarked.

And then the evening, as all evenings do, was coming to a close. Shawn walked her to the door and said simply, "I had a really great time. My car should be all ready one of these days, and we can go out then." He hadn't kissed her, just made her a promise that she clung to, yet didn't really believe.

Now it was almost the middle of December, and Shawn's car still remained in the O'Dell's back yard. Elaine and Beth had been in Armedia one Saturday doing some Christmas shopping. Elaine was actually driving that day. She could count the number of times on one hand that she'd actually driven the Hummer family station wagon, and today was one of those days.

"Want to go home a different way?" she'd asked Beth. "I want to drive around the lakebed, and see if I can find Shawn's house. It was dark when he pointed it out to me," she said. They turned left on West Lake Boulevard, and drove south past the lakebed. It was windy, and there were little dust devils swirling up from the lake.

"I miss our pretty lake," Beth sighed. "What a difference it made around here when it was full!"

"I know. It's really a shame. I wonder if it will ever have water in it again. Oh, here's his house right on this corner," Elaine added, slowing down. It was a gray shingle house that needed paint. And in the back yard, through the chain link fence, they could see Shawn's '49 Chevy, up on blocks, also in need of a paint job.

Elaine worked very hard to get her Christmas cards out early that year, and somehow she managed to accomplish that job even before the two week break from school rolled around. She had gotten Jeff's military address from Chuck and Cathy, since she thought she would send him a card that year. She enclosed a letter with the card, talking about working on the yearbook staff, and other school activities in general. He had graduated from boot camp in November, and was stationed in Long Beach for the time being. Chuck and Cathy had gone to his graduation from boot camp at the U.S. Naval Training Center just north of San Diego. Elaine had wanted to know what that was like. They told her it was mostly the different companies marching around, going through different exercises, then stopping in front of the officers, and saluting with a rifle. "It didn't really impress me," Cathy had said.

She was quite surprised to get a letter back from Jeff shortly after she had written him. Since she hadn't heard from him since she had sent him the Dear John letter nearly a year ago, she was almost afraid to open it. The message was short and sweet. *Dear Elaine, It took me a while to decide whether to send this or not. I'm sorry that everything had to turn out the way it did, and I hope it wasn't something I did that caused you to break up with me last year.*

Navy life has been really something different for me, hard to get used to it sometimes. I can't believe how short they cut my hair. And how we're outside at night scrubbing our clothes all the time and it gets colder than you would think in San Diego. (We can't use the laundromat.)

It has taken me a long time to forget you, but I hope we can still be friends. Yours truly, Jeff His brief, but sincerely written note nearly made Elaine cry. And to think that she had broken up with him so that she could be with a creep like Duane. What was she thinking??

She missed Jeff when the church youth went Christmas caroling a few nights later. She knew that if she hadn't called their romance to a halt, that maybe he would be standing here right now, holding her hand and enjoying the singing. They were singing beautiful old songs of a Joyous Event that had taken place over 2000 years ago, and had been celebrated down through the ages. But there was no joy in her heart. Why did she always feel sad at the holidays? Maybe because she wanted to share the beauty of Christmas with someone she loved. She looked at Chuck and Linda, arms around each other's waists, their eyes sparkling with love and joy. Why couldn't she have kept on loving Jeff? And even if Jeff would have been here now, it was now Shawn who was uppermost in her thoughts all the time. How had that transpired so quickly, just in a few short months? They'd had a good time at the dance. Would he have even been interested in caroling or church? She wondered what Christmas would be like at his house, and what the holiday would be like if they had been going steady. She'd wanted to make it a happy holiday for Shawn, but he wouldn't let her, so now it would be unhappy for her too.

Just two days before Christmas, Timmie came down sick. He was very cranky, and feverish. "I hope it's just a one day bug," Lois was saying, "If it's more than that, we may have to miss the big family get together this year."

"Oh, that would be awful to not go," said Elaine. "In all the years I've been growing up, we've never missed it before." She was busy in the kitchen making rice krispie treats and sugar cookies. She was thinking of all the beautiful yuletide decorations her grandmother always had all over the house, and how lacking their own house was. They still had the same, small skimpy tree over in the corner, and the same dreary decorations. Pam and Missy were at the dining table making paper chains to hang up over the fireplace. The table was a big mess with construction paper and glue and glitter, and old Christmas cards. They had made some for Missy's family, and now the girls were making them for the Hummer family. Lucky us, Elaine thought, it's definitely not worth all the mess.

She took two sugar cookies, warm from the oven, and a glass of milk to Timmie, who was lying down on the couch watching cartoons, but he didn't want anything. "He must be sick," she told Lois. "I've never seen him turn down cookies before." The next morning Timmie was all broken out. He had spots everywhere.

"It's the measles, I'm sure," Lois was saying at breakfast. "I kind of thought that's what it was because he was playing with the Loomis kids a few days ago, and they came down with measles right after that." She looked at her husband, saying "I'll have to call your mother and tell her we won't be there this year."

"Oh, man, there goes our Christmas," said Russ.

"I'm just glad we all had the measles years ago, before Timmie was born," Elaine said. "But it's just sad that we have to miss the family holiday dinner. It's always so much fun seeing everyone."

Christmas Day dawned rainy and dreary that year. They had a nice family dinner with Grandma Grace and Scottie, and gifts were exchanged but of course it didn't take the place of the big family dinner at Grandma Hummer's in Redlands, Elaine thought. There was always so much laughter and silliness among the cousins. And of course Pam and Elaine always had fun with Lynne and Annette. Elaine remembered when they had stayed with them last year right after Christmas. Elaine's blue mood continued during the entire break. She just couldn't seem to get cheered up or happy again. New Year's Eve was just around the corner, and of course she didn't have a date. But Nat called her and told her she didn't have a date either.

"Gary had duty on the base, so he couldn't get away," she told Elaine. "So maybe you and I can find something to do. Red's coming up to see Lucy, and is going with her family to see the Rose Parade this year. Lucy is just really happy with him, and says they get along so well."

"That's good. What about you and Gary?"

"He's nice, but unfortunately, there's no spark between us at all," Nat said. "So next time I see him, I'm just going to call it off."

When New Year's Eve arrived, Nat was planning to spend the night with Elaine. Vicki was also, since she didn't have a date either. Vicki's mom dropped her off down at Elaine's around 8:30 that evening. Lois and Charles had gone out to a square dance New Year's party, and Russ was at the MYF party. Pam was babysitting Timmie, who was back to his usual energetic self. Pam was teaching him a kid's version of Rummy, and the older girls were trying to figure out what to do with their evening. Nat would be driving that night. "I couldn't believe it, but my dear big brother, who is home for the holidays, loaned me his car tonight." she said happily. "The weather is better too." It had been raining off and on ever since Christmas. "Anyhow, the car has a full tank of gas! So the sky's the limit! Where do we want to go?"

"I thought maybe you guys would have some ideas," Elaine said to them. "There's nothing good on at the movies, and I don't want to hang out at the roller rink tonight. I don't really care about going to Armedia, since there are certain people I don't want to run into."

"There's a party for the youth at the Baptist Church," Vicki said. "My folks were hoping we would go to that. It's a safe bet we won't see Shawn or DJ there. So maybe we should try that party. We could cruise by there and check it out."

"You guys are just lucky you have somewhere to go," Pam complained. "I'm stuck here. I wanted Missy to come over, but Mom and Dad said no to that."

"Your turn will come, kiddo," Vicki told her.

They cruised northward to Armedia, past the Baptist Church party, but decided it looked dull, and there weren't that many cars there. "I wonder what DJ and Shawn are doing tonight?" Elaine said.

"You had to bring them up, didn't you?" Vicki asked. "Just couldn't keep your mouth shut."

"I'm sorry, wash my mouth out with soap." Just then *Save the Last Dance For Me* came on the radio, and that made her feel even worse, since that was a song that she and Duane liked. "I really feel like I need a beer," she said.

"That's funny, because I've been feeling the same way," Vicki said. "But you know they won't sell us any. Where could we get some?"

"Well, I'm not having any," Nat said. "Adam trusted me with his car, so I have to be good. But you two go ahead. I do have cigarettes with me, if you want to smoke. But just not in Adam's car. He doesn't know I've taken up smoking. And where are we going now? I can't just keep cruising around."

"The pizza parlor is just ahead. Why don't you stop there, and if we see some guys we know, we can ask them to go buy us some," Elaine said.

But as they pulled up to Tony's Pizza, Elaine saw Duane's car parked right there in front. "Oh, no, I can't believe he's here, of all people. Nat, could you park in the back please, and not under the light?" Elaine, who was in the back seat, scrunched down on the floorboards so she wouldn't be seen.

"I can do that," Nat said. "But are you just going to stay here, while we go talk to someone who will buy us beer?"

"Yeah, you bet. I really don't want to see the big fink!"

"Paul is there too, with Duane," Vicki told her. "Wonder where Beth is?"

"Her family went out of town to visit relatives, and she's with them," Elaine told her.

"Wait here, we won't be long," said Nat, as the two girls hopped out of the car. They were back in about ten minutes. "We weren't even going to talk to Duane and Paul, but they stopped us to chit chat, so we ended up asking them about the beer. They had two six packs in the car, so they just gave us two of their beers. And Duane had the nerve to ask how you were doing," remarked Natalie.

"Well, what did you tell him?"

"You'd be proud of us, Elaine," Vicki stated. "I said that you were out with a Marine friend of Lucy's, and that you were going steady with him, and he said he thought the guy had gone overseas, and we said he was back now, and that it was really serious between the two of you."

"Oh, thank you for telling him that. You think he bought that story?" Elaine asked, getting back up onto the back seat. She opened up her beer. In the last year or so, they had been making beer and soda cans with pull-tabs, which was very convenient, since the opener wasn't needed. Coors had also come out with the lighter, aluminum cans in 1960. It was a Hamms beer that she had in her hand, however. "Ohh, this stuff tastes nasty!" she said, making a face. "I've tried wine before, but this is even worse. It's very bitter."

"Well, we went to all this trouble to get it, so you have to drink it," Nat said. "You too, Vicki. I'm going to pull into this parking lot, so we can smoke, and we need to decide exactly where it is we want to go tonight." She turned off the ignition and the girls got out of the car. Nat lit her cigarette expertly with her lighter.

"I didn't know you'd started smoking," Elaine told her.

"I have been for a few months now, but mostly not around my friends, since they don't smoke," Nat said, as she blew smoke rings into the air. She offered cigarettes to the other two. Vicki had smoked once or twice before, but it was a first for Elaine. Nat told her she was supposed to inhale, but she couldn't seem to get the hang of it.

"I know where we can go," said Vicki, sipping her beer slowly. "I just remembered that the Yocum brothers are having a party. Let's head back down south."

"I don't know them all that well," Elaine said. "But don't they live somewhere in High Bluffs?"

"They do, and I've been there with Willie before, since the oldest brother was in his class. I can find their place, and we can cruise by there. I hear they usually have good parties."

"If we're going back that way, I want to stop by our house and check on Pam," Elaine told them. "And I'm going to run into this market and get cokes and a snack for them."

"Okay, but make it snappy. Time's a wastin."

Stopping by her home back on Ellington proved to be a wrong move for the girls. Once back in the car after leaving the snacks for a grateful Pam and Timmie, the girls headed up the driveway for the second time that night.

"You're driving too far to the right," Elaine told Nat "and you need to veer way over to the left because when it rains we have sort of a dip—" Suddenly the car lurched and then came to a sudden stop.

"What's going on?" asked Nat.

"I was telling you about that dip. When it gets rainy, it's very muddy there, and you can get stuck. Give it some gas." Nat tried that, but the tires were spinning.

"Well, for Pete's sake, you should have told me sooner because now we are definitely stuck."

"We'll get out and push, and maybe that'll work." Elaine and Vicki got out to try and push the rear end of the car, but that didn't help the situation at all. "Oh, no, now my shoes are all muddy," complained Vicki. "And you've got mud splattered on your skirt."

"We won't be looking too good when we get to that party," Elaine said. "I'm going to see if Dad has a shovel stuck over behind that tree," she said to Vicki. "When it rains, he keeps one out here."

Sure enough, she found the shovel, and started digging the mud out from behind the tires. They yelled for Nat to step on the gas, but that only made the tires do more spinning, spitting a spray of muddy water and dirt all over the girls. Elaine was getting more frustrated, and began to dig with renewed energy, while Vicki supervised. Since Vicki was critical of her job, she handed her the shovel. Nat finally got out of the car so see why her two cohorts hadn't been successful at digging them out. She took one look at the mud—covered girls and began to laugh. There was a little moonlight, so she could see that Vicki's French roll had come undone, and her hair and face had a few splatters of mud, as did her baby blue sweater. Elaine and Vicki began laughing too, looking at each other and finally seeing the humor in the situation.

"Just look at you two," Nat said between laughs. "Elaine, I can't even see your shoes through the mud, and your skirt has big globs of goop hanging off it. And, Vicki, you're not much better! You two would definitely make a big impression at the Yocums' party! And my brother's car is looking pretty awful! I think we'll all be washing it for him tomorrow." About that time they suddenly heard the honking of horns all over town, firecrackers popping, the yelling and screaming of kids, a couple of gunshots, and the ringing of the bell at the grammar school.

"Guess what? It's midnight already!" said Vicki.

"It's a brand new year, and here we are, stuck in mud and muck, completely spattered with it!" Elaine added. "We are one big mess!" They looked at each other and started laughing all over again. This would be a New Year's Eve they would not soon forget.

"And starting out the year like this, means things can only go uphill from here, 'cause they can't get much worse than us standing out here in the cold, looking like drowned rats! Happy 1961, girls!" laughed Natalie.

Chapter 46

""We're going to have to start working on our term papers for English pretty soon," Mary Lou was saying to Elaine, as they stood in line at the cafeteria snack bar.

"I know. They're due at the end of April. Right now it seems like we have plenty of time to work on them, but I'm not waiting til the last minute like I did with the bug collection last year. I certainly won't make that mistake again."

"We have to find a subject, and then do research at the library. It's going to take time to get out a term paper that will meet with Mrs. Teague's high standards."

"Well, I'm just glad I'm not in your English class," said Lucy, who was behind them. She was showing off her engagement ring to anyone who was the least bit interested. It sparkled in the morning sunshine. Over New Years, Red had surprised her with the ring and an official proposal, and Lucy was on Cloud Nine. She was telling everyone that they wouldn't be getting married until Red was out of the service, which would be another year. Karen was happy these days also, since she was wearing Alan Coulter's fraternity pin.

Elaine certainly didn't care about getting married and settling down, but she would be happy just to have a boyfriend, someone to go out with once in a while. Shawn had looked cuter than ever to her when she got back to school after the lonely break. Her friends were always telling her he wasn't worth all the feelings she had for him. Alma had asked her once, what she really saw in him.

"Well, he's just so witty, you never know what he is going to say next," Elaine had said. "And, uh, he is more of a thinker than any boy

I know. I don't he doesn't act like it though. He just hides his true thoughts and his true self underneath that happy go lucky act of his. Most people don't realize it, but he is very intelligent underneath."

"I've heard that he is," Alma had stated, "though it's hard to believe it because he is such a goof-off most of the time. If I had any intelligence, I'd want to show it off."

Elaine's thoughts came back to the present as they reached the snack bar counter and bought donuts and milk. Over on the edge of the square the girls could see Dennis, DJ, and Shawn, acting silly. DJ was shaking up a can of soda, and squirting it in the air. "I guess acting like idiots is a stage high school boys have to go through," Elaine sighed.

"Yeah, the way the act, you wouldn't think they had any brains at all," Mary Lou said. "Woody runs around with them sometimes, but I can't see why, since he's usually more serious than that."

"Well, I hope they outgrow it soon and start acting like seniors," remarked Lucy. "Before too long, they'll be out in the world, and then they'll have to straighten up. And I wish Shawn would stop feeling sorry for himself and take you out, Elaine. You're so crazy about him, but he just seems so ambitionless to me." Elaine took offense to that, and made no reply.

"Hey, I just thought of something," said Mary Lou. "I'm planning on going over to Woody's tomorrow night, and Shawn will be there too, I think. They're going to be working on Woody's car. I usually help when he works on it. Well, actually all I do is hand him a few tools now and then. But you could spend the night at my house, and then we'll go over there, and maybe when the boys get the car fixed, they'll take us cruising."

Mary Lou, you're a genius," Elaine cried. "It sounds like a good idea. But watch something go wrong though. You're sure Shawn will be there?"

"I'll check with Woody later today, and I'll tell him that you're coming over. He'll know what we're up, of course."

"I suppose that's no secret around here," Elaine sighed.

On Friday evening Elaine found herself seated on a rusty ice chest in Woody Stuart's garage. Scattered on the garage floor were various rusted, greasy parts that all belonged under the battered hood of Woody's 52 Buick. At the moment Woody's blonde head was under the hood of the vehicle and the only part of him that was visible was a pair of grease-covered Levis. Mary Lou was at his side, handing him various tools and holding a flashlight. Shawn was nowhere in sight.

"Man, the points are burnt pretty bad," Woody was muttering under his breath. "The condenser is shot too, the wires are bare, and she's shorting out."

"That doesn't sound good to me," Elaine said to Mary Lou.

"How about handing me that roll of black tape in the tool box," he requested of Mary Lou. Just then they heard the clunk-clunk of a car in the driveway, and Elaine's heart beat faster as she realized that it was Shawn's 49 Chevy. Shawn ambled into the garage looking surprised to see the girls.

"Well, Stuart, looks like you've got an audience."

"Yeah, it's not everybody who is lucky enough to see a real mechanic at work," said Woody. "Mary Lou is there a small screwdriver around somewhere? Never mind, I'll have to look for it." He straightened up, wiping his hands on his Levis. "Hey, O'Dell, why don't you start busting down the carburetor? We can start rebuilding it tonight."

Woody's mom came to the garage door. "Telephone for you, Mary Lou," she said.

Mary Lou was back shortly with a downcast expression on her face, and she said to Elaine in low tones, "Guess what? That was my mother, and it seems that my dad's truck broke down somewhere between here and Riverside, so Mom has to go meet him there. And she needs me to go home and babysit. That kind of spoils our plans, and I know you were counting on our scheme to work out!"

"Oh, please don't worry about that. Besides it doesn't seem as if Woody's car will be drivable tonight anyhow, and Shawn's car sounds pretty bad too." She shrugged resignedly. "Besides, this should be a lesson to me to stop scheming, since it never usually works out anyhow."

"Says who? We're going to prove your theory wrong one of these days," said Mary Lou pertly. She explained the situation to Woody, who offered to take the girls back to Mary Lou's in his parents' car. "You coming along, O'Dell?" he asked.

"Well, if we're going to get that carburetor rebuilt, I should stay here and work on it."

"Aw, that can wait," Woody said. "Come on, Shawn."

Elaine was thinking that it wasn't other girls who were her competition, it was cars. The four of them were quiet on the way over to Mary Lou's, but when they reached the Wright home, Mary Lou invited the boys in. Mrs. Wright was about ready to leave.

"I'm so sorry that you had to change your plans," she said to them, "but we didn't know my husband would have car problems of course. Ordinarily I could take the youngsters with me, but Chuckie's got the flu, and I don't want him out of the house, or even out of bed for that matter."

"Hi everybody," called a freckle faced lad from the hallway. "I'm real sick with the Asian flu. It's awful catching too. Better not get near me."

"Chuckie Wright, you get back in bed this minute," his mother told him. "Just because you're sick, doesn't mean that I won't spank you!"

Shawn was clowning again. "Oh, my God, the Asian flu!" he cried in mock horror. "We'll all be struck down by the dread disease! This house should be quarantined."

Mrs. Wright laughed. She had met Shawn before. "Don't sue me if you catch it. I'd better be leaving. The kids have already had their supper. I'll let you older ones fend for yourselves. The refrigerator is well stocked."

"Hey, swell, a home cooked meal," Woody remarked after Mrs. Wright had left. He settled himself comfortably on the sofa to watch TV. "You girls had better get busy and get some chow together. We're starved."

The girls laughed. "You mean you'd eat our cooking?" Elaine asked. "We might accidentally poison you."

"We'll risk it," Shawn said. He had seated himself in the easy chair and was talking to six year old Cindy Wright.

"Want to see my scab?" she asked proudly.

"Oh, gosh, I would love to!" exclaimed Shawn. "Do you really have a scab?"

Mary Lou and Elaine retreated to the kitchen laughing. "Shawn is so good with kids," Elaine stated. Her heart was full of love at the tender way Shawn he had picked Cindy up and put her on his lap. "Your little brother and sister are so cute."

"Oh, they can be a real handful at times. Well, what should we fix for dinner?" She found some ground beef in the refrigerator, and suggested spaghetti and meat sauce. "I'll start browning the meat and boiling the spaghetti, and you look through Mom's recipe box for the spaghetti sauce recipe," she told Elaine.

"The evening's turning out better than I had expected," Elaine said. "It'll be fun cooking for them."

The recipe for the sauce could not be found, so the girls decided to create their own, using various seasonings along with tomato sauce of course. They stirred and poured and tasted and tested until they were fairly satisfied. "It's a bit spicy," Mary Lou remarked critically.

"But it will have to do. Come and get it, guys," she called. Elaine was putting finishing touches on a green salad.

When they were all seated at the table, Shawn took a bite of spaghetti and went through the motions of choking and coughing. "Water, water," he called to Mary Lou. "Ohh—ahh, it's too hot. Bad for my ulcer!"

"Come on, it's not as bad as all that," Mary Lou said scornfully.

"No, actually, it's quite tasty," Shawn said. He added to the group, "Someday all of you will have to come over to my place and I'll fix you a pot of my famous stew." But Elaine knew that she would probably never see the inside of his home or meet his family. She was tired of his empty promises and tired of chasing him and scheming on him.

After they had eaten, Woody said he had to get back to his car. Elaine hated to see the boys leave. Mary Lou walked Woody out to the car but Elaine stayed inside, clearing the table. "Don't work too hard now," she told Shawn.

"No chance of that," he said, cocking his head and waving his hand in a brief salute. "See you." He might as well be telling me to drop dead, Elaine thought in disgust.

The following night she was at home, helping clean up after the evening meal. She hated staying home on a Saturday night. Nothing was worse in her opinion. Home life was so dull, so full of routine, she thought. Her family always ate dinner at 6:00. The girls helped Lois clean up the kitchen, and then their mother would sit at her desk to write letters or plan out her Sunday School lesson while the rest of the family watched TV. Elaine enjoyed certain TV shows like *Ozzie and Harriet, 77 Sunset Strip,* and *The Donna Reed Show,* but she didn't care for the westerns as much. Russ and Charles always liked *Gunsmoke* and *Rawhide.* She watched *Leave It To Beaver* for a while, and then retreated to her room when *The Lawrence Welk Show* came on.

Pam was in the room arranging a stack of her Kodak snapshots into her scrapbook, putting little black corners on each picture. She was concentrating hard.

"You look very busy," Elaine said to her.

"I am busy. I have all these photos, and it takes time arranging them in the album."

"Well, you have the time to do it, since you're on restriction right now."

"I know. But one more day and I'll be off. I do think that sometimes Daddy is just so unfair though," sighed Pam. The latest incident that had caused Pam to get in trouble was when Missy had come over bringing her dog. The dog was a cute little beagle, who was very hyperactive.

Charles had never wanted any dogs on his property because he always claimed that they would scare the chickens. Missy had tied up the dog while she went into the house, but he had gotten loose and ran up and down between the pens, causing a big commotion among the hens. Pam felt that she wasn't at fault, but then she had been aware that Missy had brought Snickers over in the first place.

"I know that you and Missy get along really well, but it seems like she's always getting you in trouble," remarked Elaine.

"That's true, but she is still such a good friend. She likes Billy Hathaway now, and I like Sammy Morrison. He is so cute. But I have a sore toe because of him. I tried to kick him the other day, and missed, and kicked a chair instead."

Elaine had to laugh at that one. "Well, I can see why you wanted to kick him. Boys are so frustrating, and there is one I'd like to kick. But I hope Sammy doesn't turn out to be as nutty as his brother, DJ."

"Oh, he is already nutty, but that's why I like him, most of the time, that is. I think I'll have to start writing in a diary now," Pam continued. "Because once you have boyfriends, you need to write about them. Isn't that true?"

"Well, that's one way of saving the memories," said Elaine, amused. "You might find out later on that you don't really want the memories, though, if they turn out to be bad ones." She pulled her diary out from under the mattress while Pam was concentrating on her pictures. She leafed disgustedly through the pages of the book. What a dull life she led. Nothing exciting ever happened to her. She remembered the day so clearly when she and Natalie had started their high school diaries up at Ellington's little cemetery. The two girls had both been so full of confidence and anticipation for what would be happening in the next few years. She thumbed back through the many entries she had made since that day in 1957. Many of the notes were about boys. She'd liked Warren, going into high school, but their activities together had been MYF business, not dates. Then there was Alvin, but she hadn't enjoyed his company at all. Her time with Danny at camp had been fun, but that romance was short-lived. And she'd like Woody for part of her sophomore year. Also, that same year were several fun filled weekends with Jeff recorded on the pages. Then there was the time that she had gone steady with Duane. That was one of the memories that she would like to forget about. And the most recent entries were about Shawn of course.

Maybe I shouldn't have expected so much out of high school, she reflected. Nothing has turned out like I thought it would. Looking back, she was surprised that the years had gone by so quickly. There were only about six months of school left before everyone would be graduating and going their own separate ways. A year from now I'll be away at some college, she thought soberly. Lois had left a stack of college brochures on her desk, but she had never so much as opened one. She knew that soon she would need to fill out college applications. Just maybe she had better get started reading through the college brochures, she decided.

Chapter 47

One day in late January during the midst of semester finals, Elaine arrived early to her yearbook class to start studying for her Senior Problems class. Miss Lippert had been out for two days, and they were having a study period in that class. She was surprised to see Shawn over by the blackboard, erasing some drawing he had put there. "Hello, Hummingbird, what are you up to?"

Elaine smiled at his greeting. "Same thing I've been doing all week-studying for finals."

"I don't waste my time on such trivialities," he scoffed. He grabbed her notebook. "I have to see how an intelligent person studies."

"No!" Elaine cried, knowing that his name was scribbled somewhere on almost every page. But Shawn had already opened the book and was scanning her doodling which read, "Elaine & Shawn," "Shawn 4-ever," etc. She was so embarrassed, and could feel her face turning a bright shade of pink.

"Tsk, tsk, tsk, such notes! You should be ashamed." He handed her the notebook back just as quickly as he had grabbed it from her in the first place. "Have you heard about DJ's party?" he asked.

"No, actually I haven't."

"Well, that's not surprising, since he just mentioned it to me earlier today. It's going to be Saturday night. My car is up and running, so I was thinking that maybe I could take you to the party?" Elaine's heart almost stopped. He was actually asking her out! Unbelievable!

"Well, sure, that sounds like fun," she said.

"I have to work at the market this weekend," he said. "On Saturdays I don't always get off at the same time, but I get my new work schedule on Friday, so I'll call you then to let you know what time I'll pick you up on Saturday."

Other students were coming into the room, and Elaine went to her spot at the front table. No matter how excited she was about Shawn, she had to study. She couldn't think about fun, parties, and romance. There were still two finals she had to get through before the long week was over. She reluctantly opened her book.

Thursday and Friday passed slowly, but it was such good feeling to have finals behind them, and Elaine felt that she had done fairly well in most of her classes. On Friday evening she was in her room cleaning out her desk and going through her loose leaf notebook, discarding some of her old notes, and thinking about Shawn. He probably won't call, she told herself. Maybe I just dreamed up our entire conversation the other day. The sharp ring of the phone pierced her thoughts.

"Phone for you, Elaine," called Pam from the other room. "It's Lucy." Her heart sank. Lucy was just wanting to talk. She told Elaine that Red was stuck on the base that night, but that he would be able to take her to DJ's party on Saturday. "He's an MP at the gate," she explained.

"What exactly is that?"

"Like a military policeman. I'm getting good at these military terms," Lucy said. "So are you excited about your date with Shawn tomorrow night? It's about time he asked you out."

"Oh yeah, I'm really excited, but I need to get off the phone since he's supposed to call me tonight about what time he gets off work tomorrow."

No sooner than she had gotten off the phone with Lucy than it rang again, making her jump. Again Pam answered, and it was her friend, Sammy. The clock on Elaine's nightstand read 7:12, and the second hand moved slowly around. It's just no fun being a girl sometimes, Elaine thought. Half our time is spent waiting on guys, and worrying about having a date. Boys never have to worry about that. She wished Pam would hurry and get off the phone. The house was very quiet that evening. Even the television was turned off because Charles was listening to a piano concerto on the F-M radio. Elaine could see Lois sitting placidly in the corner with her mending on her lap. Parents lead such dull lives, she thought, but at least they have a feeling of security, and don't have to worry about phone calls and dates and parties.

The clock read 7:45 and the second hand was moving slowly around, when the phone rang again, and this time it was for Lois. Elaine wished she could find something really interesting to keep her occupied. She began halfheartedly going through her college brochures again. The next time the phone rang, it was for her and Russ told her it was a guy. She dashed for the phone.

"Hello, Lainey," said DJ's voice. "What are you doing?"

"Oh, it's you," she said in disappointment.

"Of course, it's me. Who were you expecting? Elvis maybe? Or Shawn? Shawn told me your beauty and charm were just too much for him, and that you made him feel like a lowly clod and that he—"

"Quit clowning, DJ. What do you want?"

"Well, you don't need to take that tone with me. Maybe I just wanted to hear your lovely voice. No, seriously, I needed a favor from you. You see my mom, well, she is getting all involved in this party I'm throwing, and it's getting all weird. I wish she would just leave things well enough alone. She wants to have other stuff for eats besides the usual. She thought that maybe you would be willing to bring some deviled eggs."

"Oh is that all? Of course. I'm not sure how to fix them, but my mom knows how. I'll be glad to bring them."

"Okay, thanks. Now I need to call Beth about some cookies." Elaine went back to her desk. There were a couple of college campuses that actually looked pretty good to her. Finally around 8:30 the call that she'd been waiting for came. Shawn said he'd been working on his car and forgot about the time, and that he would be there at 8:00 the following evening.

When Elaine and Shawn walked in to the Morrison home, there weren't too many who had arrived yet. Mrs. Morrison was bustling around with food and drink. Elaine could tell that DJ was wishing his mother would just disappear. Usually at parties, the parents didn't hang around too much. Elaine had never had a boy-girl party at her home. She felt that her parents would be monitoring everyone the entire time. She set her platter of deviled eggs on the kitchen table. Finally more people started streaming in, and Mrs. Morrison seemed to vanish, and the music started. Elaine was quite surprised to see Natalie come into the house with Danny Kilgore. He had been a senior when they were just sophomores, but he hadn't graduated. No one was sure if he'd quit school, or had flunked a couple of classes. It was also rumored that he smoked marijuana. Elaine didn't know anyone else who did that. Nat usually told her everything, but she'd been rather secretive lately. Danny was good looking, the type that Nat always liked, with dark hair and eyes. Elaine figured she would have to have a talk with her friend at a later time.

After they had danced a couple of dances, Elaine asked Shawn a question she'd had on her mind for a while. "Are you Irish? Your name sounds like it is."

"Aye, lass, I do have a bit o' the Irish in me," he said, imitating an Irish brogue. "My dad is half Irish."

"Do you have any brothers or sisters?"

"Two miserable brats for sisters. They are always getting into my room and going through my equipment."

"What equipment?"

"Well, mostly junk. You should see my room. No, I didn't mean it that way. I mean you should see all these grotesque drawings I have all over my walls."

"Like some of the ones on your sweatshirts?" she asked.

"Yes, only uglier."

"You must have nightmares being around that all the time."

"Oh, I do. I have the mind of Frankenstein. You'd better beware."

"Like I am really scared of you," she laughed, wondering how anyone could be scared of witty, lovable Shawn. About then, Woody tapped him on the shoulder and he excused himself, along with Dennis, and DJ. Elaine caught sight of Beth and Paul and went over to talk to them.

Beth looked very happy. "I was wondering just when I'd get a chance to talk to you," she said.

"What's up?" Elaine asked her friend. Beth's answer was to hold out her left hand, which was adorned with a sparkly diamond ring. "Oh, my gosh, you guys are engaged! Congratulations!"

"I was going to put it off a little longer, and give it to her on Valentine's Day," Paul said. "But once I got the ring, I couldn't wait. I just wanted to see how great it would look on her hand. So I gave it to her tonight, right before we came over here."

"That is so exciting," Elaine told them. "What did your folks say about it?"

"They weren't home tonight. They took the kids and went to the movies." The other girls were beginning to crowd around them, oohing and aahing over the sparkling ring.

"Will this be a long term engagement like Lucy's or are you planning for a wedding sooner than that?" Megan was asking.

"Probably sooner. Maybe this summer," Beth was saying.

A new record came on and most everyone resumed dancing. The boys came back in, smelling of liquor. "Oh, not you too," Elaine said to Shawn, as they started to dance.

"I just had one can," Shawn told her, "and that's all I plan to have as long as I'm with you."

"I'm glad to hear that," she smiled at him. "I don't think I'd like seeing you drunk."

"I don't think you would either. Would you like to take a drive in my car?" Elaine was excited about the prospect of a drive with him, and thought it would be fun to spend some time with Shawn without his buddies around. They left the party by the back door and got into Shawn's green Chevy that was parked out in front. Elaine really hadn't had much of a chance to look at his car, since the ride from her house to DJ's only took about five minutes. So this is the car that Shawn has so lovingly worked on, and is so proud of she thought. He had placed a blanket over the torn seat covers. The dashboard was scratched and rusty, and a small hole had rusted through a corner of the floor. But it was obvious that the vehicle was his pride and joy.

"You're the first girl who has ever ridden in this car," he told her, "that is, since I've been the owner." He turned the ignition key, and a loud roar was heard, the car jumped a bit, and was finally moving down the street. He turned around and headed toward Ellington's main street.

"This is a good little car," she told him, trying to talk above the noise of the engine.

"It even has a radio," he said, turning it on. "And I don't use this car for a trash can, the way DJ does with his," he stated.

"Yeah, I remember all the papers and junk he had to clean out before the Homecoming Parade." After they cruised Ellington, which only took ten minutes, he turned around again, and then headed west on Oak Street toward the foothills. Stars twinkled above the dark hills.

"Do you know where you're going?" she asked him.

"Of course. This road crosses the river bed and dead ends up just past the cemetery," he told her. "I might be from Armedia, but I know my way around here too."

"That cemetery," Elaine said as they passed it, "is the only green spot in town during the summer. Nat and I came up her to start our diaries before school started. Now that seems so long ago."

"Am I in your diary? he asked, as he pulled the car off to the side of the road where it came to a dead end. *A Thousand Stars* was playing on the car radio, which was most appropriate, Elaine was thinking.

Elaine smiled at him. "Oh, I may have mentioned you once or twice."

He laughed. "We'd better lock our doors. I know Ellington has some rough characters roaming around here, not to mention the wolf man. Oh, I forgot. Your door doesn't lock."

"That's a comforting thought," cried Elaine, snuggling up very close to Shawn. "But I'm sure that you'll protect me, right?"

"You can count on that. I'll give you a wrench I have in the back seat, and then I'll run."

"I sure don't feel very safe with you," she teased. "And everybody talks about the wolfman, but I don't even know what one would look like."

"Some crazy guy about seven feet tall and covered with white hair. He has little beady red eyes in the top of his skull. DJ's seen him in this area many times. And you know his word is gold."

"Yeah, DJ never lies."

His green eyes regarded her thoughtfully. "Why are we talking about DJ, when all I want to do is kiss you?" He put his arms around her, and she was lost to everything except the feel of Shawn's warm lips on hers. She felt that it was not only their lips connecting, but that their hearts were merging, as well. The kissing went on for a few minutes, and then they pulled apart. Finally Shawn said, "I'm sorry about not taking you out lately, but you see this car just seems to take up all the money I make from my job, and, well, you know how it is."

"I get that, Shawn. I'll just be happy to go out with you whenever it works out."

"You're so understanding," he said. Their conversation turned toward who was dating whom, about school, and how quickly their four years had gone by. Shawn told her that three junior boys in his gym class had actually gotten paddled at school just that week. Elaine knew the boys he was talking about. He said that all week the boys had been flicking towels around and hitting the younger kids, and that Coach Beasley had given them warnings, but it didn't stop. "So he just lined them up and paddled them with a wooden paddle," he added. "Those guys are all football players, and sometimes they think they can get away with more than other people can. Hey, I know if I got in trouble like that at school, I would be in even worse trouble when I got home."

"Bet those guys won't try that again anytime soon," stated Elaine. They discussed the football team for a while and then went on to the basketball team. Shawn was telling her a little known fact about basketball, how it started back in the 1890's, and how different it was back then. The first game, he said, had two peach baskets nailed to each end of the school's gym, but was played with a soccer ball. It was a YMCA coach who invented the game, since he wanted to keep kids entertained during the wintertime. Once a basket was made, however, the game stopped temporarily, because they'd had to resort to using a ladder to retrieve the ball, which was very time consuming.

"I never knew that," Elaine remarked. "Seems like you know all kinds of interesting, little known facts. How did you find out about that?"

"Oh, I read it somewhere not too long ago."

Then Shawn began talking about all the plans he had for his car, which involved an exterior paint job, new seat covers for the inside, and a long list of other things. They talked about what they were going to do after graduation. "My folks want me to start seriously thinking of what colleges I want to apply to," Elaine told him. "But it's just really hard to think about that right now. Are you going to college?"

"I doubt it," he said. "Well, maybe City College, since it's not that far away, and it's not too expensive."

"Well, whatever you do, Shawn, I know you'll be a success. You're so smart and have good ideas, and I know you're really going to make something of your life." He had no answer for that, but just pulled her into his arms again.

Chapter 48

By the time February was halfway through, Elaine had read all her college brochures, and made some choices. Also on one rainy Saturday, she went up to the high school with Armedia High's other college bound students to take the SAT's. They weren't as bad as she had feared. She was feeling that she'd done fairly well, with the possible exception of the math section. It was a foggy, drizzly, dreary day, as she rode with Natalie back to Ellington.

"Where do you think you'll go to school?" Elaine was asking her friend.

"It's no contest. San Diego State is my first choice."

"It's so big, though," Elaine said. "I am looking at some smaller colleges like Pepperdine College, Whittier, or La Verne."

"Well, you know how much I like San Diego. And I can stay with my aunt and uncle, and save the cost of living in the dorms. I will have to get a reliable car though. I'm excited, and I can hardly wait to get away from this one-horse town."

"Well, so far, I haven't been able to work up that much enthusiasm," remarked Elaine. "I will miss everyone so much, especially Shawn."

"Has he been acting all weird towards you again?"

"I'm afraid so. It's been three weeks since that wonderful night of DJ's party, and he really hasn't said too much to me at school. I don't know what the deal is with him. He's just a mystery to me. And how are things between you and Danny Kilgore?"

"Oh, for now I am enjoying going out with him. He's not Ty, but he can be a lot of fun."

"But he just isn't your type. He kind of has a bad reputation. And he smokes dope. You know the saying, only dopes do dope."

"I don't know if he actually does that. He never smokes dope around me. It could be just a rumor, you know. Besides I like his bad boy image. I think it's kind of sexy. We have some great times fooling around together, if you know what I mean. Only I am more careful now, after that close call I had with Ty. Well, we're back. Do you want to stop at my house for a while, or do you have to get home?"

"I need to get busy and fill out some of the college applications." When she got home she found a letter from Ski, who was still overseas. They had written each other a few times since he had left last May. Elaine hardly remembered what he was like since she had only seen him a couple of times. He told her that were on their way back stateside, and would be docking in San Diego around the end of March, but that he might go back to visit with his family in Alabama. After that he wasn't sure where they would be sending him since he only had about four months before he would be discharged.

Later that afternoon when Elaine was out gathering eggs in the drizzle and rain, Pam came out to tell her that there was a phone call for her, and the caller sounded like Shawn. It only took her a few seconds to get back to the house. She hoped Pam was right, because he was really the only guy she wanted to hear from.

"Hello," said Shawn's deep voice. "And how are you on this dreary day?"

"Oh, doing just fine," she said casually. Fine? She was better than fine, she was wonderful.

"Hey, how would you like to go to the show tonight?" he was asking. "There's a horror movie at the drive-in. We all thought this would be a perfect night for a good old fashioned thriller to get you girls all scared silly."

""It sounds neat," replied Elaine with enthusiasm. "Who all is going?"

"It would be three couples. Dennis and Megan, DJ and Vicki, and the two of us. It will be in Dennis' car, since he has the most room. Still be a tight squeeze, but so much the better. I'm sorry to give you such late notice, but we just now decided all this." He told her they would pick her up around 7:00, which didn't give her too much time to get ready.

As she hung up the phone, she was thrilled to be going out with Shawn again, and thrilled with the world in general. She told her mother about their plan, and she gave her a big hug. Lois, who was in the kitchen starting on dinner, said, "Well, it's good to see you so happy and excited. Shawn seems like an interesting young man. But I don't know if I like the idea of you going to a drive-in. You might think I'm really old fashioned and out of it, but I know what goes on at drive-ins these days."

"Oh, Mother," Elaine protested. "There are six of us going, so I don't think that's going to happen."

"No, I guess not. I sure hope Dennis will be careful. The roads are wet and slippery tonight."

"Well, I have to finish collecting eggs and get ready." She didn't have too much time, and she was worried about her hair, which had gotten damp in the rain, and was starting to frizz up. By 7:00 she had showered, fixed her hair as best she could, and was ready in a sweater and capris. Lois was protesting over her attire, but Elaine assured her that all the girls were wearing capris. "Besides, it's enough that school rules dictate that we always have to wear dresses," Elaine said. "It's nice to be able to wear pants once in a while, and it's much more comfortable too."

They arrived on time, and were on the road back to Armedia. "Oh, I feel like singing," DJ said. "This rain puts me in a good mood. You girls will be in a good mood too after you see these monster movies." He reached up to the front seat and grabbed Megan's shoulder, and she screamed. Elaine had a feeling that the evening would be most interesting. The boys kept the girls laughing constantly. They were talking about the night of one of the school basketball games when they'd all had too much to drink.

"We got wiped out of our gourds," Dennis said. "We had a fifth of whiskey and a case of beer."

"Man, that was really a riot," DJ added. "We started drinking during the game, and didn't stop all evening."

"Well, I didn't get started drinking as soon as the rest of you did," Shawn remarked, "but I made up for it after the game."

"Yeah, I thought you guys were sort of staggering around at the dance," Vicki told them.

"We didn't dance with anybody, or we would have fallen flat on our faces," said DJ.

"I'm the only one that can hold my booze," Dennis bragged. "Megan didn't even know I'd had any."

"That's what YOU think," Megan frowned. "I knew what was going on."

"We were all in DJ's car, taking Dennis back to his car, when DJ got sick and had to stop the car," Shawn explained. "Well, just then a cop pulls up. So you know what DJ tells him?"

"I'm no dummy," said DJ. "I just said I had to check the rear axle. And I think that cop would have bought it if Dennis had just kept his big mouth shut."

"Shawn had a few things to say to him too," Dennis protested. "Don't put all the blame on me."

"Anyhow, we all got tickets," DJ finished off. "And we all have to go to court next week."

"So where do you buy your drinks?" Elaine asked. "They aren't supposed to sell you liquor."

"Oh, there are always older guys around to buy it for us," Dennis informed her. "We have lots of connections. We're very important studs around here."

They had reached the drive-in theater, and Dennis pulled the car into the last row. The two movies that were being shown were *Attack of the Giant Leeches* and *Curse of the Werewolf*. Dennis rolled his window partway down, and hung the speaker inside.

"Perfect movies for a gloomy night like this," DJ was saying. "You girls will have nightmares."

"We already have them, just from being around you," Elaine told them.

"Ohh, burn! Good one, Elaine," Vicki told her.

"All right, that does it," said Dennis. "I'm not staying around to listen to this. Come on, guys, let's leave them here." The three boys climbed out of the car and strode off in the direction of the concession stand.

"I hope they bring back lots to eat," Vicki said. "I'm starving."

"This looks like it actually might be a good show," Megan remarked as the first feature started.

"Oh, here come the clowns," said Elaine, after 15 minutes had elapsed. "They really are a bunch of nuts. And they probably won't be quiet long enough for us to watch the movie."

The boys had brought back two large pizzas, and enough drinks for everyone. "You girls like beer?"

"No," Megan wailed. "We're against drinking," she added firmly, but then she smiled.

"Fooled you," Shawn said, "We only bought cokes and Pepsis. We wouldn't drink around nice, sweet girls like you."

"No, we only drink when we're with the BAD girls," Dennis laughed. The conversation came to a halt for about ten minutes while the pizzas were being consumed.

"Hey, Vicki, quit eating so much and save some for everybody else," DJ told her.

"I hate to say this, Elaine, but I think you're sitting on the other half the pizza," said Shawn. She jumped up, alarmed.

"Joke time," Shawn laughed. He put his arm around her and pulled her comfortably against him.

"Well, I know somebody is sitting on my cigarettes," DJ complained. "I can't find them anywhere." His statement was a reminder to the boys to light up.

"Hey get a load of that hot chick over there," Dennis pointed out. "Ohh la la!"

"Get your eyes back where they belong," Megan said crossly.

"Honestly, you guys are a bunch of perverts," exclaimed Vicki.

"Did you hear that? We're perverts!" laughed Dennis. They were all three laughing as if there was a joke between them, and something more to what she had said.

"There's a very funny story behind that pervert thing," Shawn was saying. "Should we tell them?"

"Yes, you brought it up and now you have to finish," Elaine said.

"Well, the three of us drove up to the mountains a couple of weeks ago. It was right after the rain, and there was lots of fresh snow up there. We stopped at a cafe, with an open field next to it. Some kids had made a big snowman, but they were nowhere in sight right then and—"

"Let me finish this story," interrupted DJ. "Anyhow, there was that poor snowman standing there all by his lonesome, and it just seemed to us that something was missing on him. Sadly enough, he looked like he needed an extra body part, and so, being the helpful guys that we are, we made one for him. After all, it was a snowMAN."

"Oh, DJ, your mind is always in the gutter," Vicki sighed.

"Don't tell me you defaced that poor innocent snowman," giggled Elaine.

"Anyhow, after we attached the necessary parts, I was thinking that the snowMAN was looking pretty darn good, and then kids who'd made it came back with their mom. And that mom got all bent out of shape when she saw what we'd done, and she started yelling at us and calling us a bunch of perverts!" The boys all started laughing.

"See, the kids' mom didn't even know you guys, but she sure called it right," Megan told them.

Finally everyone quieted down for a little bit and watched the movie, but it was impossible for the boys to stay quiet for too long.

"Hey, look what's going on over there in that car," Dennis said.

"Where?" asked Elaine. "I don't see anyone."

"That's just it, you can't see them," Shawn laughed.

"Umm, tsk, tsk, tsk, shame on those two," DJ said. "I think I'll have to remind them that a drive-in movie is no place for such indecent behavior. The nerve of some people." He began to roll his window down, but Vicki promptly pounced on him. Meanwhile Dennis pushed back the front seat and started to roll a cigar.

"Hey, we're all getting squished back here," Elaine complained.

"Are you going to smoke that smelly cigar in here?" Vicki asked.

"No, he's not," Megan said sweetly. Dennis put it away, and pulled the front seat up again.

"This movie's getting boring," Shawn stated.

"That's because you are all talking too much and not paying attention to it," Elaine told him.

"Well, I can think of better things to do," said Dennis, as he began making out with Megan, in spite of DJ's catcalls from the back seat.

Elaine had her head on Shawn's shoulder, and she was feeling wonderfully happy, warm, and content. The evening had been full of joking and laughter. Shawn was a mixture of sweetness and gallantry at times, and then he would revert to silly and juvenile behavior. She wondered if this date would be the beginning of many lively times together for the couples, and she had a confident feeling that she and Shawn would be together for the remainder of the year. How wonderful it would be, just to be Shawn's girl, and find out what he was really like deep down inside. He seemed different, apart from the other boys somehow. Shawn gently kissed her hair. "Penny for your thoughts?" he asked softly.

"Oh, I'm just thinking about much fun it is being here with you tonight," she answered, turning her face toward his. She remembered how wonderful it had been kissing him after the party a few weeks ago, and she was definitely hungry for more. He didn't disappoint her. The car was quiet now, as each couple was engaged in a popular drive-in pastime. Elaine had a fleeting memory of telling her mother that there would be no making out in a car containing six people. How wrong she'd been.

"All right, everybody, break it up now," DJ told them. "That's enough, and the windows are getting all steamed up."

"Quiet!" said Shawn, tossing an empty pack of cigarettes at him. Everyone went back to their necking.

*   *   *

In spite of Elaine's confidence that she would be with Shawn again, it wasn't happening. The winter days grew longer, and February passed quickly into March. Elaine was working on her term paper for English. She tried to focus more on her plans for college. Her SAT scores came back, and they were good. She filled out three college applications and got them mailed off. She was glad for the extra-curricular activities she'd been involved in, for colleges were interested in that, as well as grades. She went with her parents to visit two different colleges. She liked both campuses equally well. One was newer, with lovely, modern dorm rooms, and a picturesque little chapel right there on the grounds. The student center seemed like a fun place to hang out. The other campus had much more history, with ivy covered brick buildings, a quad that was awesome and huge, and a dignified clock tower that overlooked the campus. The college activities sounded like fun; they weren't that much different from the high school activities, Elaine decided. At last, around the end of March, she received an acceptance letter from Whittier College, and it was then that she finally started feeling some excitement for higher education. That was the one campus they hadn't visited, but the pictures in the brochure looked really good, with lots of palm trees around it.

There was a Career Day at school. Representatives came from Pan American Airlines to give a talk on a career with the airlines. Most of the girls were feeling that being an airline stewardess sounded like a fun and glamorous job. Beauty School personnel came to try and convince the girls to take up Cosmetology. The Army and the Air Force were on hand to talk to the boys (and girls too) and answer their questions. Then there was a day where the seniors were assigned to help at some of the local businesses. Elaine spent a day at the Justice Court. She thought it was okay, but maybe a bit boring.

Even though she was beginning to feel a bit of excitement for college, Elaine was feeling sad that Shawn wasn't paying much attention to her at all. She kept trying to think of what she could have said or done to cause his change of heart, but she really had no clue. High school boys were the most frustrating and perplexing people on the planet.

Chapter 49

The seniors clamored noisily onto the bus that April morning in high spirits. They were going to an orientation at City College that day. The bus ride would take about an hour, and they would be spending the day at the college, hearing about the different classes and activities. Elaine and Vicki were sitting together. DJ and Woody were behind them. Elaine looked for Shawn, but she didn't see him anywhere. She somehow convinced Dennis to trade places with her, since she saw that this was her chance to talk to DJ about his best buddy, Shawn.

"So what's the deal with him, DJ? I just don't understand him. The few dates we've had seemed to go really well, but then at school he doesn't have a whole lot to say to me."

"Well, he is kind of a strange guy. He wants his situation to be just perfect if he's going to have a girlfriend, and that's not going to happen. He never seems to have extra money, or if he does, it all goes into that car of his. By the way, did you know that just this weekend, his car blew a rod?"

"Blew a rod? I have no idea what that means," Elaine said, perplexed.

"It means that his car is no longer drivable, and probably won't ever be, now that this happened."

"Oh no, that's terrible! But he's put so much time and money into it!"

"Yeah, I know. I bet that's why he's not at school today, 'cause he's probably really bummed out."

Elaine was feeling bad for Shawn after she heard that news. He had spent months working on that car of his, spending all his earnings from his job on parts for the vehicle. And now it looked as if that was all for nothing. She had a strange, sad feeling that she wouldn't be going out with him ever again.

She traded places with Woody again, since Vicki wanted to talk to Elaine. Her friend was excited about the visit to the college, since she was interested in the school's cosmetology department. "I've always enjoyed fixing people's hair, and I think I'd really like to become a beautician," she was chattering away to Elaine, who was only halfheartedly listening. Vicki then went on to tell her about DJ's latest escapade. Both Vicki and DJ were in Mrs. Gimple's sixth period Senior Problems class together, and the teacher had scheduled a mid quarter test for last Friday. It seemed that, as usual, DJ wasn't really prepared for the test, so he came up with an idea. He had read in the school newspaper that Mrs. Gimple was Teacher of the Week. In the article, it stated that she was born April 25th in Lincoln, Nebraska. So DJ had a big plan to distract her from giving the test. He somehow got into her room at lunchtime to put up a few streamers and write a "Happy Birthday" on the board. "And he had me driving to the bakery to pick up the birthday cake he had ordered for her," Vicki continued.

She had Elaine's interest now. "But last week was only the beginning of April, and wasn't even close to her birthday yet," she protested. "Besides, he could have studied for the test in the time he took for all this planning of a party. That doesn't even make good sense."

"That's true, but you know DJ. Does he ever do anything that makes sense?" asked Vicki. "And then he bought birthday candles, and asked how many should go on the cake, and I told him that I had no idea. He had two boxes, which totaled forty, and he thought he'd need twice that many."

"She may be old, but she's nowhere near eighty," Elaine laughed.

"I know. I just told him to put the forty candles on there, since it would be way better to have less than more in a situation like that," Vicki continued. "So the second bell rings, and we're all sitting in class, and we've all been clued in, and then here come DJ and Dennis, walking in the door with the cake, all the candles lit, and they are singing Happy Birthday, and we all start singing. It was classic."

"So he really pulled it off?" Elaine was asking.

"He actually did, believe it or not. The guys set the cake on her desk, and she was very surprised, and as pleased as punch, although she did mention that her actual birthday was more than three weeks away. DJ had gotten a couple of other kids, at the last minute, to get ice cream, and paper plates, and utensils. I don't know how he managed to do it, but it worked. We had a fun party, and she didn't give the test til Monday, so those who hadn't studied, had the weekend to do it."

"Amazing. If I ever tried something like that, it would backfire on me for sure," Elaine said.

They had a very enjoyable day at City College, even though Elaine thought their campus didn't measure up to the ones that she'd visited earlier with her folks. The girls visited the Cosmetology Department, and they also looked at the pre-nursing classes, since Karen was thinking about nursing as a possible career.

The next day it was back to business as usual at school. Elaine had finished her term paper for Senior English, but now it had to be typed. Her mother had an old typewriter at home, but the letter L didn't work, and there were other problems with it too. She and Karen were planning to speak to Mr. Barber, the typing teacher, about a time when they could use a typewriter in his room. Also in English, they were doing oral book reports, and everyone was nervous about that. Elaine would be reporting on *Gone with the Wind*. She had read the Civil War classic before, but Mrs. Teague didn't know that.

The Home Economics class was doing a unit on the family, and they were studying pre-schoolers, so they needed some in the class to observe. Elaine was able to bring Timmie to school with her on the bus that day. She enjoyed doing that, and the little five year old was very well behaved. He was growing up fast, she thought, and he would be starting kindergarten in the fall. She suddenly realized that she would miss her little brother when she went away to college. Timmie spent the morning hours at school until Lois picked him up at lunchtime.

In PE there was baseball again, and Elaine wasn't any better at that then she had been the year before. However, being out in right field, she did manage to catch a fly ball, much to her great surprise. Usually no one ever hit a ball out that way, or if they did, she wasn't ready. She figured she just happened to be lucky that day.

Senior Problems was still an interesting class, full of lively discussions, and informal debates. The class discussed politics, religion, civil rights, surfing, and Jerry Lee Lewis. Mr. Mauldin was even laying odds on how many of the senior girls would be married before summer was over.

World History was getting a bit easier, since Mr. Carr seemed to be letting up a bit on the class, and they had some interesting discussions in there also. Elaine had come into the classroom a couple of times to find Vicki already in the room, in deep discussion with Mr. Carr. She thought that was a little strange because Vicki hadn't liked him at all when she'd had him for Algebra.

Of course they were busier than they'd been all year in Annual class, since the deadline for everything was the end of April. At the beginning of the year Elaine had so enjoyed the class, and enjoyed flirting with Shawn, but there was none of that now. She did tell him that she was really sorry to hear about his beloved car, but all he had for an answer was "Yeah, well that's the way the ball bounces." He didn't seem to want to talk about it at all, or maybe he just didn't want to talk to her, Elaine thought sadly. He sat at his table in back of the room, and he did his work, but he didn't have too much to say to anyone. He was surprisingly quiet, and didn't seem himself at all. But Elaine tried hard not to think about him. She was very busy anyhow, arranging pictures, typing copy, and proofreading copy. Miss Lippert was on the warpath these days, and she said she was on her tranquilizers again, or she would be soon. She even planned for some of the staff to meet for a couple of days during Easter Vacation.

Vicki and Alma were talking about a last fling for the Collettes. Elaine was spending the Friday night before Spring Break at Alma's, and Vicki was there too. "I think we need to do something really big as a farewell to our club," Alma was saying. "What could we do that's something different?"

"I have no idea," Elaine said. "My mind is too bogged down with yearbook stuff, typing term papers, and the little skit for the Spring Fling."

"How about the beach?" Vicki suggested.

"That's not anything new," Elaine pointed out.

"No, I mean, what if we got together and rented a place at the beach for a week? If a whole group of us went, it wouldn't cost that much, and it would be so much fun. We could plan it for sometime this summer. But we'd probably need to reserve it now, since those rentals go really fast."

"Hey, that's a great idea, I am so stoked," Alma exclaimed. "Let's drive down there one day next week, and look into it. If we wait until summer, they'll be all booked up." The girls made plans to go on Monday, since Elaine had yearbook work on Tuesday and Wednesday. They stayed up late talking, as they usually did when they got together. Then Vicki said had some news for them.

"But this is in the strictest confidence," she said. "You guys cannot tell a soul."

"Wow, this sounds like something really important," Alma said.

"Well, it is important, and it's not something that will stay a secret for very long, but Megan is quitting school, probably around the end of this month. She's pregnant, so she and Dennis will be getting married soon."

You could have heard a pin drop in the room. Both Elaine and Alma were momentarily speechless, but finally Elaine found her voice. "Oh that is too much! It's absolutely unbelievable! She had her life planned out better than anyone I knew! She was going to college and everything!"

"I like Dennis, and he's a lot of fun," said Alma, "but he just doesn't seem like he's ready to become a father. That's so much responsibility. I simply can't picture him settling down, bringing home a steady paycheck, and just being a daddy."

"I know, that is hard to imagine," Vicki added. "But he had his fun time, and now he's going to have to get a job and settle down."

"But what about graduation?" Elaine asked. "And all the fun end of the year activities? That's so sad that Megan will have to miss out on all of that!"

"School rules," Vicki said. "She's three months along, so she can't keep on going to school. She'll start showing soon. But she's planning on going to night school so she can still graduate. She can get her diploma, but she just can't be in the ceremony with the rest of our class."

"But Dennis doesn't have to miss out on anything," Elaine stated. "That doesn't seem fair, since it's just as much his fault as it is hers."

Elaine stayed awake long after the other girls had fallen asleep that night. She just couldn't wrap her mind around what Vicki had disclosed to them. She remembered some of her dates with Duane, when it was so difficult for him to take no for an answer. She had thought she had problems, but they seemed rather minor compared to what she had just heard.

They slept late, and when they went out to the kitchen, Lenny and his dad had fixed a big pancake breakfast for them. The breakfast was delicious, but being in their kitchen reminded Elaine of the time she and Shawn had been dancing in there at Alma's party. She wished she could get him out of her head for good.

After a hearty meal of pancakes and sausage, the girls decided to take a walk across the dry lake bed. It was a beautiful day, with no breeze at all, the best kind of weather for trekking across the dusty lakebed. Everything was fine until they were about halfway across. Elaine had been wearing her sandals, since she hadn't brought her tennis shoes to Alma's, and somehow, she stepped on a bee. She felt a sharp pinch on her foot, and had to sit down for a minute. Sure enough, there was the stinger in her toe.

"Oh, I hope this doesn't swell up too much, since I am allergic to bees," she moaned.

""That's not good," Vicki pointed out. "I've heard that if you're allergic, every time you get stung, it gets worse. How many times have you been stung before?'

"Probably two or three times, but I've usually been at home."

"Well, we're closer to town now, so hopefully you can make it into town, and we'll have to find a phone, so I can call Lenny and ask him to take us back to our house," Alma said.

Her foot was hurting her, but with her friends' help, she was able to limp into town. Luckily, Alma got hold of Lenny, and he drove into Armedia and picked them up. He was teasing her. "Leave it to you, Elaine, to tangle with a little old bee," he laughed. "Your foot is starting to swell up like a football." He drove them back so she could pick up her overnight bag, and then he drove them down to Ellington. By the time she got home, Elaine wasn't feeling that well, and her foot was very swollen.

That night was the Spring Concert at school. It was called The Spring Fling this year. Elaine was supposed to have been in it. She and a few of the other girls had been practicing a song and dance number, but she felt too sick to go. She heard all about it later, and was very sorry to have missed it. The Chantells, the black singing group, sang *In the Still of the Night*. Her group had done some marching and dancing to The *Battle of New Orleans* which had been a very popular hit awhile back.

The swelling in her foot didn't go down for three days, so she had to miss out on driving to the beach with Alma and Vicki to reserve a place for the Collettes for that summer. Finally on Tuesday, she was able to get to the school for the work that they were doing for the yearbook. It was a small group, made up of Lenny, Mary Lou, Woody, and Karen, but they got much accomplished that day.

Also, during that week Beth told her that she and Paul had set a wedding date for the last Saturday in June, and she wanted Elaine, Lucy, and Nat to be bridesmaids. Her younger sister would be the Maid of Honor. Elaine was very excited about the prospect of being a bridesmaid, and the girls got together and went shopping for fabric, since they were all planning to make their dresses. Cotton candy pink was the color of the taffeta, and there would be lots of lace. She was glad they were starting early on the dresses, since between now and the end of school would be extremely busy. She was thinking of Megan, who was getting married soon, and Beth would be next and then maybe Lucy the following year. Elaine just felt that she had no desire to get married yet. There were just too many other opportunities out there. Of course she was beginning to have second thoughts about going away to college, leaving everything dear and familiar behind, and starting all over again with making friends. But her parents had already sent in a deposit, so it was too late to back out now.

Once school resumed after vacation, Elaine, Beth, and Lucy were walking up the slope from the parking lot, since Lucy had driven to school that day. Elaine caught sight of Shawn in the parking lot with a blonde senior girl named Mimi Atherton, who was in Elaine's gym class. Mimi was the proud owner of a 1960 red Corvette. She had been driving it to school for several months now. Her father owned a car dealership in town, so of course that was the reason she had the hottest car in school. She was a carefree type of girl, with a happy-go-lucky attitude.

"I wonder if there's anything between Shawn and Mimi," she mused. "Of course with all the problems with his car, leave it to him to find a girl with a really great car."

"I heard that they've gone out a couple of times," Lucy said. "But it's always in Mimi's car, sort of a strange situation."

"Well, shit, since I don't even own any car, period, I guess I'm just out of luck," said Elaine crossly.

"I never heard you cuss that way before," Beth said to her.

"There's a first time for everything," Elaine replied. "There's the bell. Let's get to class."

Chapter 50

Elaine decided that it was high time for her to have a talk with her parents about using the family car. Her friends either had their own vehicles, or had parents who were willing to let them drive their cars when they needed transportation. She realized that her folks had just paid a hefty deposit for her college, so she certainly understood that they couldn't be buying her a car also. But she felt that they should be more generous when it came to lending her the family station wagon. One evening after dinner, she approached her father with the question.

"This Friday night is the Letterman's Club Talent Show at school, and it was so good last year, and I'd really like to see it, but I need a way to get there. Nat can't use her mom's car that night, and I was wondering if, possibly, I could use our car?"

"Well, I think that maybe something could be worked out," Charles said. "You've been driving for quite a while now, and I know that you're pretty responsible. One question I have, though, is what would you do if you got a flat tire?"

"A flat tire? Well, I guess I would have to get to a pay phone, and call you, or call someone to change the tire."

"Well, don't you think a much better solution would be if you could change the tire yourself?" asked Charles. "Because you might be a long way from a phone, so it's not always practical to call someone. How about tomorrow after school, I show you how to change a tire?"

"Sure. That sounds like something I'd need to know."

The following day Elaine paid close attention as her dad showed her where the spare tire was stored, and showed her bumper jack and the lug nut wrench, and explained their functions. She placed the jack under the bumper, and pumped up the car. With some difficulty she pried the hub cap off with one end of the lug nut wrench. Getting the lug nuts to turn was quite a challenge, however, but she finally got the five of them off. "Now it's just a simple matter of taking off the flat tire, and putting on the spare," said Charles. "And since we're not actually changing the tire, you can go ahead and tighten the lug nuts now. The best way is to tighten the one on top, and then do the opposite one. And you need to use all your muscle, tightening them as much as possible. Just remember, it's Lefty-Loosie, Righty-Tightie. When you are tightening anything at all, it's the same principal." She was unable to get the hub cap to pop back on, so Charles did it for her.

"Good job, I'm proud of you, and you can plan on using the car on Friday." She happily hurried to the phone to let Nat know they wouldn't have to stay home on Friday night.

The girls enjoyed the talent show, which was as big a success as it had been last year. Nat was explaining that Danny had something else going on that evening, or she would have been with him. Elaine wanted to cruise the pizza parlor so they headed over that way, but to their disappointment, the girls didn't see any of their friends hanging out there.

"It's kind of strange, but things seem to be rather dead tonight," Elaine said. "I wonder where all our friends are. Here I have the car, and everyone has gone home early. That kind of bums me out. Do you suppose there is a party somewhere?"

"If there were, I'm sure we'd know about it. Hey, let's try the skating rink. They might be over there," suggested Nat. But when they stopped there, it looked almost deserted, and they didn't recognize the few cars that were parked out in front.

"You know, actually I'm kind of tired this evening," Nat said. "Maybe we should just head on back to your house." Elaine turned in the direction of home, wondering why everyone was such a party pooper on her big night when she had the car.

"What ever happened to Ski?" Natalie was asking. "I thought he was supposed to come back to Camp Pendleton when he got back from overseas."

"I thought I told you. The last letter I got from him said he had to go home to Alabama on leave, since his father was in the hospital, but that he would be coming back to Pendleton to finish up his tour with the Marines. But it's been about three weeks or more since I last heard from him."

Twenty minutes later they had reached Ellington, and Elaine was turning off into her driveway. As she neared the house, she saw a few cars parked out behind the trees. One of them looked strangely enough like Woody's Buick. An ominous hush was in the air. She parked the car and rushed in through the back door, with Nat right behind her. Instantly the house was ablaze with lights, and a large group of at least 30 people were yelling "Surprise!"

"What's going on?" Elaine asked, full of smiles. Her birthday was on Sunday, but she had never expected anything like this. It seemed to her that all the teen agers in Armedia Valley were here. A camera flashed in her face.

"I've never seen such a surprised look on anyone's face," remarked Beth, setting a large white cake on the dining table of front of Elaine. It was adorned with 18 flaming candles.

"Oh, my gosh, this is just unbelievable!" cried Elaine, as the group surrounding the table laughed.

"Make a wish!" someone shouted from the crowd. She closed her eyes and blew out the candles, wishing that somehow, some day, she and Shawn would be together. As Beth and Susan began to cut the cake and pass it around, she asked who was responsible for the party. Beth was beaming.

"Lucy, Nat, and I started talking about it a couple of weeks ago. Then we got together with your mother and planned the whole thing. Pretty clever of us, huh? And you didn't even have a clue. We didn't know so many would be coming, since it was by invitation only. And it turned out pretty well."

"Mom, I wondered why you were cleaning the house so thoroughly this afternoon," Elaine said, putting an affectionate arm around Lois, who had joined the girls by the table. "How did you ever manage to keep the secret?"

"It wasn't easy," Lois smiled. "I also did some cleaning every day after you had gone to school."

"Nat was designated to keep you in Armedia for a little while," Vicki explained, "so we could all leave the talent show, and get down here before you did."

"It was so funny, driving around with Elaine," Nat pointed out. "She just couldn't figure out why no one was hanging out at Tony's, or at the roller rink. And then she asked if there was a party somewhere that we didn't know about, and it was all I could do to keep a straight face. And then I made up some silly story about something I had left at her house, so she had to come by here, before she could drop me off."

"I thought that sounded kind of lame," she said to Nat. Elaine was looking around to see who all was there. She saw Lenny, Woody, Mary Lou, and DJ over by the record player. Scottie was with his girlfriend, Cheryl, and Russ was talking to them. Alma and Karen were passing out punch to everyone, and Pam was helping hand out cake. Lucy and Red were back in the corner of the room with another guy, but she couldn't tell who. Greg and his girlfriend, Wendi, were dancing, along with several others. There were plenty of other friends in attendance too. Natalie's boyfriend, Danny Kilgore was just outside the sliding door carrying on a conversation with Paul. Even though she was happy with the party, the one person who meant the most to her, was absent.

Just then Lucy came up, giving Elaine a big hug, and wishing her a happy birthday. "There's something else we haven't told you," she said, looking like she was about to bubble over. "Ski is here. He came with Red this weekend. He's been back at Camp Pendleton for a week or so, but I had Red clue him in about this surprise party, so now he is part of the surprise too. Come with me," she grabbed Elaine's hand and led her to the corner of the room, where Ski was standing, all smiles. He looked better than Elaine had remembered him, and he grabbed her in a big embrace.

"Oh, are you a sight for sore eyes!" he said. "It seems like I've been gone forever. I didn't know if I'd get stationed back here or not, so I didn't know if I would see you again. You wrote me the best letters while I was away. I really looked forward to them." Lucy and Red were dancing now, and Ski asked her for a dance.

"Well, it's really great to see you too, Ski. I certainly wasn't expecting this party or seeing you tonight. How's your dad doing? Wasn't he in the hospital?"

"He was. He had a heart attack, but is doing much better. I hadn't been planning on going home on leave, since I'm getting out next month. But then I had to go back home, when I heard about Dad."

Later when she was in the kitchen, Nat and Danny came in from outside. "Happy birthday, Elaine," Danny said "Is it sweet sixteen and never been kissed?"

"Oh, I think she's long past that," joked Nat.

""And it's my eighteenth," she told him.

"That's a milestone birthday," Danny told her. "Now you can do what you want. You're of age."

Lois came out to the kitchen and said to Beth, "You've been really busy all evening, so I'm going to take over in here, so that you can go enjoy yourself." She shooed everyone out. Elaine was glad to have the charming, good looking Ski at her side, and was introducing him to everyone who hadn't already met him. A slow song came on just then, and as they danced, Ski said he had a gift for her outside in the car.

"That is so sweet of you," she told him. They finished the dance and went outside together, since he also needed a cigarette. He reached into the front seat of Red's car and pulled out a small box. "It's something I found in one of the ports on the trip," he said. "I think it was in Yokuska, Japan."

"Oh, Ski," she cried, opening the box. Inside was a charm bracelet, and the charms were all nautical. There was an anchor, a ship, a life preserver, seashell, seagull, and a ship's wheel. "It's just beautiful and I really love it!"

As the party was winding down, Lucy wanted to talk to her privately. "Elaine," she said. "I know you weren't planning on going to the prom, but maybe now you should think about it. Ski would probably love to take you. It's only two weeks away. You should ask him about it tonight."

The next morning both Elaine and Pam slept in. The party had broken up around 1:00 a.m., and the two girls had straightened up a bit before retiring for the night. Elaine was thinking about how surprised she had been, and she how much she had enjoyed seeing Ski there. Now she had to start making plans for the prom. Later on today she would be shopping with Beth and Lucy, since she would now need a formal.

Pam woke up and started talking about the party. "I had a good time last night," she was saying. "I felt like I knew a lot of your friends, 'cause I'm always looking at your annuals to see who is who. I think Gary Okamota is really cute, and I danced with him a couple of times too."

"Did you really?" asked Elaine. "I didn't see that. He's Greg's younger brother, you know."

"Well, duh, of course I knew that. I'm getting really excited about starting high school now. I think it's going to be lots of fun. Our class took our constitution test last week, and I passed, so I'll definitely be a freshman next year. And it will be fun to meet some older high school guys, instead of these dorks around here."

Elaine suddenly could see a pattern. She had felt the same way at Pam's age. "I'm sure there was never any doubt about your passing," Elaine told her. "You're pretty smart. But are you telling me that you and Missy don't like Sammy and Billy anymore?"

"Oh, no. They're just dorks, and they act so silly all the time. They got us into trouble just the other day."

"What happened?"

"We were over at Missy's, out by the field in front of her house, and they kept riding by on their bikes and throwing water balloons at us. So Missy and I climbed the apricot trees by the road, and we were throwing green apricots at them while they were riding by. Well, then Missy's dad saw us, and got upset since we broke off a couple of branches. So he sent me home, and Missy was grounded. But those dorks started it."

The girls dressed and went out to the kitchen where their mother had oatmeal, scrambled eggs, and bacon ready. Elaine gave Lois a big hug, saying, "That's the first time I've ever had a party at our house, and it was one I didn't even know about ahead of time. You had to do all the work, Mom."

"Well, I helped too," Pam stated, wanting some of the credit.

"Yes, you did, Honey, and I think for the most part, things went very well," replied Lois.

"I don't think there was much drinking last night," remarked Elaine. "The guys seemed to be on good behavior."

"Well, I guess a few of them were drinking, because your dad found some beer cans out by the chicken pens. He and Russ are picking up around there now."

"Well, that's pretty sneaky of those guys to throw them way out by the chicken pens," Pam said laughing.

Later on that day, the girls went shopping. They drove all the way to Riverside, since there were more stores and more choices in a bigger city. Lucy and Beth already had their formals, but Beth needed shoes for both the prom and her wedding, and Lucy needed an evening purse. After looking in several stores, Elaine finally found her formal. It was a pale peach chiffon, and fit beautifully, and best of all, it was on sale for 24.99. She had some birthday money from her grandparents and her folks, and she had saved some of her allowance. She already had some heels she could wear with the dress, and her mother had a white evening bag that she had borrowed before, so she was all set.

"I heard that Dennis and Megan are getting married next week," Beth informed the others girls. The story was out at school, and now everyone knew what was going on. Beth also told the girls that Dennis would be working at the clay mining plant in High Bluffs. "He starts after graduation. Of course it really helps that his dad is a big shot at the plant, one of the bosses."

"Yeah, now I remember that we talked to him back when we were getting ads for the yearbook," Elaine said. "His dad is a very good looking man. Both Dennis and Duane got their looks from him."

"It's still just so sad the Megan has to miss out on everything," remarked Lucy. "There's the prom of course, and then Senior Ditch Day, and Graduation and Grad Night. It just doesn't seem right. Of course Dennis can go to all the events, no problem."

"Yeah, it's really the girl who has to suffer," Elaine added. "If she gets pregnant, everyone always thinks it's her fault. I mean, it takes two people to make a baby."

"Paul and I aren't planning to have kids right away," Beth said. "We both just want to have time to ourselves first, and wait til later on to start a family."

In spite of all the extra activities, school and classes still went on. Elaine got her English term paper typed and turned in. Her subject was The History of the Christian Church, and she thought the paper had turned out well. Some of what she'd studied in World History had helped, and she'd also had to write a paper for World History, and some of what she had written on her English term paper had helped on that. She and Vicki were sitting and talking one day during gym class. They had a sub that day, but she wasn't having the girls do much. They were dressed out, and on the field, but that was about it. Vicki was telling Elaine that she'd stood up with Megan at the wedding ceremony last weekend, but that it had just been very small, with just family.

"How is Megan doing? Is she really happy?" asked Elaine.

"She is, and of course she's all excited about the baby. She looks very radiant."

"Who was the best man for Dennis?" Elaine wanted to know.

"It was Duane, of course. But Bonnie wasn't there with him. After the wedding, I asked him about her, and he just shrugged like he didn't even care."

"Well, even if they got divorced, I would never go back to dating him," Elaine said firmly.

"Oh, of course not," Vicki agreed. Then she added, "I have a theory about why he married her so suddenly. I bet she told him that she was pregnant, just to trap him into marriage, because Duane was probably seeing you and Bonnie at the same time."

"Oh, I'm sure that he was," Elaine agreed. "And of course she wasn't really pregnant, so she had to tell another lie, and say she'd had a miscarriage."

"Right. I bet that's what happened. Well, it's all water over the bridge now." Then she added, "Not to change the subject, but I don't think DJ and I will be together too much longer."

"Really? But he is so crazy about you, and he has settled down some since you've been going together. He has longer periods of time where he's not so goofy," she laughed.

"When we went together last year, I broke it off, because he just seemed so immature. And then this past year when we started going together again, I felt that he'd grown up some, and I was always laughing when he was around. It's fun being with him, and I really do care about him, but I think I am falling in love with someone else."

"Oh, Vicki, this sounds serious," said Elaine. "So tell me more about this other guy. Who is he?"

"You would never guess in a million years. And you can't breathe a word of this to anyone."

"You know you can trust me not to tell."

"You're absolutely going to flip when you hear this, but, well, here goes. It's Anthony Carr."

"Nooo! You mean our teacher, Coach Carr? Are you kidding me? I can't believe it! How did this happen? You didn't even like him at all during most of our high school years. Most of the time anyone just mentioned his name, you'd have something bad to say about him. Do you remember that?"

"Yes I do, I'm ashamed to say. But when school started this year, and I had him for World History, I decided to be an adult, and let all that go. And I have enjoyed his class this year. Then a couple of months ago, I was driving out of town, doing some errands for my folks, when I had a flat tire. Well, I didn't know the first thing about changing it, and I wasn't anywhere near a phone. My dad should have made me change a tire the way yours did. Anyhow, it was getting late and I was really worried, and wondering what to do, when who should come along, but Anthony. Of course he was just Coach Carr to me then. He was really sweet, and changed the tire of course, but he was goofing around too, and we were flirting. He seemed like such a nice, normal guy, but of course he wasn't in his teaching mode at the time. So after the tire was changed, I thanked him, and he gave me a little salute and said, 'Always glad to help a damsel in distress, especially one as pretty as you are,' and then he said he would follow me back to Armedia, since it was getting dark by then." Vicki paused to take a breath. "So we've been having little talks at school, since on most days, I get to his class early, on purpose of course."

"I've noticed that you've been there early a couple of times, and both of you seem to be in deep conversation, and I kind of wondered what that was all about," Elaine stated.

"Yeah, we've had some really good conversations on just about every subject under the sun. Of course, because he is a teacher, and I'm a student, we can't date or anything, or he would be fired. But I turn eighteen in June, and I'll be out of school soon, and then we can date," she finished up. "And you know, he's not that much older than I am. He's only twenty four. We've had one kiss on a day that I got to the classroom before he did. He came in and pulled the door shut, which locked it, and he just gave me this certain look, and we both felt what was about to happen, and we came together in the middle of the room. I mean there were all kinds of bells and whistles, and fireworks that went off when we kissed. And then he said he'd been wanting to kiss me ever since he'd changed the tire, and that it was worth the wait. I could tell that he was kind of flustered when he started class that day. That was only about a week ago, and, believe me, it was the most romantic moment of my life. Megan, and now you, are the only ones I've told."

Elaine was almost speechless as she listened to Vicki's story. "Wow, Vicki, that does sound really romantic, and it's just so amazing. And your secret is safe with me. But we still have a few weeks of school left, and you're still with DJ. It's always hard to break up with someone. I've only done that once, and it was with a letter, which is much easier than breaking up in person."

"I know. That will be very difficult. DJ is planning on going to City College, and of course I'm going there too, taking that Cosmetology course. So anyhow, DJ thinks we're going to be together all next year. And prom is just around the corner, and I suppose I'll break it off some time after that."

It was the 20th of May, and the evening of the long-awaited Junior Senior Prom. It was held away from school, at the Women's Clubhouse, and the theme was "Some Enchanted Evening." Elaine and Lucy, feeling like princesses in their gowns, with their escorts, walked in to the beautifully decorated room. Ski and Red looked very handsome and debonair in their rented tuxedos.

The evening started with a banquet of appetizers, followed by a choice of ham or turkey, potatoes au gratin, a green salad, and a jello fruit salad. Dessert was ice cream and cake. Dancing followed the dinner. The music and entertainment was provided by the Hi-Hatters. And Armedia's own singing group, the Chantells were on hand to perform a couple of numbers. The girls were presented with very small program booklets that were only three by four inches. A little tiny pencil was attached to it. Inside it listed the class officers, with blanks for filling in the prom king and queen. Woody, as Senior Class president, gave a speech and thanked the Juniors for hosting such a fine event. The Senior Will was read by Lenny. Greg Okamota was crowned king, and his girlfriend, cute and perky Wendi Thomason was prom queen.

It was a night to always remember, Elaine thought. She noticed that Shawn and Mimi were not there, and she was glad for that. She saw that DJ and Vicki were sitting with Woody and Mary Lou, and thought about what Vicki had recently told her. It seemed that the last month had ushered in so many changes, and there would be many more coming. It was hard to keep up with it all. But she was having a wonderful time that evening, and she was able to forget about Shawn for a little while. Ski was a perfect date. He was sweet, and attentive, and a good dancer. She was well aware that he would be going back home to Alabama some time in June, so she knew that she would just have to enjoy their short time together while it lasted.

Chapter 51

It was a very big day for the yearbook staff, because the high school annuals had finally arrived. The tables in Miss Lippert's classroom were covered with big wooden crates, and members of the class were unloading and sorting the books. It was going to be a big job just to get them distributed to everyone who had ordered an annual. Of course before they had started on the job, they all had to glance through the treasured memory books to see how their hard work had turned out. They were also busy planning an annual-signing dance to be held on Friday, June 2nd. It was going to be a beatnik dance. For some reason, the beatnik theme usually went over well with everyone.

On Friday afternoon the students gathered in the gym to hear Elaine's very brief dedication speech and presentation of the yearbook to Mr. Nichols, the Biology teacher. That night was the dance. Red and Ski had driven to Ellington, so Lucy and Elaine were with the two Marines. It was strange, Elaine thought, how Ski had won her parents over with his friendliness, humor, and good manners. The dance had a wonderful turn-out. The admission price was only thirty five cents, and the annual staff sold snapshots that they had used in the yearbook for five, ten and fifteen cents. And since it was the last dance for the seniors, they had records from the past, representing songs from each high school year, starting with 1957, lots of oldies but goodies. Elaine was in charge of the dance, and it seemed she was doing a good deal of running around, but Ski was a good sport and didn't really mind. There was a contest for the most original "beat couple," with the students doing the judging. People kept coming up to her to offer their congratulations on the yearbook. It was the consensus that the staff had done a marvelous job. Elaine felt that a lot of the credit went to Miss Lippert, who had pushed them relentlessly. At last Elaine found some time to spend with Ski. She hadn't had the time to have anyone sign her annual, but figured there would be time to get that done the last few days of school. She knew that her closest friends would be writing an entire page for her in the yearbook, and would most certainly need more than just a few minutes. Since she was all over the place that night, she noticed that Shawn was with Mimi at the dance, so she made sure she didn't go anywhere near the couple.

"Wow, it seems that you are a gal in big demand tonight," Ski was saying to her as they finally had some time together.

"I know, and I'm sorry about that. And you're being such a good sport about it," she told him.

"Well, I do know a few of the people here, and everyone is very friendly," he remarked. "Oh, this all takes me back to my high school days like you wouldn't believe."

"Yeah, I guess schools are basically the same everywhere," Elaine said.

"I wouldn't exactly say that," stated Ski. "The colored kids that attend your school are accepted by everyone, and it seems to me that some are even quite popular. Nobody even notices the color of their skin. Back home the schools are all segregated. But hopefully that will change at some point."

He held her close as they danced. "Why is our timing always off?" he asked. "I keep thinking that I might want to stick around this area after I'm discharged, and maybe try to get a job. But then I have to realize that I'm needed by my family back home too, especially after my dad had that heart attack. He's not getting any younger."

"How much longer before you get out?" she asked.

"The date is June 12th. I have it marked on my short timer's calendar," Ski said. "That date has been imbedded in my mind for many months now. Red still has another year to go, and he is scheduled to go overseas in a few more weeks, so that's going to be hard on him and Lucy."

For the next solid week, there was something going on every single day. It was amazing that so many significant activities could be crowded into one small week. Sunday evening was the Baccalaureate Services for the Senior Class in the gym.

On Monday, all the 8th Graders from the area visited the high school. They went to an assembly where they met the student body officers, and heard a couple of songs by the Chantells. They were then given a tour of the school. Pam reported later to Elaine that she was very impressed with the school.

The Senior Ditch Day was the next event. They were going to Disneyland, which was the customary destination for many high school ditch days. Vicki rode with Elaine on the bus, since she had something on her mind.

"Well, I did what I had to do, and broke it off with DJ over the weekend," she told Elaine. "And of course, it turned out to be one of the most difficult things I've ever done. I didn't tell him that there was someone else. I just said that I really only cared for him as a friend, and that I want to be free to date other guys when I get to college, but that I hoped we could still be friends."

"Well, how did he take it?"

"I think he was really crushed. He was just so quiet, not like himself at all. You know how he's always talking and joking all the time, but it was pretty much dead silence from him. It's just sad."

"Well, I went through that feeling of rejection after Duane and I broke up, back when school started, and it was really difficult. It will take some time, but DJ will bounce back. He's with Shawn, and they're sitting way in the back of the bus, but they both seem to be unusually quiet today."

"The good news is that I'll be eighteen on the twentieth of this month, and I have a date with Anthony. We're going out to dinner. I'll feel like I'm with an adult for a change, and not a kid," stated Vicki. "I still need to tell my folks about the whole thing, but I think they'll be pretty cool with it."

The bus reached Disneyland shortly and the seniors streamed out, ready for a day of fun. Other senior classes were there too, so the park was quite crowded. But despite the long lines, they managed to ride on all the major rides and eat their share of junk food. They did find out however, that the Keystone Cops were not just park employees in uniform, but actual cops. Shawn, Dennis, and DJ, along with a few other boys, had paper cups containing liquor, and their drinking was detected by the cops, and so the boys were detained for most of the day.

"I think, with all the seniors there today, and all the partying that everyone's been doing, I bet they caught a lot of people drinking," Beth commented on the way home. "I imagine those Keystone Cops had one of their busiest days today."

"Yeah, it kind of ruined ditch day for some of the seniors," added Elaine. "They should have known better, though. Well, what's the next event on our agenda in this busy, crazy week?"

"It's Eighth Grade graduation tomorrow night, then our graduation the next night," Beth said.

The ceremony for the sixteen Eighth Graders was very nice. They were seated in a semi-circle on the stage in the old auditorium of the Ellington Grammar School. Sammy Morrison and Billy Hathaway were among them, and of course Pam and her friend, Missy, in pretty dresses. Elaine thought they all looked so young to be going into high school. She was sure she and her friends had never looked that young.

The following evening was their big night. The bleachers out on the football field were filled to capacity with proud parents, siblings, and other relatives and friends. The graduates, in their deep red caps and gowns were lining up a little ways from the portable stage. Elaine knew she would have to try very hard not to cry when the Pomp and Circumstance march began. She was in high heels, which weren't too comfortable, and she was hoping she wouldn't trip as they marched, two by two, slowly out onto the field. They were arranged alphabetically, and she was walking with Lonnie Holland, who had participated in every sport the school had to offer during his four years. He was in a good mood, and kept making wisecracks to Elaine, which was good, since it kept her from crying. Once they were up on the platform, and sitting in their assigned seats, there was whispering and wisecracking among the group, especially the boys. Also, a few balloons were being bounced around the stage.

Of course Greg and Woody were the Valedictorian and Salutatorian respectively. Their speeches went by fairly quickly, and then all the various awards were presented. Finally the diplomas were handed out by the president of the Board of Trustees. That part seemed long and tedious. Every time a graduate stepped up to receive their diploma, someone from the class would whisper, "Smile, sweetie" or "smile, stud." It had been a fad around school for the past several months now, the guys calling each other stud. At last the benediction was said, and it was all over, with the seniors moving the tassel on their caps from one side to the other, and then tossing their caps up into the air. After that everything became a madhouse, with so many people around. Elaine and a few others were trying to find their families in the huge crowd. In the meantime, while looking for loved ones, the graduates were giving and getting congratulatory hugs from their peers. Finally she caught sight of her parents. Her entire family was there, with Grandma Grace and Scottie. Then for some reason she started to cry. She had managed to refrain from doing that all evening, and now here she was crying.

"Are those tears of joy?" Lois asked her.

"You're crying?" Russ was amazed.

"I'm just very emotional right now," she told him. "Just wait. In two more years you'll be in my shoes."

"But I'll be very happy," Russ said, smiling. "Okay, it's time for a Kodak moment. Let's get the whole family with you, and then I'll get one with just you in it."

After posing for many photos, she handed her cap and gown to her mother, and went to find Lucy, since they would be riding together to the Grad Night party at the Woman's Clubhouse. The girls would be meeting Ski and Red at the clubhouse, since their dates hadn't gone to the graduation.

"This will be your last night to see Ski, won't it?" Lucy was asking, once they were in her car.

"Don't remind me," Elaine said. "I've already been crying and my make-up has been running all over the place. It seems as if it's the last night for everything. I'm just so full of emotions. And I will miss Ski, but it's not as if I'm madly in love with him. However, he has been like a knight in shining armor, showing up at my surprise party, and being my prom date. That was a pretty good surprise you girls cooked up. Maybe I'm not always too lucky when it comes to the boys, but I do have some wonderful girl friends in my life, like you, Beth, and Nat. I will miss you all so much when I go away. At least you'll be with some of the other girls we know when you go off to City College. I won't know a single, solitary soul when I go away to college. Now, here I go, crying again."

"Elaine, you have to stop that now," Lucy told her. "You'll have me crying next." The first thing the girls did when they reached their destination was go to the Ladies Room so they could repair their makeup. After that they met up with Ski and Red, and found a table. Elaine was already tired from all the excitement, and from the emotions that had been present all that week, but knew she had a long night ahead of her. She could tell that Lucy was getting emotional also, knowing that Red would be leaving soon. The two of them were planning their wedding for the following June. In the meantime, Lucy would be taking a secretarial course at City College, and would be working as a waitress at Deb's Diner, trying to save money. Ski was saying that maybe he could come back out to Ellington for their wedding. However Elaine had a feeling that she would never see him again. The entire evening seemed surreal to her.

She was thinking that she hadn't really talked to Shawn in months. She hadn't even asked him to sign her yearbook. He was with DJ and Dennis that night, and the three of them were doing a good deal of coming and going. She figured that they would all probably get very drunk. Maybe DJ had a reason to, but not the other two. But at that stage in life, who needed a reason, she thought. She hoped that they would be careful driving home. Most of their group would end the night by going out to breakfast before the last assembly at school.

She did think it was bad that Dennis was there at the Grad Night party and not at home with his new wife. She'd missed Megan these past few weeks. She was wondering if that marriage would last, with both of them so young, and Dennis so immature.

"Penny for your thoughts," Ski was saying. "You're just too quiet tonight."

"Oh, it's been a very emotional night for me," she told him. "All these changes in life, and I guess I'm not really ready for them."

"Let's not think about all that. Come on, dance with me. This is a great song, and we need to enjoy this time together tonight," he added, as they walked out to the dance floor.

She got back home about noon the next day, following the last assembly at school. She felt very groggy, and all she wanted to do was crash. It took a couple of days to feel normal again.

*   *   *

Three weeks later after all the graduation festivities, Elaine was at the wedding rehearsal for Beth and Paul. She had known Beth since they were five years old, and it was hard to believe that one of her very closest friends was actually getting married. She had given Beth a bridal shower earlier that month, That had been a fun event, and Beth had received many lovely gifts from something useful like a percolator to something fun, like a silky, sexy red teddy, trimmed with lace.

The bridesmaids were practicing their walk down the aisle, while Lois played the piano. Her mother was always the pianist for all of the town's weddings. Paul's best man was a cousin of his, and the groomsmen were Duane and Dennis, and another cousin. Elaine was going to avoid talking to Duane if she could. Chuck was directing the wedding party, and Cathy was taking some notes. She enjoyed helping with the weddings. She sought out Elaine after the rehearsing was finished.

"I have some news for you," she said, "and I wanted to tell you before the rest of this town finds out. Chuck and I are expecting a new addition to the family!"

"Oh, Cathy, that is wonderful news!'. I am so glad to hear that!" cried Elaine.

"Chuck is just about to bust his buttons, he is so excited. He thinks it will be a boy, and has already bought a football," Cathy told her. "But I think a little girl would be really nice. Next weekend we're going to his Family Reunion in Desert Palms, so we'll be making the big announcement to all of the relatives."

"Well, you are looking really good. Pregnancy agrees with you."

"Do you and Jeff still write?" Cathy asked.

"Yes we do. Last I heard from him, he was working in the ship's mess hall, and they were near Subic Bay in the Philippines."

"Well, that's good he writes to you, at least. No one else has heard from him for a while."

The following evening the church was filled to capacity. The Hathaways were known by everyone in Ellington. They were the type of people who were wonderful friends and neighbors, and could always be counted on to help out when someone in town had a problem. The sanctuary was looking beautiful that June evening. There were flowers and candles everywhere, and pink carnations and streamers adorned the end of each pew. Elaine knew that someday when the timing was right, that her wedding also, would take place in the picturesque little country church. She felt pretty walking down the aisle in her bridesmaid dress. The dresses were pink lace sheaths over taffeta. No one would guess the the frustration that she had gone through, sewing on it at the last minute, and ripping out a few stitches here and there, to redo the seams. The bridesmaids also wore tiny pink veils with velvet bands, and carried bouquets of pink carnations. Elaine reached the front of the church and the guests all stood as the wedding march began. Beth looked beautiful as she made her way slowly up the aisle in her wedding gown of Chantilly lace. Her elbow length veil was fastened with a tiara of lace embroidered with seed pearls. The couple would be living in High Bluffs, Elaine knew. Beth planned to get a job there.

As Chuck conducted the wedding ceremony, Elaine could feel Duane's eyes on her, but she wouldn't even look at him. He was nothing but a low down rat fink, she thought. It seemed that the ceremony was very short, compared to all the weeks of planning that it had taken for Beth, her mother, and her friends. Chuck was pronouncing them husband and wife, Mr.and Mrs. Paul Newberry. Paul was kissing his new bride, and then everyone walked back down the aisle. There was to be a reception in the church social hall. The wedding party stood in the receiving line for quite a while it seemed, as the townspeople paraded past. The girls felt that they must have shaken hands and received hugs from everyone in town that day. Elaine's feet were hurting in her pink dyed—to—match shoes. Old Mr. Hobbs was slowing up the entire line, since he felt that he had to carry on a conversation with each bridesmaid, and the bride and groom, and also Beth's parents.

"I never thought that being a bridesmaid could be such hard work," Nat whispered. "My feet are killing me in these shoes. I wish this line would move a little faster."

"I see Danny over in the corner looking very bored," Elaine told her. "And we still have to pose for all the wedding pictures yet. Hope he doesn't get tired of waiting for you and just hightail it out of here."

"I think Red and I will just elope," Lucy joked.

"Yeah, we have to go through all this again next year for your wedding," Elaine told her. "And maybe I'll get married the year after that, or maybe you will, Natalie."

"I'm really starving," said Lucy. "Hope no one can hear my stomach growling." At last everyone had gone through the line, and they went back into the sanctuary to pose for pictures. Finally they were done with that. Elaine and Dennis were talking as they walked back to the social hall.

"Well, it's too bad that Megan couldn't have been here today," she said to him.

"Yeah, I tried to get her to come, but she's kind of keeping a low profile these days," he remarked.

"Is she feeling okay?" Elaine asked him.

"Oh, she's fine. She's picking out baby clothes already." Elaine thought maybe Megan would feel bad that she hadn't been able to have her big wedding, since that was something that most girls dreamed of since they were just a young age. She also thought Dennis looked kind of lonesome without his buddies. She knew that Shawn wouldn't be there, but she thought DJ would have been in attendance. The rest of the Morrison family was there. Maybe DJ just hadn't wanted to see Vicki there. She certainly knew what that was like, trying to avoid certain people.

Elaine and the other girls quickly made their way to the appetizers that were being served by the women in the church Ladies Aid Society. They filled their plates with gusto. Elaine was trying to find Vicki, Karen, and Alma in the crowd. And then suddenly Duane materialized at her side as she made her way over to a chair.

"Are you going to eat all that?" he asked. "You're looking very beautiful today, and that dress fits perfectly and shows off all your curves, but it'll be too tight after you chow down on all that food."

"That is none of your business," she told him defensively. "By the way, where's your other half?"

"Oh, we're not together anymore. We're getting a divorce." He had parked himself on the chair next to her, and it looked as though he was there to stay for a while.

"Well you two sure got married on the spur of the moment, just like it was no more of a big deal than going out for a hamburger with someone. You didn't even have the courtesy to break up with me first. You just took off to Vegas with her, never thinking of my feelings at all."

"I know, I know, I have to admit that the whole sordid thing was nothing but a huge mistake on my part, pretty stupid of me actually," Duane admitted.

"You were seeing Bonnie behind my back. Everything we had together was just one big lie!" She was getting wound up now, and was so glad she had a chance to finally tell him what she thought of him. "And you made it sound like you were really in love with me, but nothing you said to me was even close to the truth!"

"Oh, I did mean every last word that I said to you," he stated, picking a pig-in-a blanket off her plate. "I thought that you and I were really good together, that we had something special between the two of us. I guess I kind of, well, just took leave of my senses for a while. I hope you can forgive me for that. And I'm hoping you'll consider going out with me again."

The nerve of him, she thought. She had a cup of punch in her hand, and she wanted to toss it in his face in the worst way, but she didn't want to make a scene. Instead she simply stood up, planning to join her group of friends over by the wedding cake. Her final words to him were said loudly and clearly, "Get this through your head, Duane, I will never go out with you again, not in a million years!"

Chapter 52

The small calendar on Elaine's desk read August 2nd, and as she looked at it, she realized that in just one more month she would be packing for college. She was so glad that her grandparents had given her a new set of luggage for graduation, since her family only owned two suitcases, and they were pretty ratty looking, in her opinion. She had been going through most of her clothes that past week, deciding what to take with her and what to leave at home. She wondered how often she would be coming back home, since she wouldn't have a car. There would probably be a bus, but then she didn't think she would like riding the bus back and forth. In a car, the college was only about an hour and a half from Ellington, not that far away. She was starting to have second thoughts about college. What if she got homesick while she was away at school? Maybe she should have just planned on going to City College for two years, like Vicki, Karen, and Alma were doing. At least she would have some friends to start out with. What if she flunked out? She'd heard that college classes were much harder.

Once in bed that night, she was tossing and turning, with many different questions running through the back of her mind. She was riding the school bus to Armedia, only there were a bunch of other, strange people on that bus, and the cops were chasing the bus. The school bus had its own phone in the back. It was ringing loudly, and police sirens kept going off, over and over again. Finally, she shook herself awake. The siren hadn't been a dream, it was real. The school bell was ringing continuously also. It was 3:00 a.m. and she heard her father's voice out in the kitchen, and she got up to find out what was going on. He was dressed, obviously getting ready to go somewhere.

"What the heck's going on?" she asked, as Russ came into the kitchen, also dressed.

"I just got a call, and the church is on fire," Charles said tersely. "I'm heading over there now, and if you want to go, get dressed, but hurry up!" She got dressed in no time, and Pam did as well, and they hurried quickly to the car. Charles was explaining that elderly Mrs. Gertrude Stiles, who lived near the church, had been unable to sleep, and had seen the flames from her window. She called the Fire Department, and then she called Reverend Chuck Graham, since their house was right next door to the church. Gertrude was a close friend to Lois and Charles, so she called them also.

"I just wonder how it started," Russ was saying. He had his camera, ready to take pictures.

"No telling, but all the building materials in it are pretty flammable," Charles said grimly. "It was built in the 1880's, and I imagine all that wood will go up in flames pretty quickly."

Elaine was thinking how Beth's wedding had been held there just a few weeks ago, and how she had always looked forward to having her own wedding there at some point in the future. They reached the site of the church, and saw that it was completely engulfed in flames. The sight was absolutely heartbreaking. The firemen couldn't save the structure from the blazing inferno that had engulfed the little country church. By now, many of the townspeople had gathered in the empty lot across the street, and there were tears on a number of faces, both young and elderly. Flames were shooting high into the sky, and the steeple came crashing down in a shower of sparks and debris. The firemen, realizing that saving the church was a lost cause, were concentrating their fire hoses on the parsonage, and because of their efforts, they were able to save it.

"How can we just stand here and watch all this?" Pam asked, weeping. "Our family has been going to this church as long as I can remember, and this is just so sad." She and Elaine clung to each other and cried.

The following day, after the ashes had cooled down and when the Fire Department declared it safe, church members, and friends, and other citizens of Ellington gathered at the site to help clean up, and see if there was anything salvageable, but the fire had pretty much destroyed everything. Elaine wept again, with Cathy, this time.

She was concerned about her friend too. "That was a lot of excitement last night," she said to Cathy, as she hugged her. "Are you sure you're feeling all right today, and is the baby doing okay?"

"We're both doing as well as can be expected," Cathy sniffed. "Mostly just extremely tired, and yet I can't seem to fall asleep. And I'm feeling so emotional, doing lots of crying."

"I know this is a tough pill to swallow," Chuck said, putting his arms around both of them. "But we'll get through this. God will bring something good from this somehow. You know, the church is actually the people, not the building. And we have a strong congregation, and we'll rebuild in time. But I am planning on having a service on Sunday. For now we can meet either outside, or maybe use the auditorium at the old grammar school. But we're going forward from here. Elaine, your dad has already offered to be chairman of the building committee, and I have great confidence in him. You'll be leaving soon, but I'm sure when you come back to visit, you'll be surprised with all the progress we will have made by then."

The congregation did meet that Sunday out on the lawn behind the parsonage. By that time, an investigation showed that it was arson that had caused the fire.

*   *   *

The very last activity for the Collette's was coming up, their trip to Balboa Beach for a week. Elaine was in great need of a fun and frivolous event to get her mind off the sadness from the loss of the church, and her apprehension about college. Only four of the girls were going. Of course, Beth wouldn't be going now that she was an old married lady, and she had found a job in High Bluffs. Lucy, also, was working. Nat had already gone down to San Diego, and had moved in with her aunt and uncle. Karen was working in Dr. Coulter's dental office. She felt that would be a good summer job, and would work out well with her ambition to go into nursing. She was still going steady with Alan Coulter, but their plans for marriage were far in the future.

On Monday morning, the four girls, Elaine, Vicki, Alma and Mary Lou were off for the beach in Mary Lou's newly acquired Edsel. They were all chattering away like a bunch of magpies.

"I can't even remember what the place looks like," Vicki was saying. "Seems like so much has happened, since that day that Alma and I went down there."

"I just remember that everything was neat and clean," Alma remarked. "It was an older place, but at least the rates were fairly cheap. Most of the rentals we looked at were pretty high priced."

"So how are things going with you and Coach Carr?" asked Mary Lou. Vicki's big secret was all out in the open now. "That still just blows my mind every time I think about it, and I just can't get used to calling him Anthony, even though we're all out of school now."

"Things are great with us, couldn't be better," Vicki smiled. "although I have instructions to behave myself while I'm at the beach."

"Oh, yeah, Woody gave me the same advice," Mary Lou stated. "But we're not going to be together much longer anyhow, since I'm going to USC to school, and Woody is going to Ohio State University."

"I heard that he was going back there, but it's just so far away," Elaine said.

"His dad is an alumnus from there, and he has lots of family living in the area," Mary Lou said. "But he couldn't get much farther away. I'm not at all happy about that."

"Oh, I ran into DJ's mother at the store the other day, and she was telling me that he just joined the army. I was really surprised to hear that," Elaine informed her friends.

"Well, if that doesn't shape him up, nothing will," laughed Alma.

It took the girls more than an hour to get to the beach city of Balboa. The little rental they had was just as Alma had described it to be, neat and clean, but a bit the worse for wear. They didn't mind that however, since they would be spending most of their time either on the beach or taking walks, or going to the little shops that were all over the place. There were two very small bedrooms, one with bunk beds. Vicki and Elaine took the bunk beds. They hastily changed into their bathing suits, anxious to be out in the sunshine, on the beach, which was quite crowded, but that was the norm for the month of August. After talking to other teens on the beach, they discovered that the place to go in the evenings was the Rendezvous Ballroom, where everyone did something called the Surfers' Stomp.

Leaving their little cottage that evening, they discovered that the whole area was wall to wall teenagers. It was hard to even walk anywhere with all the young people hanging around, but even so that was kind of exhilarating. There were plenty of cute guys everywhere, and they got invited to several parties. They weren't interested, however, since they were on their way to the Rendezvous Ballroom. The entertainment there lived up to all the hype. The group that was playing was Dick Dale and the Del Tones, and the sound they created was unlike anything the girls had ever heard. Dick Dale himself was billed as King of the Surf Guitar. The music was incredibly dynamic and extremely loud. The capacity in the huge ballroom was close to 3,000, and the energy was amazing, especially when they were doing the Surfer's Stomp, all those young people rocking out, stomping with their sandals on the hardwood floor. No alcohol was allowed on the premises, which was a good thing. It was an experience the girls would remember for a very long time.

"I don't think my ears will ever be the same," Mary Lou remarked, as they walked back, "but those guys really had a great, great sound."

"We'll have to go there again, while we're here," Vicki said. "That is if our ears can take it."

"When I was in San Diego, at the beach last summer, that surfer movement was just getting started," Elaine pointed out. "And now it seems that it's gained a lot of momentum."

Of course the week went by very quickly. The girls found a record shop where Dick Dale worked, and enjoyed talking to him and some of the band members. They were all good looking and very friendly. Elaine knew that her grandparents were at their beach house on Balboa Island, so she and her friends took the ferry over to the island, and made a short visit to see Mr.and Mrs. Hummer Sr., and also went to more of the little shops in that area.

But all too soon their week was up, and they were driving back inland, back to the warm weather. The girls hugged and said their good byes, and everyone promised to write, once they were in college, and scattered like the four winds. Elaine had that let down feeling once she was at home again. It was the same feeling she always had when she got home from a trip, or camp. But Pam, who had been over at Missy's came home and told her something that cheered her a little. "Guess who called while you were away? It was Shawn. I told him that you would be home in a few days, and he said he would call again."

"Oh, my gosh," Elaine said. "I haven't heard from him in months. I would love to see him just one more time before I leave, but I'm not even sure he'll call back."

Even as she waited, hoping he would call, she managed to keep busy. Beth had wanted her to come and spend the night with her, at their place in High Bluffs, but Elaine made an excuse. As much as she would have liked to spend time with her dear friend, she knew that Paul and Duane were still close buddies, and that he hung out with Paul at their house. Elaine didn't want to be around, if seeing him was even a remote possibility. She spent some time writing letters. She was giving her new college address to all those she corresponded with: her cousin Lynne, Ski, Jeff, and a couple of other friends.

A few days later, she did get a call from Shawn. His timing was perfect because she was planning on leaving for college the next day. "Hey, Hummingbird," he said, calling her the pet name that people sometimes had for her. "How are you doing? I heard you were down at Balboa last week." She felt that same old excitement at hearing his voice.

"You heard right. We girls rented a little place. We had a great time dancing to Dick Dale and the Deltones, and even hung out with them. Balboa Beach is one swingin' place. How have you been?"

They made a date for that evening, and he came down to pick her up in his dad's car. She was feeling a bit bashful with him, since things had seemed somewhat strained between them the last few weeks of school. "I thought we'd get something to eat, and maybe take in a flick," he told her. They ate right there in Ellington at Deb's Diner, and then drove on up to Armedia. They cruised around the town for a while, and they were both quieter than usual. Of the two of them, Elaine did more of the talking, telling him about her week at the beach, and about the church fire. They cruised by the movie theater, but neither of them were interested in the movies being shown. So Shawn drove around to the west side of the lake and up on the highway that wound around and above the lake.

"Did you hear from DJ before he went off to the army?" she asked him.

"Yeah, we did get together one last time a couple of weeks ago, and both got wasted," he said.

"Are you feeling sort of alone, now that Dennis is married, and DJ is gone?"

"Heck yeah, I can't believe all the changes that have taken place with everyone in just the last few months," Shawn said soberly. "We were just a bunch of carefree kids not that long ago. DJ wanted me to enlist with him, but I'm not really ready to do that right now." They had reached the pull-out spot just off the highway, and Shawn pulled in there. It wasn't quite dark yet, just twilight, with a few of the lights in town coming on.

"I think it hit DJ really hard when Vicki broke up with him," Shawn continued. "I never saw anyone so broken up. That was just pitiful."

"I know. Vicki told me ahead of time that it would be happening, and I told her it would be difficult. I mostly know about break-ups from a girl's point of view, of course," Elaine stated. "For some reason people don't think it's that hard on guys too, but I guess it can be."

"I think I need to apologize to you about the way I've been acting the last few months. I know I've been a real idiot lately. It's just that I was so stoked about getting my car up and running, and I put a lot of money and time into it, and it seemed like everything was coming together, and then, well, when it blew a rod, that was just the final straw."

Elaine turned to him and put her head on his shoulder and her hand on his chest. "I felt so bad when I heard about that," she said softly.

"I know you did. You tried to tell me that and I just blew you off. I'm so sorry." He leaned in toward her, and they began kissing. But then Shawn wanted to talk some more. "I could tell you felt bad way back at the beginning of last year, with all that went on with Duane," he said. "But then you and I started seeing each other, and it was really good, but I felt that my situation wasn't right at the time, to be having a girlfriend. And I know you were disappointed and upset with me when school ended."

"Well, I was, that's for sure. I never even got you to sign my yearbook. And then there was that surprise party, given by Beth and my other friends, and you didn't even show up."

"I know. Probably down in the dumps, and feeling sorry for myself," he admitted. "I think I was with DJ and Dennis, getting drunk that night. That's another thing, I'm not at all proud of. I've been drinking way too much lately, and that is going to change for sure. I need to put in a lot of hours at the market this summer, save some money, and get another car. And I want to start City College, if not the Fall semester, then in January for the second semester."

"I am glad to hear that. Sounds like a good plan." She was holding his hand and her lips brushed his fingers with a kiss. The radio was playing some really romantic songs, some of Elaine's favorites: Patsy Cline's *I Fall To Pieces* and *Can't Help Falling In Love* by Elvis. Shawn grew quiet and seemed to be deep in thought. "Okay, why so quiet?" she asked him. "There are times when I really wonder what's going on in that head of yours."

"Just thinking that because of me, the last couple months of school were kind of messed up, and I wasted that time that we could have spent together. Now our time has run out, and you're leaving for college tomorrow. By the way, what was the deal with you and that Marine?"

"Why, Shawn O'Dell, are you actually jealous? What about you and Mimi Atherton? She has a really great car, that Corvette. Probably the best car in the entire school."

"She was okay, and we had some laughs, and the car was an extra bonus. But she wasn't you, and I soon realized that."

"Oh, Shawn," she said. More kissing followed, and the sensation of his lips on hers felt so real and so right, just as everything else did on that warm summer night. And yet she'd felt the same way when she'd been with him before, and she was thinking deep down that this was probably the last time they would be together. For the next two hours they were locked in each other's arms, and lost in each other's caresses. Time seemed to stand still and the rest of the world completely faded away for Elaine. The moon was coming up in the eastern sky, and cast heavy shadows across the oak trees on the edge of the look-out point. The two of them had not even realized how much time had passed.

"It's almost midnight," Shawn remarked, looking at his wristwatch. "I'd better get you home or your dad will be waiting on the porch with a shotgun." As they parked in her driveway, they held each other once more, and she told him she would write to him from college. She was so glad that they had gotten together that one final time before she left home because it gave her some closure.

She walked into her room, with the moonlight shining in the window, and looked around. This was her last night at home, and she didn't know when she would be coming back again. Nothing would ever be the same, she thought. But she was eager to begin this new phase of life. Her suitcases were lined up on the floor, ready to make their journey tomorrow. And she felt that maybe, finally, she was ready to move on, and begin a new journey as well.

Epilogue

The plane touched down on the runway at the San Diego Airport, and slowly taxied to a stop. Laptops were hastily closed, and passengers were standing, reaching into the overhead compartments for their carry-ons. I joined the crowded line in the aisle, very impatient to stretch my legs again, impatient to be off this plane. I always felt a bit claustrophobic on plane rides. Pam said she would be waiting for me in the Baggage Claim area, and I could hardly wait to see my sister.

Once we were in the car, driving north to Ellington, of course we were talking nonstop. Pam's husband, Ed, who was driving, was listening to us, amused. It was impossible for him to get a word in.

"I don't know if you were aware of this," Pam was saying, "but the Reunion has been opened up to classes several years above your class, and several years below, which will be great because we both knew people older and younger than we are. I hear that it's going to be pretty well attended, with people flying in from all over."

"Sounds wonderful," I said. "I have so been looking forward to this."

"It's too bad that Jeff couldn't make it, spraining his ankle at the last minute," Pam remarked.

"Well, even though he'd planned on going, I could tell he wasn't that enthused about it. Reunions just aren't that much fun for the spouses who didn't attend the same school."

"Amen to that," Ed said. "I'm just glad you two girls are going together. I'll be enjoying myself back at the motor home, kicking back and relaxing, having a couple of beers.

Pam had met Ed during their college days when they were both active members of a running club. Ed was now retired from a large company in Escondido, where he had been an electrical engineer. Pam had retired also from her job as an elementary school teacher. They'd resided in Escondido for many years. Today they were driving to Ellington, where they had a 35 foot motor home, which they kept parked on the property of our family farm in Ellington.

The town of Ellington had changed drastically over the last 50 years, and was most definitely not the same sleepy little town that it had been at one time. Many farms had been sold, and the same property that once grew fields of alfalfa, wheat, and oats, now grew subdivisions. The road out to the Hot Springs, where we had ridden our bikes in our youth, was currently the home to mini malls, big box stores, restaurants, and filling stations. I was always amazed when I saw the changes.

"Oh, it looks like old Deb's Diner is getting a facelift," I pointed out. Ed was driving around town at my request. It was always interesting to see what had changed, what was new in town.

"Yes, it has gone through many owners, since Deb and Don Williams passed on and left it to their kids," Pam said. "For a while it was looking very rundown. Hopefully the new owners can make a go of it, but it's hard for these small businesses to compete with the big chain restaurants like the Olive Garden, Red Lobster, and Applebees."

Barney's General Store was no longer in business, but the building was still standing. It was now True Value Hardware. Further on down the street was Bub's Place, the old disreputable bar. It had been closed for many years, and was quite an eyesore. The city (Ellington was now incorporated) was trying to get it torn down, but there were legal issues. Main Street had been widened, and sidewalks had been put in several years ago. Striking black wrought iron streetlights added to the ambience of the main thoroughfare, and flower baskets hung from them. Most of the businesses in the old downtown area were well kept up. A few blocks to the east was Ellington's City Center with a city hall, library, city offices, and an aquatic center. Part of the property there had once belonged to the Irby family. My parents had told me years ago that when Jackie Irby left town back in the 70's, she had sold the acreage to a developer, but the land had sat idle for 15 years after that.

"When were kids, I always wished we'd had a library," I said. "Back then we had to drive to Armedia to check out books."

"That new library here is about ten years old," Pam added. "Before that a Bookmobile came through here about every three weeks. I remember that Mom used to go there all the time."

"It's so amazing that now there is a big multiplex right here in town. Back in the day, if there was a movie we really wanted to see, we'd always have to plan how to get to Armedia to the little theater."

"Well, all of us used to think this was the most boring one-horse town ever, and we couldn't wait to leave, and now it has everything, and yet we feel kind of nostalgic, and miss the old Ellington," Pam pointed out.

"Kind of ironic, isn't it?" Ed asked.

Not far from the city center was the Methodist Church, which had replaced the little, picturesque building that had burned down so many years ago. The new church was much bigger of course, and had adjacent buildings to house the Sunday School classes. The membership now, was many times larger than it had been back in the day. The Fellowship Hall had been named after our parents. Even though I'd been away at the time, I remember hearing how my dad had worked tirelessly, along with many other community members, to get the new church built.

"I'll never forget the sight of the old one burning down that night," said Pam.

"I see the old landmark grain elevator is still here" I observed, noticing the tall, gray structure a couple of blocks away, still standing proudly on the west edge of town, near the dry river bed and the mountains. "I think it closed for good back in the early 60's."

"The office buildings around it were torn down many years ago, and the elevator itself has been boarded up," stated Pam. "I remember when Scottie worked in the office that summer before he went off to college."

I asked about our cousin Scott, and Pam explained that he wouldn't be at the reunion, since he and his family had planned a trip to Italy months ago. Scott had worked in the Silicon Valley area for many years for a computer company, and had made very good money. I was disappointed that I wouldn't see him on this trip.

Ed turned around and we headed back to Main Street, and then turned into the driveway of our childhood home. "I remember when I'd go to high school football games at night and ride the bus back here," I mused. "There were no streetlights then and this place was pitch black at night, and I'd get scared silly walking home in the darkness."

"I remember doing the same thing," chuckled Pam. "Having a flashlight would have made sense, but I never thought to bring one." We both laughed at the memory.

As we drove up to the house, my eyes teared up, and I had a lump in my throat. Everything around the old farm just looked incredibly lonely and quiet. Dad had stopped poultry farming many years ago, and had decided to raise Monterey pines instead. Of course he had raised the trees with a great deal of love and care, pruning and shaping them continually, and they grew into a beautiful forest out back in the area where the chicken pens had been. During the Christmas season people came from miles around to buy one of the Hummer's trees. He staggered the replanting, so there was always a new crop of trees coming up to replace those which had been cut down. Today there was a nice little forest, which shielded the acreage from the noise of the street.

Russ and Tim both lived in the area with their wives. My two brothers came over to the property often, doing minor repairs and generally keeping the place up. In the spring when everything was lush and green, and the weeds were tall, Russ and Tim mowed the empty fields and also mowed between the trees to keep all the growth under control. We four siblings hadn't yet made a decision on what to do with the property. It would just break our hearts to sell it to some developer who would put homes on it, or construct some huge shopping center. We talked of dividing it into four parcels, with each of us building a home on our parcel. But we didn't have to decide on anything just yet. Right now it made a good place to park an RV or two. Tim, who could do just about anything, had installed electrical and water hook-ups in three different places under the some of the taller, older pine trees.

After I'd loaded my big suitcase in the RV, I walked over to our old house, and sat down on the ancient, creaking lawn swing on the porch, making sure I had dusted it off first. Pam had told me she would be along in a minute. There were so many memories around this place.

I thought about the day I had gone off to college. I'd had a real case of nerves that day. Even though I thought at the time, that I'd never have better friends than my high school buddies, I did make some great friends in college, and still corresponded with a few to this day. But I had been very restless in college, not goal oriented at all. I was majoring in Liberal Arts, but I didn't really know where I was headed, or what type of career I wanted to pursue. I felt like I was just spinning my wheels. I dated a few guys in college, but felt no spark or emotion for them. I still had feelings for Shawn even though he didn't write to me. We went out a few more times when I was home from college, but later I heard that he was seeing someone else. Meanwhile I was writing to both Ski and Jeff but after a few months the letters from Ski stopped. In the Spring of 1962, I saw Jeff again. He was still in the Navy, but was home on leave. It just so happened that his leave coincided with a Spring Formal that was taking place at school, so I'd invited him. It was the first time we'd seen each other since Thanksgiving vacation of my Junior year. We had the best time together at that dance, and felt really connected, even though we hadn't seen each other in two and a half years. Of course Jeff had to go back to the Navy base in Long Beach, but then the separation didn't seem to bother me, as much as it had in high school. I guess I had finally matured somewhat. We continued to write. Later that year the Viet Nam war had escalated, and Jeff was on an aircraft carrier which spent some time in Vietnamese waters.

After just two years of higher education, I quit school, and found a job in Whittier working for the phone company. I lived on my own for a short while, and it was good for me. My parents had not been too happy about my decision to leave school, but my mind had been made up at the time. Now, in retrospect, of course I wished that I had stuck it out, and gotten my degree. But that was all water under the bridge.

Anyhow, Jeff and I got married in the fall of 1963. The construction of the new Methodist Church had been completed just a couple of months before, and so we had been married there by Jeff's uncle, Pastor Chuck Graham. All these years it had been fun to be a part of Jeff's loud and crazy and very loving family. Chuck and Cathy were now retired, and living in Orange County. They'd had three children. Chuck was busy writing a book about his experiences in the ministry.

The next day passed quickly. That evening Pam and I entered the banquet room at the Embassy Suites Hotel. Yes, Ellington was now the home to a couple of upscale hotels. I thought Pam and I were looking pretty good. She was wearing a slinky royal blue dress, and I was wearing a slinky black dress. A vivacious little brunette ran up to us, screaming "It's the Hummer girls!" I wasn't exactly sure who it was, but she and Pam were embracing.

"It's Missy," Pam was saying to me.

"Oh, but you were a redhead last time I saw you," I told her. "And it wasn't that long ago either."

"You're right," Missy stated. "It was at your dad's memorial service. You know me, always changing my hair. I guess I'd better get a nametag on, though. And then you and I," she said to Pam, "are going to see how we can shake things up around here, get this party going."

"It reminds me of all the stunts you and Pam used to pull," I said laughing. "The two of you were inseparable when you were kids, but always getting into trouble somehow."

"Oh, you don't know the half of it," Missy said, grabbing Pam's arm, as they disappeared into the crowd.

I hoped that I'd be able to recognize people, without having to look at their nametags. I was also hoping the writing on the nametags would be big enough that I didn't have to dig out my glasses to read it. But luckily I recognized the first two ladies I saw. "Karen and Mary Lou!" I exclaimed, as we exchanged hugs. Karen had married Alan Coulter years ago. Mary Lou had broken up with Woody when they both went off to separate colleges, and she had married a distinguished looking man, someone she had met at USC back in her college days. We got caught up on each other's lives, when someone tapped me on the shoulder and I turned around to see Beth standing there, all smiles.

Beth and I had kept up with each other. She and Paul had had three children together, but they had divorced about 30 years ago. Beth had remarried, but her second husband wasn't with her this evening. "He thought he'd be better off not coming," she explained. "And I know I'll be running all over the place and visiting with everyone, and not paying any attention to him at all, so it's best this way. Isn't this great? Such a good turnout!"

"You're looking wonderful, Beth," I told her. She still had chestnut colored hair, a smooth face, and didn't at all look her age. Most of the gals were looking really good. I think our generation realized the importance of exercise, and healthy eating, and not smoking. Back in school, most all the guys had smoked, and it didn't really bother the nonsmokers. Now in California, smoking wasn't allowed in most public places. When I did smell the smoke from the occasional passerby, I wondered how I was able to stand being around it when I was younger. But it had never bothered me, even being in the confines of a car or a small room.

"How is your mother doing?" I wanted to know. Out of all the parents of friends I had known in school, Sue Hathaway was the only one still living. She was still in the same old farmhouse that I had memories of when we were kids. She had adult children, and grandchildren who lived close by and looked in on her.

"She's still going strong at 89," Beth said. "She uses a walker or a cane to get around. Her mind is still sharp as a tack, though. Next year, for her 90th birthday, we're planning on a big party. Oh, something you probably didn't know, Paul died of a heart attack about six months ago. He had remarried and lived in Arizona. So the kids and I went to the services of course."

"Oh, I'm sorry to hear that," I said. I just hated hearing about any of our contemporaries passing away, even when it was someone I hadn't seen in years.

"Right after he passed away, I started looking on Facebook for Duane and Dennis, because they were good friends to Paul, but I had no luck in locating them," Beth continued. "Their folks moved out of High Bluffs back in the eighties. Anyhow, no one has heard from Duane or Dennis for many years."

"Megan's and Dennis's marriage didn't last very long, did it?" I asked.

"No, I think they were only together about two years," Beth remarked. "But then I don't think anyone really thought it would work out. I thought it was kind of neat that later on, when Woody came back from college, he and Megan got married. Oh, here they are, coming in right now!"

Megan was one of the friends that I had really wanted to see. She and Woody hadn't been at our 30th reunion, and I hadn't been to our 40th. But she recognized me right away, and I got big hugs from both her and Woody. Megan's golden blonde hair was now white, but still looked very pretty, and her face was still unlined. She always was beautiful as a teen, and here she was, still looking fabulous at 68. Woody had put on a little weight, and he was completely bald. But he had the same teasing blue eyes, and a great smile.

"Hummingbird, it's so great to see you!" he said heartily. "And you haven't changed a bit!"

"Oh, just keep it up, I love to hear it, even though it's not true," I laughed. "And you calling me Hummingbird really take me back to our high school days."

"So what's your last name now?" Megan asked. "You married the guy from the Desert Palms football team, right?"

"That's the one," I said. "My last name is Chadwick now, and in just a little more than a year, we'll be celebrating our Golden Anniversary."

"Ohh, congratulations!" Megan said. "There are a few others who have stayed married to the same person, but more, I think, who have gone through divorce."

"Do you ever hear anything from Shawn?" I was asking Woody. "Years ago I heard that he'd married a girl he'd met at City College, but I've heard nothing after that."

"We lost track of each other when I went off to Ohio State," Woody admitted. "He was one of our classmates I tried to find on Facebook recently, but nothing turned up on him."

"I think he and his wife live somewhere around Armedia, last I heard," Megan remarked. "Oh, Lenny is about to make an announcement."

Lenny Mendoza, who had been head of the Reunion Committee, was announcing that it was time for dinner to be served, and we all sat down to a meal of either prime rib, chicken cordon bleu, or vegetarian lasagna. The dinner looked and tasted delicious, but I was so excited that I didn't really have much of an appetite. After dinner, the visiting and catching up began again. There were still people I needed to see.

I found Lenny and thanked him for all the hard work he and his committee had done to plan this awesome party. He was still the same affable guy he had always been. He was married to someone he had met in college, and she also, had helped plan the reunion. Greg Okamota had been active on the committee as well. He had changed very little. He told me he was a retired doctor, and I enjoyed visiting with him and his cute and charming wife.

I still needed to look for Lucy and Vicki. I finally found Lucy back in the corner, and we both screamed in delight at seeing each other. Of course we had written each other over the years. Her red hair had turned white, and she wore it short. She was still slim, just as she had been in school. She and Red had lived in a suburb of Dallas, Texas, and they had for many years. Red's hair was also white, and he looked as though he had trouble getting around. He was using a cane.

"Had a hip replacement a couple of months ago," he told me. "And I still need to get the other one done. Oh, it's no fun getting old. I saw a bumper sticker the other day that read 'Growing old is not for Wimps.' But isn't modern medicine amazing? I'm getting around so much better now that I've had this hip done."

Lucy wanted to know how Jeff and I were doing, and asked about our grandkids. She was lucky, since her kids all lived in the Dallas area, not that far away, and she Red saw their grandchildren frequently. "We like the Dallas area," she said. "Except this summer we've had a terrible drought. And of course we're living in tornado alley."

It was then that I noticed a pretty auburn haired gal coming toward us, and ran to give Vicki Carr a big hug. I'd had a little communication with her over the years on email, but she mostly sent out jokes. "Oh, Elaine and Lucy, it's so wonderful to see you guys!" she cried. "You both look great!" Her husband, beside her, was still good looking. She and Anthony lived in the Bay Area. They'd never had any children, but they did a great deal of traveling now that they were retired. She was explaining to me and Lucy that her older brother, Willie had passed away a last year. "His heart just gave out," she said sadly. "Did you guys know that he and Alma got married about ten years ago?"

"I wasn't aware of the fact that he'd died, or that he and Alma were married," I told her. "And I haven't seen Alma here tonight."

"She still lives in Armedia," Vicki said. "But she has health issues. However, I think she will be at the picnic at the old high school tomorrow, and we'll all get a chance to visit then. Oh, we'd better be quiet and listen. Looks like Lenny is banging on the table again."

Lenny said they would be having a brief ceremony honoring the veterans in the room. He read from a list of names, and a pin was presented to each veteran who was in attendance. "We did lose one of our own to the Viet Nam War back in 1963," he said. "And so I want to present this pin to the brother of our fallen classmate, to Sam Morrison, the brother of DJ Morrison."

My mind went back to the summer of 1963. I was living at home briefly, very busy with wedding preparations for my upcoming marriage to Jeff, when the news came that DJ would not be comIng home again. What a shock that had been for our town! Dear DJ, always joking, always full of mischief, constantly keeping those around him laughing. His family had been devastated over the loss of their son and brother. In fact all of Ellington was heartbroken upon losing one of their own. I had known him since we were both about four years old. And he had left this world way too soon. His memorial service had been held at the newly constructed Methodist Church, and there was standing room only. Vicki and I were both crying a little now, as Lenny presented the pin to DJ's younger brother, Sam. I knew Vicki would always think she was responsible, since he probably wouldn't have joined the army if they hadn't broken up. But I told her back then, that he still might have gone into the service, since the draft was in effect at that time. Lenny suggested that we take a moment of silence to remember DJ, which we did. Lenny also said that up by the podium was a list of people from our class who had passed on, and I wanted to go see that list at some point during the evening. So far, I'd been too busy visiting. I felt that I didn't really get to finished my visiting with one person before someone else would come up to me and start talking.

A good looking silver haired man was approaching. He had a nicely trimmed gray beard and mustache, and he looked vaguely familiar, and yet I could not place him. I looked for his name tag, but couldn't find it.

"Elaine Hummer," he said, giving me a big hug, "I can tell by your face that you don't remember me at all. Have I really changed all that much?"

Once I heard his voice, I knew exactly who he was. "Adam Irby!" I exclaimed. "Oh, my gosh, it is so wonderful to see you! I lost track of Natalie all those years ago. We wrote for a while, and then I got married and moved, and your mother remarried and left town. I didn't know where you were. Every time I'd come home for a visit, I'd ask about Nat, and nobody seemed to know anything! It's so awesome that you're here now!"

"Let's go sit down, and we can catch up," he said, pulling out a chair for me.

"How is Natalie, and where is she?" I asked eagerly. "I need both her email address and her phone number. It would be so great to talk to her again after all these years!"

But Adam's face looked sad, and he placed his hand over mine. "I'm afraid I don't have good news about my sister," he said. "She passed away about three years ago from pancreatic cancer."

The news hit me like a ton of bricks. I still had a mental picture of her as a young girl with a great figure and pretty blonde hair. "I am so very sorry to hear that, Adam. I had no idea, of course. I always thought I'd get to see her again one of these days. It's just really hard to hear that kind of news." I was blinking back tears again. "Well, I do need to hear what's been going on with you, and also about Natalie, how things were going in her life before she got sick."

"Well, after college, I ended up going to the Denver, Colorado area, and teaching high school. I had met someone in college, who later became my wife, and she was from there, so that's why I chose that area. But my wife's not here tonight. I flew out here myself. I just got on Facebook a few weeks ago, and was so glad I did, since I then became aware of this reunion. I really wanted to come and reconnect with people after all these years. Natalie had a difficult life, though, I'm sorry to say. I'm sure you weren't aware of this, but she was molested by my father."

"Oh, that's terrible!" I exclaimed. "No, she never said anything to me about that. Of course back in those days, no one ever talked about it."

"Exactly," Adam agreed. "She was in denial for many years. She just tried to bury it, and of course something that traumatic can't really be buried. She was promiscuous, running around with different

Edwards Brothers Malloy
Thorofare, NJ USA
July 9, 2012